WOLVES AGAINST THE MOON

JULIA COOLEY ALTROCCHI

WOLVES AGAINST THE MOON

by
JULIA COOLEY ALTROCCHI

Author of
"SNOW COVERED WAGONS"

BLACK LETTER PRESS

BLACK LETTER PRESS

First Printed in 1940 by Macmillan Co.
Reprinted 1969-70-72-73-75-77-79-94
by Black Letter Press
L.O.C. 79-103313
ISBN 0-912382-32-5

PRINTED IN THE UNITED STATES OF AMERICA

DEDICATED
TO
MY GOOD COMRADE
RUDOLPH ALTROCCHI

PREFACE

THIS story of an adventurous Frenchman on the old Northwest frontier is based in part on the brief family chronicle by Joseph Bailly's granddaughter, Frances R. Howe, *The Story of a French Homestead in the old Northwest* (Press of Nitschke Bros., Columbus, Ohio, 1907, 165 pp.), and on references in early documents. The scant biographical material has been expanded and cast in the form of a novel. The present writer has spent almost thirty of her summers a few miles northeast of the old Bailly trading post, which remains almost unchanged, with its cluster of log cabins and its picturesque original homestead, on the Little Calumet River, near Chesterton, Indiana. Through the years, the personality and the significance of Joseph Bailly have grown, until he stands beside the Calumet and passes along the fur trails from Quebec to New Orleans, a symbol of the transitions between the gallant French era along the Great Lakes, the American plowshare period and the beginnings of the rushing, commercial age. In reality, Bailly spanned all three periods and successfully adjusted the pattern of his life to each development. If he began somewhat as a flourisher of "sword and cloak," he ended as a man of the people, an American pioneer.

Many years of study of Michigan, Indiana, and Illinois history have served to place Bailly against the larger scenes in which he played his part, and to multiply his adventures. Most of the events depicted are real, most of the characters are real, even to the incredibly named captain of a Great Lakes vessel, Job Fish. (Truth is, indeed, stranger than the audacity of any author!) However, the chronicler does not wish to be held responsible by possible descendants of persons appearing in the book for every depicted action of an ancestral protagonist. The portraits are, in the main, true and provable by multiple record. But now and then the story may have required a bit of frontier ferocity or momentary lack of gallantry unproven by record. The narrator demands the freedom

vii

of action of the characters as they came to life and marched out, masters of themselves, upon the pages. The author hopes that the fictitious characters may seem fully as real as the authenticated ones. If some of the episodes seem overdramatic, this may also be ascribed to the "strangeness of truth." The author has, if anything, *underdrawn* the amazing happenings in the old Northwest.

In addition to being a story of adventure, a record of people and events of the early nineteenth century from Canada to the Gulf, and especially in the Middle Western portion of the Great Lakes region (how *could* the picturesque and exciting Middle West *ever* have come to connote the dull and the prosaic!), and a record of the passing of the Indian life and the French life and of the coming of the Anglo-Saxon frontiersman, the book also becomes a record of the vanishing wilderness of the Calumet marshes and the Indiana and Michigan dune country.

When the writer first entered the Michigan coast region thirty years ago, it was almost as wild a country as it had been in the days when the Ottawa and Potawatomi Indians made it their camping ground, when La Salle swept past on his way back from his great discovery of the Mississippi and Joliet and Marquette paddled by, when the survivors of the Ft. Dearborn massacre (of only ninety-eight years before) went past with their Indian captors, when Joseph Bailly made the shore waters his pathway from the Calumet to Mackinac Island. Thirty years ago, one could turn up Indian arrowheads after every wind storm. In those days, the herons flew past in great sky-colored flocks. In those days, far more than now, the dunes were the riotous, amazing meeting ground of the northern and the southern vegetation, arbutus and pine and oak on the north slope, cactus, sassafras, and pawpaw on the south, and the stopping point for countless unmolested birds and butterflies in annual migration. Today the shore is one long, extended summer resort, and the gulls are still there and the shadows of the gulls, and the rich memory of the procession of the past.

Several definite attributions should be made, in addition to the general indebtedness to almost a hundred historical volumes and countless pamphlets and articles read in preparation for the writing. Marie's incredible (?) power over birds and animals is adapted from Simon Pokagon's Lonidaw in *Queen of the Woods*. The beautiful baptismal prayer of Nee-saw-kee is quoted from *The Story of a French Homestead.* To Jacob Piatt Dunn's *True Indian Stories* and Isaac McCoy's *History of Baptist Indian Missions* are due the exact words of William Wells on his encounter with the bear in Chapter XIII; to the Collections of the Historical Society of Baton Rouge is attributable the remark on the Yankees and the Mississippi in Chapter XXV; to Isaac McCoy's *Baptist Missions,* the greeting of Chief Noonday in Chapter XXVIII; to the Burton Collection and the Michigan Historical Collections, Campeau's remark on property and on taxation in Chapter XXXIV; to John C. Wright's *Stories of the Crooked Tree,* the episode of the baptism of the four Indians; to Cyrenus Cole's *I Am a Man,* the basis of Blackhawk's speech in Chapter XXXV; to J. Lorenzo Werick's *Pioneer Hunters of the Kankakee* and a speech of Simon Pokagon, the basis of Leopold Pokagon's speech in Chapter XXXVII; to Gurdon S. Hubbard's article on "The Administration of Indian Justice," the end of the scene of the death of De la Vigne; to Henry R. Schoolcraft's *Oneóta,* the translation of the firefly song on which my verse translation is based (Chapter XXVII); to Barbeau and Sapier's *Folk Songs of French Canada,* the basis of the song, "The prince he would a-hunting go," and to Marius Barbeau's *Folk Songs of Old Quebec,* the translation of the song beginning "J'ai fait faire un beau navire" in Chapter IV. Phylier and his drum and his exact words are taken from Friend Palmer's *Early Days in Detroit* and from Volume XXXII of the *Michigan Pioneer and Historical Society Collections.* To these *Collections* are also due the exact words of James Abbott's and Abijah Hull's recriminations and challenge to a duel, the jokes about the mud of Detroit, Little Turtle's remark about the gout, the text of Blake's letter in Chapter XXXVI adapted from Thomas Emerson's original letter, the general scenes of the Massacre of the Raisin and the Battle of the Thames, and many small incidents elaborated into large ones in the book. History has been respected, with but few alterations of date and scene. Much has been invented, but nothing that seemed implausible.

Gratitude is due to many people and organizations for assistance, notably to Mr. George A. Brennan, whose chapter on "Joseph Bailly, Fur-Trader," in his fine book, *The Wonders of the Dunes,* first kindled my interest in the Baillys fifteen years ago, and to my old friend, Earl Howell Reed, architect, whose enthusiasm over the Bailly homestead rekindled my interest four years ago. For material by correspondence I am grateful to Mr. F. D. Baril, Office du Tourisme, Quebec; to Mr. Julian P. Boyd of the Historical Society of Pennsylvania; and to Mr. Neil H. Swanson, author of *The Forbidden Ground*, who most courteously sketched for me the return route of the voyageurs in Chapter IV. For assistance through personal rendering, to Mother Olga Rossi, Mrs. M. A. Moore, Miss Rosalie Moore, and Miss Marie Buehrle of Berkeley, who made clear certain Catholic problems; to Dr. C. Latimer Callander and Dr. Karl Meyer of San Francisco for medico-literary assistance; to Mrs. Luigi Sandri and Mrs. Tracy Crawford of Berkeley for the solution of certain musical problems; to Mr. Edward C. Bailly, attorney, New York; Miss Lena Van Genderen, secretary of the Edward K. Warren Foundation, Three Oaks, Michigan; Miss G. B. Krum of the Burton Historical Collection, Detroit; and Sister Mary Joseph and Sister Almira of the School Sisters of Notre Dame, Milwaukee, who were all tireless in their generous efforts. Also to Mr. Matthew S. Dudgeon and Miss L. M. Carter of the Milwaukee Public Library; Dr. S. A. Barrett of the Milwaukee Historical Museum; Mr. Charles Biederwolf, Chamber of Commerce, Fort Wayne; Master George Martin, former caretaker of the Bailly Homestead; Mrs. Orrill Coolidge, Niles Historical Museum; Miss Eleanor J. Conway of the Chicago Historical Society; the Newberry Library, Chicago; Mr. F. A. Blossom, Museum of the American Indian, Heye Foundation, New York; Miss Marie Wilcox of the Michigan City Public Library; the very courteous librarians of the Indiana Historical Society and the Gary Public Library; Miss Carrie S. Freret, librarian of the Louisiana State Museum; Mrs. Adele Ethridge and Mrs. Ruth B. Campbell, Library of Louisiana State University, Baton Rouge; Mr. Max Farrand, Huntington Library, San Marino; Prof. H. I. Priestley and Mrs. Rogers Parratt, Bancroft Library, Berkeley; Prof. Robert H. Lowie; and to my husband Prof. Rudolph Altrocchi, my mother Helen Wooster Cooley, and my brother Harlan Wooster Cooley, for their encouragement and wise counsel throughout the task; to my sister-in-law Elizabeth Altrocchi Swift, for valuable material relating to Berrien County, Michigan—and to my little ten-year-old son, John, who reminds me that it was he who showed me *just* how Bailly should conduct the fist fight with Rastel on Mackinac Island!

Of the books read in preparation, the most valuable, in addition to those already mentioned, have been: Sister Mary Laurentia, *The Pioneer Fur-Traders of Northwestern Indiana;* Robert Burgh, *History of the Region of Three Oaks;* John O. Bowers, *The Bailly Homestead;* Agnes C. Laut, *The Story of the Trapper;* Chief Andrew J. Blackbird, *Complete History of the Ottawa and Chippewa Indians of Michigan;* Milo M. Quaife, *Chicago and the Old Northwest,* and Henry R. Schoolcraft, *Personal Memoirs.*

Now—forget the preface and enjoy the story!

                                                     J. C. A.

Berkeley, California
1940

CONTENTS

WOLVES AGAINST THE MOON

Chapter I

MASK

THE music of the gavotte stopped. In the sudden silence, Joseph Bailly let out his hearty laugh that seemed to shake the glass lusters overhead and would have gone crackling over the ice of the St. Lawrence far below, to an echo on the opposite shores of Point Levis, if the windows of the ballroom had been open. Lord Dorchester, recognizable by his many decorations, frowned slightly above his mask as he passed, and a few of the English ladies paused with fans poised in rigid attitudes of remonstrance; but Joseph only laughed again at his partner's latest flirtatious witticism. Then:

"The jealous wolves are on my trail, you see," he said, and nodded in the direction of a group of masculine onlookers who stood in an archway at the side of the room, obviously concentrating their admiration on his partner. There was one man in particular who had never taken his eyes from her. Even under the loup mask, which hid the fine, taut muscle-wrinkles, where lies half the expression of faces, the intentness was apparent. The fellow was tall, well built, splendidly dressed in olive-green and gold, and was undoubtedly good-looking, in spite of the long, sharp nose that protruded below the mask. "Your beauty is apparent to all, mademoiselle. When you finally unmask, the slaughtered will lie about the citadel of Quebec as thick as"—Joseph paused the shade of an instant, his quick mind reviewing the sieges of the citadel, and, being French and in conversation with a French woman, he selected a French victory—"as thick as the battalions at the victory of Ste. Foye, so many years ago!"

But there was something a little too calculating about Joseph's compliment.

"Sh-sh! Not so loud, monsieur. My escort over there may overhear you. And he's as sharp of mind and sword as his piercing eyes."

I

"Good! Then I'll speak all the louder!"

"You've never been afraid of anything, have you?"

"Never—until half an hour ago, when I met you!"

Now it was her turn to laugh, with a sound quite as distinctive as Joseph's. It was a rich, contralto laugh, like her voice, which was very low and differed from the high, quick voices of the other Frenchwomen in the ballroom and the foggy voices of the English-women. It was a dangerous laugh, rich with sophistication, the kind of laugh that Circe must have spilled, as she mixed the man-into-animal brew in the bowl. Joseph listened to the sound, more affected than he liked to be.

"They say that 'fear is the beginning of wisdom.' "

"Then I shall be as wise as Solomon," answered Joseph. "But, tell me, who *is* the gentleman?"

"Oh, you'll find out sooner or later when the masks come off— won't you?"

Joseph shrugged off the thought of wolves and men with a good French shrug and guided his partner towards the gold and damask Louis XIV chairs at the edge of the ballroom. A hundred other couples were dispersing towards similar chairs or towards banquet room or smoking room. This was the New Year's Eve ball of 1793, being given in the old Freemasons' Hall in the Upper Town of Quebec by Joseph Bailly's father, the lavish Michel Bailly de Messein, whose holdings were twenty-two miles below the city, at Ste. Anne de Beaupré.

The leading guest tonight was his Royal Highness Prince Edward, the Duke of Kent, a bald, affable copy of his father, George III, and a round prefigurement of his daughter Victoria. Kent had been in Quebec for three years as colonel of the Seventh Fusileers, and his imminent return to England was a matter of universal regret, for his robust British qualities, added to very nearly the graces of a Frenchman, had endeared him to the entire population. The Duke's Seventh Fusileers were there in all their glory of scarlet coats, gold braid and gold buttons, knee breeches, and hussar jackets hanging debonairly from one shoulder, the very costume that some of the youngest of them were to immortalize later at Waterloo.

All the English officials were there, including old Sir Guy Carleton, Lord Dorchester, Governor-General of Canada, hero of the fifth siege of Quebec. A few refugee Americans, Loyalists who had fled before the American Revolution, were also present, as well as a number of French refugees swept across the Atlantic by the recent repercussions in France. Many of the old French aristocrats and their families, now loyal to the unchafing regime of the tactful British, added their Gallic gayety to the scene. A few arrivals on the last ship up the river, including the two guests whom Joseph had never seen until this evening—his present partner and the watchful man of the long nose—gave novelty and mystery to the otherwise well acquainted group.

With a lady in olive-green satin upon his arm, the Duke of Kent paused to rally young Joseph.

"You have a laugh that would make Job quake, young man! Many a bellyful of laughter to you in the New Year!"

"Thank you, your Highness," answered Joseph, bowing, for the great Cross of St. George on the Duke's bosom and the colonel's uniform would have revealed him to all the world, in spite of the mask, if his round, powdered head and spherical figure had not already proclaimed his Georgian identity. "Much laughter to you also, Sire!"

Under his breath, as Kent passed on, Joseph added to the lady in lilac: "I wanted to say: 'A bellyful to you, Sire, for your capacity is majestic.' I think he would have stood for it, too, for as the English say, 'He's a good fel-low!' "

"But, as the English also say, 'A cat may look at a king'—but not pull his whiskers, monsieur."

"I know. I know. But what an exertion it is sometimes to keep within the prescribed limits of our famous French tact! Don't you find it so? Sometimes I want to throw it all to the winds and be free as the St. Lawrence. Let's go to the window and look out."

"It's frosted, monsieur. You can't look out."

"Just a flick of a brocaded arm, mademoiselle—and all outdoors is ours! What's a bit of brocade between a ballroom and the wastes of Canada?"

"No woman, then, has the power to keep your thoughts within the borders of a ballroom?"

"If anyone, it would be you, mademoiselle, but—"

And Joseph, leaving a world of unfinished desire in the disjunctive, rubbed the orris-laced cuff of his long, yellow, brocaded coat across the thick frost of the window. The "lady in lilac" gave him a long look through the slits of her mask. Nothing is more calculated to stir the sleeping leopard in a woman than such a combination of polished gallantry and provocative indifference. The woman unsheathes her claws and prepares to dig into masculine complaisance. If Joseph had known how the consequences of that long look would pursue him to the borders of Canada and the frontiers of the Northwest Territory and the far waters of the Mexican Gulf, he would not have commented so debonairly on the view.

"Look! We're on top of the world! As high as the moon!"

"It's all as *dead* as the moon down there," murmured the lady, unimpressed.

"No, no, not dead," Joseph contradicted emphatically. "Think of the life down there—hundreds of lives down in the Lower Town, people, horses, dogs, cats, parrots. Over there at Point Levis, sentries pacing back and forth, timber wolves sniffing along the snow almost to the foot of this cliff, white foxes, white owls, skunks slinking along like shadows in the moonlight, beaver sleeping in their lodges along all the St. Lawrence creeks, fish darting around deep down under the ice. It's alive! It's all alive, that waste!"

Joseph turned his eyes from the window suddenly and caught the lady's long look of mingled interest and amusement.

"You're so very young, monsieur," she said. It was as damning a thing as a lady could say: equivalent to a pat on the head and a "Nice little fellow!"

Recovering his dignity with an assumption of still uneventuated years, Joseph remarked:

"Forgive me! I should have realized that a lovely lady is more interested in the animals *inside* a ballroom than in those outside."

The thrust went home. The sapphire-ringed hand went out to Joseph's coat sleeve.

"But I *am* interested. You seem to be quite an outdoor fellow. Tell me all about it."

"Nothing to tell. My life is that of a complete gentleman;

namely, riding around on horseback, pretending to help my father manage his estates at Ste. Anne de Beaupré, racing in the spring meets on the Plains of Abraham, fox hunting at Lorette, snipe hunting at Sillery Cove, duck shooting on the St. Charles Flats—riding around on horseback, pretending to help my father manage his estates at Ste. Anne, racing in the spring meets on the Plains of Abraham, fox hunting at Lorette. . . . Shall I repeat the round again?"

Again the strange, rich, disturbing laugh.

"No need. What is it, then, you wish?"

"The Pays d'en Haut."

"The Pays d'en Haut?"

"Yes. The Upcountry. The Indian country—fur-trading, fur-trapping, I have what the Indians call the 'sickness of long thinking,' the yearning for the wilderness."

"A gentleman—like you?"

"Parbleu! Must you say that, too, just like my father? 'A—gentleman—like—you?' Mon Dieu! I'm a *man*, not a gentleman. Must a gentleman sit in his countinghouse counting out his money in Quebec and Montreal, and let all the fellows with red blood in their veins and muscles in their arms and legs go out into the Pays d'en Haut and bring in the furs and the gold? . . . But I must stop this! What a fool I am! It's you I want to know more about, mademoiselle. You told me all too little in that last interval between dances. You are from Paris—I know that—by way of London. An escaped aristocrat, that's obvious. You are beautiful, that's obvious, too. You have blue eyes, with strange yellow circles around the centers, green where the two colors mix. Very dangerous. You have a beautiful and sinuous mouth. Very dangerous. Your nose, although I can only see the tip of it under your mask, is pointed with peril. You have the laugh of a sorceress and the voice of an angel. Very dangerous. You wield your fan with devastating skill. You have a heart-shaped, black patch on your chin, whereas all the other ladies wear semicircular or square patches. Very dangerous. But what color is your hair under the powder? Red?"

"No. Not red, monsieur. I think it is *you* who are dangerous."

"It can't be golden hair. I know that. Your voice is too rich and deep for that. It must be very black hair."

"What would you say if I told you that it *were* black hair under the powder—blue-black?"

"I should say that I had guessed correctly—and that you are irresistible."

"What if I should reveal to you, when the time of unmasking comes, a 'frosty face,' smallpox-marked, a hunchbacked nose, and a gnarled forehead?"

"I should believe in the incontrovertible beauty of your eyes, your mouth, and your voice."

"That *is* charming, monsieur, really charming." And she touched Joseph's cheek with her fan. "What a pleasant young man you are, when your thoughts are in the ballroom!"

"May I claim for you, mademoiselle, what Ronsard said to Mary, Queen of Scots?

"Je ne veux en ce monde choisir
Plus grand honneur que vous donner plaisir!"

"Delightful! May I say that I agree with your father that you belong to the world of society, monsieur, and not to the world of wolves, foxes—and skunks?"

"You think I play well at the ballroom game? I know also how to defy the rules of the game, and how to be very rude."

"Rude?"

"Yes. I *could* tell you that I've only been pretending, and that no woman has ever enchanted me or ever could, that I consider badinage a silly game of shuttlecock and love a beaver trap!"

"Mon Dieu! You're quite theatrical! Which of your two selves am I to believe?"

"Whichever you prefer."

Thick frost had regathered on the window that Joseph had recently brushed clean with his coat. The ice wastes were shut out. The moonlight gleamed in a bright blur through the pane. Joseph turned the back of his hand toward the pane, his signet ring with its seven-pointed crown of the old Bailly de Messein family of Artois projecting from it, the shield with the seven fleur-de-lis lying below the crown and the guardian griffin crouching alongside. With the points of the crown, Joseph wrote on the frost that sardonic comment that Francis I had written with a diamond, two hundred and fifty years before, on the glass of the window at Blois:

> Souvent femme varie,
> Bien fou est qui s'y fie!

"So this is the gallant sentiment our young host of Quebec inscribes for the most beautiful and trustworthy woman in all of Canada!" said a rich, deliberate voice beside them.

Joseph and the lady turned to face the man-with-the-long-nose.

"The music has begun again, mademoiselle," continued the intruder. "I am sure you do not wish to remain longer with this young provincial."

And before Joseph could make reply with word or gesture the handsome gentleman had taken the lady's arm and was stiffly escorting her back towards the center of the floor for the next contredanse. Joseph watched the two. His suddenly clenched hands relaxed, the flush of anger faded, and he smiled to himself:

"You can have her, old fellow! No entanglements for me—not yet. But just the same I'd like to slice off your fine, pointed nose and toss it to the fish in the river!"

Temporarily weary of badinage, Joseph moved towards the dining hall. The great room was as yet empty save for a few French servants moving about the enormous table, arranging the holly-wreathed bowls of distilled peaches in rum that the French called l'Eustrope, the flasks of choice wines, the trays of croquignoles, and the great platters of roast pig, roast goose, the *pattes d'ours* of chopped meat in pastry, and the hundred other delicacies.

But from another room near by gusts of hearty masculine laughter issued, and Joseph made his way towards this ladyless harbor of refuge. At the door he thought he heard his father's name spoken, and stood still.

"Michel Bailly's a gr-r-rand fellow, and this is a gr-r-rand par-r-rty; but as sure as my name's Donald M'Kenzie, he'll r-r-ruin himself yet. He'll live like a lor-r-rd and die like a louse!"

"You're a pretty good spender yourself, M'Kenzie, like all good Nor'westers!" said a voice lacking the Scotch burr.

"Yes, M'Kenzie may be a louse now, but he'll end like a lord!"

There was hearty laughter at the expense of Michel and

M'Kenzie. Joseph stepped into the room. The laughter stopped, sibilantly, like a quenched fire.

Actual firelight, from a hearth as big as a house, was turning the carved beams overhead to sunset color. Around the hearth, on chairs or stools, or lounging against the mantelpiece, were a dozen men quite different from those who were out on the dancing floor. None of them wore masks. Most of them held long pipes or pewter mugs in their hands. One carried a snuffbox. Several wore Scotch kilts. Others were gotten up in olive-green or black or brown broadcloth coats, brocaded vests, white shirts, with ruffled fronts, white cravats and stocks, knee breeches and buckled shoes. One could distinguish the French in the group from the Scotch and the English by the gold or enameled buttons on the vests, the ribbons on the shoes and the greater number of ruffles in the cravats. But every man there was alike in having the outdoor ruddiness on his face and the horizon look in his eyes.

"By God, I swear I believe Alexander Mackenzie got to the Arctic Ocean and don't know it," said one, breaking the embarrassed silence of Joseph's entrance.

"It may be so, but why didn't he put his fingers in the blasted water to see if it were salt? You'd think a child would think of that, now, wouldn't you?"

"Come, come! Don't be a blooming idiot! You're mighty unfair to him! I can explain all that!" countered Donald M'Kenzie, getting red as the checks of his plaid.

"Gentlemen! Doesn't it seem rather quibbling to criticize Alexander Mackenzie, when he's gone farther north and west than any of us and has written a more complete report than any explorer so far? It seems to me he's done a pretty fine job," remarked a quiet British voice. It was Lord Dorchester. "I have his report at my offices if any of you traders care to see it tomorrow. It's more than a report. It's an exciting and marvelous story."

"Where's Mackenzie now?"

"At Montreal. But I don't suppose he'll be there long. A man of his sort must be up and moving all the time."

"May I come also and read the report, Lord Dorchester?" asked Joseph, in French-accented English, over Dorchester's shoulder.

"Surely. But how should it interest a young beau like you?"

A few of the men laughed good-naturedly. Joseph's costume was of the richest yellow satin, and his vest, of the finest gold brocade. From the tip of his high, red, Louis XIV heel to the top of his coiffure poudrés, he was apparently the young fop just stepped out of Versailles. But as he removed his mask and dangled it in his hand something besides dandyism showed in his fine, strong face. He was, in the first place, tall and strong of build, more British than French in bodily structure and in the gusty laugh that went with it. He held his head high. His eyes were very large and very dark blue. The eyelashes and the eyebrows above them were ruddy-gold, a color which suggested masses of red-gold hair under the thick layer of powder. The forehead was higher and wider than in most French faces, and the chin somewhat larger, but the rest was French—mobile, sensitive lips, narrow, smooth-sloping cheeks, a thin-bridged, aristocratic nose, very flexible face muscles. A handsome fellow, half British and half French, one would have said, although the actual blood was entirely from Artois. A young man to watch, at once sensitive and strong, artistic yet practical, a man equally at home in the indoor world and the outdoor world. Joseph's shrug was French.

"Oh—just a young man's curiosity," he said, and dropped the question lightly down the Gallic slope of his shoulders.

"There's much more exploring and mapping to be done," continued Dorchester, "though Mackenzie's sent me an excellent map with his report. Wonderful to see the werewolves and the carcajous of the traders disappear, like the sea monsters in the Atlantic on all the maps before Columbus' time—and Indian tribes and buffalo and rivers and lakes and mountains taking their place."

"But don't let anyone tell you, Lord Dorchester, that those trappers' tales of the car-rcajous and the werewolves ar-r-ren't true," protested one of the bluff, red-cheeked men by the fire, rolling his r's as thickly as Donald M'Kenzie.

"You Nor'westers!" remarked a sardonic Englishman in olive-green, who was leaning against the mantelpiece. "If you didn't keep up your fabulous fairy tales, no one would join your ranks! Sheer legend! It's the glamour you put into your stories as well as the gold of the furs that pulls men into your ranks."

"Oh, you str-r-raight-seeing, str-r-raight-walking, str-r-raightshooting, unimaginative men of Hudson's Bay!" answered the other. "It's our imaginations that have made us the gr-r-reat Company we are!" (Washington Irving was to immortalize M'Dougal's own imagination some years later in *Astoria*.) "We'll be tr-r-rapping furs up towards the Arctic long after you've pulled up the stakes of your for-r-rts and gone down to count your pennies at Montreal!"

"Yes, brother, but don't forget that of the £250,000 worth of furs sent from Canada to England last year, £150,000 worth went out from Hudson's Bay and only £100,000 from the Nor'westers!"

"Gentlemen, gentlemen," put in Lord Dorchester pacifically. "Let us speak of something else. Of Monsieur Lafayette, for instance."

For Dorchester knew that the Frenchmen in the room would seize upon this name and toss it to and fro like a bright shuttlecock, dispersing all discussion.

"Lafayette! Lafayette!" The name became a murmur about the room.

"No one could possibly have any news, of course, since the last boat came in, ten days ago," continued Dorchester. "And according to the dispatches, he is still held by the Austrians at Olmütz."

"He will be liberated. He is too great, too much beloved, too clever, to be held for long."

It was Joseph speaking. There was a tremor of excitement in his voice. Hero worship in the young throat.

"Yes. But he has many enemies too," suggested the negative-minded man in green, over by the fireplace.

"That's true—of all great men," commented one of the Frenchmen. "And, do you know, his troubles have streaked his hair with white, already, although he's only thirty-seven? I had it from that ravishing French girl in lilac silk who's only recently come over. And the poor fellow is beginning to look old."

"Such, my friend," said Dorchester, making a diplomatic point, "is the gratitude of revolutionists."

"But Lafayette was never exactly an Apollo—like our young friend here," remarked the man in green, looking in Joseph's direction. "Rather—uh—hum—frog-faced, as I remember him."

"Oh, how *can* you, monsieur?" Joseph found himself exclaiming.

"You saw him, then, when he was in America in '78?"

"I was but four at the time, monsieur. But my father saw him. And my father has described him to me so often that his portrait hangs about my memory like a locket—strong and splendid, every feature compelling: enormous eyes to see all the misery in the world, strong nose, strong—"

"Forehead? Like a lizard's. Strong chin? Like a bullfrog's. Thick lips, like—"

Again Dorchester's smooth voice broke in, to turn the conversation from contention.

"By the way, Duncan M'Dougal, you didn't get around to telling us that story. I thought, a while ago, you had some tale to back up your belief in the trappers' carcajou."

"I *did*, sir!" roared M'Dougal. And everyone settled down to listen. "It was back in '86. A party of us, under Cuthbert Grant and Laurent Leroux, had pushed through, along the Slave River, to Great Slave Lake. We made camp at the lake and set our traps at intervals along the river. One night, Laurent and I were late in getting started back to camp and lost our way for a time in the thick woods. There was only a half-moon that we could see, now and then, where the trees gave way. There wasn't a sound except the low moan of the wind in the pines and, very far off, the howling of a pack of wolves. Yet there was something there in the night that made our blood creep. Laurent spoke first: 'Queer, but the place feels ghostly. Do ye feel it?' 'It's just the wind in the pines. Always did sound kind of human, you know,' I answered. But my flesh crawled with the lice of fear. All of a sudden, in a little clearing, something monstrous and huge, like an oversized, wolf-headed bear, stood up and waved its great arms at us. At the same instant, the most bloodcurdling yell you ever heard filled the air, like the howl of a thousand wolves. I raised my gun and aimed at where the heart of the monster should be. The creature seemed to catch something in its forepaws and throw it back towards us. 'My God! I'm shot!' cried Laurent, who was standing beside me. Suddenly there was only moonlight in the clearing. A half-mile below us, Slave Lake glimmered distinctly. Putting my arms around Laurent, I helped him down to camp. Down by the campfire, we took a bullet from his shoulder. It was the bullet from *my* gun."

There was silence and the puffing of pipes. Then the man in green broke the spell.

"Too much trader's whisky, M'Dougal. They mix it strong enough at Mackinac for a man to see dragons."

"Oh, pouf, monsieur," said a Frenchman. "That's a likely enough tale. I believe it."

"So do I," declared Joseph. "We don't know everything yet about monsters and men and mountains. I'd give the world to go on one of those trapping or exploring expeditions—the whole world on a golden platter."

"Oh, you would, would you, young man?" came a smooth voice from the doorway. A distinguished-looking old gentleman, sparkling in white satin, with gold-heeled slippers, gold fleurs-de-lis on his vest, a gold chain about his neck and a gold cane in his hand, stood there, demanding and commanding instant attention. It was Michel Bailly de Messein, Joseph's father, the host of the ball. Michel walked over to his son, and struck him half humorously, half reproachfully on the shoulder with his gold cane.

"We'll attend to this boar-headed young man later," he said, addressing the group.

"Oh, Michel, send him into the woods!" urged the Frenchman who had graciously pretended to believe M'Dougal's story. "If he were mine I'd toss him out for a time to the wolves and the bears and the carcajous. He'd come back soon enough to change his buckskin for brocade and to eat his French pastries again at the old homestead at Ste. Anne."

"If the wolves of destiny, or the real ones, didn't devour him in the meantime, Dubois! . . . Gentlemen, I came to tell you that it is almost the hour for the 'bouquet,' the unmasking and the feast. Will you be so good as to put on your masks and accompany me back to the ballroom?"

The gentlemen rose from their comfortable places by the fire, stretched their legs, put on their masks, and followed Michel back to the ballroom. The lively music of the contredanse was speeding towards its closing bars. Suddenly Michel raised his white-satined arm. The music and the dancing ceased. The doors of the dining room opened, and two footmen, in red and silver livery, came out, sedately, carrying between them an enormous platter on which, as all knew, was a charge of gunpowder and ball, concealed beneath the red and silver ribbons, and the masses of holly. The bearers advanced slowly towards the far end of the room, where a fresh fire burned brightly in another baronial fireplace. When they reached the end of the room, they paused. Michel Bailly went to one of the frosted casements and threw it open. Suddenly the sound of church bells flung across the frosty air, bells from Notre Dame des Victoires, from the Jesuits' college, the House of the Recollect Friars, the Convent of the Ursuline Nuns. At the same moment, the "Gloria in Excelsis" rose dimly from the windows of all these houses of holiness. Then the great cannons of the Fort boomed. At the signal, Michel Bailly again raised his satined arm, and the liveried footmen took the silver salver, drew it back to the fullest arc of their arms and threw its contents and all its decorations into the roaring fire. The loud explosion was almost instantaneous. Then followed laughter and greetings and New Year's wishes in minor explosions all over the ballroom. Another signal from Bailly, a strum from the fiddles, silence, and Bailly's command: "Unmask!"

Most of the men with a brusque gesture, the ladies and some of the French beaux with a flourishing gesture, took off their masks. More merry laughter, salutations, and exclamations of astonishment! Joseph was standing near the man with the long nose, who was in line opposite the lady in lilac silk. Joseph was curious to see whether the lady's beauty matched the richness and depth of her voice. He was not surprised by the strangeness of her eyes which he had studied through the mask, nor by the length of her black lashes and the supercilious trailing line of her black brows; but he was surprised at the slight uptilt of those eyes at the corners, giving a curious Mongolian, catlike twist to a face which was congruous in all other respects. The nose was straight-sloping but slightly oversized, like the noses of so many Frenchwomen. The mouth was very sinuous and long like the eyebrows. It was a strange and charming and compelling face, an unpredictable face. At times the eyes seemed to look with melting innocence directly at you; again the look seemed to slip subtly out at the corners, with sly, undisclosed inferences. A smile to match the latter look was curving now upon the lady's face. Joseph stepped towards her, ifted her hand and kissed it.

"More beautiful than I had dared to dream," he said lightly.

"More gallant than I had dared to expect," she answered, at the same time giving Joseph her more open look, lighted with real admiration, for Joseph stood revealed the handsomest of the younger men in the room. "But I have a strange feeling that you have not taken off the second mask," Joseph ventured.

"Second mask?" she asked, taken unawares.

"Yes. Second mask," he repeated, without explaining.

At that moment, the man with the long nose brushed past Joseph and took the lady's arm. Unmasked, he was even more attention-arresting than before, possessor of one of the finest, shrewdest faces that Joseph had ever seen, keen, dark blue eyes, as intense as when seen through the mask, supercilious eyebrows, two concentrated furrows in the forehead, aquiline nose tapering to a fine point, up-curling nostrils, up-curling mustache, slender lips, the lower lip projecting slightly beyond the upper, and all the fine muscles of neck, cheek, chin, and lips tensed with a long habit of wariness against life. He was tall and held himself very well. He must have been some fifteen years older than Joseph.

A look of responsive intelligence seemed to pass from this face into that of the lady. The tall man bowed low over her hand and kissed her fingers.

"Mademoiselle de Courcelles, may I have the honor of escorting you to the banquet hall, and then home?" he asked.

"Gladly, Monsieur Rastel."

The name set memory atingle along Joseph's spine. Rastel! Many a time had old Michel told Joseph of Philippe Rastel, Sieur de Rocheblave, that aristocratic old scoundrel who had disgraced the name of France all along the old Louisiana frontier and had at last been discharged by Governor O'Reilly for falsifying his accounts. Some son, or nephew, this, of old Rocheblave, the tainted blood running in his veins!

"I shall see you again," said Joseph to the back of Mlle. de Courcelles' neck, as she started away on the arm of Rastel, towards the banquet room.

"Sans doute. Without doubt," she answered, showing him an amused smile over her left shoulder.

Chapter II

SEIGNEUR OF STE. ANNE

"Malbrouck s'en va t'en guerre!"
JOSEPH dug his spurs into the flanks of his white Arab and sped up
the road from Ste. Anne de Beaupré towards Quebec. The Bailly
horses were the wonder of the countryside, for even the aristocrats
around Quebec used only the Canadian ponies. The prodigal
Michel's son, full of the joy of living on this blue afternoon of June
7, 1794, and expansive with anticipation of his rendezvous with
Corinne de Courcelles, cantered along the road, singing to the beat
of the horse's hoofs that old song of the Crusades, repopularized
during the French Revolution and repeated by French traders in
their pirogues along the creaming rivers of Canada, by lonely settlers at the far French villages of St. Louis and Vincennes and Detroit, by gay fellows in Quebec and Montreal and far, far down
the Great River to the echoing town of New Orleans:

> "Malbrouck s'en va t'en guerre;
>   Mironton, mironton, mirontaine;
> Malbrouck s'en va-t-en guerre,
> Ne sait quand reviendra.
> Ne sait quand reviendra. . . ."

All through the song, Joseph's tone continued lusty and gay,
even through the passages where Madame mounts to her tower and
sees nothing, nothing but an empty road, with no Malbrouck
returning, sees at last the page of Malbrouck riding towards the
castle, dressed in black.

Joseph was still singing as he came into the outskirts of Quebec,
where the rocky hills jutted up out of the river plains towards the
ultimate plateau of old Fort St. Louis. In twenty minutes more,
he would be at the little house that Corinne and her uncle had taken
three months before in the Upper Town. Had they taken it to be
near him? Absurd idea! And yet?

15

As if he were singing a wedding song, he shouted out:

"Quittez vos habits roses,
Et vos satins brodés!

"Le Sieur Malbrouck est mort,
Mironton, mironton, mirontaine!
Le Sieur—Malbrouck—est—m—"

At that instant, it was as if an earthquake shook the tottering world. There was a roar, a crash, a splintering of brush down the hillside. Joseph's horse shivered, snorted, and stood upright on its hind hoofs, as a great streaking sphere passed directly under its nearly vertical belly. Joseph almost lost his hold, but such was his centaurlike identity with his animal that he clung securely through the cataclysm. When the horse planted hoofs down again, both creatures were quivering. Joseph looked to the side of the road. A large boulder, three feet in diameter, had half embedded itself in the side of the embankment on the left, leaving a meteoric path of destruction down the steep slope of the hill on the right. Joseph dismounted, stroked his horse, studied the hill.

"Queer," he thought. "I never heard of a rock slide there before. Not even in spring, when the snow melts and the rocks are dislodged."

A flock of crows were noisily disputing something high up on the top of the hill. Far up, directly under their noise, a dog barked. There was as sudden a cataclysm in Joseph's mind as there had been on the hillside a moment before.

"A dog! A man! A pair of hands to push that rock! Mighty clever, old fellow—but you didn't get me that time!"

Joseph touched the gun at his belt, mounted his horse quickly, and rode on. For three months Joseph had realized that he was playing an increasingly difficult game. Rastel had moved in from Montreal to Quebec, where he was manipulating some interesting deals for the Northwest Fur Company and less ostensibly watching Corinne and Joseph's attentions to her. A month ago there had been an unexplained shot as Joseph rode into Quebec; last week a queer-looking man had followed him in the street; today a rock moved. Coincidence or conspiracy? Accident, or—

Rastel? But it was chiefly this cumulative opposition that had spurred Joseph on to his intensifying flirtation with Corinne. He had had no intention of involving himself with any woman, for it was firmly in his mind to go out into the Pays d'en Haut for two or three years of adventure before settling down to the life of a landed gentleman of Ste. Anne. Even less had he cared to involve himself with Corinne, for fascinating though she was, he recognized an element of danger in her personality. Those slant eyes, that slant look, that hint of hazard! She was far from being the demure type of French girl whom it would be charming and safe to have presiding over one's fireside and over one's children's crib; but gradually Corinne's fascination had prevailed, a blend of intelligence, exotic charm, and the allure of sex. Today Joseph threw all caution to the winds as he rode the last half-mile into town, glad that, like Malbrouck, he was not dead! Bayard clattered over the bridge across the St. Charles River and under the gray arches of the Porte du Palais and up the steep Palace Road to the Upper Town. Although most private houses were in the Lower Town (the Fort, the Bishop's Palace, the Churches, the Freemasons' Hall, and the other great public buildings occupying most of the Upper Town), Corinne had cleverly chosen a small stone house at the lower edge of the Upper Town, commanding a superb view of Cape Diamond, the harbor, and the wide sweep of the river.

Joseph exuberantly clapped the boar's-head knocker on the door of this house. A French manservant opened the door. It was characteristic of Corinne that she surrounded herself with men, down to the least important members of her staff. Joseph was bowed into the little reception room, where a fire roared on the hearth. The old uncle, who usually dozed by this fire, like all good French guardians, was for the first time absent. Joseph could not help admiring and applauding the strategy which must have arranged this. He scented danger in the unguarded room, as much danger as he had encountered from falling rock a few moments before—a danger, perhaps, of falling resolutions. But this peril he welcomed with the fearlessness of youth.

Corinne kept him waiting just long enough to tantalize him, an interval during which the servant brought him a silver cup of peach brandy. As Joseph finished it, Corinne entered, wearing a soft white muslin dress embroidered with gold stars. The last boat from Europe had brought new fashions—long, clinging, classical dresses that discarded the bouffant, beribboned effect of the old regime. Even the hair was ordered differently now, a bunch of natural curls falling over a high Psyche knot, a wave of tiny ringlets over the forehead substituting a demurer air for the imperial coquetries of wigs and powder. As Joseph had guessed months ago at the New Year's Ball, Corinne's hair, in its natural state, was a glossy, bluish black, Oriental in its thickness. Her eyebrows were of the same deep-sea shade, and dipped in long curves with a slight uptilt at the end, also Oriental in suggestion. Her lashes were long and curved and cast raying shadows on her cheeks. Her complexion was naturally pale, but Joseph suspected that she reddened the centers of her cheeks with "Spanish paper," adding to the strange artificiality of her appearance. It was always as if Corinne withheld something—a complete candor of eyes, a complete concession of color, a thorough giving of mind and heart and confidence. She always wore that accessory mask, that secondary domino. But it was this very fact, this addition of Corinne's specific enigma to the enigma of woman in general, that drew Joseph, challenged him to some ultimate discovery. The postrevolutionary curls were charming but entirely at odds with Corinne's features. They were like sparrows sitting on the head of the Sphinx.

"Joseph, my dear Joseph," she said, holding out her hand in the best European manner and letting her fingers linger in his large palm. "I am desolated that Uncle Eustache is unable to be here. A little birthday celebration for Pierre Fontaine at the 'Sign of the Three Lilies'! I forgot to tell him that you were coming!" An attempt to match the curls with a look of complete innocence!

"You expect me to believe that?"

"I expect you to believe what you choose to believe, Joseph. I've learned that you combine with the common sense of a man very nearly the intuition of a woman!"

"Flatterer! How a woman tries to throw a man off his guard with flattery!"

"Not flattery, Joseph—appreciation."

"How lovely you look—and how innocent!"

"Innocent of what?"

"Innocent of the menace you are to a man!"

"Which man?"

"You minx! Monsieur X!"

And Joseph drew Corinne to him and enjoyed a long kiss. They sat down on a brocaded sofa beside the fire.

"Be careful! Uncle Eustache—what would he say?"

"He'd say: 'Go to it, youngsters! I'm only pretending to sleep, behind the glare of my spectacles. I see it, and I approve of it. It makes my old blood tingle. Go ahead! Long life to love! Long life to love!'"

"Sh-sh! Joseph—the servants! You have such a loud voice, my dear! But come, Joseph, tell me all the newest news about yourself!"

"Well, I have one piece of news to tell you. I was almost crushed to death on the road to town. You almost received a corpse instead of a caller."

"A corpse? What do you mean?"

"About a mile out of town, as I was passing under the hills, a boulder rolled down across the road straight into my path. Bayard reared and the boulder dug itself into the opposite bank. It was quite an escape."

Joseph watched Corinne's eyes. There was no sinister presurmise in them, only surprise.

"It suggests nothing to you? Nothing at all?"

Slowly Joseph's interpretation crept under Corinne's lids into the greenish speculum of her eyes.

"You don't believe—"

"I do believe—"

"Some enemy, Joseph?"

In the wink of two subtle eyes, Corinne had banished that betraying glint of suspicion. She had been increasingly aware of Rastel's jealousy, and increasingly unwilling to criticize him in Joseph's presence. Rastel was a growing power in Montreal and Quebec and the fur trade. Plans that he had shrewdly mapped out for carrying the trade into remote and perilous western districts, combines that he had achieved, even luring some of the powerful Hudson's Bay men into the Nor'wester group, ships that he had secured to take the furs to Liverpool three weeks earlier than Hudson's Bay could get them out, had earned the respect of the fur barons and, even in this short half-year, had lined his pockets with gold. Corinne had not spoken disparagingly of him since the New Year's Ball.

"*Some* enemy?" asked Joseph, with a touch of bitterness, for he always felt Corinne slipping away from his grasp, whenever Rastel was mentioned.

Corinne wisely remained silent, and allowed Joseph to entangle himself in his own implications.

"Doesn't Rastel hunt in the hills with his dogs quite often?"

"Not so near town, Joseph. And it's pretty poor hunting at *this* time of year. No ducks and geese—"

"Plenty of quail, partridge, foxes—and other creatures."

"Doesn't it sound a little fantastic, Joseph, your supposition? Have more brandy, my dear." And with infinite grace, arched as a swan at neck and wrist, Corinne poured more brandy from a silver flask into Joseph's cup.

As a matter of fact it did sound fantastic. Against the background of Corinne's calculated silences and exonerating comments, the whole thing sounded utterly foolish. But, like any young man in love, Joseph temporarily lost his own shrewdness and floundered on.

"I suppose it does. But I wonder what I would have done, if I'd been hunting with my dogs on top of a hill and had seen my rival galloping up the road toward my lady's house—and if a nice round boulder had been very handy. I'd have *wanted* to push it over, anyway!"

"You dear, foolish young man!" said Corinne, laying her hand on his knee. "But you mustn't suspect Rastel. He's jealous, I admit, but he's a very fine fellow for all that."

"I almost suspect you of more than liking him, Corinne."

"Don't forget I've known him for a long time and that he helped Uncle Eustache and me to escape from France just as the Revolution was breaking. Very few men foresaw, as Rastel did, what was going to happen. He's as smart as a seer and as sly as a fox. If we'd waited three weeks longer, it would have been the Bastille and Papa Guillotine for us! He's been very good to us ever since. My liking is tinged with gratitude, Joseph."

"Yes, I've no doubt he's as clever as his old uncle, who made such a name for himself over here—the *honorable* Philippe Rastel, Sieur de Rocheblave!"

"Joseph!"

"Yes," continued Joseph remorselessly, "gratitude is dangerous. Sometimes it wears the mask of love."

"Don't vex yourself, Joseph, my dear. Frowns aren't becoming to you."

"Then let me hear you say you love me."

"I'm very fond of you, Joseph."

"Is that all you can say?"

And again Joseph took Corinne to him and kissed her. Whenever he did this, all sense of the danger of her personality disappeared. The flood of passion washed away all cautions, all suspicions. Corinne was beautiful. She was ardent. She was fascinating. She was overpowering. Corinne, under the same flooding emotion, acknowledged:

"I love you, Joseph."

"When will you marry me then? Surely, the summer is the time. We will go on a little journey to Detroit, and I'll bring you back to Ste. Anne while the roses are still in bloom—the roses from Artois."

"Wait a little, Joseph. Wait a little. You must have your year or two of adventure before you settle down. You would always be a discontented husband, longing for the freedom you never had had. I know you, Joseph. You must get that surge of adventure out of your heart first."

Joseph recognized the truth of this, but he could not help suspecting the sincerity of Corinne's intention. Was it for him, this sacrifice, this postponement? Why did she never wish to commit herself definitely? Uncle Eustache and Michel Bailly had already touched upon the matter, as good French guardians should, over their French pastries and Burgundy. Both were quite amenable, though neither wished, as yet, to push the matter. Joseph was only nineteen, and Michel had rather counted on sending him to France or to one of the colonies for a year or two, if things ever settled down in Europe. In the old days, Joseph would have gone to court, as a matter of course. Now Versailles was as meaningless as a

Roman ruin. But Joseph must have some gentlemanly adventure as far from the wild Pays d'en Haut as possible. When he returned, thought Michel, Corinne would make a very acceptable wife. She was beautiful, clever, a descendant of the Courcelles of Dordogne, a worthy representative of the later aristocracy. Bailly's shield went back to the fourteenth century, the Courcelles were only seventeenth century. No matter—or rather, not so much matter in the British colony of Quebec! Uncle Eustache was pleased. The son of one of the wealthiest men of Quebec, the descendant of a noble family, a charming, personable young man, was entirely acceptable in this distant province. As for Corinne, her thoughts were hidden. Joseph, in spite of himself, wondered more than once whether Corinne would be so flirtatiously responsive to him if he were as poor as a voyageur. There was always that cool, sea-green look of calculation in her eyes. Would she love him, if he were stripped of all his possessions, if he were forced to substitute buckskin for brocade? Did she love him now, utterly? Quietly he asked, as he searched her with his keen blue eyes:

"Are you thinking of me, Corinne, or—"

He hesitated to put the thing, bluntly into words.

"Or what, darling? Don't furrow your forehead—" Corinne passed cool fingertips across his forehead and cleverly brushed away the question that she dreaded. Joseph had just drawn down her hand and kissed it fervently when there was the sound of hoofs on the cobblestones outside, then a clamorous beating of the knocker on Corinne's door.

"Rastel!" exclaimed Corinne, turning pale and in that very pallor belying her previous exoneration of the man. "You must go!"

"What? Out of the back door, like a thief? I'll face him! Why shouldn't I?"

"But, Joseph! Whoever it is," said she, recovering, and her face flooding with belated crimson, "don't you realize you're compromising me? Uncle Eustache isn't here, you know."

"But the next man compromises you more than I do—especially if it's Rastel."

"Please, Joseph, please! Where have you left your horse? At Pierre's stable?"

"Yes. Then go, my dear! But come back tomorrow!"

A last embrace, and Joseph made his way to the back of the house, his heart pounding with anger and resentment. How he would love to stick a knife into Rastel and be done with it! The only safe thing to do was to marry Corinne. But why, why did she forever hold him off? She was older than many French girls when they marry, a little older than Joseph himself. She was twenty. Mon Dieu, why had he ever met her? His whole life had been in turmoil for six months. Could she ever really give him peace of mind and heart when she was settled by his fireside? He tried to think of her sitting by that fire rocking a cradle and crocheting lace at the same time, as he had seen so many French Canadian girls doing. Somehow the picture would not come. It was only a half-panel that came, with no room in it for a cradle at all—a lovely, decorative panel of Corinne in a brocaded dress, lace, jewels, and red-heeled slippers, with a fan in her hand, or a pewter cup of hot peach-brandy, which she sipped exquisitely.

As Joseph hurried towards Pierre's stable, the sound of hoofs along the cobbles came down upon him again, and then, as a house-front lantern threw its light upon him, his own name was called frantically:

"Joseph! Joseph! Wait!"

It was the voice of his brother Raoul. Joseph wheeled about as Raoul drew rein.

"What brings— What *is* it, Raoul?"

For Raoul's face showed purple-shadowed in the lanternlight.

"It's father, Joseph. He's terribly ill. You must come at once. I've ridden in from Ste. Anne in two hours. Almost killed my horse. Guessed you were at Mademoiselle de Courcelles'. She told me where you'd gone. Pray God you won't be too late! Dr. Campion gives Father only a few hours to live. But he's still conscious."

Joseph choked back a gigantic sob which clogged his throat, put his hand for a second on his brother's shoulder, then turned and ran towards Pierre's.

The long Canadian twilight had almost faded as the two brothers rode out of town. A thin streak of the day's final gold lay behind the black escarpments of the hills. A few frosty stars were emerging from the blue-blackness. Why must beauty ruthlessly come forward and attack with its keenest swords, when death lay at the end of the road? Such stars! Such glorious stars! It was as if Joseph had never realized stars before. . . .

The two brothers galloped down the road to Ste. Anne, never exchanging a word, swept forward by the same great tide of grief, feeling more like one anguished person than two separate creatures. Many candles and whale-oil lamps burned throughout the gabled château, but all was utterly quiet, save in a few corners of the house in which the womenservants wept. In the largest bedroom upstairs, Madame Bailly and Antoinette, her daughter, were suppressing the tears which would come later. Dr. Campion was mixing potions in a far corner of the room. On the great, carved bed Michel lay, like a ghost of the gay Seigneur of the New Year's dance. No powder now. No flowered brocade. His curly chestnut hair, from which Joseph derived his astonishing copper-gold, lay tousled on the pillow. His fine French face, with its delicate nostrils, surprised eyebrows, sensitive mouth, and foppish chin, lay whitened not with the powder of festivity but with the powder of death. It was obvious that to his father Joseph owed all that was worldly and gay in his nature. The mother, who stood beside the bed, undoubtedly contributed those other qualities which were so at variance in Joseph's own nature. It was she who was strongly and superbly built, who carried herself like an Amazon, who lifted her head as if she breathed the salt winds from Hudson Bay and saw, with her steel-blue eyes, horizons beyond horizons.

When his two sons entered the room, Michel's face brightened; a difficult smile tugged at the corners of his mouth and his hand moved slightly forward on the coverlet. Joseph moved quickly to the bed, knelt on the floor, seized his father's hand, and kissed it with passionate French fervor. On the other side of the bed Raoul, standing, tightly held his father's other hand. For a few moments no one spoke. Then Michel whispered hoarsely:

"Sit down, boys. I have many things to say—if there—is—yet . . . time . . ."

Joseph sat down on the edge of the bed. Raoul drew up a stool.

"I think you should know that you—face—difficulties. There is —nothing—nothing—left—except the house—and—the—stables and a few—surrounding fields."

Raoul's eyes contracted suddenly as if he had been dealt a blow. Antoinette, with a sharp, intaken breath, crumpled against the shoulder of her mother. Madame Bailly and Joseph, with precisely the same motion, stiffened their shoulders and threw up their heads.

"The horses," went on Michel, "must—of course—be sold— and most of the land—which is already—mortgaged. You'll have —to make out—for a while—with Canadian ponies—and a vegetable garden. Keep the house—for your mother—if you can. Antoinette—you must marry. Rastel is the—richest man—around here—a fine man. Set your cap for him—"

Antoinette looked excited over the proposition. A strange look came into Joseph's eyes, but he did not move another muscle.

"You, Raoul," continued Michel, "must go into—the army. It's one of the only ways out—for a gentleman. . . . You, Joseph— stay here—and build up—the estate again. With your love of— outdoors—and your good—common sense—in ten years—you'll make things—flourish again."

Michel watched his elder son closely. In spite of himself, Joseph's glance fell.

"I want you—to—promise, Joseph—to—promise—that . . ."

Every fiber in Joseph's being stiffened against this use of the merciless, deathbed promise. He waited, the blood beating against the doors of his heart, for the formulation of the promise, not assisting his father with any prompting or any sign of assent.

"I want—you—to promise"—and Michel made the effort of lifting himself up on his elbows—"to—give up that—abominable— idea—of going into the—Pays d'en Haut—and bartering for furs —like a--peasant. I want you to stay here—and live—like a gentleman."

Breathing overhard, Michel lay back on the pillows. Madame Bailly threw off the burden of Antoinette and stood tensely waiting, her own understanding of Joseph's passionate sense of freedom struggling with her deference towards her dying husband's wishes. Joseph released his father's hand and answered in a low but very distinct voice:

"I am sorry, Father, but I can promise nothing, absolutely nothing."

A low sound of protest came from Antoinette. A deathbed request in 1794 was still something hallowed.

"I will do my best, Father," Joseph went on, "to help my mother; but as for promising to stay in this little checkerboard of a place all my days—God help me! I can't do it. Besides, Uncle Baptiste could help Mother with the place far better than I could—"

"But—b-b-but—I'm *asking* you to do it. I'm *commanding* you to do it!"

The pride of the old aristocrats, the blood of the tyrants of the ancient castles of Artois, whose word was law, whose sons obeyed like slaves, surged up in Michel for the last time.

"I'm *commanding* you to do it . . ."

To Madame Geneviève Aubert de Gaspé Bailly de Messein, it seemed as if her soul and body were being torn in two. The husband whom she worshiped, the son whom she adored—with a sword between them and death over them! Her fingernails cut red crescents in the palms of her clenched hands.

"Father, believe me, I honor you, I love you, but—"

Joseph covered his face with both his hands, rose from the bed, and stumbled out of the room.

Dr. Campion returned quickly to his patient. Michel was gasping for breath, and was shutting and unshutting his right hand, as if he desired to lift it in that old biblical gesture of the father disinheriting the son. The gasps became fewer and fewer, then ceased. The look of anger in Michel's eyes suddenly vanished like a shark from the surface of a glassy sea. Dr. Campion bowed his head, crossed himself, then leaned over and closed the eyes. Antoinette and Raoul knelt down by the bed.

It was characteristic of Madame Bailly that she turned almost immediately and went to seek Joseph.

Chapter III

THE UPCOUNTRY

IT WAS the first bear trap that Joseph had ever set, but he was thoroughly satisfied. He leaned over towards the partridgeberry bush and, picking off two more branches, careful to disturb the crusted snow on them as little as possible, dropped the branches carefully over the trap. Out of the great snowy silence, a sudden, sharp "Ca-ca-ca!" at his very heels startled him. He pivoted about, to catch the gray wing flash of the Canada jay as she swept mockingly to a pine overhead. His boots must have polished the snow to glass underfoot as he worked at the trap. He slipped as he started to turn, lost his balance, fell—and with a hungry snap of great steel teeth, the trap closed over his left leg.

"This is Death," thought Joseph. He lay very still, as his mother would have done in a like emergency, and brought all the forces of his mind to bear on the problem. The chances, he decided, were quite against him.

He was seven miles from camp, and his trail was already obliterated by the snow that had fallen during the earlier part of the afternoon. No one would be sent out to search for him for four or five days, for the company had spread out in different directions to gather in the fur harvest of mink, beaver, otter, and skunk from old traps and to set new traps all along the valleys and creek beds for thirty miles in every direction. Joseph's bear trapping was a project of his own. He had chanced upon the tracks of a cinnamon bear, the lazy bruin that sleeps in the open and gets so cold that it prowls hungrily about when others are sensibly hibernating. Joseph hoped to surprise his party with good fresh bear meat after their long winter's diet of corn and tallow and beaver tail.

Night was falling, and with it the temperature. Another twenty-below spell apparently. To make matters worse, Joseph, finding his blanket coat an encumbrance as he worked, had tossed it under the pine tree upon which the Canada jay still sat, flirting her tail and inspecting the strangely prostrate man. Joseph's hunting knife lay on top of his jacket; otherwise he might have attempted to cut off his own leg as trappers had now and then been known to do in similar circumstances. His gun was within reach, leaning against the partridgeberry bush. But this was a small and ineffectual weapon against the gigantic twin traps of cold and Death. It was useless to struggle against the comparatively small and obvious bear trap, he knew. Yet, impelled by the hearty will to live, Joseph sat up and tried to pull the iron jaws apart. But his leverage was, of course, wrong. To open the jaws, he would have had to stand over them and exert all his force. He lay back, breathless, and an ironic smile flickered over his face. Perhaps his father had been right after all! His leg ached already, as if it were paralyzed, frozen at this early stage of the proceedings. He would freeze gradually, the cold creeping up from his feet until he was entirely enveloped in the cerements of death. He sat up and whipped his arms back and forth across his chest, his warm breath smoking and freezing on his new beard as he worked.

"What a fool!" he said to himself. "Gesticulating with death, like a coward, for a few more minutes of life."

He stopped and looked about him. Beautiful world, incredibly beautiful. Close in front of him, to the west, the pine woods that bordered Great Slave Lake; every branch was crusted with snow and hung with pendants of ice that began to give off a final gleam as the gold streaks of the sunset touched them off like a million candles. To the north and the south of him, the frozen hills came close with their burden of snow and laden pines. On the nearest slope were the tracks of the bear, blue hollows in the snow. For an instant Joseph played with the unctuous idea of that forfeited bear feast. Then another thought crept into his mind, something about the reversal of feasts. . . . Again he swung his arms back and forth across his chest, and lifted his right leg up and down, though each motion of the free leg sent a pain into his left thigh and the base of his spine. The gold streaks of the sunset darkened.

"If it's a last sunset, it's a damned good one," muttered Joseph, trying to choke off sentiment. But something happened to his throat, and he coughed. The sunset blurred for a moment. He remembered how beautiful a sunset could look through pear branches in bloom at Ste. Anne. This sent the memories trooping. He gave himself up to them like a Sybarite and pillowed his head on his hands in the snow, the cold creeping up to his knees, his thighs, his stomach, his breast. His mind became crystal-clear for a time, as if all the blood flowed only through his head, bringing pictures:

His first pony-ride, at the age of four, at Ste. Anne. de Beaupré. Pulling the reins out of the hands of his father, who was walking alongside, dashing off down the road, his father shouting to him to come back, Joseph pretending not to hear. . . . His first visit to Montreal—shops, a toy trumpet, a gold-handled riding-crop. . . . The red-sashed voyageurs strutting in front of Château de Ramezay. Was this where it all started, perhaps—his craving for the Pays d'en Haut? . . . His first dance at Quebec, when he was sixteen; the never-to-be-forgotten zest of it! . . . That other dance—Corinne de Courcelles! "All outdoors is ours! What's a bit of brocade between a ballroom and the wastes of Canada?" . . . God, yes! His mother at the gate at Ste. Anne, saying goodbye, her head high and not a trace of tears in her eyes—but not a trace of a smile, either: "Goodbye, Joseph. I hope you'll find the Great Adventure just as glorious as you expect it to be." . . . Corinne, saying goodbye in her house in Quebec, most exuberantly: "Goodbye, mon cher, my beloved! Three years will pass like a dream, like little yellow birds flying past. Oh, my darling, take care of yourself. . . . Of course I'll be waiting—of course. . . . Another kiss . . . and another. . . . Ah—*must* you go?" . . . The Arabian horses being led out of the stables for auction. . . . A handful of stablemen down from Quebec for the bidding, a few seigneurs of neighboring estates—and Maurice Rastel! Damn him! Why couldn't he have stayed away? Came just to torment Joseph, of course. No, by God, came to buy! Buys Joseph's own saddle horse, Bayard, and a beautiful black mare besides. Pays cash, in livres, old Quebec currency, and rides off on Bayard. . . . Joseph sailing upriver to Montreal at last, away from the Gray Rock of Quebec. Mist on the river. . . . The Fur Kings' banquet, at the Beaver Club in Montreal. Joseph sitting, proud as a prince, between the great Alexander Mackenzie and Duncan M'Dougal. . . . The rafters blue with smoke and loud with song and unsteady in the wind of many potations. . . . The fresh, clear winds of Mackinac, the turtle-backed island, and the snow-and-sapphire seas of Lake Michigan spreading far to the west and south. . . . The madcap voyageurs at Mackinac, red-toqued, red-sashed, saucy, brave, indispensable. Jean Baptiste Clutier coming up and asking to be one of Joseph's crew. . . . "But why, my good man, why do you ask to join *my* bateau?" "Because, *mon cousin*, you're as soft as a baby-otter and you need little-fox Jean Baptiste to look after you!" This had been impudent and amusing, for Joseph towered over Clutier as an elk towers over a rabbit. But Joseph, instead of getting angry, had laughed and delivered so hearty a slap on Clutier's back that it had sent the voyageur sprawling on the sands. But Jean Baptiste had jumped to his feet, laughing too, and the bargain had been sealed. Joseph felt that he had never made a better bargain. The times when "little-fox Jean Baptiste" had helped him, in emergencies and between emergencies, were numberless. Joseph's mind slipped back over a few of these occasions: that time on Laughing Fish River when the canoe had upset and Jean Baptiste had reached shore first and shoved a long birch branch into the water towards the spluttering Joseph; the time when Jean Baptiste had insisted on Joseph's moving the canvas shelter away from the base of the pine tree on the shore of Lake Winnipeg, and the pine tree had fallen squarely across the deserted site during the night; the time when Jean Baptiste had found the trail of the Hudson's Bay trappers and averted trouble in the wilderness. . . .

Other pictures, too, without any people in them at all, swept through Joseph's mind: the autumnal forests of scarlet and unbelievable gold spreading along the Ottawa River like blinding fires; the shadows of the gulls skimming along the shore of Mackinac Island; Lake Superior in November white with breakers as a Polar Sea; the snowy splendor of the Pays d'en Haut; the aurora borealis blazing like a rainbow night after night . . . A beautiful world— something to cling to, if one could. . . . "Goodbye, Joseph, I hope you'll find the Great Adventure as glorious as you expect it to be. . . ."

Joseph roused himself once more and lifted himself a little on his elbows. His eyes reentered from the world of imagination the world of reality. It was quite dark by now, and only a few stars and a fitful half-moon glimmered between drifts of cloud. There was no Aurora. But the snow showed pale, as his eyes reaccustomed themselves to the outer world, and the pine trees ahead made onyx pillars against the less dark slopes. Joseph did not remember having seen before that stubby pine tree just ahead of him, which stood out in such looming blackness. A sudden flick of the moonlight kindled two small fires in the topmost branches—like eyes! A shudder of horror went over Joseph from his constricted heart to his trapped leg. But he did not outwardly move a muscle, agonized though he was on his tensed elbows. He could hear M'Dougal speaking in Freemasons' Hall in Quebec: "Yet there was something there in the night that made our blood creep . . . something monstrous and huge like an oversized wolf-headed bear. . . . Don't let anyone tell you, Lord Dorchester, that those trappers' tales of carcajous and the werewolves aren't true . . ."

If Joseph didn't move—possibly the thing wouldn't notice him. . . . How long would his elbows hold him up? A single motion towards his gun, and the monster would be upon him, before he could aim—a clawing, smothering death. . . . Far better than this death the slow crawling of cold and sleep. . . . Perhaps this might be the Devil come to tempt him before he closed his eyes or to punish him for not praying. Very well . . .

"Notre Père qui es aux cieux, ton nom soit sanctifié; ton règne vienne; ta volonté soit faite sur la terre comme au ciel . . . and' lead us not into temptation, but deliver us from evil . . . for thine is the kingdom, the power . . . et la gloire à jamais . . ."

Peace came to Joseph and with it the recollection of the altar flame that had burned ceaselessly for almost a hundred years in the Convent of the Ursuline Nuns in Quebec, guarded by the black-veiled nuns—the white snow—the white nuns.

Joseph could not remain on his elbows any longer. They caved in and let him down. The monstrous creature took one step forward and was over him. With one unutterable last effort towards life, Joseph reached for the gun. . . . There was a vicious snarl, a scraping of claws on Joseph's shoulders, a mighty jaw opening over his head, a smothering of acrid-smelling fur, then an explosion —and blankness. . . .

●　　●　　●

The moon was riding clear in the pine-tree tops now. A fire seemed to be burning near by. And a small figure was bending over Joseph—much too small for a dream-dwindled werewolf.

"Mon bourgeois! Monsieur Joseph—parlez! Speak! Comment vous portez-vous?"

"Jean Baptiste!"

"Yes, my brother, yes. Are you all right?"

"But how in the world, Jean Baptiste—"

A twinge of pain went over Joseph's leg, yet the leg seemed to be free of the grip of the trap. There were sharp, sore places on his shoulders and under his chin where claws and jaws had viciously scraped. But he was at last blissfully warm, with his coat, apparently, wrapped completely around him.

"In a minute, mon frère, I will tell you. Here, take this crisp little piece of bear meat between your teeth, and you will soon be warm, inside and out."

"Bear meat?"

"Don't ask so many questions, mon frère. Come take it. Open your mouth."

Joseph obeyed, and Jean Baptiste slipped between the parted lips a fragment of bear meat freshly toasted on a stick.

Suddenly, Joseph began to laugh—a ghost of his former hearty laugh, but a ripple enough to shake his body and the air around him.

"Oh, Jean Baptiste, Jean Baptiste! I thought it was the carcajou or the werewolf. And—it was—only a *bear!* What a joke! What a very good joke!"

"Not a joke at all, Monsieur Joseph. It was ze most monstrous ceenamon bear I evair saw in my life! Luckily, when I shot eet, eet rolled away from you or your bones would have been smashed to splinters with ze weight of it. One more second, Monsieur Joseph, and your haid would have been a pudding in ze bear's jaws!"

"Good old Jean Baptiste! How in the *world* did you happen to arrive in the very nick of time?"

"Says I to Jean Baptiste: 'Monsieur Joseph ees in trouble. He needs Jean Baptiste.'"

"No, no, now. Tell me, Jean Baptiste!"

"Well. I was get ze camp ready for ze night only about one mile from here, and down in a snowy valley below me I see someting lumbering along in ze moonlight. Queer time for a bear to be out of ze den, says I. I take my gun and follow. There'll be leetle ones in ze cave. I follow as long what I can, says Jean Baptiste. Bear queecken his pace. I queecken mine. We come almost at ze pine woods, when bear she stop and stand up on ze hind legs. Someting's queer, I say, and I creep up behind. Den I see someting move on ze ground. Tink it's a trapped fox or someting. Better save zat fur. Bear pounce down. I shoot and bullet she go into bear's neck and bear she roll off into snow. Two more shots feenish her. Then I turn to trapped animal. You, Monsieur Joseph! You!"

Jean Baptiste wiped his buckskin cuff suddenly across his eyes. Joseph put out his hand, in spite of the twist of pain in his shoulder.

"I *know* you'll always be right there, Jean Baptiste, when anything's happening to me! I can't thank you enough—I simply can't . . ."

"Queer, n'est-ce pas?" And Jean Baptiste rose, brusquely dismissing sentiment.

"We'll make a beeg try to get back to camp at ze Lake tomorrow. I tink I make sledge for you and pull you in, if ze laig, he do not make too much of hurt. For tonight we all right, n'est-ce pas? You warm enough now?"

"Yes. Oh, yes, Jean Baptiste!"

For the first time, Joseph noticed that Jean Baptiste was wearing only his buckskin shirt and trousers. Joseph looked down at himself. His own blanket coat was under him, and Jean Baptiste's blue capote was over him. It was still twenty below zero.

Chapter IV

ADIEU, LES PAYS HAUTS!

As THE days turned towards the spring of 1798, the hearts of the trappers turned, with all the exuberance of the ice-freed streams, eastward, towards Montreal and Quebec, towards women, whisky, bread, cocks' plumes, red ribbons, and boasting. The long, ice-hard adversities of the wilderness had toughened every body and every spirit. For months there had been cheerful but none too exuberant endurance of deep snows, sprung traps, stale diet, aching backs and monotony. Now, with feet and spirits pointing towards the dawn at last, the old songs came back, the old laughter, the eternal buoyancy of the adventurer! It seemed to Joseph as if his young heart would burst the thongs of his jacket! He let out his voice reverberantly, with the voyageurs:

"Quand le printemps est arrivé,
    Les vents d'avril soufflent dans nos voiles . . .
        When spring has come,
        And the winter pales
        The winds of April ripple our sails!
        With sails unfurled,
        I shall go to my love,
        The loveliest lady in all the world!
        Who sings this song?
        A man who is young,
        A man who is strong,
        A man who is lonely sings this song.
        He sings as he sails along!
        Adieu, tous les sauvages!
        Adieu, les pays hauts!
        Adieu, les grandes misères."

More and more the face of Corinne became confused with the pattern of melting hills and scarlet sunsets and the first hepatica leaves; more and more her dark hair tangled itself in the dark

34

branches; more and more her voice sang like a siren in all the Canadian creeks along the way. Joseph had long ago forgotten every doubtful quality of Corinne and remembered only the strange beauty, the seductive smile, the charm, the wit, the utter fascination of her personality. She was the dark green sea into which he wished to plunge, utterly submerged, utterly forgetful, utterly happy. Joseph quickened his step at all the portages and invariably had to wait for the rest of the company to catch up with him.

"Ah, mon bourgeois! There is a woman at ze end of the road, n'est-ce pas?" asked Jean Baptiste.

"Yes, mon frère, and she is waiting for me, waiting to become my wife! Ah, Jean Baptiste, it's a grand feeling!"

"It's a better feeling, mon bourgeois, to have *all* ze pretty girls, white and brown, on Mackinac Island, waiting for you—and not be bound to any one of zem! If you want to be *really* happy, stay free, mon bourgeois. A sweetheart, she is a dance. A wife, she is a long march!"

"Ah, Jean Baptiste, it's plain to see you haven't met the woman of all women yet. The right woman turns the whole of life into a dance!"

Up Slave River, into the quiet loop of Athabaska Lake, they paddled, up the flooded ponds and streams of the saturated Saskatchewan country, into Lake Winnipeg, where the last snow was melting out like curdled cream, through the Winnipeg River, and into the strangely luminous waters of Lake of the Woods. Toiling along Rainy River and Rainy Lake and Lac La Croix and Basswood Lake and at last, after many a portage, down the eastward-flowing waters of Pigeon River, floated the twelve canoes, the paddles clicking in beautiful rhythm, the air reverberant with the song from sixty throats:

> "J'ai fait faire un beau navire,
> Un navire, un bâtiment.
> L'équipage qui le gouverne
> Sont des filles de quinze ans."

> "I have built a lovely sailboat,
> Oh, to sail upon the sea!
> And a jolly crew I've chosen;
> Maidens fair and fancy-free.

"Come, skip and dance with me!
Come and trip it merrily!

"Maidens fair of fifteen summers,
What a jolly crew they make!
I'm the boatswain hale and hearty,
Whistling while the whitecaps break!"

Into the Great Lakes at last! Through Superior to Sault Ste. Marie and around to the turtle-backed island again! Here M'Dougal learned that young Bailly had a hankering to get back to Quebec. Loath to let so smart a young man go, without signing him to a contract, especially since a seven years' apprenticeship was customary for clerks in the old Northwest Company, M'Dougal offered him the assistant superintendency of the post at Mackinac Island. Joseph was in a quandary. It was a good post, on the edge of the wilderness, but with just enough life passing through it to give him the human pageant he also loved. But how would Corinne fit into a tempest-swept log cabin on Mackinac Island? No mask balls, no festivals, no flirtations! A voyageur's fiddle now and then, an Indian war dance, winds, wolves, woolen dresses, long evenings of two-handed euchre, Corinne yawning and looking out of the corners of her blue-and-yellow eyes towards escape. Joseph had his first qualms since the start of the homeward journey. Would he end up, after all, on the checkerboard? A gentleman farmer, maintaining a decorative wife sufficiently near the city for her to amuse herself?

"Thank you, M'Dougal. But I shall have to consult my wife first."

"Your wife?"

"Yes. I'm to be married as soon as I get back to Quebec. And the lady might not like the island, you know."

"Joseph, my boy," said M'Dougal, looking Joseph straight in the eye and putting a strong and earnest hand on his shoulder, "Joseph, my boy, you've got to face the facts. You can't serve two white mistresses at once. If you take the white wilderness for a mistress, you can't take a white woman for a wife at the same time. It don't work, Joseph. The only flesh-and-blood wife you can take's a squaw. Squaws are the only wives for traders, God damn it! White women are about as useful as silk fans."

Joseph's insides squirmed slightly. To juxtapose Corinne and a squaw in the same set of thoughts was a barbarism. He had seen enough of voyageur-squaw alliances in the wilderness to take them more or less as a matter of course; but their relation to him and Corinne was still as remote as brocaded silk from greasy bearskin. Evidently Joseph's red eyelashes had flicked momentary superciliousness. M'Dougal took his hand from Joseph's shoulder and narrowed his own Scotch-blue eyes.

"You're not in earnest, then, about this life? You're going back to be a damned gentleman?" M'Dougal spat contemptuously.

"I don't know whether I'm going to be a damned gentleman or a damned trader!" answered Joseph, his temper flaring the color of his hair.

M'Dougal laughed. He liked the hot answer. Joseph cooled just as quickly.

"Thank you, M'Dougal, for the offer. But I can't accept it now and I can't ask you to keep the place open for me. I'll know better in a few weeks what lies ahead of me."

"Well, the offer holds. I'll be at Montreal from May to September. Let me know at the Château de Ramezay by August, will you? And remember about fans. I hate 'em. I hate to see you getting tangled up in 'em and blown around by 'em. You're too fine and upstanding a young fellow for that sort o' foolishness. You could make your fortune in the fur trade, with your brains and your body and your pluck. God A'mighty, don't go back and raise pear trees and pale brats back in Quebec. Come back to Mackinac and raise hell and your fortune!"

Joseph laughed at his earnestness, shook his hand, and turned away, sobered by many thoughts.

It was necessary to say goodbye also to Jean Baptiste. Jean Baptiste wore his cheerfulness as debonairly as his red toque, but there was a look in his small, sharp blue eyes that betrayed his feelings as clearly as pools reflect the sky.

"Goodbye, mon bourgeois. Goodbye for a leetle while. You'll be back at Michilimackinac before ze leaves begin to shake down ze gold coins. As soon as ze geese come trooping, back troop ze traders. Parbleu! You can't resist ze call of ze Pays d'en Haut once it gets in ze blood. You be back, Monsieur Joseph! Sacré! Tonnerre!"

"I'm not so sure, Jean Baptiste. Come and see me at Quebec some day!"

"I bet you a prime beaver against a gallon of prime brandy, mon cousin!"

"That I'll be back?"

"Mais oui, certainement! You bet!"

The two shook hands, Jean Baptiste's small, muscular hands crunching Joseph's larger ones with an intensity which would altogether have betrayed him had his eyes not already done so. Joseph went down the wharf and stepped aboard the sailing vessel that was to take him and a few of the men and a consignment of the furs as far as Montreal. When the vessel was finally untied and moved off, there were cheers and *Whoop-la's* and *Au revoir's* and jumping and jigs and the throwing of red toques high in the air by all the voyageurs on shore, the Ottawa Indians standing among them like motionless, disdainful statues. Gradually the shore crowd dispersed, until there was but one figure still waving his toque back and forth, back and forth, in a long red arc of farewell.

"Un bon type—a good fellow, Jean Baptiste," muttered Joseph, as he stopped swinging his three-cornered hat and jammed it back on his head.

It irked Joseph to have to stop off at Montreal, deliver the consignment of furs, and carry certain important messages and reports from M'Dougal to the partners at the Château de Ramezay. He would have been only too glad to remain on the little sailing vessel and proceed down to Quebec. But M'Dougal's errands delayed him for a week. On the last day, before boarding another vessel for Quebec, a small incident disturbed him and put an unaccountable flaw in his joyous embarkation for home, family— and Corinne. He had gone for the last time to the Château de Ramezay to answer a few final questions for the partners (oddly, they seemed to consider his own verbal reports almost as important as M'Dougal's written ones), and to say goodbye.

"My dear Monsieur Bailly, you really must consider that offer of M'Dougal's of the assistant superintendency at Mackinac," Donald M'Kenzie was saying. "We all second it here most heartily. Rastel will be back soon, and he's sure to approve also! You have every qualification. Your reports here indicate—Well, we won't go into all that, for fear of spoiling you. We simply want you to take it."

"Well, why not tell him what makes it doubly interesting?" asked Dubois, one of the few French partners.

Joseph immediately recognized in him the man who had put in a kind word for him with his father at the Mask Ball in Quebec three years before.

"Well," explained M'Kenzie, "it's a post that needs a deal of watching, Bailly. We have a suspicion that somebody is smuggling the furs out of the Arbre Croche region, for instance, and selling them independently before our agents get there. We can't put our fingers on the trouble exactly. It's a task for brains and fearlessness—for a *young* fellow. Old Angus Mackintosh has been on the job too many years to care. He just sits at his tall desk on the island, with a brazier of coals at his feet and a canister of hot toddy at his right elbow, and never does a damn thing except make out beautiful columns of figures. Takes a young fellow like you to get off the island to chase the competitors and smugglers out of the country. Adventure and responsibility—that's what you want, ain't it?"

"Yes, sir. It sounds interesting. But, as I told you, I don't know quite what lies ahead of me. I've got to get home first and see how things stand there."

Joseph had, of course, avoided all mention of Corinne in his allusions to his future, not wishing to run the risk of a repetition of M'Dougal's sort of advice. Dubois took him warmly by the hand and said:

"Monsieur Bailly, permit me to say that I think your good father would at last have approved of the career you've chosen. I hope you *will* decide to stay with us."

"Thank you, Monsieur Dubois. I've never forgotten, believe me, the encouragement you gave me on New Year's Eve three years ago. I love everything connected with the fur trade—but there are many things that I must discuss at home before I embark irrevocably. Mr. M'Dougal told me I might have until August to decide. Will that be satisfactory?"

"Oh, M'Dougal said that, did he?" M'Kenzie put in. "Seems to like you, doan't he? Well, let's say July instead."

"All right, sir. July it is. Goodbye."

"Goodbye."

"Don't you get mixed up with any frills, furbelows, flounces, or foolishness down there at Quebec, will you? No nonsense, young fellow!"

Joseph laughed, but offered no negative promise. He smiled, turned on his heel, walked out of the office and down into the street towards the wharves. As he went, he whistled "A la Claire Fontaine," utterly oblivious of everything:

> Depuis l'aurore du jour je l'attends,
> Celle que j'aime, que mon cœur aime.

> Since the dawn of day I wait
> For my true love, my mate,
> My heart is at the gate,
> For my true love, my fate.

Aboard the schooner *Jenny*, Joseph introduced himself immediately to Captain Job Fish, and began to fill the thirsting spaces in his eager young mind with all the information he could politely request and readily assimilate: how many sailing vessels were plying the lakes and the river at present, how many points of call there were, what were the chief commodities carried, how *much* lumber, how *much* copper from the Lake Superior region, whether an enormous development was to be expected in shipping, whether the lakes would not be even whiter with sails some day, covered as with gulls, how much damage those Great Lakes storms did, whether the losses were too great for the gains, whether there was good money in this business. Would the Americans push up this way, or would it always be a British river with British towns half filled with Frenchmen? What would it look like a hundred years from now?

"My Gawd, young man!" exclaimed Captain Fish, after answering a few of the more practical questions. "Ye have eyes to the future, haven't ye? And ye can ask a whale's bellyful o' questions! Now as fer me, I just sail my ship and asks nary a question, not even of meself. If my ship makes a safe voyage each time, that's all I care. How do I know what this river'll look like in a hundred years? What do I *care?* Not a blasted thing!"

Joseph watched the great woods float by the ship, and pondered the destiny of these shores. Like every Frenchman, he half hoped that some heroic figure of his own race would ultimately arise, as great in his way as Lafayette, and redeliver all this beautiful Canadian country to his own people. Not that the French were not, by this time, outwardly loyal to their British overlords, but simply that the old French fealties and the old French dream of supremacy still lingered. If he himself could be no Lafayette, Joseph hoped that he might at least be so successful a Frenchman that the cause of France would be, in a measure, served.

As he sailed past Verchères on the south bank, his memory took flame from the remembrance of Mademoiselle Marie Madeleine de Verchères, who, a hundred years before, had defended the family fort, "Castle Dangerous," in the absence of her father, with the assistance of a single old sentry and a young boy, against forty furious Iroquois. Now other French families occupied the domains of Verchères in utter tranquillity. Gone were the perilous days. Even the Pays d'en Haut seemed too safe in retrospect. Joseph knew the young man's hunger for arrowed danger, a hunger as lusty as that for red meat. Tranquil, far too tranquil and safe seemed the French ribbon farms that began again at Cap Rouge, near Quebec.

After the northward turn of the river at Sillery, the Great Rock of Quebec stood out suddenly with its fortress beauty. Joseph's heart gave a mighty bound within him. Home!

It seemed hours before the ship was tied up at the wharf. Joseph found himself foolishly looking among the crowds of wharf loungers for an elegant and beautiful feminine figure in a silk dress and a flowered hat. With an abrupt goodbye to the captain, he took up his luggage, called to a bright-eyed boy standing near by on shore, tossed him a coin, told him to take the stuff to Pierre's stable, order a horse for Monsieur Joseph Bailly de Messein to be ready in two hours and wait there at Pierre's for further reward.

Then he bounded off the deck and was away up the steep hill to the Upper Town as if the hill sloped down instead of up! People turned to stare as if he brought an unwelcome whirlwind with him. Such haste in quiet old Quebec!

Joseph brought up at Corinne's door. With hand outstretched toward the door-knocker, he stopped, as if struck by lightning! On the door was nailed a placard: "À Louer—For Rent."

Slowly, with the impact of incredulity, he completed the gesture, pulled the knocker. It resounded emptily.

"She has merely moved into a larger house," he told himself. "I'll find out."

The next house had no knocker. He attacked the door vigorously with his knuckles. A middle-aged woman threw open a casement on the second floor.

"What is it, young man?"

"Pardon me, madame, but could you tell me to what house Mademoiselle—I mean, *Monsieur* de Courcelles and his niece have moved?"

"A long way from here, young man."

"Oh, I'm sure I can walk it easily. I've just finished a walk of four thousand miles. Will you just tell me where?"

"You've just finished a walk of four thousand miles? Merciful heavens, young man! Where have you been? To China?"

"No, just to Great Slave Lake and back. I must admit we paddled it part of the time."

"Great Slave Lake? Nom de Dieu! What kind of slaves do they have there—yellow, black, red, brown, blue—what kind of slaves?"

"No slaves, madame. It's just a name. Nothing but beaver and otter and foxes and ermine and wolves and bear up there."

"Oh, a fur trader, are you? Didn't know it. You looked like a regular gentleman—a Spaniard, I should say. Suppose you're not naturally so dark, are you? Wind and sun and things like that, I suppose?"

Joseph thought of the rapids at Lachine and wondered whether he could ever stem this tide.

"Yes—yes. Yes. Could you now tell me, please, where Mademoiselle"—again he caught himself—"where Monsieur de Courcelles has gone?"

"Ah, young man! Were you caught by that baggage, too? Any woman could have told you she was pretty, *but*—"

Joseph, stiffening, cut off the ensuing adjective with all the coolness he could command.

"I'm not asking you for your opinion; I'm asking you for the location of my—friends—"

"Oh, indeed! Well, they've gone to Montreal!" answered the woman curtly, and shut the casement.

Joseph walked to Pierre's stable as blindly as he had gone that night three years ago when Raoul had told him his father was dying. He tried to respond heartily to all of Pierre's friendly effusions, and he tried to hold all his questions back. Gentlemen didn't question servants and stablekeepers concerning the intimate lives and the whereabouts of ladies. No doubt Pierre knew just when and why Corinne had gone to Montreal. But Joseph preferred to reserve his questions for the precincts of Ste. Anne. All that he wanted to know about his own family was fluently volunteered. Madame his mother was well. His sister had become lady-in-waiting to Lady Dorchester but had returned to Ste. Anne for the month of May. Raoul was with the garrison at Quebec. Mme. Bailly's brother, old Baptiste, was managing the estate and doing quite well with it, "certainly—begging your pardon, sir, as well as your father did with it." No. It was no use hunting up M. Raoul today. On Saturdays he and his friends always went riding off into the country—"goodness knows how far, Lorette, Lake Beauport, or along the Jacques Cartier River"—and never got back till late in the evening, or sometimes even until Sunday. "Better take a horse, Monsieur Joseph, and gallop right out to Ste. Anne." Parbleu! How glad the good Madame Bailly would be to lay eyes on her long-lost son again, though she'd surely mistake him for an Indian or a Spaniard at first. But she never doubted he'd come back. M. Raoul said that, whenever tales of lost trappers and wild savages drifted back from the Pays d'en Haut, Madame always said: "Trust Joseph to come out alive! The Indian hasn't been born, the wild animal let loose, the trap invented, the snowstorm brewed that can kill or maim Joseph! I'm not worrying." And she went around with her head high, like Queen Marie Antoinette, but M. Raoul said she had a strand of white hair now over her forehead, she whose hair had always been black as this mare's coat. . . .

Joseph was aching, almost bursting the silver buttons off his green coat, in his eagerness to ask one question, but the old code of the gentleman still restrained him.

"Thank you, Pierre, for telling me all this. You're a good fellow. I'm glad to see you looking so well and prosperous."

Joseph slipped a generous coin into Pierre's hand, mounted the black mare and was off down the cobbled street. Pierre watched him for some minutes before he reentered his stables.

"A fine gentleman—and a fine *man*. The best of the Bailly lot, and they're all a pretty good lot," murmured Pierre to himself as he went back to his grooming.

Joseph had to ride slowly along the well trampled road that led out from the city. There were at first many of the two-wheeled Norman carts on the road; then the vehicles thinned away. How neat the narrow French farms looked, how precise, how constrained! Could he ever breathe freely, Joseph wondered, in the narrow neatness of Ste. Anne? But how eager, how very eager he was to see his mother!

As he passed under the hill down which the boulder had descended on that summer day three years before, the unwelcome memory of Rastel returned. Would he ever be free of the man and the memory? Why couldn't you eliminate a human wolf as easily as you trapped a furred wolf? He spurred his horse past the spot. More ribbon farms. Norman-roofed houses. Thatched barns. Windmills. White oxen in the fields, yoked in ancient Norman fashion by the horns, the bright blanket paletots of the French inhabitants making color splashes against the newly turned earth. Along the Beauport Heights. Into Montmorency and past Haldimand House, where that affable Duke of Kent whom Joseph so pleasantly remembered at his father's mask ball had spent his leisure hours during his short stay in the province. Then the gorgeous spill of Montmorency Falls! The Indians always heard spirit voices in waterfalls. Ghost waters. Rather unhappy idea! If those waters were inhabited by anything, they were alive with sirens! Joseph laughed with the sheer joy of living as he rode over the bridge above the Falls! On he rode through Ange Gardien and

Château Richer, with Monseigneur de Laval's old bishopric still standing beside the mill with the flapping arms, and through Sault à la Puce and Rivière aux Chiens and at last, at last, at a gallop, into Ste. Anne! Ste. Anne on its green plain beside the St. Lawrence, with the mountain in the background and the old shrine, first put up by grateful storm-saved Breton mariners a hundred and forty years before, rising, chapel-like, in the foreground; Ste. Anne, where the great estate of the Baillys had stretched, in Michel's day, from the river to the hills.

As Joseph approached the turreted homestead, he saw his mother working at one of the rose trellises against the front wall. She turned at the sound of galloping, shaded her eyes for a moment, put down her garden basket, and very calmly walked towards the gate to await the rider's coming.

"Joseph!" she said simply as he dismounted. But the strength of her embrace told the story that her words dared not.

"How well you look, Mother!"

"And you, Joseph, magnificent! How hard and firm you are! How dark! Let me look at you. It hardens the souls of some men, the Pays d'en Haut. I want your soul firm but not hard. Let me look at you."

She looked deep into his eyes and at the corners of his mouth and eyes to discern what hardship had done to him. She was evidently pleased with what she saw.

"Firm but not hard—as I had hoped, Joseph."

Antoinette had run out of the house by now, with a shriek of affectionate rapture, and Uncle Baptiste and the gardeners were hurrying down from the pear orchard. No time now to ask that question. When would it ever get asked and answered?

It was not until late that afternoon, after food and chattering and chattering and food, that Joseph was able to get away alone with his mother. They walked far out to the end of the clôture on the pretext of seeing the pear trees again. Uncle Baptiste had already shown Joseph every inch of ground.

"And what, Mother," asked Joseph at last, "has become of the Courcelles?"

"I was waiting for that question, Joseph. I'm so glad you didn't ask it before."

Her low, restrained tone made Joseph look up from the grass
into her dark eyes.

"Yes, Mother?"

"You see, Joseph, my dear, shortly after you left, Mademoiselle
de Courcelles was married to Monsieur Rastel."

Joseph blinked as if he had been struck.

"It's unbelievable. Rastel was more—like a guardian—than anything else. . . . And he's almost twice her age. . . . And she
promised—"

"Yes. I thought she had. But the promises of a woman like that,
my dear . . . Neither she nor her promises are worth more than
the snap of your little finger."

"Mother! Don't!"

Joseph put his hand across his strangely blinded eyes.

"My dear, you will understand and be glad—oh, *so* glad—some
day! Youth takes things so enormously hard. You never knew
there was a man I thought I loved, before your father, did you,
Joseph?"

"No, I didn't, Mother."

"There was. As handsome as your Corinne is beautiful, and of a
fine old Parisian family. His name was Antoine Lefèvre. He went
off to the Pays d'en Haut, just as you did. He was gone four
years. All that time, Michel Bailly de Messein was courting me, and
word somehow got back to Antoine by the coureurs de bois that I
had married Michel. On his way home, at Michilimackinac, what
do you think Antoine did? In his despair, he married an Ottawa
half-breed woman, and then, without ever coming back to Quebec,
turned south to live at some remote trading post—down at the river
Raisin, I think, below Detroit. I thought I would never be happy
again—that my life was completely ended. Those were dark days,
Joseph, midnight-dark. But at last your father's love began to fill
my life, and I realized where my real happiness lay. I have never
regretted for a single moment, since, the misunderstanding that lost
me my *first* love. Nor will you, Joseph."

"Thank you for telling me the story, Mother. I know what it
has cost you to tell it. You've never told it before, have you?"

"No. I've never told it before. I never needed to. Look, Joseph!
Don't you think these pear trees should be thinned out a little here?"

Baptiste insists that we should not spare a single tree. But I'm quite sure that they're crowding upon each other too much, that the yield would be better from fewer, healthier trees. A little wise use of the ax, a little cutting down of the old growth that the new growth may be better. Don't you agree with me, Joseph?"

"Are you asking me a practical question, Mother, or is this by chance—a horticultural allegory?" asked Joseph, with a faint, reluctant crinkle of humor at the corners of his mouth.

Madame Bailly laughed and put her strong arm through Joseph's.

"Both, my boy—but I *would* like an answer to the straight practical question."

"I agree with you, ma mère. A little wise use of the ax . . ."

Arm in arm they walked back to the house, through the pear-tree aisles, talking of fruit and seeds and wheat, cows and horses and the pigeons on the house ridge—all of which were surface pictures on the deeper river of their thoughts.

Chapter V

RIVER OF GRAPES

A SEA GULL flying west over the shimmering valley of the St. Lawrence and southward towards the silver of the Illinois, the Wabash, and the Mississippi in 1794 would have cast its arrowy shadow over the white house fronts and steep gables of half a dozen little French settlements poised like other gulls on the river banks below the Lakes, hundreds of miles from each other and thousands of miles from the original breeding grounds in France. Across the waters of Lake Erie, the shadow would have drifted, over the sixty house fronts of the flourishing little outpost of Detroit, with its ribbon farms, its pear orchards already half a century old, the fur warehouses, the windmills, the old fort and Father Richard's newly begun little Church of Ste. Anne; then down the shore past the small village of Frenchtown on the Rivière des Raisins (or Raisin River) a depot of the Northwest Fur Company, with its thirty-five French families, and its silence preceding the storm of history; and west over Fort Wayne, loud with the altercations of the fur traders, gay with the fiddles of John Kinzie and Alexis Coquillard and the rhythmic slippers of the dancing French, then down over the "Glorious Gate," the portage and immemorial river way of the Indians and the French, Maumee River, St. Mary's River, Little River, the Wabash River, down over Vincennes, small but already important with its fifty whitewashed houses and picket fences, its gardens and orchards and the famous little rustic fort captured so valiantly for America by George Rogers Clark only seventeen years before. Then across the lower valleys of Illinois, the westward-cruising gull might have passed, weaving its shadow over old Kaskaskia on the Mississippi and Cahokia, swarming with its thousand traders and Indians, and at last to the ultimate western trading post of the French, St. Louis, the busy little river metropolis.

Many a little trading post held by a valiant Frenchman or two and their squaw-wives dotted the wilderness between. But these

48

were the conspicuous white splashes of the French villages on the great green wilderness map. Ceded they might be to Spain and back to France, to England and finally to the United States, to be comprised in the great Northwest Territory; but still they retained their Gallic flavor, their Gallic gayety and color and customs, the quick feet, the quick voices, the quick laughter, the vivacious shoulders off which the practicalities of life slipped as easily as a shrugged-off satin cloak. It was not until the strong and bitter struggle of Yankee against Briton in the War of 1812 that the Anglo-Saxon shadow was to cast itself irremovably upon the land over which the gulls traveled so lightly.

For down the Mississippi, of course, glistened the Mecca for all Frenchmen, the beautiful city of New Orleans, first under French, then under Spanish, now under Anglo-Saxon rule, but under whatever dominion, the Paris of the American continent towards which all French feet turned.

In all of these French settlements dramatic events were occurring, for danger is ever close behind the picket fences of the frontier, and where there is danger there is definite drama. But even where two or three human beings are gathered together behind the barricade of the smallest picket fence, there is always the resurgent possibility of the inner play of the emotions, regardless of the outer play of perilous circumstance.

So it was in the tiny Frenchtown on the river Raisin. A small drama of the emotions was occurring there on the morning of June 7, 1794, the very day of the events of defiance and death in the household of Joseph Bailly.

The three finest houses in Frenchtown belonged to Mr. John Anderson, Monsieur François Navarre, and the family of Monsieur Antoine Lefèvre, Northwest fur trader, recently deceased. On this June morning voices raised in anger issued from the open windows and the upper portion of the horizontally divided front door of the Lefèvre house—the bellowing voice of a man and the shriller one of a woman. Between the outbursts, there were pauses in which lower-pitched feminine tones protested unavailingly. Then a young girl's voice, musical, though racked with emotion, pleading.

Étienne Planchon, fishing for wall-eyed pike (and looking like one) in the river Raisin opposite the house, stood up and poled the boat to a place where he might catch words. Jacques Beaugrand, on the bank, stopped fitting a new handle into the head of a tomahawk and moved in the direction of the fracas. Louis Fréchette, who had just started to drive to Detroit with a dozen baskets of eggs, a crate of cackling geese, and a hamper of cheeses, stopped his Norman cart in front of the house, got out, and began to adjust the already perfectly adjusted reins of his Canadian pony.

At that very moment, the half-door opened and a handsome, loose-gowned, dark-skinned woman stepped out with a cloth bundle in one hand and a girl of about eleven years clinging frenziedly to the other hand.

"But, Maman, Maman, it's my father's house! It's *our* house! I can't go! I won't go!" cried the girl desperately, in a language which was not French but was the soft, voweled speech of the Ottawa Indians. The mother replied:

"It is no longer our house, Marie. It has been defiled—"

At that moment, above the paneled half-door appeared the features of a gaunt, red-faced Frenchman and a gaunt, red-faced Frenchwoman and, in the background, a stoop-shouldered Anglo-Saxon.

"Yes, get out, you filthy squaws!" cried the Frenchman, in his own language. "Get out and stay out! You've no more right here than a pair of bedbugs!"

"It's my father's house! It's my mother's house!" cried the girl, this time in perfect French. "It's *my* house! Oh, I've forgotten the miniature of my father, the one he had made for me in New Orleans! Maman, let me go! Let me go!"

The girl wrenched free and, ducking past her mother, flung herself full force against the door. But the man in front held the doorknob with a firm grip, and the woman seized Marie by the shoulders and held her.

"Oh, no, you don't, girl! No, you don't!"

"Let me in! Let me in! Let me in!"

"I'll take you and throw you into jail if you don't look out! See how you like that!" said the man in the background.

Louder and louder came the shrieks of entreaty. By this time Étienne Planchon was clambering up the bank from his quickly moored boat, Jacques Beaugrand was halfway to the house, and Louis Fréchette was standing as open-mouthed and unabashed as the village idiot in the middle of the road, while his geese, sensing the excitement, were cackling more insanely than ever. John and Deborah Anderson, newly married, were holding hands and listening at their open half-door down the street. Monsieur François Navarre was coming hurriedly out of his house—for once, without the gold-headed cane that he always carried like an overturned scepter, never forgetting that he was sixth in descent from the brother of Henry IV, of the House of Navarre! Antoinette Navarre was scuttering along on her high-heeled red slippers, six of her twelve children following after her, and a group of Indians from their encampment in the maple grove were moving as stolidly as shadows along the cart path towards the house.

"Oh, no, you don't!" The inimical woman at the door gave the young girl a shove which sent her backward down the three log steps to the turf below.

"What's the trouble here?" asked Navarre, coming up and speaking with authority, though he sorely missed the seignorial support of his cane.

The girl had picked herself up and stood with shining welcome for Navarre in her eyes. She was a beautiful child, fortunate in having derived the best from each branch of her mixed ancestry. From her French father and the utterly invisible French half of her mother (who looked wholly Indian) she had taken the pale skin, the narrow features, and the small body of the European; from the Indian half of her mother she had taken the thick braids of straight, black, glossy hair, the heavily marked black eyebrows and the lustrous, deep, gold-brown eyes.

"Monseigneur François! It is my father's brother and his wife just come from Paris to take my father's house from us! They're pushing us out of my father's house!"

M. Navarre made angry sounds in his throat and started to gesticulate with his lively French arms which were confined in too tight a pearl-gray broadcloth coat. But the half-door opened, spewing forth the three unpleasant people, and the man in the background came forward. With a little assertive snort between phrases, he announced.

"Mr. Navarre—ngk—I have charge of this case—ngk. The Lefèvres were wise enough to secure me in Detroit—ngk—to handle their case. This is Mr. Lefèvre's elder brother—ngk. The estate reverts to him by law. There was no will, no paper. Everything is in good order—ngk—"

"Oh, Mr. Hull, I see. You're in charge of the case? But it seems incredible that Monsieur Lefèvre left no papers, no will. No papers were found?" Navarre looked Abijah Hull straight in the eye and then shot a side glance at the brother and his wife. There was an almost imperceptible flash of guilt in each of the six eyes.

"There *was* a paper, Monseigneur François!" cried Marie. "There was a paper! I know my father wanted us to have our house, our furniture, our things! Are we not his only wife, his only child?"

"Where is the document to prove it?" asked Abijah Hull. "Squaw wife, you know. No rights."

"My mother is half French. She isn't a squaw! And you may ask Father Richard if Father Gibault of Vincennes did not bless my father's marriage and sanctify it! Ask him! Ask him!"

"Father Gibault is dead—ngk. No matter what Father Richard might say, there is no *proof*—ngk. But I do not think I need—to argue this case out of court," added Abijah, drawing up his stooped and unportentous body into a semblance of pouter-pigeon dignity.

"I think you are quite right," said Navarre, intending to help reopen the case later. "Come, Marie, there is little that I can do except to offer you a home, until you and your mother can decide upon your future course."

John and Deborah Anderson had joined the group by this time, and together they duplicated Navarre's offer.

"Stay with us, Marie!" urged Deborah. "We have a large house and no children—"

"—yet," supplemented John, looking at Deborah rakishly out of the corner of his eyes. "Yes, do come!"

"Thank you, thank you, John and Deborah Anderson. Thank you, Monseigneur François! But now there is only one thing I want; the little miniature of my father, that he gave to me when he came back from New Orleans three years ago. It's in the house. It's mine—and I want it!"

"She can't have it! She can't have it!" shrieked Marie's aunt. "The property's ours!"

"Wait a minute, my good woman," said Navarre. "How would it be if I bought the picture from you as a gift to Marie, for—let us say, the price of a double eagle?"

"A double eagle? Pouf! Too cheap!" put in Lefèvre. "I couldn't give it up for less than two double eagles. It's the only semblance I have of my dear brother."

Navarre gave the swindler one contemptuous look, then assented.

"Run, Robert," he said to one of his boys, "run to the house and bring me the buckskin coin bag from the top of the inside of the carved chest."

All the time Navarre was planning how he could place this affair in the hands of George McDougall, the only other fellow in the small village of Detroit who yet made any pretensions to a knowledge of the law. He was a smart Scotchman who had recently arrived from Edinburgh and could probably twist Abijah around his little finger.

Meanwhile, no one was noticing Marie's mother, who was standing as stolidly as a mountain, but whose emotions were kindling to the temperature of a volcano.

"Come, Marie," she said, again in the Ottawa language. "Come, don't wait in the midst of these white thieves and murderers."

"I shall come, Maman," answered Marie, in the language of her mother, "when I have the portrait of my father." And she explained to her mother the purchase that Monsieur Navarre was arranging for her.

Two of the Indians moved up to Marie and her mother, and began to speak to them in low tones. At this moment, Robert returned with the coin bag. Navarre took out the two glistening double eagles, and Marie's aunt, snatching the coins like a harpy, disappeared into the house. In a moment she returned with the miniature and flung it at Marie.

"Here you are, squaw," she said. "Can't see for the life of me what use a miniature'll be to you in a tepee!" And she went off into raucous laughter, in which her husband and Abijah joined.

Navarre put an arm about Marie and held her while she broke, sobbing.

"Shall I murder 'em for ye, Marie?" Jacques Beaugrand stepped up and asked fiercely as he flourished his new-handled tomahawk. "No. Oh, no, Jacques!"

Several Indians who had gathered about Marie and her mother cast such glowering glances upon Hull and the two Lefèvres from Paris that their laughter ceased and they slunk back up the steps and slammed the door and shut the upper panel with an echoing bang.

Then the volcanic emotions of Marie's mother broke through her Indian stolidity. With none of the gestures which the white man uses and none of the phrases of execration (the Ottawa Indians know no curses—their maledictions are silent, slow, implacable), she stood on the grass below her old home and uttered with low vehemence words which Marie was never to forget.

"Back I go," said Mme. Lefèvre, "back to my people, back to my bark house, back to Gitche Manitou, the Great Spirit who has punished me for deserting him. The God of the palefaces is a lie, blacker than the eyes of a snake, blacker than the sky of night after the panthers of the lightning have ripped it open with their claws! The God of the palefaces is a cruel god, who breaks his promises to widows and little children. The God of the palefaces is a coward who does not dare bend down and save those who have trusted him, who have burned candles to him, who have kneeled on the ground before him, who have served him like slaves and have loved him with all their hearts. The God of the palefaces is a fool. The God of the palefaces is a devil!

"I turn my back on the God of the Christians and on the Christians themselves. Never again will I set foot in a house made by the palefaces, nor eat paleface food nor wear paleface clothes. Never! Never! Nor will you, Marie Lefèvre. Come with me!"

Taking the ivory rosary with its pendent silver cross that her husband had given her, Madame Lefèvre lifted it over her head, ripped the strings so that the beads scattered in all directions and the crucifix fell at her feet. Then she turned and walked towards the Indian encampment, the other Ottawas following another path towards the encampment, in single file (for the braves never followed the contaminated steps of a squaw).

Marie did not go immediately, but looked up into Navarre's face and said firmly:

"Monseigneur François, those were my mother's words. They are not my words. I love my father. I love the palefaces who are more my people than the Indians. I love the God of the palefaces —and I shall always worship Him. I shall always worship Him, Monseigneur François! And I shall always be a *French* girl, Monseigneur François!"

"Poor child. *Won't* you come and make your home with us?" asked Madame Navarre.

"Or with us, Marie?" again echoed Deborah Anderson.

"Thank you both so much. I must go with my mother, for she is very unhappy, and she needs me. I must go with her, and try to change her again into a good Christian, though I don't think I shall *ever* be able to do it!"

"No, I don't think you will, Marie. An Indian never forgets and never, never forgives, and your mother is far more Indian than French," said Navarre. "But you are more French than Indian, Marie."

"I feel *all French!* Goodbye, Monseigneur François. Goodbye, John and Deborah. I heard the Indians offering to take my mother to some of her relatives at Arbre Croche, and I imagine that that is where we're going. I don't know when I shall see you again. And oh, I thank you, Monseigneur François, for buying for me the picture of my father. I shall pray for you and Madame Antoinette and the dear children every night—and for you, John and Deborah, and for you, Jacques! I shall pray to the God of the Christians, who is *my* God! Goodbye! Goodbye!"

Navarre kissed Marie on both cheeks, and Antoinette and Deborah kissed her full on the lips and John almost shook her hands off. Released, Marie stooped, picked up the silver crucifix, tucked it into her cotton dress, tightened her grip on the miniature, and ran, as fast as a deer, down the road towards the Indian encampment.

Louis Fréchette clucked a French "Giddy-ap" to his Canadian pony.

"Enfant de l'enfer! I wish to the devil there was something I could do to help!" said Jacques Beaugrand to Étienne Planchon as they trudged back to the river Raisin. "That's the damnedest outrage! *Don't you think so?*"

But Etienne's fish-face showed no commiseration. "Haw! Haw!" he burst out with an idiot-laugh. "I was thinkin' how funny Marie looked when that Lefèvre witch pushed her down the steps. Like a goose with its brains dashed out! Haw! Haw!"

"That's what you look like all the time, you idiot!" said Jacques Beaugrand. "Like a goose with its brains dashed out!"

Chapter VI

SERPENT COILS

MARIE had overheard correctly. She and her mother were conveyed by their Indian friends to the Ottawa villages that sprawled along the northeastern shore of Lake Michigan from Little Traverse Bay almost to the Straits of Mackinac. There Mack-a-de-penessy (Chief Andrew J. Blackbird, as he was known to the missionary priests and the French and English traders who passed back and forth along the shore) took the two women temporarily into his household. For Madame Lefèvre was distantly related to him on the French side, the same French trader and the same wilderness-bride having been responsible for the collateral ancestors of both.

Marie suffered relatively little in being transplanted to this particular Indian settlement, for it was a comparatively civilized community, and the aura of the influence of Father Marquette still hovered over the region even after a hundred and twenty years. Old Nee-saw-kee could tell tales of his grandfather's baptism long, long before, at the hands of the good Father Marquette, and the very cross of cedar which Father Marquette had planted on the bluff overlooking the villages of his converts still stood at Cross Village, venerated alike by Indians and by the voyageurs who held their red toques against their breasts and with bent heads murmured a prayer as they paddled past on the sparkling surface of Lake Michigan.

Here at Arbre Croche the Ottawa lived not in tepees but in two-story log buildings, roofed with birch and hemlock-bark shingles. In the spring they planted their gardens of corn and squash and potatoes and pumpkins. In the fall, they harvested their crops, stored them away in ground excavations, took their long white birch bark canoes, packed in their families and their provisions and their cedar-poles and bulrush mats, and paddled down to the southern shores of Lake Michigan, where they trapped for furs along the St. Joseph River, the Grand River, the Muskegon, the

57

Galien, the Calumet, the Kankakee and even as far southwest as the Chicago River, pausing in maple groves along the way for the spring sugar making, and later at the luscious blueberry marshes for the berry gathering and in the Calumet swamps where the medicine men gathered their mandrake roots and their poison-ivy leaves, their deadly sumac, their nightshade and monkshood for the decoctions which they used in their magical rituals, their wars and revenges.

For six years Marie followed these annual migrations, living, to all outward appearances, the life of a typical Ottawa Indian, and in certain portions of her being, inwardly an Indian. Few French people could have merged as completely with the natural scene as Marie or could have loved as passionately as she did the scarlet wings of the sunsets over Lake Michigan, the snowy flight of the sea gulls, the mysterious penciling of the sword grasses on the sands, the Manitou shadows of the pines creeping up the shore in the moonlight, the blue herons stalking through the blue water, the song of the thrushes in the linden trees, the thunder of the passenger pigeons descending into the beech trees. With Marie it was not merely a superficial acceptance of beauty but a merging with beauty as utterly as a being held in the pattern of mortality could merge. She not only could sit for hours with Indian stillness, melting, plantlike, into the scene, so that birds and squirrels and deer approached her, but could become these creatures in the sound of her voice and the magnetism of her summons. She could hide under a low beach juniper and, simulating a wounded gull, call the snowy flocks down out of the sky; she could mock the very mockery of the catbirds and bring these satirists of the woods within hands' reach; she could summon the squirrels into her lap; she could, so the Indians declared, pluck the wild ducks and geese out of the wind or, most wonderful of all, bring the passenger pigeons down in a great iridescent cloud all about her. Whenever the Indians of the Traverse region walked through the woods and found the birds a little more abundant than usual, they always said: "Marie has been here—Marie, the Wing Woman."

But while the Indian portion of Marie merged with all the beautiful scenes and experiences around her that portion of her which was French remained unsubmerged. As she still carried her father's crucifix on her breast and her father's miniature went with her in a waterproof deerskin packet on her long voyages to southern Michigan, so her loyalties remained French and Catholic. While she realized that the God of the Christians and the Great Spirit were closely related, if they were not the same Being, she retained the outward forms of Christian worship and welcomed the infrequent visit of whatever priests might happen to visit this distant territory. For the same fundamental reason, she was unable to entertain the idea of becoming the squaw of an Indian husband.

Neengay Lefèvre had returned completely to the savage condition and the primitive worship of the Ottawa. So far had she turned from the benevolent Christian religion and the ministrations of the priests that she had thrown herself, dark heart and soul, into the strange practices of serpent worship and black magic conducted by certain Ottawa medicine men and especially by Neoma de la Vigne, part French, part East Indian, part American Indian, who brought to this remote wilderness a European knowledge of telepathy, hypnotism, magnetism, electricity, and other phenomena to add to the strange forest knowledge of the medicine men.

In the dusk of a certain April night in 1801, six years after Marie, the Wing Woman, had come to Arbre Croche, she was hurrying rapidly up the slope of the dunes towards her home lodge. It was the rule that every Ottawa girl must be behind the flaps of the tepee or safely in the lodge before nightfall. Marie had been lingering on the shore watching the setting sun stain the waves the color of cardinal flowers and listening to the metallic cry of the sand swallows as they curveted above her head and pounced on the gnats and midges in the darkening air.

Finally she heard, far away over the bluff, the crackling of rifles and the muffled war whoop, beating on the air like the surf against the shore on a windy day; and she knew that the child that Chief Blackbird had been expecting had just been born, and that it was a son. She hurried up the bluff.

As she came into the encampment, the cries of the warriors dancing around Blackbird's lodge grew louder and louder:

"Haig—bey Oba-qua-tae,
Haig—bey Oba-qua-tae,
Za—zahe!"

As they danced, some of the painted Ottawas banged their war clubs against the logs of the lodge, and others again shot off their guns; all whooped and shouted and made as much noise as possible, in order that the child might be brave and strong and mighty. . . . Marie vaguely remembered the stillness of a French house when a French child is born.

She hurried into the lodge, thinking that her mother must still be in attendance upon Running Cloud, Blackbird's wife, but Madame Lefèvre had already returned and was wiping her hands on a piece of deerskin. She looked up, with all the reproof of a civilized mother scrawled across her face.

"You are late, Marie, and it is not well that a young girl should be outside of her lodge when the shadows are gathering. A young girl who must soon take a husband, and who is being watched by all eyes."

"I am sorry, my mother. I was watching the swallows. Is Blackbird's son a very fine boy?"

"Not a big boy, no—rather small, it pierces my heart to say. And he is quite light of skin."

"Well, if noise will make him big, he will be as big as the hill of the Sleeping Bear at Petoskey's village."

"You do not think that the noise is a good noise, a great noise?"

"I am only sure that no such noise was made when my father was born on the quiet and great rock of Quebec."

"Perverse child. Obstinate child. Obstinate as a little dog that barks at She-gog, the skunk. Pitiful as the little butterfly that floats out so proudly over the waves of Michigan and comes back folded and dead. Why will you forever set yourself against the splendid customs of our tribe, handed down from the beginning of the world?"

"I do not set myself against them all, my mother, as you know. I love our strawberry dance and our sweet-water dance in the spring and the green-corn dance in July. I love our journeys over the sea. And I obey almost all the Ottawa precepts, because they so strangely resemble the Christian precepts:

" 'Thou shalt fear the Great Creator, who is the ruler of all things.

" 'Honor the grayhead persons, that thy head may also be like unto theirs.

" 'Thou shalt be brave, and not fear any death . . .' "

Outside, above the murmur of Marie's voice, there still resounded the battering of the war clubs against Blackbird's lodge and the fierce cries:

"Haig—bey Oba-qua-tae,
Haig—bey Oba-qua-tae,
Za—zahe!"

Neengay Lefèvre lifted her voice with purposeful distinctness above the din:

"I'm glad to hear you say you feel the Ottawa blood in you, Marie, for it is time to take to yourself a fine Ottawa husband."

"Never, my mother, never. I have said it before. I shall marry a French husband, if I have to wait a hundred years!"

"Well, Marie, you have not long to wait, then. Neoma de la Vigne, the great Medicine Man, the great De la Vigne, is casting his spells in your direction. You will soon be his wife."

"Not De la Vigne! A thousand times no! Who told you this? Who told you that he is casting his spells?"

"I have seen it. I have seen it with my own eyes. Whenever he goes past our lodge, he throws a fine powder, like pollen, into the air. He is bewitching you, Marie. You can't escape. When you come into his sight, his eyes follow you, like the eyes of a hawk."

"Like the eyes of a snake bewitching a bird."

"Hush, Marie!" Neengay came swiftly and put her hands over Marie's mouth, for Marie had assailed the name of a snake and the mother feared the vengeance of Mas-ka-na-ko, the Snake God whose name had been carelessly uttered.

"De la Vigne is holding one of his magic ceremonies tomorrow at dusk a mile up the shore, near Yellow Thunder's village, and you are to go with me."

"Oh, no, my mother! I have never gone, and I will never go. They are rites of the devil, dances of the devil. It cuts my heart that you should believe in those terrible rituals."

"Tomorrow, Marie, I am to be taken into the order. I ask you to come and see the ceremony. I don't ask you to change your worship. I don't ask you to come again. I only ask you to come this time. . . ."

"Very well, Maman. But I shall hold my crucifix tight, tight, and pray God to save you even at this last terrible moment."

Late the next afternoon, Marie went to the opening in the woods on the bluff at Yellow Thunder's village. An almost circular dancing ground had been made on top of the bluff, years before, by the cutting of a few interfering birch and sassafras and pine trees. The audience of Indians was already gathering, the women in their short blue calico gowns, broadcloth leggings, and moccasins, the men, naked except for the breechclout, hideously painted with green and red stripes and zigzags, and the children absolutely naked. There was only one dressed man in the crowd, a white man. Marie noticed him as she sat down on the grass at the edge of the circular space. He was leaning against a pine tree smoking a pipe with elegant gestures. He had a handsome face, though there was a certain hardness around the lower jaw and a nothing-escapes-me look in the keen, blue eyes. But he had a pleasing smile. There was an aristocratic assurance about the whole figure, and Marie noticed how fine were the hands that made those semicircles in the air as they removed the pipe and lifted it again to the lips. The man's clothes were of the best: brown broadcloth, a white, ruffled shirt and a hat of the glossiest beaver. Marie noticed, out of the corner of her eyes, that as she took her place on the grass fifteen feet away, the beaver hat was removed and held against the breast in the right hand, almost as if in deference to her coming. Her heart skipped a beat. Here *was* a polite Frenchman!

In ten minutes the crowd was all assembled and ready for De la Vigne's performance. Chief Yellow Thunder and his braves and Chief Blackbird had taken their places, standing, across the way from Marie. A booming of the ceremonial drum began now at the edge of the trees. This noise was kept up with insistent, hypnotic rhythm for some ten minutes, until the blood of every one in the group was surging consonantly with it. Marie and the Frenchman in broadcloth seemed to be the only two spectators uninfluenced by the drum's incantation. Marie fingered the rosary about her neck and her father's silver crucifix, and murmured the "Divine Praises":

"Blessed be God,
Blessed be his holy Name . . .
Blessed be the name of Mary, Virgin and Mother . . .
Blessed be God in his angels and in his saints . . ."

From his tree, the Frenchman watched Marie; his lips curled with a delightful intention, and his eyes narrowed with the plotting of the fulfillment of that intention.

For a moment, the drum ceased, and a group of four young Indians with small green and yellow snakes painted over their bodies, their arms, and their legs, rushed in. In their hands were gourd rattles. Around and around the circle they leaped, shaking the rattles and uttering shrill cries. Indian blood curdled at the sound. Then the drums began again. The sky was saffron over the lake. The first dark feathers of dusk were falling under the pines. Then through the trees De la Vigne came sinuously dancing.

De la Vigne had a curiously yellow skin more like the Chinese than the Indian. His hair, instead of being straight, was curled like little black snakes all over his head and crisply about his neck. An odd upslant of the right eyebrow gave a curious expression to that side of his face; but he had a fine, straight nose, expressive, dark eyes, and a slender, muscular, well proportioned body. He was painted with the semblance of a monstrous green and yellow snake down the middle of his body which, splitting into two tails, ran full-length down either leg. Green parrakeet feathers were twisted into the back strands of his hair, and a pair of deer's horns was ingeniously fastened, like devil's horns, over his forehead. In his uplifted left hand, he carried a huge uncoiled copperhead snake which he stroked with a long caressing motion downward from head to tail, as he himself writhed. De la Vigne was followed by six young dancers, decorated with smaller snakes, like the gourd shakers, each holding a live copperhead and each imitating, but less effectively, De la Vigne's hypnotic motions. After these dancers came the neophytes, Neengay Lefèvre and five young women, all naked except for very short green beaded petticoats which swayed as they danced and revealed all that most Ottawa women, since the days of the missionaries, had preferred to hide. Marie impulsively hid her head in her hands and then regretted the gesture, for, when she took her hands away from her eyes, she found that the Frenchman had moved from his tree and had sat down beside her.

"Don't be distressed," he said, in Algonquin.

"I can't help being distressed!" answered Marie in perfect French.

"Mon Dieu, you speak beautiful French!"

"I ought to, monsieur. I *am* French," answered Marie emphatically, "—three-quarters French, anyway. But I don't happen to know who is addressing me," she added, rebuking the stranger with the sophistication of a Montreal belle.

"Pardon, mademoiselle." The stranger rose, bowed with mock-ceremony, took Marie's hand, kissed it, and presented himself. "*I am Monsieur Maurice Rastel, Sieur de Rocheblave—at your service, mademoiselle.*"

"And I, monsieur, am Marie Lefèvre, daughter of Antoine Lefèvre, once fur trader of the Rivière des Raisins."

"Parbleu! I have heard of him. A fine gentleman, they say. And your mother? I never happened to meet her."

"There—over there!—is my mother," answered Marie. "That first woman-dancer." Although she tried to betray no emotion, her voice broke.

"I understand," said Rastel, with apparent sympathy, and he sat down so close to Marie that she could feel the warmth of his body and moved an inch or two away from him.

"You see, monsieur, I am a Catholic. My mother was once a Catholic, too, but something happened—I cannot tell you—and she has taken up—these Indian rites."

"I am sorry, mademoiselle." Again Rastel used that rich, vibrant, throaty tone which always brought Frenchwomen to his feet, and into his arms.

"Thank you, monsieur."

Rastel now attempted to place a hand over Marie's hand. To her own surprise, she allowed the covering hand to remain for one warm instant, before she slipped her own from under it.

The gourd shaking, the yells, and the dancing were now becoming so violent in front of them that Marie and Rastel could no longer converse. They watched the wild rites, Rastel every now and then stealing a glance at the surprisingly beautiful, troubled

face of the French-Indian girl beside him. De la Vigne was twisting like a contortionist, bending body and arms backwards so far
that the snake in his hands almost touched his heels, then straight-
ening up; then bending frontwards and looking between his legs
and up, so that the snake almost touched the back of his neck. The
men followers were also twisting into unbelievable shapes and the
women neophytes were writhing with such wild agony of gesture
and such distorted faces that Marie felt sure that De la Vigne had
bewitched them. The drums boomed. The gourds shook in the
electrified air. The beaten sod resounded. The dancing became
wilder and wilder.

At last the men and the women neophytes began to draw closer
to one another in the wild and weaving tortuousness of the dance.
A frenzy of passionate excitement swept, like fire, over dancers
and spectators. The ancient serpent rites, as old as earth, returned
again on this American plateau, in their symbolization of all the
sinister things of the black ground: abysmal passion, animal birth,
eternal death. All the orgiastic figures that ever passed along the
moving frieze of time took shape again in these mad dancers of the
dunes. The men and the women intertwined, embraced, swayed,
interlocked, leaped up and down and back and forth, now as individuals, now in coupled bodies. De la Vigne and Neengay Lefèvre
often came together.

The spectators sat throbbing, mesmerized. This was like no
other Ottawa dance, in which the men alone usually performed
or the women danced apart, in imitation.

Marie, head down, counted her beads. She felt as if the caval-
cades of the devil were careering over the dunes. When at last
she looked up, a new horror struck her eyes. Her mother, older
than the other women neophytes, was showing signs of exhaustion.
She had left the dancing-embrace of De la Vigne and was swaying alone, her contortions becoming weaker and weaker, her arms
and legs describing smaller and smaller arcs. At last she fell writhing on the grass not twenty feet from Marie, wriggled on her back
and lay there quivering, like a half-crushed snake. Marie rose from
her place, screamed, and tried to push towards her mother. But
there were dozens of Indians packed closely together in front of
her, and the strong hands of Rastel reached out and pulled her back.

"No, no, mademoiselle, no!" he said commandingly. Then, as he pushed her down again: "It's no use. She's been drugged, but she'll be all right. Sit where you are."

A new dread now held Marie to the spot. De la Vigne began to serpentine around and around the open space, making smaller circles each time, with the prostrate figure of Neengay Lafèvre as the center of his convolutions but with Marie at the focus of his eyes. Bending on his knees, then leaping into the air, his eyes gleaming in the last yellow of the twilight, he began to shriek:

"Mas-ka-na-ko, Great Snake Spirit, possess me now! Snake of Birth-out-of-the-Ground, Snake of the Never-Dying, Snake of Eternal-Passion!"

The circles became smaller. De la Vigne ceased shouting, his eyes glittering now on Neengay Lefèvre, his body and his hands weaving such hypnotic circles that even Marie felt herself passing under their spell. At last De la Vigne reached the tormented body of his victim. Now he stood motionless over her, compelling her with his black flame-centered eyes. She in turn looked back at him unwinking, gradually stiffening in every muscle. When the hypnotism was complete, De la Vigne lifted his hands slowly and Neengay rose stiffly to a sitting position, then to a kneeling position, then stood up. As De la Vigne backed towards the dark pine woods, she followed him like a doomed sleepwalker.

Marie shook off the vapor of enchantment, uttered a weak scream and tried to rise. But she must have fainted, for when she recovered her senses she was lying in the woods some three hundred yards away from the dancing ground—with her head in Rastel's lap. Through the haze of dusk and returning consciousness, Rastel's expression looked singularly like the last expression that Marie had seen on De la Vigne's face. But Rastel's words were adroitly, gallantly reassuring:

"I'm so sorry that all this had to happen, my dear. Are you all right now?"

"Yes—but my mother?"

"The rites are over. She is—ah—thoroughly initiated. She has been taken to Yellow Thunder's cabin. She will be perfectly all right very soon."

"You must have carried me here, Monsieur Rastel!" said Marie, getting up.

"Yes, mademoiselle. I am here to help you—and to make you happy."

"I am very grateful, monsieur. You seem to be a good man."

"Thank you—Marie, my dear. May I call you Marie?"

Chapter VII

GOING IN FIRE

ALL the next day Marie Lefèvre's heart was in wild tumult, as if she had been in the very center of one of those terrific storms that sweep over Lake Michigan in September, when the water is lynx-eye green and the sky is a swirl of purple clouds and the gulls scream and turn and retreat upon the blasts like shreds of thistle-down, and the trees are bent eastward and the sword grasses lie, shivering silver, against the dunes.

In the first place, everything in her French and Catholic inheritance revolted against the pagan rites of the serpent worship and the surrender of her own mother to this fearful cult. Then, for the first time, Marie had become aware of the desire of men. On the previous night, that desire had looked out of four eyes, kindled with the singular, burning, bone-penetrating scrutiny that Marie had never fully experienced before. From De la Vigne's eyes she fled like a frightened hare before a forest fire; but Rastel's eyes had something in them almost equally terrifying. Rastel, however, was a Frenchman and a gentleman, and perhaps, she told herself, his look was merely one of intense admiration. Marie made up her mind that the only thing she could do was to escape from the magician into the arms of Rastel, if he should ask her to marry him.

While she was sitting in the doorway of the lodge, sewing porcupine quills on deerskin moccasins and thinking these things, and her mother was busying herself about the lodge in the background, Marie heard the sound of a flute in the pine woods at the edge of the encampment. It meant that some young brave was serenading the girl of his choice, luring her with his music as surely as any bird resorts to serenade for the same purpose. Nearer and nearer came the sound of the flute. A panic thought flashed across Marie's mind. She picked up the moccasins, scattering porcupine quills in all directions, and retreated into the shadows of the house.

"Shut the door, Mother, please!"

"No, we shall shut no door. Sit down in that patch of sunlight in the middle of the floor."

"No, Mother, no. Please don't ask it."

" 'Honor the grayhead persons, that thy head may also be like unto theirs.' "

"Yes, Mother."

Marie sat down in the patch of sunlight, from which she could see everything that happened, if she lifted her head. And she did, in spite of herself, lift her head. But at the same time she began to finger her rosary and whisper:

"O God, I am under his spell. He has bewitched me. The snake and the bird—the snake and the bird . . . 'Ever glorious and blessed Mary, Queen of Virgins, Mother of Mercy, take pity, I beseech thee, on my necessities . . .' "

Into the open ground in front of the lodge came De la Vigne, prancing to the sound of his own flute. Over his head and back were fitted the head and hide of a wolf, the ears of the wolf pricking above the crown of his head, the wolf-tail dragging behind him. But the front of him was completely clothed in the white man's fashion, as a concession to Marie. His red calico shirt was ornamented with brass buttons, such as were used on some of the British officers' uniforms, but fastened differently, in four or five parallel jingling rows. His trousers were of blue military cloth. His belt was of deerskin. The scalps which usually hung from it were noticeably absent. Over his wolf-skin shoulder hung a large pouch containing some heavy things which bumped against his back as he jumped about.

The sound of the red cedar flute was in itself not displeasing. If it had been played by some halfway acceptable lover, Marie might have found herself touched by the plaintive melody, repeated over and over again, like the diminutive, poignant song of the vesper sparrow. But played by such a petitioner, master though he was of the magic of the flute and of all other magic, the instrument struck no chord in Marie except that of fear. When De la Vigne had played for a half hour, he stopped suddenly, leaped with a single bound into the lodge, released the deerskin pouch from his shoulder, and threw it at Marie's feet.

"Open it, Marie!" urged Madame Lefèvre.

Marie shut her eyes and lowered her head.

"Open it, Marie! It is the gift of meat."

Marie lifted her two hands, palm outward, before her face, in the gesture of sending someone away.

De la Vigne straightened up, fury upon his face. This was the gift of meat which every lover gave to his beloved, to prove his prowess as a hunter and a provider. In De la Vigne's packet was buffalo meat which he had recently journeyed two hundred and fifty miles, to Parc aux Vaches (Buffalo Park), to procure. (Slowly the great herds had been moving towards the vast sunlit prairies of the west, and only a very few stragglers were left now around the southern loop of the lake.) De la Vigne had expected Marie to receive it joyously and, with its acceptance, accept him.

Looking like the wolf whose hide he wore, as he stood there in the doorway, his face dark with anger, De la Vigne uttered a single parting threat:

"Look out, Wing Woman. Take care lest I go in fire and you turn to a small white ash, or a cold dead bird. Take care for your life, Wing Woman!"

Neengay Lefèvre flung herself at De la Vigne and with shrieks of terror begged him to take back the threat. For among the Ottawa this "going in fire" was a rite which never failed to wither and destroy one's enemies.

"But I am one of you!" cried Neengay. "I belong to the snakes! You would not destroy a snake's daughter! No! Oh, no!"

But De la Vigne pulled himself away from the Wing Woman's mother, picked up the packet of meat from the floor, and leaped out of the lodge. As Neengay watched, with tears streaming from her eyes, she saw De la Vigne turn suddenly, face the lodge, pick up a handful of dust, and scatter it with a high, scornful gesture into the air. Guessing all too readily the symbolism of the act, Neengay turned, and collapsed on her daughter's shoulder.

"Comfort yourself, my mother. I shall marry the Frenchman, and he will protect me."

"No one, no one in the world, can protect you from the spells of De la Vigne. Oh, my daughter, my daughter, already you are but a handful of dust!"

So all the Ottawa village thought. No one ever survived the spell of "going in fire." The evil-doer who performed the ceremony always let the choice of his victim be known, and the power of the lethal idea shared by the entire community was sufficient to wear down any superstitious Indian spirit, however warlike or stoical, into disease and death. Rarely, if ever, was a woman chosen for these demonstrations. A rejected suitor practiced evil usually upon himself, not upon the object of his love. The warrior Neoma, whose name De la Vigne had adopted, had thrown himself from the Crooked Tree (Arbre Croche) when Wa-wass-ko-na, his beloved, was abducted by Motchi Manitou, and Weosma had committed suicide when he was unable to marry Enewah. But De la Vigne, the sorcerer, was about to practice his arts upon a woman!

All day the Indians surged about Marie's lodge, some with pity, some with potent herbs to help Marie resist the spell, but almost all with condemnation that she had not chosen to accept the wisest and most powerful man among them.

De la Vigne did not wait for several days, as did most goers in fire, in order that the ointments for his body might be prepared and the psychological effect might be slowly and venomously produced. His solutions were at hand, and he counted upon his own powers to produce the desired effects almost immediately. In that strange way in which Indian news passes from mind to mind as effortlessly as pollen traveling on the wind, the news that the great sorcerer, De la Vigne, was to practice his art of going in fire the very next night at the encampment at the Crooked Tree, passed twenty miles down the wigwam-crowded shore from the Straits to Little Traverse Bay and sent the Indians trekking south from Cross Village and north from Wequetonsing on silent, hurrying feet.

The long June twilight of the selected day lingered like prairie fires in the West, and the stars emerged slowly along the Pathway Traveled by Departed Braves, which white men call the Milky Way. At last the darkness lay thick as Indians' hair under the pine trees. On the bluff at Arbre Croche, hundreds of Indians stood silently against the tree trunks or sat along the sides of a great cleared oval space about five hundred feet long which skirted the bluff at one side and the rows of lodges and wigwams and pine trees on the other. There was no hilarity among the Indians, and very little talking. All were deeply superstitious and felt the awesomeness of the impending spectacle. No campfires burned, for the impressiveness of the rite depended upon the surrounding, unbroken depth of night. But a lynx-keen eye might have distinguished in the faint starlight the seminaked Chief Blackbird and his brother Shabanee against adjoining trees and near by, comfortably seated on the ground, the well clothed figure of Maurice Rastel, smoking a pipe. Somewhere in the darkness, near the lodge, sat Neengay Lefèvre, surrounded by consoling relatives, among whom was Running Cloud, already recovered from the birth of her baby. But Marie was not there. She was inside the closed lodge, kneeling before a little shelf on which she had placed the silver crucifix which had belonged to her mother and a pewter dish in which a pine knot instead of a candle burned. This was as close as she could come to the creation of a Catholic altar. Before the small shrine she bowed her head and murmured, with all the fervor she could summon, the Catholic prayers and her own passionate personal prayers to a Deity whose power for good, she felt sure, could outweigh the powers for evil leagued against her.

Outside, the first intimation of the beginning of the ceremony came when Asa Bun, one of De la Vigne's assistants, walked slowly around the edge of the assembly, shaking a medicine gourd, to enforce silence and prepare the minds of the watchers for the mysterious rite. When he came to Rastel, Asa Bun leaned down, took Rastel's pipe from his mouth, shook out the ashes against the gourd and returned the pipe to the astonished Frenchman. Chief Blackbird came forward and explained in a combination of French and Ottawa that there must be no fire except *the* fire. Three times De la Vigne's assistant circled the silent group, shaking the seed-filled gourd and mesmerizing the susceptible Indians with the small, mysterious crepitation of the magic seeds as surely as the East Indian mesmerizes his audience with the insistent rhythm of his flute and the swaying of the spellbound snake. In the still darkness —for even the lake was smooth and soundless tonight—the tiny sound seemed magnified until, up and down the long rows of huddled figures, all hearts shivered in the living gourds of the palpitating Indian bodies. At last, when the nerve-quivering effect had been achieved even upon Rastel—whose cynicism gave way to a reluctant shiver—the vibrating hoot of an owl, that other sound calculated to put an Indian's nerves on edge, broke out under the trees at the south end of the oval.

De la Vigne was obviously appearing with his feathered head-dress in the guise of an owl. Although little could be seen but a dark figure dancing up and down against deeper darkness, every Indian there was able to see, as if with night-penetrating eyes, the red-and-green-striped naked body, the scalps dangling on a thong about the waist, the silver bracelets, the fierce, handsome face, the enkindled eyes, and the owl eyes and ears and feathers surmounting it all.

When the owl sounds had been rhythmically and resonantly and shiveringly given over and over again for some five or six minutes, De la Vigne began in a monotonous, nasal voice which mounted in scale and in fury as he went on, to intone a spell against the Wing Woman:

"As I burn with a swift fire, so she shall burn with the same fire, like the prairie grass in the fall, like a leaf in the flaming forest, like ash in the wind—burning and blown, burning and blown—ashes—ashes—dust—dust—dust . . ."

Three times De la Vigne repeated the incantation. Darkness lay under the pine trees. Darkness, scattered with fine star dust, lay on the cleared space. Darkness lay in the five hundred pairs of brown eyes. Darkness and the small flames of mesmerized expectancy running like underground fire from bedeviled mind to mind.

Then suddenly the dark figure of De la Vigne leaped into action. A hundred and fifty feet it ran, black against the deeper blackness. All at once, the whole body of the sorcerer broke out phosphorescently, then trailing plumes of fire against the night, so brilliant that the bead-eyes of the owl glinted and the silver bracelets and the silver nose ring gleamed and De la Vigne's teeth flashed in a cruel smile as he fled past. Then darkness again. Then, a hundred and fifty feet farther on, again the phosphorescence and the flame! The whole multitude cried out in one great exclamation of horror. Children screamed and hid their faces against their mothers' blankets. Women murmured. Even the warriors groaned.

At the far end of the oval De la Vigne, again dark, paused, repeated the incantation once more, and returned flying on his intermittent wings of fire. The light enkindled him for the fourth time just as he reached Marie's lodge. Before the flames faded away, he checked himself, stooped, and repeated the act which had so horrified Neengay Lefèvre in the morning. Picking up a handful of dust, he threw it with a shriek high into the air, while his body darkened. Another groan went over the assembly.

Inside the lodge, Marie raised her voice in frantic entreaty, for the pine-knot candle had suddenly gone out: "Délivrez-moi, ô Seigneur, de l' homme méchant. . . . Deliver me, O Lord, from the evil man, rescue me from the unjust man. . . . They have sharpened their tongues like a serpent; the venom of asps is under their lips. . . . Keep me, O Lord, from the hand of the sinner. . . . O Lord, overshadow my hand. . . . Thou art my God. . . . hear, hear, O Lord, the voice of my supplication. . . ."

The lodge door was pushed open, and Rastel entered. As he did so, he fastened the thong latch, so that no one else could enter until his business was finished. Surely this moment of high emotion was the one in which to declare his love for the beautiful French-Indian girl and to ask her to become his (temporary) squaw. The business of deerskin bartering with the mother could come later. Only the last red ashes of the pine torch showed where Marie still kneeled, murmuring: "Écoutez, écoutez, O Seigneur . . ."

Rastel crossed the room lightly and laid a vigorous arm around Marie, his fingers pressing, at the end of the semicircle, into her soft breast. Before she could disentangle herself, he lifted her to her feet, his arm still around her, his blue eyes shining even in that faint light, close above her eyes. He made his voice shake with emotion, a trick that always worked wonders with French-women:

"Marie—Marie—my own! I have come to rescue you. You are mine. . . . You shall be my squaw—my wife—"

In spite of the glow in the eyes which seemed struck from the identical fire that burned in De la Vigne's eyes, Marie allowed herself to remain in the encircling arm and to look steadily into a face which was completely French.

"I shall be your wife—like a French wife?" she asked, her gaze searching his.

He turned his head slightly away from her and laughed a little harshly. "Why, yes, my little Wing Woman—surely!"

"To follow you when you go back to the French settlements? To be your wife, not your squaw-for-a-season? Not like Wakona, left behind with her white child—Wakona, straining her eyes for the canoe of Jacques Lacolle who never comes again? Not like Wakona? Look at me, Rastel!"

"Surely, little Wing Woman. To be my wife. I will go away only for short seasons. This will be our home, here, at Arbre Croche."

"I will go with you wherever you go. I wish to go to the French towns."

"We will talk about that later. Very soon I will talk with your mother. It is all very quickly arranged. Tomorrow I shall bring all the necessary furs and beads to your mother, and tomorrow night, my little Marie, you will be my—my *wife*."

Again Rastel tightened his grip around Marie's waist, drew her face to his and covered her lips, her cheeks, with kisses.

Some deep, strange thing within Marie recoiled as much as if De la Vigne himself had been embracing her. Here was her Frenchman at last, her own French husband. Yet something was wrong. She was not happy. She drew away.

"This is wrong—Monsieur Rastel. You must not kiss me—yet. You should not be in my lodge alone with me. Please open the door. My mother will soon be coming."

"Very well, my darling. À demain! Till tomorrow! To-morrow!"

Rastel opened the door and slipped out into the darkness. The Indians were talking in small, excited groups all over the camping ground. Rastel felt prime. The prettiest girl of the Ottawa would soon be his to use for the season. He had no fear of Marie's revengeful relatives whom he would leave behind, for he had almost exhausted this territory and was not likely to return. Rastel was already dreaming of rivers farther south, of the Grand River, of the

Wabash, even of the affluent tributaries of the Mississippi, and of the great golden Mississippi itself. New Orleans beckoned. With Corinne at his side and the fur trade in his pocket, the social and financial conquest of New Orleans would be easy!

There was a sudden twanging sound and a sharp pain in Rastel's left arm. Instantly his right hand went to the place, and found an arrow stuck through his broadcloth sleeve. He made his way swiftly to his own wigwam and in the darkness carefully pulled out the arrow. It had merely grazed his skin, inflicting only a slight wound. As he touched the shaft, he was aware of a piece of birch bark dangling from it. It was a laborious process, with one arm still stinging badly, to light a fire with his flint, steel, and punk; but he did not wish to call in any of his Indian servants. When the fire was at last lighted, he undid the small thong that attached the birch bark to the arrow shaft, and held the piece of bark towards the light. Scrawled across it in red paint were these words, in French:

Leave the Wing Woman alone, or the next arrow will reach your heart.

DE LA VIGNE.

So De la Vigne knew that he had entered Marie's lodge! It would have seemed to require magic indeed to make such a discovery in the utter darkness, especially when De la Vigne, at the time, should have been busy removing the oily solution of putrid bone, the crushed fireflies, and other phosphorescent substances from his body, in the remote sanctity of the medicine man's lodge. Rastel unconsciously rendered the tribute of one shrewd man to another. Possibly he could make use of such a man. But he had no desire to add a scalplock to De la Vigne's interesting collection. How could he compass the seduction of Marie with complete safety to himself? It occurred to him that Marie would soon be going over to Mackinac Island with the other Indian women to barter their bead and quill work. Possibly he could follow, make his arrangements with the mother, and live with Marie on the island for a few days before returning to Quebec. He could send the fur packs that he had collected on Traverse Bay ahead of him down the lakes with his own Indians. He certainly did not wish to stop at Mackinac with his furs, for if the other traders found out that he had made a clean sweep of the Traverse region, they would send boats after his boats, make trouble for him, or even murder him. Yes, a few unencumbered days with Marie on Mackinac Island was the thing!

Rastel washed his wound with half a flask of water and bound it with a cambric handkerchief. Then he threw the piece of birch bark into the fire. As it blackened over the words of the threat, there spurted suddenly into Rastel's mind the memory of that day on the hills above Quebec when the stone he had rolled down on Joseph Bailly for the sake of Corinne had missed its mark. After all, De la Vigne's motives and Rastel's were the same; but Corinne was worth a dozen Indians! As he thought of his final triumph over Bailly and of his pending triumph over De la Vigne, Rastel's fine lips curled back in the flickering firelight for a second, like the lips of a hungry wolf.

Chapter VIII

THE GHOST FADES

JOSEPH BAILLY sat in his office on Mackinac Island, drumming on the desk in front of him. He had had a busy day, supervising the thousand and one details of the fur establishment, interviewing clerks and voyageurs, checking lists of furs, going out frequently to the beating ground to see that the furs were properly whipped free of dirt and moths and lice, sorting the packs, settling the quarrels of hotheaded French Canadians, writing letters to Montreal, to Quebec, to London, to Liverpool, to Marseilles. Yet to keep busy was a good way of forgetting the emptiness of life. Joseph was now, in the early June of 1801, twenty-seven years old, handsomer than ever because of the filling out of his body and the color that three years of the Pays d'en Haut and four years of the gales of Mackinac Island had whipped into his cheeks. He had acquired, too, the self-assurance of the man of business. He was the chief representative of the Northwest Company on Mackinac Island, with a territory covering the Upper Peninsula and most of the Lower Peninsula of Michigan by agreement between the British and the United States Government. As a result of natural energy, resourcefulness and ambition, he now had a comfortable annual income; but he was far from being satisfied. He dreamed of becoming an independent trader and a potentate of a far greater fur kingdom than this.

Then, some day—the cities again, the balls, the festivals, the brocaded vests, and the silken ball gowns! He longed to be free to spend six months of his year in the cities and six months in the wilderness, thus satisfying the swinging poles of his nature.

As he looked out on the white breakers of Lake Huron scurrying towards the island, the picture of Corinne de Courcelles floated like a white ghost riding towards the shore. It was a picture that Joseph feared would always haunt him, for she was the most enchanting woman that he had ever seen, and all her treacheries, all her deceits dissolved in the mere presentment of her beauty. He knew that she was not altogether good nor safe, and that she might have burned away his happiness in the end; but his thoughts were moths to her candle, still.

Jean Baptiste Clutier entered the room. To Jean Baptiste, Joseph had long ago paid the lost wager of a gallon of prime brandy on the basis of his return to the wilderness.

"I believe ze Indians from Arbre Croche, zey coming in, Monsieur Joseph," said Jean Baptiste.

"So? I can't see them."

"Yes, Monsieur Joseph. Come to ze door. Zose leetle white sails to the west. You watch zem now?"

"Look like gulls, don't they? Yes. I guess they *are* sails."

"It's ze women coming over to trade. Some day ze most beautiful woman of zem all will come, ver', ver' beautiful."

Joseph did not even ask a question, but shrugged his shoulders and turned his back to the door.

"You don't believe? Wait and see, monsieur."

Merely out of courtesy to Jean Baptiste, Joseph asked the expected question:

"Who is she, Jean Baptiste?"

"She is Marie Lefèvre."

"Marie Lefèvre?" Joseph only half listened.

"Yes. Much French. Only leetle bit Indian. Her father Antoine Lefèvre, reech fur trader, Rivière des Raisins. Died seex years ago."

"Six years ago? . . . *My* father died six years ago— Hold on! What did you say the name was?"

"Lefèvre—Marie Lefèvre."

Joseph suddenly remembered his mother and the pear orchard —and the story she had told him of her youthful love affair. Surely that was the name—Lefèvre, Antoine Lefèvre. Joseph was, all at once, exceedingly curious about Marie Lefèvre. But he tried to make his voice casual:

"Tell me a bit more about her, Jean Baptiste."

"Well, Marie, she been living with Ottawa mother in Ottawa villages near Arbre Croche, las' seex years. Ottawa call her Wing

Woman because she pull to her all ze birds out of ze sky and all
ze animals out of ze woods. But other tribes call her Lily of ze
Lakes because she ees so white and so ve-ry beautiful."

"Why haven't I seen her before?"

"Because her mother keep her pretty close in lodge, and because,
last summer and summer before zat, zey went south to Ottawa relatives on la Grande Rivière."

"I'm not interested, Jean Baptiste. But thank you for telling me."

Jean Baptiste began to talk of other things and did not refer
again to the sails as they grew larger and larger and finally skimmed
the waves like snowy herons close to shore. The Mackinac Indians and traders ran down to the water's edge, and some plunged
into the water to steady the canoes as they rode in to the beach.
There was great excitement, laughter, talking and shouting. About
twenty boats, with four or five people in each, chiefly squaws with
a few braves thrown in for protection, grounded at last on the wet
pebbles. The little sails were pulled down; the Indians jumped out
and the unloading began.

Jean Baptiste persuaded Joseph that he had better come down
and see that all was well with the Arbre Croche contingent before
dusk settled down. As soon as the two men left Joseph's office
Jean Baptiste, with his keen wilderness eyes, detected Marie
Lefèvre in the group. Her white complexion, which she had never
painted, shone out, an evening star among the sunset faces of
the squaws. Jean Baptiste beguiled Joseph's footsteps slowly towards the Lefèvre canoe.

"Let me help you, Neengay Lefèvre," urged Jean Baptiste in Ottawa when he had come within hearing distance.

"Ah, Jean Baptiste, good evening! Thank you," muttered Neengay.

Marie, lifting out a canvas-wrapped bundle, straightened up and
looked into the face of Joseph Bailly. Joseph's jaw dropped in
amazement, for on the Mackinac beach before him stood a girl so
much more beautiful than Corinne de Courcelles that the memory
of Corinne became suddenly like a crow flying behind a sea gull.
The girl's brown eyes were enormous, filled with an incandescence
which was not sunset light alone but a light from very far within.
Her perfectly shaped face had none of the Mongolian features of

the Indian face but some of its fullness. Her nose was straight and sensitive with narrow nostrils, and her mouth was full and red and smiling. Jet Indian hair swept back in braids from the startlingly white forehead. There was depth in this face—but no mask. Her Indian dress seemed inconsistent with her physical characteristics and bearing.

"This is Madame Neengay Lefèvre—and Marie Lefèvre," said Jean Baptiste with assumed indifferent bluntness. "Monsieur Joseph Bailly—fur-trader."

"Madame Lefèvre," replied Joseph, giving a swift, punctilious look at the mother and a brief bow. "Mademoiselle Lefèvre!"— holding out his hands to Marie and keeping her hands so long within them that Madame Lefèvre's eyes began to burn like coals.

"Won't you both come up to my house for a cup of tea?" asked Joseph. "The evening winds are cool. I'm sure that Jean Baptiste will help you put up your wigwam a little later."

"I think we put it up now, monsieur," replied Madame Lefèvre curtly.

"Come, come, Neengay," urged Jean Baptiste. "Monsieur Bailly will be one of your best purchasers tomorrow. Suppose we bring up a packet of the moccasins right now to Monsieur Bailly's house? What do you say?"

Madame Lefèvre's eyes glinted with cupidity.

"All right."

Jean Baptiste shouldered the packet and took Neengay's elbow to assist her up the beach. This left Joseph to accompany Marie.

"You have never been here before, Mademoiselle Lefèvre?"

"Oh, yes! I've been to the island several times."

"But I have never seen you before."

"I have never seen *you*, monsieur."

"I hope that you will come over often hereafter."

"I doubt it, monsieur. You see, I am to be married and I hope to go away to Quebec. All the arrangements are to be made by the French gentleman with my mother, in the Indian way, but I want to go with him to Quebec to find a priest to marry us in the *right* way, the Catholic way. He wants me to stay at Arbre Croche, but I am sure I can persuade him to take me away to Quebec when he goes in a few days. Do you not think so, monsieur?"

Joseph was astonished at the complete somersault his heart took under his cambric shirt. He felt suddenly as if it had leaped and then stopped dead within him. Why, nom du ciel, did the girl have to look up at him with such appeal in those glorious eyes of hers? Antoine must have been devilish handsome!

"I don't know," he answered mechanically.

"You see, I'm really French, just as much French as Indian—but I feel, oh, so much *more* French than Indian! I shall love Quebec."

"I think you will. It is my home too. My mother is there, and my sister and brother. Your father came from there too. I have heard my mother speak of him—"

"You have, really? How strange!"

"It *is* very strange indeed. Yes, Quebec is a beautiful city!"

"I'm sure it is. I long to see it."

"What is the name of the man you are to marry? I've been away from Quebec for seven years, but I may have heard the name."

"Monsieur Maurice Rastel."

Joseph stood still, his face whitening, his mouth tightening.

Marie looked up in surprise.

"What is the matter, monsieur?"

"Did Rastel say he was going to marry you?"

"Why, yes!"

"Do you love him?"

"I like him very much. He seems to be a good man. Now I do not have to marry the magician, De la Vigne."

"Do you *love* him?"

Marie dropped her glance.

"I don't know, monsieur. I think I do. I am very grateful to him."

"He does not love you, mademoiselle, as he should love you. He already has a wife in Quebec."

"Oh, monsieur! How do you know?"

"Because I know his wife."

"Then he was going to make me his squaw for a little while and desert me—as Jacques Lacolle deserted Wakona? Oh, merciful God! What am I to do? Monsieur Rastel is coming to the island tomorrow."

"You and your mother shall stay at my house. I will deal with Rastel. I know him—and he knows me."

Such a fierce look came into Joseph's eyes that Marie laid her hand on his arm.

"You will not kill him, monsieur?"

"No. I will not kill him. I will let his own ways of doing things kill him some day."

"We must tell my mother and quiet her down if we can. Her anger is terrible sometimes. My Indian friends would tear Monsieur Rastel to pieces, if they knew what he had planned to do to me. We must let him get away, before we tell the other Indians."

"You don't want him torn limb from limb?"

"No. I am a Christian."

"I fear *I* am the Indian in this case!"

At noon of the next day Rastel's canoe grated on the gravel of Mackinac Island beach and his Indian servant, Weosma, helped him out. Rastel went immediately to the Indian encampment. Bailly had left word with all the Indians that Marie was to be found at the white house three doors down from the Nor'west trading depot. He was curious to see whether Rastel would really have the temerity to claim Marie under the Indian law of exchange or whether he would slink away when he was shown up, like the coward that he assuredly was under all his bravado. From Bailly's window, Joseph and Marie and Neengay Lefèvre who, in revenge against a paleface, was at last breaking her vow never to enter a paleface house, watched Rastel land, watched him go to the encampment, watched a squaw point out the white house and saw Rastel swagger confidently up the wharf road towards the middle terrace where Bailly's house stood.

"You open the door, Mademoiselle Lefèvre, and talk to him for a few minutes. Let him say everything he can to incriminate himself. Then I'll come out. I don't promise to restrain myself. . . . And you, Madame Lefèvre," he continued, speaking in Algonquin, "come with me. You must not be seen at all yet. Come!"

"I may not crush his breath out?" asked Madame Lefèvre, making a slowly strangling gesture with both hands, her eyes burning as fiercely as on that day of her first betrayal by a Frenchman, at the Rivière des Raisins six years before.

"No. Come! Please, Madame Lefèvre."

There was a loud, assured knock at the door. Joseph and Madame Lefèvre left the room. Marie opened the door.

"Ah, my *dear!*" and Rastel, bending low, kissed Marie's hand. "Are you alone, my dear?"

Marie hesitated the fraction of a second, for she was unimpeachably honest.

"You see—" she said.

"That is good, my dear. You have taken this little house for us? How charming! I shall be here for a week. I have brought half a pack of beaver, a pail of beads and several beautiful silver ornaments for your mother, my dear; so I am sure she will not hesitate to bestow you upon me. Prime beaver like mine is selling for one English pound per pound weight. Forty pounds! You see how I value you, my dear. I could not find your mother at the beach just now. No one seemed to know where she was. But we can arrange all that later. How beautiful you look, Marie!"

Rastel approached Marie—who had already recoiled—with eyes narrowed, wolflike.

"And now a *real* kiss for your husband, my dear."

Marie thrust him off with both hands.

"I just want to ask you again a most important question," declared Marie.

"Yes, yes, my dear."

"You intend this to be a *real* marriage—with me as your one and only wife, now and forever?"

"What a foolish question, my darling! Come, kiss me."

Rastel seized Marie and kissed her violently upon the mouth.

Instantly Joseph and Madame Lefèvre were in the room, and a strong arm was wrenching Rastel away. Before Rastel could take in the situation, Joseph had pulled two pistols out of Rastel's belt, depriving him of any chance to shoot.

"Oh, *you!* What the devil!" exclaimed Rastel.

"So you were going to deceive the girl? And what about Corinne?"

"Haven't you ever heard of squaw-wives? What is it to you, you damned interloper?"

"It's just this. This is an honorable French Catholic girl who was expecting an honorable marriage. And I'm here to protect her. And what's more, I see now who's been tampering with the trade at Arbre Croche. You're not working for the Nor'westers. You're working for Maurice Rastel! As superintendent of this region, I order you to get off the island. Get off the Straits. Get off the west Michigan coast. If I ever catch you slinking around here again, I'll kill you—and I have a good mind to kill you now!"

"You pompous young fool! What proof have you for these accusations against a partner in the Nor'west Company? Look out for yourself!"

Rastel whipped out his hunting knife and made a quick stab at Joseph, who moved to one side in the nick of time.

"So that's it!" cried Joseph. "All right. Come on!"

Joseph could have used his own hunting knife, but he preferred to wrench Rastel's away and then pommel the life out of him with his fists. By agile dodgings Joseph worked his way into an advantageous position from which he finally ducked down; then, as the knife slanted for the blow, he put his hand up, seized Rastel's wrist, pushed him against the wall, and wrenched the knife out of his hand. Stools, benches, chairs, vases, candlesticks were overturned. Marie and Madame Lefèvre huddled speechless in the inner doorway. The two combatants were near the outer door.

"Now, Rastel!" Joseph gave Rastel a punch on his fine, long nose—something he had always longed to do. Rastel staggered and cried out:

"You backwoodsman! Can't you fight like a gentleman? I'll fight you with swords or foils, as all gentlemen should!"

"You're no gentleman!" cried Joseph. "We'll fight like *men*, with raw fists!"

Joseph stepped back to give Rastel a sporting chance to get ready. Rastel turned suddenly, unlatched the front door, and bolted.

"Oh, no, you don't! I'm not through with you yet!" Joseph leaped after him and caught up with him.

In the street the battle became fiercer still. There was another street at right angles to the main road along the terraced hill, along which the bales of fur were carted down to the wharves. Along this, the fight continued, the two men pommeling, twisting and turning, and moving steadily towards the wharves and the wharf taverns and the shore—Joseph usually the pusher, but Rastel now and then becoming the momentary aggressor.

People came out of their houses and out of the taverns and up from the beach to watch. Jean Baptiste came running from a tavern, and followed the fighting pair, cheering Joseph along with a steady stream of exhortations: "Fight! Fight, Monsieur Joseph! Maudit chien! Heet him! Heet him hard! Good. By gar! Make him ze squashed worm! Make him ze jellyfish! Sacré crapaud! Sacre tonnerre! Good!"

Rastel was becoming more and more breathless and pale, while Joseph seemed to grow redder and stronger, the perspiration pouring out from under his red hair. Rastel now kept barricading himself with his hands, trying to get in a few jabs at Joseph, but Joseph's flailing hands were everywhere.

"Ah, diable! Heet him! Bien! By gar! Good! Good!" shouted Jean Baptiste.

A left jab to Rastel's jaws, a feint and a right cross to Rastel's chest. Rastel trying to cut in under Joseph's quick, strong defense. "It would be different with foils," thought Rastel. "I'd fix him!" But even as he admitted the thought he doubted it, for Joseph seemed as shrewd as he was strong.

"You dog!" muttered Rastel breathlessly, and was able to land a smart, glancing blow at Joseph's chin.

"You carcajou!" said Joseph.

Rastel tried to rouse himself to final aggression but he was a dying wolf. Down, down Joseph backed him straight on to the Nor'wester wharf! As Rastel became aware of the water, he cried out:

"That's enough, Bailly. That's enough! I give up! I kiss—your —hand—my dear—Bailly."

"*I* haven't had enough—not till I knock your handsome face into a pulp, my dear Rastel!"

With that Joseph gave the breathless Rastel an upper cut to the jaw which knocked him flat on the wharf.

"Now!" Joseph gave Rastel a purple nose.

But Rastel was soon up again and trying to maneuver Joseph over the side of the wharf into the water. The two clinched, were close to the edge. They both slipped over.

Joseph clung to the boards with strong fingers and pulled himself back to the wharf. Rastel fell into the water with a plop. Most of the people on the wharf laughed and shrieked and jumped up and down with delight, although a few had been cheering for Rastel. Rastel floated a minute, then feebly stroked himself back towards the nearest pile.

"Weosma! Weosma!" he called to his Indian servant.

Weosma, on the wharf, sidled away, pretending not to hear.

"Weosma! You devil! Five gold eagles if you pull me in!"

"Yi! Yi! Five eagles!" Weosma picked up a coil of boat rope from the wharf, threw one end of it into the water, and fished Rastel in.

"Biggest shark of the year!" muttered Joseph, as he walked away, brushing the dust from his torn ruffled shirt and broadcloth trousers.

"Yes, by gar, biggest shark of year!" echoed Jean Baptiste.

Madame Lefèvre and Marie were waiting for Joseph in his house.

"Oh, Monsieur Joseph, are you hurt?" The question was Marie's.

"No. No. Well, I guess you won't be bothered by *that* suitor any more!"

"You were a great brave, great brave!" declared Madame Lefèvre, her eyes glittering with savage, reminiscent joy.

"I thank you with all my heart," Marie said simply.

She put out her hands to Joseph, who held them between his own. A long look passed between the two young people that needed no translation into language. Then Joseph stooped and kissed Marie's hand. He looked up to see her eyes filled with tears.

"We must go now and leave you to recover," said Marie. "We must go back to the beach. Thank you again for everything you have done."

"*I* shall *never* recover," said Joseph, enigmatically.

Joseph watched Madame Lefèvre and Marie walk slowly down the wharf road to the beach. When they turned towards the Indian encampment and disappeared, Lake Michigan for the first time looked clear and luminous and empty of its haunting ghost. For the life of him, he could not remember the pattern of the face of Corinne de Courcelles.

Chapter IX

WILDERNESS WEDDING

JOSEPH found an extraordinary lot of work to do at Arbre Croche that summer. He left Toussaint Pothier, as clerk, in charge of his desk at Mackinac and Jean Baptiste in charge of the voyageurs, and paddled the forty miles through the Straits and around the northwest shoulder of the Lower Peninsula once or twice every two weeks.

"Monsieur Joseph, he ees mad," shrugged Jean Baptiste to Pothier, "—madly in love. Too bad. Such a good fellow, too! Goodbye, la liberté—goodbye!"

But Joseph was not suffering over the prospect. For the first time in his life, he was completely, gorgeously happy. Marie Lefèvre seemed to supply every need in his nature. Here was a girl of the wilderness as wild and free as himself, yet possessing many of the graces and certainly all of the beauty of a French girl of his own social group in Quebec. Dress her in a ball gown, and Joseph was sure that she would outshine all feminine competitors; even Corinne de Courcelles would look tinsel and tawdry beside her! The better he became acquainted, the greater the variety of surfaces she revealed and the more he admired that blend of native shrewdness, integrity, deep, poetic feeling, quaint humor, surprising naïveté and equally surprising sophistication, physical and moral courage, delicacy, and passion, which made the often inconsistent but always delightful Marie. Joseph was sure that his own mother would heartily approve of her, and for him this was the ultimate seal.

Marie, whose heart had never been completely possessed before, had taken far less time to fall in love with Joseph. The once-burned Joseph went so cautiously that Marie openly avowed her love for him even before Joseph spoke the entangling words.

Joseph and Marie were sitting on a dune terrace at Arbre Croche late one July afternoon. The sun was setting, and the long path

88

on the water ended in scarlet waves that broke with a small song on the shore far below. The sand was taking on that unearthly rose color which lasts, like the Alpenglow, for only a few indescribable moments. Across the luminous background of the sky, a moving frieze of herons passed southward on the way to the wild rookery at Little Traverse Bay. For long moments Joseph and Marie said nothing, absorbed in the outward beauty.

"I suppose you could even call the herons to you if you wished, Marie?" Joseph questioned finally.

"I've never tried, Joseph, but they allowed me to watch their spring love dance once—and not many people have ever been allowed to see so rare and beautiful a thing as that. No other living person I know has seen it—not even Nee-saw-kee, who has lived twice forty years."

"What was the dance like, Marie? Do tell me about it."

"Well, it happened one misty March morning three years ago. I came down at dawn to watch the fog break up over the lake. I was sitting with my knees hunched up, down there among the sword grasses. Thick gray mist was all around me. As I looked towards the lake, I seemed to see darker gray forms moving through the mist, circling, passing, repassing. I strained my eyes to see. Circling, circling, went the figures. As the sun grew stronger and turned the mist to pale gold, I saw it was the herons, Joseph! A dozen of them, moving in two circles in opposite directions, weaving in and out, around and around, the wings half spread, slow, stately, like solemn dancers—so strange, so beautiful. Even when the mist was gone and I could be seen there, so close, they did not flap their wings and go away. They finished their dance—like people, Joseph, bowing, circling. And then—"

"It was the love dance, you say?"

"Yes."

Marie laid her hand on Joseph's knee. The touch set him tingling, even as Corinne's touch had always done. But, remembering the scorched hurt of other times, he did not at once lay his hand over Marie's, nor look at her. He pretended to watch the homeward-flying gulls, as they swooped now and then into the water for an unwary silver-glinting minnow or drifted, on held wings, along the unseen waves of air.

"I love you, Joseph," said Marie, very simply.

Joseph looked into her clear, uncalculating eyes, and drew her to him with all the vigor of his arms, and kissed her with all the slow-gathered strength of his passion.

"Marie, my beloved."

"I'm so happy, Joseph."

"Happy!" shouted Joseph, throwing caution to the winds. "Happy, my Marie! That's a foolish little word! There's no word big enough for the feeling, Marie! No word big enough! It needs a giant of a word! *When* will you marry me?"

"When? Oh, Joseph, when? The priest—"

"It must be a wilderness marriage, Marie. We can have it confirmed by Father Richard, later. Now, Marie, now! Soon!"

"Oh, Joseph, look! The sun is almost down! Hurry! I must be in the lodge before sundown."

They stood up. The sand was deep rose, on the point of fading. The gulls screeched joyously, overhead.

Joseph seized Marie and kissed her again and again. The whole world seemed small, and he a giant, because of his enormous happiness!

"Let me go, Joseph! I love you—but let me go!"

As Joseph released her, Marie ran up the slope, sandpiper-fast. The dune sang beneath her feet. Joseph ran a little less swiftly behind her. Neengay Lefèvre was waiting at the door of the lodge.

"Madame Lefèvre," said Joseph breathlessly, "I want—I want—"

"I know what you want," declared Madame Lefèvre, a little grimly.

"I want to marry Marie—"

"I love him with all my heart, Mother!" announced Marie.

After a pause, Madame Lefèvre spoke.

"I never thought I would give my daughter to a white man. Never! Never! The Great Spirit forgive me—but I cannot help it. I think you are a good man, Joseph Bailly."

Ten days later, an oddly assorted group stood in the little living room of Joseph Bailly's house on Mackinac Island. The sun poured in through the south windows, making bright squares on the rough floor and on the reed-woven Indian mats. It shone on the simple maple chairs, a fine carved walnut sideboard, a brass-handled hair trunk, a French landscape, a magnificent elk's head, and a framed map of Hudson Bay on the wall, and two silver candlesticks on the mantel. It enveloped the guests in its brightness.

They stood, packing the small room, Madame Lefèvre, Madame Laframboise of the island, both in their bright Indian clothes, Joseph Laframboise, the trader of Muskegon Lake, Chief Blackbird and his wife, Running Cloud, several Indian girls from Arbre Croche, friends of Marie, Michael Dousman, Duncan M'Dougal, two Nor'westers in Scotch plaids and skirts, two or three clerks, half a dozen voyageurs, a few of Joseph's Indian servants, and Toussaint Pothier with a fiddle and Jacques Phylier with the drum that he had used in Napoleonic campaigns, in the very hearing of the great general.

When Jean Baptiste Clutier had admitted the last guest, Jacques Phylier gave a low, preliminary rumble on his drum, and then Toussaint Pothier began to play on his fiddle the "Venite Adoremus". It was the only hymn he knew, and Marie had begged Toussaint to be religious. But being a merry fellow, he speeded up the tune so that it sounded far more like a gavotte than a hymn. Marie, in the next room, put her hand to her forehead in despair, and Joseph, standing with his arm around her, gave a French shrug and reassured her with:

"Never mind, chérie, his intentions are of the best. Come, let's go, even if we have to dance into the room!"

Joseph slipped his arm from Marie's waist to her elbow, and together they entered the crowded room. Jean Baptiste cleared a path for them to the mantelpiece, by swinging his red toque from side to side, and there the two young people took their stand.

Joseph was very elegant in a sky-blue broadcloth coat, snowy ruffled shirt and cravat, blue and gold brocaded vest, buff knee breeches, buff stockings, and buckled shoes. His unruly red-gold hair was clubbed back with a blue ribbon. Marie was beautiful in a white deerskin jacket and skirt richly embroidered with colored beads and porcupine quills, a white cambric waist, and white moccasins. Her hair, in deference to her French husband, was brought up from her shoulders and braided in lustrous black coils about her head. Above the shoulders, she might have been the beautiful Lucrezia Crivelli of Leonardo da Vinci's famous painting; below the shoulders she seemed altogether American Indian.

The two young people stood facing each other in front of the mantelpiece, until all echoes of drum and fiddle and whispers had ebbed away. Then Joseph took both of Marie's hands into his hands and, looking straight into her eyes, declared:

"I, Joseph Bailly de Messein, in the invisible presence of God the Father, God the Son, and God the Holy Ghost, and in the visible presence of your mother and of these many friends and witnesses, and in the absence of any officiating priest, but with all due reverence and with full intention of having these simple wilderness rites confirmed by Holy Church as soon as it is possible so to do, do take you, Marie Lefèvre, as my beloved wife."

Marie repeated almost the exact words after Joseph, in a full, clear voice:

"I, Marie Lefèvre, in the invisible presence of God the Father, God the Son, and God the Holy Ghost, and in the visible presence of my mother and of these many friends and witnesses, . . . do take you, Joseph Bailly de Messein, as my dear, beloved husband."

Joseph drew Marie to him and kissed her. Then pandemonium broke loose. Jean Baptiste and the voyageurs cheered and cheered, and threw their toques into the air, and the Indians let out wild whoops. The cheers and whoops were echoed in the small square of grass in front of the house and in the cobbled street, where a hundred more of Joseph's well-wishers had gathered. Then Joseph threw open his front door and presented Madame Bailly to the assembled voyageurs, Indians, clerks, and traders outside. Inside the house, Toussaint Pothier struck up the saucy, romantic tune:

Dans mon chemin j'ai rencontré,	On my way I've met
Rencontré Mime, rencontré Fine,	Jane and Joan and Jean;
Rencontré Jacque-Jacqueline,	I've seen Jacqueline,
Tra la la la la la la la,	Tra la la la la la la la,
Rencontré Germinette,	On my road I've met
Celle qui vend des chopinettes,	Lisette and Germinette,
J'ai rencontré ma reine,	And Anne and Antoinette,
Celle qui mon cœur aime!	On the road I've met
	The loveliest lady yet,
	The mistress of my heart,
	My dearest and my queen!

Toussaint fiddled, and Phylier beat his drum, and everyone who knew the song—which meant all except the Indians—sang it at the top of his voice! The voyageurs, at the same time, began to dance round and round, and down the steps and into the yard; finally the dance caught infectiously, and all the crowd began to twirl in swinging, singing couples!

As new mistress of the house, Marie directed Joseph's Indian servants in the distribution of the wedding refreshments: French croquignoles and baskets of fruit, and glass on glass of wine, white and red and gold. Gayer and gayer became the crowd. Louder and louder screeched the fiddle and boomed the drum. Phylier was remembering his great days under Napoleon. Only the year before, he had been wounded in the shoulder, at the battle of Marengo. His wielding of the left drumstick was never quite so vigorous as his gay tattoos with the right, for just that reason. For the fiftieth time, the voyageurs were chaffing poor Phylier about that wound. They were swarming around him now.

"Say, Phylier, how did you get that wound?" cried Réaume Rouleaux.

"I tell you! I tell you! Joost as I shall say, 'Vive mon Général! Vive Napoléon! I receive a ball!"

"And what did you say, then, Phylier?"

"I shall say joost ze same, all ze time, wot I been say before: 'Vive mon Général! Vive Napoléon!' Great man, Napoléon! He be king some day! He be emperor of ze world!"

"Listen to him! Listen to him! He doesn't know that France is a Republic!"

"He be King! He be Emperor! Vive Napoléon!"

"No, Phylier! No, no! Not today! Today it's Joseph Bailly, Seigneur of the Great Lakes. Vive Joseph Bailly! Vive Joseph Bailly! Vive Marie Bailly, Lily of the Lakes!"

The cry was taken up and carried out to the cobbled street and down to the wharves and all over the singing island.

"Vive Joseph Bailly, Seigneur of the Great Lakes! Vive Marie Bailly, the Lily of the Lakes!"

It was only the red sun setting through the Straits of Mackinac and the quick dusk at last that stilled the shouts and the songs and muffled Phylier's drum and muted Toussaint's fiddle.

Chapter X

MESDAMES BAILLY

"QUEBEC, my Marie! Quebec!"

The fur barge rounded Cap Rouge, the voyageurs rested in their poling and their maneuvers with the sails long enough to swing their toques for joy, and Joseph stretched out his hand towards the lofty town that he loved. Marie, on a bale of beaver in the stern of the boat, exclaimed:

"It's beautiful, Joseph! It's taller than you are, Joseph! It's beautiful, but it frightens me."

"Frightens you?"

"So many houses, Joseph. So many windows, like eyes staring down."

"The eyes will love you, Marie—and so will my mother!"

Joseph could hardly wait to show Marie to his mother. And Marie could hardly wait to see her husband's mother and his home and to have their wilderness marriage confirmed by a priest. A month before, they had said their vows as solemnly as any frontier settlement could demand. But with all her Catholic soul Marie longed for the priest's confirmation.

In half an hour the boat was tied up at the Nor'wester wharf, and Joseph and Marie stepped on shore—Joseph in his blue broadcloth coat and buff trousers and Mackinac boots; Marie in her typical Ottawa costume of blue waist, red petticoat, embroidered apron, moccasins, and beads, her hair in two long braids again, the only un-Indian garment she wore being a blue broadcloth cape scalloped with cream-colored braid, which Joseph had bought for her on a merchant vessel from Montreal. Marie was arresting not only for the brightness of her clothes but for her beauty and the whiteness of her skin.

Joseph had given directions to Jean Baptiste Clutier about the boat and the luggage and had just taken Marie's arm to conduct her to the Upper Town when he became aware of individuals in the little group at the wharf, first among them Pierre of the livery stable, who immediately stepped forward and asked:

"A cariole, Monsieur Joseph? Or a horse?"

"Not just now, Pierre. Good to see you! I'll walk to the Upper Town, and stretch my legs a bit. But prepare three horses for us for the journey to Ste. Anne this afternoon."

"Yes, Monsieur Joseph."

Joseph did not care to present the new Madame Bailly to Pierre here. That might come later, if necessary, when they went to obtain their horses. Joseph became aware of the first onset of embarrassment. "My wife. This is my wife. Let me introduce my wife." If an eyebrow went up so much as a millimeter, Joseph was sure he would reach for his hunting knife, which he still carried under his fashionable belt, and shave those taunting eyebrows off clean! For the first time he realized that Marie was overbrightly dressed, like a sauvagesse. He must get her some new clothes at Quebec, clothes like those of the lady with the green parasol. The parasol shielded the lady's face, but there was something vaguely disturbing about that long green silk dress and the green, very pointed slipper that just showed, like a poised humming bird, beyond the ruffle of the dress. Joseph clutched Marie's arm so tight that she looked up at him quickly and seemed to guess the confusion in his mind.

"Joseph! Ah-h-h, Joseph Bailly!" came in the most musical tones directly at him from under the green parasol.

Joseph stopped. The green parasol lifted, and Corinne extended a green-mitted hand to him.

"Madame Rastel! A pleasure!" And Joseph, in the most courtly manner, bent over the green-mitted hand (which he found to be scented with a delicate, lilac perfume) and kissed the protruding fingertips.

"For how long, mon cher ami, are you to be in town?" asked Corinne. "Long enough to take a cup of tea or a sip of cordial with me? Maurice is out of town, alas!"

"Thank you for inviting us," answered Joseph, pointedly using the plural. "But we're here for only the shortest possible time. We are on our way out to my mother's at Ste. Anne de Beaupré."

"How charming! Taking the prettiest possible Indian maid-servant from the upcountry to your mother, I see! Ah, Joseph!"

Joseph flushed red to the roots of his red hair. Marie, at Joseph's use of the name Rastel, had turned pale.

"I have the honor," said Joseph, in a voice that shook with poorly suppressed anger, "of taking Madame Joseph Bailly de Messein to meet Madame Michel Bailly de Messein."

"My *dear* Joseph, may I congratulate you? I *beg* your pardon," rejoined Corinne, effusively, extending her hand to Marie. "I did not know of Joseph's *great* happiness. Will you translate this into Algonquin for her, Joseph?"

In her most exquisite and careful French, Marie replied:

"The pardon is granted, Madame Rastel. Nor did I know of Monsieur Rastel's 'great happiness' two months ago, when he asked me to marry him at Arbre Croche. May I congratulate *you?*"

Both Joseph and Corinne flashed a look of astonishment at Marie. For a moment Joseph could not tell whether Marie had made the remark innocently or intentionally; the thrust was so unlike her. Her face was absolutely impassive. But Joseph delightedly guessed at a new defensive depth in her which he had not suspected. She was a match even for a woman of the world! Corinne bit her lip, gave her parasol a nervous twitch, got herself under control, and lied valiantly:

"There is more than one trader who masquerades under my husband's name, so enviable is his power. My husband happened to be at Montreal two months ago."

"How fortunate!" pursued Marie. "For my husband set his seal on the one who was at Arbre Croche two months ago, a purple seal on the fine, long nose, a purple seal on the blue eyes. I am so glad it was not your husband, madame."

"*My* husband's influence is of the mind, not the fists. He can be a powerful friend and a powerful enemy—and I can be even more friendly or more unsparing, Joseph, than Maurice!" declared Corinne, ignoring Marie and piercing Joseph with her flame-colored eyes.

"I have no doubt of it, madame," replied Joseph.

"Perhaps I can make your trading troubles easier for you if you will come up and discuss them with me over a glass of *cordial*, Joseph. *Cordial* relations are possibly what you need."

"Possibly on our way back from Ste. Anne, madame. Not today. We have several errands in the town. Thank you."

"Very well. Remember that cordial is good for the health." Then, in an intimate whisper, "I *do* congratulate you on your wife. She is even brighter than her clothes!"

As Corinne shot a jade look at Joseph from under her parasol, he bowed low, and Marie noted a second deep flush on his cheeks, deeper than any mere bending at the waist should induce. Corinne turned and walked quickly away along Chemin St. André.

Marie took Joseph's arm, and the two walked a little way, in silence, towards Mountain Street and the Upper Town. Then, very quietly, Marie said:

"You loved her once, Joseph. It is like mandrake poison. It is still in your blood."

Joseph felt pierced in a vital spot by the deadly combination of his wife's feminine intuition and her Indian intuition. He hesitated for some time before he spoke.

"I am not sure, Marie, that you could ever have called it love. I was bewitched; but I am no longer under her spell."

"She is also bewitched by you, Joseph. She is only pretending to hate you. She wants you to love her."

"She wants all men to love her."

"She is dangerous, Joseph. And with Rastel! They are a deadly combination—*unless they destroy each other!*"

"I know they're dangerous. I've known it for a long time."

"You've disposed of him, but I'm not sure that you've disposed of her."

"Perhaps not."

"We must be very careful. Do you think we *should* go to her house? Or perhaps you should go alone, Joseph. If you think best, I am willing for you to go alone and pretend to—to—to be *cordial*, Joseph—"

"Marie, my Marie! You're an unusual woman. Yes, very unusual. You gave me a wonderful start when you mentioned Rastel's 'proposal' to you! That was very shrewd indeed. It was the sort of thing that women in the world of cities say."

"Have you never thought, Joseph, that women of the wilderness may not be so very different from women of—what you say?—women of the world? Open up the breast of an Indian woman of Arbre Croche and open the breast of a white woman of Quebec—and the heart is the same, and the quick words of the heart are the same. I am a little sorry now that I said what I said. I shall ask Mary, the gentle-spoken Mother of our Lord, to forgive me. It was a savage thing I said."

"It was a splendid thing you said. I'm proud of you for saying it. Mary was a woman, too. I'm sure she'd understand. She'd say: 'Go to it, Marie! Go to it!' "

"Joseph, Joseph! How disrespectful you are! You're only a tiny bit Catholic, I'm afraid. I must talk to your mother about it."

"I'm just Catholic enough to slip past St. Peter. He'll slap me on the back and say: 'Joseph! You meant well! And you had a saint for a wife! Come in!' "

Joseph's laugh echoed against the graystone house fronts. The habitants in their blue blouses and the townspeople in their long coats turned and looked at the hearty, handsome visitor and his exotic wife.

"Shall we go to the priest first or the cloth merchant? Dresses for our souls, or for our bodies first? I know what you'll say, my little Marie."

"The priest, please, Joseph. Oh, Joseph, listen! How lovely!"

It was midday, and the bells in all the spires and towers in town had begun to ring—pontifical bells in the Bishop's palace, sea-deep bells in the Cathedral, quick bells in the monastery of the Recollect Friars, bells as faint as sheep bells in the convent of the Ursuline Nuns on Palace Hill.

"Yes, I knew you'd like this town, Marie. Many windows, yes. But many singing towers. There is music of some kind or other in this town all the time: music of the organ, chanting of the nuns or the friars, altar bells, the sound of the big bells overhead, the laughter of French fiddles, gay songs, and solemn songs. Quebec is made of stone and song."

"That is like *you*, Joseph. *You* are made of stone and song, I think."

"God bless you! Look, Marie, over there is the Convent of the Ursuline Nuns. Did you know that an altar flame has been burning there every minute for over a hundred years? It was lighted by Marie Madeline de Repentigny when she became a nun there, after her fiancé died. Beautiful to think of that light guarded by the black-veiled nuns night and day. I've often been aware of it. Many a time I thought of it in the Pays d' en Haut."

"Yes, very beautiful, Joseph. Very beautiful. But I'm glad *I'm* not a nun!" Marie gripped Joseph's arm hard.

"*I'm* glad you're not a nun too!" asserted Joseph loudly, to the amusement of several French Canadians, who heard the indirectly amorous remark and repeated it over their brandy several hours later.

It was not long before the travelers came abreast of Freemasons' Hall. Joseph tried hard to forget the New Year's Ball of seven years before, but it beat, with all its pageantry, against his brain.

It took time to find the priest. Joseph had been sufficiently far-sighted to bring all the data concerning his own and Marie's baptism and confirmation, and the little paper signed at Mackinac at the time of the exchange of their marriage vows. Father Martin was well acquainted with Joseph's devout mother and, after looking over the documents, arranged to perform the desired ceremony upon the young couple's return from Ste. Anne in a week or ten days.

Joseph then took Marie gayly down Mountain Street to the British cloth merchant in the Lower Town, and selected a bolt of yellow silk and a bolt of green broadcloth which his mother and Marie might fashion into a dancing dress and a riding habit. There was a French shop across the street which displayed the new drooping bonnets from Paris, fastened with enormous bows of satin ribbon, and a few smaller riding hats, trimmed with ostrich plumes. Joseph and Marie enjoyed much laughter as the bonnets were tried on over Marie's coal-black braids.

"Monsieur. Pardon my suggesting it, but would it not be better for the young lady to loop up her hair on top of her head, if she is to wear one of these hats?" asked the milliner.

"Yes. Yes, I suppose so."

"Comme ça?"

"Yes. Yes."

"You see, she looks almost French now."

"I *am* French, monsieur. I look what I *am!*"

"Yes, madame," agreed the milliner, with deference, catching the emphasis both of the reproof and of Marie's personality.

Drawing her cloak tight about her and fastening its braided loops across the front, to conceal the Indian dress underneath, and cocking her green ostrich-feather hat with a saucy air, Marie did indeed look French (with a difference—a dash of an exotic difference which gave her added charm).

"Ah, voilà, monsieur!" exclaimed the milliner. " C'est une Marquise enfin!" Then he added: "All she needs now, monsieur, is a pair of dancing slippers!"

"Oh, *red* slippers!" cried Marie. "Like Madame François Navarre's!"

"Red dancing slippers it shall be," declared Joseph, "if we have to look all over the continent of North America for them!"

Joseph did hunt all over the Lower Town for them; but when he finally found them they proved to be much too small for the free, wide-soled, moccasined feet of Marie. In spite of himself, Joseph's mind flashed a picture of those hummingbird feet of Corinne's!

"I'm afraid I'm not a lady after all, Joseph. Not even as much of a lady as Antoinette Navarre, who never let her red slippers off her feet, no matter how much they hurt her! They were her symbol of elegance, like the chief's eagle feather—"

"Or the cavalier's sword! You *are* a lady—after my own heart, Marie!" averred Joseph gallantly. "And we'll have a pair of red slippers *made* for you!"

He gave orders, then, to the best shoemaker in Quebec to have a pair of red slippers of the right size ready for Marie in ten days, and left the man shrugging his French shrug, the shrug which says, "C'est impossible," and holding his hands palm upward in the gesture of futility protesting against fate.

It was time now for a bite at a tavern and the ride out to Ste. Anne. The two travelers refreshed themselves with a venison pasty and a glass of white wine at Antoine's "Sign of the Lilies of France," attracting much attention as they sat there, for Joseph was still as good-looking as any man in Quebec, and Marie quite the most beautiful Indian girl that these French Canadians had ever seen, if indeed she were Indian with that pale face and those delicate features.

"But look at the hair, mon cousin," they whispered to one another. "Blue-black Indian hair, sans doute."

"But her face like a pearl—"

"Half-breed, doubtless. But what a beauty!"

It was early afternoon when they met Jean Baptiste at Pierre's stable. Pierre knew nothing this time of the whereabouts of Joseph's brother and sister, had seen neither of them for a long time. Joseph presented Marie to Pierre, who was properly respectful, and whose eyes bulged over Marie's loveliness.

When Joseph and Marie and Jean Baptiste started on their journey to Ste. Anne, Marie took off her cloak and tied her bonnet to the saddle, then rode free as an Indian, cross-saddle, as she had always ridden. Her black braids and her ribbons flew straight out behind her, as she swept down the road.

As they came within view of the many-gabled, white farmhouse and the pleasant fields and orchards of the restored Bailly de Messein estate, Marie slowed down her horse and leaned across towards Joseph.

"Joseph, would you like me now to put on my cloak and my French bonnet?"

"No, my darling! My mother will love you just as you are!"

"But your brother and your sister?"

"I don't know whether they're at home. If they are, you can dress up for them later, à la Parisienne. But you shall come home just as you are, and be loved for yourself, Marie!"

As they rode towards the house, Joseph caught sight of his mother standing at the open door. She came out of the house, shaded her eyes with her hands, then moved quickly towards the picket gate. Her face was more radiant than Joseph had ever seen it.

"My son!" was all she said, as Joseph walked into her arms.

When Marie jumped from her horse, Madame Bailly took her by both hands, looked searchingly into her face, then drew her close, and said, simply:

"My daughter!"

Then, releasing her, Joseph's Mother looked again into her face. The memories of over thirty years before sprang up in Madame Bailly's heart.

"Yes. You do look like him—like your father," she said. "The same deep eyes that hold the earth and the sky—and what is beyond the sky. You are very beautiful, my child. But you are good too. Goodness is in your eyes. I am well pleased. I am happy for Joseph's sake."

"Thank you, Madame Mother. I shall try to be good for Joseph's sake, and for your sake. Joseph is as easy-going as a sea gull, and as strong as a red-shouldered hawk. I love him very much. He is as my father was, strong and good. Is it not strange that you—you knew my father?"

"Yes. It is very strange."

"And yet I am glad that Joseph is not my brother."

Madame Bailly gave Marie the same kind of quick look that Corinne had given her a few hours before, for the same reason—the subtlety of her simplicity.

"And this, Mother," announced Joseph, bringing up Jean Baptiste, who had ridden deferentially in the rear and had just arrived, "this is my very faithful comrade Jean Baptiste Clutier, who saved me from the bear's clutches up at Great Slave Lake."

"Jean Baptiste, I'm glad to meet you face to face. I've blessed you in my thoughts many times for what you've done for my son. Thank you, Jean Baptiste, and may God keep you from all harm."

Jean Baptiste stood, embarrassed, his head bent, his toque crunched in his hands, and was only able to stammer:

"M-m-m-madame—"

Madame Bailly, realizing that Jean Baptiste's forte lay in deeds, not words, smiled and briskly changed the subject.

"Well, children, come into the house. You're just in time for supper. I'll have Nicolette beat up an extra omelette for you and open a bottle of Burgundy to celebrate. Uncle Baptiste is the only one at home. Raoul has gone off down-river to camp with his company and Antoinette is visiting Cécile Marteau at Montreal. But they'll both be here in a few days, and then won't we have a celebration! Joseph, are you yet married by a priest?"

"Not yet, Mother. But Father Martin will perform the ceremony for us at Quebec next week."

"Then I'll give you separate rooms, Joseph."

Joseph laughed till the house rang, and pinched his mother's cheek.

"Don't you know what a wilderness marriage is, ma mère? It's a *real* marriage! How a few priestly mumblings and rumblings can make it a better marriage, I don't see, by St. George!"

"Joseph! Joseph!" remonstrated the two women, looking at him with eyes in which reproach ill concealed their separate adorations.

It was only when the four of them went out into the pear orchard after supper, Uncle Baptiste taking Marie by the arm with a great show of elderly gallantry and Joseph walking with his mother, that Madame Bailly put the question:

"Joseph, how *did* you do it?"

"Do what, Mother?"

"Find the one wife in all the world for you?"

"Thank you for saying it, Mother. I'm *so* happy, if she pleases you."

"She pleases me enormously. She is good, wise, beautiful—and devoted. The fine old Parisian part of her will understand the French of you; the Indian will understand that wilderness part of you—which you and I alone in all the family possess. She is perfect for you Joseph. And she is Antoine's daughter . . ."

"Do you remember, ma mère, what we were talking about when we walked under these same pear trees the last time?"

"Yes, Joseph, I remember."

"You were right, Mother. I saw Corinne in Quebec this morning, and I was thankful that I hadn't married her. But she is still fascinating . . ."

"She has you still a little under her spell, Joseph?"

"Perhaps. I don't know what it is about her. I've known all along what she was really like—beautiful and dangerous as a cat. But you simply can't forget her. She's there in the deepest woods sometimes, far away in the upcountry, or down in the oak openings at Parc aux Vaches or in the pines along the lakes—there like a green-eyed lynx, paddling along, pursuing, pursuing."

"You'll shake off that vision now that you're married, Joseph. She may be the toast of Quebec, as Raoul says she is. She may be the champagne at all the banquets. But you couldn't live on champagne, Joseph. For a steady diet, red wine is best."

" 'Red Indian' wine, ma mère, 'red Indian' wine!" And Joseph laughed his hearty assent!

Chapter XI

AT THE PLACE OF BUFFALOES

THERE was excitement at the Place of Buffaloes. So few pale-face travelers ever found their way along the old Sauk Trail that the coming of a white man was still a major event. To be sure, the traders, Joseph Bailly and John Kinzie and Antoine Le Claire and old Bertrand from two miles up the river, and William Burnett from twenty-five miles down at the outlet of the St. Joseph River into Lake Michigan, and Alexander Robinson and Joseph Chandonnais passed to and fro, but they had become accustomed figures to all the Indians. Here were different men. American soldiers, sixty-seven of them, in all their glory of blue uniforms, gold buttons, gold braid and aiguillettes, who had arrived today, July 25, 1803, under the command of handsome young Lieutenant Swearingen, and had set up camp by the river.

The Indians had already begun to crowd around the cabin of Joseph Bailly, where Marie Bailly had been serving a supper of roast deer and Indian corn cakes dipped in maple syrup to several of the travelers and to John Kinzie and his wife. The news of the soldiers' arrival had spread, Indian-fashion, faster than prairie fire.

Chief Topenebee, or Quiet Sitting Bear, had been the first to arrive from his village across the river. He was sober, but doubtless expected something to allay his sobriety. His subchiefs, Leopold Pokagon, Weesaw, and Shavehead, arrived shortly from their different up-river encampments: Pokagon of the huge aquiline nose, the vast dignity and the fine intelligence which were to yield him leadership for fifty years; Weesaw, the son-in-law of Topenebee, orientally dramatic and majestic, with the scarlet turban, the scarlet sash, the silver rings in ears and nose, the monstrous silver amulet on his breast, his leggings tinkling with silver bells; and Shavehead, with the mere ferocity of his expression for ornament, disporting only one tuft of hair on his head, the stiff, up-

104

right scalplock tied with a thong, while the scalplocks of his enemies dangled from his rawhide belt. (It was said that he carried the tongues of ninety-nine white men on a string beneath his belt!) At the heels of the chiefs, came the throng of young braves, curious squaws, and papooses.

Down at the grove encampment, Joseph's voyageurs were already making friends with the soldiers by means of broken English, gestures, and whisky.

Joseph came to his door and, inviting Topenebee and the three subchiefs to come in, handed out a large package of plug tobacco and a pan of white man's bread, which the Indians adored, to be divided among all those for whom there was no room in the cabin.

Joseph presented the chiefs to Lieutenant Swearingen and Surgeon William Smith and Sergeant Louis Pettle with all the dignity which he could command. He feared that the light-hearted Americans might take these forest chiefs a trifle casually unless he set the keynote of dignity. Two of the travelers had made considerable sport at dinner of the frontier life, the damned Indians, and the helluva fix they were getting into themselves, coming out to the wilderness where they'd have Injuns for friends and coyotes for dancing partners! The Lieutenant's disapproving eyebrows and boot kicks under the table had been insufficient to stop the flow of merriment, induced more by Joseph's stock of French brandy than by the soldiers' realization of their distance from the nearest white settlement at Fort Wayne. The Lieutenant had guessed that, in spite of Marie's white skin and French features and linsey-woolsey dress, she must be a half-breed. Those jet-black braids and the fathomless brown eyes betrayed her. Besides, these French Canadian men were all "squaw men." Kinzie, the Scotchman, seemed to have married an American, but not Bailly. But what a beauty the girl was! So Swearingen had kicked his men under the table, and they had gone on laughing at Indians. Marie had quietly continued her waiting upon table, though a scarlet flush on each cheek showed how the blood must be racing underneath.

Now, with this group of wildly colored Indian chiefs in the house, there was still greater need for curbed tongues. Fortunately, the surgeon was growing sleepy-lidded from excess of brandy; but

Louis Pettle was still alert, with a curl of laughter lurking around his lips. He even refused to extend a hand to the chiefs until Swearingen said sharply in his ear: "Shake hands, Sergeant Pettle!" He shook hands then, and gave Weesaw a playful tap on his silver nose ring and Shavehead a jocose pull on his highly prized scalp belt. The two chiefs looked at each other and then at Pettle as if they would instantly have set about skinning him alive. Shavehead's hand even moved instinctively to his tomahawk. Then Joseph said something to Shavehead and Weesaw in Algonquin and the two sat down on a buffalo-robe-covered bench near by, while Pokagon and Topenebee took their places in the walnut chairs which Bailly indicated to them. Marie poured very small glasses of brandy for the chiefs. She knew Topenebee's weakness too well to pour liberally.

Then, in English, Joseph began to direct the conversation, interpreting now and then in Algonquin, in order that his guests (none of whom, with the exception of the keen-witted Pokagon, knew subtleties beyond traders' English) might understand. It was an additionally delicate situation, for the reason that, however friendly these Potawatomi chiefs might be, they must inevitably feel this invasion by sixty-seven white men as symbolical of yet greater invasions to come.

"It is an interesting undertaking, my brothers," said Joseph, addressing the chiefs, "on which our American friends are setting out, an undertaking which will bring great benefits to us all. We are all eighty miles from the protection of an American fort here and two hundred miles from the great trading and military post of Detroit. Our friends are sent here into the wilderness to build a fort on the piece of land that General Anthony Wayne purchased from you eight years ago at the mouth of the River Checagou."

"Me there! Me there, Greenville!" proclaimed Topenebee, drawing himself up proudly so that the silver medal on his breast flashed out an extra ray or two in the candlelight.

"Yes," said Joseph, expanding the idea to satisfy the chief's vanity, "Chief Topenebee was present at the making of the Treaty of Greenville and set his mark on the document. You are responsible, then, Chief Topenebee, for the building of this splendid new fort in the wilderness!" (Another sop to his vanity, thought Joseph.)

"Me, me and Great Wind Anthony Wayne," continued Tope-nebee, warming with brandy and vanity and puffing out his brown chest like a fighting pheasant: "*Me! Me and Anthony Wayne!*"

Louis Pettle gave a snort that wakened the surgeon from his after-dinner nap. Louis too was getting drunk.

"God! What was that?" exclaimed the surgeon, sitting upright.

"A bad dream!" flashed Joseph, quickly.

"He laugh at me?" inquired Topenebee, narrowing his char-coal eyes.

Again Joseph made some answer in Algonquin, which seemed to placate the chief. Marie and John Kinzie, who understood, smiled a bit. Joseph had said that the man's stomach was sick, that there was an evil spirit jumping up and down inside it—and that he had meant no harm.

"You call Fort, Fort Topenebee?" persisted the chief.

"No, the Great Father at Washington has ordered us to call it Fort Dearborn," explained Lieutenant Swearingen.

"Deer? Deer-born? Not so many deer born there now. Jean Baptiste Point du Sable, Ouilmette, Alexander Robinson, many, many white traders they kill, kill, kill almost all the deer. Buffalo gone too."

"Dearborn is a man."

"A man? A chief?"

"Yes. A war chief."

"Great war chief as—Topenebee?"

"No, not so great as Topenebee."

"Then why they call him Fort Dearborn?"

Pokagon answered the question in dignified, almost perfect English:

"Because the Great Father at Washington orders it, Chief Tope-nebee. Dearborn is the Great War Secretary, or war chief of the Americans. . . . It will be different, very different now," contin-ued Pokagon, turning towards the tableful of palefaces. "Not so long ago, we used to lead our warriors around the bend of Lake Michigan to hunt the buffalo. No more thunder of buffalo now!

Only the hoofs of the waves pounding up the beach at Che-ca-gou!"

"He says Che-ca-gou as if he were spitting it!" remarked Pettle.

"He *is* spitting it!" corroborated Bailly. "That's the Indian pronunciation. Checagou means Ill Smelling Place—ugh!—Place of the Wild Onion, or Place of the Skunk."

"Skunktown! Listen to that, boys! By Gad, we're going to live in *Skunktown!*" roared Pettle.

"I for one am glad I'm going to live at Checagou," declared Kinzie, glowering at Pettle, "though I'll miss the Baillys like hell! Beg pardon, ladies. It'll be a damned good post. Plenty of passing to and fro there now, plenty of trade, plenty of life! Jean Baptiste Chandonnais is going too."

"You go too?" asked Topenebee of Joseph.

"No. I'm staying here, Chief Topenebee. This is a good place. But I'm glad of the fort. It's a great step forward for all of us."

"Are you really glad to go to Checagou, Elinor?" asked Marie of Mrs. Kinzie.

"Oh, I've had so many adventures, Marie, that one more adventure is just a perfectly natural part of my life. I'll miss you good people very much indeed. But you'll be riding over to Checagou very often, I'm sure. It's only a hundred miles away. That isn't very far."

"It'll be very exciting, won't it," remarked Marie, "with all those soldiers? They'll be bringing their wives out later, won't they?"

"Oh, yes!" answered Swearingen. "Major Whistler, you know, is on the schooner *Tracy* right now, with his wife and fourteen children. Young Lieutenant Whistler is bringing his fifteen-year-old bride, Julia Fearson, along from Detroit. The bride's a beauty, though not half the beauty her sister-in-law Sarah Whistler is. *There's* a girl for you! And that girl *you* left behind you in Detroit, Pettle, that Irish queen! Not half bad! A wonder! I'll bet you'll be bringing her along one of these days, eh?"

"To Skunktown? Dublin Castle isn't good enough for her!"

"Well, other wives will be coming along soon enough, after we get the fort built," asserted Swearingen.

"How exciting it all is!" exclaimed Marie.

"Dear Marie, what a quiet life you've lived!" put in Elinor. "All this doesn't seem exciting to me at all . . ."

"Mrs. Kinzie was taken in an Indian raid near Fort Pitt, as a child," explained Kinzie to Lieutenant Swearingen. "She was brought up with the Senecas. Later she was released and married Dan McKillip, of Butler's Rangers. Then Dan was killed in the Battle of Fallen Timbers, and Elinor went into Detroit to live, where I found her. Quite a bit of territory and experience, she's covered, you see."

"Yes, I see," agreed Swearingen, looking at Elinor Kinzie with new interest. (Yet no one in the room realized to what adventure, far more exciting than anything she had yet encountered, Elinor was now going out with her second husband, nor how half the people there in Joseph's cabin were to be swept into the very centre of the coming cyclone of circumstance.)

"Taken by the Senecas, eh?" asked Louis Pettle, drunkenly. "Treat you well?"

Elinor shied away from the subject visibly, but replied:

"Oh, yes, yes indeed! I was adopted as a sister by Chief Cornplanter."

"Sister?" asked Pettle, with an insinuation of which, had he been sober, he would never have been guilty.

Kinzie got up so suddenly from the table that his chair crashed backwards. His fist was doubled for a blow, but Shavehead, coveting his own vengeance, had risen at the same instant, and stopped the blow with his left hand while he reached for his tomahawk again with his right. He had not understood the insult, but he had read Kinzie's gesture perfectly.

"Me do it," cried Shavehead, and lifted his tomahawk, the candlelight flashing along its cutting edge.

Joseph rose instantly and seized Shavehead's tomahawk hand, holding it stiffly and talking rapidly again in Algonquin until the flames in Shavehead's eyes subsided and he was ready to lower his arms.

"Wilderness life," muttered the Surgeon sleepily.

"Pettle didn't mean anything, Mr. Kinzie," defended Swearingen. "He's a fine fellow, really. Only a bit of a bad actor when he's had too much drink. Shake hands, Pettle."

"Yes, sir. Sorry, Kinzie. See you in Che—in Skunktown!"

"Well, Mr. Bailly, we thank you kindly for your hospitality," said Swearingen, rising and giving a stiff little military bow.

"I'm glad to have had you here, Lieutenant. Our cabin is always open to travelers on the trail. Come again. And I'll be riding in to see you one of these days, when your fort is up. Sure you can't spend the night here with us?"

"No, sir. Tents are already up, down by the river. Thank you just the same."

"You leave in the morning?"

"Yes. Thanks to your supply of boats, our baggage will be off down the river at dawn, and the rest of us will be taking the trail to the lake soon after. How long do you make it to the lake exactly?"

"About thirty-five miles. It's a well worn trail: Indians, traders, La Salle, Joliet, Marquette, Father Allouez, Father Hennepin, Charlevoix—"

"Good Lord, man! Do you read books out here on the frontier?"

"Couldn't get along without them. Send to Montreal and Quebec for them. But then, the legends still live out here, you know. The Indians still tell stories about all those fellows, especially about Père Marquette, and the Grand Seigneur, La Salle—stories handed down from hundred-year-old squaws to little grandsons. Why, we know an old Indian, Nee-saw-kee, up at Arbre Croche, whose grandfather was actually baptized by Father Marquette—"

"You don't say?" That far-away look of diffidence had come into Swearingen's eyes.

"Well, good night," said Joseph again, putting out his strong hand.

It was a little over a year later, the autumn of 1804, at the Place of Buffaloes. The midday sunlight filtered down in long shafts through the red oak leaves to the yellowing grass below. The oaks grew in solitary clusters with smooth parklike intervals between, in that majestic, ordered fashion which had given to so much of the country along the St. Joseph and the Kalamazoo rivers the name of the Oak Openings. Here, in these open spaces the buffalo had recently browsed on the luscious, river-dampened grass. The buffalo wallows were still warm, and Indian children still played with buffalo skulls at Parc aux Vaches. Here an occasional elk still found its antlered way. Here the deer still browsed abundantly.

Down by the St. Joseph River, the smooth grass gave way to a riot of grapevines, and now, in this autumn season, to the full fire of twenty varieties of goldenrod and the varied purple of ironweed, blazing star, asters and vervain. Here and there, the fireweed lifted its torches, and the Indian pink, or "painted cup," that fades before the settler's ax, still blazed magnificently.

In an "opening" some four hundred feet back from the river, the autumn light fell upon two large cabins, a few bark wigwams and several small log structures. All these buildings now belonged to Joseph Bailly, for Joseph had bought Kinzie's cabin, his blacksmith shed, his storage sheds and his voyageurs' camping grounds. Joseph Bailly was now the ostensible "seigneur" of Parc aux Vaches but in reality of a far greater territory, with his fur-trading lines spread out, like a spider's web, in all directions over the southern Michigan Territory and the whole of sparsely exploited Indiana Territory as far south as Vincennes. His dream of becoming an independent trader had been realized. He still bought some of his supplies of the Nor'westers; but his license was his own, his profits and his developments were his own. On the north, his domain stopped at the Manistee River, to which point the Nor'westers operated thoroughly. On the west, the Chicago region and Wisconsin, with its great trading post at Green Bay were thoroughly covered by rival companies and traders. But Joseph had pushed his men to remote tributary streams in middle and southern Michigan, off the main trade routes, and south through the prairies and forests of Indiana Territory to the very waters of the Ohio, gathering up furs in unexpected places, giving gifts of good quality and establishing friendly relations through his French tact, his perfect use of the Indian dialects, and his strong, courageous personality. In three short years, through his gift for management, through a beaverlike capacity for work, through Marie's assistance in making valuable Indian connections, and through the good will of the Ottawa of Arbre Croche and their Potawatomi allies of southern Michigan Territory, Joseph had built up a business which already ran into thousands of pounds annually.

In the spring, when the voyageurs returned from the trapping grounds or the Indian posts, and in the earlier fall when they set out, Parc aux Vaches was alive with color, sound, and excitement. Usually Joseph set out with a group of voyageurs in the fall, or went with Jean Baptiste and one or two other chosen men to open up new markets with fresh groups of Indians. This fall, Joseph was lingering, for Marie was expecting her first baby.

In the Bailly cabin, Marie had just swung the huge soup kettle over the hearth fire for the midday meal, and Joseph was oiling his guns for a hunting expedition with Jean Baptiste.

"Oh, Joseph, Joseph!" exclaimed Marie, stirring the fire again under the kettle. "I can hardly *wait* to see a white woman again, in our cabin! We've seen them at the little post of Checagou, of course, but not a white woman has been *here* since Elinor Kinzie left. Oh, *when* do you think they'll be here?"

"My little Marie, do you realize that you've asked that question precisely twenty times since breakfast?"

"Really, Joseph? How accurate you are in all your accounts! Martens, 344 at 75 cents apiece; beaver, 300 at one eagle per pound; raccoon, 200 at two quarter-dollars per pound—wife, twenty questions per hour! Joseph, do you *count kisses?*"

Joseph crossed the cabin floor and delivered a number of the commodity in question.

"Did you count them, Marie?"

"N-n-n-no, Joseph. You almost sm-m-mothered me!"

"Are you going to ask that question again?"

"N-n-n-no, Joseph—but I *want* to know!"

"You little minx! If I knew the answer, I'd tell you. But I should say the Abbotts ought to put in an appearance today or tomorrow. Mr. Abbott went through here six days ago. He was traveling at such a clip in his eagerness to meet his bride that he probably reached Checagou in about two days. They'll travel more slowly on the return trip, no doubt, to make it easy for the new Mrs. Abbott."

"Oh, what a couple they'll be: she so beautiful and he so fine with his great gold watch and his great ruby ring! But I think he's rather stern, Joseph, don't you? They'll live like lords and ladies in Detroit, won't they?"

"Yes, they will. Next to our old friend Joseph Campeau, he's the richest man in Detroit, as I told you. Tell me, Marie, my darling. Is that the way you'd like to live—like lords and ladies, I mean?"

"Oh, no, Joseph. I'm perfectly happy! Our house here, and our visits now and then to Checagou and Fort Wayne and Detroit. You've been good to take me with you so many times. I love the forts and the towns, but by and by they smother me, Joseph, just as you tried to smother me a little while ago! I'm always so glad, so very glad to come back here, where I can breathe and sit very still just like a stone, and listen to the river and the passenger pigeons thundering by and the, oh, so lovely song of the brown thrush and the, oh, so funny gobbling of the wild turkeys! And, oh, Joseph, the flowers here! Even at Arbre Croche, the flowers weren't so lovely. . . ."

"I'm glad you love it all, Marie. So do I. But I think I like the cities a little more than you do!"

"Yes, Joseph. Do you remember how you bought me at Quebec those high-heeled red slippers like Madame Navarre's? And, oh, Joseph, how I suffered in them at that dance at Fort Dearborn! I was in agony! And still I had to smile and smile! How good the moccasins felt afterwards! That is like me! I feel so very French sometimes, like Papa, red slippers and gold rings and all! And then—pouf!—moccasins, and I am just an Ottawa girl again from Arbre Croche. Listen! . . . What is that?"

"I didn't hear anything."

"No. You never hear until five minutes *after* I do! That is because you are *all* French. Joseph! Don't you hear it now? It is some one giving the 'call of approach.' And it is a white man, not an Indian. A white man's voice always sounds so hollow, like a reed. Why, Joseph, it *must* be the Abbotts!"

"Of course it's the Abbotts! Hurrah!"

They both rushed to the door. The few Indians left behind by the fall trapping expeditions had also heard the call, and Jean Baptiste had risen from beside the kettle of soup that swung from a tripod in front of his cabin, and was striding rapidly towards the trail.

In a few minutes the Abbotts rode in, followed by an Indian leading a pair of pack horses. Abbott got off his horse a little heavily, for rich living in Detroit had already given him, at twenty-eight, the full figure and round face which were to be his always. The fashions of our great-grandfathers had also added to his apparent age and dignity, for he wore whiskers up to the line of his ears. His eyes were blue, his hair tawny, and his expression, as Marie had indicated, was usually stern, his lips compressed in the manner of one who gives frequent and precise orders and expects them to be rigorously obeyed. Sarah Whistler Abbott, daughter of Captain Whistler of Fort Dearborn, was a genuine beauty, as Lieutenant Swearingen had declared at the Bailly house the year before. She was only eighteen, with hair as black as Marie's but curling, with eyes as blue as Lake Michigan on an August day, and with cheeks as red as partridgeberries. A deep dimple in her chin and a constant upcurve of mouth added to her general attractiveness and made a complete contrast with her straight-lipped young husband.

Abbott helped his wife ceremoniously from her horse, while Marie made haste to greet her guest.

"Oh, Madame Abbott! Madame Abbott! I'm so glad to see you! I'm *so* glad to see you!" And Marie threw her arms enthusiastically around her guest.

"And I'm so glad to see *you*, dear Mrs. Bailly!"

Sarah Abbott wore a long riding habit of brown broadcloth, with amber buttons down the front, and her hat was a small-brimmed perky brown felt upturned with a brown ostrich feather. Mr. Abbott had brought the outfit with him from Detroit. It was the most attractive costume that this oldest daughter among fourteen children of a United States Army captain had ever owned. She was riding out to wealth, and she knew it. Yet no luxurious prerogative could turn her sensible head.

Jean Baptiste Clutier took the Indian guide to the best tethering place for the horses, while the Abbotts followed the Baillys into their cabin, and Marie, with the apologies characteristic of hostesses of all races and times, set before her guests pewter plates of delicious venison broth, Ottawa tamales, St. Joseph River pickerel, wild salad, and pewter cups filled with Joseph's best Madeira.

"To the bride and groom!" toasted Joseph, and the occasion was celebrated in the wilderness cabin with as much enthusiasm and savor as if a valet with powdered wig had been standing behind every chair.

"To the Baillys!" replied Abbott, with raised cup. If he had been French, he would have added, "To this generation and the next!" For he had not failed to observe Marie's promising condition. Toasts ended, Bailly asked:

"And how did the ceremony go off?"

"Well. Very well. John Kinzie, as Justice of the Peace, had all the dignity of a minister of the gospel—"

"And, oh, James, do tell about the two fifers!" interrupted Sarah, relating the story herself. "One of the fifes had been lost. So the two fifers at the Fort alternated on the one fife, while one of the drummers drummed on a real drum and the other on a rawhide stretched over a barrel, Indian-fashion. If it hadn't been so solemn, it would really have been very funny, especially the way those fifers snatched the fife out of each other's hands and puffed and tootled and puffed and tootled! They *all* took it *so* seriously, as if it had been a funeral! And the music was so *excruciatingly* bad! But it wasn't half as bad as the Indian powwow afterward. James had to treat to whisky, of course, and all the Indians along the Checagou River were howling at the tops of their voices when we left. I hope there weren't any murders—"

"I hope not," assented Joseph rather solemnly, for he knew a good deal about Indian firewater murders.

"And everyone's well at the Fort?"

"Oh, yes, though we all have the ague now and then, till the pickets rattle and the flagpole does a jig! The boys all love it there, wolf- and fox-hunting, fishing, trapping, skating and racing. But I sometimes wonder about Mother and the other women in the fort, the ones who come from big places like Albany and New York and Detroit. They're busy, too, but they have much more time to think than the men. You catch tears in the women's eyes sometimes."

"Well, there'll be no more weeping now for you, Mrs. Abbott," remarked James, with kindly pomposity.

"No, James, no more weeping." And she put her fingers affectionately on James' plump, ruby-ringed hand.

"And how is Surgeon Smith?"

"Fine. Keeps busy with the cases of fever and ague, and sick Indians, and hunting accidents now and then."

"And Louis Pettle?"

Sarah answered: "He's the happiest man you ever saw, since he brought that lovely Irish girl from Detroit to be his wife. She's changed him entirely."

Abbott added: "They say he hadn't touched a drop of liquor for a year—until our wedding! But he did loosen up then, all right. That wife of his certainly *is* a beauty. Don't blame Pettle for lov—for liking her."

"He's a fine fellow, but I'm sorry to say he got drunk—and showed small tact towards the Indians the night he dined at our cabin on the way through last year. We almost had a scalping here!" supplemented Joseph.

"Why, he even tried to pick a quarrel with *me*," continued Abbott. (Joseph smiled inwardly, for Abbott's reputation at Detroit included its own implications of quarrelsomeness.) "Said I was—"

Abbott caught the first look of domestic reproof he had ever received, from under the long lashes of his young wife. He stopped, not in obedience, for that ingredient was not in his composition, but in sudden realization of the wisdom of self-protection. He coughed and reached for his pewter.

"Damned good wine! Where do you get it, Bailly?" The label on the flask stared him in the face. Besides, Abbott, being a merchant as well as a fur trader, knew every liquor that ever reached American shores.

But Joseph politely answered:

"I ordered quite a stock from Montreal before we left Mackinac Island. Besides, my friends Joseph Campeau and Pierre Desnoyers gave me so many bottles the last time I was in Detroit that I shan't need to resupply for some time. They like their little 'quelque chose,' you know. Bons vivants! But I'd like to look over your stock at your supply store the next time I'm in Detroit, if I may, Abbott."

"I hope you will. I have a splendid line, Bailly. Your French friends in Detroit are my best customers. Probably these very flasks came from my store. Yes, they did! Look!" Abbott held high one of the bottles, on whose base was pasted the hand-written label, "Abbott's Supply Store, Detroit." "The French certainly know how to live!" continued Abbott. "Fancy having an elegant meal like this way out in the wilderness! And in Detroit your French friends are the despair of my life! Such cooking! Such service! I couldn't teach any of my blacks or Indians to come within a hundred miles of that cooking. Finally, I got a young French girl and had her just at the point where everything was delicious and I could give quite admirable banquets once a week— when up the young flippet gets and marries a soldier from the fort! And she wasn't even pretty! Sharp-faced little witch—but with that twinkle-eyed French way with her, you know, that gets 'em. When French eyes start flashing, you don't notice the sharp nose or the gimlet chin or the mouth that goes from ear to ear—"

Sarah started the covering laughter, and Abbott came to a tardy realization of his faux pas.

"Damn it, Bailly, you may be French, but I always think of you as an American."

"I am—almost. It's all right, Abbott. Go ahead."

"Well, well, I'm foisting the culinary troubles on Mrs. Abbott now. Ann Wyley, my best black, does pretty well, but she lacks that French touch, that je ne sass— What is it you call it, Bailly?"

"The je ne sais quoi?" Joseph laughed, ringingly.

"Yes, that's it!"

"How much has been laid at the door of the French with that little four-word phrase!" exclaimed Joseph.

"It means everything charming and beautiful that we Anglo-Saxons lack!" said Sarah, gracefully making amends.

"My dear Mrs. Abbott, you contradict yourself in the very utterance of so courteous a remark," answered Joseph.

Sarah found herself embarrassed by a sudden fear that her husband might resent the compliment, and rushed in to remark:

"My dear husband worries me. He's used to such high living, and I'm used to such simple living that I don't see how I can ever keep house to suit him."

"I know you will," said Marie simply. "If he loves you, he will love everything you do for him." And she gave her own husband a look that revealed the remark to be not merely theoretical.

"Is that the secret of *your* success, my dear?" asked Sarah. "I rather think it is. Imagine your preparing such a banquet as this all by yourself!"

"It's all very simple. I have hardly enough to do to occupy myself, as it is."

"She won't hear of having any assistance yet," said Joseph. "But next year we're enlarging our house, and Marie is going to have several Indian servants and sit back and act the part of the grande dame that she really is!"

"Oh, Joseph, how bored I would be!"

"We shall see! We shall see!"

For a fraction of an instant, a picture of Corinne flashed across Joseph's eyes, a picture of her in a bouffant flowered silk dress, her hair done up in tight curls, rings on her fingers—Corinne presiding over this table. Would Corinne have been able to prepare this delicious meal? No, hardly. Would she have been gracious and kindly to the squaw who would necessarily have had to prepare it? No, imperious and brusque. How would she have carried a child? Joseph could not, by any effort of the imagination, bulge out, in thought, that wasp-slim, tight-laced figure with the corpulence of motherhood. He sat back in his chair, well content with the fullness and beauty and serenity of his wife. His conscience pricked him sharply even for his momentary dalliance with the remembered image of Corinne. Strange that she came back now and again with such sharp insistence.

"Have I not a lovely wife?" he asked suddenly, with that French revelation of the innermost thought alien to the Anglo-Saxon—so alien that Abbott had not even paid his brand-new bride the smallest compliment since their marriage.

"Oh, yes, Mr. Bailly!" exclaimed Sarah earnestly, her heart missing a beat over this charming French gallantry. "How delightful of you to say so! How long have you been married?"

"Three years."

"James, do you think you will be able to say such pleasant things to me after we have been married three years?"

"Nice place here, Bailly," said Abbott, ignoring his wife's too personal question. "You've fixed it up like a house in Detroit or Quebec. Wager there aren't many cabins in the wilderness, a hundred miles from nowhere, that have a carved walnut sideboard, a canopied bed, a gold-framed mirror, and a solid silver tray and tea service."

"Oh, well," said Joseph, "I have to have something to remind me of old French elegances. The tray and tea service are from my old home at Ste. Anne, my mother's wedding present; the bed and sideboard were shipped by sail from Montreal to Mackinac and then by one of my fur barges down here; and the gold mirror I bought down at Vincennes. Marie had nothing but the St. Joseph River to mirror her pretty face in! We'll have it fixed up nicely here some day!"

"You intend to make this your permanent home, Bailly?"

"For the time being at any rate. It's a pretty good center for my trading activities. It's on the Sauk Trail that runs all the way from the Missouri to Malden. Big Indian villages near by. Not far from Fort Dearborn. Not too far from Marie's old home at the Crooked Tree. And it's a beautiful place."

"I guess it's the practicability of it that appeals to you, Bailly. You're a pretty good calculator. Pretty neat business you've built up out of brains and beaver. Almost like an American!"

"Mon Dieu! Funny how many people say to me: 'Almost like an American,' 'Almost like a Yankee.' My French blood used to boil, but now I know that they mean it as a big compliment. Yankee push! Yankee grit! Yankee go! Yankee brains! I'll have to become a naturalized American in self-defense! Mon Dieu! As if a Frenchman had no brains! Sacré tonnerre! I'm going to make them say before I die: 'Smart as a Frenchman! Smart as Joseph Bailly!' "

"Don't misunderstand me, Bailly. It isn't a question of brains with the French but of method. You must admit that those dear old Frenchmen in Detroit, all except Campeau—I take my beaver hat off to Campeau!—are living now in exactly the way they lived in Cadillac's time: same old methods of farming, the few of them who do farm, same way of yoking steers, same way of fishing, same way of pressing the furs, same way of *not* paving the streets, same slow, everlasting, leisurely ways."

"Yes. But they're happy, Abbott. What difference does anything make if you're happy? Dream and be happy. Hurry and be dead!"

"But you hurry—and are happy! Is it not so, Joseph?" asked Marie with a sly smile.

"Yes, my Marie! And now I'm going to do a most extraordinary thing!" declared Joseph, pouring fresh Madeira into the glasses. "I'm going to propose a toast to myself! Hear, ladies and gentlemen! Here's to a Frenchman on the American frontier! May he thrive like the devil!"

"Which, being interpreted, means," amended Sarah with a mischievous smile, "may he thrive—like a Yankee!"

"May he thrive like a saint!" reamended Marie, with a twinkle that redeemed the wish from righteousness.

"Like the saint that he ain't!" climaxed Abbott with a touch of jocosity that astonished even his wife.

Chapter XII

FIRE AT THE NARROWS

"REMINDS me of the last time we rode into Detroit, eh, Jean Baptiste?"

"We deedn't ride, Monsieur Joseph— We swam! 'Member ze fellow way out ze end Ste. Anne Street, walking into town, up to ze meedle in mud? Mud in ze eyes, mud in ze ears, mud in ze nose, mud in ze mouth?"

"Do I remember?" Joseph assented, with a laugh. " 'Sir, will you tell me how far it is to Detroit?' says he. 'Sir, you are already *in* Detroit!' say I. 'In God's name, then, sir, will you tell me how far it is to shore?' Bon Dieu! I'll wager Campeau's story isn't so far off the truth, after all!"

"Wheech story? Monsieur has as many stories in hees pate as he has pelts in ze storehouse."

"Oh, you remember! About the hat he saw floating in the mud on St. Joseph Street? And when he stooped to pick it up he found a living man's head under it. Sacré! Pauvre diable, let me help to pull you out!' says Campeau. 'Thank you, sir,' says the man, very solemnly, in English. 'Thank you kindly. I shall come out all right, for I have a good horse under me.' "

"Oui. Zat ees one of Monsieur Campeau's stories, all right. But zis ees true. With zeese eyes I saw ze whole Campeau family, except Papa Campeau, get out of zeir windows right on ze horses' backs and ride across ze leetle narrow street to St. Anne's Church."

"Oh, it's a grand village, Jean Baptiste. We ought to ride crocodiles instead of horses into Detroit! But it's June now, and maybe the place has dried up a bit since spring. Perhaps some day they'll cobble the streets like Quebec. Qui sait? But they'll never cobble this swamp. Mon Dieu! What a swamp!"

Joseph and Jean Baptiste were riding across the Thirty Mile Swamp that stretched eastward from the future site of Ypsilanti to Detroit (Joseph's mount was a black Arab, Rabican, successor to Bayard.) It was a lush stretch, interrupted only by a very few patches of timber and the winding mirror of the River Rouge that looped across its leagues of cattail and arrowplant, cinnamon ferns, wild rice, pond lilies, and rose marshmallows. Flocks of red-winged blackbirds rose before the travelers as they plodded on.

"But it's beautiful—if one can stop cursing for a minute," asserted Joseph, his love of nature coming to the top. "The rose marshmallows will be in bloom pretty soon! Look! They're already in bud—dark crimson."

"Can't see anything but ze mud," said Jean Baptiste, prosaically.

They squudged on towards Detroit. About five miles out of town, where the lower and upper Rouge joined, they came to a plateau covered with pines and oaks. As they pulled towards the higher ground, they heard a sudden sound of galloping and saw a herd of Canadian ponies taking flight before them. The ponies soon recovered from their alarm and took their stand among the trees, betraying their recent disquietude only by an occasional nervous snort or a flung mane.

"Campeau's ponies!" exclaimed Jean Baptiste. "See ze letters 'J. C.' branded on ze flank? How many ponies he have?"

"Oh, forty or fifty, I should say."

"How many slaves he have?"

"Eight or ten. I don't remember. He's always buying new ones of the Indians that raid them off the Kentucky plantations."

"Beeg man, Campeau. But not so beeg man as Monsieur Joseph!" affirmed Jean Baptiste loyally.

As they came to the eastern edge of the wooded plateau, Joseph drew rein.

"Wait a minute, Jean Baptiste. Let's take a look."

"What for you look?"

"Why, it's a fine view, Jean Baptiste. Don't you think so?"

Actually it was, for the plateau overlooked Detroit, only two miles away. The most conspicuous buildings in the village were old Fort Shelby on the north side and the two-story "King's Palace" of stone near the river, rising high above the tall white pickets that surrounded the place. Pricking above the pickets also was the belfry of the little log church of St. Anne. The steep, dormer-windowed roofs of the sixty whitewashed log cabins clustered about the church. Here and there, the green of trees overshadowed the roofs, the line of tall sycamores along the banks of Savoyard Creek below the fort, the old Pontiac Tree on Jefferson Avenue, the ancient pear trees, down by the waterside, which had grown big since Cadillac's time. Outside the border of the picket fence lay scattered farmhouses, ribbon farms, more trees and the picturesque old windmills on the banks of the Detroit River. Across the blue-brown water, around Fort Malden, clustered more white houses, more windmills, and the Huron Mission Church. To the north stretched a few low hills, a few man-made mounds of the ancient Indians, and the woods where their descendants camped. It was an altogether attractive scene; and much as Joseph jested at the mud and the simplicity of the place, Detroit gripped his heart almost as Quebec and Ste. Anne did. Here were many French people whom he loved, and here was the stir and the hum of the fur trade in which he delighted. He always took joy in remembering that here the adventurous Frenchman Cadillac and his handful of soldiers and settlers had sowed their little colony a hundred years before.

When Joseph had had his fill of the sight, he and Jean Baptiste trotted down the hill towards the west gate of the town.

"Ho! What's zis?" exclaimed Jean Baptiste, reining in his horse as they came up to the gate, on the pickets of which two posters were nailed. "What do zey say, Monsieur Joseph? Zey say we can't go into town?"

"Let's see!" Joseph drew up. "Enfant de l'enfer, what's this, what's this? Mon Dieu! Mon Dieu! Heaven preserve us!"

"What is it, Monsieur Joseph? Read zem aloud, vite, vite, please!"

"Jean Baptiste, you won't believe it, but they say this: The first one:

"June 1, 1805.

"In a scurrilous piece published this day by Abijah Hull relative to myself, I observe several falsehoods, consequently think it necessary to inform the public that the said Abijah Hull is not only a liar but a perjured villain, and as such will be treated by

"JAMES ABBOTT."

Whew! The second one reads:

"June 2, 1805.

"James Abbott, Esq.:
"Sir;
    "The language which you used respecting me in your publication of Saturday last, imperiously demands satisfaction. As I conceive that no legal redress can give adequate compensation to injured character and insulted honor, I shall expect you to give me the satisfaction due to a gentleman by meeting me at seven o'clock tomorrow morning at the windmill on the Petite Côte, on the other side of the Detroit River.

"ABIJAH HULL."

Joseph whistled again. "Well, Jean Baptiste, we'd better go to Campeau's later, and see first whether we can offer our services as seconds to our war-like friend, Mr. Abbott! I'd like to help, for I believe that that same Abijah Hull was the lawyer who helped Madame Bailly's uncle and aunt to take her home away from her. Parbleu! *I'm sure it was!*"

"Good! Let us keel him! Look, Monsieur Joseph!"

As they rode through the gate, Jean Baptiste pointed to two similar posters nailed to the inside of the gate.

As they moved on slowly through the narrow streets, which were no longer marshy but only slightly soggy, as Joseph had predicted, they paused frequently to greet friends. Of the four hundred inhabitants, they knew over half by name and almost all by sight. Slowly they edged through the market-place, where the whipping post stood and into narrow Ste. Anne Street. As they rode towards Ste. Anne's Church, they noticed a crowd collected in the street, all faces turned upwards towards the little belfry.

"It's that darky Crow! Look at him! Look at that monkey!" exclaimed Joseph. "Campeau ought to send him to the whipping post, but I've an idea Campeau eggs him on, hating churches as he does!"

Jean Baptiste was laughing so hard that he didn't hear a word Joseph said, for there at the top of the little belfry, like a living weathercock, poised Crow, Campeau's favorite slave, doing gymnastic tricks. Crow was dressed in his usual brilliant scarlet livery. so that his ridiculous motions stood out against the blue sky. First, he clung to the slats of the belfry with his bare feet, and, hands on hips, swung to right and left. Then he held on with his left hand and left foot, and lifted his right foot above his head, like a ballet dancer. Then he bowed. Then he thumbed his nose, first at the crowd, below, then skyward as at God himself!

The women in the street shook their heads. The men laughed. The children shouted. Some one said: "He sure is celebrating! He's marrying Abbott's slave girl, Ann Wyley, today. Feeling his oats!"

Shortly, the church door opened and Father Richard stepped out. All sounds ceased. Father Richard looked up and saw Crow transgressing once again, for this was an old trick. Joseph, a hundred feet away, could see the smile that flashed across Father Richard's face, and his quick suppression of that smile as he called out, with apparent severity:

"Come down, you young sinner, come down!"

"What'll you gib me if I do, Massa Richard?"

"A box on the ear—and a guinea for a wedding present!"

"Oh, ah's comin', ah's comin'!"

Crow nimbly climbed down the belfry, clutching the little eaves of the bellvents, slid down the low roof, and jumped the remaining ten feet to the ground. To Joseph's amusement, Father Richard gave exactly what he had promised, a cuff on the ear, and a guinea which he drew from the folds of his cassock.

Knowing that he would see Father Richard later, Joseph cut down Ste. Honoré Street, towards the wharves. There, most of the well-to-do traders and merchants had their warehouses, and their homes were conveniently near by. Jean Baptiste drifted off towards Campeau's, where he might find a voyageur or two left behind from fall expeditions. Joseph proceeded to Abbott's house. It was more pretentious than its neighbors, two stories high, with leaded windows, a large brass door knocker incised with the owner's name, and window boxes which Sarah must have added to the front of the house, for Joseph had not seen them before. Sarah, too, was probably responsible for the cobbled walk from the picket fence to the door and for the variety of currant bushes and climbing roses planted on either side and at the end of the garden, screening off Abbott's adjacent flour mill, distillery, and store.

A hearty use of the brass knocker brought Pompey, a negro slave

in an emerald-green uniform, to the door. Yes, Mis' Abbott was
at home, and Massa Abbott was at the warehouse, from which he
could be summoned presently. Sarah came in a moment, as lovely
as she had been as a bride, but fuller of face and fuller of body, for
she was obviously on the point of contributing an American to
the preponderantly French Detroit.

"Monsieur Bailly! How delightful! And how is Madame
Bailly?"

"Very well, madame. We have a little daughter since you came
by last year, Agatha, as sturdy as a bear and as pretty as a deer.
We're expecting another child very soon, and I must hurry back
as soon as I can, after laying in a few supplies, and talking over
a little business with Mr. Abbott and Monsieur Campeau."

"How wonderful! Do you wish for a son this time?"

"I wouldn't be quite honest if I didn't answer 'Yes'; but we shall
be thankful for son *or* daughter. Marie and I thought we were
perfectly happy before Agatha came—but now we know we had
only *begun* to be happy!"

"How nicely you always say things!"

There was an almost imperceptible edge of wistfulness in Sarah's
remark. She was taking breath to say something else when Abbott
blustered in, bringing competent hospitality with him.

"Bailly, my friend! Well, well! Welcome! How go things at
Parc aux Vaches?"

"Splendidly! Splendidly! And with you?"

With true French tact, Joseph was determined not to mention
the affair of the duel unless Abbott referred to it first himself.

"Oh, business goes well enough, but there are household troubles.
I should tell you, Mrs. Abbott, that I caught that nigger Ann
Wyley an hour ago with six guineas in her apron—stolen off my
desk at the warehouse. I'm going to have her tied up to the whipping post!"

Sarah grew pale. "May I see her?" she asked.

"No. I've had her locked up in one of the fur sheds. Forget
about her."

"Oh, what will poor Crow do? Have you forgotten that Father
Richard was coming to marry them this afternoon?"

"*There won't be any marriage.*" Then Abbott continued,
addressing Joseph as if nothing had happened: "I've got other

troubles too, Bailly. There are some rascals in town, damned rascals. Detroit isn't what it used to be. Filling up with scum."

Joseph lifted his reddish eyebrows interrogatively and shrugged his shoulders.

"Scum's everywhere, my dear Abbott. Even out my way, in the deep woods: traders that'll try to undersell you and lie about you to the Indians—"

"But this is scum of scum, Bailly," pursued Abbott, warming to his subject. "Cussed ignoramus called Hull, Abijah Hull, petty lawyer commissioned by the Government to survey the old French farms and confirm the titles. Doesn't know a thing and is as lazy as a stinkpot turtle. Sits on his haunches all day at Dequindre's Tavern and plays euchre and slops toddy and then has the impudence to say my warehouse is halfway across Campeau's line. Campeau and I understand each other. But Hull says I've got to move the warehouse. I'll send him to Pontiac before I move the warehouse—"

"James! James!" remonstrated his wife.

"Mrs. Abbott, go tell Ann—I mean go tell Pompey to bring us some claret and cakes immediately," said Abbott brusquely.

"Yes, James. But, oh, James, I can't believe you'd actually consent to encounter such a fellow—"

"The claret and cakes, Mrs. Abbott."

"Yes, James." Sarah curtsied to necessity and left the room.

"Fellow challenged me to a duel."

"Yes, I saw the posters," admitted Joseph finally.

"Oh, you did?"

"Yes. I came to say that if you're going to fight and need a second, sir, I'll be delighted to serve you."

"Thanks, Bailly. I'll take it under consideration. But I'd rather use the backwoods method and punch the fellow's block off! Seems to me I've heard you're pretty good at that yourself, Bailly!"

Joseph laughed. "Thanks! I'll be glad to handle this scoundrel too! I have special reasons for hating him."

Abbott ignored Joseph's troubles and went on with his own.

"I've got still other troubles too, Bailly. There's a fellow cutting in on my fur business in a big way—scaring off my Indians, buying off my voyageurs, stealing my goods. I run into him south of here all the time."

"Oh, we all run into that. Can't get away from it in a rich business like ours. Burnett on the St. Joseph and Pélégor on the Grand River are my bêtes noires."

"My 'bait new-war,' as you call 'em, is a fellow by the name of Rastel, fellow from up Montreal way. Smarter'n ten foxes and cussed as twenty wolverenes. I lay most of my troubles to him."

A sudden crimson flash crossed Joseph's face.

"Ciel! I wonder if he could be putting Burnett and Pélégor up to *their* tricks, way off in west Michigan Territory—after the thrashing and the warning I gave him, too!"

"That's his method. He's poisoned the whole country around here. Yet you can't ever lay your hands on him. Works through undertraders. Uses them as decoys. Sits and pulls the strings. And takes in the cash!"

"*There's* a man I'd like to run a sword through! And the Nor'westers still keep him, though they've been warned of his tricks—"

"You know him all too well, I guess."

"Yes, I *know* him." Joseph shut his lips tight on the rest.

Sarah was heard coming back from the rear of the house. Abbott had just time to ask, before she and Pompey entered the room:

"How are the beaver holding out, your way?"

"Fairly well. Better just now on the Grand River than the St. Joseph. Too much passing to and fro by Indians and whites along the St. Joseph."

Sarah's return interrupted the talk of business. Very charmingly she poured the claret from a swirl-glass decanter, while Pompey passed the individual glasses and the cakes. For one twinge-sharp moment, as Sarah bent over the decanter, the picture of Corinne pouring peach brandy at Quebec came back to Joseph. Both Sarah and Corinne curved slightly forward, with arched neck, conscious smile and graceful wrist. Marie always sat very straight, in her hospitable dispensings, with straight wrist and elbow and no thought at all of the pattern she might be making.

"I am sorry my wife could not come with me this time," said Joseph, suddenly compunctious.

"We're sorry, too. I imagine she will be very busy with the little ones."

"Little ones?" asked Abbott. "I thought you had but one child, Bailly."

"We have one child, and are expecting another very soon, as I told Madame Abbott."

"Oh, I see!" Abbott frowned in the direction of Mrs. Abbott, rebuking not Bailly for his French laxity but his wife for her immodest use of the plural. He could not help wondering whether they had gone so far as to discuss *his* imminent progeny.

"I am very eager to have Father Richard baptize our children—our child," Bailey hastened into the breach to remark; "but it will be impossible for Madame Bailly to travel this way for some time, and of course we cannot expect Father Richard to come our way very often on his missionary travels."

"No. Father Richard is very preoccupied here just now with his little Church of Ste. Anne," said Sarah. "How he loves that church, and how charming he has made it! He's just imported a beautiful altarpiece from Paris and several exquisite altar cloths and silver vessels that were thrown out into secondhand shops by the Revolution. Have you heard the little organ and the new set of bells—from his own town of Saintes in France? And have you seen the printing press he's so proud of?"

"No. Not yet. I was going to the church to see Father Richard a little later in the day. I came to you first of all. You see—"

Joseph was on the point of mentioning Crow's escapade, but thought better of it. Fortunately Abbott intervened with:

"That's right, Bailly, to come first to us. That's right. More claret?"

"I don't know anyone who's more loved than Father Richard," continued Sarah.

"He's feared, too," supplemented Abbott. "I like his courage. He's a real man. And that's a tribute from me, a Protestant and a Freemason. When a parishioner's acting badly, getting drunk or neglecting his family, Richard isn't afraid to bear down on him pretty hard. And can he tell stories? Ripsnorters, like other men! He's had his share of regular, rough adventures, too. Did you ever hear how he got that scar across his cheek?"

"No. I never did, but I always wondered," answered Joseph. "It looks like a dueling scar."

"No. Not that. I asked him about it one day, a straightforward question, and I got a straightforward answer. Seems he was a young priest in France when the Revolution broke out. One day he looked out of his front window and saw some soldiers coming, then heard them asking for him at the house next door. Knew what that meant. Jumped out of a rear window of his house. Cussed woman, a Revolutionist, threw a teapot at him. Broke on his cheek. He ran as fast as his priest garments would let him. Jumped into a ditch where some men were digging. They threw a vest and a coat over him, and he went to digging with 'em; and the soldiers passed him by. Richard dug in that ditch until he got a chance to slip on a vessel and come to America. Quite an adventure, eh?"

"Yes, indeed. Young Desnoyers, too, you know, who works for Campeau in the silversmith shop, is a refugee from the Revolution."

"Oh, yes, don't we know!" said Sarah. "All the little boys in the neighborhood, when they want to tease young Desnoyers, march behind him and call out 'A la lanterne! A la lanterne!' and pretend to cut off his head with wooden swords. He's a nice young fellow and carries out the game all the way to Campeau's door. But I sometimes wonder whether he likes that game quite as well as he pretends to. He probably remembers a lot of horrible things that he'd like to forget."

"Undoubtedly!" corroborated Joseph. "How lucky we are to have been born over here! By the way, how do you like Hull?"

Abbott scowled frightfully.

"Oh, I mean the new Territorial Governor William Hull, not your friend Abijah," laughed Joseph.

"Oh, the Governor hasn't arrived yet. But he's due any day now. I have letters from the East that describe him as a pretty good fellow. Was a captain in the American Revolution—Yankee from Derby, Connecticut. It'll seem like the edge of the world to him out here, I guess."

"Oh, Detroit's a *fine* town!" asserted Joseph.

Abbott raised his eyebrows. "Perhaps. But imagine holding together the whole of Michigan with all its savages and trappers and Frenchies—"

"James!" remonstrated Sarah, in an almost inaudible voice.

"Beg pardon, Bailly. I mean it'll be like holding together a half-dozen islands strung out in the ocean a thousand miles apart."

But Joseph had again caught the implication. In that single alien word "Frenchies" lay the whole wide world of difference between the Latin races and the Anglo-Saxon. It was obvious that the jealous and aggressive Anglo-Saxons would be closing down, with their absorbing characteristics, on all the little French settlements that lay stretched so indolently and so gayly along the oak openings and the riversides of Michigan Territory. Joseph was himself a sufficiently good business man to admire the American "hustle," of which he had encountered so many instances at Michilimackinac, Checagou, Fort Wayne, Detroit, and elsewhere; but he was also a sufficiently good Frenchman to sense the racial difference and the racial antipathy, however slight. That one word, "Frenchies," revealed the attitude of Abbott and his confreres as completely as if he had stood on the Esplanade in front of Fort Shelby and delivered a two-hour tirade against French characteristics.

Joseph saw the flush of embarrassment on Sarah's kind face and her effort to think of something newly palliative to say. But the situation was resolved when the door knocker sounded and Pompey opened to Father Richard. The priest was wearing the straw hat lined with green silk which he always wore to protect his eyes from the sun, and had his indispensable cotton umbrella. Out of his black cassock, Father Richard would never have been taken for a priest. He was slim, tallish, a bit ungraceful. He had a lively, humorous face, small, quick, coal-black eyes, high-arched, very mobile eyebrows, a large, pointed French nose, and wide, thin lips almost saucily curved with a sudden straight upturn at the very ends. The deep scar across the left cheek added but another accent to an already highly accented face. He was thirty-eight years old, keen, practical, full of a thousand plans for his parish and for the whole Northwest. Although he had come from Illinois to Detroit only seven years before, he had, in the meantime, erected his church of Ste. Anne and had become adored and respected throughout the whole Northwest Territory. Joseph had met him only a few times before, but Father Richard greeted him like a cousin, addressing him first in French, then, in deference to the Abbotts, in his slightly French-accented English.

"Joseph Bailly! Joseph Bailly! What a joy to see you in our part of the world! Come, tell me how it goes with the little Madame? Everywhere I go, Michilimackinac, Arbre Croche, Rivière des Raisins, there are tales of her beauty and her strange powers. Is she as lovely as ever?" And he smiled, with his sharp, faunlike smile.

Joseph was immediately at ease, sunshine flooding his recently troubled mind.

"Encore plus belle! More beautiful than ever," he remarked quietly. "Some day we want you to baptize our children, Father Richard."

With a French priest in the room, Joseph now found it altogether easy and natural to use the plural. "We have a daughter, Agatha, and are shortly expecting another child," he explained.

"If I can possibly come your way, Bailly, I will come. But my good people here at Detroit and up Mackinac way keep me terribly busy. However, I'll bear you in mind, Bailly. Indeed I will."

"Possibly you've been to Arbre Croche since we've been there," said Joseph, "or since we've had news from the Ottawa Indians who come down from there in the spring? How are Madame Neengay Lefèvre—the Snake Woman, they sometimes call her now—and Chief Blackbird and De la Vigne, the magician? Have you heard anything of them?"

"Chief Blackbird is having his troubles with De la Vigne and the Snake Woman and all their followers, and so am I. I've done my best to preach the word of God to those poor souls, but they are sunk very deep in their black magic and their pagan rituals. I'm begging for other missionaries to be sent out to re-establish the old mission of Arbre Croche. Those poor souls have been forgotten since Father Marquette's day. De la Vigne is as smart as the devil."

"Yes, I know," said Joseph.

"Much of his work is sheer trickery, sleight of hand, hypnotism, jugglery. I've seen the queer people of the East do things like that in Paris at the bazaars—"

"That 'going in fire'! Did you see De la Vigne do that?"

"No. But it's just a question of stuff rubbed on the body to produce a glow like the phosphorescence of wet wood at night. I saw De la Vigne stick a small arrow through his tongue, heard it squish as it went through the flesh—quite a trick that—and I saw him in one of his josakeed, lodge-shaking exploits. Strange voices came out of the billowing tepee and denounced me, called me an evil spirit, told me I would be punished for trying to oppose De la Vigne, told me my 'lodge with bells' would burn and all the lodges in my village would burn until nothing but black dust was left. Funny, isn't it?" Father Richard laughed. "That was last June."

"Your lodge with bells? I suppose he meant your church?" asked Joseph, suddenly solemn, for he had heard too many of Marie's tales of De la Vigne's prophecies not to place some reluctant bit of faith in them.

Father Richard gave a French shrug. "By the way, I was at Rivière des Raisins recently and the whole Navarre family were asking about you and Madame Bailly. François Navarre was planning to ride up to Detroit in a few days. You may see him before you go. How long will you be here?"

"Three or four days, Father, depending on how my business with Abbott and Campeau goes."

"Oh, Bailly's a quick fellow—knows what he wants and usually gets it. I tell him he's almost like an American," doggedly reiterated Abbott.

Joseph, from under his red lashes, caught yet another troubled look from Sarah and decided to meet the thrust with gayety:

"As for Abbott, I've always thought him *almost* as logical as a Frenchman—eh, Father Richard?"

Abbott scowled, and Father Richard smiled placatingly. Joseph changed the subject.

"And the Lefèvres of Rivière des Raisins? How are they, Father?"

"Not getting along so well, Bailly. Disliked by all their neighbors, who've never gotten over the way they treated your wife and her mother! Tried to take over old Antoine Lefèvre's fur business around there, you know, but even the Indians don't like those two. The Indians and the French always get along well, but somehow these Lefèvres are different. Lazy, cowardly, scornful, poor managers. Too bad."

"I know, for a fact, Rastel has tried to use them," said Abbott. "They're his kind. But even *he* can't get anything out of them."

"Well, it's just as I thought," said Joseph. "When I began to make a few extra pounds, I thought I'd come down here to Detroit and set about prosecuting, through McDougall, to have Marie's property restored to her. But Marie didn't want the property; it would have taken months of complicated business to get it back, and, as for punishment of the Lefèvres, they're getting all the punishment they deserve. Living like rats, so the Indians told me long ago. No. The evil people in this world *do* sometimes get what they deserve, right here!"

"Well, I'm willing to put in a few blows for sinners, with my good right arm!" said Abbott. "You've heard about *my* troubles, Richard?"

"Yes. I hope you're not going to pay any attention to *that* fellow, Abbott."

"That's what I tell him, *exactly*, Father!" exclaimed Sarah.

"No! I fully intend to go down to the Petite Côte tomorrow and give him a basting—swords if he wishes; but I prefer my good right arm!" Abbott extended his arm and swelled out the muscles under the brown broadcloth coat until a flush came to his cheeks.

"Oh, no, Abbott, don't!" urged Father Richard. "I'm not pleading on any Christian or biblical basis, but simply on the basis of human understanding. I know the fellow. He's just a blattering bullfrog. Pay no attention to him and he'll finally splash in, and the little waters will close over his head. Much more dignified to pass right by and pay no attention to him. McDougall can lay your case before the Government surveyor's office, and that's all there is to it."

"Oh, no, Richard! Don't deprive me of the pleasure of running a sword or an arm through the fool."

Sarah restrained the "Don't be ridiculous, James!" which would have been the conjugal comment of nine wives out of ten, and merely shook her head slightly, her eyes meeting Father Richard with a look that said: "Dissuade him, Father, dissuade him."

"It's not worth fretting over, Abbott. The man's beneath your notice."

"But I can't retreat as a coward."

"A man who runs away from a skunk isn't a coward!" put in Joseph.

"That's right," assented Father Richard. "That's common sense. Put up your sword, Abbott, and fight with a quill pen. I don't mean posters. I mean letters to Washington."

"I've already written to the Government surveyor's office," said Abbott. "I'll follow the letters up in person, if necessary."

"How would you like me to go to Hull myself and have a talk with him?" suggested Father Richard.

"An excellent idea, Father. How very kind of you!" assented Sarah.

Abbott frowned in Sarah's direction. Why should women always be meddling in men's affairs?

"I can't see that it would do any good!" he declared.

"May I not tell him that you are carrying the matter to higher authorities and don't care for any local encounter under the windmill at the Petite Côte?"

"Yes, Father! Yes, Father!" urged Sarah.

"No, Father! *No*, Father!" bellowed Abbott. "Tell him that I'm carrying the matter to higher authorities and that I *do* care to meet him at the Petite Côte at seven o'clock tomorrow morning. Joseph Bailly will act as my second, you will be my chaplain, McDougall will be my lawyer."

"And what doctor—if you were *wounded to death?* Oh, James, you *cannot* mean this! You simply *can't* mean it," cried Sarah, rising and putting her arm around Abbott's shoulder.

"I *do* mean it!" proclaimed Abbott, getting up, so that Sarah's arm fell limp from his stiffened neck.

Again Sarah shot a glance of entreaty at Father Richard, from behind this bulwark, and Father Richard responded with a sly little look which said: "Madame, I will do my best!"

"And now, how about Ann Wyley and Crow?" asked Father Richard. "Are you bringing them into the parlor, or shall I go out to the slave quarters?"

At this moment Crow himself burst into the room, shaking with terror, and threw himself at Abbott's feet.

"Oh, Massa Abbott, Massa Abbott! Ann, she didn't do n-n-n-nothin'! Oh, M-M-Massa, let her out! *Please* do! She gwine be mah wife, mah g-g-good, g-g-good wife!"

"Get up, you stammering idiot! Get up! Your Ann Wyley

stole six guineas from me! I'm going to have her tied up to the whipping post for the night, and then we'll see what the justice of the peace will prescribe for her! Get up, Crow! She isn't the last nigger in the world!"

"Oh, F-f-f-father!" sobbed Crow, crawling over on his scarlet-cloth knees to Father Richard. "Oh, g-g-good Father Richard, save mah wife! Save mah wife!"

Father Richard lifted Crow up gently. "Get up, Crow. Don't take on so. We'll see what we can do. Are you sure about this, Abbott?"

"Sure?" roared Abbott. "I found the guineas in her apron, I tell you!"

"Can't we overlook this first offense?"

"I'm not sure it's the first. I've been missing lots of little things from the warehouse, and Sarah can't find a gold locket she had on her dresser, and—"

"May I go out to speak to Ann?"

"Yes. But don't let her think she's going to get off without being punished."

"You wouldn't let me perform the ceremony today as we'd planned it—and punish her *afterwards*?"

"No, as her master, I won't give my consent. Bad policy. Bad policy! Get out of here, Crow! Stop blubbering! Take Father Richard to see your thieving Ann!"

Father Richard took Crow's arm and said a brief and troubled goodbye to Bailly and Abbott.

"Don't worry, Sarah," urged Abbott. "I have to frighten those cursed niggers, you know. I won't let them use the 'cat' on her, if I can help it."

"Thank God, James. I know you mean to be kind."

"Discipline, Bailly, discipline."

"Yes. I understand, sir."

Sarah paused long enough to ask Joseph: "You couldn't make our home your inn while you're in Detroit?"

"You're very kind. But Campeau knows I often turn up at this season, and he always expects me to roll up in a buffalo skin on his floor or oust one of the children from a trundle bed, whenever I come. Thank you enormously, just the same."

"Perhaps dinner tomorrow night here with us?"

"I'd be delighted."

Sarah followed the slave and the priest out of a rear door, and Bailly shook Abbott's hand firmly and went off to Campeau's.

Campeau's was four strips down from Abbott's, on property once owned by Cadillac, in whose Company Campeau's grandfather had come to Detroit. The estate was on the water front, and a very busy place it was. While Abbott had built up an efficient business after the American pattern, with neat, up-to-date offices, storage houses, and various kinds of barges tied up at the private wharf, Campeau engaged in an even greater variety of enterprises, shrewdly but less tidily conducted. He was a cabinetmaker, a distiller, a fur trader, a manufacturer of silver goods, a dealer in real estate, and a dealer and experimenter in livestock. In addition to the various shops and buildings and stables devoted to these enterprises, there were Campeau's blacksmith shop, machine and repair shops, and the quarters for his workers and his ten slaves. The fine old log house itself, set back from the crowded river front on Jefferson Avenue, was of the usual French type, a story and a half high, steep-roofed, with dormer windows and the divided front door, the upper part of which opened separately to enable the house owner to lean with comfortable elbows and look out upon the passers-by. But Campeau revealed his originality not only in the multiplicity of his enterprises but in the tint of his house, which stood out among the whitewashed log dwellings of Detroit in its glowing goldenrod yellow. Campeau himself might dress always in black broadcloth, swallowtail coat, vest, and trousers with immaculate white ruffled shirt and snowy cravat, but his house sang out with spontaneity! As an additional touch, on any fête-day there could always be seen hanging from the outside beams of the house huge poster pictures of Campeau's two great heroes, George Washington and the Marquis de Lafayette.

Today again the posters swung in the south wind, though Joseph could not guess what obscure holiday it might be in the calendar or in Campeau's festal mind. On the roadway in front of the house some eight or ten Indians sat hunched over the gambling game of "moccasin," grunts or cries of excitement now and then interrupting the singsong of the player who manipulated the ball. Other sounds of excitement and rejoicing and the scrape of a fiddle issued from a near-by warehouse and indicated to Joseph the bibulous vicinity of Jean Baptiste Clutier and his comrades.

Joseph struck Campeau's knocker, a large fleur-de-lis of wrought iron. Immediately the upper half of the door opened and MacNiff, Campeau's clerk, already bent after only ten years of desk service, looked out. He had a watery blue eye, a sharp chin, a sharp ruby nose, a quill pen stuck over his left ear, a dusty, long-coated suit, a stock and ruff of saffron color, whether from the dye of butter-nut bark or from the tincture of time it would have been difficult to tell.

"Eh? Eh? What? Who is it? All the cussed slaves have gone to that black wedding at Abbott's! Who is it? Who is it?"

MacNiff's mind seemed to come back slowly from columns of comprehensible figures to the incomprehensible pattern of reality.

"Greetings, MacNiff!" said Bailly, laying a hearty hand on the angular shoulder. "It's Bailly—Joseph Bailly from Parc aux Vaches. Is Campeau in?"

"Yes. Oh, yes, yes, Monsieur Bailly! So glad to see you. He'll be delighted, I'm sure. Step this way."

But Campeau had already heard Bailly's resonant voice and came out of the office at the left of the doorway.

Joseph Campeau was a small man but straight-standing, which seemed to add the Old Testament cubit to his stature. His skin was olive, almost Italian in its darkness. Against it shone perfect, small, dazzlingly white teeth. The lips were thin, supple, expressive. The black eyes, though not large, were so full of the incessant sparkle of a shrewd mentality that they seemed to occupy a far larger space than, in reality, they did. There were already many fine wrinkles, born of astute calculation, about the corners of the eyes, although he was only thirty-five years old. Campeau's head was a French version of the similarly shrewd, small head of his contemporary, Thomas Jefferson.

"Ah, que tu es le bienvenu, mon cher Joseph!" he exclaimed joyously, and opened the whole door to his friend. The two embraced, French-fashion, and kissed each other smackingly on both cheeks. As it was almost six o'clock, MacNiff was dismissed for the day and Joseph was led past the store at the front of the house, into the countingroom at the back, with its two high desks, high stools and the deal tables and chairs which had been made in Campeau's own cabinet shop; with its bear rug on the floor, the beaver blanket thrown over the window bench, the stuffed otter glaring down from one of the desk tops and the elk's head projecting from the whitewashed log wall, and the wall shelf with its beautiful specimens of Carolina parrakeet, cardinal, bald eagle, whistling swan, and passenger pigeon.

In this room, the two Josephs spent an hour discussing fur-trading business problems. A casual listener might have thought Campeau the shrewder, with his clever face, brittle voice, quick manner and sharp decisions. But Bailly, who looked the handsome, bland, and hearty gentleman, kept all his wits at work behind his large blue eyes and his charming smile so that, in the end, he had revealed far less and learned far more than his good friend Campeau and had struck some excellent bargains in the exchange of furs for needed supplies.

When the two finally came out of the office in response to the dinner bell, Madame Campeau, as small, quick, and dark as her husband, hurried towards him to tell him in French of the Crow tragedy.

"Crow is so upset, Joseph, that I've had to order him to bed. If I should let him wait on table tonight, he'd break every glass he touched, he's trembling so badly. He begged to be allowed to go out to the market square to stay all night with Ann, if Abbott carries out his threat to tie her to the whipping post. I've forbidden him to leave the house, but I wouldn't be surprised if he slipped away during the night! It's awful!"

"Parbleu! That ees a fine kettle of fish! That man Abbott, he ees a fine man, a clever man, but he ees too severe. He has no heart. Ze Americans, they are all mind, all plan, no heart."

"Oh, yes, he has a heart!" defended Bailly. "But he can't show it. His severity is part of his success. You couldn't let a girl who'd stolen six whole guineas go free, could you? Most Englishmen and half the Americans would hang that girl without a second thought, or have her whipped with the cat. Abbott's a fine man, Campeau, and don't you forget it!"

"Mebbe. But this ees Crow's wedding day. And Crow ees a

fine fellow. Well, well, well! A fine kettle! Tomorrow I will see that Abbott!"

They went into the dining-and-living room where a long deal table was spread with good linen and good pewter. Half a dozen children, who had been laughing and shouting a moment before, stood suddenly quiet behind their chairs as their parents entered the room. A parrot in a cage on the mantel above the fireplace greeted Campeau with a high-pitched "Vive Lafayette!" and the uproar began again.

Dinner was a tumult of conversation and a succession of foods which would have been delicious if they had not been burned. The cooking had been done in the separate kitchen which Campeau's house boasted, by a negro cook who had just returned from Abbott's house, too distraught to attend properly to the preparation of the food. The serving was fitfully performed by Mullet and Tetro, two other blacks, who displayed as much nervousness as Crow would have shown, and dropped knives, forks, and dishes right and left. It was apparent that Crow's tragedy was deeply felt by his fellow blacks.

Later, after Campeau had sent Mullett out to bring in some of the French cronies, the enjoyment of the evening began, in a gradual atmosphere of peach brandy, Jamaica rum, pure Monongahela whisky, tall stories, pipe smoke, and song.

The cronies who dropped in, one after another, were Campeau's cousins, François Navarre of the River Raisin and Peter Navarre of Detroit, Antoine Beaubien, Jacques Beaugrand of the Raisin, and Pierre Desnoyers, the young refugee from the French Revolution.

Desnoyers was something of a dandy with his brass-buttoned lavender coat, white cravat, many-ruffled white tucker, his fine, curly, ash-blond hair tied back with a lavender ribbon, a silver love-knot brooch in the cravat, and on his aristocratic fingers two richly embossed silver rings which he himself had made in Campeau's shop. He had the manners of a gentleman, and an unusually melodious voice. Very rosy cheeks, two deep dimples, excellent teeth, and blue eyes with slightly drooping lids which, in a woman, would have been considered insinuating completed the picture of a young fop driven from Paris by the Revolution and forced to seek his living by the fine jeweled work of his hands.

Peter Navarre (to use the form of his name by which he was known to the Americans) was a fine, physical specimen over six feet in height, slender and straight as an arrow, and swift and active as a panther. He was, however, a homely fellow, with a large, pointed nose, a pointed chin, and eyes much too close together. But his smile was rollicking.

Antoine Beaubien, brother of Jean Baptiste Beaubien, Joseph Bailly's representative on Grand River, belonged to the old Cuillerier family of Canada and of Detroit. His first Canadian ancestor was said to have been a follower of La Salle, related to La Salle's faithful Tonty. Antoine was vigorous, though already filling towards stoutness, with dark blue eyes, ruddy cheeks, and light brown hair.

Jacques Beaugrand was still the freckled fellow whom Marie had known at the Raisin, with sandy hair, mocking blue, devil-may-care eyes, and a manner somewhat more rural than that of the others.

François was the oldest of the group, being thirty-eight and Peter Navarre, the youngest, was twenty. Joseph Bailly was thirty-one.

It was a tight little French group. MacNiff had gone home to his lean Scotch wife or to the tavern where he recovered from the sight of her. Mullett and Tetro had cleared the table, pushed it to the back of the room, and set it with all kinds of flasks and decanters and with plates of croquignoles and bread and cheese. Madame Campeau had whisked herself and the six children to bed. The seven Frenchmen drew up to the fire in their deal chairs, and smoked their pipes and drank their good drinks, and talked—in French.

The two events of immediate interest in Detroit, of course, were Abijah Hull's challenge of James Abbott to a duel and the imminent arrival of the new Territorial Governor. The tragedy of Crow, the slave, was a comparatively minor affair.

The matter of the duel seemed to amuse them all.

"It's a great joke," chuckled Campeau, "better than a play at the Orleans Theater in New Orleans, or a duel at Ponton's afterwards. We haven't had such excitement in Detroit since Anthony Wayne came through!"

"Oh, the fight will fizzle out!" exclaimed Peter Navarre, disgustedly. "These cold-blooded Americans have too many second thoughts. A Frenchman rushes out and fights! An American sits calculating and cools off!"

"Not if he's like Aaron Burr," amended Campeau. "Burr did rather a quick and complete job on Hamilton last year!"

"So he did!" put in Beaugrand. "Now if *I* had the chance, I'd run a dagger in no time through both Abbott and Hull and skewer 'em on the same dagger, if I could."

"Why, what harm have they done to you, Jacques?" asked Antoine.

"I've wanted to send Hull to hell for years! You know I was there when he drove the Lefèvres out."

"So was I. I feel just as fierce as Jacques!" added François.

"And I—I guess you all know how *I* feel," exclaimed Joseph, exhibiting a clenched fist. "But what's the matter with Abbott, Jacques? I don't see that."

"I don't like his looks. Abbott looks like a frog, and Hull looks like a lizard. But that isn't what I mean. You know what I mean. They're Americans."

"Yes," explained Desnoyers. "They're cold and domineering, and they don't care a damn about anything except the pewter money. And they have no manners. And they have no time for dancing and singing, or even laughing or being polite. I do like their independence and I do like their country. But they're a different breed of men from us."

"I think the Americans are terribly smart," said Joseph. "We'd better take care, or while we're dancing and singing they'll take our trade and our properties away, even though we pretend to be naturalized Americans—just as they've taken the lands of the Indians out from under them. I admire them. And I'm even half American in *feeling*."

"So am I!" corroborated Campeau. "Vive Georges Vashington!"

The parrot untucked its head from its wings at this familiar salute and half-heartedly squawked, "Vive Vash-ton!" At which everyone laughed. When the amusement had subsided, Campeau continued, seriously:

"As an example of good American business, look at Abbott's

flouring mill, distillery, and warehouses. Neat as a convent, busy as the docks at New Orleans—"

"See here, Campeau, why are you talking so much about New Orleans?" questioned Bailly. "You make me wilder than ever to go. I've been trying to get down there for four years, and I've been so busy up around the lakes I haven't been down yet."

"A Frenchman in this country who hasn't been to New Orleans is like a Frenchman in France who hasn't been to Paris. I've been telling you you ought to go, Joseph. More reasons than one. There's a grand opportunity for fur trading down there. Plenty of room. People are a bit lazy down there, you know. A bit more interested in sugar cane and fruits and shipping than they are in furs. Creeks and bayous are still full. Indians from the West bring in furs, too. Your eyes would open bigger'n mill wheels, if you went down."

"Why don't *you* develop something down there, Campeau?"

"I? Too much tangled up here in too many things. Furs are a secondary interest with me. But you think about it, and I'll give you some pointers. Baton Rouge—that's the place for your post: just above New Orleans; high ground; on the river; Indian settlements; Indian trails crossing. Old Jacques Jombeau has a little post there, but he's as lazy as a sheep tick. Make your fortune there, Joseph!"

"As if he didn't have a fortune tucked away already," suggested Antoine Beaubien, chuckling. "My brother Jean Baptiste thinks you're a great man, Bailly—smarter than twenty red foxes. Seigneur of the Great Lakes he calls you!"

"It's Jean Baptiste who's made the post at Grand River what it is," said Bailly. "Jean Baptiste is worth at least twelve of those twenty foxes. We've got some fellows to deal with up there who burrow underground with all sorts of tunnels and trickeries. But Jean Baptiste is equal to them. He's a wonderful fellow, your brother—a real Cuillerier, worthy of the name."

"Thank you, Joseph."

They all smoked and sipped reflectively for a few minutes. Then Joseph remarked:

"This Governor Hull is another fellow who's going to have his hands full. I don't know how much you city fellows know of what's going on out in the Indian country all around us. But strange things are brewing. Have you gotten wind of anything?"

"I think I know what you mean, Bailly," confirmed Campeau. "The Shawnee Prophet."

"Yes. The Shawnee Prophet," said Bailly. "He's a great man. I have absolutely no doubt of that. He's drawing the tribes together slowly in a great confederation. Tribes that have fought against each other all their lives are pulling together. The Prophet forbids the Indians to buy whisky. Some of the traders who bought furs chiefly with whisky are having a bad time of it. I still find your silver ornaments, Campeau and Pierre, pretty good stuff for purchases. By the way, I'll triple my order this time, instead of doubling it, as I told you."

"Bien! Bien!"

"You see," continued Joseph, "the Prophet teaches the Indians to go back to their own way of life, the old Indian customs. So far, so good. But he urges them to have as little to do with the white man as possible. And for some Indians such doctrine spells danger. There might even be a great united Indian uprising some day, as in Pontiac's time."

"You think so?" asked Peter and Pierre, simultaneously, with eagerness in their young voices. War—action—excitement! It was what they wanted more than anything else in the world.

"Yes. I do think so. The Prophet is sending scouts all over the country, to the Ottawa villages on the Grand, to the Ottawa at Arbre Croche, and even among our Potawatomi at Parc aux Vaches. I wouldn't have known *all* about this, but the Indians tell Marie everything."

"Does she think the matter serious?" asked Campeau.

"Yes, she does, rather. One of our chiefs and one of our wildest young braves, Topenebee and Shavehead, have been pretty seriously affected by all the talk. Shavehead has hated the whites, ever since he lost his brother to a white man's gun. That way danger lies, grave danger—"

"Shavehead's the fellow that comes swinging into Detroit with all the scalps dangling at his belt, isn't he?" asked Campeau.

"Yes. And Topenebee's rather susceptible—susceptible to whisky when it's around, and now susceptible to the Prophet's scouts. It's a hard battle he's waging inside himself, between the Prophet and whisky."

"I thought the Prophet advised the Indians to leave this Territory to the whites and go West," remarked Campeau.

"Yes. He does. But you can't wrench the Indians from their old hunting grounds, their old camping grounds, their sugar bush, their rice fields and especially their sacred burying grounds, by just urging them to go. Our Parc aux Vaches has been a buffalo-hunting ground for hundreds, perhaps thousands of years, and the villages have been there for just as long. The river banks are mounded over with burial grounds as thick as anthills."

"You feel then that the Prophet is a Pontiac come to life?" asked Beaubien, who was nephew of Pontiac's great friend.

"Not quite. He doesn't work so fiercely, so destructively. But the result may be just as destructive in the end."

"Tonnerre! I'll be ready for them!" cried Peter.

"Slowly, my boy! We don't want bloodshed," remonstrated Joseph. "I'm just mentioning all this to show you some of the problems that Governor Hull has before him. It won't be just quietly sitting down at a frontier post and sipping claret and playing euchre and watching the soldiers drill at Fort Shelby."

"No! Not by a long shot!" agreed Campeau. "Things haven't quieted down yet between the English and the Americans. There are a lot of little boilings over, here and there."

"Things never seem to boil when I'm around, damn it!" exclaimed Peter again.

"I say damn it, too!" chimed in Beaugrand.

François clapped his younger brother on the shoulder.

"You'll have your chance before you settle down. Don't worry!"

"By the way, when *are* you going to settle, Peter?" asked Pierre Desnoyers, smiling slyly.

"When *you* do, Pierre!"

"Which will be *never!*" chaffed Antoine. "Pierre doesn't want to lose the advantage of having every marriageable girl in Detroit in love with him!"

"*Marriageable* only? Ah, we should drink to love, Pierre!" Peter poured a glass of Madeira and recited with sweeping gestures, the first verse of "Je Me Suis au Rang d'Aimer":

"Partons, allons, chers camarades;
    Partons, allons vider bouteille!
    Allons y boir' de ce bon vin
    Qui met l'amour en tête!"

(Let's drink the good wine
        That puts love in the head!
    Let's empty the bottle, revelers mine,
        Let's empty the bottle that sends us to bed!)

"Ah, wouldn't it be a grand sight to see Peter and Pierre dueling for the same lady! Mon Dieu, I wouldn't know on which chap to lay my wager!" exclaimed Antoine.

"By the way, are we all going out to see that farce of a duel in the morning, that Abbott-Hull affair?" asked Antoine.

"That duel of words at twenty yards? That duel that won't come off?" echoed Peter.

"Come, fellows, don't be so sharp. Abbott asked me to serve as second, if it *does* come off," confessed Bailly.

"He did? Oh, my! Oh, my!" Peter went off into gales of laughter.

As Joseph tightened his lips and the fires darted to and fro under his red hair, Campeau saved the situation by reverting to the uneventuated toast.

"What about that toast to love, Peter?"

"Oh, yes, oh, yes!" cried Peter, rising. "Come on, gentlemen. Up and drink a toast to love! À l'amour! À l'amour!"

They rose in various stages of hilarity and drank, "À l'amour!" while the parrot screeched incoherently, for apparently "love" was outside its vocabulary.

"Ah, that's too general!" protested Desnoyers at last. He lifted his pewter cup filled with a third pouring of Madeira and clicked it against the cup of Peter Navarre. "Here's to Peter Navarre, descendant of the kings of France, prince of lovers, king of good fellows!"

"And here's to Pierre Desnoyers, the beau of Michigan Territory—and hero of the Revolution!" laughed Peter Navarre, his devoted friend, the only one in the group who would have dared to touch this still sore point in Pierre's history.

"And here's to Joseph Campeau, sovereign of the Northwest!" cried Joseph Bailly.

"And here's to the Marquis of Michigan and the Seigneur of the Great Lakes, Joseph Bailly de Messein!" cried Campeau, effervescing like an opened champagne bottle.

"And here's to the great name of Cuillerier and Beaubien!"

"And here's to François Navarre, ruler of the Raisin, gentleman and good friend!"

"And here's to Jacques Beaugrand, hunter, trapper, and prince of good comrades!"

"Messieurs," cried Campeau, when the names of those present were exhausted, "I give you—Monsieur le Marquis de Lafayette!"

The little group responded instantly and clinked pewter mug against pewter mug and raised French voices with enthusiasm:

"À Lafayette! À Lafayette!"

Here in America, for this little group of well born Frenchmen, Lafayette represented all the grace of the aristocracy and all the spacious joy of freedom. For them he was a double symbol, whereas the Americans applauded him for his gesture of freedom alone. Even the Navarres, descendants of the kings of France, delighted in the courage and the charm and the democracy of Lafayette.

"Vive Lafyette! Vive Lafyette!" rasped the parrot, flapping its green wings excitedly. Then, in quick sequence: "Vive Vashton! Vive Vashton!"

"And Napoleon?" asked Joseph Bailly, while they were still standing. "Are we not to toast Napoleon, too? Marching towards Austria! Let's wish him well—and a great victory against Austria and Russia!"

"And England!" exclaimed Peter Navarre. "He's at war with England, too!"

"Oh, well, let's just wish him a great victory!" said Joseph, for he had only the kindliest recollection of the British regime in Canada.

"À Napoléon! À Napoléon!" Again the pewter mugs were raised.

"Vive Lafyette! Vive Vashton!" screamed the parrot, for "Napoleon," too, was outside his vocabulary.

At last the celebrants sank into their chairs, in a pleasant confusion of wine and patriotism.

As soon as he had sat down, Campeau, whose head was swimming, so that the sharp edges of his shrewdness were submerged, remembered something of which the parrot had reminded him.

"Ah, mes amis! Mes amis! One more thing! One more toast, mes amis!" He filled his cup once more. Tottering slightly, he rose and proclaimed in a high, shrill voice:

"À Georges Vash-ton!"

Those who could still rise, got up, with varying degrees of physical and spiritual resilience, and pledged George Washington, although their hereditary zeal was a little less for George than for the other two heroes.

"And, my friends, while we are still standing, some of us—and are still *able* to stand," suggested Bailly, still quite lucid and in command of himself, "how about our President, Mr. Thomas Jefferson, and our new Governor William Hull?"

"Une bonne idée, Bailly—very good." Campeau poured again, a little more haltingly than before, and the toast was drunk, a little more exhilaratedly.

Then, above the noise, Joseph lifted his large, melodious voice:

> "La belle Lisette
>   Chantait l'autre jour.
>   Les échos répètent:
>   'Qui n'a pas d'amour,
>   Qui n'a pas d'amour,
>   N'a pas de beaux jours!' . . .
>   Vive l'amour!
>   Vive la fleur-de-lis!"

> (Lovely Lisette
>   Sang the other day,
>   And the song echoes yet:
>   "Who knows not love,
>   Knows not the sun above,
>   Knows not the shining day,
>   Nor joy nor ecstasy!" . . .
>   Long live the heart no longer free!
>   Long live love!
>   Long live the fleur-de-lis!)

This started the music in the gay little French group.

"The fiddles! The fiddles!" cried Campeau. Tottering to the mantelpiece, he took down two fiddles. "Who's not too tipsy to play?"

"I can play! I can still see straight!" said Bailly. "Give me a fiddle!"

"I'll take the other!" chimed in François Navarre.

Joseph began fiddling and singing and tapping his shoe on the plank floor:

> "Du vin dans ma bouteille,
> Je n'en ai bien quand je veux.
> Ce n'est point du raisin pourri,
> C'est le bon vin qui danse!
> C'est le bon vin qui danse ici,
> C'est le bon vin qui danse!"

> (In my bottle, wine!
> I have it
> When I want it!
> But it isn't merely wine,
> The juice of the vine.
> It's the sun's glance!
> It's the fluid that enchants;
> The felicity of France!
> It's laughter, it's the dance!
> It's the dance of the wine!
> It's the dance of the wine!)

"Dance! Dance! Dance!" cried Desnoyers, and he pulled Peter Navarre out of his chair. The two began to sway into the figures of a contredanse, Desnoyers ludicrously impersonating the woman partner, with all her smirks and flirtatious gestures of the fan. The other Frenchmen clapped and sang. The fiddles squeaked. Those who were fit, intermittently got up and danced and jigged. The house shook.

The yellow light of dawn was breaking over the dormer roof before anyone made a motion to go. It was the weary Francois who at last started the exodus. Campeau assisted his more or less helpless guests in finding their beaver hats. Then he opened the door.

A blast of heavy, smoke-laden air came in.

The candles in the pewter sconces on the mantelpiece blew out, and black ashes from the fireplace scuttled across the floor.

"Bon soir! Bon soir! Good night! Good night!" The guests hurried out as fast as they could. Joseph remained behind to enjoy Campeau's hospitality for the night.

"I don't like that smoke, Campeau. Let's investigate!" suggested Joseph.

"Let's go to bed," said Campeau, shutting the half-door, and pulling Joseph away.

If Campeau's mind had not been slightly blurred by too much wine he would have leaned out of his half-door and studied smoke and fire and wind. Likewise, the five departing guests might have noticed something odd in the atmosphere if Pierre, linking his arms with Peter and Jacques, had not started singing again, at the top of his voice:

"Vive l'amour!
Vive la fleur-de-lis!"

It was only twenty minutes later when the bells of Ste. Anne's began to ring frantically, louder and more hysterically than they ever rang for early morning mass. The first streaks of red in the sky were mingling with sinister streaks of red lapping at the houses along Jefferson Avenue. The southeast wind was still blowing, picking up the sparks from the stable of John Harvey, the baker, where the fire had started.

As the flames devoured the little log houses, the sound changed from a crackling to a low roaring. Soldiers rushed out, half-uniformed, from the barracks and began to form a bucket brigade to and from the little river Savoyard. Citizens poured out of their houses down near the wharves, the old part of town, the crowded part of town, the teeming little business part of town. Furniture was thrown out of windows, looking glasses, feather beds, rose-wood clocks, gold Louis XIV chairs, everything, anything.

Abbott rushed out of his house, fully and competently clothed, a gun in his right hand, a sword in his left. He had been preparing for his journey to the dueling ground! Gesticulating with the gun, he roared to the swarming, frenzied people in the street:

"Keep calm! Keep calm! Save my house, and you save the

town! Come! Come! A fine reward to every man who works! Buckets! Buckets! To the river! Sarah! Sarah! Pompey! Pompey! Pompey, you black devil, where are you?"

That reminded Sarah of something.

"Pompey's not here, James! Oh, James, James, what will happen to Ann Wyley? You must run and set Ann free! She'll burn to death! Where's the key to the padlock of her chain?"

"That's right. It's on the mantel. But we've got to finish getting the children off first. Hurry Mullett and Tetro off in the cart with them to the Indian mound. Then you run and let Ann loose. She's had enough punishment, I guess. She's probably frightened to death, this minute. I'll stay here and see what I can do about saving the house!"

With much scampering of black slaves and white children Abbott's orders were obeyed, and little Sarah, Madison, Bill, and Robert were soon bobbing over the stones in a two-wheeled cart, while Tetro cracked his whip as loudly as the flames, over the frightened pony. Mrs. Abbott, with the key in her hand, rushed out of the house. As she passed Campeau's house, she saw Joseph Bailly helping Campeau to organize a bucket brigade.

"Help! Help me, Joseph Bailly!" Sarah called out when Campeau's voice had subsided.

Campeau had been calling for Crow as Abbott had called for Pompey in the emergency: "Crow! Crow! You rascal! Come here, thees meen-it! Crow! Crow!"

Bailly ran towards Sarah with a bucket in his hand. "What may I do for you, Sarah?"

"Help me save Ann Wyley's life. You can be back in just a minute. I'm so nervous I don't think I could unlock the padlock alone."

Bailly, torn between two duties, set down the bucket and called out to Campeau:

"Back in a minute, Campeau. Work like the devil, boys!"

Joseph and Sarah ran to the market place. They met Pompey humping along towards home, looking at the ground and murmuring: "Oh, Lawdy, Lawdy! Oh, Lawdy, Lawdy!"

"Run home, Pompey! Run! What's the matter with you? Mr. Abbott needs you!" cried Sarah, as she fled past.

Arrived at the almost deserted market place, they hurried to the whipping post, where tragedy was huddled. There lay Crow, at the foot of the post, screaming like a madman, while Ann's relaxed body hung from the chains attached to her wrists.

"She daid! She daid! She scairt into de ground! Oh, Gawd! Oh, Gawd! Oh, Gawd!"

"Give me the key, Sarah. Stay back!" said Joseph.

He took the key, unlocked the padlock, and Ann's literally frightened-to-death body fell into his arms.

"Was she afraid of being whipped or afraid of the fire, Crow? What happened?"

"Afraid the Jedgment Day. All de smoke. All de fire. Afraid de Debil come get her. Oh, Gawd! Oh, Gawd!"

"Come, Crow, come! You must get out of here! The fire's coming this way!"

"I not leave Ann. She comin' wid me. She mah wife!"

Joseph had already stooped over Ann and ascertained that she was not in any African trance or coma, but was indeed dead. Now Crow leaned down, lifted Ann over his shoulder, her black hair, dress, and arms lying solemnly over his scarlet costume, and ran like a stricken animal before a forest fire.

Joseph, supporting Sarah by the arm and murmuring, "Never mind! Never mind! It couldn't be helped. Buck up! Buck up!" hurried back to Campeau's.

The little Frenchman, with an efficiency similar to Abbott's, but not so bellowing a voice, was continuing to organize his bucket brigade to drench and preserve his own house and the Church of Ste. Anne across the way. Now he was speaking in his broken English:

"Here you all! Frenchmen to ze buckets! I geev you seexpence! I geev you seexpence!"

Campeau's parrot, which seemed to have been forgotten and yet to have sensed danger and commotion, could be heard screeching wildly about Lafayette and Vash-ton and indeterminate people and things. Sarah rushed on to her own house, and Joseph began to work desperately again keeping the line of frantic Frenchmen in order, scooping up huge bucketfuls from the river and even looking up now and then to pat some frightened girl on the sleeve and say:

"There, there, Annette! Don't take on so! We'll be all right!"

"All right, monsieur? Look at those flames. We'll all be burned to death! Look! Let's run!"

"Not yet! Not yet!"

Father Richard had set a little boy to continue ringing the bells, while he carried from the church the precious vestments, the altar cloth, the silver vessels, and packed them on the backs of two Canadian ponies loaned to him by Campeau. These were driven off shortly to the Indian mound by one of Campeau's slaves.

At the Desnoyers house and the Beaubien house similar activities were going on. The various young men, who had recently come from Campeau's house and had begun to undress for bed, had roused themselves from the fumes of the grape at the sound of Ste. Anne's bells and were now doing their best to save their separate properties, while their guests from the River Raisin assisted. None of them looked quite so handsome as the night before. Pierre Desnoyers' blond hair was unclubbed and scattered over his shoulers, and he was bare to the waist, having taken time only to pull up his trousers before rushing out. But several girls in his neighborhood had gathered near him and, completely forgetting the fire, were whispering to each other and exclaiming on the glory of his shoulders and the muscles of his back.

"Mon Dieu, he is beautiful! A young god! I thought he was beautiful in his clothes, but—"

"He needs no clothes!" Wild giggles.

"Come, you little witch!" The mother of the last commentator gave her a resounding spank. "Go, get your belongings together! Even your young god can't save us! Run!"

At this moment, an even more surprising sight than Pierre Desnoyers' half-nakedness opened the girls' eyes wider. For now an entirely naked man ran out of a near-by house and sprinted like the very devil down Ste. Anne Street, a shrill-voiced woman pursuing him with a broom.

"Get out, you worthless sot! Run the other way! Run *into* the fire! Sold your clothes for rum again, did you? Turn around! Burn up, MacNiff! Burn up and roast to a crisp!"

The girls paused, saucer-eyed, on their doorsteps before disappearing into their houses in a renewed burst of giggles. MacNiff's sprees were well known in Detroit. It was Joseph Campeau, of course, who always had to buy him a new suit of clothes after these Godiva gambols.

Meanwhile, Abijah Hull was trotting out of town on his brown mare, a whole armament of guns, swords, and rapiers tied to his saddlebags. So intent was he on his revengeful journey to the Petite Côte, so coiled in his own emotions, that he did not even turn to look behind him, was not even aware of the flames that were licking over the southeastern part of town nor of the smoke that was eating into his nostrils. It was only when four men on horseback came galloping along the road towards him that he looked up. The leader drew up so suddenly, seeing Abijah, that his horse reared.

"Man! Man! Is that Detroit?"

"Huh?"

"I say! Are you deaf? *Is that Detroit?*"

Abijah came out of the swirl of his emotions, out of the duel that he was already furiously enacting, and turned, absent-eyed, in his saddle.

"My Gawd! My Gawd! *I hope Abbott's roasting!*"

"The man's crazy," said the leader, and started on.

"It *is* Detroit! Who are *you?*" called Hull after him.

The last man on horseback, as he galloped past Abijah, shouted: "Governor Hull!"

"Governor Hull! Governor Abijah Hull! That man's got the *right idea!* I *may* be Governor if I go back and take matters in hand! Governor Abijah Hull! Hooray!" And Abijah turned and rode back towards the blaze.

By this time, all efforts to save Abbott's house had proved vain. Blackened and singed, Abbott had been the last to leave the premises, hoping against hope that the wind would change. Sarah had followed the slaves and the children, on horseback, down the river road. She had had time to take with her only a miniature of her father, Captain Whistler, a silver coffee urn, and a few provisions. Now Abbott, having competently ordered a barge to be loaded with flour, sugar, whisky, and furs and poled down the river, had at last jumped on his horse, and was rushing away, the flames almost licking his coat tails.

Campeau had also sent Madame Campeau and his children off in carts and on horseback, while he and Bailly and a dozen friendly

Frenchmen worked against wind, flame, and time. The flames, gathering momentum, were now roaring down narrow Ste. Anne Street.

"C'est fini, mon ami. It is finished," said Campeau, at last. "The bells of Ste. Anne's have stopped ringing. Let us see what else we can do to help."

Most of the young men and boys, and half of Campeau's slaves who had been helping, were now running down the street. Father Richard was kneeling in front of the church door. Campeau and Bailly stood still, their eyes suddenly blurred. Already the air was hot and loud with the voice of fire, the falling of timbers, the crackling of dry moss on roofs, the swish of red wind through the narrow streets.

"Come, Father," said Bailly gently, touching Father Richard on the shoulder. "You must go."

"Yes," said Father Richard. He turned upon Joseph a look which Joseph was never to forget as long as he lived—the look of a man whose only child has just been murdered. Yet, in the eyes as black as cinders, the faith of the zealot still burned.

"Yes," he repeated, "I must go. My 'lodge with bells.' My 'lodge with bells.' Your De la Vigne was right, Bailly."

As Joseph lifted him to his feet, he could feel Father Richard's body quiver down its entire gaunt length. It was dangerous to stay longer. Joseph kept his arm through Father Richard's and fairly carried him along, with the rush of his own strong body, through the street. In the deep wells of space, where, a moment before, the bells of Ste. Anne's had resounded, only the flames crackled loudly.

Campeau caught up with Joseph and Father Richard and together they ran out of town, to the east gate where Campeau's horses were waiting. Slowly they rode towards the Indian mound, which was swarming with human bees. Almost a hundred people were gathered, with their pack horses, wicker baskets, bird-cages, silver coffee urns, family portraits, pigs, chickens, babies—whatever of value or of no value had been carried away at the last impulsive, undiscriminating moment. An imperious-looking man on horseback was riding back and forth at the foot of the mound, calling out orders. With him were several of the soldiers from the fort.

"Who's that?" said Joseph to Campeau.

"Never saw him before. Who in the world?"

"Acts like the commander of the fort, or the general-of-all-outdoors. Sure he isn't one of the officers of Fort Shelby?"

"No. Who's he to shout out orders like that?"

"Why, Campeau, it must be Governor Hull!"

"Sure enough!"

"Sit down, everybody!" shouted the Governor. "Keep cool. Have courage! Guard your belongings!"

Everyone was trying to obey these injunctions when Crow, in his brilliant scarlet uniform, carrying the body of Ann, came hurrying out of the smoking city towards the mound. Running, tumbling, and moaning, Crow made his way to the mound, went a little way up the slope, the astonished group opening up before him, then dropped himself and his burden on the ground. Father Richard and Sarah Abbott immediately hurried towards him.

Apart from the group, on a lower terrace, comedy rather than tragedy ruled, where sat the abject MacNiff huddled in an Indian blanket, his wife standing guard over him like a frozen Fury.

As Joseph and Campeau wriggled their way towards Campeau's family, they saw James Abbott walking slowly along, beside his horse, towards his own family. At just this moment, Abbott suddenly looked up into the face of Abijah Hull, who had dismounted from his own horse and was somewhat enviously watching the maneuvers of the real Governor Hull, whose identity had at last been made clear to him. Pierre Desnoyers and Peter Navarre, standing near by, nudged each other, winked at Campeau and Bailly, and all four edged nearer to this encounter. The faces of the two would-be duelists underwent the various changes of amateur actors trying for the part of villain in a play. Then Abbott said:

"Well! Hell fire! I suppose we'd better shake hands!"

"Yes, I sup-pose—we—might—as well," drawled Abijah. "But you can thank—this—fire—James Abbott—that you ain't sprawled down by the Petti-coat, as full of holes—as a pepper pot!"

Abbott dropped the halter of his horse and said firmly:

"You go to Pontiac—and the devil!"

"So that's it, is it? To hell with *you*, you fat puff-guts, you bacon-faced fool! I'll fight you right now, to the death—and cre-mate you—in the blaze of De-troit!"

Abijah started to let fling with his right fist, but Joseph Bailly gripped his arm from behind.

"Keep out of this, you ginger-pated fool!" shouted Hull, screwing to look over his shoulder. He was unable to complete another invective, for Bailly had sent him sprawling, flat as a fish.

Father Richard had stopped his ministrations to Crow at the first loud sound of Abijah's voice.

"What's the use, Abbott? What's the use, Bailly?" he asked quietly. "The fire's wiped out everything: houses, farms, surveyors' lines, boundaries, and the pattern of all quarrels."

Father Richard helped the giddy Abijah to his feet, and held him, while he slowly recovered himself.

"'If any man's work shall be burned,'" murmured Father Richard, "'he shall suffer loss: but he himself shall be saved; yet so as by fire.'"

Sarah, in consternation, had also worked her way to the scene and now, as Abijah finally opened his lizard-eyes, urged:

"Shake Abijah Hull's hand, James. Do!"

"Shake the damfool's hand?" asked Abbott incredulously.

"Yes. Please do."

Abbott finally put out a reluctant hand.

Then Joseph extended his right hand, but held his nose significantly with his left hand as he did so, as from the propinquity of a skunk. Father Richard gave Joseph a look in which reproof struggled hard with a twinkle, and Pierre Desnoyers and Peter Navarre laughed outright.

After these small interruptions, the crowd settled back against the hill and watched the red-edged, black smoke rolling over their homes. From here and there on the hill came the sound of weeping. Crow still moaned incoherently near the foot of the mound. Even Governor Hull had ceased his encouragements and was silently watching the smoke.

Joseph, resilient, rebelled against the general helplessness.

"Pierre! Peter!" he called out. "Let's sing! Let's cheer them up a bit! Come on, let's sing!"

And he broke into the recently popularized "Marseillaise":

"Allons, enfants de la patrie!
Le jour de gloire est arrivé!"

Pierre and Peter joined in. The rest were slow to follow, resenting this loud, youthful burst of joyousness. Hearts ached too much. But gradually Joseph's infectious enthusiasm prevailed; the song took hold, and French voices were lifted one after another.

"Allons, enfants de la patrie!"

When the "Marseillaise" died away, Joseph said to his two friends:

"How does that song of the Americans go—that Doodle song?"

"Oh, yes," said Pierre, "that's a good one. I like that little idée: 'And with ze girls be handy!'"

"That's your motto, Pierre, isn't it?" laughed Joseph, giving his friend a slap on the back. "Let's see: 'Yankee Doodle,' that's the name! We'll start the song, and the Yankees will finish it for us! Come on, everybody. Let's sing 'Yankee Doodle'!" And Joseph shouted enthusiastically, so that everyone on the mound could hear: "Then tomorrow we'll go in, every last Frenchman and Yankee Doodle of us, and build a greater Detroit than Cadillac ever dreamed of! Come on! Come on and sing:

> "Yankee Doodle, *keep it up*,
>   Yankee Doodle dandy;
> Mind the music and the steps,
>   And with the girls be handy!"

Chapter XIII

RUMBLINGS AT FORT WAYNE

THE little village of Detroit rose gradually, log by log, dormer by dormer, slowly recovering from its fire. But there were other fires abroad in the land, unseen fires, sending their nostril-filling, brain-beclouding smoke ahead of them over the whole Northwest. The Indians were uneasy, the British were restless, and the French and Americans were stirring to the fumes in the air.

To all outward appearances, Joseph Bailly resumed his life quietly at Parc aux Vaches, but he was more than ever alert, aware, and busy. He felt the keenness of the pressure against him on all sides, and he could not attribute it solely to the strategy of an indi-vidual competitor by the name of Rastel. Others were reaching into the fur lands, and there was a discontent everywhere. Trader was pitted against trader, trader against Indian, Indian against trader; the British were subtly working everywhere against the Americans; the quota of furs was diminishing; and there was a feeling of general tension among the races, making a situation which called all of Joseph's abilities into play.

Joseph moved about continually from one of his posts to another. His carefully documented ledgers were full of entries from "La Fourche de la Grande Rivière," "Les Rapides de la Grande Rivière" (Grand Rapids), "Venture au Kinkiki," "Venture aux Illinois," "Poste à Vincennes," and so on. Joseph, apparently, had reached the peak of affluence in 1804–1805. For, in a dusty case in a dusty room in the old fort at Mackinac Island is a "Livre d'Emballage de Pelleterie" with a revealing page from the year 1804 in Joseph's fine French handwriting (and with his own spelling):

Chats	2759
Chevreuilles	1469
Ratmusquies	2170
Castores	221

Louttres 132
Oursses 59
Ourssons 8
Peccants 89
Renards Grands 197
Loups 56
Renard roy 8
Loups Cerviers 4
Martres 344

103,834 Livres.

Le 15 Aoust, 1904. Jos. Bailly.

Thus Joseph may be imagined for several years after the Detroit fire, busying himself with his various trading posts, riding over the old Indian trails, or paddling down the St. Joseph, the Grand, the Kankakee, the Wabash, the Checagou, packing his goods, managing his voyageurs, conferring wisely with his Indian friends, counteracting at every point the stratagems, the green words, and the definite underbidding of his hidden rivals. All his French shrewdness and all his "American" enterprise were combined in these affairs. Pélégor and William Burnett (agents, he felt sure, of Rastel) found their trading power gradually diminishing, under Bailly's tactful handling of the surrounding Indians. The bales of gold-brown beaver, packed on the backs of ponies or heaped in the long canoes, found their way to Bailly's central posts and filled his cabins with their soft mintage. A better quality of goods and a greater variety and quantity helped to turn the trick: silver ornaments by the bushel from Desnoyers' workshop at Campeau's in Detroit or John Kinzie's workshop in Checagou; blankets from Montreal almost as beautiful as the thick, five-point blankets distributed by the old Hudson's Bay Company; rifles ornamented with silver, odd trinkets and musical instruments from New Orleans (purchased at Vincennes, for Joseph had not yet visited the Gulf)—and always whisky. For Bailly could have achieved nothing at all without the customary distribution of whisky, which most of the Indians still craved with a fiery zest, in spite of the Shawnee Prophet's warnings. But Joseph's was a light brew compared with that dealt out at Fort Wayne, at Mackinac, and elsewhere. (The recorded recipe for this was, "Two gallons of whisky or unrectified spirits, thirty gallons of water, red pepper enough to make it fiery, tobacco enough to make it intoxicating." The cost of this hellish concoction was five cents per gallon, and the retail price to the Indians fifty cents a quart.)

During these busy years, which were moving towards the crescendo of later events, Bailly's private affairs were also prospering. The child born shortly after Joseph's return from Detroit was a second daughter, Thérèse, pale, with a fair skin, ash-blond hair and pale blue eyes. She looked as if she had not a drop of aboriginal blood in her and was as complete a contrast as could be imagined to her sister Agatha, who in the darkness of her eyes and skin so much resembled her grandmother, Neengay Lefèvre.

Joseph was, by now, ready for a son and stoically tried not to betray the slightest disappointment when, in 1809, Marie gave birth to a third daughter, Rose, a minute replica of Joseph, even to her copper-gold hair. Rose was born at the post at Grand Rapids in the very same week in which Jean Baptiste Beaubien's Indian wife gave birth to a handsome son, Médor Beaubien.

Joseph might have gone on living indefinitely with his increasing household at the wilderness post of Parc aux Vaches, if events had not begun to swirl like gathering dust storms along the unresisting prairies and through the portals of the oak openings. For ten years now, the Shawnee Prophet, Elkswatana, tall, ugly, and squint-eyed, brother of the famous warrior Tecumseh, had been binding together the Indians of the Northwest with his fervent preaching, prophecies, and warnings. From his village on the Wabash River, he had sent out his impassioned emissaries along the shadowy Indian trails, along the green waters of the rivers, and far up along the wave-white coasts of the Great Lakes. Around remote campfires, the words of the Prophet were repeated:

"The Great Spirit has made two different races, the red and the white. Let the white men worship in their own way. Let us continue to worship the Great Spirit after the manner of our forefathers. Let us continue in the old ways, the old customs, to eat only the meat of the deer and the buffalo, only the Indian corn, to dress only in skins and furs, to drink only water, to shoot only with arrows. The old ways are the good ways. If we displease the Great Spirit, he will shake the earth!"

Strangely enough, in the year of the first pronouncement of that prophecy, the year 1800, there had been two earthquakes in the region of the Great Lakes.

Gradually, the Prophet's words began to take on a greater resentment, a greater belligerence, as the white men crowded along the trails and pushed the frontier forward with greedy feet and hands. Fire crept into the words:

"The Great Spirit gave this great land to his red children, he planted the whites on the other side of the big water; they were not contented, but came to take our lands from us. They have driven us from the sea to the lakes. We can go no farther. . . . But the nation of the seventeen fires can be pushed back. . . . The nation of the seventeen fires shall be pushed back. . . . The nation of the seventeen fires shall be extinguished."

Down towards Parc aux Vaches, Indian opinion was divided. Then, on a day in 1807, something happened to sharpen the divisions and deepen the emotions. For Tecumseh himself, tall and splendidly built, powerful and persuasive, his coal eyes smoldering with those flames which were to kindle him into "The Shooting Star" and the "Torch of the Northwest"—Tecumseh, with three of his sub-chiefs, came riding on a black pony into the oak openings.

Tecumseh camped at Topenebee's village, on the Sauk Trail, a few miles west of the St. Joseph River and of Parc aux Vaches. There a great council was held. Indians came riding on their ponies or walking, from all directions, raying towards the centralizing power and eloquence of Tecumseh. For days, Tecumseh harangued the brown gatherings, his clear, sharp voice ringing out under the oaks, his eyelids squeezing down over the black eyes that became fiercer and more burning as they narrowed. Topenebee was utterly swept away by the force of Tecumseh's eloquence and rose over and over again from the ground to exhort his band to join with the great warrior-leader and with his brother the Prophet, the "Messiah" of all the Indians. Shavehead echoed the voice of Topenebee and added his special brand of animosity to the scene, his head, bald except for the upstanding scalplock, gleaming like the head of a vulture on its craning neck, the nameless scalps swaying from his belt as he gesticulated.

But it needed the moderation of Chief Leopold Pokagon to subdue the intensity of the situation. In long and carefully planned and very astute speeches, Pokagon opposed the great Tecumseh. He pointed out to his brothers how the white men had pushed ever and ever forward towards the west in an uncontrollable multitude, how the Indians had fought on those first frontiers by the eastern sea, in the valleys, over the mountains, by the lakes, everywhere, everywhere unsuccessfully. It was the will of the Great Spirit that the white man should come. If the red men were to survive they must shake hands with the white men, follow their ways, adapt themselves to the new world:

"Listen. The Great Spirit looks down and hears what I say. Listen to me. In the old, old days, tradition says, a crippled, gray-haired sire, Au-tche-a, the ancient Ottawa prophet, told his tribe that in the visions of the night he was lifted high above the earth, and in great wonder beheld a vast spider web spread out over the land from the Atlantic Ocean towards the setting sun. The old man who saw the vision claimed that it meant that the Indian race would be caught in the net of the pale-faced stranger. No, we cannot stop the weaving of the web nor the flight of the wind from the east. We might as well attempt to stay a cyclone in its course as to beat back the on-marching hordes of the paleface towards the setting sun, as they come sweeping over the Indian villages, the rice-marshes, the blueberry swamps, the forests, the hunting grounds, until nothing is left but black stubble. When the cyclone comes, do you rise and shake your tomahawk at it? No. No."

"Ho-ho. Ho-ho," murmured the Indians.

"No. You lie down flat and let the storm pass over you."

When Tecumseh rode out of the village a few days later, he went without the promise of the definite alliance which he had hoped to secure. The words of Pokagon, repeated over and over again in various forms, with great calmness, with great eloquence, with great force, had prevailed even against Tecumseh. Topenebee and Shavehead had been able to muster only a few of the wildest young braves to Tecumseh's side. The majority of the Potawatomi voted, for the time being, with Pokagon on the side of moderation.

Joseph discussed the matter with Pokagon.

"Well done, mon ami, Pokagon," he said. "But it is all a very bad business, isn't it? There are evil spirits stirring in the air."

"Yes, my brother. Motchi Manitou is very busy in the woods

and the prairies. Tecumseh and the Prophet are great men, but they have listened to the wrong voices. The Great Spirit does not speak with the voice of the tomahawk and the singing arrow. He speaks with the voice of the birds and the rivers and the rain."

"Yes, Pokagon, that is true. But there are many who listen to the wrong voices, many white men and many red men. Tell me, Pokagon, with Topenebee's young braves aroused as they are, do you still think it safe for me to live here with my little family?"

"They are all friendly towards you, Monami Bailly." (Pokagon and several other Indians had fallen into the habit of slurring Joseph's own oft-repeated phrase, "mon ami," into an Indian-resembling name for him, not unlike the Indian tribal names "Menominee" or "Miami.") "They all know that the Great Spirit has looked down on you."

This, Joseph knew, was the very highest tribute that an Indian could pay to a white man.

"Thank you, Pokagon. You are quite sure there is no immediate danger?"

"If any sign of danger arises, I will let you know, Monami Bailly."

"Suppose Topenebee plots something all by himself? Is that not possible? With Shavehead to help him?"

A flicker came and went in Pokagon's very deep eyes.

"It is possible. But I will let you know what I know. Do not be troubled, Monami Bailly."

Pokagon clasped Bailly's hand with bone-crunching strength and stalked away through the leaf shadows.

For three more years the Indians simmered and simmered under the influence of Tecumseh and the Prophet.

In early June of 1810, Joseph made the eighty-mile journey to Fort Wayne, riding alone. The first summer colors were sweeping over the prairies. The lakes of lupin, as if washing in from the blue waters of Lake Michigan, were flowing over the open country. There was the lesser surf of the yellow arethusa, and the coral-pink prairie phlox. On the fringes of the many little glacially gouged lakes and ponds, and along the sluggish creeks, the showy lady's-slipper was in full, cool marble bloom. The birds were equally abundant, meadow larks, cardinals, thrushes, wild pigeons and, now and then, in the groves along the St. Joseph and the Lake of the Woods, the tropical flash of the Carolina parrakeet. Now and then Joseph startled a covey of partridges as he rode, or a flock of quail or a few awkward prairie snipe. Now and then a deer bounded through the prairie grass. Now and then an Indian from one of the St. Joseph or Tippecanoe villages passed along the trail.

As Joseph reached the Tippecanoe River and the thick cluster of woods and lakes, Winona Lake, Lake Wawasee and Tippecanoe Lake, the signs of animal life became more abundant, a great timber wolf slinking to cover, a whole herd of deer browsing together, a multitude of wild turkeys.

At the river bank, Joseph dismounted to rest for a few moments and to enjoy the packet of deer meat and Indian-meal bread that Marie had put up for him. He loosened his horse for browsing, and sat down under some sumacs and vines, not far from the fording place, where he could watch the unhurried, green-brown Tippecanoe River flowing by, and rest his eyes on the tangle of fox-grape vines and elderberry bushes, wild roses and cardinal flowers on either side of the well worn Checagou and Fort Wayne Trail, where it dipped up out of the water, some sixty feet across the way. As he sat munching and watching, his attention was caught by a sudden agitation of the grape leaves and then a great, black-furred back. Then an enormous black bear padded out onto the trail and turned towards the water; Muckwah, the giant bear, whom the Indians loved to describe in their tales as "taller than the highest wigwam and longer than six canoes placed end to end." Joseph shuddered slightly, remembering a certain night in the vicinity of Great Slave Lake, and reached for his gun. But, before he could take aim, the sound of another gun split the air. The bear stopped short, jerked up its huge head, rolled over on the trail, and set up a pitiful whining, like a woman in agony.

Then the grape leaves were again shaken and the man with the gun came into view. He was a strange-looking man, apparently white, though greatly burned and weathered, with large, dark eyes set so wide apart that they seemed to stand almost at the edge of his face and with thick, black, bushy eyebrows that curved down and then swerved sharply up in a Mephistophelean manner; but so kindly were the eyes and so jovially upturned the mouth, in a matching curve, that the diabolical suggestion was completely neutralized. The man's costume was as contradictory as his face. He wore pioneer boots, cotton trousers, a red cotton shirt, a buckskin jacket embroidered in beads with the figures of the white-crane totem of the Miamis and the black and yellow turtle; there was a black ribbon tied around his short queue, and he was adorned with various spectacular ornaments, large silver discs dangling from his ears, silver bracelets on his wrists, and three brightly colored bead necklaces. His costume was a compromise between that of the pioneer and that of the Indian—which was understandable, for the man was William Wells, who had been stolen as a child from his Kentucky home, by the Miamis, later became Anthony Wayne's scout, and was now the son-in-law of his captor, the great Miami chief Little Turtle, and the Indian agent at Fort Wayne.

Joseph was about to call out from his vine and bush shelter when Wells began talking to the bear as if it had been a human being. In the quiet summer air above the soundlessly slipping water, every word, spoken in the Miami tongue, was distinct. Joseph realized, as he listened, that this was the Indian half of Wells speaking.

"You must not whine like a woman, no," said Wells. "I know I have broken your back, brother bear, but that is the fortune of war. It was decreed that one or the other of us should fall. It is you whom Gitchi Manitou lets fall. No use protesting."

More whimperings from the bear. With the ramrod of his gun, Wells struck the animal gently on the nose and continued:

"No, no, I say. Do not whine like a squaw. You ought to die like a man. You belong to the great bear tribe that is so much like the man tribe. Do honor to the tribe to which you belong. If you had conquered me, if I had fallen into your power, I would not have disgraced my nation, as you are doing. I would die with silence, with courage, as becomes a true warrior. Die like a brave, brother bear. Be still."

Again Wells struck the bear admonishingly on the snout. Gradually, the agonized whines eased into smaller and smaller whimpers and finally dwindled into silence. When there was no more sound in the air, Joseph rose to his feet. Wells instantly caught the slight rustle and rammed the rod into his gun. Joseph waved his arms and called Wells' name.

"Oh, you? Joseph Bailly!" came the answer.

"I'll cross to your side, Wells. I'm on my way to Fort Wayne."

"Good! We'll ride back together. But I must attend to brother bear first."

Joseph went after his horse, and mounted and rode through the shallow water to Wells, who was already kneeling beside his quarry.

Before the two men rode away at last with the bear haunches and the hide tied to their saddles, Wells performed one more Indian rite. He took the paws of the bear and some small pieces that were left, gathered them together under a large sycamore tree, dug a hole, buried them all, and covered the strange grave with brush and leaves.

"This I do, as you know, Bailly," he explained, drawing the last leaves over the small mound, "because the shape of the bear so much resembles the shape of man that there must be some relationship between men and bears. Therefore it is necessary to observe ceremony in the funerals of bears."

When the last leaf was satisfactorily in place, Wells stood up and, as solemnly as any white preacher, uttered his Indian sermon over the grave:

"I have now, brother bear, with deepest respect, performed the last services, for the dead. I would have you understand that I cherish the good will which has long existed between the family of the bears and the family of the Miami, and I earnestly hope that no offense will be taken on account of what has happened in this case."

Touching the mound once more reverently with both hands, and also touching the protecting tree, Wells finally walked away from the scene of his killing and mounted his horse. The two men rode away together towards Little Turtle's village on the trail to Fort Wayne. En route, Joseph learned something which surprised him. He had merely asked the casual question as to how things were going at Fort Wayne.

"Oh, trouble, as usual, Bailly, of one kind or another. My father, Little Turtle, has grown very old with trouble this last year. Many wrinkles. Many sad looks. Much gout. Feet like pumpkins, all swelled out."

"What special worry, Wells?"

"Oh, many mean traders at Fort Wayne, you know. Much whisky. Much fight. Much throwing fur pelts around. But more than that. Real trouble. Little Turtle is afraid his son, Black Loon, is joining Tecumseh, and also his subchief, Bluejacket."

"Oh, that's so much talk, Wells. There's no real danger. Our Potawatomi friend, Pokagon, assures me there's no danger. It's just a little excitement that means nothing, he says."

"Pokagon is so friendly to the whites that Topenebee doesn't tell him what's going on."

"What *is* going on?"

"I'll tell you, Bailly, for your wife is partly Indian and you are one of the men upon whom the Great Spirit has looked down. There is trouble brewing, and if I were you, I would take the Wing Woman and your children away from Parc aux Vaches for a little while."

"What harm could come to Parc aux Vaches?"

"It is on the trail from Fort Wayne to Checagou, and there may be many Indians with red tomahawks running to and fro on the trail before very long."

"I can't believe it."

"There has been a plot forming between the Chippewa, Ottawa, and Potawatomi to attack all at once, as in Pontiac's day, Detroit, Fort Wayne, and Checagou. It is true, my brother. Little Turtle has been working to try to prevent the Miami from joining, but his own son, Black Loon, is a renegade and, as I said, Bluejacket bears watching."

"I can't believe it. I usually hear all these things. They all come to me."

"Have you no enemies, who might include you in this plot and keep you from hearing of it?"

Joseph bit his lip, remembering.

"If such an appalling thing were to happen, how soon do you think that it *would* happen?"

"Six months, a year, two years—who can tell? The confederation is not yet strong enough, but it may be soon. From Lake Superior down to the Ohio, it is all like a swarming wasps' nest. Do you not hear the buzzing, my brother?"

"Yes. But I thought it was only the meaningless buzzing of a summer's day."

"It has meaning, my brother. Take care of yourself. It is hard for a friendly Frenchman to realize the danger—"

"It is all very strange—"

"Do you not see the red-coated wasps working among the rest?"

"Red coats? You mean the British who are helping to stir up the trouble?"

"Yes. They have spies at Fort Wayne. And there are silver medals passed out among the Indians. Black Loon wears a silver medal with the image of King George, as large as the moon, on his breast."

"I suspected something of all this. But it has all been so peaceful at the Place of Buffaloes, so very peaceful."

"Peace is a moth that flies against the storm," said Wells.

It was not until the following day that the riders came within sight of the trees that grew along Eel River near Little Turtle's village. Here the old chief lived among his Miami in a comfortable house that had been provided for him by the Americans after the Treaty of Greenville. Bailly and Wells found him already receiving guests in his well furnished sitting room. He was resting on a couch spread with the magnificent robe of sea-otter skins which had been presented to him by the Polish patriot, Kosciusko, thirteen years before, in Philadelphia, in the presence of George Washington. The costume worn even in his illness was imposing: a military blue cloth coat with gold buttons, a buff waistcoat, a red sash, blue pantaloons, deerskin leggings and moccasins, a red feather in his cap, gold rings in his ears. Little Turtle was not a large man, but there were great power and keenness in his small eyes, his long, thin, tight mouth, his entirely unpainted, copper-colored, wrinkled face. He was sixty-three years old.

Two subchiefs—the Shawnee Logan and Bluejacket, who had been the defeated commander of the Shawnees against Mad Anthony Wayne at the Battle of Fallen Timbers—and two American traders were sitting near Little Turtle, smoking and chatting. Little Turtle greeted his son-in-law and Joseph with placid enthusiasm, and motioned to them to be seated with exactly the same gesture with which a white host offers a chair.

"I am sorry, my father, that you have not been so well lately," began Wells.

"Thank you, my son. It is hard to be off the feet that have carried me over the earth for so long. But the Great Spirit knows best. Perhaps it is time for me to walk into those other trails where the stars grow instead of the yarrow."

Bailly was again astonished at the perfection of Little Turtle's English, which, combined with his qualities of leadership, had gained him so much respect on his visits to the Legislatures of Ohio and of Kentucky and even at the National Congress in Washington.

"Is there any other physician whom I could bring to you, my father?"

"No, my son. We have tried all the medicine men between here and Detroit and Louisville. You have been very good to me."

"There was once a josakeed at Arbre Croche named De la Vigne who claimed—" began Wells.

"He claimed too much. He is a very evil man," said Little Turtle, looking narrowly at Bailly, "—as you very well know, my brother."

"Yes, I know," answered Bailly, surprised at the extent of Little Turtle's information. "Is he still in the Lake Superior country, as I know he has been recently, or at Arbre Croche?"

"He is again at Arbre Croche. He is now a very good friend of a certain fur merchant whom you also know, a man whom he once hated. It is a bad combination, my brother." Again Little Turtle's long, deep look gave Joseph all the information that he needed. The ears of the two traders sharpened like fox ears, but the conversation was deftly swerved by Joseph.

"I'd trade my feet for yours, if I could, Chief Little Turtle."

One of the traders took out his disappointment in this small conspiracy of silence, with an impertinence.

"I thought," he said, with an unhearty laugh, as he rose to go, "that the gout was supposed to be a disease of fine gentlemen!"

Joseph caught his breath. Wells put his hand automatically to his hunting knife, while Logan and Bluejacket touched their tomahawks. But Little Turtle answered promptly and quietly, though his dark eyes shot fire:

"I have always thought that I *was* a gentleman."

"You are right," said Bailly, with held vehemence. "I never knew a finer gentleman. President Jefferson thought so, too, as I remember it."

"And I believe General Anthony Wayne died of gout," remarked Little Turtle, with piercing gentleness.

The trader was belatedly alarmed: "Oh, I was only joking, Chief. You didn't think I meant that, did yah? No harm in a little joke, is there?"

"No harm in a harmless little joke. Little Turtle will prove that he *is* a gentleman by forgetting what you said."

With this, Little Turtle extended his copper-colored hand to the trader who, discomfited, shook it and quickly left the lodge. The other trader excused himself a moment later, leaving Joseph, Wells, and the three Indians alone.

"Let me kill him, Michikinaqwa," muttered Bluejacket, using the Indian form of Little Turtle's name.

Bluejacket's eyes were very small and narrow, his lips so thin and tight that they were almost invisible, and three wrinkles ran from beside each tense nostril to the chin. He had shifted from British to American and American to British partialities more than once and was well known for his treacheries and his cunning. Like Little Turtle's face, however, Logan's was inclined towards pleasantness, with an upgoing mouth and crinkles of past laughter about the eyes. Logan was simply dressed, with few ornaments, but Bluejacket wore the kind of blue coat which had given him his name, a red shirt, a silver necklace with a silver disc as large as a saucer on his chest, many bangles and armlets and anklets that jingled as he walked, and a red and blue toque with an eagle feather stuck into it at a rakish angle. Joseph had never liked or trusted Bluejacket, and he could not help wondering just how loyal Bluejacket might be to Wells, for instance, whose bitter enemy he had been at the Battle of Fallen Timbers. Little Turtle looked so calmly and steadily at Bluejacket that the subchief's angry gaze dropped before the level intelligence of the old man's eyes.

"No. No killing," said Little Turtle. "He meant no harm. He is a fool—and the Great Spirit protects fools."

Under this Indian logic, by which the red man believes the abnormal person actually to be under the care of the gods, Bluejacket subsided.

"Too many of these fellows are impudent," said Wells. "It makes me ashamed, sometimes, of my American blood. Your French trader may be a bit hilarious at times, but he's always polite, Bailly."

"Thank you," answered Joseph. "I'm afraid there are exceptions to that. But there are old European traditions of courtesy among the French, of course, and a feeling of warm sympathy which makes them genuinely *like* people and want to make them comfortable."

"That's one reason why the French and the Indians have always understood each other," explained Little Turtle. "The Englishman says, 'Dog of an Indian.' The Frenchman says, 'Mon ami.' The two races were meant to be good friends. I think my son Apekonit is like a Frenchman, so kind, so sympathetic, so adaptable."

"Thank you, my father," said Wells, by whose Indian name Little Turtle had just referred to him.

"As for the British, they are stirring up more and more trouble, Monami Bailly. Look out for them. Such big storms come up sometimes—over Lake Michigan."

"That is what Wells has been telling me. Is it really so serious?"

"More and more serious. Is it not so, Bluejacket?"

Bluejacket stirred uneasily and nodded his head, the single eagle feather putting an exclamation point on the silent affirmation.

"So many young braves are so easily stirred up, so quick to respond to bad whisky and good silver, to ear wheels, medals and finger rings, to vermilion by the ounce and beads by the gross, and to redcoat lies and promises. For me now, the only good colors for coats are blue—and black," said Little Turtle, referring to the American soldiers and the Catholic priests.

"Yes. But red and black mean war," put in Logan, referring to the colors of the paint assumed by the Indians when they started out to war.

"There was a time," remarked Little Turtle, smiling reminiscently, "when we all fought against the Americans. But we are as hummingbirds battling the eagles. The strength is no longer in us to hold back the inevitable—the Americans. We are as sword grass blunted and battered by the waves of Lake Michigan. Long,

long ago our prophets saw the multitudes of white people marching across the beautiful hunting grounds of America. The time has
come."

Bluejacket rose and walked to the window, his bangles tinkling
slightly as he walked. There he stood, very still, looking out on
the river, and concealing the strong emotions which might be
working on his face, through the mask of Indian control. Joseph
was able to guess what were the vehement emotions of this man
who had led the desperate Indians at Fallen Timbers, this man who
lacked the mellowness and wisdom and acquiescence of Pokagon
and Logan and Little Turtle, and who was so loath to relinquish
Indian sovereignty. A wave of pity swept over Joseph for this
doomed, defiant savage. For an instant he felt a certain kinship
with Bluejacket, the relationship of the Frenchman in America
who also had lost his racial right to the soil and had been driven
from the sovereignty of Canada and of the beautiful lake country,
and at last from the vast reaches of the Mississippi country, the
water-hyacinth bayous and the old French plantations of Louisiana. Joseph felt an almost uncontrollable desire to walk over and
put his hand on Bluejacket's shoulder and say to him: "We've
both lost out, Bluejacket. But never mind. It is for us, as individuals, to fight for a sovereignty which our people have lost. Gird
yourself, Bluejacket, and be a *person*. I'm beating them, beating
them all, not so much as a Frenchman, but as Joseph Bailly, fur
trader. We've lost out as races, but not as *men*, Bluejacket."

But what Bailly said was:

"If you had to go to battle again, Bluejacket, how many men
could you muster?"

Bluejacket turned from the window, the tight, down-drawn
lips the only remaining sign of the inner battle he had waged, considered a moment, and answered:

"I think we could raise two hundred warriors here on the Eel
River. Don't you, Michikinaqwa?"

"Not quite so many, Bluejacket."

"But with Bluejacket leading them into battle, and Little Turtle
directing, they'd seem like twice as many, wouldn't they?" With
this touch of French courtesy, Joseph imparted the hint of a
smile to Bluejacket's lips.

"I may not live to see this last stand-up of the British and Amer-

icans," said Little Turtle; "but Logan and Wells and Bluejacket
will carry on, until the redcoats are pushed back across the sea and
all this territory is in the hands of the Long Knives."

"You will live to see it, my father. You *must* live to see it," declared Wells.

"I have seen many things, Apekonit—so many things that my
eyes are tired."

"I do not see how I could walk across the earth without you,
my father."

Little Turtle drew his hand from the sea-otter robe and placed
it on Wells' hand in the old patriarchal gesture of paternal affection.

"You are tired now, my father. We must go."

"Not before Nau-ga-ooh brings you some food."

After partaking of the bowls of rice and wild strawberries, Wells
and Bailly, accompanied for a short distance by Bluejacket,
trotted off, on the old trail to Fort Wayne. In the late gold afternoon, they came within view of the groves that lay along the
famous three rivers.

The farther outskirts of Fort Wayne were the level river
meadows. The tall groves rose up half a mile from the rivers.
There was no upstanding structure to be seen from a distance as at
Detroit—only the overshadowing trees and the horizontal lines
of the log cabins of the old French village on the west bank of
the St. Joseph River, the bark lodges and bright tepees of the
Miami village on the east bank, and the stockade and unpretentious
fort of Anthony Wayne on the west bank of the Maumee River,
formed here by the joining of the St. Joseph and the St. Marys,
whose tortuous windings from the sodden glacial lakes of Michigan and Ohio it continued serenely towards Lake Erie. The rivers,
with the magnificent oaks and elms and the park-smooth green-
swards of Fort Wayne, made a beautiful picture. The place seemed
predestined for great events, even apart from its possession of that
brief, historic portage to the Wabash, which had made it for
centuries the "Beautiful Gate" of the Indians and the traders.

Joseph and Wells rode slowly along, greeting Indians and voyageurs on the way, their path echoing with the soft bonjour of
the voyageurs and that harsher imitation, the boozoo or boojoo of
the Indians.

Wells owned a farm and farmhouse on the eastern side of the village, and towards this the two men rode.

"After only three days away," said Wells, "I'll be glad to see my wife and my niece. You've never met my niece, have you, Bailly?"

"No. I didn't even know you had one."

"If you knew me better, you'd realize right well I had a niece. I'm proud of Becky. She's the daughter of my brother Samuel Wells of Louisville, Kentucky, and a finer, brighter, sturdier girl you never saw. She's been visiting us for three months, and my brother's beginning to get impatient. Seems she doesn't want to go back to Louisville just yet!" Wells struck his thigh and laughed.

"I don't wonder she likes you and the place," remarked Joseph.

"Oh, that isn't it! All the men in the garrison are courting her, but it looks as if Captain Heald were winning out. He's quite desperate, because he's been ordered to take Captain Whistler's place at Fort Dearborn, and must make the transfer in a few days. He's older than Becky's other suitors—about twelve years older, I think. But he's a fine fellow and I'm all for him!"

"Yes, he is a fine fellow. I ran into him once or twice at Vincennes, when he was at the post down there. An upstanding chap and a good soldier, I should say. Just the commander for Fort Dearborn, until all these British-Indian commotions are settled."

"I think so, too. But we'll miss him at Fort Wayne. Hope Captain Rhea, whom they're sending in, will be half as good. I'll be interested to see how Becky chooses."

"Would you mind her going to Checagou?"

"Not a bit. Becky looks like a Louisville belle, but she has the hard fiber of a good frontierswoman, under all the flounces and furbelows. I've been riding her all over the country these last few weeks, and she can ride like a cavalryman and endure like a Miami brave. She's a grand girl. Wish you weren't already married, Bailly. You might be in the running too."

"Thanks, Wells, but I'm well fixed. My wife, too, has everything that a fine lady and a brave Indian should have!"

"Yes. You're lucky. Her reputation carries far. The Indians love her, and so do the whites. But why haven't you got any sons yet, Bailly? Three daughters. Fine! But what you need is a son."

"Well, I'll raise a few grandsons, if I can't have sons," said Joseph, with a well summoned laugh.

But the remark hurt just the same. Joseph wondered more and more, deep within him, why, in the plentitude of his strength, he was not able to plant the seeds of sons.

The two men, after passing the Miami village, with all its hubbub of squaws, braves, papooses, dogs, tame foxes, and ponies and after fording the Maumee, came out into open country and into sight of Wells' large, whitewashed farmhouse, surrounded by cornfields, wheat fields, orchards, and neat truck gardens. In the corn three Indians were at work at the weeding. Under the apple trees, which were still in late bloom, two people were walking, a man in blue regimentals and a woman in white. Wells shaded his eyes for a moment.

"It's the captain, all right," he said. "Off duty at this time in the afternoon! It must be serious." And he chuckled again.

Rebecca Wells, seeing her uncle in the distance, left her lover flat and came flying across the fields.

"Oh, Uncle Will, Uncle Will! How good to have you back! Did you have a good time?"

The two riders dismounted. Wells kissed his niece, then announced portentously:

"Rebecca, this is the Seigneur Joseph Bailly, of Quebec, Mackinac, Vincennes, Arbre Croche, Kankakee, Grand River—"

"Mademoiselle," interrupted Joseph, laughing, "I am simply Monsieur Joseph Bailly of Parc aux Vaches. Your uncle exaggerates. I am delighted to meet you, for I have been entertained for the last fifteen miles with a description of your many charms."

"But, as you say yourself, monsieur, my uncle exaggerates!"

Joseph was delighted with the quickness which could overtake his own French gallantry, but he made the perfect amends.

"Your uncle exaggerates only masculine virtues. I see he underestimates the feminine."

Joseph, who had mistrusted the praise of a doting uncle, could, in all honesty, make this statement. The girl who stood before him in a white muslin dress and flower-laden straw bonnet, a medallion portrait of her father, Samuel Wells, around her neck, was undeniably handsome—handsome rather than beautiful, for

Rebecca was built more on the strong, masculine than on the feminine pattern. She was tall, with square shoulders and a face inclined to be square, with largish cheekbones and a determined jaw relieved by a beautifully undulating mouth, an infectious smile, and healthy teeth. Her cheeks were red as vermilion paint, her eyes very large and brown, her eyebrows thick and black, coming almost together above the nose; and there was a faint down between upper lip and nostrils which might some day develop into the feminine mustache so much admired by certain Europeans. Joseph noticed all these characteristics minutely and was surprised that the composite of so many rather graceless elements could be so effective and instantly likeable. The girl gave the effect of going out towards the world with all her healthy heart, and yet of possessing great reserves of reticence and strength behind the squares of her pattern.

"Come, Bailly, don't spoil my niece. She's a terribly spoiled baggage already."

"Speaking of baggage, what have you brought home from the hunt, Uncle?"

"Bear meat, my dear. Bear meat for a change."

"Did you have to go forty miles for bear meat, you old rascal? There are bears in the woods all around Fort Wayne! He said he ought to go on a hunting expedition, Monsieur Bailly. But I think he went on some mysterious business connected with Indian-agenting—or perhaps he just wanted to get away from my aunt and me. Indian, you know—and solitude!"

"Aren't you neglecting your caller? He seems very desolate, leaning against that apple tree," suggested Wells.

"Oh, it's good for him to wait for me! He's too impetuous anyway. Men always are! They don't know the charm of waiting! What do you think, Uncle? He actually wants to take me away with him to Fort Dearborn *right now*."

"Well, why not? Why don't you go?"

"Indeed not! Without allowing me to go back to Louisville and consult my own mind, not to speak of consulting my father and mother?"

Joseph sensed that poor Heald had a long wait ahead of him, if indeed his lady were not slipping through his fingers altogether.

He also sensed again the rectangular quality of the lady's character.

"Suppose he should find some raving beauty at Fort Dearborn to fall in love with?" asked Wells, with mischief in his eyes.

"There aren't any more raving beauties at Fort Dearborn since Sarah Whistler went away with James Abbott. The other Whistler girls are leaving with their mother on a lake steamer for Detroit, before Nathan gets there; and all the rest of the females are married women and children. I've already investigated that!"

"Well, scalp my head!" exclaimed Wells, surprised, himself, at his niece's strategic surrounding of the captain's situation.

Joseph put his hand to his mouth, as if to brush away a bothersome gnat. He was greatly amused at the thought of the stern and soldierly Heald being so completely outmaneuvered by a woman.

The three now began to walk towards the farmhouse, and Captain Heald, who had not wished to interrupt the first phases of the family reunion, started in their direction. He walked erectly as a wooden soldier, more than a little on the stiff side. At close range, he was a good-looking man of thirty-five, with blond, bristly hair, straight-seeing blue eyes and a tight, fine-drawn nose whose nostrils could undoubtedly distend when he exerted a little of his potential authority. He smiled a straight smile, bent a little from the waist, and extended his hand to Wells.

"Glad to see you back, sir. Good luck at the hunting? Oh, how do you do, Bailly? Haven't seen you since Vincennes!"

"How do you do, captain? Congratulations on your new post. You'll be a neighbor of mine."

"You're still at Parc aux Vaches? Good! What's in your packets, Captain Wells?"

"Oh, just a lot of bear meat. I had a good time, though. Stopped in at several of the villages, scouted around a bit—and learned a few things."

"Good news or bad?"

"Oh, same old story. I'll tell you more about it later. British at their old tricks. Tecumseh and the Prophet at *their* old tricks. Plenty of bubbling around in the kettle but no boiling over just yet. How soon do you leave for Dearborn?"

"Tomorrow, sir. I'd like to stay longer, but Harrison's orders are that I should be at Checagou by the 12th."

"When does Captain Rhea arrive?"

"Today, sir."

"Don't you need a longer time—to—show the new captain around?"

"I dare not stay, sir—although I'd give a good deal to be able to stay. Orders are orders."

"You're a good soldier, Heald. Has my niece been behaving herself?"

A troubled look crossed Heald's face, but he made a stiff little attempt at a smile and answered:

"Yes—and no."

"Oh, see here, captain," said Rebecca, putting her arm through his, and smiling up at him tantalizingly, "I've been behaving charmingly."

"You're always charming, my dear Miss Becky."

"But women can be charming and outrageous at the same time, can't they, captain?" suggested Bailly, with a smile.

Mrs. Wells had heard the voices, and now came down out of the farmhouse, Although she was dressed in white woman's cotton frock and apron, with a frilled cap on her jet-black hair, Little Turtle's daughter wore Indian moccasins and three sets of beads around her neck. She had a broad and ready smile, eyes that were almost shut in by the crinkles of affability, and was as dark as an acorn.

"Apekonit! Apekonit!" cried Mrs. Wells, using Wells' Indian name, and drawing his face to hers with an odd nuzzling kiss.

The two exchanged several questions and answers in the Miami tongue, and then Mrs. Wells greeted Joseph warmly:

"Bo jou, Monami Bailly. You stay with us, as always? Good! Dinner almost ready now. Come in. You come, Captain Heald?"

"Not this time, Mrs. Wells. Thank you very much. I'm needed at the Fort. There's much still to be done before we leave in the morning, and several of the officers are dining with me to discuss important matters. I really should not have been wasting—ahem— spending so much time here this afternoon."

Rebecca had caught the resentful word and could not refrain from picking it up.

"Wasting, captain, *wasting?* That isn't a very gallant thing to say!"

"I'll discuss that participle with you another time, Miss Becky. Perhaps you can walk down to the edge of the orchard with me, as I'll not have time to say goodbye in the morning?"

"I'll consider it, captain. I'll consider it," said Rebecca, with a mischievous look in Joseph's direction.

Joseph was the last to say goodbye to Heald:

"Well, goodbye and good luck, captain. I'm sorry I'm not to be at the Park when you pass through; but be sure to use our camping grounds and any provisions you need, and let Madame Bailly give you one of her delicious dinners. She'll be glad to do anything she can for you. And give her my love!"

"Yes. Thank you, Bailly. Your place is already famous as the only real home between Fort Wayne and Checagou and the most hospitable one in the whole Northwest—with the single exception of Captain Wells' house."

"You're good to say so. It's our joy to make it so. Be *sure* to stop off whenever you come through. I'll see you, then, at Parc aux Vaches—and at Checagou!"

"I hope you'll come over often to Checagou. It's far out on the frontier—a bit lonely, I guess."

"It wouldn't need to be lonely. May I be permitted to say that I shall look forward to seeing a *Mrs.* Heald there with you some day? Checagou could be a most romantic place—a place for peace and leisure and love!" suggested Bailly, with a dash of Gallic guile.

Heald could not blush, but he looked so flustered, and stumbled so much in the effort to say something sensible, that Rebecca took pity on him.

"Come, captain," she said. "I'll walk down to the end of the orchard with you!"

Chapter XIV

THE ASTORIANS

As soon as Joseph returned from Fort Wayne, he began to arrange for transferring his family to Mackinac Island. Joseph Bailly was no coward, but he did not wish his family to remain in the path of any oncoming human storm. Mackinac seemed to him the best fortified and the most opportunely situated post, and Marie was more than willing to pick up the family and bundle them off to the safety of the island, in a region which she knew and loved so well.

By the 10th of July, the necessary household belongings were packed on two Mackinaw boats, and Joseph, Marie, the three little girls, and two Indians embarked in a smaller birch-bark canoe. The little fleet made a bright picture, with the colorful Bailly family and the red-sashed voyageurs flashing red paddles, as it moved down the St. Joseph River and into the smooth waters of Lake Michigan.

William Burnett came down to the shore as if he had been the most loyal friend in the world, and waved goodbye with a group of the St. Joseph Indians until the boats disappeared behind the next dune-promontory. His eyes gleamed, for he regarded Joseph's decamping as an admission of defeat, little realizing how often Joseph planned to return on reconnoitering and trading journeys and to keep his hands as closely as ever on beaver traps and southern Michigan Indians. Burnett's muttered "Won't Rastel chuckle now?" would have changed to an unwilling "Won't Rastel be surprised?" if he could have read correctly the determination in Bailly's vanishing silhouette, as he sat shading his eyes and looking ahead towards the wooded promontory where the Kalamazoo River poured into the lake.

There was only one day of rough lake, when the canoes had to be drawn ashore and the family camped under the pines and made merry, while Bailly and the Indians hunted for fresh venison and the voyageurs, useless for hunting, smoked their pipes, wrestled, and fiddled and danced, and the children explored the beach for crinoids, translucent stones, green beetles, and drowned dragonflies. Marie reveled again in the beauty of the wide white shore which she had so loved in its upper reaches at Arbre Croche. Here were the same white gulls, the same cliff swallows and sandpipers and snipe, the same beautiful blue heron that marched with stately tread along the moist, scalloped sand or moved cautiously through the shallows in search of minnows. Because of the exultant noise of her children, Marie was not able to call the birds about her as she had done in the quiet, childless days, but she watched with delight from a distance.

At Grand River, Bailly borrowed a horse from an Indian and rode up to his post at the Rapids, and beyond to his post at the junction of the Grand and Maple rivers. He found reason to suspect that Rastel, by way of Pélégor, had been tampering there, for Jean Baptiste Beaubien reported the defection of six voyageurs, very poor furs recently brought to the post by the Indians, and his own discouragement, so profound that he threatened to leave and establish himself in Checagou. Bailly spent a half-day cajoling Beaubien, talking of Detroit and of Antoine Beaubien and the old associations of Baillys and Cuilleriers, and complimenting him, with a sincere enthusiasm, on the beauty and alertness of five-year-old Médor. Joseph did not fail to offer constructive advice, promised to come down to the post later and have a heart-to-heart, coin-bag to coin-bag talk with Pélégor and to send down in the meanwhile six of the best voyageurs from Mackinac and a little group of the Ottawa from Arbre Croche to mingle with and influence the Ottawa of Grand River during the coming autumn. By the end of the afternoon, Beaubien had become his old cheerful, optimistic self, and Joseph left with a smile and a curse—a smile for Beaubien and a curse for the shrewd husband of Corinne de Courcelles. Joseph would have given one of his fine front teeth to know of just how many of her husband's intrigues Corinne was aware, and just how glad or sorry she would be to have him damage Joseph's prosperity. He was not yet able to figure the thing out. The face of Corinne came back to him like the face of the

Sphinx, malevolent or benevolent according to the shifting impression of the shifting self.

It was the 20th of July, a beautiful blue day with the whitecaps running high through the Straits of Mackinac, when the travelers rounded McGulpin's Point. With the waves rising, sails had been hoisted, and the canoes had swept straight past Arbre Croche, Joseph promising Marie that she should pay her mother a visit as soon as they were settled on the island.

Joseph felt a thrill as he sighted the Great Turtle again, sleeping in its gray bed of gravelly sand, its green-black head and forepaws stretched out towards the western horizon, and the snow-white walls and turrets of the old fort jutting up from its mid-back: a sturdy place for sturdy men, where gales blew from three of the Great Lakes and from the blue ice of Hudson's Bay, making a frozen fortress of the island for five months of the year. Snow, hurricane, solitude. Yet, in its live months, nothing could be more alive than Mackinac with its mobs of strutting voyageurs, its jingling Indians, and the sailing vessels coming up from Montreal as plentifully as gulls. A man's island! Joseph's chest expanded a little. He looked at Marie and realized that, if there needed to be a woman, she was just the woman for the place. No little white-lace-capped French girls from Vincennes or Ste. Anne de Beaupré would fit in here, no British soldiers' daughters from Quebec—no brocaded Corinne. Marie would fit into the island as a gull into its nest. And the children? A rough place for them, but Agatha and Rose, the baby, were as sturdy as wild geese, and Thérèse, with Marie to guard her, would set her pale wings against any storm.

As Joseph peered towards the beach—it was characteristic of him never to screw up the flesh around his eyes in the contortions of curiosity or calculation, but to stare, open-eyed, straight ahead—he caught the images of many people moving to and fro, making a bustle greater than the usual midsummer stir of returned trappers and Indians. Marie also noticed it.

"Something happens, Joseph."

"Yes, Marie. The island's all turned out to meet you!"

"Really, Daddy? How wonderful!" exclaimed Thérèse, clasping her hands and looking eagerly towards the beach.

"Oh, no, goosey!" protested Agatha. "Don't you know when

Daddy's joking? Can't you tell? If you weren't sitting with your back to him, you could see his mouth turn up at the corners—just like this canoe! But you can hear his voice turn up anyway. Can't you? Besides, why should they all be coming to meet us, as if we were the people of a chief or a king?"

"Why shouldn't they?" answered Thérèse quietly. "Daddy *is* a chief—a white chief! He's a very great man!"

"Sh! Children! Sh! Sit very still," said Marie.

The two Indians were taking down the small sail by which the canoe had been carried over the crisp waves of the Straits, and were getting ready to negotiate the inner sand bars, with the paddles well timed to the rhythm and reach of the bucking waves.

The canoe had already attracted attention on the beach, and the crowds were darkening towards the point where the prow of the canoe was to cut the shore. Joseph could make out the usual proportion of voyageurs, Indians, and soldiers; but all seemed to be in holiday attire and in the state of hilarity that usually preceded an expedition into the Pays d'en Haut in September. Many of the voyageurs were wearing their cloth berets, into which were stuck at jaunty angles all kinds of flaunting feathers: eagle feathers, cockscombs, cardinals' wings, parrakeet wings. The best red sashes with tassels were in evidence. The Indians also were in full regalia of feathers, paint, beads, and silver bangles. The Nor'westers wore their Scotch plaids, kilts, dirks, and proud Nor'wester buttons. In the group were several Americans in dark broadcloth suits and ruffled shirts whom Joseph had never seen. But he recognized a sufficient number to make the home-coming seem rather pleasant after nine years' absence except for brief trading visits.

Marie, in the bow of the boat, was the first to be recognized and was loudly acclaimed by a group of Arbre Croche Indians. Then the voyageurs acclaimed Joseph:

"C'est Joseph Bailly! Bailly! Bienvenu! Holà! C'est le Seigneur Bailly!"

A dozen Indians plunged into the water and pulled the canoes safely in.

The voyageur Toussaint Pothier was the first to accost Joseph.

"Ah, comment ça va, Sieur Joseph? Mon cousin Jean Baptiste, where is he?"

"He'll be along in a few weeks. He's taking care of things down at Parc aux Vaches. Did you get the house ready for us, Toussaint?"

"Yes, Monsieur Joseph. The tenants move out last week. Everything in fine shape."

"But tell me, Toussaint, what is all the stir about?"

"Oh, some crazy expedition going across the country," answered Toussaint in French, "all the way to the Pacific Ocean. As if there weren't enough beaver around the lakes! They probably expect to find beaver out there as big as buffalo!"

"Who's in charge of the expedition? What is it? Tell me all about it."

"Oh, I don't know much about it. They can't get *me* to go. Look at those crazy fools with feathers in their hats—all going! Or so they say. Their bones'll be making a track as white as the Milky Way from here to the Columbia! Look at 'em! Bird brains, all of 'em!"

"But who's in charge, Toussaint? What's the purpose of it?"

"Monsieur! It is the grandest expedition ever planned! Toussaint, he is jealous," said a voyageur over whose shoulder trailed a plume of the snowy egret as white as the waves that were breaking on the beach.

"But will no one tell me what the expedition is and who is in charge?" asked Joseph, addressing the group.

A young man (in blue swallowtail coat with brass buttons, fawn-colored vest and trousers, and beaver hat) whose gold-headed cane was a quarter buried in the beach, as he leaned elegantly upon it, gave the answer.

"Pardon my answering the question, sir, since I have not the pleasure of knowing you, but this is the John Jacob Astor expedition to the Pacific in conjunction with another expedition by sea. Purpose: to establish a fur post at the mouth of the Columbia, Leader, Mr. Wilson Price Hunt. Mr. Hunt is standing over there by the house of Madame Laframboise, talking to Mr. Ramsey Crooks who, with Mr. Donald M'Kenzie, is also joining the expedition."

Joseph liked the compact answer of the young man, even while the news itself startled him. The manner of giving it was briskly American, though there was a slight British accent, and a tailored splendor about the informant more London-British than American.

"Thank you, sir," said Joseph. "That was a complete answer indeed. And from whom have I the pleasure of receiving this information?"

"Edward Biddle, sir, late of Philadelphia, now of Mackinac, at your service."

"And I am Joseph Bailly."

"Monsieur Bailly, the well known fur trader?"

"Thank you for the adjective, monsieur."

The two shook hands. Joseph felt fairly certain that his new acquaintance must be the brother of the well known Philadelphia banker, Nicholas Biddle, of whom he had read and heard more than once, but his Gallic delicacy forbade his asking a question which someone else would answer for him in due season. Besides, there was no time for asking any more questions now. Old Mackinac friends were crowding around—Samuel Abbott, Collector of the port and brother of James Abbott of Detroit, Michael Dousman, who had fought with Pierre Desnoyers in Wayne's army and now owned a large farm at the north end of the island, and various Nor'westers, traders, voyageurs, and Indians. Joseph was busy for several minutes with gay greetings. Then Marie, who was so surrounded by friends that she, like him, was momentarily separated from the children, clutched him by the arm.

"De la Vigne!" she said, in a low voice.

Thérèse, who was standing at Biddle's feet, suddenly flung herself at him, wrapping her arms tightly around one of his legs.

"Oh, don't let him look at my mother like that! Oh, monsieur, don't let him!"

"Why, what's the matter, little one?" asked Biddle, looking down and laying his hand on the child's head.

"That man! Oh, don't let him come near my mother! Can't you see, in his eyes, that he wants to do something dreadful to her? Can't you see?"

At this, Agatha came, made a little curtsy before Biddle, then stood up very straight, and said:

"Forgive her, monsieur. She has *such* an imagination! She would make a serpent out of a—sandpiper, and a carcajou out of a caterpillar! Come, Thérèse!"

Biddle threw back his head and laughed.

"By Jiminy, I'll not forget that! I'd say you had quite an imagination yourself, young lady! What is *your* name?"

"Agatha. Agatha Bailly."

"How old are you?"

"Almost eight."

"Just ten years younger than—your humble servant! Do you often make remarks like that?"

"Like what, monsieur?"

"Oh, never mind. Do you often make remarks—"

"No, monsieur. I'm not at all remark-able."

Agatha's dark eyes flashed with such premature coquetry that Biddle was amazed. He murmured something to himself about these "half Latin" children and decided that he must see more of Bailly and his interesting family.

Marie and Joseph had moved down closer to the boats, to supervise the unloading, and De la Vigne had slipped away, upshore. The Baillys finally moved together up the wharf road, towards their new home. Still more people came out of their cabins and log houses to greet the newcomers. Among these was Madame Laframboise, to whom Joseph gave a heartfelt greeting. She and her husband had belonged to the pleasant group at Grand River, and Joseph had not seen her since her husband had been murdered by the Indian, White Ox, in a drunken rage, on the banks of the Grand the year before. But he knew that Madame was valiantly carrying on her husband's fur business as if nothing had happened, an extraordinary feminine figure of dominance in that frontier world of men. She was a half-breed, dressed like a squaw, yet she acted with the grace of a Frenchwoman and the business acumen of an American.

"Madame Laframboise, I'm glad to see you. I know you guess what is in my heart concerning your husband, for he was my comrade too. I'm so sorry. And I'm so proud of you for carrying on his work so splendidly."

"Thank you, Monsieur Joseph. You were always a great fellow, and my husband admired you. And now let me present Mr. Wilson Price Hunt of New York, who is in charge of Mr. Astor's great land expedition to the Pacific. Think of it, Monsieur Joseph! To the Pacific!"

"It takes my breath away, sir! I'm proud to meet you!"

"Glad to meet you, Mr. Bailly. It *is* going to be a grand expedition. Wish you could go with us!"

"It does tug at my mind. I wish I could. But I'm all tangled up with interests here—and a family, as you see. I wish I could hear more about it."

"Drop in tonight at my house, Monsieur Joseph. I'll have Mr. Hunt and Mr. Crooks and Mr. M'Kenzie there, and you shall hear all about it," suggested Madame Laframboise.

"With *great* pleasure. Thank you. Au revoir."

Joseph continued his journey up the wharf road. In the little taverns fiddles were scraping, and voyageurs were dancing and singing and shouting, and Indians were reeling. But the house at the end of the wharf road was quiet and peaceful and full of welcome for Joseph, returning now with a wife and three children.

Joseph had to summon all his powers of reason and resistance that evening, as a result of the over-stimulating conversation at the home of Madame Laframboise. At thirty-six, he found his blood still young and coursing with the color of adventure. It was like a stream pouring westward towards new scenes, new enterprise. But his French logic held him back. Who knew whether this adventure would end in success or disaster? The stakes were high, but the peril-edged chances were equally high. Joseph still had a sure thing in the fat flow of beaver in all the creeks and rivers of Michigan Territory. It was a flow that would diminish, but meanwhile Joseph could take and take and, with his fine French thrift, save the shimmering coins that the shimmering furs brought him. No other trader in the region knew how to handle the Indians so well, to play his gifts so well, without overspending, to lay by the increasing gold so well. Even Rastel, who played his game shrewdly and tried to cut into Joseph's profits so cleverly, undoubtedly could not claim the net gains that Joseph's ledgers showed. Let Rastel, let the Nor'westers and Hudson's Bay, let Astor play their huge stakes—Joseph was coming along mighty well, in his own independent way.

It had been at once pleasant and painful to see Donald M'Kenzie again, whom Joseph had last encountered in Freemasons' Hall in Quebec on New Year's Eve sixteen years before. It reminded Joseph of his father and of the poignant remark M'Kenzie had made that evening about the certainty of Michel Bailly's living like a lord and dying like a louse. It also reminded Joseph of his first vivid meeting with Corinne. Corinne must be thirty-seven years old now. Joseph had casually ventured a question about her. Yes, she was still beautiful, M'Kenzie answered, beautiful in a hard, emerald kind of way—and M'Kenzie had slurred seventeen Scottish "r's" into the word "emer-r-r-r-ald." Everyone knew that she hated Rastel and that he had come to hate her; but some strange, magnetic bond held them together. And together, by their wits and their riches and their power, they ruled their little worlds at Quebec, at Montreal, at New Orleans. They had even gone back to Paris once; Rastel had come home with a bronze medal from Napoleon, and Corinne with such a supply of Parisian dresses and hats and ribbons and jewels as perhaps had never been seen on the American continent.

"Yes, continent—I said continent," M'Kenzie laughed over a poor joke.

Joseph had flushed scarlet, he could not understand why.

It had been unequivocally good to see young Ramsey Crooks again. Joseph had caught several glimpses of him in the old days at Mackinac, when Ramsey was a raw young clerk for the Nor'-westers and had not yet adventured out, as an independent trader, to the Missouri. Joseph recognized in him qualities similar to his own: a sense of high adventure, business ability, and square character surrounding the pleasant circularity of laughter, and joviality. Ramsey's face was rounder than ever; but his bulging brown eyes, drooping eyelids, surprised eyebrows, wide, mobile mouth, and long pointed nose on a face that seemed to call for a short, full nose were, of course, unchanged. Ramsey had at last explained in full Astor's plans for the expedition, or rather the two expeditions, for the ship (with Alexander M'Kay, Robert Stuart, David Stuart, and Duncan M'Dougal) had already sailed from New York to meet the land party in Oregon. And he had recounted, with reminiscent hilarity, many of his hairbreadth escapes from the Sioux and many adventures with competitive traders at the little frontier post of St. Louis. If health and gusto and a sagacity beyond his twenty-three years could carry a man to the Pacific, then Ramsey would reach his goal safely and come back with a packet of furs and fine tales!

It was with something of envy and a great deal of hearty well-wishing that Joseph stood on the beach the next morning and saw the great canoes push off for their journey to the west. Voyageurs splashing in the water and laughing like children, Indians wading in to give an extra push—it was all very hilarious and exciting! At last the old familiar starting cry, "To boats all!" rang out. The voyageurs took their places, the red paddles flashed in the sun, the canoes leaped into life. Hunt and Crooks and M'Kenzie waved till their arms almost fell off, and the full-throated boat song gave rhythm to the flight:

> "A la claire fontaine,
> M'en allant promener,
> J' ai trouvé l'eau si belle
> Que je m'y suis baigné.

> "Depuis l'aurore du jour je l'attends
> Celle que j'aime, mon cœur aime,
> Depuis l'aurore du jour je l'attends,
> Celle que mon cœur aime tant."

> (Since dawn of day I've waited
> For the one I love, the one my heart loves.
> Since dawn of day I've waited
> For the one I love so much.)

Marie, who had been standing a little way up the beach with Rose and Thérèse and Agatha, moved down to where Joseph stood and slipped her hand into his. Joseph knew all that her half-Indian silence implied, every word that she meant to say. The adventuring ache in his heart was momentarily forgotten, as he smiled down into Marie's face and, with French volubility, repeated gayly the last line of the boat song:

> "Celle que non cœur aime tant!"

Without waiting to watch the boat out of sight as it glided towards the shining Straits, Joseph dutifully turned his eyes away and, flanked by his wife and children, walked up the beach to his chosen home.

Chapter XV

TURTLE WITH A RED COAT

JOSEPH BAILLY, in his office in an ell of the house on Mackinac Island, sat tapping his quill pen on the open ledger in front of him. It was eight o'clock of the morning of July 17, 1812. Joseph should have been knuckling right down on the list of receipts in front of him:

Venture au Grand Portage :	£	1,000
Venture au Kinkiki		1,500
" aux Illinois		3,000
" à Détroit		2,500
" au Wabash		4,000
" à Muskegon		3,000
" à la Grande Rivière		7,000
" au Parc aux Vaches		8,000
		—————
	£30,000	

But his eyes went racing over the whitecaps outside, and his thoughts went tumbling over many memories. It was now eleven years since he had looked idly out of the window and Jean Baptiste Clutier had told him of the boats coming over from Arbre Croche and of the mysterious "Wing Woman" who would some day come with them. Joseph smiled. It was a pleasant memory and a full and a rich life that he and the Wing Woman had already lived together. There were four children now. Esther had been born shortly after their arrival on the island—another little girl, of course, and never the son of Joseph's strength, the tall, splendid son that his dreams designed. Four daughters—more than a little good-looking, all of them; the dark Agatha, the pale-gold Thérèse, the copper-haired Rose, and the brown-haired Esther. They should all have the best education that the continent of America

191

afforded; they should travel; they should wear Paris fashions; they should marry successful men. If he couldn't create a fine son, he could at least select fine sons-in-law! Joseph laughed a bit of his large laugh to himself. That *was* stretching the imagination! Already planning the husbands for his girls, the oldest of whom, Agatha, was only ten!

Well, business was coming pretty well still, in spite of the new American Fur Company, which was trying to swallow everything in sight. The Mackinaw Company and the Nor'westers were hard pressed, and Astor's agents had been after Joseph to sign up with them. But Joseph still preferred to handle his own business as an independent trader, under the aegis of the Nor'westers, in his small but astute and thrifty way. Late in the fall he went off to his posts, leaving Marie and the children alone on the island or at Arbre Croche, with Neengay Lefèvre; and in the spring he came back, his boats loaded with furs, of which he himself disposed at Montreal.

Joseph had intended to go down to his dreamed-of Mecca of New Orleans this year to investigate the possibilities mentioned by Campeau seven years before, but the whole continent was still in the process of boiling over. The British-American-Indian troubles were simmering. Only eight months before, groups of discouraged, weary Ottawa had dragged in from the battlefield of Tippecanoe, four hundred miles to the south, and had told of the complete defeat of Tecumseh and his brother, the Prophet, at the hands of General Harrison and the Americans. But Tecumseh was arming again, and the redcoats were stirring everywhere. The air was full of rumors. Here on the turtle-back island there were seventy-nine Americans in the strong little garrison. But, whatever happened, Joseph was comparatively safe. As a Canadian, he would be protected by the British. As a law-abiding citizen in Michigan Territory and on the island, under the Stars-and-Stripes, he had little to fear from the friendly Americans. He could be a witness but did not need to be a participant in the conflict. In the deepest heart of him, he was still French and an independent fur trader. Mackinac had probably been a wise choice for his home, though the garrison at Detroit was a trifle larger.

His thoughts wandered, for a moment, to Checagou and the little garrison there. On the visit to his post at Parc aux Vaches the previous autumn, he had ridden his black horse, Rabican, over the old Sauk Trail, the dune-ridge, and the beach to Checagou for a brief visit. He had stopped a night on the Little Calumet River with Alexander Robinson, that Scotch-Irishman with the pale blue eyes and corn-colored hair and eyebrows who traded with the Indians and had so endeared himself to them that people scarcely remembered at all that he was a white man. Joseph let his mind remember how beautiful the Little Calumet River had been, with its sun-colored water and the great trees bending over, and the colors of goldenrod and ironweed and asters and vervain reflected in the water, like the shimmering silks and brocades that Corinne used to wear. Deer bounding away from the river brink, turkeys by the hundred, pheasants, squirrels, foxes, wolves, bear, ducks, and geese crowding the Calumet marshes between the river and Lake Michigan—a perfect Garden of Eden! Joseph was inclined to think that it was even more beautiful than the Place of Buffaloes. And the same Sauk Trail that passed through Parc aux Vaches passed directly along the Calumet Ridge. If the world ever calmed down again to safety, the Calumet region would be a beautiful place in which to settle.

Alexander Robinson, leading a string of pack horses, had ridden to Checagou with Joseph. (Alexander collected corn every year from the Indians of the Calumet, packed it to Checagou, and got shrewd Scotch prices for it from the soldiers of the garrison.)

It had been good to see the log walls of the old fort again looming up in the distance from the prairie and the riverside. Joseph had wondered, as he rode along the sandy beach, how Captain Heald might be making out in the wilderness, and what had happened to the lady of his heart, Rebecca Wells. Was Rebecca pining for him back at Fort Wayne or consoling herself with Heald's successor, Captain Rhea, or was she back in her Louisville home, the belle of every ball and the breaker of every heart? Joseph had ridden into the fort enclosure, and the first person upon whom his glance had fallen had been—Rebecca!

Joseph had leaped from his horse, taken off his beaver cap, bowed very low before Rebecca, with French court ceremony, and remarked, with a smile which the protraction of his bow only partly covered:

"My homage, mademoiselle. But what may you be doing here? Are you visiting the fort with your uncle, Captain Wells? And for how long, mademoiselle?"

"I am visiting the fort permanently, Monsieur Bailly. Your poorly concealed smile tells me that you know exactly why I am here."

"I cannot guess! The last time I saw you, you were scarcely conceding a walk to the end of the orchard to a very charming officer of my acquaintance! Can it be that you conceded a ride as far as Fort Dearborn?!"

Rebecca had laughed.

"I took something far more serious than a ride! I took his name, monsieur!"

Then Joseph had noticed something in Rebecca's contour that decided him against further jesting—a visible proof that the name had not been taken in vain.

"I'm glad, Mrs. Heald—glad for you both," he had said simply, and had gone with Rebecca to pay his respects to the captain.

On the way, Rebecca had introduced him to two extraordinarily pretty women: Mrs. Louis Pettle, quite evidently the dark-haired Irish beauty about whom Lieutenant Swearingen had chaffed Pettle at the Place of Buffaloes nine years before; and Mrs. Simmons, wife of Lieutenant Simmons, a plump, flaxen-haired picture who, like Rebecca, was big with child. Mrs. Pettle already had two mischievous little boys clinging to her skirts. Joseph remembered thinking that Checagou was evidently a successfully "romantic place," as he had suggested to Heald that it *could* be.

Heald had seemed even more serious and much older than the year before. Things were apparently a little difficult at the new post. Louis Pettle, on the contrary, was lighter hearted, more affable. Apparently the responsibilities and charms of an unusually attractive family had turned the trick.

At the lovely, white, poplar-bordered home of Joseph's old friend, John Kinzie, just across the river from the fort, all had been carefree gayety! The laughter of the four Kinzie children, Elinor's radiant hospitality, and Kinzie's fiddle made the house resound from morning until night.

Joseph was startled from these pleasant memories by the sound of people running down the gravel road in front of his house. There was a babel of voices, low outcries. He went rapidly towards the front door; but before he reached it there was a loud knock, and he opened the door to Edward Biddle, whose face was as pale as his stock.

"It's the English, Bailly, the English! You're safe enough, but I wanted to tell you. Look out for the little girls! Where's Agatha this morning? At home? The English, my God!"

"What do you mean, Biddle? *What is it?*"

"They've crept onto the island during the night. They're on the heights above the fort. They've got a thousand savages with them. Michael Dousman's been sent to bring in all the Americans. Stay where you are, but, for God's sake, look out for yourself! You're all safely at home?"

"Yes. Thank you a thousand times for stopping to tell us, Biddle. It's just like you."

"I've got to go!"

Joseph stood stupefied as Biddle hurried along the street behind all the other Americans whom Dousman had been sent to corral. There they went, westward, in the direction away from the fort, following after Dousman like frightened sheep and surrounded by British redcoats, while their wives stood in the doorways, looking wildly after them or weeping into their aprons. How could such a thing have been accomplished so quietly? Not a sound from the cannon at the fort, not the smallest shot from the smallest gun.

But if the Americans should resist, should shoot off a single gun, Joseph feared not only what British bombardment might do, but what those thousand savages on the heights might do. He knew well enough the bloody history of his own Quebec and of the little American settlements, creeping westward over a pulp of mashed bodies and scalped heads, and he was sufficiently well acquainted with the contemporary Shaveheads and Topenebees, Asa Buns and De la Vignes, Bluejackets and Black Loons, to realize what might happen to Mackinac Island on this surcharged, sunny day if the least wrong move should unleash the wolves of disaster.

Marie had slipped into the room in time to see the last retreating figures and to catch the import of everything.

"I'm going, Marie," he said.

"Yes, I think you might be able to help a bit, Joseph. There may be hundreds of our friends from Arbre Croche up there. You could try to stop a few of the chiefs if—"

"Nothing could stop them. Not Blackbird and Wing and Chusco and Pokagon, and all the chiefs put together."

"I'll come too. I might be able to help a very little. No, Agatha, you may *certainly not go*. You must stay here with Magama and look after your little sisters."

Marie gave a few hurried instructions to Magama, one of the squaw-servants, picked up half a loaf of bread from the oven shelf in the kitchen, threw an Indian blanket over her shoulders, and hurried out with Joseph, who had put on his best white beaver hat and his olive broadcloth coat. Marie's effort was to look as Indian as possible, while Joseph was trying to appear British. Both had a dramatic feeling that, if death were to be dealt to them from the guns at the fort, they would be dying hand in hand, as they should, in an effort to serve their own household and the larger island group of which it was a part. Marie slipped her hand into Joseph's.

"I don't know quite where the British are taking the Americans —probably to the old distillery on the west side of the island. But we won't follow that small British guard. We'd better push up towards the hill—don't you think so, Marie?"

"Yes, Joseph."

The cobbled street that ran parallel with the beach and at right angles to the wharf road was absolutely deserted. The Americans had gone, and the British had hastened, at the earliest rumor, to-wards Captain Roberts' camp on the heights. The French Canadians were prudently staying indoors, behind their lace curtains and parrot cages. Now and then the pink blur of a vanishing face showed at a window's edge.

The Baillys did not take the stair path straight up to the front of the well guarded fort, but slipped behind, up the grassy slope, past the west and north blockhouses. There was tense quiet on the other side of the walls. The American flag still flew in a stiff Huron breeze from the flagstaff just inside the walls, near the north blockhouse; but the portcullis of the north sally port, which

Joseph had never seen closed by day before, was down. He came to a stop on the level sward outside.

"Marie, I don't want you to go any farther. This is utter folly. Look at the gate, and then look up there! We're in a devilish bad situation!"

From this point, they could see the steep, tree-crowned hill that commanded the fort so strategically from above. The mouths of two cannon caught the slant rays of the morning sun on their polished rims. The woods were thick as Autumn with splashes of scarlet, and Joseph thought that he could make out the darker forms of the Indians, although their bodies blended with the tawny and green summer foliage. Sharp glints here and there, like day stars, on the hill, showed where the rifles gleamed.

"There are a few sea gulls here, as usual," remarked Marie.

Joseph, anxiously scanning the hill, wondered why Marie should bother about the triviality of sea gulls at such a moment: there were always a few birds on the parade ground inside the walls, and always a few here, pecking away at worms in the rich grass. It was only when Marie gave a perfect gannet's cry, beside him that Joseph realized that she was going to attract *more* sea gulls. But why?

"No, no, Marie, you *can't* do this!"

"Oh, yes, I can, Joseph. I'll stand here and attract as many gulls as I can, and then the Ottawa will know that the Wing Woman is here, and they'll quiet down a bit and won't start any trouble in *this* direction."

"But the British don't care a sou about the Wing Woman! You're as naïve as a child, Marie. Come along with me quickly towards the British camp. No doubt Lieutenant Hanks has already signed the surrender, but we're not safe until the British flag is up and the Indians have gone."

"Give me just a few minutes, Joseph, in which to signal the Ottawa, and then I'll come."

"You notice that all the American soldiers have had the prudence to retire inside the walls? There isn't a single guard outside."

"I know this seems silly to you, Joseph—and dangerous. But, *please* just go over there and leave me alone for ten minutes."

Joseph retreated under the pine trees, and Marie set about her strange work. She started by throwing crumbs of bread over the grass, with the gesture of the sower. But, as she threw, she lifted up her head and gave the exact, metallic cry of the gull. Wheeling overhead, at first, in wide, suspicion-slanted circles, the gulls spiraled lower and lower, their gray and white wings sheer as snow against the sunlight, their orange legs tucked up under their bodies, their orange beaks brilliant against the blue sky. Down came the birds, settling about Marie on the grass, closer and closer, she now standing motionless as a tree and giving the unhuman cry. Down from the highest sky and up from the beach far below they came—herring gulls, little white terns, Bonaparte gulls. More and more of them, closer, closer, until several of them came to rest on Marie's moccasined feet, on her blanketed shoulders.

Then at last a cry from many savage voices on the hilltop, and Marie knew that she was recognized! For only she could have summoned the gulls in such snowy numbers. Doubtless many of the birds she had often called at Arbre Croche were in these very flocks. The others responded to her crumbs, her call, and her strange powers. Satisfied at last, she took a step forward, and, with a whir and flapping of wings and multiple cries, the gulls rose, circled, and flew off towards the white shores of Huron and Michigan.

"Well done, Marie!" cried Joseph, emerging from the pine trees. "You never drew them so quickly. A beautiful feat, my little Wing Woman. And did you hear how the Indians cheered you?"

"Yes. I hope I put friendly, peaceful thoughts into their hearts for a moment."

"I hope you did, Marie. Shall we see how far we can get by the back trail to the summit?"

They had not gone more than a half-mile through the woods when they met a small company of men, three redcoats, one of them carrying a white flag of truce, three hostage Americans, and two Indians, one of whom proved to be Chief Blackbird.

Blackbird dropped behind just long enough to say to Marie, in his own language:

"It was like holding seven hundred dogs on a leash until you showed yourself, Wing Woman. The Indians are thirsting for

American blood, thirsting, thirsting! Asa Bun and De la Vigne are like mad dogs. De la Vigne is so excited that he almost fired at *you*, Wing Woman. Take care, Monami Bailly. Take care. The British will be good to you—but take care, just the same."

Up the back trail that led from the Indian village southwest of the summit to the fort the Baillys climbed, then pushed through thickets towards the top, the highest point of the old "turtle back." For a quarter of a mile below the summit, the woods were full of savages and of redcoats on guard. Joseph took his old Nor'wester license and his more recent independent trading license from his pocket and showed them to each guard in turn, as proof of his British citizenship.

The few British of the island were gathered together in an opening of the woods to the southwest of the summit, under the surveillance of one of the underofficers. They were standing about, nervously chatting together, smoking pipes, and watching the Indians who passed to and fro like sinister shadows. A few of the island British had brought guns and swords from their homes and were ready to enter into active conflict, but Captain Roberts had sent word that there was no need for this.

Marie made it her business to move quietly among as many of the Ottawa as came down to this lower plateau. Redcoats, of course, blocked the path to the operations on the strategic top of the hill.

"Carry this message to my brother, Asa Bun," she said to one of the Ottawa. "Tell him that this is the Wing Woman's island, that the Americans are her friends. Tell him that American scalps are not good scalps."

"Carry this message to my brother, Chief Wing," she said to another, repeating almost the same words, and so she proceeded in her self-appointed mission.

During this message giving, Marie wandered some little distance from Joseph, who stood talking with the British officer on guard. For a moment alone, she leaned a bit wearily against an oak tree, wondering how much her stupid words would avail against seven hundred Indians painted for war. A brilliant carmine toadstool just beyond the reach of her left foot attracted her attention. As she stooped suddenly to examine it, a cracking thud resounded from the tree just over her head. A tomahawk had lodged in the bark at the very point where her head had leaned the split fraction of a second before. Even her quick Indian turning of the eyes to the logical location of the thrower did not reveal the assailant; but she knew very well that the tomahawk was still warm from De la Vigne's hand. Word had evidently filtered up to him on the summit that she was here trying to dissuade the Ottawa from ferocity. The new resentment added to the old had directed the attack. De la Vigne was undoubtedly equipped with a rifle, too.

Darting to one side, then to the other, in order to make a poor target, Marie bounded down the slope and rushed into the group among whom Joseph was standing. Motioning him to one side, she told what had happened. Joseph turned white with rage.

"Give me your gun, Simpkins," he said to one of the islanders.

"What for?" asked a British officer, putting a hand on Bailly's shoulder.

"A private grievance, sir."

"No guns are to be shot off without orders from Captain Roberts."

"Of course, sir. Sorry. I understand. The private grievance must wait." Bailly clenched his hands.

"We must have news here," said the officer, looking down-trail.

The group with the truce flag were returning. Although the message must first be delivered to Captain Roberts, it was perfectly obvious from the truce bearer's unworried face that he carried a surrender. There was silence in the group on the hill for some fifteen minutes. Then a trumpet on the hilltop rang out, and drums began to beat, with a happy, triumphant rhythm. The British were marching down the hill.

In as regular a formation as they could manage on an ill defined trail among trees and shrubs, they came, a company of British soldiers, then a company of Indians, then British, then Indians— the savages prudently wedged in between the watching British. As they went by, Joseph and Marie marveled at the obedience and orderliness of the Indians and the quiet dignity of Captain Roberts and his men. Many a smile of recognition went out to Joseph and Marie from passing Ottawa and Chippewa and Potawatomi, but Asa Bun and De la Vigne averted their eyes. At the end of the procession, Marie and Joseph joined the little group of island British.

The portcullis of the north sally port was open now. American soldiers stood grimly on either side of the gate. The American flag, visible over the wall, was still high, and horizontal in the Huron breeze.

The whole company entered the fort grounds. Under the flag-pole stood Lieutenant Porter Hanks and his seventy-nine men, all at attention. Hanks' face was as pale as the flag's white stripes.

It was exactly noon, the sun standing straight over the flagpole, when the drummers rolled the long signal and two British soldiers stepped forward, loosened the rope from the staff, and hauled down the flag of the fifteen stars and the fifteen bars. Then the cannon roared out, frightening the sea gulls, and at last trumpeters and drummers together blared out "God Save the King," every man standing at attention while the Union Jack slowly rose to the top of the flagstaff and caught the breeze with its scarlet crosses.

Neither Joseph nor Marie realized how that imperial flag and the news of its floating, carried by canoe and Indian runner, was to change the lives of their friends in all the forts of the old North-west, and how it was to alter the pattern of their own lives to the very end.

"Well," said Joseph when the islanders had been dismissed to their homes, and he and Marie turned away from the hill, "the old turtle of Michilimackinac is wearing a red coat now."

"What a funny picture, Joseph!" Marie's laughter rang out for the first time that day. "I must tell the children what you said! A turtle with a red coat!"

Chapter XVI

SKUNK WITH A RED COAT

AUGUST 15, 1812. A cool wind from far-off Hudson Bay stiffening the scarlet and blue and white folds of the British flag on the flagstaff of Fort Mackinac. The same dwindled wind from Hudson Bay fluttering the fifteen stars and the fifteen bars of the American flag on the flagstaff at Fort Dearborn three hundred and fifty miles to the south. Quiet at Fort Mackinac. Fear and trouble and suppressed excitement at Fort Dearborn.

At nine o'clock the gates of Fort Dearborn are thrown open. A low roll of drums, the thin sound of fifes and the Dead March from "Saul" lift solemnly over the walls of the fort and go quivering down to the sandy edge of the river Checagou and the lupine-colored lake beyond.

The first person to issue from the gates is Captain William Wells, who has come voluntarily all the way from Fort Wayne to escort the niece whom he adores, Rebecca Wells Heald, along the trouble-packed trail from Checagou to Fort Wayne. The Indians are at fever pitch of excitement everywhere in the old Northwest. Tecumseh and the British have stirred them to the boiling point. They are unrestrainedly eager to sink their tomahawks into American scalps. Governor Hull of Detroit has ordered the evacuation of Fort Dearborn and the transfer of the scant fifty-five soldiers and their families at Checagou, ninety-three people in all, to Fort Wayne. Lieutenant Helm has pleaded against it. John Kinzie has pleaded against it. But Captain Nathan Heald is too good a soldier to disobey orders from a superior officer. He carries out instructions to the letter, though they be loaded with death. Wells, with all his knowledge of Indians and Indian susceptibilities, is gravely anxious about the outcome of this journey. There is an unconfirmed rumor that Fort Mackinac has been taken by the British, and Wells has seen a few of the Ottawa of Arbre Croche mingling with the Potawatomi around the fort. If the news of Mackinac is true, it will give courage to every Indian in the region and strength to every tomahawk-swinging hand. Besides, these Indians are surging with extra hatred because Heald has thrown all the extra muskets and whisky into the water.

Wells is unrecognizable, disguised as an Indian in death paint, with black stripes running diagonally up and down his bare chest, and thickly over his face. An edging of dark green gives a lurid effect to each bar. But he wears a frontiersman's hat, the buckskin jacket with the bead designs of the crane and the turtle, and long deerskin trousers. His short queue, as always, is tied with a black ribbon. In his belt he carries a pistol, a knife, and a tomahawk. There is a rifle in the crook of his left arm. He is astride a black pony. Behind him ride twenty-five painted Miami warriors from Fort Wayne.

Never were Indian eyes or eyes of the foxiest white man more burningly alert than are the eyes of Wells as he moves out of the gate and along the sandy edge of the river, southward. A circle of eyes seems to glow all the way around his head. For he is watchful of treachery from behind, from the beach, from the prairie, from the forest skirting the prairie, from the pine knoll a mile and a half ahead. Excitement is in the air. Suspicion. Danger.

Captain Heald, with his bright blue uniform and red sword sash rides behind the Miami. A little distance behind, rides Lieutenant Helm. The fifty-five regulars of the garrison are on foot. The twelve Chicago militia are on foot. Alexander Robinson walks with these. Mrs. Helm (Mrs. Kinzie's daughter by her first marriage) is mounted, as is Rebecca Wells Heald, whose horse is a handsome bay mare. In the rear creak two covered wagons containing children and valuables. Foot soldiers flank these wagons. A few of the mothers also walk beside the wagons, as do Jean Baptiste Chandonnais and John Kinzie, who might just as well be paddling along in the canoe in which his wife and children are edging along the lake on their way to Parc aux Vaches, but who has chosen instead to use his strong personal influence with the Indians, for the protection of the Americans and of Margaret Mc-Killip Helm, his wife's daughter. A very small band of Potawatomi, only a fraction of the expected friendly escort, rides along on either side of the little caravan. Black Partridge and Topenebee are in the lead, on horseback, very solemn, very erect. At the extreme end of the procession ride twenty-five more of Wells' friendly Miami warriors, headed by Bluejacket, whom Wells has purposely put in the position of trust.

Music. The jingling of harness and spurs and swords and bayonets and muskets. The creaking of the wagons. The subdued cries of children in the wagons. A cloudless sky overhead. A smooth, sparkling lake at the left. A small caravan of soldiers, settlers, and Indians retreating from one frontier post to another a hundred and fifty miles back, towards tenuous civilization.

The eyes of Wells continue to glow like torches at the back of his head, at the side, in front. Suddenly he turns those torches to the right. The band of Potawatomi has dashed away westward, to the rear of the sand ridge that begins to skirt the lake. Wells notes a blade here that is not a sword grass, a plume there that is not a feather of prairie grass, a brown knob that is not a stone. The whole ridge is thick with Indians peering over the edge!

Wells' heart sinks within him. The moment has come! He is not afraid for himself. He has the Indian's fatalistic attitude towards death. Let death come at its own chosen moment, and may there be good hunting in the happy hunting grounds! It will be good, very good to meet Little Turtle again, who died at Wells' farmhouse at Fort Wayne only a month ago. "Such big storms come up over Lake Michigan sometimes!"

But Rebecca is not ready to go. Rebecca is still young and beautiful and in love with life. Rebecca is not ready, as an Indian is ready. Wells gives one flicker-swift look behind him. Rebecca is tossing her head back and actually laughing at some remark made by Margaret Helm, who is riding behind her. How beautiful Rebecca is! More beautiful now as a woman, and not as a girl is beautiful. She must be allowed to live and have more children— fine children to carry the good blood of the Wellses and the Healds. Too bad that first baby had to die at birth three months ago.

Wells takes off his hat and swings it around and around his head as a signal to Heald that the company is surrounded by Indians. Riding back quickly, he says to Heald:

"Indians everywhere, back of the ridge. Let's push on and take the highest point, where the pines grow thickest!"

Heald shouts out his orders:

"Indians on the ridge! Take the pine knoll! Charge!"

A hundred shots ring out from the ridge. Five hundred yells slash the quiet August air. Five hundred Indians rush down like fiends out of hell, tomahawks and muskets and white teeth shining, with a fierce dazzle, in the sun! Down on the white men, who are charging towards the ridge. Too many Indians. Too few white men.

The "friendly" Miami, headed by Bluejacket, have rushed off the scene, at the first sign of trouble. A few of the soldiers manage to reach the pines, but they are quickly surrounded. The militia around the wagons are hacked down like grass under the scythe. Only James Corbin and Sergeant Louis Pettle, wounded and left for dead on the sand, and John Kinzie, erect and untouched, because of his friendly relations with the Indians, remain alive among the men defending the wagons.

But the women have seized the swords and guns of the fallen, and fight with the fury of desperation to protect their children in the wagons. Mrs. Simmons, her flaxen hair flying, her face a mass of blood and sweat, her seven-months-old baby in her arms, her five-year-old boy clinging to her skirts, is taken alive by a savage who admires her golden beauty and her courage. He tomahawks the little boy, but allows the baby to remain in her arms. Mrs. Corbin and Mrs. Pettle, in the rear doorway of one of the wagons, fight off the savages who try to climb up. But, meanwhile, Shavehead, eager for more easily procured scalps, climbs stealthily up over a dead horse, over the driver's empty seat, through the front of the wagon, his tomahawk lifted. Sergeant Pettle, unable to move, watches, like a man in a dream, his eyes wide as moons with horror. Corbin, wounded in hip and thigh, heel and shoulder, tries to get into a crawling position, but is as helpless as Pettle. Pettle's two small sons and Corbin's little girl are in that wagon! Shavehead appears triumphantly at the back archway of the wagon, pulls Mrs. Corbin and Mrs. Pettle down inside, then jumps to the ground, with their two scalps of long dark hair and six or seven scalplocks of the fine, short hair of children in his bloody hands. Pettle faints away.

Out in the open, events are happening as swift as flying arrows to the friends of Joseph Bailly. The carnage is thickening around

William Wells. He is surrounded by half a dozen savage Potawa-tomi. Black Partridge and Topenebee circle around and around, trying to distract the infuriated young warriors, trying to draw them off. But it is like trying to draw off hungry wolves from a dying buffalo. Wells is summoning all his energies. Rebecca has courageously ridden up close to him. He must fight for them both. He must live. He must live!

"Father, I want to live!" he calls out to Topenebee.

"You *shall* live, Apekonit! You *shall* live! Off, you dogs! Be off!"

But Topenebee's voice is carried away by the mad yells, like the hum of a gnat in a hurricane.

They are closing in on Wells. He has shot down three of the Indians, one with his rifle, two with his pistol. He has stabbed another in the breast with his hunting knife. But he has received a bullet in the lungs, a bullet in the shoulder, and slashes all over his body. Blood is foaming from his nose and mouth. Rebecca has been slashed in the side and bullets have lodged in her left shoulder and right arm. Heald has reached the ridge, and there are many surging groups between the husband and the wife. Rebecca cannot get through, but she still sees, through the mêlée, the uncle whom she adores. She has only her riding whip for a weapon, but she is lashing with it in all directions.

"Fight, Uncle, fight!"

"I'm done for, Rebecca. Ride off—if you can! If you can't—die—like a—soldier!"

Strangely, the memory of that bear Wells killed near Fort Wayne the day he encountered Joseph Bailly, comes back to him. The bear must have felt just as he does now. "Die like a brave, brother bear. . . . This is the fortune of war. . . . Die like a brave." . . .

"Fight, Uncle, fight! Don't let them kill you! Fight! Fight!"

" 'Die like a brave—brother bear!' "

Wells' wounded horse quivers and gives way under him, pinion-ing one of his legs. But Wells is able to load his pistol and bring down two more Indians. Rebecca snatches at the flying black hair of an Indian as he passes her, and half pulls him from his horse. He reaches back and slashes her across the breast, cutting her dress open. Her horse rears and plunges. Rebecca's hair is down. Her hand, holding the riding-whip, hangs limp. Again she tries to reach Wells. But it is useless. The pack is closing in. Some one shouts, in Algonquin:

"Me, me, let me kill him!" The pack gives way a little, and De la Vigne, the magician, appears in the opening, the wolf skin over his head and back, the front of his bare body painted in zigzags of scarlet and green. He lifts his tomahawk. Wells is too weak to reload his pistol again. Wells lifts himself to a half-sitting position, stiffens his shoulders, points to his breast, then, with a grim smile, circles his head with his forefinger, indicating the ready scalplock.

"Goodbye, Rebec—"

But the blow cuts off the last syllable. Wells falls back against his horse, the ironic smile still on his lips. Yells shake the air:

"Apekonit! Apekonit! Apekonit!"

In an instant De la Vigne has cut off the scalplock. Then he plunges his knife into the warm flesh of Wells and digs out his heart. He holds up the bleeding heart. A dozen hands are stretched towards it. A dozen warriors claim a morsel of the brave flesh, to increase their own bravery. De la Vigne takes one reeking bite and passes it on to Shavehead, who screams, "Apekonit!" and rips off another morsel. The bleeding fragment is passed from hand to hand, until there is no fragment left for the last warrior, Asa Bun. Asa Bun licks the hand of Black Loon, in whose palm lay the last morsel. The remorseless Shavehead bends down, severs the head of Wells and holds it up in triumph.

After the death of Wells, the fighting diminishes. There is a lull, during which the Indians send the half-breed Le Claire forward to Heald (who is still on the ridge), with a request to surrender. Heald offers, through Le Claire, a hundred dollars ransom for every white man still alive. The fighting draws to a standstill, though there is many a small residual skirmish.

A group of Indians crowds around Rebecca to take her bay mare. The reins are seized by De la Vigne, who, indifferent to the mare, discovers almost as beautiful a specimen in Rebecca as he thought he had once found in Marie Bailly. He waves off the other Indians. Marie Bailly's escape from him has made the passionate De la Vigne doubly cruel to all women. He stares down at Rebecca as, overcome with pain and horror, she rides beside him. She has recognized her uncle's scalp-lock dangling from De la Vigne's headgear.

Her cheeks are white. Her mind is a torture chamber. She shuts her eyes tight, till they are red with their own blood, as she goes past the wagons, outside of which the bodies of women and children lie in confusion. Rebecca is thankful now that the little son, born at the fort three months before, did not survive to suffer the frightful death of this day. De la Vigne jerks at her reins to attract her attention. She does not respond, but rides on, stately as a dying queen, towards Fort Dearborn.

"Bien jolie! Pretty girl!" says De la Vigne. "Only one girl prettier in all Great Lakes. Marie Bailly leetle bit prettier. But not so pretty breast, I tink!"

Catching the direction of his obscene look, Rebecca suddenly discovers that the slash across her dress and the motion of riding have disclosed one of her breasts in its entirety. She tries to lift her left hand to cover it but, for a moment, is unable to complete the gesture. De la Vigne laughs lewdly.

"You are the vilest man I have ever known!" declares Rebecca.

"Look out, my pretty one!"

And De la Vigne raises his scalping knife flashingly in the air. With the very same gesture used by her uncle a few moments before, Rebecca stiffens her shoulders and lifts her head proudly:

"You are coward enough to kill a squaw? I am not afraid—dog!"

De la Vigne quivers with rage at the intolerable epithet, but his eyes flash a glint of admiration. He lowers his scalping knife and makes a slash down Rebecca's leg. She is forced to drop her head with the new pain, but, remembering her uncle's "Die like a soldier, Rebecca!" lifts it up quickly again, her lips trembling and her eyes washed with tears. A new humiliation awaits her at the gates of the fort. A group of squaws are out on the sandy river bank, awaiting the return of captives and booty. One of the squaws, with a yell, takes hold of Rebecca's saddle blanket, and tries to pull it out from under her. With an arm which shoots pain from shoulder to wrist, Rebecca lifts her riding-whip and lashes at the squaw, vehemently. The squaw bends her back away from the blows and runs off, stooping, while De la Vigne, in spite of himself, cries out the tribute to Wells' niece:

"Apekonit! Apekonit!"

The cry is repeated around the fort, in the midst of laughter over the discomfiture of the whipped squaw.

De la Vigne is just putting his brown arm around Rebecca to lift her from her own horse to his when hoofs thud on the river trail behind them. Jean Baptiste Chandonnais rushes up. He has been urged by Mrs. Kinzie, who has been watching everything from her canoe, to hurry to Mrs. Heald's assistance.

"Your captive, De la Vigne?"

"My captive."

"I give you a new musket for her."

"Pouf!"

"I give you a mule."

"Pouf! I like her. She has a pretty breast."

Flushing, Rebecca painfully lifts her riding-whip hand and draws the torn dress together again.

"I give you a mule and feefty dollar and a gallon of firewater!"

"Take her! How soon you give firewater?"

"At fort. This afternoon! Come, Mrs. Heald. I take you to Mrs. Kinzie's boat."

"Goodbye," sneers De la Vigne. "No matter. Mule better. Fifty dollar better! Firewater better! You not so pretty as Marie Bailly!" And De la Vigne turns and rides back to the battle ground for new pickings.

There, on the field of massacre, the surviving white men are gathered together and marched or ridden back towards the fort. Kinzie has already hurried back to join his family. Black Partridge is keeping a watchful eye on the younger men, for half the fun, to most Indians, is to tomahawk a captive or torture him before scalping. Shavehead's tomahawk is still in his hand, and there are eight new scalps dripping from his belt. He is still insatiable. Heald is riding, as erect as he can, in spite of two wounds. His reins are held by Topenebee who rides beside him. Lieutenant Helm is also mounted, but his left hand is over his eyes, for he has just passed the wagons and believes that he has seen the scalpless body of his wife stretched out beside the wheels. Louis Pettle and Fielding Corbin are lying as limp as sacks of wheat across the back of a horse led by Alexander Robinson. There is a grim look in Alexander's eyes. He had done his best to avert the tragedy. Yesterday, he had been paddling in a big canoe, with the season's first corn from the Calumet region, when a group of Miami had signaled to him from the shore, and urged him not to go any farther but to camp with them:

"Big storm coming up tomorrow. Big storm, Checagou. Better stay here, Calumet."

Alexander had thanked them, pushed his canoe out into the blue water again as fast as he could, and paddled without stops to Checagou. Back of the fort, he had found the Indians in their final council and had pleaded in vain for the garrison.

"If you *must* have blood, kill me first!" he had said, and had opened his blue shirt-front to the thirsting knives. But no one had stirred, not even Shavehead.

So Alexander rides in, with his burden of wounded flesh. At the fort gates, Jean Baptiste Chandonnais greets Heald.

"She is here, Chief. She is here."

"Thank you, Chandonnais, for bringing in her body."

"*Body?* She's *alive,* captain. Wounded, but alive. I bought her for you from De la Vigne."

"That magician? I've heard of him from Little Turtle and from Joseph Bailly." Heald shudders slightly, places his hand over Chandonnais' hand, and says:

"You shall have the ransom and a reward besides, Chandonnais. I'm endlessly grateful."

"I didn't do it for reward, sir."

"I know you didn't, but you shall have it just the same."

"You're wounded, sir. May I help you?"

"I'm Topenebee's captive."

"Oh, I'm sure, Chief Topenebee, you'll let the captain join his wife at Kinzie's house," says Chandonnais, turning deferentially to Topenebee.

"No. No. I take captain to my camp, Parc aux Vaches, then on to British camp, Mackinac, or British camp Detroit, for ransom."

"But those are *not British camps!*" says Heald, stiffening in his saddle, and speaking in a voice which rises above the high chatter of squaws' voices and the low rumble of Indian braves who have taken possession of the interior chambers of the fort.

"I afraid they *are* taken, captain," asserts Topenebee. "Fort Mackinac already taken seventeenth day of Month of Deer, fort at Detroit taken today, tomorrow, Fort Wayne too! All forts British now. American council fires—pouf! Gone out. Black ash. Americans—Americans . . ." And he encircles his head with his right forefinger, signifying "scalped," "finished."

"*It can't be possible.* I don't believe it."

"It's true, sir," says Chandonnais. "The Americans have hung up the fiddle!"

"Never! Take me to Kinzie's house."

"No! You my captive!" announces Topenebee, jerking the reins, to show his mastery. Chandonnais begins to use his oratory on Topenebee, expatiating on the bravery of both Heald and his wife and on the fact that Mrs. Heald is an Apekonit, and that such a warrior husband and wife should be allowed to be together. Topenebee at last grunts assent and with a "Me go, too" follows to Kinzie's house.

Lieutenant Helm follows at a short distance, bowed over his horse so that his head almost rests on his animal's neck. In this way, they ford the river to Kinzie's house. Just as their horses reach the top of the bank, the riders are forced to witness another incident of the massacre. Sergeant Burns, badly wounded, has been brought in by a brave and dumped on the river bank. A squaw from the encampment has snatched Kinzie's pitchfork which has been left in a heap of grass outside the house, and brings it down, full force, into the abdomen of Burns. At that instant, a woman standing on the porch of Ouilmette's little house back of Kinzie's, screams, and Helm turns from the hideous picture of the murder of Burns to a picture which he had never dreamed of seeing again. The woman is his wife. Mrs. Helm has been saved from a scalping Indian by Black Partridge, who rushed her down to the lake shore and held her almost entirely under water, until her assailant stopped looking for her.

Heald is helped to dismount and, with the aid of Chandonnais, goes slowly across the veranda into Kinzie's house. There, lying on a bed in a small room off the main room, with John Kinzie, Elinor Kinzie, and their servant, Josette Laframboise (daughter of Madame Laframboise of Mackinac Island), in attendance, is Rebecca Heald. Spartan all through the massacre, she has given way at last, and hot tears are pouring down her cheeks.

"No, I shall never see him again. Never. Never," she is repeating over and over again.

"But I tell you, he is riding in, perfectly safe and sound," asserts John Kinzie. "I saw him only a half-hour ago. The bloody battle was over and Topenebee had him as his captive."

"I couldn't get through to him. . . . I couldn't get through to the ridge. And I couldn't save my uncle either. . . . And Topenebee, Topenebee will kill my husband in one of his drunken fits. He's probably halfway to Parc aux Vaches already. . . . I shall never, never see him again."

"No. No. Topenebee will come back here to see me. I'd arranged with him to take my family to Parc aux Vaches, you know. But I'll tell you this, Mrs. Heald: You're the one to be worrying about. Mrs. Kinzie's fixed up your cuts all right, but there are two bullets to be taken out. And if the captain doesn't come in pretty soon, I'll have to cut them out without waiting for him."

"He—won't—come. If Topenebee doesn't kill him—De la Vigne will, or Shavehead. A thousand scalps wouldn't be enough for either one of them! Oh, Nathan, Nathan! . . ." And from under closed eyelids, the tears burn their way down Rebecca's cheeks.

"Rebecca! Rebecca!"

Heald has entered the room just in time to hear Rebecca's last words. Chandonnais helps Heald into a chair beside her bed. Husband and wife forget their wounds as they lean towards each other in a desperate embrace.

Topenebee towers darkly in the doorway. He approaches the bed and says to Rebecca:

"You say I keel the captain? You say I keel like De la Vigne or Shavehead?"

"Oh, no, no, Chief Topenebee! Forgive me! My wounds have made my mind sick. I know you would not. I know you are a kind man!" answers Rebecca, still striving for her husband's life.

"Yes. Topenebee brave chief, good man. Me, me and General Harrison!"

A wan smile crosses the faces of those in the room.

"Then, if you're a good man, Chief Topenebee, you will allow my husband to travel with me?"

"Yes. Yes. We all go Parc aux Vaches, eh, Chandonnais? Then Mackinac, to British general? Ransom?"

"All this can be arranged later," interposes Kinzie. "The thing of greatest importance just now is to get the bullets out of Mrs. Heald's arms. The Surgeon was killed in the battle. Are you well enough to extract them, captain?"

"No, Kinzie. I believe I've got a couple myself. You do it, Kinzie. You're unharmed. My blessings on you."

"Are you ready, Mrs. Heald?"

"Ready."

Kinzie takes his knife from his belt and wipes it off a bit on his trousers. Mrs. Kinzie has already removed the slashed and tattered dress sleeves from Mrs. Heald's arms and covered her shoulders and chest with an Indian blanket. Heald holds Rebecca's right hand, while Kinzie, sitting on the bed, begins digging at the flesh of her left shoulder. He is very deft, but it takes three screwings of his knife to dislodge the first bullet. Rebecca tightens her lips, but makes no other gesture except that her right hand digs into her husband's hand. Topenebee, at the foot of the bed, looks on, arms crossed, a faint spark of admiration in his somber eyes. While Mrs. Kinzie washes and binds the left arm, Kinzie exchanges places with Heald, in order to remove the final bullet imbedded in the right arm. He finds the right even more limp and helpless than the left arm.

"You cannot move the hand or clench your fingers, Mrs. Heald?"

"Not just now."

"Ciel! I see her take a whip on a squaw with zat hand just half an hour ago!" proffers Chandonnais. "She have bullet in zat arm?"

"Yes, a big one," says Kinzie, who has just begun to dig.

"Ciel! Mar-ve-lous! Squaw come up. Try to take saddle blanket away. Mrs. Heald, she take whip, and she whip—and she whip—and she whip! Squaw run. Everybody at fort laugh till walls fall down! 'Apekonit!' they yell, 'Apekonit! Apekonit!'"

Rebecca is about to give her first anguished groan, but the word "Apekonit" and the remembrance of her uncle still her voice and steel her lips. Kinzie digs out the last bullet, and the spectators file out of the little bedroom to leave Rebecca to the ministrations of Mrs. Kinzie and to the memories of a bitterly memorable day.

The night and the following day are only a little less poignant than the day of the massacre. All night long, the Indians in their encampment near the fort shriek and sing and beat their drums and torture their victims. The Healds in Kinzie's house and the Helms in Ouilmette's house snatch scarcely an instant of sleep from the terror of the night. For it cannot be at all certain that the friendship of the Indians for the Kinzies and the peaceable efforts of Black Partridge and Topenebee can protect all the guests within the house. The blood-maddened, torture-hungry younger Indians may burst in at any moment, with the raised tomahawk splitting the shadows. But the night passes in safety. No hostiles pass the threshold, where Black Partridge and Shabanee stand with guns crossed in front of the door.

On the next day, a new sight and a new sound sweep through the closed windows of Kinzie's house. The Indians have set fire to the buildings of Fort Dearborn. The old walls, that Captain Whistler and his men so stoutly set up against Indians and wilderness nine years ago, crackle and blaze and swirl out to the lake in blood-colored clouds. Rebecca, lying on her bed, shuts her eyes against the sight, but she cannot close her nostrils against the acrid smoke of death.

News of the massacre has spread, with that strange instantaneity of the wilderness, from Indian village to Indian village, through the prairies of Illinois and the dark pine woods of northern Indiana and the thickets of the Wabash and along the white-horned beaches of Lake Michigan. All day long, more and more Indians have been thudding in on their swift ponies or padding in on almost equally swift moccasins—Potawatomi, Miami, Chippewa, Ottawa, and at last, the desperate Ouabache from Tecumseh's own village of Ouiatanon on the Wabash. Dark as cinders, they stand and watch the blaze, or encircle it with the mad swirls of the death dance.

In the Kinzie house, nerves become raw as torture, and the shadow of death comes down like the shadow of the turkey buzzard over every soul. Indians have crowded along the pathway to the two houses, Indians have peered in at the windows, and, finally, with death in their eyes, they have stalked into Ouilmette's house, where Mrs. Ouilmette has hidden Mrs. Helm behind a feather bed. Disappointed at finding only half-breeds and Indians, they stalk into Kinzie's house, past Kinzie and Robinson and Chandonnais and Black Partridge and Shabanee, who are now all on guard with guns on the porch, but who no longer dare to stop the visitors for fear of a new massacre. Black Partridge has practically given up hope of saving the surviving palefaces. Every Indian is painted red and black and armed with some instrument of Indian or pioneer destruction. They steal through the few rooms of the Kinzie house like stealthy coyotes, they peer down at Rebecca on her bed, they glower at Captain Heald on his couch in the main room, they form a grim, blanketed circle on the floor.

Mrs. Kinzie, her heart thumping wildly against her ribs, goes about her supervising of Josette, her own work, her waiting upon Rebecca, with smooth competence and with as calm a face as she can possibly manage to smooth out to the keen gaze of the savages. For she has lived long enough among Indians to know that they are like wild animals, ready to pounce on the smaller animal at the first motion of panic or the faintest emission of the odor of fear, but likely to pass by a statuelike, odorless, unalarmed creature. So Elinor Lytle Kinzie, stolen by the Senecas as a child, adopted as a daughter by Chief Corn Planter, neighbor to Indians at Fort Pitt and Fort Defiance and Fort Detroit and Parc aux Vaches and Fort Dearborn, composes her face, and moves about her house, speaking in a low, comforting voice to her four terrified children, dusting her shelves, baking her bread, spinning her flax, changing the bandages on her wounded guests, and smiling at the Indians sitting in a circle of death on her parlor floor, as if she were entertaining angels instead of devils. When the bread is finished at teatime, she enters the parlor and hands out a fresh warm piece of this coveted white man's delicacy to each Indian. Brown hands reach out greedily, but there is not even a grunt of appreciation.

Black Partridge comes into the house and says to Mrs. Kinzie, in a low voice:

"Mrs. Kinzie, we have done all we can to save you. I am afraid we can do nothing more. The Indians' minds are made up."

Mrs. Kinzie answers nothing, and continues to distribute bread.

The evening comes down. A thin smoke still rises from the charred timbers that were Fort Dearborn. With the time of shadows, the atmosphere becomes more and more gloomy. More Indians have crowded into the room. They have taken Heald's sword from his belt. They have taken his red sash. One of the savage Ouabache is cutting off the gold buttons from his coat. Heald's eyes shine balefully, but he is helpless to resist.

"Why don't you get down your fiddle, John?" asks Mrs. Kinzie, who is passing through the room from Rebecca's bedside.

"No use, Elinor, no use," mutters John, meaning that such a gesture would only madden the Indians and cause them to break his instrument or start the new massacre at once.

Another Indian enters the door. It is De la Vigne. He looks around the room, with eyes as quick as the tongue of an adder. Rebecca Heald is not there. De la Vigne goes towards the bedroom. John Kinzie pulls down his fiddle from the mantelpiece and starts playing a polka, as if the life of everyone in the household depended upon it. Might as well try it now. Death's close anyway. A slight outcry is heard above the music from Rebecca's room. She has recognized De la Vigne and his intentions. But first he cuts from the ribbon around her neck the medallion portrait of her father, Samuel Wells. Then he stands gloating over her for an instant, before the attack of passion.

Suddenly, his expression changes. His ears turn fox. A loud, prolonged call is heard from the direction of the river, the "friendly arrival" cry of an Indian or a trader. Then another and another call, sturdy, unafraid. The lust slips out of De la Vigne's eyes, giving place to fear. He turns towards the door and glides out. The Indians in the parlor have stiffened. Their ears also seem to stand visibly erect, pointed, listening. Kinzie goes on fiddling, very low. Black Partridge slips out of the door and in the glowing darkness goes down to the river Checagou.

The smell of the acrid smoke is stronger tonight than the smell of the wild onion growing pungently at the river's edge. The smoldering fires of the fort reveal three Indian figures disembarking from a large canoe. Numbers of Indians crowd down towards the canoe, hungry with curiosity about these new arrivals, as to whether they may be friends or enemies or possible victims. Those nearest the canoe raise the cry, "Sauganash! Sauganash! Sauganash!"

The Sauganash—"Englishman," or Straight Tree, as some call him—is a half-breed greatly loved, feared, and respected by the Indians, an especial friend of the Potawatomi. He is dressed like an Indian, even to the eagle feathers in his hair, and is accompanied by two Indian servants. But he was born William Caldwell, the son of Colonel William Caldwell of Amherstburg, a British officer in the recent Revolution, and of the sister of Tecumseh. Unlike many of the rough traders of the day, he is a highly educated gentleman, having been sent by an ambitious father to schools both in Canada and in Scotland. Like Joseph Bailly, he has the double aptitudes of the parlor and the wilderness. He is a giant of a fellow, absolutely fearless, and owns a tongue with a twist of laughter at the tip, an additional quality which endears him to the Indians, whose sense of comicality is far more highly developed than most intimidated settlers realize. But Billy Caldwell, the Sauganash, is not amused or amusing tonight. Down in the Illinois country, where he has been hunting and making trading arrangements with the Indians, he heard of that same "storm brewing at Checagou," of which Alexander Robinson had heard as he cruised along the southern edge of Lake Michigan. He has hurried up the wide reaches of the Illinois, up the bark-brown Des Plaines, up the rippling snake of the Checagou, his Indians paddling night and day, for, like Alexander, Billy the Sauganash knows what "storm" means. Worse than the Water Panthers and the Thunder Birds of the Potawatomi battling in streaked splendor over the fiercely mirroring surface of Lake Michigan, worse than the hurricanes of September, could be this autumnal storm at old Checagou. Billy has picked up the news all along the watercourses, Indian tongues clacking more furiously, Indian eyes lighted with more sinister flames all along the way. At last he has picked up the grim message of the massacre. He has paddled on and on, furiously. His friend John Kinzie lives near the fort. He must rush to see if anyone remains alive to be saved. He trusts, with a frosty margin of doubt still left, to his own popularity with the Indians and to the fact that he is known as "the Englishman." England is again triumphant on the Northwest frontier.

Shouts and a murmur of welcome greet the Sauganash, as he steps ashore, a murmur edged with a blade-thin gleam of hostility. Black Partridge immediately takes him by the buckskin arm, and in a low voice says:

"You've come just in time, Sauganash. Shaw-nee-aw-kee * is in danger, bad, bad danger. Hurry."

---

* John Kinzie.

The Sauganash leaves the boat to the boatmen and, followed by the glances of a hundred eyes, glinting lynxlike in the darkness, he hastens on quick moccasins to Kinzie's house. He enters the house. Kinzie stops fiddling. The Sauganash looks about him in the smoldering firelight, with the utmost calm, then says, in a deep, steady voice, with a touch of chaffing in the tone:

"Good evening, friends, good evening. The Sauganash is glad to see you. But why do you look so solemn, my Indian friends? Why have you painted your faces with the discouraged color of black? Is it because you are mourning your friends who died in the battle? A great battle! The victory was yours! The Great Spirit smiles on you! You are brave soldiers!

"Are you here because you wish blankets in which to wrap your dead? John Kinzie will be glad to hand them out to you. When has he let an Indian, living or dead, go unclothed, or unsheltered? Or are you here because you are hungry, perhaps? Good! Our old friend John Kinzie has never turned away a hungry Indian, or done harm in all his life to any Indian. You have come to the right house—*haven't they*, Shaw-nee-aw-kee?"

Kinzie, hollow-eyed, standing by the fireplace, with his now silent fiddle in his hands, answers in a voice less steady:

"Yes—Sauganash—you're right. They've come to the right house."

Slowly, the abashed Indians rise from their places on the floor, and without looking at Kinzie or the Sauganash slink out of the door like lashed hounds. In a few moments the house is empty of all Indians except Topenebee. Elinor Kinzie, standing by Rebecca's bedroom door, suddenly brings her apron to her eyes and sobs with relief. The four children, peeping from behind her skirts, follow the dramatic clue and wail aloud. Kinzie takes the Sauganash by the hand and almost crushes it:

"Billy, Billy! Thank God you came! You saved us, Billy. No question—one minute more and this place would have been a shambles."

"Glad I got here in time, old fellow. When can you get out of here?"

"We have two wounded people with us. How about you, Captain Heald?"

"Thanks enormously, Caldwell," says Heald. "As for me, I'm well enough to move. I don't know about Mrs. Heald."

"I'm well enough," comes Rebecca's voice from the bedroom. "If I had no arms and no legs left, I'd crawl from Checagou on the stump of my body!"

"I'll take them in my canoe to Parc aux Vaches or beyond," volunteers Alexander Robinson.

"All right. Fine!" says Kinzie. "That's where Chief Topenebee expects the captain to go for the present anyway, on the way up to Mackinac, isn't it, chief?"

"Yes. Yes. You ransom? Big money?" says Topenebee.

"I'm going to take my family up to the Parc, just as we'd planned it, chief. When we all get together there, we can arrange the details of ransom and reporting to the British commander, and all that. We're all too sick and tired now to think of anything except getting to a safe, quiet place. It'll be strange not seeing Bailly at the Parc. Hope he came through the siege of Mackinac all right."

"Oh, surely, Jo Bailly's smart enough not to get flattened out in any storm. He's all right!" assures the Sauganash.

"He'd jump out of trouble—like ze deer from ze ring of fire!" adds Chandonnais.

"Nathan, oh, Nathan!" calls Rebecca's voice again. "Do you remember what Joseph Bailly said about Checagou? about Checagou's being a most 'romantic place—a place for leisure and love and peace?' I must tell Joseph Bailly about Checagou some day!"

Chapter XVII

REFUGEES

THREE weeks later, Joseph Bailly was striding down to the beach with Jean Baptiste Clutier and a few of his Indians, to look over his Mackinaw boats and get them into condition for the autumn trip to the Grand River and the St. Joseph. He was thinking of bales of fur and prices at Montreal, but Jean Baptiste's mind was pleasantly empty and his eyes were outward.

"Boat coming in, Monsieur Joseph."

"You always see them, don't you, Jean Baptiste? Eyes of a gull, that's what you have."

Joseph looked up from the gray gravel of the beach. A black line topped the water in the distance, and four red paddles flashed like tanagers' wings against the green.

"Indians from Arbre Croche?"

"What you t'ink?" asked Clutier of the Indians who were following after him. "Ottawa?"

The Indians stopped for a moment and focused their keen eyes on the distance. They watched without speaking, then one of them shook his head.

"Mebbe one, two Indians. Mebbe three white. Indians tired. Paddle slow."

"Traders?"

The eagle-eyed Indian paused again, until the infinitesimal figures broadened a trifle in the retinas of his eyes.

"One white squaw."

"A white woman? Are you sure?" asked Joseph, surprised.

All three Indians nodded their heads.

"One white squaw. Yes."

"That's strange—a white woman paddling up this way, from the south, at this time of year. Well, let's get on, down to our boats."

The little group moved down the beach, towards Joseph's boat shelters. On the way, he and Jean Baptiste talked of the coming journeys and whether there would be any reverberations of the British-American troubles to deter them, farther along the lakes. A sailing vessel from Detroit had come in with supplies for the British at the fort a few days before, and the astonishing news had winged its way over the island that Detroit also had surrendered to the British, that Governor Hull had capitulated almost without a struggle. Joseph wondered how the change of government would affect all his friends at Detroit. As little, he hoped, as the change had affected the Mackinac Islanders. Except for the fact that the bars instead of the stars flew from the flagstaff of the fort, and that scarlet coats made gay splashes against the white walls of the fort and the whitewashed houses of the town, and that familiar British tunes floated over the walls, and that Biddle and Abbott and other Americans were politely watched prisoners-at-large, life went on exactly the same. No word of massacre had as yet reached the island. There was only a sense of a general quiet taking-over of the old Northwest by the British. The Ottawa of Arbre Croche had not yet brought over the alarming news, nor had even that invisible, inaudible, inexplicable signaling of the wild conveyed its messages to the island.

"Pretty soon we start south for the old adventures, Jean Baptiste. What do you say to our going far, far south, below Vincennes, this year?"

"How far south, Monsieur Joseph? Jean Baptiste eager for ze adventures, new ones!"

"What would you say to New Orleans?"

"I say, zat would be heaven!"

"We'll see! I feel a bit adventurous myself!"

"Monsieur Joseph, ze people in ze boat—they wave at you."

"Che-che-bing-way! Che-che-bing-way!" exclaimed Bailly's Indians, delightedly, using the native name for Alexander Robinson.

"*Is* it? Is it Alexander?" asked Joseph excitedly. "At *this* time of year? Really?"

"The lady, she wave at you, too, Monsieur Joseph!" added Jean Baptiste. "Ah, Monsieur Joseph, killer of every lady's heart!"

Joseph put up his hand to shade his eyes, but could not yet make out the identity of the five figures. He turned towards the point where the boat would cut in to shore. A few more paddle sweeps, and Alexander appeared in full Indian regalia, with his half-breed wife Catherine Chevalier dipping the other paddle. At the rear of the canoe sat two men in Indian dress—fringed buckskin leggings, open buckskin jacket, feathers in the hair, beads about the neck and color splashed across the chest and cheeks; but something about each was un-Indian, the complexion under the paint, the slump of the shoulders, the low roundness of cheeks, the casualness of attitude. With them sat a thin, white woman, unpainted but also wearing Indian dress and beads. Although she lifted her hand again in salutation to Joseph, he failed to recognize her. The boat slipped in to shore. Joseph and Jean Baptiste went a little closer. Alexander stepped on shore. Joseph gripped his hand.

"Good to see you, Alexander!" boomed Joseph in his hearty voice. "What brings you here, at this time of year?"

"Death," said Alexander, holding Joseph's hand and looking into his eyes significantly.

"Death?"

"Fort Dearborn wiped out. Massacre."

"Mon Dieu Seigneur!"

"I bring you Captain and Mrs. Heald and Sergeant Pettle."

"Captain! I did not know you!" exclaimed Joseph, turning to help him out of the canoe. "And Rebecca!"

Rebecca bore only a scant resemblance to the laughterful young girl whom Joseph had encountered at Fort Wayne two summers before. The ruddy color had dimmed from her cheeks, the pleasure from her eyes. The squareness of her mouth, her chin, her cheeks was emphasized by the withdrawal of the healthy curves of happiness. Rebecca allowed Joseph to help her from the boat and, in a flat voice, said merely:

"Thank you."

Sergeant Pettle stepped out. He too was a statue, without a word. His eyes were those of a blind man, with no recognition in them, his mouth was tight.

"You will all put up at my house, of course?" asked Joseph. "My house is ready and open with a great welcome."

"Thank you, Bailly," answered Heald. "We're to report here to the British commander of the fort. Sergeant Pettle and I will doubtless be housed at the fort, but I entrust Mrs. Heald to your care and Madame Bailly's, with all my heart."

"Sure you can't be our guest, Pettle?"

Pettle merely gave a slight negative nod of the head.

"And you, Alexander?"

"Thank you, Joseph, but I think Catherine and I will camp on the beach as usual. We must be turning south again, soon. But we'll go up and say 'How do you do?' to your wife."

Joseph left his Indians in charge of the canoes and the luggage, and the rest of the group moved up the beach slowly, two by two, the Healds, the Robinsons, Pettle and Jean Baptiste. Jean Baptiste started a running fire of talk with Pettle, but came up against a stone wall of silence. Joseph went close to Alexander and gripped him by the elbow.

"Tell me, Alexander. Tell me. Are the Kinzies all right?"

"Entirely all right. They paddled up to Parc aux Vaches, then took the trail to Detroit."

"Who else is safe? The Helms? The Simmonses? Pettle's handsome wife? The surgeon?"

Robinson reported on each one, then summed up: "Only about thirty-five are left, Joseph. About fifty were killed. It was the most God-awful massacre you ever saw: a wagonful of babies, a wagonful of women; five hundred raging Indians against less than a hundred whites. Even Topenebee and Black Partridge and Shabanee and Wells couldn't stop them."

"Wells? Was Wells there?"

"Yes. Wells was there." Alexander hesitated. Something in his silence made Joseph look at him searchingly.

"Was Wells wounded?"

"Killed, Joseph. Fought like a demon, to the end. Six savages beat him down, yelling, 'Apekonit!' They thought enough of his courage to eat his heart. He's at peace with Little Turtle."

"*Is Little Turtle dead?*"

"Yes. He died of the gout at Wells' house at Fort Wayne, just before Wells set out for Checagou."

"My two old friends, Wells and Little Turtle. . . ."

Joseph put his hand over his eyes and missed a step or two.

"Wells' niece was just as wonderful as he was," continued Robinson. "She had only a riding whip in her hand, but she used it as fiercely as a tomahawk and stayed close to her uncle, trying to beat off his enemies. De la Vigne dragged her off the field."

"De la Vigne? My God! He was here at the taking of Mackinac only four weeks before!"

"Oh, yes, your Arbre Croche Indians came down in full force; Blackbird, Asa Bun . . . But none were worse than De la Vigne—and Shavehead."

Close on the utterance of the name "Shavehead," a groan came from behind Alexander. It was almost the first sound that Louis Pettle had made since the massacre.

"Oh, yes!" whispered Alexander to Joseph. "I forgot to tell you that it was Shavehead who scalped Pettle's wife and children. You mustn't mention Shavehead's name to Pettle. I'm almost afraid Pettle's in the way of losing his mind."

"I don't wonder," said Joseph. "Odd, but Pettle and Shavehead didn't get along any too well when they first met at my place at Parc aux Vaches. If Shavehead was taking revenge, he certainly did a thorough job of it. . . . Terrible. . . . That beauty of a wife and those two little fellows. . . . By the way, didn't Mrs. Heald have a baby? What happened to it?"

"Luckily, the baby died at birth, in May."

By this time, they had all arrived at the threshold of Joseph's house. Marie, who had caught a glimpse of the group through the window, came welcomingly to the door.

"It's the Healds and the Robinsons and Sergeant Pettle of Fort Dearborn, Marie. Mrs. Heald is not very well, and she is going to make us a long visit," announced Joseph in a firm, loud voice. Then, going close to Marie, he said in a quick, low whisper:

"Don't ask any questions. I'll tell you all about it later. *The skunk of Checagou is wearing a red coat!*"

Chapter XVIII

SURVIVOR

ALL through that autumn and winter of 1812, refugees from the various battlefields of the Northwest climbed up to the safe back of the Turtle of Mackinac Island. Joseph was increasingly glad that he had chosen the old Turtle for his own place of refuge, and that he had postponed the perilous journey to New Orleans. Everything was calm and controlled on the island, under the British flag. But the ravens of dark news and the refugees continued to come, adding a black edge to the red coat of British surveillance.

Shortly after the departure of the Healds by sailing vessel to Quebec and the ultimate release by General Proctor, news came of the attack on Fort Wayne, and the gathering of the forces of Tecumseh, the delay in the arrival of General Harrison's soldiers from their headquarters at Cincinnati, and the bravery of Major William Oliver, of the Shawnee Logan, and of young Peter Navarre in pushing ahead, scouting, discovering the condition of the besieged and getting messages out to Harrison in time to save the garrison. Joseph Bailly's heart expanded with pride over these exploits of young Peter, who was getting his share, at last, of longed-for adventure! And Marie delighted in the renown of this brother of her own good friend, François Navarre.

In early October came the double news of the attack on Fort Harrison and of the Pigeon Roost massacre in southern Indiana, twenty miles above Louisville. The burning breach in the wall at Fort Harrison at Terre Haute, the carrying of buckets, under fire, and the valiant repairing of the breach under the direction of Captain Zachary Taylor, were all described by the roundabout word of captains of lake vessels, traders, and vagrant Indians. But the tales of the Pigeon Roost were even more harrowing. They told how twelve Shawnees, at the time the unsuccessful attack was being made on Fort Harrison, had ridden off in fury, a hundred miles to the southeast, and had killed twenty-two American settlers on the tiny hilltop of the Pigeon Roost. Among these was Mrs. Henry Collings, who, as she was crossing the fields from Mrs. Jeremiah Payne's, had been seized, tomahawked, and scalped. Then her unborn baby, slashed from her body, had been laid across her breast. And there was Mrs. John Biggs, who, to keep the cries of her baby from attracting the lurking Indians, had held her shawl so tightly over its mouth that she had smothered it, and had stumbled on to the blockhouse, with the dead child in her arms. Only two of those outside the blockhouse had been taken alive by the Indians, so the reports said: a ten-year-old boy, Peter Huffman, and a golden-haired little girl, Ginsey McCoy, cousin of Mrs. Jeremiah Payne and niece of the Baptist missionary, Rev. Isaac McCoy, whom Joseph Bailly had met at McCoy's Wabash mission on every journey that he had made to and from Vincennes. Joseph remembered having heard McCoy speak very often of his brother at the Pigeon Roost and of Ginsey, the only child, who was to be sent to McCoy's mission school as soon as she was old enough. This slight connection with a victim seemed to bring the Pigeon Roost affair close to Joseph and made him hug his own four little girls very tight. His friendship towards British and Americans, French Canadians and Indians alike, brought no sharp cleavage in his attitude but only a general, abounding sympathy and gratitude that the Turtle, with the British astride it, was still safe.

One evening in January, when frozen waters had apparently stopped the flow of refugees, Jean Baptiste brought a strange bit of news. Joseph was sitting by the fireside, playing "Sur le Pont d'Avignon" on his fiddle and tapping his booted foot, while his four little girls, in their nightgowns, were dancing around and around to the tune. It was such an attractive sight that Jean Baptiste delayed his news for a full half-hour, while he stood deferentially by the door, his cap off. Agatha and Thérèse were taking each dramatic motion of the dance very seriously, doffing their imaginary plumed hats at the proper words, making their obeisances, delightfully. Joseph, with all his memories of the ballroom, had trained them well to the various elegances of the steps. Auburn-haired Rose was watching Agatha with great earnestness, and imitating, a step late and a gesture late, each time. Plump Esther, two years old, was merely turning around like a top, tangling in her nightgown and tumbling over at every attempt at a bow. Marie, sewing beads on moccasins, watched with delight, laughed, and now and then glided from her place and lifted Esther to her feet. The thought flashed across Jean Baptiste that Madame Joseph grew more beautiful with the years. The deep happiness in her face made her look like—something that Jean Baptiste had seen in some very beautiful place once. Could it have been a priest's place —a chapel somewhere? Yes—it was a picture over the altar in the Chapel of Ste. Anne de Beaupré to which Monsieur Joseph's mother had taken him. Jean Baptiste hadn't been in a chapel for a dozen years. That picture! Why, it must have been the Mother of God! La Madonne—that was it!

> Sur le pont d'Avignon,
> L'on y danse, l'on y danse;
> Sur le pont d'Avignon,
> L'on y danse tout en rond.
> Les bell's dames font comm' ça,
> Et puis encor comm' ça.

At "Les bell's dames font comm' ça!" Esther fell headforemost and turned a complete somersault. Joseph's hearty laugh broke out and he stopped fiddling.

"Bon soir, Jean Baptiste! Bon soir! Good night, little girls, good night! Dance to bed!"

After a smothering of kisses, the little girls let go of Joseph, and Marie shepherded them to bed.

"Sit down, Jean Baptiste," said Joseph.

"No, thank you, Monsieur Joseph. I just came to tell you a leetle piece of news. A party of Indians came across ze ice from Arbre Croche just now—not Ottawa, but Shawnee. Zey been walking all ze way *around* ze lake from Green Bay. Zey got a white woman and a white baby with zem, taken in ze massacre at Checagou. You should see ze poor woman. She is ze walking skeleton—"

"What is her name, Jean Baptiste?"

"I think—Mrs. Symes—Mrs. Simms—Mrs.—"

"Mrs. Simmons!"

"Oui. Mrs. Simmons, zat is it. She must carry ze leetle, leetle baby, all ze way, six hundred miles. Her shoes, they are in pieces. Her dress, it is a rag. You go see her now?"

The picture of the lovely, robust, flaxen-haired Mrs. Simmons, whose beauty had so strikingly set off the dark beauty of Louis Pettle's wife, at Fort Dearborn, came back vividly to Joseph. He remembered also his thoughts about the fecundity of Checagou on seeing both Mrs. Simmons and Rebecca Heald big with child.

Joseph immediately went to Marie, took her aside, and told her of the new refugee. Together they made up a bundle of peace offerings for the Indians and warm clothing and bread for Mrs. Simmons. From his office desk Joseph took a bag of coins. Carrying these articles under his arm, he left the house with Jean Baptiste, Marie promising to come down as soon as the children were sound asleep.

A campfire was burning at the west end of the beach, where the pine trees came down almost to the water's edge. Four tepees had already been set up. The supper kettle still hung over its tripod. Four braves and two squaws were sitting by the fire, in silence. A very thin woman with a baby strapped to her back could be seen moving slowly about in the shadows, a hundred feet or more away from the fire. Every now and then, the woman stooped to pick up whatever driftwood protruded from the snow on the beach.

When he was within easy hailing distance, Joseph gave the "sau-sa-quan," the "joyful greeting." One of the Indians jumped up and came forward to investigate. Joseph stuck out his hand and said:

"Bon jour! I'm Bailly, the Frenchman, the trader, husband of the Wing Woman of the Ottawa and a friend of Shawnee Logan."

"Boo, joo," said the Shawnee.

"I bring tobacco," said Bailly, "and bread."

Joseph sat down by the fire and distributed the tobacco. The Indians reached out their hands hungrily for the tobacco and for the white man's bread. No one thought of calling to the woman in the shadows. Joseph knew that he must thoroughly placate the Indians before speaking about Mrs. Simmons or to her. He brought out his calumet, his flint, steel, and punk, placed a little tobacco in the pipe, struck fire, lighted the tobacco, took a few slow puffs and passed the pipe to the Indian nearest him. There were many prolonged minutes of smoking before the woman in the shadows returned, limping and dragging, with an armload of driftwood which she carefully set down near one of the squaws. No one looked at her, nor did she look at any one. As she stooped, and her face was, for a flashing instant, etched in the firelight, Joseph momentarily lost his self-possession, and exclaimed, under his breath:

"Sacré nom de Dieu!"

The savages glanced at him fiercely under their contracted brows, and Jean Baptiste, who had been sitting at the edge of the group, coughed a warning to Joseph.

"Sacré! But it is cold," said Joseph, bringing his shoulders forward in the pantomime of a shudder, then realizing the contempt which that remark also would bring down upon him, he added: "Cold as the legs of a squaw who falls through the ice," and the low guffaws swept away both the suspicion and the contempt.

The firelight had revealed, as Jean Baptiste had suggested, a skeleton. The dark parchment skin hugged a tight nose, jutting cheeks and lips so thin that they were drawn rigidly back revealing the set of square, fine white teeth. The eyes were sunk like lava in deep craters. Only the yellow hair flowing in uncombed strands over the forehead and shoulders and the perfect teeth suggested the beauty that had once belonged so lavishly to Mrs. Simmons. Joseph noted also, as they let go of the driftwood, the hands that were like claws. He could not yet see the face of the blanketed baby, but it whimpered continually.

Mrs. Simmons turned away to gather more driftwood, and Joseph used every moment for ingratiating himself with the surly Indians, addressing them as "cousin" and "brother," asking them, in as much of the Shawnee dialect as he could possibly remember and filling in with Algonquin where he could not remember, about their long journey, then telling them of some of his own adventures, ending as dramatically as he could, with much use of gestures and of the sign language, with his encounter with the "carcajou" at Great Slave Lake.

By this time, Mrs. Simmons' baby had begun to cry more piercingly, the wail slivering the vast cold night, like the thin cry of a trapped hare. Mrs. Simmons returned with another burden of driftwood, laid it down, said something to a squaw, who grunted to a brave, who grunted something in reply. Mrs. Simmons sat down between and a little behind the two squaws, for they made no room to enable her to come closer to the fire. Then she loosened the carrying strap which fastened the baby to her back, brought the baby forward, opened her dress, and approached the mouth of the baby to the flattest, emptiest breast that Joseph had ever seen. The baby itself looked like a small mummy.

At leisure, for the first time Mrs. Simmons glanced across at Joseph. Her eyes widened slowly with recognition and her lips fell open with astonishment. Joseph gave an almost imperceptible, negative nod of his head and put his fingers admonishingly to his mouth, as if he were rubbing chapped lips.

Ten minutes later, Joseph had reached the point where he could ask the leader of the Indians if he would be willing to sell his captive.

"No. No sell. Take to Fort Mackinac, British commander. Pay ransom. French no pay. British pay good money."

"I will pay good money."

"No. Sell commander. Always have good luck British. British give good presents, good money."

Joseph decided to let the subject drop for a few minutes.

"Would you allow me to give your captive a little present from the Wing Woman? Would you promise to let her keep it? This is for the white squaw and her baby. Not for the Indian squaws."

The Indian hesitated.

"See, I will give you these gold coins, if you will let the white squaw keep these warm clothes and eat what remains of the bread."

Joseph opened the package of warm clothes, so that the Indians could see them, then dropped two gold coins on the heap of cloth.

"Yes. Yes. You give white squaw old clothes," said the Indian leader, eagerly grasping the gold coins.

"May I talk to your captive?"

"Yes. Yes," grunted the Indian.

Joseph crossed the small, lighted area and sat down beside Mrs. Simmons. The two Indians who had made no place for Mrs. Simmons made a place for Joseph. Joseph laid the bread and the warm clothes in Mrs. Simmons' lap. It was the first kind thing that had been done for her for four months.

After she had watched the murder of her older child in the wagon, and of her soldier-husband in the battle of Checagou, the

Indians had dragged her (while she held tight as an octopus, every moment, to her seven months-old baby, for fear its brains would be dashed out against some tree along the way) all the agonizing distance to Green Bay. There, for the entertainment of the Indians, she had been forced to run the gantlet with her baby in her arms and, by some miracle, had raced past the tomahawks and the cudgels and the battle axes, with bruises but not with death for the ending. Then she had been dragged back again, in the general movement of the tribes towards the scene of conflict on Lake Erie, all the long way to Checagou, on bleeding feet, past the ashes of the fort and the yet unburied remains of the victims of the massacre. Then, with the Shawnees' hope of ransoming her at Mackinac as the final impetus of the journey, they had moved north, up the bleak shore of Lake Michigan, up the cold Ottawa trail to Arbre Croche, and across on the ice to Mackinac. Like a ghost she had walked, carrying her child, curving over it with the eternal arch of motherhood, that arch which is more durable, more dependable than all the vaults and spans in all the builded world.

When, therefore, after all these months, Joseph laid the package in her lap, the tears that had been frozen in the caves of her heart were suddenly loosened, and Mrs. Simmons wept—silently, for she was even yet afraid of reprisal from her captors.

"My husband and my little son were both—killed—you know—at Checagou—"

"Yes. I know."

"Have any other—survivors—come this way?"

"Yes. Captain Heald and Mrs. Heald and Louis Pettle. They were paddled up in a canoe by Alexander Robinson and his wife last September. They went on to Detroit."

"Dear Rebecca Heald. She was well?"

"Yes. She had been wounded several times, but all the wounds were healed. But she looked much older."

"And Louis Pettle, poor man?"

"Could not say a word. Like a man who had lost his mind."

"I don't wonder. Louis's wife—and children—were killed by the same monster—who killed my little son. I can't forget that Indian, night or day. No hair on his head but the single clump of the scalplock—"

"Shavehead!" exclaimed Joseph, above a whisper.

"Shavehead!" echoed the leading Indian, overhearing. "Great man! Great warrior, Shavehead!"

"Yes! Great, great warrior!" echoed Joseph, placatingly.

Mrs. Simmons hugged her remaining child to her suffocatingly. Joseph rose and went over and sat down behind the leading Indian. It was a part of his French tact to conceal himself in the shadows behind the Indian, in order that Mrs. Simmons should see as little as possible of the transactions which he was about to resume on her behalf.

"Look!" said Joseph to the Indian. "Good gold!"

The Indian looked over his shoulder, uttered a grunt of astonishment and screwed himself completely around. Joseph had dumped out on a piece of deerskin fifty gold half-eagles, which gleamed alluringly in the firelight.

"That buys many ponies," suggested Joseph, "many silver muskets, many good blankets, many beads, many silver ornaments. Give white squaw to me. I give you these. I will get her parole from the British commander. Take all these. You come to my trading house, up the hill, take all you want for these gold coins; or go to any trading house you please. The gold is good anywhere."

"Whisky? Good Mackinac whisky your place?"

"I'll give you a gallon for you and your men, that's all. But you can have anything else this gold will buy—"

"British commander—"

"British commander will not give more."

"No," proclaimed the voice of Marie, who had just arrived at the edge of the firelight. "British commander will not give more. That is enough for three white squaws! Take it and thank the Great Spirit for the trader Bailly!"

The Indians looked up at the firm-voiced woman, who was using so perfectly their own Shawnee idioms.

"You Wing Woman?" asked the leader of the Shawnee. "Great Wing Woman of Ottawa?"

"I am the Wing Woman."

"Wing Woman right. I take gold. You take white squaw."

"And white baby," added Marie, with emphasis.

"More gold for white baby. *More* gold."

"No," declared Joseph with finality, getting up and towering over the huddled group. "Absolutely no! That is enough for three squaws and three babies. Go ask the British commander! He's at the fort now."

"You are lucky Indians. Gitchi Manitou has smiled on you," said Marie. "He has thrown beautiful gold in your path. Look!"

Marie picked up a handful of gold and let it cascade like a shining river through her hands to the blanket again. The sight was too much for the rapacious Indians. Their leader grunted assent.

Then Marie and Joseph walked quietly over to where Mrs. Simmons drooped over her baby. Marie touched her on the shoulder.

"I am Joseph Bailly's wife. And I've come to take you home."

As the sunken face of Mrs. Simmons looked up at her, Marie's eyes filled with tears.

"Home?" asked Mrs. Simmons, blindly.

"Yes, Mrs. Simmons, you are going home with us," assured Marie.

"Thank you. . . . I can't believe it."

As Marie helped her to her feet, the Indian leader began to toss coins up into the air with a "Hi-yi! Hi-yi! Hi-yi!" and all the braves began to dance about the heap of gold.

"Oh, how good you are! How good you are!" repeated Mrs. Simmons over and over again. "My people in Kentucky will re-pay—"

"We don't want any repayment, Mrs. Simmons," declared Joseph emphatically, as he took hold of her other elbow.

"Oh, I'm sorry if I said the wrong thing. I don't know what to say any more. I've lost track of everything. I don't even know what day it is. It's January, I know. But long ago I lost count of the days—"

"It's the 22nd of January," said Joseph.

"The 22nd? The 22nd of January? Why, then it's my baby's birthday. She's one year old today!"

"Then, we'll give her a birthday feast at our house. May I carry her?" asked Marie.

"Oh, no, no thank you. I've carried her six hundred miles. She's fastened to the *outside* of me now, I think."

Without so much as a goodbye or a backward look at her cap-

tors, Mrs. Simmons, supported on either side by her two libera-
tors, trudged away into the darkness.

Jean Baptiste followed the little group. When Marie had helped
Mrs. Simmons into the house, Jean Baptiste paused on the door-
step before going to his quarters at the rear and detained Joseph
to ask:

"Zere anyt'ing Jean Baptiste can do to help zose poor creatures,
Monsieur Joseph?"

"No, thank you, Jean Baptiste. Not now. Perhaps later, you
can help by escorting Mrs. Simmons back to her relatives in Louisville, Kentucky. But I want her to look and feel more like herself
first."

"What she look like once? I can't remembair ever seeing her
at all at Checagou."

"Why, Jean Baptiste, she was that flaxen-haired beauty, that
rosy, round-cheeked young beauty at the fort. Don't you remember? The prettiest blonde woman at Checagou?"

"That—No, really? That gold—that golden angel?"

"Why, yes, Jean Baptiste."

"Sacré tonnerre! How she change! Only François Fortier,
whose eyes were clawed out by ze bear, would marry her now,
by gar!"

Chapter XIX

WINE OF DEATH AT THE RIVER OF GRAPES

BUT the end was not yet. While Mackinac Island lay peacefully sealed in its fortress of ice, with only the dog-sled runners bringing in news from the world outside, that world was still raging with the hurricanes of hatred and the whirlwinds of war. Tomahawks and rifle barrels flashed in the pale January sunlight. Red pools lay on the snow that bordered the Great Lakes.

While Joseph and Marie sat by their quiet fireside and talked of the places they held most dear, Quebec and the River Raisin, Arbre Croche and the Place of Buffaloes, and while their children danced and sang, the hurricane was blowing down on the little French settlement beloved of Marie and once beloved of the man who had loved Joseph's mother.

Across the snow from Ohio, the troops of Governor William Henry Harrison were plodding towards Detroit. The new governor had been eager to retrieve the error of the governor who had surrendered, and the proud Americans rallied to his cause. Detroit must be recovered. The city at the passage of the Straits had been logically American and must be American again. Leading the Kentucky division, sent ahead to the River Raisin, General Winchester, by blunder of the War Department, replaced General Harrison. Far ahead rode Winchester's scout, Peter Navarre, in buckskin and boots and coonskin cap, the tails of the cap flying behind him as he rode his swift Canadian pony, or falling slack as he reined in and cautiously cut across the lead trail.

Adventure lay both behind and in front of Peter; and his sea-blue eyes gleamed with the luster of it. There was a more determined set to his chin than usual, for he had taken part, only five months before, in Hull's retreat from Canada and the surrender of Detroit. Retreat and defeat were not acceptable to Peter's lusty young temperament and he was as determined to wipe out his own personal ignominy as General Harrison was to wipe out the stinging American defeat as a whole. With his usual cunning, Peter had escaped over the palisades of Detroit and past the British lines, just in time to avoid the humiliation of witnessing the actual ceremony of surrender and the marching of the British soldiers into the garrison, and the wide-eyed, unweeping wonder of the French girls, half of whom were his sweethearts, and the wild tears of the three or four American girls in the settlement and of pleasant Mrs. James Abbott.

As if aware of his coming, the hostile Indians, who feared him and regarded him as being as unkillable as Tecumseh, fled before him almost to a man and disappeared into the forests beyond the harassed settlement of Frenchtown on the River Raisin. Only two Miami twanged their arrows at him along the way, and then fell back into the thickets, amazed at the futility of their aim. The wily Peter dashed to his own home, told his father to prepare his house for the coming of General Winchester, and dashed back to Winchester, before a single bullet of a British scout could find his flying heart.

On the 19th of January, Winchester and his thousand men marched to the north border of the village of Frenchtown and camped, Winchester and two of his officers finally riding a mile south, under Peter's escort, to take up quarters in the old Navarre house, which had been St. Clair's headquarters twelve years before and Anthony Wayne's nine years before. For three days, rumors kept coming in that the British general, Proctor, was advancing from Malden and Detroit over the snow, with a large body of Indians. Peter rode north until he saw the red coats and the brown feathers, and brought back confirmation. But Winchester refused to be alarmed, believing the force a small one and Harrison's arrival imminent. Peter rode east to hasten the coming of Harrison.

At four o'clock in the morning of January 22nd, Colonel François Navarre, who shared his brother Peter's anxiety, rather than Winchester's laissez-faire attitude, was wide awake, listening to the wolves that were howling around the American campfires, where the odor of Frenchtown roast pig still lingered. Suddenly, the wolf-sounds ceased, and the sharp reports of the sentinels' guns ripped the moonlit air. Then the dull boom and swish of cannon ball and shot swept into the room, followed by the distant yells of Indians. Navarre leaped from his bed, tripping over Antoinette's red slippers on the floor and stumbling up the stairs to Winchester's room in the dormer. It took many shakes to rouse the general, drowsy from Navarre's good dinner and assortment of wines; but, finally roused, Winchester put on his boots and, leaving his military coat over the back of a chair, rushed downstairs with Navarre and the other two officers, and into the yard. There they mounted four of Navarre's horses held ready by young Robert.

At the camp, slaughter was going forward. General Winchester and Colonel Lewis and Colonel John Allen rode around and around the field, trying to rally, trying to give orders; but their frosty breath was wasted on the air of confusion. The few bleeding survivors fled. Colonels Lewis and Allen rode off and were shot down south of the village. Colonel Navarre escaped towards his house. Winchester, in his retreat, was captured on Woodchuck Creek by the Indian chief Split Log, and taken to the quarters of General Proctor. With what tattered dignity he could summon, he surrendered himself and his maimed forces, but with the guarantee that the wounded and the captives should be carefully protected from the fury of the Indians. Meanwhile, the Indians were wild with excitement and whisky and the sub-rosa promise of eight dollars for every American scalp.

It seemed as if all the gathering fury of the Indians poured itself out in a flood of purple intoxication on the River of Grapes. Perhaps the presence of Tecumseh himself on the battlefield, swirling his followers into a frenzy of madness, perhaps the recoil from the repulses at Tippecanoe and Fort Harrison and Fort Wayne, perhaps the blood in the eyes of the warriors who had so recently enjoyed the glory of slaughter at Fort Dearborn, perhaps the ferocity of the yet undistinguished but wild young Black Hawk with his contingent of braves from the Rock River, or the sight of the blood of Winchester's "fallen," and the indifference of General Proctor to the usual horrible Indian sequels, or the frenzied combination of all these elements, fermented the grapes of intoxication and helped to create such scenes as had not been witnessed since Pontiac, such horrors as were to lead to the American battle cry

of "Remember the Raisin!" and to the final American victory at
the Battle of the Thames.

In all the welter of blood and confusion, several scenes were
acted out on the red stage by people whose lives were closely
coiled in with those of Joseph and Marie Bailly. While Marie sat
by her Mackinac Island fireside, the night after Mrs. Simmons'
rescue, singing songs of the great Algonquins to her four small
daughters, and Joseph smoked his long pipe, thinking the forbidden thought that it would be wonderfully fine to have just
one son to whom to sing of those great deeds, the descendants of
the Algonquins were performing these not so glorious deeds three
hundred miles down the Peninsula.

The first little subsidiary scenes took place the night after the
battle, in the store and the home of Colonel John Anderson. Anderson's regiment had taken part in the fatal engagement, and,
after the rout he had escaped to the village. Most of the excitement was at General Proctor's camp two miles north of the Raisin,
on Sandy Creek. Only a few Indians were skulking around
Frenchtown, but Anderson feared that, unless General Proctor
were able to hold them in check, hundreds might soon be there to
investigate the possibilities of the village. To be sure, the Indians
were friendly to the French population, and John and Deborah
spoke both the Ottawa and the Miami dialect and were considered
exceedingly good friends of the Indians. But there were strange
Indians here from far places, and this was war; and, with such diabolical excitement abroad, Anderson knew there was no telling
what might happen. The first thing for him to do, after looking
in at his family, was to empty out all the whisky barrels in the
store.

He tied his horse to a tree on the outskirts of the village and
made his way past the whitewashed French houses. Several of
them were unlighted, the inhabitants having taken flight or pre-
ferring to risk concealment in basement or closet or behind secret
panels. But candles burned brightly in the Lefèvre house, the
Navarre house, the Beaugrands' and in his own home. In the
Navarre yard, under the French pear trees, two large sleighs were
drawn up close to the house, and Anderson could see horses tied
to the hitching posts and figures moving about. He dashed on to

his own house and knocked gently on the door. There was a long pause.

"Let me in Deborah! Let me in! It's John!"

Deborah came to the door, a candle in her hand.

"No time even to kiss you, Deborah. I'm dashing over to the store to empty out the whisky barrels. I'll be back here in a few minutes. Safer to stick it out here, don't you think? It would be hard to get you and the children past the lines into Detroit."

"The Navarres and the Beaugrands are all going up to the city. Robert Navarre is driving them in, and Peter's scouting for them."

"Is Peter back here already? He's a flying devil! I think it's foolhardy to try for Detroit. Safer to stay here. Sit tight. Little Seth and Linda all right? Every door and window locked? Everything all right? I'll be back soon."

"Yes. And Nanette and Oneota and I have a gun apiece."

"Good! Give me the shop keys."

Deborah took the keys from the mantel and gave them to her husband, who with a quick, "Goodbye—take care!" hurried down the steps and along the shadowy street as fast as his heavy boots and clanking saber and gun-loaded belt would allow him to go. The little shop stood at the very end of the village street, half a mile beyond his own home. He thought he could hear muffled howls and yells from the direction of Proctor's camp, like the baying of wolves on distant hills, and he could most certainly see the red glow of dozens of campfires on dark treetops far away. He reached his shop door, fumbled in the shadows, found the lock, opened the door. Reaching for his tinderbox, he spent two or three minutes making a light, then touched off a candle and hurried belowstairs. For one reluctant instant, he stood and surveyed his supply: ten barrels of pure Monongahela whisky, ten barrels of rum, six of brandy, three small casks of Madeira and six of wild-grape wine made by himself under good old French instructions from François Navarre—a small fortune in beverages. He heaved a deep sigh, as of a man forced to lighten his ship of the ballast of a chest of gold, then stepped stanchly to the first barrel of Monongahela whisky, opened the bung, and let out the acrid liquid. The hard-packed mud floor sipped it slowly. With another heavy sigh, Anderson tipped the barrel forward. The liquid splashed back on his military boots. The work went too slowly. He seized an oak staff from a corner. One after the other, he stove in the casks and barrels, holding each one far forward, until the last thin stream sprayed out. By the time he had reached the Madeira, he was standing in two inches of assorted beverages such as had never been mixed in any tavern on this or the other side of the Atlantic. He began to wonder whether the point of the floor's absorption had been reached. It looked as if bedrock must underlie the mud. He began to be afraid that the lake of drinks might prove far more tempting than the bunged barrels, but decided that, before any Indians could arrive, the liquid must surely seep away somewhere. The fumes that rose from that lake of alcohol seemed of themselves intoxicating. Anderson breathed deeply. He concluded that it might be wiser to dump the small barrels of Madeira in the back yard. That Madeira! That exquisite Madeira!

He reached for a gourd that hung on the wall near by, and poured himself a draught. Hm-m-m! It suggested the sunlight falling on ten million crystal grapes and on the silver olive-slopes and on the far-rippled Mediterranean and on brown-skinned, dark-haired, laughing-lipped girls—the kind of scenes that Navarre had so often described to him in a similar state of titillation. Anderson took another gourdfull. Then he put his arms around the barrel, snickering softly to himself in the thought that she was rather a hard proposition, this girl, a bit resistant—yes, a leetle bit resistant. He took a few steps, remembered the candle, put the barrel under one arm, took the candle in the other hand, and stumbled up the stairs, a thin purple stream marking his ascent. He had forgotten to replace the bung. He set the candle in the back storeroom, unlatched the back door, and stepped out into the night. His wits were not so befumed that he did not immediately recognize that something was definitely wrong with the night. The trees were too full of artificial owls and whippoorwills. Every branch seemed vocal. There was the sound of ponies' hoofs beating wildly down the road from Proctor's camp; and the wild yells that had been like the baying of distant wolves circled Frenchtown now like intermittent fire. Under the stress of death, Anderson's brain began to function again. He stepped back, blew out the candle, set the keg of Madeira down on the floor and stood for an instant making a brave effort to drain his thoughts of grapes, sea waves, and brown girls and to see clearly what he should do. The shop was dangerous. He must not stay there. Could he possibly get back home to his wife? Probably not. But he would try. Taking a pistol from his belt and holding it tight in his right hand, he crept out of the house and down close to the stark, ice-hung shrubbery edging the River Raisin. Creeping like an Indian along the black tangle of elderberry bushes, blackberry bushes, grapevines and bittersweet, squeezing between this shrubbery and the end pickets of the white fences that outlined the old French enclosures, Anderson had just reached the river end of the Lefèvre place, when a movement across the faintly starlit snow arrested his attention. He was only a few enclosures away from his shop and a quarter of a mile from his own home. He stopped in the shelter of one of the Lefèvre sheds and strained his eyes to see. Four shadows, like four wolves, were skulking horizontally along the snow. The shadows crept up to the house, then became vertical: Indians looking into the dimly candle-lit Lefèvre house. Anderson began to feel the need of a more secure shelter for himself. As he squeezed up to the outside of the shed, the heels of his boots discovered a hole considerably larger than a woodchuck hole at the base. He leaned down, felt his way along it with nervous hands and found that it was likely to be large enough to admit a man. No use shooting at four Indians. He'd be dead in a minute if he did, and so, shortly, would all the other citizens. There were probably a hundred more Indians near by, ready to pounce, at a shot. Feeling unsoldierly but prudent, he dug himself backwards into the hole, like a sand crab or an ant lion, so tightly that there was not a millimeter to spare. He had just drawn in his head when the four Indians, who had probably detected some small sound, came down close to his hiding place. In the Ottawa dialect, familiar to Anderson through many years of trading, they stopped for a moment to talk.

"Noise down here? No. Nothing but fox or woodchuck."

"Some one escape?"

"Why some one escape? All French. French not afraid."

"John Anderson not French. Barney Parker not French. Sam Ewing not French."

"All good men. Indians' friend."

"What we want, whisky. Whisky in white men's cellars."

"This not good house. This Lefèvre house. Wine here. Not whisky."

"Lefèvre? Lefèvre? That bad uncle Marie, the Wing Woman? I want Lefèvre wine. Wine Lefèvre blood. Lefèvre scalp—"

"No. No, Blackbird. Enough scalps. Whisky!"

"Whisky, Anderson's store. We go Anderson's store."

"Yes. Yes. Anderson's store. Whisky! Whisky!"

The four Indians padded away, and Anderson lay still with a beating heart. It became clear that other Indians had been struck with the same idea at the same time. The yells that had been encircling the town seemed to be converging in the direction of the store. It was possible to picture everything that was going on. There would be short silences as new groups entered the store, then diabolical outbursts as these groups, satiated with their lapping-up, rushed out again. Anderson realized that the lake in his cellar was being diminished by something far more serious than seepage. He tried to extricate himself from the hole, but before he could do so, he was roused into new attention by the sound of more low talking near by, this time in French. It did not take him long to realize that the two Lefèvres were standing near by discussing a pressing matter. He did not need to urge them to escape, for they already seemed to be planning that very thing.

"But we *must* get out!" said the woman. "We must save ourselves and these bags of coin—all your brother's savings for fifty years and ours for twenty. We can walk down the river ice and then come back in two or three days, when all the trouble is over."

"If we're killed, it's your fault, you gabbling goose! We're safer where we are!"

"Safer where we are? Listen to that yelling, you old fool! Is that safe? Go see if it looks perfectly clear up and down the river."

A sound of Lefèvre scrunching down the little private wharf steps to the landing. No use calling out a warning to the Lefèvre woman, Anderson told himself. The Lefèvres would figure it out all right. Yet, even as the thought passed across his mind, he wondered guiltily whether the hatred for these thieves and interlopers which he had shared with the entire community from the very day of the eviction of Marie Lefèvre and her mother held him back. A good French oath from Lefèvre interrupted the exercise of Anderson's conscience. Then the scrunching steps of Lefèvre returning.

"A thousand devils! There's a party of savages coming down the river. That's settled. We'll have to wait. No escape by the river yet."

"Oh, God! Nor by land! Here they come!"

Madame Lefèvre dropped the coin bags close to Anderson's head and started to run towards the river bank. But the padding of Indian feet was loud on the snowy ground behind her. In an instant, the Indians had caught up with both Lefèvres. Blackbird's voice could be heard again, harshened with drink:

"You Lefèvre?"

"Yes. Yes. I'm French. Leave me alone. Good friend of Indians. Good friend. *Good friend*, I tell you!"

"You—friend of Marie Lefèvre?"

"Marie Lefèvre?"

"Yes. Little Marie, brother Antoine's daughter? You *good friend?*"

Lefèvre began to see the drift. Even in the pale starlight, one might have seen the shadows of terror deepen on his face, sharpening the resemblance of the hollows to skull sockets.

"Yes. Yes. I send her money. I give *you whisky!* I give you so much gold you never see before! Let go! Let go!"

A man's shrill scream and a woman's yet shriller scream cut the frosty air. There was a snapping of icy twigs as the bodies fell into the bushes. Then—triumphant yells as two new dripping scalplocks were lifted in the hands of Chief Blackbird, against the dim background of the sky.

As soon as these newest yells receded, Anderson crawled out of his hole. Taking the dropped coin bags, he shoved them far into the opening that he had just left, hoping that the trail leading to the shed would be less interesting to Indian passers-by than the bodies newly left in the snow and any accouterments they might still possess. It was Anderson's honest intention to give the money to Marie Bailly, to whom it rightfully belonged, if he should ever get out of this bloody mess alive. Just now it was his purpose to run the gantlet of the hundred different varieties of death that were undoubtedly lined up ahead of him on the trail to his own house. He must make a superhuman effort to reach Mrs. Anderson and the children. Certainly, not even all the tact and friendliness of Deborah Anderson could hold out against such hellhounds as were abroad tonight. He crouched again and went over the trampled, bloody snow, past the two bodies askew in the blackberry bushes like spiked vultures, and crept down closer to the river bank. He strained his eyes along the starlit ice of the river. There seemed to be no moving shadows now in any direction. Again he stooped, and keeping as close as possible to the overhanging branches of trees and bushes, and yet not so close as to scrape against them, to make any sound for sharp brown ears to hear, he moved along, lifting each foot high, like an oversized heron. Anderson's sense of hearing was projected beyond his flesh, as if on long, quivering antennae. He was aware of every patch and plot of sound against the January stillness: a swirl of screeches from the direction of the whisky pool in his own shop, a swirl of screeches from the group who were swinging the Lefèvre scalps, a swirl of screeches on the highroad, a swirl of howls ahead of him—from the direction of his own house!

While Anderson was stepping along the frozen River Raisin, things were indeed happening within his own house. Just ten minutes before, Shavehead and a group of young Potawatomi and Ottawa, and Blackhawk of the Rock River and a few Sauk, all drunk as dervishes, had joined together unpremeditatedly on the Anderson lawn, and made a rush at the house. It was not long before Blackbird's scalp-carrying group also joined them.

Deborah Anderson, an hour before, had pried up two puncheons of the living-room floor, and laid her ten-year-old son Seth and her little three-year-old girl Linda, wrapped in bear rugs, on the cold ground two feet underneath the floor. She had instructed Seth to keep Linda quiet at all costs, should any commotion waken the child, to gag her, if necessary, with one of his father's handkerchiefs, which she gave him for the purpose. Then she had fitted down the puncheons again, without replacing the wooden pegs, so that Seth could get out with Linda, even if the rest of the

family perished. Nanette, the little French nurse-girl, pale and
stammering with terror, had long ago fled to her dormer room and
had rolled herself up in a blanket on the floor, underneath her
bed. Oneota, the Ottawa servant, had come down out of her adjoining dormer room and was now sitting hunched up by the
Anderson fire, in an attitude whose lax curves belied the intensity
of her attention to all the sounds outside.

Deborah Anderson sat down on a carved walnut chest against
a side wall not far from the fire and began to knit. Long living
with the Indians had given her the same familiarity with the savage
respect for courage and the casual attitude, which Elinor Kinzie
of Checagou had acquired. Though her knitting needles chattered
like teeth with fear, and though her blood ran as cold as the
Raisin River outside, Deborah continued the pattern of Linda's
jacket. The carved chest on which Deborah sat contained all of
her own and her husband's valuables.

It occurred to her belatedly that it was strange for Oneota to
have come down from her attic and sat down by the fire with
never a by-your-leave. Oneota had never taken such a liberty
before. She was probably frightened to death.

But was she? Over her knitting needles, Deborah cast a swift
look and caught the strange, full gaze of Oneota upon herself. It
was such a gaze as she had never seen in those eyes, savage, cruel,
scorching with hatred, the concentrated detestation of the Indian
for the white. A veil went over the eyes as Deborah looked, but
not quickly enough. Deborah tried to continue her knitting.
She wondered whether Oneota knew that she had taken the children out of their beds and hidden them. Her fingers had only just
caught their rhythm again when an owl trilled in the yard, then
another. Oneota rose and went swiftly to open the door. Deborah dropped the knitting, pulled a pistol from the belt beneath
her apron, stood up, and said:

"If you open that door, you are a dead squaw!"

Oneota took one more step towards the door, then glided back
to the fire.

"No, not there. Upstairs! Upstairs, I say, to your room!"

Oneota shrugged her shoulders, turned and went up the stairs.
By this time, the yard was a pandemonium of owl trills, whip-

poorwill shrillings, catcalls and undisguised whoops. As she stood by the fire, Deborah began to feel the serpent flame of Indian eyes darting in upon her through all the windows. Very quietly, she resumed her place on the chest and picked up her dropped knitting. As she did so, she heard Linda start to cry underneath the planking. Deborah began to drown out the sound by singing, in a voice that vainly strove to deny the tremolo of terror, the first lusty song that came into her head, realizing only after she had begun it the ironic appropriateness of the words:

> "Scots, wha hae wi' Wallace bled,
>   Scots, wham Bruce has aften led;
> Welcome to your gory bed,
>   Or to victorie!
>
> "Now's the day, and now's the hour;
>   See the front o' battle lower;
> See approach proud Edward's power—
>   Chains and slavery!
>
> "Wha will be a traitor knave?
>   Wha can fill a coward's grave?
> Wha sae base as be a slave?
>   Let him turn and flee!"

The tomahawks were already cutting into the door, but Deborah thought she could detect that Linda's outcry had stopped. She too stopped her ironic song. On and on her fingers flew over the knitting, though her arms felt like bars of lead that might fall helplessly into her lap at any moment. Though she did not look up, she could follow the shivering progress of the war hatchets and tomahawks through the door. Splinter! Splinter! Splinter! Crash! Crackle! Smash! Crash! With a howl, the first Indian leaped through the opening. Then a second and a third. . . . Deborah looked up—and smiled.

She recognized Shavehead from the descriptions, though she had never seen him before. His eyes burned like devil's eyes. His bald head reflected the firelight like a hazelnut. From his belt, new scalps dripped blood on the clean oak puncheons. His scalping knife cut the air with light, as he held it high in his right hand. A dozen drunken Indians were in the room by now.

Deborah sat smiling, while Shavehead and half a dozen Indians approached her, and while the others were throwing down upon the floor a mass of grisly specimens which Deborah recognized as more scalps. As Shavehead, watching her every change of expression, moved down upon her, Deborah met his eyes with such an unflinching look that he paused within a yard of her. Again he began to move, his eyes and lips narrow with hatred. Suddenly, below the din of savage yells and whoops, Deborah heard again the tiny whimper of Linda. Raising her voice to the loudest pitch, she shouted at Shavehead and his comrades, in Potawatomi:

"Shame on you, Shavehead! Shame on you, braves! Does it take so many to kill a lone woman? You are a great warrior, Shavehead, a great warrior! You are all great braves! Leave the women to the petticoat men!"

Shavehead and the others stopped for a moment as if shamed. He had again raised his arm against her when it was seized by a splendid-looking, hawk-nosed Indian who had just walked through the slit in the door. Deborah recognized Pokagon of the Potawatomi.

"No, Shavehead!" said Pokagon. "No! There's better game than this. Let the little American faun alone."

Shavehead jerked his arm away and said:

"Let her get up then! There must be something in that box! Get up! Get up, white squaw!"

Deborah again picked up her knitting, lowered her eyes, and went on with her work. All the Indians in the room except Pokagon and Shavehead were by now dancing and thumping and yelling in a driving circle, around and around the heap of scalps in the center of the floor.

"Hi yi! Hi yi! Hi yi! Wa-hoo! Wa-hoo!
Hi yi! Hi yi! Hi yi! Wa-hoo! Wa-a-hoo!"

Wilder and wilder, faster and faster. Shavehead was whirled into the circle. Shavehead stooped down, picked up a gory mass and hurled it at the spinning-wheel in a corner of the room. Then another clump was hurled at a blue glass vase on the mantel. Then the candles were blotted out with blood. In a moment, the Indians were picking up the scalps and hurling them indiscriminately at every object in the room, and daubing with scarlet the whole length of log walls, log ceiling, and puncheon floor. Several fell into Deborah's lap, and calmly she allowed them to remain there. Things were becoming worse instead of better. Could even Pokagon, who stood at her side, command such hysteria as this?

Suddenly, a shot went off at the side of the house, then another at the back, then another at the other side of the house. Three-quarters surrounded! American soldiers! The Indians leaped for the opening in the front door and tumbled out in a mad scramble, all but Pokagon. The Indians dispersed over the countryside, their yells sounding fainter and fainter. Everything was comparatively quiet. Oneota, no longer afraid of her drunken friends, crept down the stairs and paused on the last step. To Pokagon she said:

"There are children here. Two children hidden. Good scalps."

At the last words, Colonel Anderson stepped through the broken front door.

"Yours, too, is a good scalp, my girl. Go out and join your brothers! Go before I shoot you!"

Seizing her by the neck and belt of her dress, Anderson placed her exactly in the door slit, took one quick step back, and then kicked her, with all his strength, into the snow. Then he went quickly over to his wife, who now sat slumped on the chest, all power gone from her.

"Deborah! My darling! And the children? Safe?"

"Safe, dearest!"

"Thank you, Chief Pokagon! I imagine you saved my wife's life."

"No, I imagine it was you and your friends' shots that saved your wife."

"Friends? I was alone—but I ran fast from place to place, to make it *seem* like a squad."

"All shots yours? Wonderful! Good work, Colonel Anderson!"

"Deborah, what *are* you doing?"

Deborah was down on the floor, plucking at one of the puncheons with a tomahawk.

"I'm getting up the children! Help me!"

For a moment, Anderson thought his wife's mind had been affected. But Deborah pried up the loose plank and lifted it.

"Are you all right, Seth? Are you all right, Linda? Seth! Seth!"

No answer.

"Light the candle, John, quickly! Or bring a brand from the fire!"

Anderson strode to the fire, picked up the tongs and seized a small brand. Brought to illuminate the opening in the floor, it revealed Seth lying with his hand over his sister's mouth and a look of fixed terror in his eyes. His father reached in and shook him.

"Seth! Seth! They've all gone! Everything's all right! Get up! Come up!"

"Wait a minute, John. We'll pry up the other puncheon, as I did before."

Even then Seth made no motion to come up, and at sight of Pokagon on the edge of the flooring he fainted dead away. His father leaned over and lifted him and his sleeping sister into the room. Both children were placed near the fire to recover.

When the children were at last carried to bed, and Pokagon had gone and the yells of the marauding Indians had all quivered into the distance towards Proctor's camp, Colonel Anderson told his wife of the fate of the Lefèvres and of the bags of coin left in the Lefèvre shed.

"It's wicked of me to think it," commented Deborah, "but I almost believe those Lefèvres deserved their fate. I'll never forget as long as I live, that awful day when they drove Marie and her mother from their own home."

"Nor I, Deborah. They deserved what they got. I couldn't help them."

"No. I wonder if the Navarres got safely through to Detroit. And the Beaugrands. I wonder if Jacques Beaugrand got through the battle alive. His first battle, poor fellow!"

"It won't help much if he got through the battle alive—and was taken prisoner, you know—"

"Yes, I know. . . . And how about *you*, John? You're still in great danger—"

"I must try to get back to the main army as soon as possible, now that things have quieted down around here. The worst is over. I'll scout around a bit and see just how many of our friends are left here, and then I'll cut across country. . . . God! How I wish Peter Navarre were here to scout for me! He'd find his way between seven devils and seven deep seas and come out on the other side of them every time, with a 'Bon jour!' and a bow and a laugh."

But Peter Navarre was not doing much laughing that night. After leading his family to the outskirts of Detroit, he was riding madly east to hasten the march of General Harrison. Nor was Jacques Beaugrand doing much laughing. Jacques was a captive of Proctor, along with many others from Winchester's unfortunate army. All night he had stood up, leaning against a tree at Proctor's camp and steadying himself against the trunk with his hands, in spite of slight wounds in the left shoulder and the left leg; for the Indians were scalping all the wounded, all the horizontal ones, and Jacques was doing his best to maintain a vertical position. He had frozen a devil-may-care smile on his face. Leaning against a neighboring tree was Étienne Planchon, the fish-faced fellow who, along with Jacques, had watched Marie Lefèvre's expulsion from her home so many years before. At close range, these two witnessed the atrocities which the Navarre family watched at a distance, creeping past in the night, on their way to Detroit—atrocities which Robert Navarre would never be able to describe without tears.

Drunk with whisky and blood, the Indians set fire to the houses in which many of the wounded lay, throwing them back into the flames as they crawled out, and torturing with knife, with fire, with arrow, with tomahawk, those prisoners who lay on the open ground. When at last the Indians began to scalp, they abandoned their usual quick method and, instead, cut a shallow line around the top of the victim's head, put a foot on the prisoner's neck, clutched the hair on the top of the head, and pulled off the scalp by main force. Over and over this was done, the moans and the screams of agony mingling with the shouts of the remorseless Indians. Fair-haired boys from log cabins in Ohio out on their first and last great adventure, six-foot giants of the breed of Daniel

Boone, out of Kentucky, dashing officers, like Colonel John Allen (whose wife's pathetic candle was to burn in the window of the home near Louisville for two years after the Raisin, on the chance that he had been captured, not killed by the Indians), striplings, and seasoned campaigners who had fought the Indians on the ever-westering frontier for forty years—all were butchered alike at the red camp of Proctor, until the slaughtering hands wearied.

Jacques Beaugrand and Étienne Planchon, clutching at their trees, and eight other Americans remained alive when dawn poured over the landscape. Almost all the Indians had dropped to the ground, exhausted with the orgy, mingling their blanketed bodies indiscriminately with the dead Americans. All was silent at last. Even the Michigan timber wolves that had bayed louder and louder and nearer and nearer, towards dawn, were silent at last. But Beaugrand knew that they were lurking near for the reeking feast that would be theirs when camp was moved. To make a feast for wolves! Was this what he had been born for? Was this what his youth, his strength, his joy of living, his power of loving were for? If he only had the full use of that left leg, he would make a dash for it! The British sentries at Proctor's camp a quarter of a mile away looked half asleep, as they leaned on their muskets or ambled lazily back and forth from post to post, and the Indian guards here were fierce but befuddled. God help me to live to avenge this night, thought Beaugrand. God let me live! I'll fight like twenty demons the next time!

Most of the Indians slept until evening. No food was passed out by the British commissary to the Americans. These were left to understand that they were the prisoners and the property of the Indians who had so nobly supported the British cause. Let the Indians feed them, if they could. At least the Americans had something to drink. They were able to assuage the burning of their throats by scooping up the compound of mud, filth, blood, and snow close around them.

When the sun was again casting a blood-red light at evening, the Indians began to stir. They woke up suddenly, and with the first waking the snakes of triumph slipped back into their eyes; but now the effects of the whisky and the blood had somewhat worn off. The Indians huddled together and began discussing how to dispatch the remaining prisoners to their own utmost enjoyment. Not all together, like last night. No. That was grand while it lasted, heap grand. But these last ten prisoners—these must serve for some time, give as much long-drawn-out, tortured pleasure as possible. One by one! One for each day! That was it! One man a day. And let all the other prisoners see the one man die. And save for the last, the man that seemed to suffer most.

Asa Bun apparently took charge of the gruesome arrangements. Followed closely by Round Head and Split Log and a dozen of the three hundred Indians, he moved towards the ten American survivors standing or seated around a small campfire.

"Up!" said Asa Bun, making the lifting gesture with his hands. "Up! Up!"

The Americans were a pitiful-looking lot. The Indians had torn from them every button, every bit of braid, every ornament, their belts, their knives, and, of course, their guns. Some were without their coats in the January winds. All were muddy, ragged, bruised, blue with cold, and hairy, little resembling the spruce regiment that had gone out a few days before to meet the British and Indians. As they stood up slowly, they tried to read in their captors' faces the nature of the death which was being prepared for them. But there was only the familiar general menace in the grim brown faces.

"Here! Here!" directed Asa Bun. "Line up—like soldiers! Yes—like soldiers!" And he emitted a laugh.

The ragged Raisin River and Ohio and Kentucky boys, their helpless hands clenched with eagerness to tear the nearest brown throat, formed a pitiful line from an oak tree to a maple tree whose trunks were momentarily reddened in the light of the setting sun. Asa Bun now called Shavehead to him, and slowly they walked the entire length of the line, studying each face keenly. At the end of the line they paused for a moment's discussion, then walked slowly back again, consuming the faces with hungry eyes. Another brief discussion, then the two Indians stalked halfway down the line and came to a halt in front of the youngest and most attractive member of the group, a sensitive-looking, blond boy. David Montgomery, of Louisville, was about seventeen years of

age, and his every feature indicated fineness of nature and of background. Although his lip quivered, he held his head high and
stepped forward when Asa Bun directed him to leave the line.
Next to the boy stood a tall, lanky frontiersman from Kentucky,
William Simpson, with amiability and kindliness written all over
his face. He seemed to like the boy, for he had passed remarks to
him in a low, gay, reassuring tone while the Indians were making
their inspection. This the shrewd Indians had noted. This spelled
his doom.

"Now," said Asa Bun, in a shrill voice loud enough for all to
hear, and in perfectly distinct English: "Now, we take one life
each day. One bad American life. Maybe we save two, three
lives at end. Brave men be saved. Now we begin. Weak boy first.
Hi yi! Hi yi! Hi yi yi! You come here!"

With this, Asa Bun pulled the lanky Kentuckian from the line
by the front of his buttonless army coat, and shoved him close to
the boy. He then gave the Kentucky frontiersman a tomahawk.

"Now kill boy!" said Asa Bun to Simpson.

"You hellhound! Not on your life!" cried Simpson.

"Look back of you!" warned Asa Bun in the same shrill voice.
"It's you or boy! Make choice!"

Looking over his shoulder, Simpson saw Shavehead with a huge
battle-ax raised to cleave his skull, should he prove refractory.
Never had any instrument seemed so monstrous, so imminent—
yet so avoidable. Simpson turned toward the boy again. The
boys' face was whiter than the snow, but he managed to say:

"Don't flinch, Bill. Kill me. Your life is worth ten of mine.
You've got a family. But tell my m-mother. . . . Oh, go ahead,
Bill! It'll be over in a minute!"

Simpson wanted to be alive to catch the boy, if he fainted.
He wanted to be alive, *alive*— He turned swiftly, in an attempt
to lodge his tomahawk in Shavehead's chest, but the great cleaver
descended before he had completed the turn. A tall body fell to
the ground.

Howls broke from the Indians. The fair-haired boy keeled over
in a dead faint. Not a soul moved to touch him, until Asa Bun
dragged him back by his heels to the line of horrified Americans.
The Indians began their whoops and dances around Bill Simp-

son's body and only when the last whoop was whooped and the last dance danced were the Americans allowed to return to the campfire to try to choke down a few portions of bear meat. As each American lay on the ground that night, he wondered just what he would do when the tomahawk was placed in his hand and he was ordered to slay a comrade. To murder or not to murder? To live or not to live. . . . Who except Indians could have devised such inconceivable torture? It was almost dawn when Jacques Beaugrand at last fell asleep.

It took two more afternoons to kill the fair-haired boy, David Montgomery. The next afternoon a young Kentucky lieutenant, Arnold McAfee, was led up to face him. McAfee lifted the tomahawk as if to strike, then let his hand fall. If the boy's eyes were not so blue—why were his eyes so blue!

"One more chance. Just *one more chance!*" shrieked Asa Bun.

Again Lieutenant McAfee, shutting his eyes, lifted the tomahawk. But the color of the boy's eyes leaped into the darkness under his own lids. He let the tomahawk fall to his side. He heard the first shouts of savage triumph, before the lightning of pain struck him into the unlistening darkness.

The eight remaining men grew a little more insensitive, a little more obdurate, more desirous of life each night. It surprised only a few of them, for only a few of them would have failed to do the same thing by now, when, on the third evening, Étienne Planchon took the tomahawk from Asa Bun, his face absolutely expressionless, and brained the boy with one swift crack. The Indians made much of Étienne. He was a hero for an hour. They stuck a chief's eagle feather behind his ears. He was bloated with pride.

Jacques Beaugrand was made so sick by the whole sight that he vomited. The minute he did it, he knew that he had singled himself out for the next performance. As he lifted his head, he caught the cunning gleam in Asa Bun's eyes. Shavehead had been too preoccupied with dangling the beautiful, fair scalp of the boy, to be looking in Beaugrand's direction, but Asa Bun had been scanning the line of Americans for any signs of weakness or sensitiveness. Étienne now returned to the line of his seven comrades and took his place beside Beaugrand. Every bit of Beaugrand's flesh recoiled from Étienne, but the man on Étienne's left, a big ape of a fellow from Ohio, gave Étienne a resounding whack on the back, and said: "Well cracked, Captain Hackem! Well hacked!" And he went off into guffaws, which shortly became hysterical.

Jacques wished that he might never wake up from the night that followed, that some Indian might steal upon him and brain him before the dawn rendered reality so brutally distinct. If only, by some miracle, General Harrison might come up during the night and effect a general rescue—or Peter Navarre, whose name was dreaded by the bloody-backed British from loop to loop of the lakes, might slip into the lines and spirit him away! He kept dreaming of his old friends, Peter Navarre and Pierre Desnoyers and Joseph Campeau and Joseph Bailly, and of the gallons of brandy and claret they used to consume and the miles of stories they used to tell. But twice he sat up suddenly in the night, a cold sweat breaking out all over him, clutched by the clammy feeling that he had already been killed and that the black earth, the black black earth through which no moon-gleam, no star-gleam, no eye-gleam could ever, ever find its way, had already been mounded over him. Suddenly he saw the moon. He was alive! . . . A white icicle of a moon shining between the leafless branches of the trees. Death. . . . Life. . . . Death. . . . Life. The two thoughts beat through him like the rumble of an everlasting drum.

When day finally came, Jacques Beaugrand was actually ill, with a raging fever and red-gold dreams more horrible than those of the night. He sat up with his back against a tree, trying to seem vigorous. He didn't want to be the one to be tomahawked. . . . He didn't want to tomahawk. . . . He didn't want to be tomahawked. . . . He didn't want to tomahawk. The everlasting drum. . . . He wanted to live . . . to live . . . to live . . .

At five o'clock, when the sun was setting in a yellow sea of sky, the Indians marched the Americans into line again. Jacques shivered and half shut his feverish eyes, and stood as straight as he could. Asa Bun came and took hold of Étienne Planchon and pulled him out of line. Jacques could hear a low moan of entreaty to the Blessed Virgin whom Étienne had probably not implored since his childhood thirty years before:

"Bonne Vierge! Mère de Dieu! O bonne Vierge! Ayez pitié de moi!"

Then, Asa Bun came back and took Jacques tight by the arm and pulled him out into the open space, facing Étienne. . . .

The courts of Detroit wanted to know later just how it happened, and Jacques Beaugrand had the greatest difficulty in remembering. It was all like a part of the feverish dream. . . . He could only remember that Asa Bun placed a tomahawk in his hand . . .

Chapter XX

TWO INDIANS BY THE FIRE

THE LAKES were no longer blue as water and free as air. The red glare of war lay across the under blue. Indian runners and traders coming in their long pirogues down the old safe way along the Ottawa River or slipping past enemy schooners on the upper lakes brought the news of one battle after another to the solid old island of Mackinac.

News of the Raisin came across the packed ice with little groups of Ottawa from Arbre Croche. But it was not until March that Leopold Pokagon brought the detailed story to the Bailly fireside at Mackinac Island. Grimly he sat and told the whole fearful tale, watching the holly-leaf flames of the fire, and not once looking into the tense faces of Joseph and Marie, until he reached the Lefèvre episode. Then he looked up, eaglelike, into Marie's face.

"There were two at the Raisin who loved you not, Wing Woman."

The pupils of Marie's eyes dilated with the pressure of a remembered hatred, but she did not utter a word.

"What of them, Pokagon?" asked Joseph.

"Their scalps hang from Shavehead's belt."

Marie drew in her breath with a rasping sound.

"But it was Blackbird who slew them for your sake, Wing Woman."

"I had long ago forgiven them," said Marie, bowing her head.

"They left behind them two bags of gold, Wing Woman, which John Anderson, who was hiding near by, picked up and saved for you."

"But why?"

"Because some of it was your father's money and some of it was their money—and all of it is yours."

257

"No. It should be my mother's. I want no money. I want no scalped men's money."

"Here it is, Wing Woman. You can do more good with it in the world than ever the wicked Lefèvres could do. And your mother would have no use for it."

Pokagon drew the bags from under his blanket and laid them on the floor at Marie's feet. Marie sat unmoving, her head still bowed, the ends of her two long black braids touching her knees.

"Take them, Marie, and thank Pokagon," said Joseph gently. "You and your mother can divide the gold between you, later."

"Are you going back to Parc aux Vaches by way of Arbre Croche, Father Pokagon?"

"Yes, Wing Woman."

"Will you take one of the bags to my mother?"

"Yes, Wing Woman. But she does not need it."

"You are an honest man, Father Pokagon, and a true friend. And John Anderson is an honest man. You must have a share and John Anderson must have a share, . . . and some we shall send to Father Richard for the beautiful new Ste. Anne's Church he has been so long building at Detroit. Don't you think so, Joseph?"

"Yes. And some for pretty dresses from Paris for my little Marie, if the boats ever get through again!" declared Joseph.

"Not now, Joseph. There are too many people in need just now. No, no, Joseph. I don't think I can ever look at a pretty dress again! Tell us more, Pokagon, everything about all our friends."

"You knew Jacques Beaugrand?"

"Yes, oh, yes! What about him?"

Pokagon proceeded to tell the story of Beaugrand, until every bit of color had left the cheeks of both his listeners. Joseph stood up and clenched his hands and strode back and forth across the room.

"God! Why did he do it? Why did he *have* to do it? Why did they *put* him in such a ghastly, devilish situation? I hope they killed him afterwards. How could a man live on and on with a picture like that burning behind his eyeballs forever?"

"No. They didn't kill him. They gave him back to the British. He's a British prisoner in Detroit."

"God! I wish this war would end!"

Even Joseph's mother, in far-away Quebec, was witness of the ebb-tide incidents of war. In September, 1813, a letter from her came through in the red-tasseled toque of a voyageur:

Dear Joseph,

It gives me great comfort to think of you on the safe, well guarded island of Mackinac. I thank the good God for the red coats of the British. Stay on the island, Joseph. Give up the trading until the war is over. The wolves of war are skulking, far beyond the lines of battle. I'm sorry for all the victims of war, Joseph. God forgive me for being sorry even for the Americans. I rode over to Quebec last Monday and saw such a sight—a little group of *skeletons*, Joseph, being driven by the British soldiers up the hill from a schooner from Detroit. They were supposed to be twelve men and two women, who were left alive from that massacre down your way at Checagou. I was so horrified that I'm afraid I stood with my mouth wide open! Then I came to my senses and it occurred to me to ask the names of some of the prisoners and to find out if they knew you. The faces of several of them lighted up like skulls with candles in them, when I spoke your name. They were Captain and Mrs. Nathan Heald, Lieutenant and Mrs. Helm, James Corbin and Louis Pettle. Mrs. Heald may have been beautiful once. Was she? She has such enormous black eyes . . . I couldn't get much out of Louis Pettle. He doesn't talk much . . . I didn't ask any questions, so I don't know exactly what happened to each one of them. They all spoke so splendidly of you, Joseph! And of Marie. You seem to be, from their accounts, quite the nicest people in the Northwest! The American agent at Quebec is arranging the transfer of all these friends of yours to the American army at Plattsburg, so there seemed to be nothing I could do for them for your sake.

And now for home news. Raoul may be called into active service any day. He is still on guard at the citadel, praise be! But there are rumors of more big battles to be fought along the lakes, and every man will be needed. Thank Heaven, Antoinette's husband is a civil, not a military, officer! Your uncle is well, and the harvests are good this year, wheat never better, sale price sixteen shillings one penny sterling per bushel. The pear crop is excellent, Joseph. A little wise use of the ax was very good—for those trees.

I send a few ribbons for your dear Marie and the children, hoping they will get through to you all right, and my blessings to all.

Your most devoted

MOTHER.

In October, 1813, came the epic news of Perry's victory on Lake Erie. The British soldiers in the fort at Mackinac paced grimly to and fro, and men walked, with heads down and hands behind their backs, along the cobbled paths. Only a few, like Edward Biddle and Samuel Abbott and Michael Dousman, rejoiced behind closed shutters. Things were coming to a grim pass. The sturdy Americans were regaining their foothold. How long would it be before they reappeared on the island to fling up the Stars and Stripes to the stiff Mackinac breeze again?

In November, 1813, boatloads of red men touched at the island, told their sorry tale, and passed down the coast like disappointed ghosts to Arbre Croche and the Rapids of the Grand River, Parc aux Vaches, and other Potawatomi and Ottawa villages.

Late one gusty night in November, when Joseph opened the door to a knock, Blackbird entered without a word, sat down before the fire, and wrapped his brown blanket tightly around him. For a long time, he looked into the flames, still as a bronze statue of despair, then spoke:

"It is over—like forest fire. The long dream—is buried, and Tecumseh—is buried beneath the ashes of the leaves."

Joseph and Marie both breathed the sibilant word "Tecumseh!" with astonishment, for this was the first news of Tecumseh's death.

Joseph brought from the mantelpiece a red sandstone calumet and a deerskin pouch of tobacco, which he offered to Blackbird. The Indian took his own tomahawk-pipe from his belt, stuck it into a crack of the floor in front of him, took a piece of Joseph's tobacco, grunted thanks, drew from a pouch of his own a fingerful of kinni-kinic, rubbed it with the tobacco in the palm of his hand and placed the mixture in the head of the tomahawk-pipe. There was no need to draw out flint and steel, for Joseph now handed him a small, burning pine stick from the fire.

For fully half an hour the silence remained unbroken, while the thin coils of the smoke from the pipe of friendship, alternately smoked by Blackbird and by Joseph, rose and disappeared under the dusky beams of the low ceiling. Marie remained, with folded hands, watching Blackbird's face and hands. She was quietly suffering one of those inner storms, those spiritual struggles born of her partially Indian, partially French heritage. Try as she would, she could not keep her fascinated gaze from Blackbird's hands, and her mind from repeating over and over: "Those hands killed my uncle and aunt. Those hands held aloft their scalps—those quiet, tense brown hands. Those hands avenged my father. Those hands avenged my mother. They avenged me. Forgive me, Mother of Jesus, for not hating those hands . . ."

For Blackbird, the Lefévre incident had been almost entirely obliterated by the fearful events of the recent battle of the Thames, in Upper Canada. At last, the battle reenacted itself in the light of the fire and in the mesmerism of the pipe smoke, and he began to speak, slowly, in a droning voice, then more and more vehemently, with sharply varied inflections and swift, angular gestures.

"In a swamp—we lay behind tree stumps. Eighteen hundred of us, still as sleeping lizards. Tecumseh in the middle. Tecumseh. His hawk-eyes watching all. Tecumseh, in fringed hunting shirt and red leggings. Silver ring in nose. To side of us, out in front, British regulars. At rear, Proctor, British general, and a thousand redcoats waiting, waiting. Guns and bayonets glisten in the sun. Red coats shine, like blood. Then a noise like thunder. Then six hundred Kentucky men—black hunting shirts, gray hunting breeches—come galloping, galloping after the British, shouting, shouting! They shout, all together, over and over they *shriek:*

" 'Remember the Raisin! Remember the Raisin! Remember the Raisin!' "

Blackbird shut his eyes and clenched his hands, as if the sounds once more surged over him, then covered both his ears with his hands. When that portion of the storm of memory had swept past him, he let his hands fall from his ears, and resumed:

"They gallop like demons. Proctor's redcoats fall and turn and turn and try to escape, like red beetles under buffalo-hooves. Shrieks of horses, shrieks of men, and sharp, sharp cry like million snakes hissing:

" 'Raisin! Raisin! *Remember the Raisin!* Remember the Raisin! Raisin! Raisin!'

"British redcoats fly. Redcoats get down and beg for mercy. Blood, blood and red coats everywhere. Proctor turn and gallop away . . . British fly . . .

"We wait in swamp—rifles cocked . . . Tecumseh in middle,

behind tree. We wait Tecumseh give signal. . . . Americans now come after Indians in swamp. Colonel Richard Johnson, on big white mare, lead twenty men into swamp. . . . Brave men ride into death to draw fire. . . . Everything still—still as autumn day. Then Tecumseh call out loud and strong: 'Fire!' Twenty men, twenty horses go down, but Johnson ride on, left hand torn with bullets. Now hundreds Kentuckians come galloping, marching in. Tecumseh yell, shriek, like great demon. Shrieks, guns, screaming horses. Terrible battle. . . . Terrible battle. . . . I see men you know fight, fight. I see Noonday fight in swamp. I see Sauganash in red coat with British. I see Peter Navarre, in blue, fight like demon! I see John Anderson! I see Colonel Johnson ride over to where Tecumseh stand. . . . Tecumseh stand up taller, taller, shriek out orders. Tecumseh see big general on big white horse. . . . Tecumseh shoot. . . . Johnson reel on saddle—but Johnson let go reins and take pistol from own wounded left hand. Tecumseh's gun empty. Tecumseh reach up with tomahawk. Brass pipe on head of tomahawk gleam like little sun. Johnson shoot. . . . Tecumseh—Tecumseh—fall . . .

"We bury him deep in forest, deep, deep dead, where no paleface ever find him. . . . We bury the long dream—deep—deep . . ."

Blackbird wrapped the blanket around himself, bowed in the immemorial arc of grief, as old as suffering humanity itself.

Joseph took Marie's hand tightly in his own, and the two watched the stricken figure by the fire. So had the dreams of Tecumseh failed the race of the red men, even as the dreams of Pontiac had failed them. The last burning hope of a reunited and triumphant Indian race had flickered out. The blanketed Blackbird seemed to symbolize the final despair of the Indian as he sat there, crumpled in the curves of defeat.

Chapter XXI

ARRESTING INCIDENT

FROM the night of Blackbird's visit, Joseph Bailly began to feel the slow strength of the tides that were turning against the British, Perry's victory, the Battle of the Thames, the death of Tecumseh. These young Americans were full of vigor and spirit. Any day they might land at Dousman's farm again and invade the island. Joseph began to speak to Marie about moving the family away from the island.

"But where, Joseph, where?"

"South."

"Into American territory?"

"Yes. My business is south. My trading license is still good on American territory. The streams are still fresh and full of beaver to the south: golden streams, Marie, filled with golden fur."

"Parc aux Vaches again, Joseph?"

"Perhaps . . . But how about exploring the Calumet region with me in the spring, Marie?"

But the war dogs were still loose in the spring, and there was trouble all along the lakes. Among a thousand other rumors, one especially winged its way into the island that held a particular interest for Joseph. It reported that Ramsey Crooks had returned from the long Pacific expedition on which Joseph had seen him start out; that, after a thousand deadly adventures, he was again unweariedly rushing into the face of death; that he had recently set out by schooner from Detroit to try to retake Mackinac Island for the Americans, but that he was next heard of at the bloody battle of Lundy's Lane, near Niagara, helping Generals Jacob Brown and Winfield Scott to score yet another victory against the British.

Joseph Bailly longed for the peaceful days again when Ramsey Crooks might return to Mackinac Island without the uniform of

263

a soldier or the torn buckskin of an explorer, and sit quietly by the Bailly fireside and tell of all those far-flung adventures.

Summer went by. Then on August 4th, cannon and shot rang out on the island once more. Colonel Croghan and Major Andrew Holmes and Captain Arthur Sinclair had landed with a small force on the island, where Dousman's farm came down to the water's edge, but were stoutly met and resisted by the British commander and his Indian allies, Major Holmes was killed, sixty-three men were wounded, and the survivors were driven back to their boats.

The sound of the guns had frightened Marie and the four little girls, and Joseph made up his mind, then and there, that it was certainly time to go. By the end of August, the Baillys had taken much of their baggage and their four children to Arbre Croche and had put them in charge of old Madame Lefèvre.

Then Joseph and Marie, with Jean Baptiste Clutier, took three saddle horses and three pack horses, and started south on the old Indian trail that ran from Arbre Croche through the length of Michigan down to the Wabash River, the "hunting path" of the Ottawa, pointing towards their distant hunting grounds in the Miami-Wabash country.

In six days, the travelers drew rein before Joseph's trading post at the junction of the Grand and Maple rivers. Jean Baptiste Beaubien came running, in answer to their halloos:

"Oh, Monsieur Joseph, you come leetle too late!"

"What do you mean, Jean Baptiste? What's the trouble?"

"Monsieur Rastel and his man, De la Vigne, been at ze Injuns again. They camp joost across ze rivair, and zey harangue Noonday and his Ottawa. Zey hand out ze six-foot muskets and make contract for all ze beaver zis season. I t'ink Noonday promise, too. I talk to Noonday till I purple in ze face, and I make ze offer six-foot muskets, silver trimmings, and everyt'ing you t'ink of, but— Pouf! Rastel, he got much whisky with him and it no use, Monsieur Joseph. Zat fellow got us by ze t'roat. I t'ought he gone somewhere else to stay but he certainement keep ze hands on t'ings here too!"

Joseph's cheeks had turned blood-red, and Marie's eyes glowed. Joseph was once more astounded at Rastel's ubiquity.

"How long did he camp here? When did he leave?"

"Left two days ago. Camp five days, Monsieur Joseph. He

t'ink he got zem fixed. Drinking, shouting, devilment every night. Tonight, too. You see. Whisky not all gone yet. Oh, one more t'ing, Monsieur Joseph. Ze second night, zey invite me over across rivair. T'ought I might as well cross over see what go on. Rastel try to get me away from you, offer me just a leetle more money. But I no take. No, don't say, 'Good for you, Beaubien!' How could I trust heem to pay, even if he promise? Then, says Rastel: 'Zat all right, Beaubien. I admire your loyalty. But you'll live—or die—to regret it.' Zen De la Vigne hand me gourd of whisky. Zat leetle remark, 'You'll live—or die—to regret it,' put notion in Beaubien head. Mebbe zey go put Beaubien out of way. Mebbe zey go try to keel Beaubien right now, so it won't look like zey *had* keeled heem. I take zat gourd o' whisky from De la Vigne, and I watch hees eyes—and I t'ink I see a snake in zem. I lift zat gourd and I mak' ze throat go *cluck, cluck, cluck,* and I mak' ze throat ball go up and down, and zen I hold gourd to one side, and I see sharp look which say, 'I got you now,' in De la Vigne's eyes. Zen he walk away, and I pour whisky on grass beside me—and toad in grass, he lick, he tak' one hop and stretch long legs and lie still, turn to toad of stone—daid. Pretty soon I get up and say: 'Goodbye, Rastel, goodbye, De la Vigne,' and zey shake hands hard and glad, and say: 'Goodbye! Goodbye, Jean Baptiste Beaubien! Mebbe you be sorry you doan' sign up with Rastel. Jo Bailly soon be beggar. Rastel be prince!' "

"We came just in time, I see, Beaubien. This is indeed pretty bad," commented Joseph.

"Oh, Joseph, you don't suppose De la Vigne will give our children anything to drink, do you, when he gets back to Arbre Croche?" asked Marie, in terror.

"No, no, Marie. Don't imagine dangers. The children are under Chief Blackbird's protection, and you know what that means. Besides, your mother will take care of them."

"But Esther is only three."

"Don't worry, Marie. Esther is old enough to understand what she should do and what she shouldn't do. Besides, De la Vigne is probably going to a dozen other posts with Rastel, before he returns to Arbre Croche. We've another problem on our hands, just now."

"Yes, Joseph. What are you going to do?"

"I'm going to the powwow tonight."

"Oh, no! Joseph, wouldn't it be better to lie low until the effects of the whisky have worn off?"

"No, indeed! I'll go and put the matter squarely up to Noonday and his braves tonight."

"Oh, no, no, Joseph! Keep away. Handle it afterwards. For my sake, do!"

" 'For my sake, do!' How many cowardly acts can be traced to just such wifely importunities as that! No, Marie, I *will* go. The British and American armies put together couldn't stop me!"

Joseph waited that night until the drumming and the howling across the river had reached their height. Then he and Jean Baptiste and Beaubien and Marie pushed out in a canoe in the smooth water above the Rapids. They beached the canoe and went quietly to the scene of the powwow. In spite of the drunken noise around him, Noonday was delivering a speech, in which the name of Rastel figured frequently. The only moderately sober listener seemed to be Pélégor, the rival trader on the Grand and the probable tool of Rastel who stood, leaning against a tree, with an amused smile on his lips.

Suddenly Joseph, tall and splendid, stepped into the circle of the firelight. He waited in silence while the drumming and the yells, the moans, the hysterical laughter, and all the other sounds of drunkenness subsided in ebbing waves around him. Joseph spoke, in his loudest voice:

"I hear that you have been listening to the voice of Motchi Manitou, the Evil One. I hear that he sent two of his creatures disguised as men to talk with you, and that you listened. Is that so?"

Not a sound except uncontrollable drunken hiccoughs here and there. Guilty looks in the eyes. Heads lowered.

"Is this so?"

"Ugh."

"Is this not Monami Bailly's trading ground? Why have you let a stranger come in to steal the furs of Monami Bailly?"

No answer.

"Has Monami Bailly not given you good gifts of silver, good guns, good whisky all these years?"

"Hoh! Hoh!" (Yes! Yes!)

"Let me see the gifts of Motchi Manitou's men!"

Noonday went, without a word, to the edge of the encampment and brought back six muskets.

"Six guns for a hundred braves!"

"He give more guns later, Monami Bailly. He give much whisky now."

"How much whisky is left?"

"Two keg, Monami Bailly."

"Six guns and two kegs of whisky left after two days! And you trust such men? You think they pay you more, and better than Monami Bailly? Fools! Squawmen!" Joseph's voice resounded against the tree trunks.

"Beaubien and Jean Baptiste, take away these guns of the false traders and bring Monami Bailly's trading goods."

The two men went down to the boat and brought up two handsome, silver-mounted muskets, half a dozen silver-handled hunting knives, a package of vermilion, a Hudson's Bay blanket, a small keg of whisky, tobacco, and a bag of gold coin.

"These are but samples of the goods that Monami Bailly carries to trade. Is this musket better than the muskets of Rastel?"

"Hoh! Hoh!"

"Are these blankets better?"

"Hoh! Hoh!"

"Are these silver-handled knives, made by the Indians' good friend, Monsieur Campeau of Detroit, better?"

"Hoh! Hoh!"

"Have you been children and fools?"

"Hoh! Hoh!"

"Are you Monami Bailly's friends from now until the sun is old and tired?"

"Hoh! Hoh!"

"Very well. Monami Bailly is going south to the Little Calumet, where he plans to set up a new trading post. Monami Bailly will be back in the spring, with many pack loads of trading goods— and with many boot loads of kicks for Monsieur Rastel!"

The Indians rolled on the ground with laughter. Noonday made a speech, repudiating Rastel and acclaiming his old friend,

Monami Bailly, and very soon the tipsy Indians came and shook Joseph's hand and gave him kisses, in the French manner, on both cheeks, and made blubbering protestations of their loyalty. If it had not been a situation so full of serious implications, it might have been comical. At least Pélégor seemed to think it comical, for he was smiling broadly as he slipped away into the shadows.

As Joseph and Marie walked down to the river, Marie said:

"I'm a little worried, Joseph. Why did you have to tell them exactly where we're going? It seemed to please Pélégor a little too much."

"What an idea, Marie! I'm not afraid of Pélégor or Rastel or De la Vigne or the whole crew of them together!"

"I know that, Joseph—but still I wish you hadn't told."

"Why not? Rastel's a coward at heart. Men of that kind always are. And the Indians around here are all more friendly to us than to him. However, Jean Baptiste and I can take turns guarding at night, for a while, if you're really worried."

"Yes, I wish you would."

"Don't worry, my little Marie. Remember that some day 'every fox must pay his skin to the furrier.' And don't forget the good old Hudson's Bay motto, my dear: *Pro pelle cutem!*—'A skin for a skin!' That's mine for my good friend, Rastel!"

"Oh, Joseph, not so loud, not so rash, please!—There are reasons why I want you to be especially careful just now—"

"Why, especially careful?"

"Chiefly, for the sake of—of—our—our—son."

"*Our son?*"

"Yes, Joseph, that is what I said."

"Marie! Marie! Are you with child again?"

"Yes."

"Are you sure? How—how wonderful!"

"I'm sure. And this time it *will* be a son, Joseph. I am sure of that, too. I have prayed to God and the Great Spirit and to all the saints in heaven. It *will* be a son!"

Joseph had halted Marie in the path, and now threw his arms about her jubilantly. After almost smothering her, he asked more gently:

"How are you feeling, Marie?"

"Tired, Joseph. A little tired, that's all."

"We must get you back to Arbre Croche, Marie. Jean Baptiste shall take you back, right away."

"Oh, no, Joseph! We're only sixty-five miles from the Calumet. I must see our home—and our son's home—first!"

After ten days at the Grand River, during which Joseph bent all his efforts towards securing the unswervable devotion of Noonday's Indians, and then dispatching them along the various tributaries of the St. Joseph for furs, the Bailly family pulled up the tent-stakes for the southward journey. Joseph had set a few Indian spies to watch in the four directions for any return of the wolves of danger; but the disappearance seemed complete, and gradually the very thought of risk vanished in the September haze. Joseph rode slowly, for Marie's sake. The three travelers camped under the dusky pine trees or by deer trails in the oak openings. Joseph and Jean Baptiste brought in rabbits or raccoon or deer or wild turkey to the campfire pot, and Marie cooked as savory meals as were ever prepared beside Indian fire or pioneer hearth.

The trail lay straight south from the rapids of the Grand, across the shallow, westward-flowing streams, Rabbit River, Gun River, Kalamazoo River, Portage and Pigeon rivers. Four days south from the Grand, they forded the St. Joseph River, considerably to the south of Parc aux Vaches, deciding to visit their old home site on the return journey. As they looked down into the green-brown waters of the St. Joseph, Bailly asked:

"Any longings for the old home at the Parc, Marie?"

"Yes. We were very happy there. I can't admit that the Calumet is more beautiful."

"More beautiful. Far, far more beautiful, and much more important as a crossing place of the trails. And nearer to Checagou, which will surely be built up again some day. And nearer to the lake and all the facilities for the fur barges . . . Well, there are many reasons why I think it a good location, Marie."

"I trust your judgment, Joseph. And I'm glad it is a beautiful place. I want our son to live in the most beautiful place in the world!"

They swam their horses across the St. Joseph River and paused

on a small, grassy plateau, encircled with shrubbery and grapevines, to take account of wet baggage and wet clothing. As the
three stood there, preoccupied with their horses, there was a
sudden movement in the vines, a thickening of shadows, and the
three looked up to find themselves surrounded by a squad of
United States Cavalry. In the rear, astride a horse, sat Rastel,
smiling, with malicious joy.

Joseph touched his raccoon cap with a semimilitary salute, and
managed to give his most ingratiating smile. But the officer-in-
chief, without returning the salute, sternly asked:

"Joseph Bailly, British citizen?"

"Yes, monsieur."

"Joseph Bailly, I have here an order for your arrest."

"Arrest, sir? On what grounds? I have here my trading license
which I have always used in going through to my trading grounds
on the Grand River and the St. Joseph. It is duly signed by the
British authorities and by Governor Harrison. There must certainly be some mistake."

"No mistake. There are serious charges against you. The United
States and Great Britain are at war, you know. Come along."

"But the charges? There *is* such a thing as false arrest, sir."

"There are also penalties for resisting an officer! A true copy of
the charges will be furnished you by the Judge Advocate, before
you come to trial. Everything will be in good order. Come along!"

"Where, sir?"

"To Detroit!"

"But my wife?"

"No charges against her."

"She may be permitted to go with me?"

"Gad, no! No extra baggage allowed! Though she's a pretty
piece of baggage!"

In spite of the coarse laughter of the soldiers, Joseph, in a low
voice, made one more plea:

"She is in a delicate condition, captain. I dare not leave her."

"Delicate or indelicate, raped or unraped, virgin or squaw-wife,
she can't come!"

Jean Baptiste sidled up to Joseph, and scarcely moving his lips,
remarked:

"Go along, Monsieur Joseph. Everything will be all right. I shall protect Madame Bailly with my life."

"Who is this fellow," roared the captain, "and what is he saying?"

"He is my voyageur—and my friend; and he tells me to go along with you—"

"Well, come along then—both of you! I arrest the servant for collusion!"

"You don't think we *could* take on the baggage, sir?" asked one of the younger officers, sidling up.

"No, Higgins! No! Sorry I can't oblige you. Orders are only for the monsieur. The squaw'll find her way in the woods all right. Mount your horse, Bailly—and you, too," he told Clutier. To Marie: "You won't need one. You'll be able to find your way in the woods all right."

It was obvious that Rastel must have referred to Marie as being Indian, for she was wearing a new, very stylish Quebec riding habit of brown cloth trimmed with beaver, and a red waistcoat, and looked in every way French Canadian, except for a little over-ornamentation in the way of bracelets and for the fact that she had tied her plumed hat to the saddle and was wearing her black hair freely down her back.

"Shouldn't he be disarmed?" suggested Rastel.

"Certainly! Disarm him, Higgins," ordered the officer.

Then Joseph put his arms around Marie and held her, desperately, until Higgins and two other soldiers tore them apart.

"Mount your horse, Bailly!" commanded the officer at last.

Joseph's eyes darted flame.

"I shall be all right, Joseph. You *must* go," urged Marie.

"She'll be all right, Monsieur Joseph. I guarantee it," whispered Clutier. He mounted his horse, with apparent difficulty, so that the delay made him the very last of the group. He said something, in Ottawa, to Marie, then started his horse, as the soldier who had been placed in charge of him roared: "Hurry up, there, you fool 'breed!"

Joseph had mounted and, as he moved off, was looking back at Marie, who stood in the middle of the trail, one hand, palm back, against her forehead, the other still held out helplessly towards

Joseph. Higgins, who was now riding beside Joseph, enjoying his marital misfortune, stretched out a boot and kicked Joseph's horse in the belly. The horse reared, and Joseph turned from the last glimpse of Marie, to control his animal.

"It'll be many a day before you see *her* again," remarked Higgins.

"Just what *I* was going to say," echoed Rastel, a horse or two away.

Chapter XXII

MARIE'S ODYSSEY

THE autumn twilight was coming down like a flock of black-winged butterflies over the woods that fringed the St. Joseph River. The color was going out of the copper leaves that clung so valiantly to the oak trees, out of the gold leaves that tinkled about the sassafras trees, out of the berry-red of the maple and the hawthorne and the sumac. The color was ebbing from the trees as the hope was dying out of Marie's heart. She had trudged west, down-river ten miles, in the direction of Parc aux Vaches, since Joseph had been snatched from her and Jean Baptiste had spoken the reassuring words to her, promising to slip away from his captors and to meet her on the outskirts of Topenebee's village. She was not to reveal herself to any Indian, man or woman, until he came (for there was danger abroad, even in the friendly Indian settlements). Marie had great faith in the cunning of Jean Baptiste. He would not be watched, as Joseph was watched. Officers were surrounding Joseph on all sides as he rode away. There was but one petty soldier in charge of Jean Baptiste, who had already maneuvered for the rear position, before he had half started. Yet all this had happened four hours ago, and there was no sign of Jean Baptiste.

Although Marie tried to avoid worrying about Joseph and to believe that Joseph's integrity and good sense and influence would stand him in good stead in this strange dilemma, her heart gave way at the thought that, at this most important period of their lives, Joseph should be wrenched from her. She stopped walking and leaned against a tree. She was very tired. Her feet ached, her head ached, and a nausea came up from the pit of her being where the new, exigent life lay. She dared not sit down, for if she did she would yield to absolute exhaustion. She must try, in a minute, to push on towards Topenebee's village, still more than ten miles away. She flung both arms against the tree, as if to draft upon the strength that it drew up from the earth. An owl chirred, a short distance behind her. A chill went through her, stabbing the child that lay within her. Was that cry from a bird or from a human throat? Was it a Potawatomi or some hostile Indian who had discovered her, and mistook her for an enemy paleface? Although she trembled in every muscle, she clung as still as a lichen to the tree. The owl spoke again. Certainly, the sound was human. There was something too smooth, too resonant about it. It lacked the blurred, bosky quality of the real owl's throat. She could do better. She could be the very owl itself. She gave the soft, chirring sound, with no human tautness in it.

She turned and knew Jean Baptiste by the short, low-shouldered bulking blackness of his figure.

"Jean Baptiste!"

"Madame Joseph!"

"Oh, Jean Baptiste! How did you manage it? I was so afraid you would not come!"

"I lag behind; zen—pouf! In ze woods, I turn, and away I go! Zey chase me. Zey shoot. Zey shout. I let my horse go. I climb into oak tree, high, high up. Zey hunt. Zey not find me. Zey curse. Zey go back. Zey swear zey come back with whole battalion to get me. I walk. I cross leetle creeks. I hide my trail. I come."

"Good, clever Jean Baptiste. And Joseph, how is he? What do you think they will do to him?"

"Not'ing. Not'ing at all. Monsieur Joseph is smart man. He cannot escape yet, I t'ink. They guard him like beeg bag of gold. But mon cousin smart man."

"Where do you think they are taking him? Detroit?"

"Yes. Detroit, I t'ink. But Monsieur Joseph, he has ze friends everywhere."

"Monsieur Rastel has shot the arrow too far this time, I think."

"Yes. Rastel! Wolf!"

"Half fox, Jean Baptiste."

"Monsieur Joseph fox, too. Monsieur Joseph *good* fox! Rastel bad fox. Now, Madame Joseph, you in my care. Jean Baptiste take good care of Monsieur Joseph's wife."

"I know you will, Jean Baptiste. I trust you, absolutely. Now what shall we try to do? Reach Topenebee's village tonight?"

"No, too far tonight. Indians maybe drunk. Bad Indians maybe in woods. No. We camp here tonight. Eat wild grapes, black walnuts for supper. No fire. No signal. Get good rest. Jean Baptiste has leetle plan for tomorrow."

"Good! I'm sure it's a clever plan. But now about eating. Couldn't we roast that signal owl for supper? I'm terribly hungry!"

But Jean Baptiste only chuckled and went down to the river to gather the wild grapes and the nuts. A little later, he made a pine-bough bed and shelter for Marie, offered her, in vain, his buckskin jacket for a covering, and then went off and curled himself up like a hedgehog under some spicebushes.

Although she had cried herself to sleep, Marie woke with new hope to the golden flood of the October dawn. Jean Baptiste, too, was optimistic and explained his plans.

"Now, you must stay here very quietly, Madame Joseph, while Jean Baptiste go to the Potawatomi village. Jean Baptiste get you Indian clothes. Not safe for you to travel in paleface clothes. Too many soldiers. Too many war-crazy Indians."

"Yes. You are right, Jean Baptiste. And you, too, should be dressed like an Indian, I think."

"Yes, Madame Joseph. Jean Baptiste make good Indian, ver' good Indian."

"Here, Jean Baptiste. Take my silver riding crop and my boots, and—just a minute! I'll give you my red waistcoat. These will help to make the squaws give you everything you want."

It was some five hours before Jean Baptiste returned. He was now a complete Potawatomi, in a red calico shirt, deerskin jacket embroidered with porcupine quills, fringed deerskin leggings, a red blanket slung over his shoulders, a red calico handkerchief wound, turban-style, around his head. His beaded belt carried the usual accouterments of sheathed hunting knife, tomahawk, powder-horn and tobacco pouch. Jean Baptiste had also purchased a rifle, for he had been deprived of his arms when arrested. To make his Indian semblance complete, the giggling squaws had even painted a large vermilion moon on each of his cheeks.

To Marie, he also brought a complete Indian costume: blue broadcloth leggings, a blue calico gown, red blanket, and beaded moccasins. When Marie had retired into the shrubbery and made the change, Jean Baptiste added the finishing touch to her appearance, by rubbing over her cheeks the juice from the hulls of walnuts. She wept copiously during the process, streaking the stain with her tears and making it necessary for Jean Baptiste to apply the juice over and over again. So much did he spread over her betrayingly fair face that the marks of it were to remain for months. With these changes, Marie looked almost the perfect picture of a Potawatomi girl. Yet there was something still so delicate and un-Mongolian about the nose, the finely molded, slimly sloping cheeks, the sensitive mouth, that a close observer might have noted the contradictions. And there was a brilliance of eyes and a beauty of expression that few Indian girls possessed.

"Now, Madame Joseph, you and I, of course, are two Indians traveling together. Brother, sister, we say?"

"Yes, Jean Baptiste"—without lowering her eyes at all.

"We speak Algonquin, eh?"

"Yes. Always."

"Now, Madame Joseph, we go down around Lake Mitchigami and up to Wisconsin, n'cest-ce pas?"

"Oh, Jean Baptiste, no, no! Why *there?* That carries me farther from Joseph—and from Arbre Croche!"

"The squaws say white soldiers come t'rough here more zan once in last few months. Come from north and east. Woods full of zem. May come galloping after us! Better go around lake, far from Fort Shelby, Fort Wayne. Up Wisconsin way. Menominee friendly. Zen go from zere across lake to Arbre Croche."

"Yes, I see. I see it is the wise thing to do. But hard to do, like so many wise things. I'm ready, Jean Baptiste."

"I tell squaws we go straight back up north to Arbre Croche. Zen, if soldiers come, squaws send zem on trail to north. Good idea, n'est-ce pas?"

Marie laughed for the first time: "Yes! A very good idea, Jean Baptiste."

"I t'ink we better hurry. Madame feel ready good long walk, t'ree hundred, four hundred mile, maybe? Maybe we can't get horse. Horses all gone with braves on hunting trips. Only old horses zere at Topenebee's village, old skeleton-horses, die before zey reach Checagou. We try again, Calumet Indians. We try Checagou."

"All right, Jean Baptiste, I'm ready, even to walk four hundred miles."

"First we have real food, Madame Joseph. See here. Jean Baptiste buy for Madame one roast duck, leetle corn cakes, and bite of maple sugar."

They ate ravenously, Jean Baptiste with the clutching fingers of a trapper, Marie with the daintiness of a Frenchwoman, even in this unimplemented wilderness.

Then began the long trek around Lake Michigan. Little by little, traveling at first mostly by night, lighted by the hunter's moon, feeling their way along the Niles-Checagou section of the hard-beaten old Sauk Trail that ran all the way from the Missouri to Malden, Canada, they went; following the great south bend of the St. Joseph River, then west across Terre Coupée and Rolling Prairie and the moonlit grasses of Door Prairie, along Trail Creek and past the little Potawatomi village and the abandoned trading post of Jean Baptiste, Point du Sable. Here, the Sauk Trail left the creek and followed along a sandy oak ridge inland, above the winding ripples of the Little Calumet River, and above the great set-back marshes, between the river and the shore dunes—marshes that were filled with ducks and geese, blue cranes and trumpeting swans and snowy egrets and bald eagles and muskrats and beaver and otter, and teeming with a plant and animal life that had made them famous among Indians for hundreds of years.

Here the vast prehistoric Lake Chicago, vaster than Lake Michigan, had made a silver link with the Atlantic Ocean, laying down its coral and shells, its salty deposits that turned to white deer licks later, its beach plum and beach pea and arrowgrass, as perennial reminders of salt-water occupation. Here the glaciers had halted millennia before, pouring their melted waters down to make the lasting ooze of the marshes. The Sauk Trail followed along the Valparaiso moraine top, above the ancient Calumet beach, grooving deeper the trail of the vanished elk and the more recent deer.

Marie looked down on the teeming marshes to the west, and

the deep forests and the gold-brown windings of the Calumet on the east and exclaimed:

"Monsieur Joseph is right. This is beautiful, very beautiful, Jean Baptiste—perhaps even lovelier than Parc aux Vaches."

"Yes, Madame Joseph. Ze Indians call it 'ze happy hunting grounds,' and ze trappers call it heaven—all ze way from La Rivière du Chemin to ze Lake of ze Calumet."

They halted for several days in the Calumet region, and feasted, for they knew that many a foodless day lay ahead. Jean Baptiste, with his Potawatomi rifle, brought in fat geese and ducks, turkeys, and raccoons, and Marie gathered the tart wild cherries and whortleberries and wild grapes.

Jean Baptiste visited the Calumet camps, but there were no horses fit to travel. Snow fell before the end of October. The travelers dared to walk by day now, for the Calumet Indians were friendly and there was no news of any pursuing parties. They tried to quicken their pace, but the going was very slow. Marie, in spite of herself, could not maintain her old quick rhythm, and even the first light snowfalls retarded them both. So they left the trail along the river, and struck the shore at the foot of Lake Michigan. Marie was happy to be out again on the continuation of that shore which she had so much loved at Arbre Croche—with its dazzling sand, the snowy-shouldered dunes, the dark crowning of the pines, and the copper and gold of sassafras and pawpaw and oak and maple, the silver creeks winding down to the purple lake, and everywhere the gulls whitening the air with beauty.

It was mid-November when they rounded the lake and turned north towards Checagou. A few miles beyond the turn, the dunes dwarfed down into low sand banks; the pines disappeared, and the prairies swept up to the very brink of the lake, the blue prairie grasses touching blades with the gilded sword grasses of the sand. Here had spread the buffalo hunting grounds of Chief Pokagon and the Potawatomi before the buffalo had thundered farther west.

As they approached within two miles of the Checagou River, Marie inadvertently shaded her eyes for a glimpse of the log towers and the picket fence of the old fort. She had known Fort Dearborn and its occupants so well that she quickened her step as if to go forward to meet the Whistlers and the Kinzies, the Helms and the

Healds. But no towers or walls were visible at all, only the dark trees by the river.

Jean Baptiste took her arm suddenly.

"Let's go up over the pine knoll, Madame Joseph."

"But the sand is so much firmer down here on the beach. Such hard walking up there through the soft sand— Oh!"

Marie came to a sudden stop, seeing what Jean Baptiste had seen—midway up the beach, a little ahead of them, a huddle of weathered wagon wheels, a few rusty metal rims, and a human skull staring against the tawny sand.

"Fort Dearborn people!" murmured Jean Baptiste. "Zees way, Madame Joseph: Up ze ridge—a leetle—*please*."

Wind and wave and sand had mercifully mounded over most of the vestiges of that tragic battle by the wagons, most of the traces of that desperate fight on the pine knoll, and long ago the Indians had removed such tokens of humanity as guns, swords, bright buttons, and buckles.

With eyes half closed, Marie followed Jean Baptiste in a long arc around the mounds of battle.

They trudged in silence the remaining two miles to the Checagou River. The fort was a mass of charred timbers overgrown with willow bushes, bittersweet, and tumbleweed. But across the river the Kinzie house was still standing cozily inside its white picket fence, as were Ouilmette's house and a few log-cabins near by.

Marie and Jean Baptiste stood and hallooed on the river bank. At first they thought that the little settlement was deserted, but presently someone appeared on the porch of the Kinzie house. It couldn't be one of the Kinzies, for they had been living in Detroit since the massacre. A moment later the familiar figure of Alexander Robinson came running towards them.

"Bon jour! Bon jour, Alexander!" shouted Marie. "It's Marie Bailly and Jean Baptiste Clutier! Can you come and get us?"

"Bet your moccasins!" shouted Alexander. He jumped into a canoe among the dried sedges and wild-onion plants on the river bank, loosened the fastening, and dipped his paddle in the muddy water.

Alexander and his Indian wife, Catherine Chevalier, took the two travelers into the cabin and gave them rest and warmth and food for an entire week. The little settlement by the river had dwindled sadly since the time when the fort had been lively with the soldiers and their wives, and the sound of Kinzie's fiddle had floated over the river every night. Ouilmette and his squaw were still in their house, raising corn and pumpkins and pigs, or, at times, trapping, and ferrying the infrequent traders and travelers across the river or carrying their goods up the South Branch of the Checagou River and across Mud Lake to the Des Plaines. Mrs. Lee, now Madame Du Pin, was there, quietly settled in a tiny cabin after terrible adventures. Mr. Lee had been killed in his cabin up the river, just before the massacre. She had come to Fort Dearborn, and had escaped death in the massacre because Black Partridge had wanted her as his squaw; but the trader Du Pin had offered enough goods for her to satisfy Black Partridge, and had married her himself. The trader was away at his trapping grounds on the Des Plaines just now, and Madame Du Pin and Marie spent many an hour by his fire, talking of the old days at Fort Dearborn and of the more horrible days that followed. Madame Du Pin had much to say of Captain Wells' calm and heroism on the day of the catastrophe. She and Catherine Chevalier and Arcange Ouilmette begged Marie to remain at Checagou during the winter, under their care; but Marie felt a little better and stronger after their hospitality, and was eager to push northward and to cross the Lake to Arbre Croche before spring and the new birth should overtake her.

On a November morning, when a fresh snow lay upon Checagou, against which the few patches of uncovered sand looked like old gold, Marie and Jean Baptiste set out with one horse, given to them by Alexander Robinson, and with a pack in which were two warm blankets, and a supply of salt pork, deer's meat, and parched corn to last for many days.

Slowly, Marie on horseback and Jean Baptiste on foot beside her moved north along the Green Bay Trail, following along the clay bluffs that had been the white, shining beacons to so many traders and explorers in canoes. Not once but many times, Marie thought of Mrs. Simmons dragging along this trail three years previously with her Shawnee captors, her baby in her arms. Her martyrdom seemed to make her own going easier.

For the sake of caution, the travelers avoided the Indian villages as much as possible, and the trading post at Mil-wâ-kee. But they returned to the main trail near Whitefish Bay, proceeding slowly, and at night whenever there was a moon. They were getting near the country of the Winnebago tribes that were especially fierce and inimical. The Menominee, farther north, were apt to be much more friendly. When they did encounter roving bands of Indians, they posed as two Ottawa who had suffered in an encounter with the whites and were on their way home to Arbre Croche. If the band proved to be friendly to the Americans, the strategic Clutier's talk was all of misadventures with the British; if they proved to be friendly to the British, his loyalties were shrewdly reversed. Marie kept as quiet as possible in these conversations, her integrity and her sympathy for both sides preventing her from declaring any open hostility. If it became necessary for Clutier to go into camp to beg for food or to buy it with the coin and beads loaned by Alexander Robinson, Marie stayed away, disliking the scenes of wild dancing and guzzling which went on in most of the camps that lay on the traders' paths. She preferred a quiet bed on the pine boughs, under the starlight, though December was now coming down with its tomahawk-cold.

Deeper and deeper grew the snow, slower and slower the going, more desperately chill the air. They began to come upon coveys of dead quail, and once they stumbled on a deeryard with two dead deer lying in the trampled snow. These Jean Baptiste cut up and slung over his back. The frozen meat lasted until the travelers reached the falls of the Sheboygan, which were now cliffs of crystal. After the dead-deer feast, no other animal, dead or alive, appeared in the snowy wastes. Jean Baptiste began to scrape the dry moss from the north side of the pine trees to make an imitation meal for himself and Marie. Where, now and then, a wild rose thrust its topmost twigs above the snow, they feasted on the dried hips. Down along the creek beds, they knew, were the wild iris, with the succulent tubers loved of the Indians, but these were hidden too deep and were impossible to locate. The horse nibbled bark and was able, where the wind had blown the snow, to paw down to grass, but he already looked like the horse on which Death rides.

One evening Jean Baptiste said:

"Madame Joseph, what you t'ink? We keel ze horse? What would be better for Madame Joseph: ride and starve, or eat and walk? I do what Madame Joseph t'ink best."

"I don't know, Jean Baptiste. I'm so tired, so tired. Let's wait another day. I can't bear to think of killing the horse to eat. I'd almost rather die myself— No! No! I *must* not die. I must live—for the sake of the little son. Perhaps tomorrow I shall be brave enough to let you kill the horse. One more day, Jean Baptiste. Let us see."

That night was bitter. Although Jean Baptiste was able to make a pine-branch fire which gave a little warmth, Marie suffered so much from cold and hunger and pain that she scarcely slept. Through the trees, the "dancing spirits" of the Indians crackled and shimmered and flashed their nocturnal rainbows. The Great Bear glimmered faintly through the radiance. In the near distance, the hungry wolves howled.

As the night advanced, the wolf sounds came nearer and nearer. The horse, tethered to a pine tree fifty feet away, snorted uneasily. The fire was dying down. Jean Baptiste was fast asleep. The fire, Marie told herself, was still bright enough to keep the wolves away. No need yet to call Jean Baptiste. How beautiful the northern lights were! The dancing spirits of the Indians . . . the dancing spirits . . . Marie fell asleep.

She woke with a start. The yelping of the wolves was at hand! In the light of the aurora, she could see their black, leaping forms around the horse. The horse whinnied wildly. The single, large black bulk plunged upward, tugged, pulled, broke away. Then off across the crusted snow galloped the horse, with the wolf pack at its heels! Jean Baptiste's gun broke the silence a second too late.

"There goes our food for a week, Madame Joseph!"

The two stricken people stood in silence, the great lights sparkling mercilessly over their heads. After a long time, Jean Baptiste said:

"It would be easier, Madame Joseph, to go to the Winnebago village at the foot of Green Bay, but I dare not take you. We might never get out of there alive."

"Yes, Jean Baptiste, I think I prefer starvation to the torture of the Winnebago."

"Then we must push on to Sturgeon Bay along the lake. There we will cross on the ice, towards the sunset, ten or fifteen miles to the Menominee villages. You are a brave woman, Madame Joseph. I know you can get there."

"Yes, I know I can get there!" And to herself, she whispered: "Nin-gwis! Nin-gwis! My son! My son!"

Half starving they dragged along the picturesque Door Peninsula, only dimly realizing how beautiful was the world about them. The high snowy ridge on which they walked overlooked an oceanic view of Lake Michigan to the east. The lake was frozen solid as far as the eye could see, in tumultuous wave formations near the shore, where the vehement water had long resisted immobility, but in a vast smooth, snow-covered Arctic waste beyond. The trees along the trail would have been, to less afflicted eyes, rarely beautiful, for the rich lime soil of the peninsula had lifted the white cedars to heights of fifty or sixty feet and they carried their burdens of snow magnificently. Against their darkness, the slim stems of the thousands of white birches leaned in bright contrast.

They came at last to Sturgeon Bay. It was frozen solid, with the wind-blown snow only a little above the glare ice. When they were six miles from the nearest Menominee village, Marie, overburdened as she was with her unborn child, slipped on the ice in her eagerness to arrive and sprained her ankle. She felt sharp twinges in her womb, and was agonizingly sure that she would have a miscarriage. Jean Baptiste carried her for a short distance, then, at her entreaty, left her and hurried on to the Menominee village for assistance. Marie was drawn in, on a sledge, just in time, for the Menominee squaws found her nearly dead of starvation, exhaustion and cold.

"Save my son! Save my son! Nin-gwis! Nin-gwis!" Marie kept imploring. "Never mind about me. Save my son! My husband is a great trader. He will reward you!" The Menominee squaws understood.

The child was not to have been born until April. With the prospect of reward from the great trader, and out of genuine sympathy for Marie, the squaws resorted to their best remedies, their best care. They succeeded in saving her from the loss that she most dreaded. It would be an April child, after all.

It was February before Jean Baptiste dared to leave Madame Joseph. It was his plan to walk across the frozen lake from Sturgeon Bay to Sleeping Bear Bay and up the Ottawa Trail to Arbre Croche. As soon as the ice was out, in the spring, he would return with the Ottawa in canoes, to carry Marie back to her children in her old home at the Crooked Tree.

Marie lay propped up on deerskin robes in the doorway of a Menominee lodge and watched Jean Baptiste prepare to set out on his journey.

"Bon voyage, Jean Baptiste. Find out about Monsieur Joseph if you can. You have taken good care of me. I shall never forget it. You are a good man, Jean Baptiste."

"Any man who deed not serve you well, Madame Joseph, would be a dev-eel!" answered Jean Baptiste.

Turning, he set his feet sturdily towards the rising sun and the white glare of Green Bay.

Chapter XXIII

BIRTH

ON A morning in early April, Marie was sitting on the same deer-skin robes in the doorway of the same lodge, watching the ice floes drifting like swans over the indigo water. Soon, if no misadventure had befallen Jean Baptiste, he should be returning with a pirogue from Arbre Croche. The floes made the crossing still a little dangerous. But a few more such days of thawing sunshine would end all danger. Marie hoped that Jean Baptiste would hurry. The child within her was as ripe as an autumn apple ready to slip from the tree. Her son—at last. All during the long, terrible journey from Parc aux Vaches, she had prayed for a son. All during the last three months of unaccustomed weakness and illness, she had prayed for and dreamed of a son. Surely only a son could have suffered with her such incredible hardships, and lived and prospered through them all. It must be a strong child, a man-child indeed that lived within her, that kicked against her so sturdily that she winced, smiling even as she winced.

"Nin-gwis!" she repeated. "Nin-gwis!"

"Yes. It *is* a son," muttered old White Sky, who was sitting behind Marie, and had guessed rather than heard the murmuring. White Sky was so old that she was often able to penetrate the veil of the Great Mystery and bring back visions of what lay, about to be revealed, behind the evening star.

"Yes, it is a son, Wing Woman. A beautiful son, but not strong, Wing Woman. He is weak from the cold and the snow, the hunger and the distance. Take care of him. . . . Take care. . . . He has— I see him plainly, Wing Woman—he has black hair, like your hair—and black eyes, blacker than the rain-washed pines . . . Does the father of the child have darkness hair?"

"No," said Marie. "Sunset hair. I would have the child resemble his father."

A withered smile crossed the face of old White Sky.

"He will resemble his father, Wing Woman. As a man resembles a man. But he will be like you also. He will have a strange, gentle spot in his soul. He will talk to the animals."

Overcome with emotion, Marie closed her eyes. She was not to realize for many years that the strands of the old woman's prophecies were crossed and confused, that she was combining two visions.

When Marie again opened her eyes, the ice floes seemed to have multiplied, and moved. Marie brushed away the tears with her deerskin sleeve, caught the glint of vermilion paddles and cried:

"The boats! The boats!"

"Sure enough, Wing Woman. Risky business to come so early, with the ice still in the bay."

In a few moments, three long birch-bark canoes slid up the shining shore, and Jean Baptiste and a dozen Indians jumped out. Marie was not well enough to run to meet them, though her spirit raced ahead of her bound feet.

"Oh, Jean Baptiste, brave, good Jean Baptiste! How is Joseph? And my little ones? And my mother?"

"Good news, Madame Joseph. Monsieur Joseph will be on hees way home soon. Jean Baptiste went on snowshoes to Detroit. Will tell you all 'bout it later."

The truth of the matter was that Joseph's case had not yet come to trial at the time of Jean Baptiste's visit to Detroit, but the voyageur had thought it best, for Madame Joseph's sake, to seem optimistic.

"God be praised! And those at Arbre Croche?"

"Well, very well, Madame Joseph. No accidents, and only a leetle illness during the winter. All ees very well."

"And De la Vigne, has he been there at the Crooked Tree?"

"Yes. But Blackbird, he had ze eyes on heem all time, till he went away to trapping grounds. Then young Weeliam Blackbird kep' hees eyes on De la Vigne after zat. Young Weeliam has strange power, lak priest. De la Vigne afraid like dev-eel of young Weeliam. Young Weeliam look—De la Vigne crawl into grass. I t'ink your leetle Thérèse love Weeliam."

"Oh, Jean Baptiste, she's only ten, and William is only fourteen! How well I remember the day he was born!"

"Mademoiselle Thérèse leetle saint, too. Angels marry—I t'ink!"
Jean Baptiste chuckled.

The Indians from the boats had come up by this time, and
Marie greeted them all joyously by name.

The Menominee braves, who had just come back from the trapping grounds, and the squaws of the village gathered around, and
urged the visitors to stay for a feast and celebrations. But old
White Sky whispered in Jean Baptiste's ear:

"Better hurry back across the lake with Wing Woman. Child
to be born soon, soon. Hurry, or child will be born in canoe.
Wing Woman will have hard time, very hard time at the birth, like
poor foolish white women at Fort Howard, Green Bay. May die.
Somebody die. White Sky speaks the truth."

Jean Baptiste's face paled at the prophecy. Unfortunately, it
was necessary to stay for the feasting, for Indian etiquette would
have tolerated no refusal. But Jean Baptiste passed the word along
to the Indians that they must start back on this same day. The
wind was freshening from the south, so that it might be possible
to set the small canoe sails and make better time.

After the banquet of beaver tail, whitefish, corn soup, and fresh
maple sugar from the spring sugar camps, the Indians hurried down
to the shore and rigged up the sails. Marie was carried down in a
blanket stretched on tepee poles, and laid in the largest canoe as
tenderly as Father Marquette had been handled by his Indian
friends, over a hundred years before, for his final journey up the
opposite shore. The squaws and the wrinkle-faced men and the
young braves crowded down to the shore and showered their fare-
wells and friendly wishes upon Marie. Tears stood in many slow-
to-weep Indian eyes, for Marie had won these alien Menominee
hearts.

The journey to Sleeping Bear Point that ordinarily required
eight good hours of paddling was accomplished in five hours
before the wind. The canoes slid up the shore at sunset, and camp
was made among scrub willows on the first terrace of the dunes.
Marie was exhausted by the journey and was able to sip only a
little fish broth heated over a beach fire by Jean Baptiste. It was
necessary to allow Marie a day's rest, and the condition of the lake,
beaten up to a froth by a stiff wind, made it necessary to wait
another day. On the third day it was possible to use the sails again,

and to start the seventy-mile journey north along the coast to
Arbre Croche.

The shore was as familiar as childhood to Marie, from Sleeping
Bear Point to Arbre Croche; but the dull thud of pain had begun
within her, and she was scarcely able to turn her head to recognize
the Indian villages along the way, the looming shadows of the
Manitou Islands to the west, the black and white promontories of
Pyramid Point and Cathead Point, the gap in the white shore
where Grand Traverse Bay swept away southwards like an inland
sea, and the smaller sea of Little Traverse Bay. She could only
watch, in rhythm with her pain, the gulls trooping overhead, swimming, with their inimitable white grace, against the wind.

But when Jean Baptiste and the Indians at last pointed far ahead
to one of the two most conspicuous landmarks of the coast, Marie
raised herself a little from her deerskin bed and looked, for there
was home. The Crooked Tree! The great pine with the storm-
bent top that had given the Indian settlement the same bent-tree
name in Ottawa, in French and in English. Seven miles beyond,
Marie could almost see that other loved landmark, the great cedar
cross erected so long before by the good Father Marquette.

As they slipped towards the land and skirted it closely, Marie,
even through the blur, thought that she had never known a shore
so beautiful: the dark looming of the pines against the snowy sand,
the flush of the maples prefiguring their autumn glory, the tight
red buds of spring, and the hundreds of birds, those winged flowers
that precede the fastened flowers, filling the trees with color and
with song.

When they were within a mile of Blackbird's village, Jean Baptiste gave the call of peaceful approach, and he and four or five
Indians who had brought rifles held them close to the water's
surface and discharged them, thus redoubling the sound and sending it echoing, in a heralding volley, to all the listeners in the
village. In a moment dozens of brown figures began to run down
the sand slopes; and by the time the canoes reached shore the entire
village, the chiefs and braves who had just returned from the winter's hunting and trapping, squaws, children, and puppies, were on
shore to greet Marie. Her anxious eyes sought out first the four
little girls from whom she had been absent eight months: Agatha,
the tall, dark girl of twelve; Rose, the rollicking, red-haired six-

year-old; Esther, the brunette baby, now four, and Thérèse—
where was she? Thérèse was a little apart from the others with
young William Blackbird, her pale-gold loveliness standing out like
a birch tree against his pine-darkness. The children all looked
brimming with health, and to Marie they seemed the most beautiful
children in the world. They shouted with welcome. There was
affection in the eyes of Marie's old mother, and genuine pleasure
in every face except that of De la Vigne, who lurked somberly in
the background. Then Chief Blackbird and his son came down to
the canoe to offer their official welcome. Marie, looking into the
young boy's face, saw that he had developed from a child into a
man, and she noted the expression that the undevout Jean Baptiste
had so shrewdly remarked. It was very different from the dark
earth-aware glance of his father, Chief Blackbird. If only *her* son
might look a little like young William!

Jean Baptiste and the squaws carried Marie up the dune slope in
her blanket-litter. No Indian male would suffer the contamination
of a woman in labor, and those who had been in Marie's canoe had
already plunged into the ice-cold lake to wash off the feminizing
and polluting effects of their recent propinquity. Madame Lefèvre's cabin had been prepared for Marie, but now, in the active
condition in which she was found to be, she was carried immediately, according to the old Indian custom, to one of the wigwams
outside the village set apart for women in the monthly phase and
in childbirth.

Strangely enough, the adjoining wigwam was occupied by another woman in labor—Enewah, who had transgressed the rules
of the tribe but, so far, had refused to name her seducer. Madame
Lefèvre and Chief Blackbird's wife, Running Cloud, who was one
of the midwives of the tribe, followed Marie into the wigwam.
The other squaws retired and Madame Lefèvre and Running Cloud
arranged a pack of deerskins for Marie to lie on and heated a
drink made of boiled gentian root and whortleberries. Marie had
never felt so close to death before.

"O great God, if You save me," she vowed inaudibly, "I will
dedicate myself to Your work. I will teach Your word to far-away
Indians who worship other gods. I promise. Not for my husband
and my children alone will I live, but for others. I promise."

When the pains came at ten-minute intervals, the two women

forced Marie to get down on the hard ground, on all fours, in the posture of an animal. Marie was so weak and dizzy and flayed with pain that she could not maintain this old, required Indian posture, but fell moaning on her stomach, the words, "Nin-gwis, nin-gwis," now and then emerging from her incoherence. Her mother and Running Cloud, with the best of intentions, raised her by force and held her in that most difficult of positions. They could feel her quiver in their arms, with every surge of agony, like a deer that gasps out its life in a hunter's lap.

"Wing Woman suffer like white woman," said Running Cloud. "Real squaw not suffer like this. Wing Woman dance too much in the red slippers, walk too much on the hard roads of the Turtle Island, read too much in the white man's Book. Bad for squaw. Bad for papoose."

The squeezed top of the small head was already protruding from the held woman, when the two midwives felt a great spasm pass over the body of the mother; then all motion and all moaning ceased. They quickly let Marie down and laid her on her back. Then, in the most primitive fashion, Running Cloud placed her bare hands deep in and around the protruding head of the child and began to work it out of Marie's body.

"Child maybe die. Wing Woman die, too, maybe."

"No, no!" cried Madame Lefèvre distractedly. "I go get strong medicine."

Running Cloud, scarcely aware that Madame Lefèvre had run out of the wigwam, went on with the crude extrication of the child. In a few minutes, Marie's mother had returned with the "strong medicine" out of her herb collection. Raising Marie's head, she tried to force the draught down her throat. But as there was scant sign of life, it was necessary to lay her down again, force her teeth apart, and pour the liquid into her mouth.

At this moment, Running Cloud brought forth the child, a boy. With an ordinary unwashed hunting knife, she cut the umbilical cord and tied it with a small deerskin thong from her dress. She quickly held the child upside down and shook it. Instead of a lusty cry, it gave only a faint whimper and a gasp.

"Child die soon," declared Madame Blackbird, rubbing it over the heart and the lungs and massaging its little legs. It was a beautifully formed baby, with huge expressionless blue eyes, reddish eyebrows and tufts of red hair already growing above the ears. The mouth was drawn up at the corners in a strangely sweet smile. Suddenly Marie stirred.

"Alive! Alive! She lives! She lives!" cried Madame Lefèvre.

"The red comes back to her cheek. She will get well," declared Running Cloud. "But the baby, the baby grows purple. The baby is dying."

"If it dies, Marie will want it to go to the white man's heaven!"

"Then it should be—what they say?—baptized."

"All nonsense! All wickedness!" declared Madame Lefèvre. "But I will do as Marie would wish. Yes. I will do as she would wish! Marie may die, too."

A struggle greater than the words implied was taking place in Madame Lefèvre's soul, a struggle between the hatred she had long felt for all Christian ceremonies, and her great love for Marie. She bowed before the latter, and went out of the tepee and into the enclosure of the village. Crossing the grass plateau, she made her way quickly towards the cabin of Chief Blackbird. On the way, she passed the cabin of De la Vigne, who was sitting cross-legged in his doorway, pounding something in a mortar-stone. De la Vigne gave Madame Lefèvre a quick, under-the-eyelid look. Madame Lefèvre hurried on.

On the ground, in front of Blackbird's cabin, old Nee-saw-kee was sitting, also cross-legged, his white head bowed over in sleep (for it is ever as if the earth pulled down towards her inevitable self the inclined heads and the arched shoulders of the very old). Madame Lefèvre touched Nee-saw-kee gently on his brown-blanketed arm.

"Come, my father, come with me! I need you. Hurry! It is life—and it is death."

The old man, after a first baffled look, recovered his clarity and rose slowly, with Madame Lefèvre's hands under his arm crotches helping him up.

"A child is dying, my father—Marie the Wing Woman's child. Can you help us say over it the white man's words of Baptism, the Black Robe's words? Do you remember them?"

"Remember them? Remember them? Oh, so long ago, my

grandfather was baptized by the good Father Marquette. I have
heard him tell the words long, long ago, and Father Richard has
used the same words."

"Yes, I know. I know. That is why I came for you. Come
quickly, my father. Come."

"Perhaps I can remember a little—just enough to get the little
one into the white man's heaven."

Slowly the two crossed back over the grass. De la Vigne had
disappeared into his cabin. When they arrived within two hundred feet of the birth wigwam, Nee-saw-kee stopped under a pine
tree and said he would go no nearer the pollution.

"Bring baby here," he said.

As Madame Lefèvre approached Marie's wigwam, she heard
the voices of the two other squaw-midwives issuing from the adjoining birth wigwam:

"You are dying, Enewah. Tell us. Tell us who is the father of
this child. The Great Spirit will forgive you, if you will give up
your secret."

"I am afraid. I am afraid!"

"You do not need to be afraid. You are dying. You must tell
us."

"You promise to be good to the baby, no matter what I tell
you?"

"Yes. We will be good to the baby."

Madame Lefèvre half caught the name "De la Vigne" as she
hurried by, but in her great anguish she did not receive the name
into her mind as the answer to the question that had preceded it.
The meaning came to her much later.

As she entered Marie's wigwam, the voices of the neighboring
midwives rose suddenly in the death lament:

"She is dead. O Great Spirit, receive her! She is dead! Enewah
is dead! But the baby lives! The girl, the child of sorrow, the
child of death! Dark as the midnight, strong of limb! The child
without father or mother! Enewah, Enewah is dead! O Great
Spirit, receive her!"

Madame Lefèvre leaned over Running Cloud's shoulder.

"How are things going?" she asked.

"Dying," answered Running Cloud.

"O Great Spirit!" exclaimed Madame Lefèvre, uttering the Indian cry of astonishment, in the belief that Running Cloud referred to Marie.

"Oh, the Wing Woman lives! But the baby is gasping for breath."

"Nee-saw-kee is outside to baptize it. Take it to him quickly, quickly. I will stay with my daughter. And you must take water. They do something with water in the ceremony, I think."

Running Cloud picked up the naked baby, wrapped a deerskin around it, then a blanket, scooped up a little water in a birch-bark dish from the kettle that hung on a tripod just outside the wigwam, and hurried towards Nee-saw-kee, who was still standing under the pine tree, his thin old arms raised now towards the high, unreachable place where lie both the white man's heaven and the Indian's happy hunting grounds.

"Quickly, my father, quickly!" urged Madame Lefèvre.

The old man slowly got down on his knees, lifted his arms again and in a thin, earnest voice began to pray:

"O God of the palefaces, forgive an old Indian that he has forgotten Your Names. Nee-saw-kee knows that You have three names, O God of the white men, for he remembers that his grandfather whom the good Father Marquette baptized, told him long, long ago of the three Names. Perhaps Nee-saw-kee is not worthy to remember. But if Nee-saw-kee is not good, forgive the child, for the child is not at fault. It is Nee-saw-kee who is sinful. The mother of the child is a good woman who prays to You by day and by night. The father of the child is a good man. Bless the child, O God of the Three Names!"

Then old Nee-saw-kee took the gasping baby in his arms and sprinkled water three times over its forehead from the little birch-bark dish which Running Cloud held down towards him.

Each time he repeated as gently as any Catholic priest could have spoken the words, yet in the alien Ottawa tongue:

"I baptize thee, Little White Fawn, in the name of the God with the Three Names. May he be kind to thee, papoose, and let thee run with living feet into the white man's heaven as freely as if the good Father Marquette had baptized thee instead of old Nee-saw-kee."

As he spoke, the child ceased gasping and slipped away into the eternal painlessness. Nee-saw-kee gave the little body back to Running Cloud.

"How can we tell Marie? She is *so* sick! It will break her heart! How can we tell her?" asked Running Cloud.

Just then the midwives came out of the other wigwam, bearing Enewah's newly born child. At the same moment, Neengay Lefèvre emerged from Marie's wigwam.

"The Wing Woman's child is dead," announced Running Cloud.

"O Great Spirit, she is asking for her child! She will die, she will die if she knows the child is dead!" wailed Madame Lefèvre.

"Let us lay the new child in her arms," suggested Running Cloud. "It shall be her child. It is the will of the Great Spirit that the child shall be hers. The mother is dead. The father is unknown. We will tell no one except Chief Blackbird what we are doing. We six shall keep the secret. It is the will of the Great Spirit. Is it not so, father? Tell us out of your wisdom. Are we not right?"

"Yes. It is the will of the Great Spirit and of the God with the Three Names," pronounced old Nee-saw-kee. "The Wing Woman's life must be saved with the life of this child. Was the name of the father spoken before Enewah died?"

"No," answered the two midwives, looking at the ground, afraid for the present to yield the secret which they later revealed to the others in this strange conspiracy.

So it happened that when Marie woke to complete consciousness, she found a living baby lying against her arm.

"Nin-gwis? My son? My son?" she asked faintly.

"A daughter, a beautiful daughter," answered Madame Lefèvre, although the child, with its yellowish skin, blotched cheeks, and coarse curly black hair already thick on the top of its head, did not yet deserve the adjective.

"A daughter?" asked Marie. Then, after a pause: "I dreamed that it was a son."

Chapter XXIV

COURT-MARTIAL

IT WAS mid-morning of March 1, 1815, but the light that came through the foot-square barred window in Joseph's cell in the military prison at Fort Shelby, Detroit, was a dim, cobwebby light. Joseph had not had the strength to wipe off the square with his frayed sleeve for the past three weeks, and no soldier had washed off the outside of the building for years. For the first time in his vigorous life, Joseph, the man of energy, lay listlessly, reclining on the army cot, his hands under his head in the place of the missing pillow. The vultures of despair were at last sitting upon him, plucking out the flesh of his spirit.

Joseph had been poorly fed for months in spite of basket gifts now and then, from his friends. He was bony, yellow, and unrecognizable. He had grown a red beard. His trial, unlike the courts-martial of officers and soldiers of the army, which are run off very quickly, had been postponed for five months, no doubt because of the machinations of Rastel.

The following day was at last set for the trial. The articles of the charges had been duly sent to the accused by the judge advocate, and Joseph had filed his response in writing. He had had time to summon a few witnesses, but Peter Navarre and Major Heald and Captain Swearingen and others whom he had wished to call in, were still involved in the war, and from a few possible key witnesses he had received no reply at all.

James Abbott, one of the most influential of his friends, had been in poor health since his recent imprisonment by the British in Canada. George McDougall, one of the best lawyers in Detroit, had been in New York for the last six months, and Joseph had decided to defend himself. The eloquent arguments and gestures of his French friends, who had several times visited Commander Butler and the judge advocate, Major Kittle, had only

antagonized the American authorities, who were already beginning to slam the doors of influence in the faces of the good old
French citizens of Detroit. The dog-sled runners who had taken
messages to his friends of the Northwest Company at Mackinac
and Montreal and Quebec had brought back the astonishing news
that the Northwest Company was no more, that John Jacob Astor
of New York had been buying it out and taking over all its posts,
boats, agents, and properties. There was no word from Duncan
M'Dougal nor from Ramsey Crooks, who was probably off adventuring again in the Pays d'en Haut, but a fellow by the name of
Robert Stuart wrote:

Sorry, Bailly. I've heard of you. But we're so busy on the island
under the new regime that I can't spare a man to help you. I hear
you're clever. You'll get out of the scrape. I enclose an affidavit
as to your character signed by six of us. Good luck!

Joseph thought it strange that he had had no word from Edward
Biddle. He was saddened too by a letter from his sister Antoinette,
who told him that the news of his imprisonment had been withheld from his mother because of a recent serious illness. Antoinette
was with her, and Raoul was with the troops, so that Joseph could
not have the heartening presence of any member of his family,
who would otherwise have journeyed across endless snowy wastes
to be at his side.

To make matters worse, Joseph had heard through Campeau
that Rastel was again in Detroit, waiting to testify at the trial and
that, long since, he had hooked up with Abijah Hull, who had
helped to eject Marie from her father's home so many years before. Hull and Rastel had collected all sorts of unreliable witnesses
and influential names that would count against Joseph. Rastel had
shrewdly taken out American citizenship papers ahead of Joseph.
He had also, so Campeau reported, been spending money lavishly
on the officers, in all the taverns of the town, so that the members
of the military tribunal were all undoubtedly friendly towards
him, in spite of his being French. He was obviously preparing his
final coup to take over all of Joseph's trading grounds.

It's meant to be the end of me, thought Joseph. I'll be hanged as
a spy, no doubt, on arguments concocted by Rastel.

He thought of Marie and wondered whether she were still alive and whether his son were yet born. Jean Baptiste Clutier had come through, on snowshoes, in December, with the news of Marie's safety in the Menominee village on Green Bay and had cheered Joseph tremendously. But in January Jean Baptiste had returned to prepare for the rescue of Marie, and for her journey over the Lake to Arbre Croche.

The thought of Marie made Joseph's heart gentler, so that the vultures tore less fiercely. He remembered that, in this strange life, the deepest disasters sometimes precede unexpected good fortune. He might be able to make so strong a plea at the trial as to be saved. It might be that le bon Dieu—who had listened to him before, in two emergencies of his life, once when he had been caught in the bear trap at Great Slave Lake and Jean Baptiste Clutier had delivered him, and when he had been caught in the fox trap of Corinne de Courcelles's charms and Marie had delivered him—would yet save him a third time. Lying there on the cot, with eyes half closed, he made a vow:

"Bon Dieu, if You save me once again, as, in your infinite mercy, you have saved me twice before, I promise to dedicate my life to some service which shall please You well."

He paused a moment, wondering what that service might be. What could he do to help? The poorest people he knew were the Indians, especially those who were led astray by the white man's whisky, the white man's trickery. In some remote place where no good white men ever came, perhaps he could help. Into his mind came the memory of the Calumet Indians and the beautiful marshes and dunes of the Calumet country towards which he and Marie had been making their way when he was arrested. What place could be more perfect for all his unwordly as well as all his worldly schemes? His lips scarcely moved as he made his vow, identical with Marie's:

"Bon Dieu, Notre Seigneur, if You save me, I promise to save the Indians, to spread Your name among them. I promise to help You, even as You have so often helped me."

He lay quietly for a long time, thinking. No food had been brought to him the day before. None would probably be brought today. Why should the thrifty Yankees feed a man who would be hanged tomorrow? Well, it would all be over soon. He thought again of Marie, of his ailing mother at Ste. Anne de Beaupré, of his four little daughters. Then he tried not to think, but to let time pass over him, as the Indians do, the old Indians who are half asleep most of the time, like misty-eyed old Nee-saw-kee at Arbre Croche or the Indians in ambuscade who can become as unmortal and motionless as trees for forty-eight hours at a time.

As Joseph lay unthinking, a tap sounded on his grated door. He let the sound become a part of his drowse. Again, the tap as of wood upon iron and then the kindly voice of Father Richard:

"Joseph, my son."

Joseph lifted his aching limbs off the cot and exclaimed, with an echo of his former heartiness:

"Come in, Father, and make yourself at home!"

The guard unlocked the door and allowed Father Richard to slip through the narrow opening. Then he shut the door with a peremptory bang, took up his station outside, and remarked through the grating:

"No treasonous talk. No French talk allowed. Speak English. Them's orders."

"Certainly, my good man," said Father Richard. "We're delighted with your company." And that worldly twinkle which had endeared Father Richard to all sorts and sects of men lighted up his black eyes and set the crow's-feet dancing at the corners.

"What news, Father? Any news?"

"I've talked again with the Commandant and many of the other officers, Joseph. They won't commit themselves, of course. Won't say a thing. But the Commandant, Butler, seems to be a good sort of man. Listened attentively to all I said and took notes. But remarked: 'There are two sides, you know, to every question, Mr. Richard, and in time of war we must investigate every kind of accusation, no matter how impossible it may seem.' "

"He called you *Mr.* Richard?"

"It's all right, Joseph. I'm used to it from the Protestant Yankees. They think it compromises their religion to call me 'Father.' So, of course, I answered: 'Yes, Mr. Butler. But there's only one *true* side, *Mr.* Butler.' Butler looks at me under his shaggy brows, and breaks out into a laugh! Laughter helps, Joseph. I think you'll come out all right."

"I don't think there's anyone left in town who hasn't been bribed by Abijah Hull either to testify against me or to hiss against me in court."

"I know. But those accusations are absurd, too absurd."

"Yes. They are *too absurd*. I thought Rastel was shrewder than those articles of the charges show him to be. But I rather imagine that that fool Hull is chiefly responsible for the way the bill of accusations is drawn up. Probably Rastel decided to let him go the whole hog, and trusted to the power of his own personality to put the thing over in court."

"I've wondered about that too. That must be the way of it. By the way, Madame is in town, has been for a week."

"What Madame?"

"Rastel's Madame! And isn't she a beauty! You should see the men following her down the street, at discreet and indiscreet intervals. It's a regular procession!"

"I'll wager it is!" said Joseph, emphatically.

"I even saw poor Jacques Beaugrand stealing a look. He's such a pitiful fellow now, Joseph, even though the courts did pardon him. People avoid him on the street as if he had the cholera. I think I'm the only one who ever says a word to him. Ah, well, to get back to Madame Rastel. I saw your friends Campeau and Pierre Desnoyers following the lovely lady too. Didn't see me at all. They should be too old for such things now, the rascals, with their children growing up!"

"It seems to me you took everything in yourself, Father."

"Paternally, my son, paternally." But the betraying twinkle spread again out of Father Richard's eyes.

"Madame Rastel is up to some mischief, you may be sure," declared Joseph. "Her husband sent for her either to serve as a witness at the trial or to entertain the prospective jurors. And she's as clever as seven devils and beautiful enough, as you see, to befuddle a roomful of judges."

"How did you know she was clever? Had you been acquainted with her before?"

"Oh, yes, I knew her quite well," said Joseph. "I narrowly escaped marrying her."

"Mon Dieu! Does she not, then, retain a little affection for you that could be turned to your advantage?"

"I doubt if she knows what affection is, Father. She knows only ambition. And at present it suits her ambition to stick to Rastel."

"I can't believe, Joseph, that the powers of evil will triumph. You're a good man, and you will be vindicated and released."

"If I *am* released, Father, I think it will please you to know that I've vowed to combine my life as a fur trader with missionary work of some kind among the Indians."

"God bless you, Joseph."

"When the time comes, if it comes, you will help me to map out a plan, Father?"

"Yes, my son."

"But I do not expect to escape, Father. I am caught in a trap worse than a bear's trap."

"Have faith, my son."

Father Richard kneeled down beside Joseph's cot, and began to repeat the ninety-first Psalm in the language to which he was accustomed:

"Celui qui demeure ferme sous l'assistance du Très-haut, se reposera sûrement sous la protection du Dieu du Ciel. Il dira au Seigneur: Vous êtes mon défenseur et mon refuge—"

"Here! Here! Treason! Treason!" shouted the guard, shaking the door violently. "No more o' that furrin language! Speak English, I say!"

"We are *praying* in French."

"Pray American!"

"Very well, monsieur!"

And Father Richard continued in a very loud voice, from the point where he had left off, in his slightly French-accented English:

"Surely He shall deliver thee from the snare of the fowler, and from the noisome pestilence.

"He shall cover thee with his feathers, and under his wings shalt thou trust: his truth shall be thy shield and buckler.

"Thou shalt not be afraid for the terror by night; nor for the arrow that flieth by day."

At this moment, there came the sound of voices at the door, the jingling of the keys in the lock, and Joseph's door swung open again. Father Richard made the sign of the cross and rose to his feet. Joseph's eyes widened as he beheld in his doorway—Corinne Rastel. She was wearing a long blue muslin dress, too flimsy for the season, blue satin sash, wrist bows and flowing bosom knots at the low-cut, almost-all-revealing collar. Her cape was of pale blue cloth, trimmed with a deep border of beaver fur. Her Oldenburg bonnet, tied under the chin, was a dainty mass of blue ostrich feathers and velvet ribbons. She carried a sea-blue silk parasol and wore blue half-mitts.

The guard was holding the door open with a sickeningly infatuated expression on his boiled-walrus face. Corinne showered upon him over her shoulder one of her most irresistible smiles, as she said:

"Thank you, monsieur. You are *very* kind!"

"Kind as a cougar!" laughed Joseph, a bit hoarsely, as he rose to receive his caller. Under his breath, to Father Richard, he muttered:

"What the devil do you suppose she means by coming here?"

Then, bowing low as a courtier at Versailles, his hand on the bosom of his soiled, ruffled shirt, Joseph greeted his caller:

"Welcome, Madame Rastel!"

If Corinne was discomfited by this overdisplay of courtliness, she did not betray it. Nor did she betray the slight revulsion she felt at Joseph's grimy ruffles and ragged red beard.

"My dear Joseph! And you, Father, my homage!"—in a tone that carried more ice than homage.

Father Richard answered mildly:

"Good day, daughter. Joseph, I must be going."

"Oh, no, Father! Stay with me, won't you?" asked Joseph, trying to detain him by the arm.

"But I have very *secret* matters to discuss with you alone, Joseph," put in Corinne, with undiplomatic haste.

Father Richard was already at the door, murmuring something that sounded very much like: "The *secret* of the Lord is with them that fear Him." At the door, he turned back towards Joseph, the gay sparkle and merry crinkles coming back into his face. While Corinne was seating herself in the single chair by the bed and, with deft touches of her mitted hands, arranging the folds of her dress to the most artistic advantage, Father Richard waggled a warning forefinger at Joseph, smiled, shrugged his shoulders, then turned his back, said through the grating, "Let me out, Monsieur Guard, if you please," and went out of the immediately opened door. The guard held the door open long enough for a procession of cardinals to pass out, then at last deprived his ogling eyes of the sight of Corinne.

"My dear Joseph!" exclaimed Corinne again. "What a situation for you to be in!"

"You never would have guessed it!" rejoined Joseph, staring through her various masks with such a level, deep look that Corinne's eyelashes flickered and she dropped her glance to her parasol.

"I am desolated."

"Yes. You look like the very picture of Niobe in our old French schoolbooks! Niobe—with a blue parasol!"

"Joseph! I wouldn't—if I were you!" Corinne looked up, quick, alert, catlike, her claws showing. "It's not so shrewd of you to take this attitude! I might have helped you! In fact, I'm going to do one thing to help you anyway. I'm going to remind you that they'll probably ask you to show your trading license. Have you got it with you?"

Joseph made an involuntary movement towards his shirt pocket, then changed the gesture towards his coat pocket, from which he brought out his handkerchief. The first reflex gesture had not escaped Corinne.

"It's better not to enumerate my possessions, I think, Madame Rastel."

"It would have been shrewder long ago not to have opposed my husband."

"You think his methods of absorbing other people's trading grounds will succeed—indefinitely? I'm not sure but that he's overshot himself this time. And then—two or three plausible charges would have been so much more effective than eight or nine spurious ones! Don't you think so?"

"I'm not discussing the case." Joseph knew by Corinne's eyes, before the green shutters went over them, that she was smart enough to agree with him this time and not with Rastel, or Rastel-advised-by-Attorney-Hull.

"He may be enjoying his little patch of sunlight at his den door at the moment, but he'll go running, like the hunted wolf, with his tail between his legs some day; and I'll live to see the chase and take part in it!"

"You're still very fearless, aren't you?"

"I'm certainly not afraid of either of you."

"You *were* afraid of me—once, Joseph. Weren't you?" Corinne laid her mitted hand warmly on his knee, expecting the old passion to course through him. Joseph was not unmoved by that mesmerizing touch, but something deep and cool within him, and the sudden, amused memory of Father Richard's waggled forefinger made him toss back his head with a laugh.

"It won't work, Corinne. It won't work!" Then: "By the way, what do you want with me, anyway? You and Rastel have me just where you want me, haven't you? What is it you want, then? Did you come here hoping to see me squirm—or what?"

"No. I'll tell you frankly."

"Frankly? Ha!" Joseph's laugh resounded, until the guard shook the door in warning.

"Yes. *Frankly.* I'll lay my cards on the table. Sometimes, it pays. If you in your pleading tomorrow will leave the reputation of my husband alone, I, in my turn, will not testify against you. I have an influence with men, you know. I could send you to death —with the twist of this parasol!"

"I have no doubt of it, madame!"

"Are you not afraid of death, Joseph?"

"Mon Dieu, no! It's just the last journey—to the Pays d'en Haut!"

"You're a good actor, Joseph! Then you plan to testify against my husband, to say all manner of blasting things against him?"

"Why not a blast for a blast, Corinne?"

"It won't do any good, you know. The members of the court are all—"

"Primed," said Joseph.

"Joseph! Very well. Instead of being friends, we are enemies?"

"That is scarcely a new role for you, madame. You have been my enemy, I believe, for the past ten years."

"How can you say that, Joseph?"

"Do you think I don't know how closely you and Rastel work together?"

"Do you think you have guessed everything, Joseph? You might be surprised if I told you how many times a little suggestion of mine here, a little hint of mine there has deflected Maurice from really serious injury of you or your business. Do you think I don't care for you a little still, Joseph?"

"Oh, what's the use of all this?" Joseph cried out, and he began to stride up and down the room like a cougar caught in an empty cabin. He felt suffocated with petticoats and intrigue.

"Joseph!" The word was spoken dulcetly.

"Oh, damn!" exploded Joseph. "Tête d'escabeau! Sacré crapaud!"

"Tch! Tch! Tch! Tch!" came from outside the door, in amused remonstrance.

The key scraped in the lock, the door swung open, and there stood Joseph Campeau and Pierre Desnoyers who had apparently trailed the lovely lady straight to Joseph's door. They were bowing from the waist, their beaver hats held to their bosoms, almost touching the floor as they stooped.

"Welcome, friends! Welcome! You saved me from disgracing myself before a lady! Madame Rastel, let me present my old friends, Monsieur Campeau, Monsieur Desnoyers."

Both gentlemen stooped and kissed the lady's mitted hands. The mitts were exquisitely tinctured with oil of cinnamon.

When the "grand honneurs" and "grand plaisirs" had died away, Campeau pursued the previous subject, in French:

"I should say you had *already* disgraced yourself, Joseph!"

"English, gentlemen!" growled the guard through the small iron grating in the upper part of the door. "Speak English! Them's orders! French's treason!"

"We have merely been greeting each other, Monsieur Guard, in the politest language in the world," observed Corinne, covering the irony with one of her most devastating smiles. "You can be ten times as polite in French as in English—can't you, gentlemen?"

"Oui! Oui, madame!" Campeau and Desnoyers bowed again, almost turning a complete somersault.

"Stop that wee-weeing! Stop it! Do ye hear me? We've had

enough of treason around here! Orders are to put out any people suspected o' plotting. Talkin' furrin is plottin'. Do ye hear me?"

"No, we didn't hear you. Won't you say it again?" asked Joseph, with mock courtesy.

"You—you—you—" spluttered the guard.

Corinne gave Joseph a quick, penetrating look, wondering whether his bravado were genuine, or "poudre aux yeux" tactics. Then she rose, asked the guard to unlock the door, placed one mitted hand on the arm that held the door open and with the other mitted hand slipped a silver coin into the guard's anger-clenched left hand.

"Thank you, Monsieur Guard, we *did* hear you. And now you will leave us to ourselves for just a moment, won't you? We're old friends. We're not plotting any treason, or planning to help the prisoner escape. We're just talking."

The guard's face swam in rapture as Corinne smiled on him, and again he slowly shut the door. Corinne seated herself once more in the only chair, with much rearranging of muslin and ribbon cascades, and the three men sat down as gracefully as they could on the cot.

"Madame came to pay me a final call," said Joseph, "before the hanging. Was it not gracious of her?"

"Hanging, Joseph? Are you not a leetle pess-e-mees-tic?" asked Campeau.

"Oh, no!" declared Joseph briskly. "Nothing pessimistic about that! Might as well face the truth—and the rope!"

"Quite a hero—don't you think?" asked Corinne. And the sparkle of her eyes and the flash of her very white smile completely blinded two of the Frenchmen to the cutting edge of her remark.

"How is it, dear madame," asked Desnoyers, "that you have never visited our little town before? Ah, let me answer the question myself. It is because we are but a rude frontier town, and you are accustomed to all the gayeties and advantages of the great cities. N'est-ce pas?" He leaned forward earnestly, the same beau of a Desnoyers that he had been ten years before, slightly heavier but still handsome, still well dressed from his ruffles to his buckles.

"Ah, but I do not consider Detroit a frontier village—when it can produce such char-r-r-r-rming gentlemen!" exclaimed Corinne, spreading her hands expressively and lifting and letting down her shoulders in Gallic exclamation points.

"Oh, we're not fools exactly!" said Campeau.

"Ah, we're not fit for the society of angels!" added Desnoyers, sighing obnoxiously.

Revolted, Joseph rose from the bed. He began to fear that Corinne's charms were already ruining his cause for the trial, even with his friends. At this moment he was fully aware of those charms himself. The enchantress! Could he never cast off the spell!

"Desnoyers has always been romantic!" Joseph retaliated. "His exploits are famous! You must know, madame, that, like a second Leander, he once crossed the Detroit River without a boat to visit a sweetheart on the opposite shore. He paddled himself across in a wheelbarrow!"

Desnoyers was quick to catch the irony, and the reproof of his old friend; but he found himself saying, to his own astonishment:

"I would do as much for Madame!"

"Char-r-r-rming! Char-r-r-r-rming!" commented Madame.

Low tones outside the door announced yet another visitor on this last day before the trial, when the strict visitors' rules had been relaxed. The door opened, and Sarah Whistler Abbott, in a black bonnet and a black dress with collar and wristlets of white lace, entered. There was a basket covered with a napkin under her arm. She was the same gracious and beautiful woman that she had been on her wedding journey eleven years before, with the same vivid coloring, the same black hair, the same sea-blue eyes, the same appealing cleft in her chin. But a sadness had taken the place of the old sparkle in her eyes. The death of her brother John in the war, the death of her little daughter Sarah, and the recent imprisonment and illness of her husband had deepened her thoughts and her expression. Although she still had the three wild little boys, Madison and William and Robert, the loss of the only daughter remained almost unbearable.

It was characteristic that Corinne did not rise when she was presented to Mrs. Abbott, but merely put out her hand and surveyed Sarah coolly. The three men jumped to their feet.

"Sarah!" exclaimed Joseph. "How kind of you to come, how very kind!"

"I may only stay a moment, Joseph, but I brought you some delicacies from the house which I thought might vary your military diet a trifle: a pigeon potpie—Pompey went hunting on Sunday—and some johnnycake, and two bottles of sherry."

"Oh, Sarah, you've saved my life! Nothing ever sounded so good since Elijah famished. God bless you, Sarah! Let's have the sherry now, all together."

"No, as donor I forbid it, Joseph. That's for you alone, to put you on your mettle for the trial!"

"Thank you, Sarah! You've restored my soul!"

Corinne looked keenly at Joseph's enthusiastic face and flicked her glance across Sarah's. She suddenly felt tigerishly jealous of Sarah.

"I'll bring you a basket next time myself, Joseph—if there *is* a next time," she said, rising. As Joseph rose, also, she stood close to him and fumbled coquettishly for several seconds with the ruffles of his shirt front, her enveloping blue cape not quite concealing the gesture. But Joseph looked ignoringly past her at Sarah.

Sarah felt herself bristling like a hen in defense of its chicks: "A *next time*? You don't believe that Mr. Bailly will be released, madame?" She crimsoned as she realized that she was addressing the wife of Joseph's accuser.

"He prefers the rope!" cried Corinne, laughing, with cool ripples, over a joke which no one else seemed to appreciate. "Goodbye, Joseph!" she said, without extending her hand. "Goodbye, mesdames et messieurs! Open, guard!" And she moved quickly and dramatically out of the room.

Exactly twenty-four hours later, Joseph sat in the room set aside at Fort Shelby for military tribunals. It was a long room with high barred windows as dusty and webby as those in his cell. The atmosphere was decidedly gloomy. But Joseph, always sturdily ready for battle, had, in spite of temporary physical weakness, recovered his natural pugnacity. The visits of his friends the day before, Sarah Abbott's pigeon potpie, the two bottles of sherry, the fact that he had had his beard shaved off that morning, and his own natural resiliency had turned the trick. As a final spur, the sight of Abijah Hull standing at the prosecutor's table, of Higgins at the jurors' table, the sight of the whole court glitteringly arrayed against him, had aroused the redheaded indignation, the old courage, the moral force of the unjustly arraigned prisoner. Joseph rose from his bed of despair and was a man.

The guard led Joseph to the small prisoner's table opposite Hull's. A long table, covered with papers and uncomfortable weapons and dimly lighted from the grilled windows, stood with one end toward the spectators. On the left of this was Major Andrew Kittle, acting as judge advocate, with Joseph behind his right shoulder and Hull behind his left and an orderly beyond them. On the right of the long table were the president of the court and, at his left and right, the twelve acting members of the court (officers in various degrees of gold-braided, gold epauleted eminence—infantry in blue trousers and white stripes, artillery in scarlet and gold). The only juror whom Joseph recognized was Lieutenant Higgins, who looked quite as unfriendly as on the day of Joseph's arrest.

Joseph allowed his eyes to pass slowly over the hundred or so spectators. Among the soldiers, the rabble of Detroit, the "claque" of Rastel, and Corinne, who was seated on the center aisle, in the very front row, he was immensely warmed to recognize a handful of his stanch old friends: Father Richard, with his green-lined hat and green umbrella; James Abbott, a thinner version of his former self; Sarah Abbott; Deborah Anderson and Antoinette Navarre from the River Raisin; Elinor Kinzie, still living, with her family, in Detroit since the Checagou massacre; Pierre Desnoyers, Joseph Campeau, and his clerk, old MacNiff; Antoine Beaubien and poor Jacques Beaugrand, whose own exonerating but humiliating trial had taken place only a short while before, and who sat huddled in a far corner of the room, apart from all his old friends, a colorless and pathetic figure. Peter Navarre, still serving his country as scout, and Colonel François Navarre, also on duty, were missing. In an adjoining room were several more good friends who were shortly to serve Joseph as witnesses for the defense, the court procedure forbidding the witnesses to listen to any of the possibly prejudicial proceedings and the testimony of the others. Two of Joseph's witnesses had arrived unexpectedly that very morning, one by the first boat of the season from Mackinac Island, the other by sleigh-coach from Louisville.

When Joseph had been conducted to his place near the judge advocate, and the whispering and stirring which had followed the handsome prisoner like a summer wind across a wheatfield had subsided, Major Kittle read the Commander in Chief's order for convening the court:

"Headquarters, Detroit, February 20, 1815.
"The General Court Martial of which Colonel Hepburn is President, will meet at ten o'clock on Monday morning, March 1, 1815 at the assembly room at Fort Shelby, to consider the case of Mr. Joseph Bailly, British citizen of Mackinac Island."

Major Kittle then read out the names of the officers of the court in the order of their rank, those of highest rank having already taken their standing positions nearest to the president of the court, the rest arranging themselves, in order, down the table. The judge advocate then addressed Joseph:

"Has the defendant any objection to make against any member of the court here standing? If so, let him herewith make his challenge."

Joseph felt mightily like challenging Higgins, for he knew that "suspicion of prejudice" was a legitimate cause of challenge; but he feared that the suspicion might seem cowardly and preferred to trust to the justice of the other members of the court. After a slight pause, during which he steadied himself, he answered in a firm voice:

"No objections, Your Honor. The defendant is satisfied with the personnel of the court."

Joseph's eyes passed quickly from Higgins to Abijah Hull. The same look was on both faces.

The judge advocate gravely delivered the words of the charge, while the court still stood:

"You shall well and truly try and determine, according to evidence, the matter now before you."

Major Kittle then administered to each of the thirteen members

of the court the solemn oath required by the Articles of War, each
officer holding up his right hand and repeating the words after the
judge advocate:

I, ——— [name], do swear that I will well and truly try and determine, according to evidence, the matter now before me, between the United States of America, and the prisoner to be tried;
and that I will duly administer justice, according to the provisions
of "An Act establishing Rules and Articles for the Government of
the Armies of the United States," without partiality, favor or
affection; and if any doubt shall arise, not explained by said articles, according to my conscience, the best of my understanding,
and the custom of war, in like cases: and I do further swear, that
I will not divulge the sentence of the court, until it shall be published by the proper authority; neither will I disclose or discover
the vote or opinion of any particular member of the court-martial,
unless required to give evidence thereof as a witness, by a court of
justice, in a due course of law. So help me God!

After the president of the court had administered a somewhat
similar oath to the judge advocate, the court was seated. Major
Kittle then rose from his seat and rapped his sword loudly on the
table to call the court to order, and the proceedings of prosecution
against Joseph began.

When every murmur had subsided and the last theatrical swish
of Corinne's petticoats had rustled into silence, Major Kittle
cleared his throat and in a resonant voice read the document containing Rastel's charges:

"To Major A. B. Kittle, Division Advocate, Third Division of
the Militia of Michigan Territory: Detroit, October 10, 1814:
The Complaint of Maurice Rastel, Sieur de Rocheblave, merchant
and trader throughout the American territories, American citizen,
against Joseph Bailly, British citizen, and independent trader in
Michigan and Indiana Territories, respectfully represents that
said Joseph Bailly is responsible for the following treasonous acts
against the United States of America:

"1. That on July 17, 1812, he met Lieutenant Roberts and his
army of attacking British soldiery near Michael Dousman's farm
on Mackinac Island and guided them to the heights above the Fort,
thus enabling them to take possession of the Island. That he and

his Indian wife gave signals to the British from the grassy plateau near the Fort.

"2. That he carefully and successfully plotted with the Potawatomi of Parc aux Vaches the destruction of Fort Dearborn and its inhabitants, supplying to them, through his agents, five Mackinaw boatloads purportedly containing furs but actually containing rifles, tomahawks, spears and knives, which went down the St. Joseph River to Checagou on July 28, 1812. That he led the Potawatomi in the disguise of an Indian, on the day of the massacre, August 15, 1812, in their attack from the pine-ridge on the helpless caravan.

"3. That he has stirred up the Indians from Mackinac to Vincennes against the United States, causing the enlistment of many Chippewa, Ottawa, Potawatomi, Miami and Wea Indians, otherwise friendly to the United States, against the United States in the war with Great Britain.

"4. That he carried to success, through his and his wife's Indian connections and his presence on the scene, again disguised as an Indian, the River Raisin massacre of January 22, 1813.

"5. That Chief Blackbird was seen in consultation at the Bailly house on Mackinac Island, before the Battle of the Thames and is known to have received supplies of gold for the purchase of ammunition from said Joseph Bailly.

"6. That, just previous to arrest, that is, in mid-September, 1814, said Joseph Bailly was supplying guns to the Indians on Grand River for an attack on Fort Wayne.

"7. That said Joseph Bailly was traveling through American Territory without a legitimate license.

"8. That said Joseph Bailly forcibly resisted arrest on September 23, 1814.

"9. That the said Joseph Bailly is a dangerous enemy to the United States, in whose territory he lives and operates, and is subject to the penalties stipulated in Articles LVI, LVII and CI, Section 2, of the Articles of War.

"Wherefore your Complainant requests that charges and specifications may be preferred against the said Joseph Bailly for the offenses above mentioned and that he may be otherwise dealt with as the law, in such cases, provides.

"(Signed) Maurice Rastel, *Sieur de Rocheblave*."

A red fire flowed over Joseph from head to foot. Although, in the quiet of his prison, he had been served with a copy of the gen-

eral order and the charges and specifications preferred against
him and had prepared his defense, according to the privilege of the
accused in court-martial, the enormity of the allegations, as they
issued out of the living mouth of the judge advocate, poured over
him like molten lava. Such atrocious absurdities! Surely the crude
Hull and the handsome, outwardly suave nephew of old Philippe
Rastel had overshot themselves this time! No one would believe,
no one *could* believe such perjured preposterousness, such Gar-
gantuan lies! And yet, if the jurors were all of the caliber of Higgins, and if Rastel and Hull and Corinne had worked their wiles
upon them, and perhaps even on the judge advocate, there was no
telling what might happen, in this military tribunal which was
supposed to be the ultimate court of objective truth, impersonal
justice. Joseph leaned forward with the impulse of jumping to his
feet, and clenched the arms of his chair till the knuckles showed
white. But when the judge advocate addressed him with the customary question, "Mr. Joseph Bailly, are you guilty or not guilty
of this matter of accusation?" Joseph, having gotten himself under
control, rose with dignity. His flush of anger gave a momentary
healthy glow to his thinned face. He replied firmly:

"*Not guilty!*"

"Then we are ready for the first witness for the prosecution,"
announced the judge advocate as Joseph sat down.

Abijah Hull motioned to the orderly who stood near. The
orderly went out of a door to the left and rear of the jurors' table,
and returned shortly with a man immediately recognizable, but
so incongruously dressed that Joseph's mouth began to twitch
with suppressed laughter even in the midst of his discomfiture. It
was Neoma de la Vigne, whom Rastel had clothed in the latest
fashion: a ruffled shirt, a stock so high and stiff that the French-
Asiatic-Indian looked like a totem pole, a white vest, a long, brown
broadcloth coat, brown cloth trousers of elegant cut, and buckled
shoes. De la Vigne's black, curling-serpent hair had been oiled
back into the semblance of a short but unruly queue tied with black
satin ribbon. His skin was squash-yellow against the white shirt
and brown cloth. His supple figure was completely concealed. His
walk did not fit his clothes. He should have minced. But he glided
with that smooth Indian step that seems to remain motionless, while
the earth slides backward under it.

When the judge advocate had first sent him the list of witnesses, Joseph had thought of challenging the legality of this witness, who was part Indian; the thought recurred to him today, but he desisted for three reasons: because he did not approve of the law that refused to accept the testimony of Indians; because De la Vigne claimed to be far more French than Indian and was certainly trying to look the part today; and because Joseph wanted to sit back, as an amused and amazed spectator, and see what the fellow might dare to say.

De la Vigne took his stand at the left of the judge advocate, close to Hull and facing the courtroom. Joseph saw Hull poke him in the back and heard him whisper: "Bend down, fool! Bow!" De la Vigne made a low, awkward bow, letting his hands fall limp at his sides, without lifting his right hand even halfway to his bosom, in the gesture of courtesy. Joseph could hear people in the courtroom whispering, and thought he could make out a multiple echo of the phrase: "Queer-looking duck!"

De la Vigne was made to place his hand on a Bible resting on the table beside the judge advocate, and to swear that "the evidence I shall give in the cause now in hearing shall be the truth, the whole truth and nothing but the truth, so help me God." Joseph's mind went back, with his unwearying sense of humor, to the wild dances at Arbre Croche, the spirit-shaken lodge, and the demoniacal worship of Motchi Manitou and the serpent god by this man who was now swearing a solemn oath on the white man's Bible!

Abijah Hull coughed and squirmed in his eagerness to conduct the prosecution himself as in a civil trial. But in the military tribunal the judge advocate is both prosecutor and attorney for the defense, and the civil counsel of neither the accused nor the accuser is expected to address the court or to interrupt the proceedings except in notes occasionally passed between himself and the protagonists or between himself and the judge advocate. Abijah felt that it needed only his guiding voice to damn Joseph utterly.

The judge advocate cleared his throat, consulted a note and said:

"I understand that you are one of the accuser's most valuable witnesses, Mr. Neoma de la Vigne, a respected trader, trapper, interpreter, 'known and venerated alike by Indians and whites throughout the Michigan Territory,' according to the notation I have here."

"Yes, monsieur."

"Yes, *Your Honor!*" corrected Abijah in a loud whisper.

"Yes, Your Honor."

Pierre Desnoyers jumped to his feet, from the floor of the house. The act surprised no one, for Detroit had not yet formalized in its civil procedure and scarcely in its military procedures, the spontaneous freedom of the frontier.

"Your Honor, is this man to be accepted as a witness, who is an Indian medicine man, jossakeed, and sorcerer—a man who has fought with the British against the Americans in half a dozen battles and has scalped untold numbers of our fellow countrymen? How can—"

"Order! Order!" shouted Major Kittle, rattling his sword on the table. "This is a military court."

But the informal frontier atmosphere still prevailed and there was another interruption from the floor. From the very back of the room, Jacques Beaugrand rose and kept his body from shaking, by grasping the back of the bench in front of him.

"Your Honor—I saw him—I saw him—with my own eyes— murder Americans—at the River Raisin—Bon Dieu!" Jacques fell back limply on his bench.

"Order in the court!" cried the judge advocate, rising. "No further interruptions from the floor, if you please. The court has, you may be assured, already gone into the matter of testimony, and the defendant has not challenged this witness. This witness is French, of French ancestry, French name. His former British sympathies are no more prejudicial to the just consideration of this case than the former British sympathies of the accuser himself, a recently naturalized American citizen, operating with an American trading license, who is supposedly seeking abstract justice equally removed from British or American partisanship. All these matters have been well considered by the president and judge advocate of this court, before convening the court. We will now proceed.

"Mr. de la Vigne, what detailed evidence can you give in support of any of the nine specifications of the charge brought against Mr. Joseph Bailly? Were you present at the capture of Mackinac, the Fort Dearborn massacre, the Raisin River massacre or on any

of the occasions upon which Mr. Bailly is said to have given assistance to the enemies of the United States?"

"Yes! All of them! All of them, Your Honor! And he was in
center of all! At Mackinac Island, he met Captain Roberts' boats
in early dawn of July 17, 1812, and led British soldiers by secret
path back of fort to heights above fort. I was camping on beach
and saw all, and his wife, Wing Woman, gave signals with gulls
and Lieutenant Hanks had to surrender. Bailly's fault.

"At Checagou, he rode a bay horse, color of his hair, and led
the Potawatomi and Ottawa. Murder! Murder! He was there all
right! Killed Captain William Wells, killed Surgeon Smith, killed
Lieutenant Simmons. Saw with own eyes.

"At River Raisin, was aide General Proctor. Told General
Proctor let Indians massacre Americans. Best way.

"At Grand River, Bailly gave Indians muskets to attack Fort
Wayne.

"Heard from Chief Blackbird all about Bailly plan to supply
guns, gold at Battle of Thames. Saw big bag of gold Bailly gave
Blackbird."

"Is that all, Mr. De la Vigne?"

"Could say much more. Bailly bad, bad man!"

"If there is nothing definite, that will be all."

Joseph noticed, with reassurance, smiles leaking out of the corners of the mouths of several of the jurors and realized that the
spectacle that Hull and Rastel were putting on wasn't going so
very well. The judge advocate apparently did not even consider
it worth while to cross-examine this perjured witness.

After De la Vigne had retired, through a whispering that
amounted almost to a hissing, Rastel, through Abijah Hull, summoned six or seven witnesses who mechanically gave evidence on
one or another of the counts. But Joseph did not become interested
until William Burnett, the jealous rival trader on the St. Joseph,
was summoned and sworn in. Major Kittle put the question:

"Mr. Burnett, have you any knowledge of the activities of Mr.
Bailly at Parc aux Vaches relative to the Fort Dearborn massacre?"

"Yes. I have. He is a close friend of Blackbird and Topenebee,
Shavehead and Weesaw, who were all murderers at the Fort Dearborn massacre; and it was Bailly who supplied them with guns and

ammunition and stirred them up to the plot. I stopped one of Bailly's barges on its way out of the St. Joseph River to Checagou on August 10, 1812, because I suspected something was wrong, and under the sacks of Indian corn and bales of fur were piles and piles of guns and bags of powder. I asked the half-breed in charge where they were going. He said: 'Mind damned business!' But an Indian rower said they were going to the Calumet to supply all the Indians there with guns, and that there was going to be a 'big storm' in Checagou."

As Burnett was concluding, Abijah Hull passed him a note. Burnett resumed:

"Moreover, Your Honor, Bailly's an illicit trader. Ask him if he has a trading license."

"Certainly. That question should have been asked in the beginning. Can you produce your license, Mr. Bailly?"

Joseph put his hand to his shirt pocket, under the long cravat. Then he got up and fumbled about in all his pockets.

"It is gone, sir. I have kept it at hand, all these months, and I had it yesterday morning in this high, front shirt pocket. Could an orderly be sent back to my room to search for it?"

"Yes. That can be done."

Major Kittle gave the commission to an orderly at the back of the room.

"But surely, Your Honor, this accusation is too absurd," continued Joseph. "It would take me only a few weeks to have my license reconfirmed. And may I take the liberty of saying that I hope soon to be operating as an American citizen, if I am cleared of these charges? I have already written my preliminary application to President Jefferson."

There was a stir of approval in the room. Then Sarah Abbott clapped her hands, and there was a round of applause. Joseph smiled, bowed, and continued:

"And may I, at this point, protest against Mr. Burnett's use, in his declaration, of the testimony of an Indian against me? I have every respect for the Indians and deplore the law which rules out an Indian's testimony as unacceptable, but since this *is* the law, I demand the rights of having Mr. Burnett's quoted testimony of the supposed Indian on my fur barge on the St. Joseph River struck out.

I moreover declare that no such barge went out of the St. Joseph on August 10, 1812. It must be a fact well known to all of you, that by August all furs are already shipped, and that corn is not shipped until October. On August 10, 1812, I was on Mackinac Island with all my voyageurs, and my Indians were at the Galien River gathering rice."

"This is all very well, Mr. Bailly, and may be brought out later in your plea. But your inability to produce your license is serious," declared Major Kittle.

As Joseph sat down, he suddenly remembered Corinne's question about his license and how flirtatiously she had fumbled with his shirt front just before her quick exit from his room on the preceding day. He had wondered all along how Rastel had dared to make that seventh charge about his lack of a license. The plan had probably been to steal the license all along. Finding that Joseph kept it always close to his person the accusers had brought in Corinne for the special purpose (among others) of stealing the license. That, then, accounted for her visit of the day before! He rose hotly.

"Your Honor!" he said, in a resounding voice. "My license has been stolen—by my accusers!"

"This is not the time for counter accusations! Sit down," roared Kittle, again rapping his sword on the table. Joseph cast a sidewise glance at Corinne, who was poking a crack in the floor with a gold-and-ebony cane and looking devilishly beautiful. She had fixed herself up to kill—the jurors. She was wearing the type of dress and hat recently made fashionable by that dashing Parisian sympathizer with Napoleon, the Duchesse d' Angoulême. It was a high-waisted, long-skirted morning dress of military blue broadcloth, with a small round cape of the same material, bordered with a six-inch trim of the richest sealskin (exhibit of a fur trader's wife! thought Joseph). The cuffs were trimmed with gold braid, and Joseph was amused to note gold epaulets on the shoulders, Corinne having thrown one flap of the cape back. The hat was a feminized imitation of the stiff officer's hat, blue, but touched off with brilliant red braid and with a gold cockade sticking up saucily in the center of it. Corinne must have ordered the outfit months in advance from Paris for this very occasion! Shrewd, a little too shrewd. Joseph wished, nevertheless, that he had adopted other tactics with Corinne the day before. It would have been less honest on his part, but more farsighted. The orderly, of course, would not find the license in his room.

Abijah Hull passed a note to Major Kittle, and the judge advocate asked Lieutenant Higgins to rise.

"While we are waiting for the return of the orderly from Mr. Bailly's room, we will continue with the testimony of the witnesses for the prosecution. Lest any one should protest the summoning of a member of the court as witness, let me affirm that such summoning is entirely within the limits of procedure. Major Alexander Macomb, in his authoritative *Treatise on Martial Law and Courts Martial,* which I have here, states that 'the judges of the court and the jurors may be sworn as witnesses for any of the parties; for they have no interest in the issue of the trial, and no bias of any kind to give evidence against the truth.' "

Joseph hid a smile behind his hand.

"Lieutenant Higgins," continued the judge advocate, "may I ask whether you found any suspicious amount of ammunition on Mr. Bailly's pack horses on the day when you arrested him?"

"Decidedly, Your Honor," replied Higgins promptly, but unspecifically. "Enough to supply a small army."

"And did the prisoner resist arrest?"

"Yes, sir, most objectionably, Your Honor."

"Very well."

After Pélégor, Joseph's rival on the Grand River, had been sworn in and had supported De la Vigne's testimony as to the muskets distributed to the Ottawa of Grand River just before the arrest, the star witness of the prosecution was brought in, Monsieur Maurice Rastel himself. Rastel was beautifully clothed in dove-colored broadcloth with a vest embroidered with lavender flowers. His shirt sleeves, long and lacy under the tight waistcoat, suggested the courtly days of the Louis's as did his manner and his bow. All that was lacking was a gold-headed cane. He was undeniably handsome. Before Rastel had had time to pledge his word upon the Bible, Father Richard rose from his place.

"May I ask a question, Your Honor?"

The sympathetic manner in which the judge advocate gave his

answer was testimony to the esteem in which Father Richard was held by Protestants and Catholics alike in Detroit.

"Why, certainly, Father Richard."

"May I rise to ask Your Honor, whether it is permissible for the prejudiced accuser to give evidence against the accused?"

Major Kittle again consulted the medium-sized leather-bound volume on the table before him:

"Your question, Father Richard, which is the question of 'bias, prejudice or malice, propter affectum,' is again answered by Major Macomb, where he definitely states that 'in cases of a criminal nature, and when the object is not gain, or the avoidance of loss, but the punishment of a crime, the informer or prosecutor is allowed to give evidence against the party accused: one principal reason for such practice being the necessity of circumstances; for otherwise, many crimes would escape punishment for the want of evidence."

"Thank you, Your Honor." Father Richard sat down with a wry little smile.

Rastel was sworn in and introduced with some ceremony by the judge advocate, as the Sieur de Rocheblave, illustrious fur trader and descendant of famed fur traders, now an American citizen. The introduction had no doubt been written by Rastel himself and handed to the major by Hull. Rastel bowed very low, his hand on his ruffled bosom.

"Mr. President, Your Honor, the Judge Advocate, Gentlemen of the Court, and friends. It would hardly seem necessary for me to add more evidence to the evidence of the esteemed gentlemen who have preceded me in order to brand Monsieur Joseph Bailly as an unlicensed trader (I will not stoop to speak of his innumerable poachings on my own licensed territory, for this great patriotic cause on which we are embarked is far greater in its importance than any petty personal cause), also as a spy, as a traitor, and as one guilty of sedition against our beloved United States of America—therefore, I am sorry to say, as one triply guilty of death. But I have evidence even more damning than the evidence already presented, which has come into my hands too late to present before this moment. I have, for instance, self-accusatory letters written in his own hand: a letter written to Captain Roberts setting the date and making the arrangements for the attack on Mackinac Island; and a letter to Captain Rhea at Fort Wayne written one month before Monsieur Bailly's arrest, urging Captain Rhea to send out a detachment from Fort Wayne to round up some supposedly dangerous Miami who were threatening a handful of settlers in the direction of Detroit—an obvious stratagem to render resistance weak at Fort Wayne, when Bailly and his Indians should attack. You already have in your files the letter I handed over to you several weeks ago, that significant message from Bailly to Captain Nathan Heald at Fort Dearborn, strongly advising evacuation of the fort on August 12, 1812, at the time when John Kinzie, Lieutenant Helm, and others cognizant of the danger were urging Captain Heald to remain safely in the fort. This points directly to Bailly's responsibility for the Fort Dearborn massacre.

"If further evidence were needed, I have here the signatures of some forty witnesses on all the assertions which I presume have already been made by my illustrious fellow witnesses. A more damning bundle of evidence could scarcely be brought together."

Rastel turned to Abijah Hull, who unfolded and handed to him some long papers which trailed the floor as the transfer was made. Rastel held them conspicuously before the court. From where Joseph sat, he could see that the names had been written in a handwriting five times as large as ordinary writing, in order to take as much impressive space as possible.

"This paper," continued Rastel, "concerns the accusations connected with the River Raisin. Since you may be more familiar with these neighboring esteemed gentlemen than with those at a greater distance, I will read off the names of a few of the former who have irrevocably involved Monsieur Joseph Bailly in the massacre of the Raisin: Mr. James Kidney, Mr. Barney Parker, Mr. Seth Billups, Mr. Cyrenius Black, Mr. Ebenezer Smith, Mr. Horace Butler, Mr. Wilford Parrott. It is scarcely necessary to go farther. You already know the standing and ability of these men."

"Coquins! Voleurs! Thieves and rascals!" exclaimed Campeau to Desnoyers in so piercing a whisper that everyone in the court heard him.

"They all testify," continued Rastel, only momentarily perturbed, "that Bailly was in Proctor's camp on the night of January 22, 1813, and that it was he who incited the Indians to their atrocities!"

"Hear! Hear!" cried out Campeau, rising. The excitement in his voice was at odds with the clerical dignity of his black swallow-tail coat and snowy ruffles. "This is too—ri-dic-u-lous! I can testify that my good friend, Joseph Bailly, was on Mackinac Island all t'rough ze winter of 1812 and '13. I have ze letters from him to prove it. He order t'ree barrels of Madeira wine of me, two barrels Monongahela whisky—"

The court began to titter pleasantly.

"Where *are* the letters?" asked the judge advocate. "They should have been brought in as evidence."

"Well, well, they must still be in ze files at ze office. I never t'ought to bring them—never t'ought the honesty of my good friend Joseph Bailly would be so questioned by ze bunch of rascals."

"That will do, Mr. Campeau!"

James Abbott rose.

"I too have letters, Your Honor. Mr. Bailly divided his orders between me and Mr. Campeau. All this is obviously absurd. It is outrageous! Mr. Bailly *was* on Mackinac Island all during that winter. This whole list of accusations is absurd. How such a fantastic case was ever allowed to come to trial I don't see!"

Abbott was becoming ruddier than usual, with indignation, while Sarah pulled energetically but to no effect on his coattails. Kittle rattled his sword, but Abbott, who was afraid of no man, not even of a military tribunal, merely lifted his voice loudly above the rattle, to make his final contribution:

"Why, Joseph Bailly is innocent of *all* these cooked-up, outrageous, preposterous accusations!"

"I am sorry to remind you, Mr. Abbott, that this is a military tribunal, in which no talking from the floor should be tolerated, nor any indefinite evidence admitted—"

"How about presumptive evidence?" threw in Abbott.

"The letters must be produced to constitute evidence. Sit down, Mr. Abbott."

Major Kittle spoke with less severity than he would ordinarily have used, for James Abbott was the most influential and respected non-French citizen in Detroit. Abbott's emphatic words had produced an obvious impression on every one present.

Joseph made a sign with his lips to Abbott and Campeau, "Never mind—it doesn't matter," for he had living evidence for that date which was far better than any epistolary evidence could possibly be.

"You may proceed," signaled the judge advocate.

"In conclusion," continued Rastel, with a flourish of his hands, "I would say that this illicit trader, this poacher, this traitor should not be allowed any longer to run wild, causing theft, murder, conflagration over the whole Northwest. Your Honor!" With a bow, he walked backwards, bowing still, as from the presence of royalty, through the door at the rear of the jurors' table, into the witness room.

Joseph sat back at his ease. Rastel's attempts at eloquence had been ineffective indeed. Abijah Hull could scarcely have done worse. The effects, if any, had been gained with lace-sleeved gestures and elaborately aristocratic enunciation. Even Corinne looked embarrassed, as if her grand seigneur had not come off quite so well as she had expected. Joseph, genuinely sorry for her discomfiture, smiled at her. To his surprise, she smiled radiantly back at him. A gilded weathervane, thought Joseph, blowing to and fro with the *prevailing* winds. Or is there a little of the old love for me still in her heart? Or did she ever love me? Strange woman—Always the woman-mask and the Corinne-mask!

As for Rastel's charges, Joseph thought that surely they must sound as preposterous to the jurors as they sounded to him. He supposed that only the necessity of investigating every suspicion of spying had permitted such an obviously factitious case to come to trial. He was glad that he had not availed himself of the privilege of counsel or "amicus curiae." He felt that with his witnesses, especially the newly arrived ones, he could handle the case. The vultures of despair had flown out of the window!

"Does the prisoner wish to question the witnesses further?"

Joseph rose.

"No thank you, Your Honor, I believe that the testimony of my own witnesses will serve to correct or nullify the testimony of the accuser's witnesses."

Joseph's simplicity, sincerity, and lack of acerbity were in pleasing contrast to the previous speaker.

"Very well. In that case, the court also will postpone its privilege of questioning the witnesses. Will you summon your exculpatory witnesses? Wait a moment! We will get a report on the trading license."

At this moment, the orderly who had been sent to Joseph's quarters to hunt for his trading license was returning down the center aisle towards the jurors' table. Everyone involuntarily turned his head to see. At this moment of general preoccupation, an oblong document fell into the aisle in the path of the advancing orderly. Only Joseph was quick enough to catch the slight motion of Corinne resettling her hands in her lap and the look in her eyes, suddenly devoid of the mask, suddenly revealing, for one quick instant, as in the long-forgotten days at Quebec, a genuine, unaffected emotion. Something more than his gratitude went out towards her.

The name "Joseph Bailly" lay across the folded sheet in the aisle. The orderly advanced, stiff-chinned, undeviating, to within six feet of it. Father Richard, across the aisle from Corinne, suddenly understood many things. He stooped over and picked up the sheet from the aisle. As the orderly came into line with him, Father Richard handed the paper to him with the words:

"Is not this, perhaps, the document you were looking for?"

The orderly paused, unfolded the paper, then advanced to the table and handed it to the judge advocate.

"Yes. This is Joseph Bailly's trading license," announced Major Kittle. "How did it happen to be lying in the aisle?"

No one stirred.

"Well, never mind. That is an irrelevant matter. The relevant matter is that the trading license of Joseph Bailly is found, and appears to be in good order, in every respect. Very well. Summon your witnesses, Joseph Bailly."

Joseph spoke to the orderly, who left the room and shortly brought in John Kinzie. Major Kittle swore him in, then asked:

"You were at the Checagou massacre, were you not, Mr. Kinzie?"

"Yes, Your Honor."

"What can you tell us of the activities of Mr. Joseph Bailly at the massacre?"

"*Activities*—of Mr. Joseph *Bailly?*"

Kinzie was always of a quick temper. The red was already flushing over his face at the implied accusation.

"But, Your Honor, he wasn't anywhere *near* Checagou at the time! I believe he was up at Mackinac Island."

"You have no proof that he was at Mackinac Island?"

"Proof? Good God, Your Honor, I *know* he wasn't at the Checagou massacre!" bellowed Kinzie. "I was *there!* I know every man, woman, and child who was at that massacre, and what happened to every one of 'em. I know every Indian. Jo Bailly was no more there than *you* were there! The last time I saw Jo Bailly at Fort Dearborn was in October, 1811, when he came down to his old post at Parc aux Vaches and rode into Checagou with Alexander Robinson. Bailly stayed at my house, and we played the fiddle and sang French songs and had the hell of a good time! I remember it well, for it was one of the last good times we ever had at old Checagou!"

"You don't remember seeing him ride a bay horse at the massacre?"

"Hell, no! He had a black horse the last time I saw him, and he wasn't at Checagou, I tell you! I could get forty people to swear to that—forty of 'em. I saw everything, I tell you! This is an outrage. Why, Jo Bailly's the most God-damned innocent man in the whole Northwest!"

"If you will please to remember that there are ladies, and military judges of great dignity, in this court, and use language a little less violent, Mr. Kinzie."

"Yes, Your Honor."

"Does the prisoner wish to examine the witness further?"

"If you please, Your Honor. Mr. Kinzie, did you see Captain William Wells killed?"

"Yes, I did, Jo—er—Mr. Bailly—"

"Who killed him?"

"Neoma de la Vigne, the Ottawa medicine man."

A gasp went over the room.

"Who killed Lieutenant Simmons, Mr. Kinzie?"

"Shavehead, a Potawatomi."

"And Surgeon Smith?"

"Neoma de la Vigne."

"Thank you. That is all I wish to ask, Your Honor."

"Very well," concluded Major Kittle. "That will be all for the present, Mr. Kinzie."

Joseph, planning his refutations carefully, next handed the judge advocate a newly arrived letter which he asked him to admit as evidence. The judge advocate read aloud to the court:

February 1, 1815.

"Major A. B. Kittle

"Fort Shelby,

"Detroit, Michigan.

"MY DEAR MAJOR KITTLE: This is to testify that Mr. Joseph Bailly was not present at the Checagou massacre and was, to my knowledge, in no way involved in it or in any other disturbances on the Northwest frontier. Furthermore, I never received any letter from him urging me to evacuate Fort Dearborn in August, 1812, or any letter other than of a purely personal, friendly nature unrelated to business and military affairs. On September 6, 1812, three weeks after the massacre, Mr. and Mrs. Bailly received my wife and me in their home on Mackinac Island and rendered us every possible assistance. I have known Mr. Bailly for many years and can testify to the utter integrity and kindness of his character, as can hundreds of others who have been entertained, helped or cheered by him, throughout Michigan and Indiana Territory.

"Yours very sincerely,

"NATHAN HEALD

"FORT HARRODSBURG, KENTUCKY."

The letter produced an audibly favorable impression, for Major Heald was well known to many of the soldiers at Fort Shelby and to many of the spectators.

"I have here also," said Major Kittle, "an affidavit as to Mr. Bailly's character signed by Mr. Robert Stuart of the Northwest

Company and five other members of the company: William Mc-Gillivray, Thomas Thain, Aeneas Cameron, Charles Chaboillez, and Kenneth Mackenzie:

"This is to certify that Joseph Bailly has always proved himself honest, honourable and trustworthy, to the highest degree, in all his dealings with us. We can find no flaw anywhere in his personal or business record."

Joseph then requested the orderly to summon Colonel John Anderson, on leave from campaign duty, who was duly sworn in and questioned by Major Kittle:

"You resided, as I understand it, Colonel Anderson, at French-town at the River Raisin at the time of the massacre there?"

"Yes, sir."

"Was Mr. Joseph Bailly there at the time?"

"No, sir. He was not."

"Are you sure of that?"

"I'm sure, Your Honor. He always came to see us at our house whenever he made a trading visit. And he didn't come that autumn or winter at all."

"He couldn't have been at the British camp?"

"Why, no, sir! He had no ax to grind. He was always as friendly to the Americans as he was to the British. French Canadian. Absolutely neutral. Bailly's a trader, not a soldier."

"He couldn't have stirred up the Indians to that massacre?"

"Why, no, sir! That's absurd. It was the British who let the Indians do as they pleased. Joseph Bailly had no more to do with it than I had. I know all that went on in the British camp, through my friend, General Winchester."

"Very well. Was Mr. Bailly a friend of some of those Indians at the Raisin?"

"Why, we traders all know those Indian leaders. I know them just as well as Bailly knows them."

Joseph passed a note to the judge advocate, asking the privilege of putting a question. Permission granted, Joseph asked:

"Colonel Anderson, will you please tell the court how it came about that I gave a bag of gold to Chief Blackbird to carry to Arbre Croche? The whole story, please."

John Anderson began at the beginning, then, and told the story of Marie Lefèvre, of the Lefèvre aunt and uncle, the bag of gold dropped on the snowy ground on the night of the massacre, the murder of the Lefèvres by Chief Blackbird, and Anderson's own part in conveying the gold to Marie and Joseph who, in turn, conveyed their share, through Blackbird, to Marie's mother at Arbre Croche. At only one point did Anderson alter his story; and Joseph smiled, with an inward smile, at one more manifestation of human vanity. For Anderson did not sketch himself as he had done to Joseph; in all honesty, as working backward like a crab horizontally into the crevice of a shed but as standing, with vertical military dignity, in the shadow of the building. The court listened, in thrilled silence, to Anderson's simple, stark narrative. The explanation of the giving of the bag of coin to Chief Blackbird sank in, with full force.

For his next to the last witness, Joseph summoned Edward Biddle, who, to his great joy, had arrived unexpectedly that very morning. Biddle made an instant impression, with his handsome face and figure, sartorial elegance, straightforward speaking. He was eager to help Joseph, not only for Joseph's own sake but for the sake of Agatha Bailly, for whom he was already making almost as many journeys on snowshoes or dog sled to Arbre Croche as Joseph had once made by canoe to visit Marie Lefèvre during a summer of long ago.

After the formalities of the oath, Major Kittle, consulting the notes given him by Joseph, asked:

"Mr. Biddle, you were on Mackinac Island at the time of its capture by the British on July 17, 1812?"

"Yes, I was, Your Honor."

"Did you see Joseph Bailly on that day?"

"I did indeed, Your Honor. I knocked on his door as soon as I learned of the situation, at about half past eight on the morning of July 17, to notify him and his family of the attack."

"You found Mr. Bailly at home?"

"Yes indeed, Your Honor."

"Did he seem surprised at your news?"

"Yes, sir, very much surprised. He thanked me for telling him about the situation."

"Was it known that he helped the British in any way at that time?"

"Helped the *British*, sir? On the contrary, Your Honor. It is a well known fact that Mr. and Mrs. Joseph Bailly were responsible, through the signals that they gave to the Indians from the grassy plat near the fort, and through their talks with several Indian leaders in the British encampment, later, for preventing a general massacre of the Americans by the Indians on that dangerous day! Every American on Mackinac Island knows to whom he owes his life since the seventeenth day of July, 1812!"

Sudden, deafening applause swept the courtroom. Edward Biddle retired, there being no further questions, and Joseph summoned his last witness, who had come by Ohio River boat and then by stagecoach all the way from Louisville, Kentucky—not at Joseph's behest, for he had not thought of summoning her, but because (through Rebecca Heald, who was living with her father at Louisville while Major Heald was away at the war) she had heard of Joseph's court-martial and longed to repay the debt she owed him. Rebecca would willingly have come with her, had she not been about to give birth to her second child.

The woman who preceded the orderly from the witness room and came and stood at the judge advocate's table was thin, with a pretty mouth, pale cheeks, large, serious eyes, and masses of beautiful, golden hair billowing under a dove-gray, flowered bonnet. Her suit was a gray cloth edged with black braid, simple, but dignified. She carried a gray cloth muff. She nodded her head slightly in response to the judge advocate's query as to her name:

"Mrs. Simmons? Of Crescent Hill, near Louisville, Kentucky? Widow of Lieutenant John Simmons?"

"Yes, Your Honor."

"I am sorry to have to recall painful scenes to your mind, Mrs. Simmons. But would you tell us, please, whether you know who was responsible for the death of your husband at the Fort Dearborn massacre?"

"Yes, Your Honor, I do know." Mrs. Simmons' low voice vibrated distinctly to the end of the deathly-still courtroom. "It was an Ottawa medicine man, by the name of Neoma de la Vigne!"

"And your child? I am so sorry, Mrs. Simmons."

Mrs. Simmons paused a moment, then answered, less audibly: "A Potawatomi named Shavehead."

"Do you happen to know who was responsible for the death of William Wells? Did you happen to see him meet his death?"

"I did not see it, Your Honor; but I have talked of the incident many times with the niece of Captain Wells, Mrs. Nathan Heald. She was close to her uncle all during the massacre. He was scalped by Neoma de la Vigne—who also—cut out—his heart—and ate it—"

Again a deep murmur went over the courtroom.

"Did you see Mr. Joseph Bailly at the battle?"

"Why, no, Your Honor. Mr. Bailly was not at the battle at all. Mr. Bailly was at Mackinac Island." Mrs. Simmons' voice rose from its low pitch to a challenging distinctness and resonance. "And Mr. Bailly was at Mackinac Island *five months later*, when I was dragged there by my Indian captors, with my starving baby in my arms. It was Mr. Bailly who came down to the snowy beach and dickered with my captors and purchased me from them and took me to his home and, with his good wife, saved my life and the life of my only remaining child. He had *nothing* to gain by such an act. He merely proved that he is one of the kindest men that ever lived. . . . I have come three hundred miles to testify to the goodness, the kindness of Joseph Bailly. If this earthly tribunal unjustly condemns him, I know that before the tribunal of God he will stand guiltless—God bless him—" She broke down and wept.

The orderly was about to lead her back into the witness room when Joseph suddenly leaned forward and asked the judge advocate for permission to ask a question.

"Ask your question, Mr. Bailly."

"Mrs. Simmons, do you happen to remember what month and what day it was when I—when you—saw me on the beach of Mackinac Island—"

"Let me see. It was January. Wait a minute. . . . Yes, I remember exactly—for it was the day that my baby was one year old. It was January 22, 1813."

"January 22, 1813," Joseph repeated, and waited for the date to sink into the minds of jurors and spectators.

Abruptly, from the back of the room, Jacques Beaugrand cried out:

"Merciful God! The day of the Raisin River massacre!"

The judge advocate cleared his throat.

"Well, well! You have apparently successfully disproved Mr. Bailly's presence at the River Raisin massacre, Mrs. Simmons. Thank you. That will be all. . . . And now, Mr. Bailly, is there anything that you yourself wish to add in your defense?"

"Thank you, Your Honor. . . . Mr. President, Your Honor the judge advocate, and gentlemen of the court: It hardly seems necessary to offer any further refutation of such absurdities as these accusations that have been brought forward today by a highly prejudiced rival fur trader of twenty years' active hostility who has attempted, by these final stratagems, to take over all of my trading grounds. Believing that truth will prevail, I prefer to state quite simply that, throughout all the recent disturbances, I have remained a fur trader and a neutral, that I have taken no active part whatsoever in any of the enterprises connected with the war, that I have remained a British citizen because I happen to have been born a British citizen at Quebec, but that, as I have said before, I have every hope of becoming an American citizen.

"May I point out that the first article of the charge, accusing me of participation in the attack on Mackinac Island, was disproved by Major Nathan Heald and Mr. Edward Biddle; the second article, accusing me of participation in the Fort Dearborn massacre, was handled by Mr. John Kinzie and Mrs. Simmons; the third, with regard to the general 'stirring up' of the Indians, is too vague to have deserved admission to consideration; the fourth, concerning the Raisin River massacre, was refuted by Colonel John Anderson and Mrs. Simmons; the fifth, concerning Chief Blackbird's interview with me on Mackinac Island, by Colonel Anderson; and the seventh, charging me with possessing no license, by *the discovery of the license*"—here Joseph flashed a look at Corinne. "The ninth, denouncing me as a dangerous enemy, is again too vague and preposterous to consider. As for the eighth charge, that I resisted arrest, I admit that I exercised my right to ask the reason for the detention, but that, in spite of the fact that my wife was cruelly torn from me and left unprotected in the wilderness, in a delicate condition, *with child*, I followed, almost immediately and with obedience, the officers making the arrest. As for the sixth charge, concerning the guns at Grand River, I appropriated six guns illegally distributed to the Indians on my own trading grounds by Monsieur Maurice Rastel and gave out two in payment for future deposits of fur as could be attested by Jean Baptiste Beaubien, whose brother, Monsieur Antoine Beaubien, is in the room."

"Oui, oui, c'est vrai! That's true!" cried Antoine, getting up excitedly. "My brother wrote me all about it in a letter. And that letter—it is here."

An orderly went to get the letter and handed it to the judge advocate.

"Proceed, Mr. Bailly," said Major Kittle.

"Apropos of letters," continued Joseph, "may I suggest that the members of the court be so good as to compare the handwriting of the letters submitted by Monsieur Rastel, and supposedly written by me, with my actual handwriting as submitted by me on the respondent's answer filed with the judge advocate six weeks ago, —and also with the handwriting of Mr. Abijah Hull."

"May I also point out that several of these accusations refer to supposed occurrences of more than two years ago, contrary to the statute of limitations and the eighty-eighth Article of War: 'No person shall be liable to be tried by court-martial for any offense whch shall appear to have been committed more than two years before the issuing of the order for such trial.'

"May I also point out that my esteemed accuser has failed to enumerate my machinations at Fort Harrison, at the Pigeon Roost massacre, and at the battle of Lake Erie, in the present war; at General Harmar's defeat twenty-five years ago, General St. Clair's twenty-four years ago—and in Pontiac's conspiracy *fifty-two years ago!*"

Joseph's booming laughter rang out with the general laughter that swept the room after so much tense solemnity. Even the stiff-mouthed jurors had a twitching at the corners of the mouth or suddenly had to pull handkerchiefs out of their pockets. In the midst of the merriment, Joseph sat down.

All his friends continued to chuckle, for they felt that Joseph's amiable attitude had saved his neck. Corinne's cheeks were bright crimson, and her eyes were on Joseph.

When the laughter had subsided, the judge advocate gathered up his papers and gave a solemn and careful recapitulation of the material presented by accuser and accused. It would have been impossible to tell from this evenly accented survey just where the sympathies of this judge, this incarnation of abstract justice, lay. When all the material had been sifted and re-presented, the judge advocate ordered the courtroom to be cleared. The defendant, prosecutor, and lawyer retired into the witness room, under guard. The spectators filed out and distributed themselves along the corridors outside, to await recall for the verdict.

A half-hour had passed when a guard opened the door of the courtroom and rang a town crier's bell, to reassemble the crowd. Just as the spectators had settled themselves for a verdict and the judge advocate was about to rise from his place, a soldier loudly demanded entrance of the guard at the door.

"State your business. Important case being considered," said the guard.

"This is more important, my man, than any ten thousand cases put together! I have an urgent dispatch from Washington relayed by Commander Butler, for Major Kittle!"

"Pass!"

As the soldier hurried down the aisle, he was seen to be gray with the dust of long travel, from cap to boots. He reached the jurors' table, saluted, and handed Major Kittle a dispatch. The major broke the seal, read the dispatch, and placed it on the table with no change of expression. Then he asked Joseph to rise.

"Mr. Joseph Bailly, the court having considered the charges and specifications preferred against you and the evidence adduced by the judge advocate in support thereof and also the answer and evidence furnished by you, do adjudge you, *on the whole count,* Mr. Joseph Bailly—Not guilty! . . . Silence! Silence! Silence in the court!

"Rise, Mr. Maurice Rastel!

"The court, having considered the charges and specifications preferred by you against Mr. Joseph Bailly and the doubtful testimony brought in by you and your witnesses, finds you guilty and deserving of severe censure for the 'frivolous and vexatious accusations growing out of personal ill will and animosity.' Were it not for this unexpected dispatch just received, the court would retain you for further questioning. But in view of this great news the case is dismissed, with all questions appertaining thereto."

There was not a sound in the room as the judge advocate paused for dramatic effect, turned to the document, mumbled a paragraph of it, "All prisoners of war taken on either side, as well by land as by sea, are to be restored as soon as practicable", then stood, lifted his hand and ringingly announced:

"Congress has confirmed the Treaty of Ghent! The War with Great Britain is over!"

Pandemonium!

Chapter XXV

AMERICAN PARIS

BECAUSE of complications of orders and release, it was not until the 15th of March that Joseph Bailly rode out of Detroit, with a valuable document in his coat pocket:

DETROIT, 14 MARCH, 1815.

To all Officers Acting Under the U.S.:

The bearer of this paper, Mr. Joseph Bailly (Ba-ye), a resident of Mackinac Island, has my permission to pass from this post to his residence aforesaid. Since Mr. Bailly has been in Detroit, his deportment has been altogether correct, and such as to acquire my confidence; all officers civil and military, acting under the authority of the American government will therefore respect his passport which I accord to Mr. Bailly, and permit him, not only to pass undisturbed, but if necessary yield to him their protection.

H. BUTLER,
Commandant Michigan Territory and its dependencies and the Western District of U. Canada.
To all officers of the American Government.

American flags were flying from every house in Detroit and from the mast of every ship in the river. The *Queen Charlotte*, the British man-of-war captured by Commodore Perry, was almost entirely concealed by banners and was continually surrounded with excited throngs. Joseph accepted the rejoicing but could not enjoy the banners derisive of England which flew from a few windows: "Goodbye, you Bloody Backs!" "Britannia rules—the Graves!" "Crawl—you Lobsters!" "Britannia, Bite the Dust!"

A great Pacification Ball was to take place at Woodworth's Hotel in a few days, but Joseph did not care to stay for any such dubious rejoicing. He hurried, as fast as he could board a sailing vessel (now that the lakes were free of the smoke of war), for Mackinac Island. Arriving there the 5th of April, finding his house

334

closed, and hearing from the Indians that the Wing Woman was still at Arbre Croche, he took a canoe and paddled through the Straits and around to the Crooked Tree.

Beaching the canoe, he asked the first Indian he encountered about Marie.

"Wing Woman? She been very sick. Better now. Got baby."

"Is it a boy? Is it a boy?" asked Joseph, shouting the question, seizing the startled young Indian by the shoulders.

"Boy? Don't know. Just come back maple-sugaring trip. Don't know. Who you?"

"Don't you know me, Ke-po-tah? I'm the boy's father!" cried Joseph, running up the dune slope, a meter at a step.

He scarcely took time to greet the Indians he knew, as he rushed like a great whirlwind through the village. The Indians, in their turn, hardly recognized him, so gaunt had he become, so hollow of cheek, so thin of arm. Only his red-gold hair under the beaver cap betrayed him, and a few Indians set up the shout: "Monami Bailly is here! Monami Bailly's come home! The Wing Woman's 'brave'!"

No Marie came running to greet him. Joseph pushed on to Madame Lefèvre's cabin. Outside, two little girls were playing with stick-and-cloth dolls.

"Rose! Esther! My darlings!" cried Joseph, lifting four-year-old Esther off the ground, and up into the air, above his shoulders.

The only response was a burst of tears and shrieks from Esther and the flight of Rose into the house.

"Don't you know me, little Esther?"

"Bad man, let me down, let me down!"

Joseph, astonished, released the child. Immediately Agatha and Thérèse appeared in the doorway. Their recognition was instant.

"Papa! Papa! Oh, Maman, Papa's come home!"

Joseph gave them each a quick hug and hurried into the house. Marie lay on a low couch in one of the inner rooms. Her pale face and the deep shadows under her eyes were accentuated by the two thick braids drawn down close to her cheeks, over either shoulder. Beside her, on the deerskin roll which served for a pillow, lay a baby. But Joseph turned to his wife.

"Oh, Marie, my darling! How are you? How are you?"

"Almost well! And you, Joseph—so *thin!*"

"Oh, never mind! That's soon thickened! My darling!"

After they had clung to each other for the greeting, Joseph lifted his head and turned towards the baby:

"And this, *this is our son!*"

Marie's eyes opened very wide.

"Son, Joseph? No, Joseph. God has given us another daughter."

Joseph sank on his knees beside the couch and hid the grief of his face from Marie. When he had sufficiently composed himself, he said, with a trace of resentment towards the Almighty Apportioner: "It's devilish hard, sometimes, to say, 'God's will be done.'"

"Say it, Joseph."

"'God's will be done.'"

"Is she not a beautiful baby?"

Joseph looked down on the homeliest, yellowest infant he had ever seen. She had an odd up-slant of the right eyebrow. The only assets seemed to be the black, curly hair, already luxuriant at the age of two weeks, and the large, expressive, dark eyes.

"Beautiful hair, hasn't it?" commented Joseph.

Marie noted Joseph's struggle for tribute and looked up with a reproving smile.

"She'il probably be the beauty of the family."

"Oh, no, Marie, no matter how many daughters you give me, dozens and *dozens* of them, *you* will remain—the beauty of the family!"

There were many things for Joseph and Marie to discuss—all their past adventures, all their future plans; but Joseph waited for several weeks, until Marie was almost herself again, before he opened up the really practical aspect of the future. To their awed surprise, they discovered that they had both made, under the stress of misfortune, identical vows. They decided that the Calumet region, upon which they had already set their hearts, would eventually be the very best place in which to carry out their plans for Indian welfare, as well as to continue the independent fur-trading business. But Joseph would not consider going until Marie should have recovered her former strength.

In the meantime, it would be necessary for Joseph to visit all of his establishments. In his six months' absence, with the British and American troubles sweeping over the whole Northwest, it was inevitable that his trade should have suffered. He decided, moreover, that the time had come for him to visit New Orleans and to study the question of extending his operations in that direction.

As soon as he could leave without undue anxiety, Joseph set out on his journey of survey. August found him floating down the Wabash from Vincennes on a flatboat which carried dried venison hams, corn, flour and a few passengers to New Orleans. Six flatboats traveled together, for protection against the river pirates farther south.

Joseph was as excited as a boy over this first visit to the "Paris of the south." When the boat slipped into the Ohio, the scope of the adventure widened with the river, for here were more vessels than he had ever seen on the Detroit River and the lakes, all released by the termination of the war, and moving southward in an almost steady fleet: flatboats, sailing vessels, Indian pirogues, dugouts, and two of those amazing new contraptions with the constant eruptions of smoke and noise—steamboats.

The Mississippi was all that Joseph had imagined it to be, in its broad reality and in its vast vistas of suggestion. He had read sufficiently under the tutelage of the priests in Quebec, under the instruction of his own mother, and later by himself, to know something of the historic events that had taken place along the Great Waterway, and to remember the explorations of some of his French predecessors. The shore of Arkansas, particularly, suggested to his mind Marquette and Joliet, who had turned back from their great exploration at the junction of the Arkansas River and the Mississippi, and La Salle, who, somewhere inland near that same Arkansas River, had come to the end of his stupendous dreams. No one on the flatboat had ever heard of any of these Frenchmen, and, after putting out a few conversational feelers, Joseph relapsed into the more popular talk of river traffic, steamboats, and northern and Southern produce. The boat was operated by Yankees, and the three other passengers were Yankees.

"No wonder they get ahead so fast!" thought Joseph. "They think, talk, eat, breathe, and walk business! There's not one minute left for thinking of the past. There *is* no past for them. There's *only* the future!"

As the boat slipped by Baton Rouge, Joseph was all attention, for he had held in the back of his mind for ten years the pointer that Joseph Campeau had given him on the night that Detroit had burned to the ground: "Baton Rouge—that's the place for your post, Joseph: just above New Orleans; high ground; on the river; Indian settlements; Indian trails crossing. Make your fortune there."

"Not much of a place to look at from here," thought Joseph. "But Campeau probably knew what he was talking about."

The little village was situated on an elevated plateau above the river and consisted of a small fort, a little, close-crowded settlement of some sixty cabins adjoining the fort and six or eight frame houses, on ribbon farms, on either side along the river. Thick woods surrounded the clearing. There was a rough cart path leading down to the river and a small wharf. Willow bushes and feathery grasses leaned over the water, and a few live oaks trailed their silver moss in the stream. There were other southern trees that Joseph failed to recognize but with which he was to become well acquainted later, the magnolias, glossy and rich now with their clusters of maroon berries, the feathery locust trees, the silvery myrtle. From the shore, the song of the mockingbird could be distinctly heard above the ripple of water and the talk of the Yankees. Joseph had to admit that Nature had done well by the place. Perhaps the very fact that the village was small left him opportunities to develop a post there. But his heart was set towards New Orleans. It was like going to Paris! *There* was the field for his endeavor! A trader at New Orleans: what could be more wonderful, more desirable, than that?

It required another day to reach New Orleans, eighty-three miles farther down the river. The vegetation became even more subtropical at every turn of the river. Unrecognizable trees. Brilliant berries. Dazzling autumn flowers. Birds brighter than the Carolina parrakeets flying from nameless tree to tree.

The flatboat landing at New Orleans, just off the Tchoupitoulas Road, was even more bustling than Joseph had expected it to be. It took a long time to find a berth for docking. There were countless sailboats at anchor, fifteen hundred flatboats, and five hundred barges wedged along the banks. Negroes stripped to the waist were unloading cargoes of bananas from Santo Domingo. Yankees were hauling off their freight of corn and furs from the North. Frenchmen, Spaniards, Cubans, Indians, flatboat men, trappers mingled in a great, noisy, parroty throng. Commands—curses—laughter—confusion.

Joseph took his portmanteau and decided to walk into town. At Quebec, he would have hired a boy to carry it and show him the way, but he was so full of excitement and curiosity that he did not wish to be bothered even by a servant. He walked zestfully along the Tchoupitoulas Road above the river bank, towards the old city. As he approached, he saw men at work demolishing the city walls in a great cloud of dust, and other men dumping dirt into a canal just outside the ramparts.

"It's certainly a growing city!" remarked Joseph approvingly to himself.

Aloud, he accosted two elderly Frenchmen who had paused to chat together on the embankment.

"Pardon, messieurs, but will you tell a stranger where he may find good lodgings in your town?"

"Certainly, sir. At Maspero's Exchange or the Hôtel des Étrangers on Chartres Street. There are dozens of other places, of course, but those two are hotels run by Frenchmen in the heart of the old city. But perhaps you like *new* things—hotels run by damned Yankees, for instance?"

Joseph laughed. "Oh, not necessarily! The Yankees are apt to do everything up in fine style, but I'll take the French hotel this time. Is it the Yankees who are tearing up your city yonder?"

"Yes. It is, by Heaven! Ruining everything. They've come down here like a plague of locusts, or rather, like a stampede of wild horses, since the Cession, and now Jackson's victory!"

"Yes. It's the end of everything," said the other old fellow. "Why, twelve years ago, there were only about eight thousand peaceful souls in New Orleans. Now look at it: *thirty-three* thousand! Six thousand flatboatmen in the city at one time! Why, you can't move! And now they're tearing down our beautiful old walls, leveling the Fort, filling up the old canals. It's outr-r-rageous! It's wicked. It's blasphemous!"

The old man's voice quavered.

"Yes," added the other. "New Orleans used to be beautiful—peaceful—like the edges of Paris. But now it's hideous."

"No doubt it will be far more healthy and prosperous now," remarked Joseph, provocatively.

"Young man, you blaspheme!" The man who had called it "outr-r-rageous," raised his cane and brandished it at Joseph.

"Forgive me, messieurs! Good day!"

As Joseph, chuckling heretically to himself, started to walk away, he heard the emphatic old man address the river in a voice that still rattled:

"Well, old river, you're still running down towards the sea. The damned Yanks haven't changed your course yet—but they will, they *will!*"

Joseph walked over the half-filled canal on a temporary planking and entered the famous "Old Square" of the original city, outlined by Canal, North Rampart, Esplanade and Old Levee streets. The newest traveler from the North fell in love with the city from the first moment of setting foot in it. He hurried to the Hôtel des Etrangers, six blocks or "islands" away on Chartres Street, registered, deposited his bag, and swung out again to view the enchanted city, looking at everything with the zest of the young man that he no longer was, but that he felt himself to be to the end of his days. The utterly foreign look of the place, the out-Frenching of everything French that he had ever seen, added to the Spanish touches, delighted him beyond words—grilled windows, iron lacework, flirtatious balconies, courtyards summoning with flowers and fountains, steep gables, green shutters, palatial brick, gay stucco, stone-and-marble churches, gardens, vines, luxury cafés from which strange savors issued, shops from the "Arabian Nights," people from all the world over, a conglomerate hubbub of talk, gayety, laughter, song, street cries! This was not Paris! This was heaven!

Joseph paused in front of an armorer's shop in the Rue Royale: "Amédée Fortier—Armurier." The entirely masculine display fascinated him. There had been too many perfume shops and drapers, wig shops and pastry venders along the street. Here were muskets, swords, poniards, crossbows, pistols, and foils, old instruments of curiosity and instruments of modern defense. Joseph found himself dramatizing situations with one weapon after another wielded in his own hand—always pursuing Rastel, pinning Rastel to the wall of the shop with that gleaming, silver-hilted poniard, slashing him into fine bits with that keen Toledo blade in the corner, piercing one of his blue eyes with that little Moroccan dagger! The various guns did not interest him. They were too remote of operation. They lacked the clamorous vigor of a personal encounter.

His eyes strayed to a small perfectly shaped sword, with the silver-wrought figure of a naked boy leaning back along the curve of the handle. It must be a dwarf's sword, or—no, a child's! thought Joseph, and with the thought an unexpected pang went through him. How he would love to take that sword home to his *son!* He shrugged the thought away, set his shoulders straight, and turned from the window.

He decided that very soon he ought to begin talking to the Indians and finding out from them and from the traders all that he could learn of the fur business of the region. So, turning down St. Philip Street from the Rue Royale, he made his way to the old French Market on St. Philip and Decatur streets. For over a hundred years this particular spot had been the gathering and trading place of the Indians, the trappers, the farmers, the hunters of all colors and varieties. It stood at the end of the old two-and-a-half-mile Indian portage from Bayou St. John to the Mississippi. It had heard all kinds of talk and witnessed all kinds of swapping, plotting, fighting from Bienville's day, when the Indians merely squatted on the levee and transacted their business, to the present day when the chatter resounded loudly under the new "Halle de Bouchers."

Joseph loitered about the market for some time, unobserved but observant, watching the venders and traders of goods and deciding at last upon those whom he wished to draw into conversation. Under the shelter of the building were the numberless French, Spanish, and German farmers and their wives from all the plantations along the river. Their stalls were piled high with lemons, oranges, figs, pomegranates, bananas, sweet potatoes, almonds, pecans, pistachios, bags of sugar, rice, and tobacco, eggs and cheeses. Cotton occupied one snowy corner of the market, with negroes in bright kerchiefs presiding over the bales. Chickens, ducks, geese, and wild birds occupied another corner. Fish and oysters claimed several stalls. And the butchers themselves, for whom the building was named, spread their reeking wares over a full half of the entire space. Against one wall a few trappers leaned, laughed, and smoked, with their bales of furs, including many packs of sealskin from the distant Pacific, spread out at their feet. On the sidewalk in front, twenty or thirty Choctaw Indians sat displaying their woven baskets, their bows and arrows, their silver and bead jewelry and their pounded leaves of sassafras for seasoning, the "kombo" or "gumbo."

Joseph decided not to talk as yet to the traders. He did not wish to make them suspicious through his questions. He veered inevitably towards the Indians, wondering how best he might make an approach: through the Algonquin speech, which might carry a few sounds to their ears more familiar than any European language, or through the sign language, or through French, of which they might easily understand more than a few words. He decided that making a purchase would naturally be the best beginning, but he preferred to select a person rather than an object—an old fellow, if possible, wise in the ways of the wilderness and the world. Quite at the end of the row of Indians, he noticed just such an old fellow, with wrinkled, walnut skin and shrewd, piercing eyes. His old squaw sat beside him doing the active displaying and trading, while he remained watchful, putting in a word of advice in Choctaw at strategic moments in the bargaining.

As Joseph came and stood over them, he noted that his choice had been a wise one in every respect, for, spread out on an alligator skin in front of them were some of the loveliest pieces of semi-precious and precious jewelry that he had ever seen—far more elaborate than those offered by any other Indian, and certainly not Indian in workmanship. There were silver crucifixes set with rubies. There were gold bracelets studded with pearls, gold lockets, silver-and-pearl earrings. There was a most exquisite likeness of the Madonna on an enamel pendant hung from a heavy gold chain. Surely no shop in Paris or Madrid could offer anything lovelier than that Madonna. Joseph could not, for the life of him, understand how such treasures could have come into the hands of two Choctaw Indians. Being a good trader himself, he did not at once indicate the Madonna, but pointed to one of the crucifixes and asked, by a shrug and raised eyebrows, "How much?" The squaw mumbled something that Joseph did not quite catch, and he was ready enough to turn with his question to the old man.

"She say cinq francs," said the Choctaw in a broken but understandable French.

"And this?" asked Joseph in French, delighted that the conversation could be carried on in something besides gestures, pointing to a small, undistinguished silver necklace.

"Un peso," momentarily returning to the not so long vanished Spanish regime and coinage.

"And this?"—indicating the Madonna indifferently.

"She say five dollar. She very beautiful."

A third coinage! How confused things were down here still, in spite of the Americans! Well, everything would be dollars and cents soon, no doubt of that!

"Yes," said Joseph. "She's quite attractive. Where did she come from?"

"Qui sait? Who know?" said the squaw, shrugging and turning to her husband with a knowing smile.

All at once, the explanation flashed through Joseph's mind.

"Fruit of the sea?" He smiled disarmingly.

The two old Indians unfearingly returned the smile.

Joseph made a proposition: "You're asking far too little. I'll give you eight dollars for it!" This to serve the double purpose of easing his conscience and of rendering the old people voluble. They were, of course, his servants from that moment.

As he took the Madonna locket and put it into his wallet, he remarked, this time with an even bigger smile:

"Mon Dieu, but Monsieur Lafitte is a great artist!"

"Ah, Monsieur knows him?" asked the Choctaw.

"No. But I admire him—for many things. I should like nothing better than to meet him!"

"He has left town, monsieur."

"Again?"

"For good, monsieur. It is very sad. Great man, Lafitte. Good to Indians."

"Yes. So I see," said Joseph.

"Where you come from?"

"I come from Quebec, and Mackinac Island, up North—way, way up North. Will you smoke a pipe with me? Good northern tobacco I have."

The Indian nodded affirmatively, and Joseph sat down beside him, drew a pouch of tobacco from his pocket, and filled the old man's pipe with it. The two sat smoking for a long, long time. Joseph was in no hurry to put his questions. He knew very well the prolonged evasions of the Indian mind and the old powwow and treaty methods of beating all around the bush for days without coming down to the bush at issue. But, to his amazement, the old Choctaw himself precipitated the answer to some of Joseph's most important unasked questions:

"Montreal up North too? By Quebec? By Island of the Turtle?"

"Yes. Not far."

"I know great man, Montreal."

"Yes?"

"Yes."

"You haven't been to Montreal?"

"I? Oh, no, monsieur! I been west to setting sun, not north to Island of the Turtle."

Joseph did not care to disturb the old man by clarifying his geography. The Choctaw puffed at his pipe for a few minutes, apparently recapturing in the smoke of his pipe the drifting memories of his westward journeys. Joseph was not particularly eager to continue the Montreal association. He was more eager to learn of the fur situation here in New Orleans than of the situation which he knew so well up North. But the old Choctaw returned after a while to the subject.

"Great man Montreal here," he said.

"Um-m-m," said Joseph.

"Yes. He and Monsieur Lafitte great friends. One he Chief of the Sea. Other he Chief of the Bayous!"

"Mon Dieu! *What's his name?*" asked Joseph suddenly.

The old Indian watched him closely, as he answered:

"He Monsieur le Marquis Maurice Rastel."

Joseph never had greater need of controlling himself.

"Oh!" he said, shrugging his shoulders and recovering his pipe, which had fallen to the ground. "Yes, I believe I *have* heard of him up North. What does he do down here?"

"Do? He Big Man of the Furs. Used to be four, five other traders down here. He wipe them all out—like *that!*" The old man crushed a passing spider with the heel of his moccasin. "All trappers work for Big Him now."

"Yes. He and Lafitte *must* have been *good* friends," muttered Joseph, rising to his feet and brushing the New Orleans dust from his trousers. "I must be going now, but I'll come and smoke with you again some day."

"Your name, monsieur? You did not tell old Chenko the name."

Joseph thought quickly.

"My name," he said, "is Monami d'Artois."

"Goodbye, Monsieur d'Artois. Come again, and buy some more —what you say?—more fruit of the sea!"

Joseph strode away without ever pausing to chat with Rastel's trappers in the Halle de Bouchers. His fury mounted with each step. The universal wolf again! Strange that, on so huge a continent, he must always be running into Rastel. Uncanny! Except that their ambitions were identical. Well, that seemed to finish his plans for New Orleans. He certainly wasn't going to do to Rastel what Rastel had done to him—poach on his grounds. He was enough of a fighter to want to stay and drive Rastel out by his own shrewdness, but the strong moral streak from his mother denied the fighting blood, in this particular instance. He must go out and find his own independent field—not like a whipped dog with his tail between his legs but like the heads-up explorers of the old Northwest Company, Alexander Mackenzie and Duncan M'Dougal and Ramsey Crooks and Robert Stuart faring forth to new and untouched fields. He went down to the wharf and dickered for a place on a flatboat going up the river the next day.

It was twice as slow a journey going up, for poling against the current was a backbreaking job. Ten miles a day was the average. In eleven tedious days Joseph was again at the little settlement of Baton Rouge. Of the two inns, he chose Madame Le Gendre's— a neat whitewashed cabin close to the river bank, where such delicious meals were served and such good wines set out that it had long since become a meeting place for fashionable plantation owners from miles around. This suited Joseph's purpose exactly. The very first night, he made some acquaintanceships that were to become lasting.

He was quietly drinking his white wine and eating his broiled red snappers with their delicious French sauce, when the plantation owners began to drift in, a group that ate, drank, made merry and played euchre at Madame Le Gendre's every Saturday night. For a long time Joseph watched them quietly, before making any move. He ate slowly, pretending at intervals to read the latest issue of the *Moniteur de Louisiane;* but every moment he listened, and every other moment he watched over the rim of his paper until he knew the name, the nature, the interests, and the attitude of every man there.

Of the eight men, five drew his interest particularly, for they were the most interesting-looking and the most voluble of the group. The oldest was a gentleman who looked as if he had just stepped out of the court of Louis XV, for he deferred not a bit to modern styles. He still wore the powdered wig, the buckled knee breeches, the flowered waistcoat, the lace sleeves of his father's day, and he pinched his snuff with elegance. But he was obviously more than a fop. He was keenly interested in crops, slaves, commerce, and all that directly or indirectly touched the prosperity of a plantation. His name was De Boré. He appeared to be well along towards seventy years of age, but the others ranged between forty and fifty-five. One, whose first name was Léon and whose last, infrequently used, seemed to be Bonnecaze, apparently held some official position. He was dark and thick of hair as a Spaniard and held his shoulders back with considerable dignity. Even more aware of his importance was Alexander Cousso, who wore a starry order on his breast, had a booming voice, and jammed a four-inch-thick chunk of French bread into his mouth all at once, with gigantic impressiveness. Dr. Lanzin, a sharp, quizzical little man with spectacles, given to rubbing his hands together with a frequent, apologetic gesture, was the complete antithesis of Cousso.

Joseph liked best the Conte de Duplantier, who was full of laughter, full of witticisms that stopped just this side of malice, and who loved his wines as unashamedly as Pierre Desnoyers and Peter Navarre of Detroit. There were six different bottles in front of him before the second course was over.

"Come, Lanzin, another glass!" urged Duplantier. "It won't do you a bit of harm!"

"Oh, yes, it will, Duplantier. It will do you harm, too, mark my words! You should see what it does to the liver, my boy! Shrivels it up like a dried fungus!" Dr. Lanzin bunched his claw-fingers together illustratively.

"Listen to the doctor, will you? Come, doctor, this isn't a death house. This is a tavern! Cheer up! What's the matter with you tonight?"

"Well, I was trying to postpone the news, but since you ask me, there *is* something the matter. I don't want to spoil the party. But have any of you seen the papers brought in from Europe three days ago, on the *Star of the Sea?* I was in New Orleans. Galloped home in two days. Just got in today. When did you leave the city, De Boré?"

"Oh, I've been here for five days now. My news from Europe is a month old. Let's have it, Lanzin, let's have it!"

"Well, it concerns Napoleon!"

"Good God, what's happened? A month ago, we heard he defeated Blücher at Ligny! A great victory! What happened?"

"Well, two days later he was—he was—*defeated* by the Duke of Wellington at a place called Waterloo!"

A little chorus of "Mon Dieu!" quavered in the air, and every hand was still. Eating, drinking, laughing, almost breathing, were suspended. Joseph dropped his paper, which did not yet carry the news, and frankly looked and listened.

"Yes," continued Dr. Lanzin, "but that isn't the worst of it, mes amis. That isn't the worst of it. The great Napoleon has been sentenced by the British to some terrible island called St. Helena. C'est fini, mes amis. It is finished."

"My God! What will become of *me?*" exclaimed Bonnecaze. "Have the British taken over France? What kind of government has been set up?"

"Nobody seems to know exactly. But Britain certainly hasn't taken over France. It's time for Louis to come back, and he probably will!"

"But where *is* this island of St. Helena?" asked Duplantier.

"I looked it up in an old atlas of mine as soon as I got home," said Lanzin. "A little speck of a place way off in the Atlantic Ocean about a thousand miles west of Angola, Africa. Nothing else near it. The English have certainly fixed it so that Napoleon can't get away!"

"Here!" exclaimed De Boré, the old-time Royalist, raising his glass of white wine. "Here's to Louis XVIII! May he come back, and all good things with him! Vive le roi!"

Though the group smiled benevolently, no one joined the toast to the old regime.

"To Napoleon! To Napoleon!" shouted the youngest member of the party, Duplantier. "To Napoleon! To Napoleon!" echoed around the table, as glasses were clinked.

Joseph, across the way, also lifted his glass. It only needed Campeau's parrot, he thought, to duplicate that other scene of old French fervor, far north, at the edge of the great lake! ten years before, on the night of the Detroit fire.

Monsieur de Boré and Monsieur Duplantier both noticed Joseph's lifting of his glass. Monsieur de Boré said something in a low voice to the other gentlemen, then addressed Joseph:

"Won't you join us, monsieur? You seem to be in accord with— some of us." The merry crinkles at the edges of his eyes reminded Joseph of Father Richard.

"Gladly indeed, monsieur."

A chair was drawn up for Joseph, and presentations were made all around.

"Are you a gentleman of leisure, monsieur, or are you engaged in some business or other?" asked De Boré.

"I'm a fur trader from Mackinac Island, monsieur, with posts as far south as Vincennes."

"Fur trader? Good! Then you've come to take over old Jacques Jombeau's post?"

"Jacques Jombeau's post? I know nothing of the situation here, sir. I merely came to find out what I could about possibilities here."

"You've come in the nick of time, monsieur. Old Jacques Jombeau died last month. He had a fair business here, but I always thought a younger man could do better. But old Jacques was much loved around here. No one would have allowed any outsider to step in and take old Jacques's trade away from him. But he's dead and he's left no heirs. You'd better step in, Monsieur, and get things started before a certain trader down at New Orleans gets wind of the fact that old Jacques is dead."

"I will, monsieur. I *will!*" declared Joseph with an emphasis that was startling.

"Good!"

"Heard a queer story about that trader in New Orleans the other day," said Dr. Lanzin. "Dr. Antommarchi told me. Seems the fellow gets more jealous of that beautiful wife of his all the time. Stopped her nursing of the American soldiers, during Jackson's siege last year. She'd turned the house into a hospital, you know."

"Sorry to be suspicious, but I was always a bit doubtful of her motives there," remarked Alexander Cousso. "She's the kind of a woman who wants a houseful of men, don't you think? Any kind of men, invalids or healthy ones, maimed or unmaimed, all the time, eh, n'est-ce pas?" and he enjoyed a gust of unvirtuous laughter.

"Why, the young man's blushing!" exclaimed Bonnecaze, looking at Joseph's flaming cheeks. "Come, Cousso! You mustn't talk of the ladies like that. The young man is gallant. He'll be after you with the sword." (Apparently, to these middle-aged men sturdy Joseph still seemed young.)

"Besides," suggested De Boré benevolently, "Madame Rastel may have undergone a change of heart. She may also have real kindness. She's certainly suffered enough with that husband of hers. But what was your story, Dr. Lanzin?"

"Well, it seems Monsieur Rastel challenged a young American to a duel the other day. Found the American coming out of his house. The young fellow claimed he'd merely gone to sell Madame Rastel some woolen blankets, woven up in Massachusetts. Had a portmanteau or samples with him, in fact."

"Did you say blankets? *Blankets!*" Cousso indulged in another spasm of inexplicable laughter.

"Blankets, Cousso, blankets! Well, the young American says this dueling is a foolish business, all right, but he can handle a gun as well as anybody. Rastel, reversing the rights of the challenger and the challenged, insists on foils. Very well, says the Yankee, he'll pink the life out of Rastel! They go out to the Dueling Oaks. The young American gives Rastel a devil of a swipe across the cheek. Rastel merely flicks the young fellow's ear. The fight is over. But in an hour the young American is dead."

"Dead?"

"Yes. Dr. Antommarchi told me he performed the autopsy himself. The young man died of poison. The foil tip had undoubtedly been poisoned. Scarcely honorable, you know! Devil of a scandal!"

"Well! How will Rastel live *that* down?"

"As he does everything else. He tried to bribe Antommarchi not to tell. Offered him a thousand pounds, I mean five thousand dollars. Antommarchi wouldn't take the bribe, of course. But the newspapers will. And if the story *does* get out, why, all the Rastels have to do is to give another dinner and ball at their house, the grandest party since the days when the Duke of Orléans himself was entertained in the city—and all Rastel's sins will again be forgiven and forgotten. A charming couple!"

"You have to admit they're clever as the devil, and that she's still a raving beauty at— How old do you suppose she is? Certainly thirty-five. Rastel first came down here eighteen years ago, I distinctly remember."

"Oh, she's the age of all enchantresses at the time of their greatest victories—Cleopatra, Helen of Troy, Diane de Poitiers, Ninon de l'Enclos—forty exactly!" declared Bonnecaze.

"Forty-one!" said Joseph, to the astonishment of everyone, including himself.

"How do *you* know, young man?"

All eyes glittered upon him.

"Well, you see," said Joseph, trying desperately to appear casual, "I met her in Quebec twenty-one years ago. Her uncle told my father at that time that she was twenty."

"I'll bet *you* flirted with her!" declared Cousso.

"Oh, we all did," said Joseph, with a shrug. "But I went away to the Pays d'en Haut soon afterwards. That's how I became interested in the fur trade. Now, about this post of Jacques Jombeau's . . ."

Chapter XXVI

THE WHOLE CYCLE

It was two years after the visit to New Orleans. Things were going fairly well for Joseph Bailly. All of his posts were prosperous, from Arbre Croche to Baton Rouge. The beaver and other furred creatures would never be as plentiful as they had been when he started out at Parc aux Vaches fifteen years before, but there were still enough to keep the traps crunching and the lake and river vessels sailing to Quebec and Montreal and New Orleans with cargo for Marseilles and Liverpool and St. Petersburg. The quality of the fur had been prime, as a result of the phenomenal cold of the previous year—frost in every month: the year referred to not as 1816 but as "eighteen-hundred-and-freeze-to-death." In 1816 also, Joseph had become a naturalized American citizen. This not only was a shrewd business step (for, as it happened, that very year saw the enacting of a law excluding foreigners from the fur trade in the United States), but was honorably in accord with his American sympathies and progressiveness, although the very deepest heart of him would probably always be French. The American Fur Company under John Jacob Astor had bought out all the other companies, and Joseph continued, as an independent trader, under its auspices. His headquarters were still at Mackinac Island, for it had taken Marie over a year to recover from the bitter journey to Wisconsin, and now that she was expecting her sixth child it seemed unwise to make the change until she and the child were strong enough to brave another frontier.

Joseph sat in front of his hearth on Mackinac Island late on the last afternoon in November, 1817. He was trying to concentrate on the issue of November 21st of the *Detroit Gazette*, which had been brought in by schooner the day before. It was hard for Joseph to keep his mind on the paper, for Thérèse was playing a game of dolls with Lucille at the other end of the room and, up-

351

stairs, Marie was already in labor. Surgeon William Beaumont of the fort was in attendance, and had summarily dismissed Joseph from the room an hour before. Edward Biddle had taken Esther and Rose to the beach for a sunset walk. Biddle had become almost a member of the household. He was still devoted especially to Agatha, drawn to her as he had been on that very first day on the beach at Mackinac, when the Astorians were gathering and he had met Bailly for the first time, and when her remarks had made him laugh so heartily. But at present Agatha was away at school in Philadelphia.

After hours of nervousness, Joseph tried to sit back and read that strangely illegible newspaper. No use allowing that absurdly recurrent idea to slip into his mind again! Of course it would be another little girl. *Six* little girls! What would the next one be like? Certainly Thérèse and Lucille, the youngest, were as different as two sisters could possibly be. Thérèse with her pale gold hair, pale blue eyes, and ethereal expression; Lucille with her dark, curly hair, dark eyes, and amber skin. Marie loved Lucille with a desperation born of the shared difficulties of that long journey around the lake. Joseph loved her too, of course, but there was something disquieting about Lucille, something deeper even than her streak of childish malice. Even now she was saying something unpleasant:

"Don't touch Lucille' doll, Thérèse! Lucille' doll! Don't touch it!"

Always that old ogre of human possessiveness, thought Joseph: "Get off our grounds, you Nor-westers! We're the Gens de la Baie!"

"But I was only trying to arrange your doll's dress, Lucille," Thérèse was saying, in the most conciliatory way. "You mussed it, you know, when you spanked her. See how much better she looks now!"

"Lucille go get papa's hatchet."

"Come, come, Lucille!" remonstrated Joseph. "Thérèse was only trying to help you."

"Awfu' Tess! Lucille not like!"

"No, no, that's a bad thing to say, Lucille. You mustn't speak so loud, either! Mamma has gone upstairs to get you a new baby. Now won't *that* make you happy?"

"No! Don't want baby. Lucille is 'nough baby. No more baby! No!"

"Come, Lucille—I'll sing you a song," suggested Thérèse soothingly.

"Aw wi," said Lucille, quieting. "One 'bout burned baby! One 'bout burned baby!"

Thérèse flashed a disturbed glance at her father and then began to sing the required, macabre song, beginning:

> "Ah! c'était la nourrice,
> La nourrice du roi,
> Un jour s'est endormie,
> L'enfant entre ses bras.
> Dieu, aidez-moi!
> Douce Vierge Marie,
> Saint Nicolas! . . ."

All was peaceful now in the room, and Marie was making only a few low moans upstairs. Joseph tried to return to his reading: There was a conspiracy at Lisbon. Well, that wasn't particularly interesting. There were always conspiracies in Europe. . . . A sea serpent sighted off Cape Ann, New England. A marine carcajou, thought Joseph. . . . A dwarf, Peter Louvrill, of Charleston, South Carolina, who had predicted the War of 1812, now in 1817 was predicting:

1. Two prosperous years, then a nine months war with England.
2. Twenty-five years of prosperity.
3. In 1819 Bonaparte, in an extraordinary manner, will again become Emperor of France.
4. In three years the Island of Santo Domingo will sink and be swallowed up by an earthquake.

Nonsense, thought Joseph. And yet why did I read it? Because we're all superstitious, and like to believe extraordinary things. Maybe the dwarf's right, at that! Ah, here's another reference to Napoleon:

Subscriptions will be taken to aid the escape of Bonaparte.

Parbleu! I think I'll send a contribution. Yes, in the name of my newest child! It ought to be a boy. No, I mustn't think that!

Napoleon's little son, l'Aiglon, is six years old now. Joseph, you're a fool! Come, let's look at the advertisements:

Dancing Academy: Mr. Tobias respectfully informs the Ladies and Gentlemen of Detroit that his Dancing School will commence this afternoon at Mr. Whipple's Hotel.

I'd like to send my girls to that. They must all go away to school and learn to be ladies, all six of them—yes, all *six* of them!

For Sale. A Few Buffalo Robes by the Pack. Cheap. Can be seen at H. Berthelet's Esq. in Detroit.
Auction. James Abbott Auctioneer at James Abbott's Vendue Room. Groceries. Hardware. Dry Goods.
James Abbott will sell newly arrived mococks of Maple Sugar from Michilimackinac cheaply.

Joseph basked for a moment in the pleasant thought that the Abbotts were prospering. All was well with them, except for the loss of little Sarah, over which they would never cease grieving. . . . Only daughter. . . . Strange how God—or the Great Spirit or whatever you chose to call It—allotted children: the Abbotts with three sons, and the Baillys with five—*six*—daughters . . .

There was a little commotion upstairs, a thin, small cry. Joseph's heart stopped beating. In a few moments, creaking footsteps on the stairs. Dr. Beaumont, with a broad smile on his face, stood in the doorway.

"Well, Mr. Bailly," he said. "Do you want to come upstairs and meet—your son?"

"*Son?*"

"Yes, yes, Bailly! Son! What are you staring at? Can't you believe it?"

"No—I can't—" said Joseph, biting his lips, for he was afraid he was going to sob aloud. He dashed the blur from his eyes with his knuckles—followed Dr. Beaumont up the stairs.

It was a year and a half before Robert Bailly could be baptized. But the event enlarged itself to include several other baptisms and a wedding. Few such gala events had taken place on the island since the Bailly wedding eighteen years before.

The Bailly house had been extended, and the living room was now almost double the size of the original room in which Joseph and Marie had been married. There were no longer Indian mats on the floor, but instead a handsome rug from Ste. Anne de Beaupré. Gold-framed pictures of French court scenes hung on the walls. An ormolu clock from New Orleans stood on the mantel. There was a rosewood pianoforte diagonally across one corner of the room, and to the sturdy, handmade chairs of the earlier Bailly period had been added half a dozen chairs and an Empire sofa covered with French brocade. The only reminders of a rougher life preceding the later elegances were the magnificent elk's head at one end of the room, with a bow and arrow beside it, a buffalo robe folded over the arm of the brocaded couch, and the brass-handled hair trunk on the floor at one side of the fireplace. The tongs and andirons, Joseph had ordered from France. They were of brass in the fleur-de-lis design. Though the winds of Superior, Michigan, and Huron might rage outside, Joseph had created a tiny French château on the American frontier.

As the large room filled with people on that June afternoon of 1819, the furniture became gradually obscured. There were many guests who had been present at the Bailly wedding eighteen years before and many later comers to the island. Madame Laframboise was there again, and Michael Dousman, Jean Baptiste Clutier, Toussaint Pothier with his fiddle, Jacques Phylier, white-haired now, with his drum, Reaume Rouleaux and two other old voyageurs. Among the newcomers were the illustrious John Jacob Astor from New York, on an investigating visit to his establishments on the island, Ramsey Crooks of the Astorians, now representative of the American Fur Company on the island, his partner Robert Stuart, and old Uncle David Stuart, who had weathered a thousand storms from the coast of Labrador to the Pacific and could tell stories such as no other yarn-spinner in all the world could tell. Young Gurdon Hubbard, who had just signed up with the American Fur Company and was to make history at the foot of Lake Michigan as a founder of the great city of Chicago, was there; Dr. William Beaumont; Samuel Abbott, port collector and notary public and brother of James Abbott of Detroit; the Reverend David Bacon, Protestant missionary; another visiting missionary, Dr. Jedidiah Morse of Morse's Geography, and his son, Samuel Morse, who had come to the island the day before on the famous ship *Walk-in-the-Water*. Madame Lefèvre had come over from Arbre Croche, also three young Indians in their best regalia who were to receive baptism and Chief Blackbird and his son, young William, now a tall, handsome fellow of eighteen. Josette Laframboise, daughter of old Madame Laframboise and a survivor of the Fort Dearborn massacre, stood beside her new husband, Captain Benjamin K. Pierce, commandant of the fort. But, dearest presence of all to Joseph, among the guests, was Madame Geneviève Bailly de Messein, his own mother, who had come on the swiftest boat from Quebec as soon as it was learned that Father Richard would be in the vicinity of Mackinac Island in the middle of June to baptize young Robert and to perform the marriage ceremony for Agatha Bailly and Edward Biddle.

Father Richard had been moving slowly up the west coast of Michigan, visiting all the Indian settlements. Only a few days before, he had set up once again the storm-toppled cross at the mouth of the Père Marquette River that marked Marquette's first burial place. Now, the light of his good deeds past and present shining in his eyes and the merry, mundane twinkle crinkling at their corners, Father Richard stood in the Bailly parlor, exactly where Joseph and Marie had made their simple vows. An improvised altar had been placed in front of the mantelpiece, a table with a lace cover, lighted candles, the chalice, silver bowls of water and of salt, the Bible, a bell.

Now, again, Jean Baptiste Clutier cleared the path with his red toque, in a more dignified manner since almost twenty years had been added to his boisterous youth. At the piano sat Mrs. Robert Stuart, for Marie had requested that the ebullient Pothier and old Phylier should reserve their gayer melodies for the wedding. The baptism of the long awaited little son should be as solemn and dignified as possible. Mrs. Stuart began to play "Holy, Holy, Holy!" and Joseph and Marie slowly entered the room, leading between them little Robert, who had just begun to walk.

Robert's face had the delicacy of Marie's, with her pale olive complexion, but he had Joseph's deep sea-blue eyes. His wavy hair was brownish black, and his dark eyelashes were long and cast starry shadows on his cheeks. The set of his chin was reminiscent of Joseph's. But the beauty of the child lay under the surface, in the strength and sweetness of his expression, the depth of his eyes, the look of wisdom far beyond his few months. He was dressed in a white linen suit with lace collar and cuffs, and in white shoes and stockings.

Lucille, also in white except for a blue bow on top of her head, walked on her mother's left side. Her black, curling hair billowed closely about her face, a long loop of it concealing her right eyebrow. She had a sprightliness, an impudent flash of black eyes, and a grace of bearing that attracted attention.

Marie was dressed today in a French muslin dress of saffron color that harmonized with Lucille's bow. Her hair was done in a coronet about her head. Joseph was splendid in pearl-gray broadcloth, a long coat, and the new fashionable long trousers just showing the tips of the black shoes without buckles. The parents were closely followed by the godparents, Madame Laframboise in her bright Indian clothes, Samuel Abbott, Mrs. Ramsey Crooks, and Ramsey Crooks, very dignified in black broadcloth and ruffled shirt. Three Bailly daughters stood at the left of the mantelpiece with their grandmother from Quebec. Agatha, the bride, remained as yet in the other room with her prospective husband.

As the two children about to be baptized approached Father Richard, his face took on an expression even more beautiful than usual. Taking Robert into his arms, he held the child affectionately for a moment, then dipped fingers into a small, silver bowl of water on the altar table, made the sign of the cross over him, placed a bit of salt on his lips, signifying the gift of wisdom, held the lighted candle before him, representing faith, anointed him with oil on chest and back, adjured him in the beautiful Latin words: "Receive this white robe and see that thou carry it unsullied before the judgment seat of God"; and baptized him, "in the name of the Father and of the Son and of the Holy Ghost, Robert Michel Antoine Bailly." Then, bowing his head, Father Richard added, in French, a brief personal prayer:

"Robert Michel Antoine Bailly, long awaited, most welcome and well beloved child, may the great Maker of all things watch over you and make your life strong and beautiful and very good and very long. God bless you!"

Father Richard then set Robert down and laying his hand on Lucille's head, sprinkled her also with the holy water, gave her the holy salt and the oil and the light of the candle, and confirmed upon her the name given aloud by Mrs. Crooks, "Lucille Geneviève Bailly," then in French pronounced over her a simple "God bless you." Only Joseph noticed in Lucille's black eyes the flash of jealous resentment over the benediction, briefer than Robert's.

Then, in Algonquin, Father Richard asked those Indians who wished to be baptized to step forward. The three young Indians from Arbre Croche shook the floor as they majestically marched towards the hearth. All were fully clothed, as Bailly had warned them to be, two of them in calico shirt, blanket-cloth leggings, moccasins, blanket across the shoulders, turban with feathers, and many silver bracelets and ornaments, bead necklaces, and tinkling bells. The third, Sassaba, or the Count, a Chippewa chief, wore a scarlet uniform with gold epaulets and carried a sword in his belt. Captain Pierce and Mrs. Crooks, who understood neither French nor Algonquin but were both pleasing to the Indians—one on account of his splendid uniform, the other on account of her kindness in nursing sick Indians—had been chosen to stand sponsor, and presented the three young braves to Father Richard. But Father Richard chose to speak directly to the slightly bewildered Indians rather than to their sponsors.

"Well, Sassaba," asked Father Richard, first in Algonquin, then in French, "what Christian name do you wish to have bestowed upon you?"

In broken French, Sassaba replied:

"Me want Sacré Crapaud!"

"*What?*" asked Father Richard. "What *name*, Sassaba? What *name?*"

"Me want name *Sacré Crapaud!*"

"Are you trying to joke, Sassaba, to make laughter on such a solemn occasion?"

"Joke? No joke. Me want name Frenchmen say all the time! If Frenchmen say name all the time, must be *good name:* Sacré Crapaud!"

Father Richard turned towards the hearth, his shoulders shaking. The whole roomful of people began to chuckle.

Father Richard, fearing that the Indians, who were as sensitive to laughter as the palefaces, would not understand, spun around again, only a ghost of a twinkle still lurking around his eyes, and addressed Sassaba:

"You see, Sassaba, the good people are laughing because the words 'Sacré crapaud' are bad words. They are swear words of the palefaces. They mean 'cursed toad.' You are too good a man, Sassaba, to have such bad words for a name. How would Simon do? Simon is a good name. You understand, don't you, Sassaba?"

"Ye-e-es. But Simon not sound so good as 'Sacré Crapaud'! Big thunder in name 'Sacré Crapaud'! Little wood-mouse squeak in name Simon. But Sassaba do what good Father Richard say."

"All right, Sassaba. The name Simon is satisfactory to the god-parents? Very well. . . . In nomine Patris et Filii et Spiritus Sancti . . . I baptize thee Simon. . . . Amen."

When Father Richard had completed the ceremony of sprinkling and christening, he turned to Petosega.

"And you, Petosega. What name have you chosen?"

"Enfant de l'enfer!"

"I beg your pardon?"

"Me Petosega—Enfant de l'Enfer!"

Again the room shook with laughter.

"See here, my Indian friends. Is this a joke you are playing on me?"

"No. No joke. Good name! French palefaces say 'Enfant de l'enfer!' many, many times. Good name! Thunder name!"

"But that, too, my dear Petosega, is a swear word, an evil word. It means 'child of hell.' You want to be child of hell—child of Motchi Manitou?"

"No, no! Me no want."

"Very well. We'll get another name for you. How about you, Wab-she-gun? I wonder if you too have chosen paleface devil words. What name have you chosen, Wab-she-gun?"

"Me? 'Tête d'Escabeau.' That all right?"

"*That* means 'Blockhead'!"

Father Richard, this time, unashamedly, joined the general

laughter. It was impossible to remain dignified, prelatical, any longer. In a voice that shook, as he wiped the tears from his eyes, Father Richard announced:

"It is impossible, under the circumstances, to baptize the rest of you today, my good Indian friends. If you will come back to me tomorrow morning, here at Mr. Bailly's house, where I am staying, you and your sponsors, we will select good Christian names for you and I will baptize you. You will come back?"

"Yes. Yes." The Indians themselves had begun to laugh, slapping one another on the back and doubling up until their plumes shook in the wind of laughter. This was well, for anger on their part might have been a serious matter.

When they were a little subdued, in order that they might not feel cheated of all ceremony, Father Richard repeated for the three Indians the Lord's Prayer in Algonquin:

"Nossimaw Wawkwing, kitchiwa Kiaia anosowin. Ki ogimaw-win ondass, Ki inendam aia apine ogid Aki binish pindg Waw-kwing. . . ."

Then, Father Richard turned to Mrs. Stuart.

"Now, Mrs. Stuart, will you please play some good solemn Christian hymn in order to restore the religious atmosphere here, before we proceed with the wedding ceremony?"

With chuckles still sputtering in various parts of the room, Mrs. Stuart began to play "O Come All Ye Faithful." It required several verses to restore a semblance of reverence and solemnity to the group. Then the musician moved into the strains of Handel's *Largo*, and to this music Agatha entered the room on the arm of her father.

Agatha, who, all her life until she had gone away to school in Philadelphia three years before, had preferred the comfort of the Indian costume, was dressed today in the best Paris fashion, a long white muslin dress with a soft white satin sash, a white satin coronet ribbon bound about the coils of her Indian hair, and a veil of point d'Alençon lace falling over her shoulders.

Edward Biddle followed, like Joseph elegant in a long-trousered suit, buff-colored, with a buff and lavender brocaded vest and the usual snowy, ruffled shirt. Edward was a tall, brown-haired young man, with ruddy cheeks and a twinkle in his brown eyes. Even on this solemn occasion the twinkle effervesced on the surface, like bubbles on a vat of wine. Edward was very proud of his clever and beautiful wilderness bride, but he was thinking with amusement of how that eighth fraction of Indian in her blood had seemed to nettle some of the aristocratic Quaker relatives in Philadelphia. His brother Nicholas, the Philadelphia financier, had magnanimously written:

We had all hoped, my dear brother, that, after having your fling at adventure in the wilderness, you would have come back to join the ranks of civilized society. But since you seem to have cast your lot on the frontier, it would seem that you have chosen a suitable bride for the situation. Tales of Joseph Bailly's astuteness and prosperity have reached even as far as financial circles in Philadelphia. Any man who can handle a hundred thousand dollars' worth of furs annually, as an independent trader, is worthy of respect. I am also glad to note in Chazot de Montigny's *Dictionnaire Héraldique*, which I happened to see in the Harvard Library on a visit to Cambridge a few days ago, that the Bailly de Messein family is of authenticated, noble lineage. The later tincture of the American aboriginal in the blood, through the mother, is but small—and the girl is doubtless as beautiful and as devoted as Pocahontas. My blessings, my dear brother. Should you ever return for a visit to Philadelphia, be assured that our door will open to you and Mrs. Biddle.

The effort that this broad-mindedness must have cost the dignified Nicholas was revealed in another letter, plainly expressive of general family feeling, which Edward had received from his eighteen-year-old sister, Cynthia:

My Darling Ned,
Before you take this rash step and marry a squaw, won't you come home and get your bearings? On bended knees, we beg you to come home just for a short, short visit! Diana Gwathmey and Calista Todhunter enquire about you almost every day. Diana is more beautiful than ever! You should see her in her new flower-brocaded, blue silk dress from Paris! She looks like an angel—like an archangel! Oh, Ned, Ned, what can you be thinking of? I think at least a dozen members of the family would sink into their yawning graves with mortification, if you should step out of a carriage and walk up the steps of their houses with an Indian

bride! And your children, Ned,—my nieces and nephews!—
papooses, that's what I'll have! Papooses! Oh, dear! Oh, dear!
The family is *horribly* upset! Some of them threaten never to
speak of you or write to you again! Aunt Rebecca fainted when
your letter came and has been practically in a swoon ever since!
Darling Ned—do come home—*alone!*

Edward smiled over the family's panic, over the yawning graves,
and the papooses and Nicholas's consulting the book on heraldry
(he had undoubtedly ridden to Cambridge for that very purpose)!
Edward was very like Joseph in his common sense, his scale of
values, his unclouded vision and his gusty sense of humor, and an
almost brotherly relationship had sprung up between them since
Joseph's return to the island in 1809. Edward was well pleased, as
he followed Agatha and Joseph through the little aisle of spectators
and took his place, facing Father Richard, in front of the fireplace
where Joseph and Marie had made their unconventional vows,
without benefit of clergy, eighteen years before.

This time, the beautiful old formulas, so similar in the Catholic
and in the Protestant churches, were repeated by a genuine priest.
Afterwards, with no other cleric to help him and no acolytes,
Father Richard conducted a simple version of the Low Mass of the
nuptial ceremony, with its poetic words, its praises of God, its
admonitions to the new husband and wife, its tracing of the cross
with the sanctifying hand, the elevation of the Sacred Host, the
consecration of the chalice before the improvised altar, the Holy
Communion, the sprinkling with holy water, the nuptial blessing
and the final prayer:

"May the God of Abraham, the God of Isaac, and the God of
Jacob be with you and may He accomplish His blessing upon you;
that you may live to see your children's children even to the third
and fourth generation and afterwards have eternal life, by the aid
of our Lord Jesus Christ who liveth and reigneth with the Father
and the Holy Ghost, world without end. Amen."

The ceremony was at last over, and solemnity was at an end for
the day. Joseph turned towards the circle of his friends with a
beaming face and called out, in a voice that could have been heard
all over Mackinac Island:

"To the fiddle, Toussaint! To the drums, Phylier! To the
dance, mes amis!"

Toussaint began with a much accelerated "reel à huit," and Agatha and Edward led off. Joseph went to Marie and swung her out, laughing and protesting, upon the parlor floor. Mr. Crooks claimed Mrs. Crooks, and Captain Pierce his wife Josette. Old David Stuart, whose limbs creaked, but creaked gayly, bowed low before Madame Geneviève Bailly de Messein, and carried her into the dance. Dr. Beaumont swung out with Madame Laframboise. Young William Blackbird took Thérèse with awkward grace. Mr. Robert Stuart had a pious streak which prevented his dancing. Almost all the rest of the guests were men. Some jigged off with men. Others retired to a corner to smoke and chat and watch.

After the first dance, Joseph swung open the door of his house, in order that those outside might share the music and the joy and, a little later, the refreshments. There were cries from those outside for "Le petit enfant!" and "Les nouveaux mariés!" Joseph rushed into the house, picked up his little boy and carried him to the door in his arms, quite as proudly as Napoleon had carried his lace-covered "Aiglon" to the windows of the Tuileries eight years before for the roaring adulation of the crowd.

"Vive le petit Robert! Vive l'enfant du Grand Seigneur Bailly! Vive l'enfant de notre cousin Joseph Bailly!" cried the voyageurs and the mixed French Canadian group outside.

"Hurrah for Robert Bailly! Three cheers for little Bobby!" cried the English and Americans.

"Penaci! Penaci!" shouted the Indians, for this was the name they had bestowed on the Wing Woman's son, almost as soon as he was born. "The Bird! The Little Bird! The Little Bird!"

It was only when Marie came up from behind and, touching Joseph on the shoulder, asked wistfully, "And Lucille—aren't you going to show the newly baptized little girl to them, too?" that Joseph was reminded of his latest daughter. But Lucille had already pushed between her father and mother, had stepped in front of Joseph and was bowing and curtsying, tossing her black curls and widening her wide little mouth into an extremely self-satisfied smile.

The crowd renewed its plaudits with less enthusiasm: "Vive la petite! Vive Lucille!" Lucille prolonged her ecstasy until her father took her firmly and gently by the shoulder and led her inside. The bride and groom who took her place received thunderous shouts of joy.

As soon as Joseph set Robert down inside the house, Lucille vented her newest resentment against him (fruit of the circumstance that he had received ten times the amount of acclamation that she had received) by giving him a slap on the cheek. The mark of her hand showed red, and the cries of Robert resounded above the loud music of the dance.

"*What is* the matter with you, Lucille?" asked Joseph. "Do you want me to take you and whip you before the entire company?"

"Yes! Why don't you?" challenged Lucille, her dark eyes blazing.

"I'll attend to you later, young lady. Meanwhile, your grandmother will look after you. But if you so much as lay the tip of a finger on Robert today, I *will* whip you in public! Do you understand?" Joseph laid such a grip on her shoulder that Lucille bit her lips, but she allowed no weak betraying sound to pass through them.

Madame Geneviève Bailly was sitting on the sofa now, talking with John Jacob Astor. Joseph set Robert in her lap, with a whispered word, and placed Lucille on the other side of Astor. Then he stepped away and called out to Pothier and Phylier for a good Yankee jig, "Turkey in the Straw"!

For over an hour the dancing continued, hornpipes and reels and square dances and even an old French minuet, all managed with echoing enthusiasm by Joseph. Then Joseph shouted out:

"The banquet, ladies and gentlemen! The wedding feast! Make room! Make room!"

As there was no separate dining room in any private house on the island, most of the cooking still being done, pioneer-fashion, at the hearth fire, Joseph's living room had to serve as dining room also, though he had gone so far as to install a spacious kitchen at the back of the house. From this kitchen there now came a procession of squaw-servants who, in the twinkling of an eye, set up, on deal horses, long tables of planking, covered them with fine linen tablecloths, silver, and glassware, set candles and pine sprays and bouquets of marigold in the center and shortly brought in the "coups d' appétit" on large silver trays, the brandy for the gentlemen, the cordial for the ladies, and, at last, the wedding repast.

It was the happiest banquet of Joseph's life. The recollection of the New Year's ball and banquet at Quebec, of almost a quarter of a century before, passed through his mind more than once. On that long-ago night, he had been a troubled young man, uncertain of his future, amiably scorned by the older adventurers, bewildered by that masked minx, Corinne de Courcelles. This evening he was a successful man, surrounded by a handsome, happy family and by delightful friends. His oldest daughter was marrying into one of the best families in America. His son, his *son* was here!

To his mother sitting on his left (the bride was on his right), he said:

"I was just thinking of that last New Year's ball at Freemasons' Hall in Quebec, Maman—when I was nineteen. Do you remember?"

"I've been thinking of it all afternoon and evening, son. You've come a long way since then."

"I'm not half through, Maman!"

"Bien! Your father would have been proud of you." (Which was Madame Geneviève's quiet way of saying, "*I'm* proud of you.")

"Do you think, by this time, he would have forgiven me for going to the Pays d'en Haut?"

"I think he forgave you long ago, Joseph."

"He would have liked the grandchildren, n'est-ce pas? His name will go on now, through little Robert Michel! Something to be enormously thankful for, isn't it?"

"Yes, son—énormément!"

After Father Richard had blessed the food, Joseph asked for the toast to bride and groom, and crystal glasses of white wine were clinked, as Mr. Astor rose and toasted:

"To the great future of the children of two great men!"

"Thank you, Mr. Astor. And now—a toast to my grandchildren!" cried Joseph, visioning the procession of the Bailly generations spreading out ahead of him in endless glory. But, as he spoke the word "grandchildren," the grandfather picture struck him with the sudden impact of the realization of venerability. After all, he was only forty-four years old. He had *felt* like twenty all his life! He still felt twenty; but forty-four is only six removed from fifty, and fifty is—half a century! His hand paused in lifting his glass, but he completed the gesture. How *old* Phylier, down at the other end of the table, looked—withered and bent and crinkled, with only a small Gallic twinkle left in his eyes! *Must* one look as old as that some day? Joseph looked *past* Phylier, straightened his shoulders, and repeated emphatically:

"*To my grandchildren!*"

The rafters rang with the toast, and with the din of the merry conversation that followed. The accompanying banquet was one of the most lavish that had ever been served on the island. Every delicacy that the island afforded and a few that Joseph had ordered from long distances appeared on his table that memorable night; whitefish and pickerel and pike of the neighboring waters, but also codfish from the banks of Newfoundland, served with the tangy French sauces which Marie and Madame Geneviève had taught the Indian servants to prepare; partridges stuffed with chestnuts; a whole roast pig, complete with filling and spices and the ultimate apple in the mouth; a platter of buffalo tongues from the western plains; pattes d'ours; headcheese; onions and corn and potatoes grown in the Indian village, wild salads, and, for dessert, that old adapted French dish dear to Charlevoix a hundred years before, sagamite (cracked-corn mush with maple sugar and cream), and croquignoles (French doughnuts) and fruit preserves.

It was towards eleven at night when the heavy-laden guests rose from the table.

"More dancing, friends?" asked Joseph. "Come, Toussaint and Phylier, just a little more music to end the day!"

Most of the guests were too weary now to dance; but Edward and Agatha, Thérèse and William Blackbird, and Josette and Captain Pierce pirouetted to the final music, after the tables were removed, while the older people stood about and watched them. It was observed that William and Thérèse looked at each other with glances quite similar to those that passed between the bride and groom. They were a startling couple, those two unmarried ones, Thérèse, pale and flaxen as a Madonna, William dark and handsome as a young St. Anthony of the wilderness.

"Why don't they marry now?" came the murmur of whispers.

"They're madly in love with each other. That's plain to be seen."

"She's only fifteen. And he's going to the Baptist Seminary at Hamilton, New York, to study to be a missionary to the Indians. They'll marry when he comes back."

"But I thought he was going to be a priest."

"No, not a priest. A teacher of the Indians. He gave up the priest idea after he fell in love with Thérèse Bailly. They're beautiful young people, aren't they? So are Agatha and Biddle, in a more dashing, worldly way! Handsome children, those Bailly children—even that youngest girl, who's so different from the rest of the family."

"A bit of a devil. She's always making trouble."

"Well, you have to have some fly in the ointment. She's the fly."

Jean Baptiste Clutier and three of Joseph's oldest voyageurs, who had also been present at Joseph's own wedding, were standing beside Toussaint and Phylier, after jigging around the room several times with one another. The imp of mischief seized them, along with a recollection.

" 'Member how we tease old Phylier at Monsieur Joseph's wedding? Let's tease 'im again! 'Member how he say Napoleon be king, be Emperor some day? Poor Napoleon!"

Phylier caught the words above the rattle of his drum, and his white old face flushed an angry red. He beat a double tattoo on his drum.

"Say, Phylier!" shouted Reaume Rouleaux in Phylier's ear. "How did you get that wound?"

"I tell you! I tell you!" shrieked Phylier above the music, shaking out the words with the beat, "Joost as I shall say, 'Vive mon Général! Vive Napoléon! I receive a ball!'

"And what did you say then, Phylier?" shouted all the voyageurs at once.

The dancing couples ceased their dancing, the talking stopped, the music came to an abrupt end. Everyone listened. Phylier got up, as if in brittle sections, from his chair, stood erect and shouted, with defiant pride and with every ounce of his energy:

"I shall say joost de same all de time, wherever Napoleon be,

on battlefield in Europe, in Paris, in Rome, on leetle island in de sea
—I say wot I been say before: 'Vive mon Général! *Vive Napoléon!*'"

The cry was taken up by all the Frenchmen in the room. The reverberant echo carried to the ends of the island.

But, in the silence that followed the shout, old Phylier crumpled to the floor, his drum falling under him with a booming thud. There was a moment of soundless consternation. Joseph crossed quickly over to where Phylier lay, leaned down, turned the old drummer over on his back, bent his head down to the heart, rose, crossed himself, and announced:

"Old Phylier is dead."

Father Richard took charge, murmuring the last prayers, while Joseph quietly dismissed his guests.

As Joseph kissed the bride good night before she left for Biddle's house, he said:

"I'm sorry for the last event, my dear. But don't be troubled or superstitious about it. Just feel that, at your wedding, you encountered the three greatest human experiences—baptism, marriage, death."

Chapter XXVII

WOLVES AGAINST THE MOON

"Wait a minute! Oh, Papa, please wait! The moon's coming up over that great big dune that hasn't any trees on it! I want to watch!"

"But we must be getting on to the camping place, Robert. All good travelers try to camp before dark. We're late. I'll give you three minutes. Then, en avant, marche! On we go!"

"How quiet it is! Just that little ripple of the lake—and those wolves baying, Papa. They're so near. Should we be afraid?"

"No, Robert. A big hungry pack of them in the winter might be dangerous, but not those two you hear. Those aren't the big timber wolves anyway. Those are the dune wolves, half timber, half prairie. Wolves are shrewd animals, but we mustn't be afraid—of anything."

The Bailly cavalcade had stopped on the beach, at the edge of Rivière du Chemin, which, as Trail Creek, winds today through Michigan City, Indiana. Two great dunes stood guarding the entrance of the river, one at the south covered with pines, one at the north, a barren moving dune. It was early evening of the 15th of July, 1821.

Joseph had taken another step forward in his shrewdly advancing career. He was about to settle at last on the banks of the long anticipated and insufficiently exploited Little Calumet River, forty miles from Checagou—"forty miles from Skunktown," as Louis Pettle would have put it—and to trade with and help the Indians according to his and Marie's vows. The Bailly house at Mackinac Island had been turned over to the custody of Agatha and Edward Biddle, the needed household furniture and utensils for farming, trapping, and trading were to be shipped down in September, in the care of Toussaint Pothier, on the same schooner that was to carry the autumn supplies to Fort Dearborn.

369

Joseph believed that he was entering Michigan Territory, the southern tip of the peninsula he loved so well, and that the site of his new home was to bear that same name of pleasant association. (But the later surveys of the recently created State of Indiana were to shunt the boundary of the old ordinance of 1787, ten miles north of the southernmost shore of Lake Michigan, in order that the new state might be given a bite of the Lake and its potential harbors. In this strip, then, of the future Indiana, Joseph was placing his destiny.)

Joseph was not at all unaware of the strategic position of the site, at the end of the great old Indian Trail coming up from the Ohio River and the Wabash, crossed at right angles by the important Sauk Trail from the Missouri to Malden, Canada, and lying close to the irresistibly impending developments of white settlement at Fort Wayne, Checagou, and Detroit.

Joseph, in all probability, considered these things as well as the harbor potentialities of the mouth of Trail Creek itself, as he paused on that midsummer evening of 1821 to humor the whim of his son. Robert sat in front of his father, on the saddle of Veillantif, the beautiful chestnut Arab which was the third successor to Bayard. Marie and Rose were mounted on fine black Arabs. The rest of the group rode Canadian ponies—Esther, Lucille, Jean Baptiste Clutier, Magama, and two Indian menservants. Several pack horses led by the servants brought up the rear of the little procession. Thérèse was not with the group. She had, at her own request, been sent to a Catholic school in Quebec rather than to the Philadelphia boarding school which her father would have preferred for her.

"Oh, look, *look!*" cried Robert. "How fast the moon comes! It's almost over the dune. Oh, it's so beautiful I can hardly stand it! La beauté m'inonde!"

Joseph and Marie exchanged a significant parental glance across their horses' heads. Of all their children, Robert, more than any other, inherited their own and Geneviève Bailly's feeling for the beauty of out-of-doors. Thérèse had something of it, refined into a mystic essence that lay beyond the borders of the sensuous. Roes had it, in a pagan, exuberant, riotous way. Esther was entirely an indoors, doll-playing, spinning, domestic little person, and

Lucille seemed entirely without feeling for nature, people, or animals; for anything except dramatic situations and her own physical comfort (which could always be enhanced by any discomfort which she might be able to create in the situation of those in her immediate vicinity). This latter peculiarity Joseph had recently begun to observe; but when he had once suggested its existence to Marie she had denied it with such passionate maternal protectiveness that he had subsided into solitary conviction. It was Robert who seemed to combine all the qualities that Joseph and Marie most admired and had scarcely dared to hope for in their only son: sensitiveness of nature, strength of character, warmth of heart, sturdiness of body. He looked more like Marie as he grew older (he was five at this time), though his eyes and his chin were his father's. He had that faintly Italianate look that Marie had: the exquisitely oval face, delicate nose, very pale olive skin, finely penciled dark eyebrows low over the deep-set eyes. The eyelashes were still very long and starry like Marie's, casting rayed shadows on the cheeks. The hair was still brownish black, not the Indian blue black of Marie's, and was not as thick as hers. It curled slightly at the temples and the nape of the neck. There was the glow of intelligence over the whole fine little face.

The little group were beginning to get restless, and attention was wandering to the gilded lake or to horses' bridles and reins when Robert cried again, in a loud whisper:

"Look *now*, everybody! Look!"

Everyone turned to see what the child was indicating, and remained motionless in surprise. Two wolves, to whose nostrils the west wind had carried the smell of man, had come to the summit of the barren dune to investigate. As they paused, alert and watchful, their lean, dark bodies were silhouetted, for one perfect moment, against the golden disc of the full moon. The coincidence and the picture were so unusual that no one moved or made a comment. Then the wolves vanished as if they had been a dream. A horse snorted suspiciously. Joseph dug his heel into his Arab's flank, shook the reins, and the procession turned landwards up the north bank of Trail Creek, where many Indian moccasins and many ponies' hooves had grooved a path. After several minutes, Joseph said:

"There's a fording-place three miles east of here, and a Pota-watomi encampment. We can probably camp near there for the night. Best to make friends with our new neighbors. I haven't seen them for two years. It's an Indian village, Robert, so old that there are Indian mounds there, no man knows how ancient. And the Indians there will tell you how Father Marquette camped with their great-grandfathers a hundred and fifty years ago on the very spot where we shall probably spend the night. You see, there is a beautiful spring there, as old as time, and salt licks near by. The Indians still call the spring Marquette Spring and believe that its water is 'good medicine.'"

"Then Father Marquette must have gone along this very path, didn't he, Papa?"

"Yes. Or else he paddled up this very river in his canoe. This is all interesting country. Big battles were fought near here too, only forty years or so ago, in the Revolution."

"Are there any battle places near our new home?"

"Oh, yes, indeed! There was an old French palisaded fort near the shore, not far from where we're going to be. And there were battles there too, battles between Pontiac and the British, between the Spanish and the Americans and between the British and the Americans. And there are many Indian mounds there too. It's a wonderfully interesting place, Robert, and very beautiful. I smell smoke, do you? The smoke of Indian campfires!"

"Not yet. Your nose is so much better than mine, Papa! Is that because it's bigger?"

"No. Just older, son. Just older and wiser," answered Joseph, laughing.

Back of the ridge of dunes, there was marshy country; but the path along the river embankment was close-packed and firm. About four miles from the shore, the flat marshes were relieved by a few low, wooded glacial mounds and the lower mounds made by the prehistoric Indians, giving an overturned-bowl effect to the landscape. The contours showed darkly against the moonlight. The marsh stars, the fireflies, flashed faintly but continuously. The wisps of smoke from Indian campfires could be smelled rather than seen. When Joseph was within a quarter of a mile of the camp, he gave the friendly halloo call, which Jean Baptiste and the two Indian men echoed long and loudly. By the time they came into camp, there was a bustle of preparation for the guests. Two or three of the headmen had come out to the edge of the encampment knoll to welcome the travelers into camp, and the squaws were hastily piling new wood on the fires to reheat the left-over corn soup and boiled deer meat for their refreshment, for Joseph had been immediately recognized and every hospitable effort was made to make him and his family feel at home. He noted at once, with pleasure, that the scenes of drunkenness so frequent at Indian camps were lacking tonight. Evidently no trader had passed through for some time. The squaws, overcome with interest in the feminine members of the Bailly household, helped Marie and her daughters to dismount, and passed their hands over every bit of their guests' clothes, hair, hats, ribbons, and ornaments, as if the sense of touch were the gateway to some kind of possession. Marie noticed, almost immediately, a young girl in Indian dress, standing motionless as a tree and consuming the proceedings with eyes that burned with curiosity. The fire haloed her with light and showed her hair to be pure gold.

Within fifteen minutes, Jean Baptiste and the three Indian servants, at the insistence of the headmen of the Potawatomi, had set up tepee shelters for the night, at the edge of the Indian encampment, and the entire Bailly family were seated around the campfire pots.

It was only then that Joseph also noticed the golden-haired girl. She was busying herself with the other squaws in handing out gourd-dishes of hot soup and deer meat. She never said a word, but paused for a second in front of each successive guest, consuming each white face with her great, searching, brown eyes. When she came to Joseph, he asked her, in Potawatomi, what her name was.

"Ne-wa-quir," she answered, in the same language.

"The only name?"

"Squaw of Op-wa-gun."

"This is a very pleasant village, isn't it?"

"Yes. Very nice."

"You like it?"

"Yes, I like it."

"You speak French or English too?"

"No."

The girl dropped her glance, whether from fear or the effort of protective prevarication or from some vague, deeply stirred memory, Joseph could not tell. He was, of course, certain that she had been taken in some Indian raid, but whether as an infant, with no memories of paleface life at all, or as a child with troubled recollection, he could not guess, although he felt inclined towards the latter surmise. Certainly, she spoke Algonquin as if she had always spoken it. She wore the blue calico short gown of the Potawatomi women, the blue broadcloth leggings, exquisite flower-beaded moccasins, armlets, bracelets, and earbobs. Evidently the young brave who had married her was eager to cover her with many solid symbols of his esteem. The girl's face was painted with two bright spots of vermilion, and the golden hair was drawn, Indian-style, in two thick braids over her bosom. She was not a pretty girl. Her nose was too large and her mouth too wide. But her hair and her hazel eyes were conspicuously fine. Joseph decided that, like nine out of ten of the captive palefaces, the girl was happier with her adopted people than she could ever be in returning again to the suffocating life of a stationary plantation of white relatives. Nevertheless, he was vaguely uneasy about her and more than eager to know from where she had come. He was concentrating on this particular anxiety when, far in the distance, came the halloo of greeting which he had himself given half an hour before. Other travelers too who had not yet settled down for the night? Strange. Most wayfarers, white or Indian, of course made camp before the sun went down. This country was marshy and difficult, besides, and there were many giant bears and pumas, wild cats, coyotes, and wolves roaming about, between whom and all travelers it was just as well to place the barricade of fire before nightfall. But the full moon had rolled up over the marshes to the east and was spilling through the oak trees. It was yet very light along the trail.

Again the Indians began to simmer with imminent hospitality. The Bailly household had evidently emptied the soup pot. Another bark pail was filled with water from Marquette Spring, and twenty or so Lake Michigan perch were quickly scraped and thrown into the pot, heads, fins, tails, and all.

It was ten minutes before the new visitors climbed the low wooded mound to the brink of the encampment. An Indian on ponyback came first, greeted the headman with signs and guttural speech, and announced the coming of the white cavalcade which he was guiding through the wilderness. The Indian was followed by a lanky man on horseback whose feet almost touched the ground, and whose slouched, disappointed-dreamer contour suggested to Joseph an engraving of Don Quixote that he had seen years before in a volume in the priest's house at Quebec. Two small children rode on the saddle against the concave arch of their father's front. Then came a younger, stiffer man with two more children riding on his saddle. Then a fellow, poorly clothed, who might be a servant, and a woman draped in a long mantle which fell part way over the horse's sides after enclosing in its ample folds a tiny child held in the mother's left arm. Finally, on two mangy horses at the end of the line, two boys of about eleven and thirteen rode in, driving a dozen cows and half a dozen pigs. It was not until the long, lanky man descended from his horse and shook the hands of the head chief, announcing in a cavernous, vibrant, pastoral voice, "Name's McCoy, Reverend McCoy," that Joseph recognized the Baptist missionary to the Indians, Reverend Isaac McCoy, whom he had seen at Terre Haute several times on his journeys to and from Vincennes.

"Well, how do you do, McCoy!" he exclaimed heartily, rising from his place.

The white Indian girl, Ne-wa-quir, was on the point of handing Joseph a second plateful of soup. As he rose, she dropped it, spattering his trousers and his arms and hands with the hot liquid. Two of the squaws came over and began a noisy tirade against the girl.

"Never mind! Never mind!" protested Joseph. "It's all right. Leave her alone. It wasn't her fault. I got up too suddenly."

Joseph strode over to McCoy and greeted him and his family cordially, then presented his own family. At last the McCoy household was seated with the Baillys, in an immense circle around the campfires. The squaws began to pass around the bark dishes of soup and fish. Ne-wa-quir came to McCoy. He looked up at her casually as he was taking his hunting knife from his belt, and paused in mid-gesture. Ne-wa-quir looked back at him with deep, troubled eyes.

"Good evening, my child," said McCoy, in English.

The girl did not answer.

"Good evening, my child," repeated McCoy in Algonquin.

"Good evening."

"Won't you sit down beside me? I think I could find a little present for you somewhere in my pocket, if you'd sit down."

The missionary fumbled in his trousers pockets, brought out a two-yard strip of scarlet ribbon and handed it to the girl.

"Me-gwuck, She-mo-ke-mon" (Thank you, white man), said Ne-wa-quir, still standing.

McCoy took the dish of soup and placed it on the ground in front of him.

"Do sit down. There may be more pretty things in my pockets."

In the light of the campfire, two persons watched intently: Joseph, sitting on the right of McCoy, and a young brave leaning with casual curves against a tree, but with every nerve taut—the husband of Ne-wa-quir, who had bought his bride of a band of Shawnee the year before and had never had occasion to see her with a group of palefaces before. McCoy moved closer to Joseph, and Ne-wa-quir sat down on his left.

"Now, let's see what else we can find."

McCoy rummaged in his pockets a minute longer, and drew out a silver thimble, which he handed to Ne-wa-quir. Again, she repeated the formula:

"Me-gwuck, She-mo-ke-mon. Me-gwuck."

Then, McCoy, mindful of the repast and of his benedictional duty, rose to his feet and, in a hollow, sermonic voice, called for silence. Several repetitions of his pious admonition were necessary before the chattering of squaws and the squeaks and laughter of children, both white and red, were silenced. Then he bowed his head and, in Algonquin, spoke the grace:

"Great Father of all men. We thank Thee for this food that Thou hast prepared on Thy wilderness table for us, and we thank Thee for the peace and friendship of all these people who have gathered on this little hilltop to eat together. Bless this food, and bless all these Thy people, the white and the red. Thy will be done forever and ever. Amen."

McCoy sat down again. Ne-wa-quir was looking at him intently.

"You come from where?" she asked.

"From Terre Haute, my child," he answered. "A long way from here, to the south." Then, in the same tone, level and casual, he asked: "And you, where do you come from?"

"From—here."

"But not always from here. Where, *before* here?"

"From—a long way to the south—where the Shawnee live."

McCoy looked up quickly from his soup. His eyes widened, with a sudden thought from the far back of his mind.

"And—*before that?*"

"Before that?" The girl's eyes wavered.

"Yes—before that, child? Tell me, tell me what you remember."

Ne-wa-quir lowered her eyes and her voice.

"I remember—I remember—a hilltop—with a big wooden house with two towers—where there were men with guns—and wooden houses—and thousands of pigeons roosting—"

"Let me look at you, child. Let me look at you!"

McCoy set down his dish, seized Ne-wa-quir by the wrists, and searched her painted face. At last he spoke, and his deep voice trembled:

"Ginsey! Ginsey McCoy!"

A tall, earth-colored young man stood suddenly over McCoy. Joseph rose quickly and spoke to the young Indian, restraining him by the arm.

"It's all right. It's all right! The man happens to be kin and friend of your squaw. But he's not going to try to take her away. Don't worry. I'm your friend. Here!"

Joseph placed several pieces of shining silver in the young brave's hand. The brown fingers closed over them with the ferocity with which they would willingly have shut over McCoy's throat or a tomahawk handle a moment before. The brave returned to his tree to watch, with smoldering eyes.

The dazed look in Ne-wa-quir's eyes was clearing little by little, like mist before the sun of dawn.

"McCoy . . . McCoy . . . Ginsey McCoy . . . Yes, that was it. *That was it!* . . . I've been trying to remember that name for years. Then, when you came tonight—something happened way back in those caves in my head. Something stirred—like a little fox—in a den. . . . Yes—I *remember*. . . . I remember more now. I remember a tall man, tall like you—and a woman with kind arms. I remember how their bodies looked that day—like porcupines, with arrows stuck in all over them. I remember—everything . . ."

"Do you remember me, Ginsey? I've seen you only twice, once when you were two years old, once when you were four, just before the Shawnee came."

"I almost—think—I do. Was it you who brought me a little French doll with a pink dress? You must be related to me. Are you?"

"I'm your father's brother, Ginsey. I'm your Uncle Isaac. And I brought you the doll from Vincennes. I'm so happy to find you again. Will you come home with me—be my daughter?"

"Oh, no, no, I couldn't! I have a husband. This is my home."

"Are you happy here?"

"Oh, yes, I'm very happy. I'm happy to be what I *am*. But I'm so glad to know now who I *was!*"

"Will you come and visit me, then, some time? I'm going to live at Fort Wayne."

"Yes."

"Say, 'Yes, Uncle Isaac.' "

"Yes, Uncle Isaac."

"I remember you when you were just as tiny as those children over there."

McCoy nodded across at a little group of Indian children, who had begun to dance around the fading campfires, reaching out their arms as if to catch something forever escaping them, and singing the firefly song of the Chippewa and Potawatomi. Even in the flicker of the campfires and the pour of the moonlight through the trees, the countless fireflies flashing back and forth on the mound top could be plainly seen, the inspiration of the children's song. The only white child to join the group was Robert Bailly, whose mother had taught him the song long before, and who loved it with all his heart. Joseph watched the joy of his gestures and of his face as he danced and sang with the Indian children, and rejoiced that his child, like himself, was equally at home with the red people and the white:

Wau wau tay see!
Wau wau tay see!
E mow e shin
Tshe bwan ne bann-e-wee
Be-eaghaun-be-eaghaun ewee!

Wa Wau tay see!
Wa Wau tay see!
Was sa koon ain je gun
Was sa koon ain je gun.

Dancing light fireflies,
Glancing bright fireflies,
Little white lightnings over my head,
Come fly before me and light me to bed!

Dreaming white glowworms,
Gleaming bright glowworms,
Wings of the night-things over the grass
Give me the flames of your stars as I pass!

"Is that your son, that little fellow over yonder, dancing with the Indian children?" asked McCoy.

"Yes, that's my son," answered Joseph proudly.

"Fine little boy! I've lost three sons."

"Lost three sons! My God, how do you endure it?" asked Joseph, with sudden gigantic compassion.

"The Lord giveth and the Lord taketh away," answered McCoy, deep in the throat, in the monotonous tone of pious acquiescence.

Good God, I wonder if I'm religious after all, thought Joseph, I wonder if I could ever take the Lord's givings and withdrawals with such abject submission!

"I'm going to start a missionary school at Fort Wayne, Bailly," continued McCoy, after a moment, "for Indians and whites both. Perhaps you'd like to send a few of your children to us later, after we're well started?"

"That sounds like a good idea, McCoy. I'll keep in touch with you. My wife and I are going to do a little teaching of Indians ourselves down on the Little Calumet. But I think I'd like to send some of my younger children to you at Fort Wayne for a while. I don't want my young people to lead too solitary a life down here in the wilderness. I want them to know the wilderness and the world *both!*"

"Well, my life's the wilderness. I can't say it isn't hard and bitter and lonely at times, but it's the Lord's will. The text I've taken for Mrs. McCoy's life and mine is from Isaiah: 'The wilderness and the solitary place shall be glad for them; and the desert shall rejoice, and blossom as the rose.' "

"I'd forgotten that old Isaiah said that! That's fine!"

An hour or so later, Joseph and Marie were settling to sleep in their tent. The night sounds had almost ceased in the camp, the champing of horses, the yelp of a puppy or two, the grunting of pigs, the cry of a restless papoose. But the frogs were piping in the marshes below, and, far out on the dunes, a pack of wolves were howling to the moon. At that distance, the sound was like a faint, pleasant melody.

"I feel as if we were far from all our enemies, Joseph, our Rastels and De la Vignes—and Corinnes—all our troubles, and all intrigues, don't you? It's so beautiful and peaceful here, the dunes, the marsh, the moon—"

"I think you'd like the verse that McCoy quoted to me from Isaiah."

"What was it, Joseph?"

"You'll remember it: 'The wilderness and the solitary place shall be glad for them; and the desert shall rejoice, and blossom as the rose.' "

"The marshes of the Calumet, Joseph, and the dunes 'shall rejoice, and blossom as the rose.' "

"I hope so, Marie. Yet—listen, listen to that baying. There are always wolves of some sort or other—wolves against the moon."

"Not human wolves, Joseph. Not here."

"I hope so," said Joseph, with a man's unsentimental reservations.

Chapter XXVIII

SHADOW OF POKAGON

"OH, PAPA, don't chop that tree down! Please! There's a cardinal's nest in the top of it!"

"Wait a minute, Jean Baptiste," said Joseph. "I've got to explain this to the child."

Joseph dropped his ax, stalked over to Robert, who stood looking up into the treetop, kneeled down so that he could look on a level into his son's face, took one of the small hands in his, and said:

"See here, young man! I've got to explain this to you again, I see. You know what we're doing, I suppose?"

"Cutting down birds' nests!"

"You little rascal! What are we *really* doing?"

"Murdering trees!"

"Enfant de grâce! Murdering trees! Did you hear that, Jean Baptiste? We're murderers, you and I!"

Jean Baptiste's dark olive face wrinkled with the chuckle that finally spilled over into shaking sound.

"He t'ink ze trees have spirits—like ze Indians t'ink."

"They *have* spirits, Jean Baptiste!" declared the child. "Haven't you ever heard them speak? Haven't you ever heard them sing? Haven't you ever heard them *shriek*, Jean Baptiste?"

"Shriek? Ze trees shriek?"

"Why, yes! In a *storm*, Jean Baptiste!"

"Zat is good. Shriek! So dey do. Well, zen, what you t'ink when your Papa keel ze animals? bring home ze beaver and ze otter and ze muskrat? What you t'ink den?"

"I think it's horrible, Jean Baptiste. I have bad dreams sometimes. I dream that all those skins come alive again, and the animals inside them come and stand around my bed at night. It's awful, Jean Baptiste. I wish that you and Papa wouldn't do such things! Perhaps, down here on the Calumet, you'll do something else instead."

"Funny little boy you are, Robert. So much like your mother at times," said Joseph. "It's all right for women, but not for men. You've got to get used to killings and fighting and cruelty. That's what life is! You mustn't act like a little girl, son."

"Little girls don't act that way. Lucille doesn't."

"No. Lucille doesn't. But she's different from most little girls."

"Well, I want to be different from *her*. She likes to hurt animals. The other day, she chopped the wings off of—"

"Never mind about Lucille. Now, about these trees, Robert. We're going to build a *house* here, you know."

"Well, why not build it down in the flat land below, where there aren't any trees?"

"Why, Robert, that's all marshy down there. And besides the river overflows sometimes. This is the right place for the house, in this beautiful grove of oaks and maples on the dry land above the river. This is where our home *must be*. And we'll have to cut down a good many of these trees, even though they *are* beautiful and alive—not only to make room for our house, but to use for the logs to *make* our house. In a way, the trees will still be very much alive, for our house will be a *live house*. Don't you see?"

"Yes, Papa. But if you didn't cut them down, I'd climb to the top of each one and reach up and take a piece of blue sky and bring it back to you and Maman!"

Joseph hugged the child to him, and muffled his huge laughter against the little deerskin jacket; but when he stood up at last he offered one more masculine remonstrance.

"You understand now, son? No more complaints. No more talk about murderers. You must learn to be a man. A strong man, a brave man. You've got to see a lot of cruel, bloody things in this world."

"Suppose the tree bleeds?"

"It won't! Come, come, don't be foolish any more."

Joseph picked up the ax and strode towards the tree.

"You've forgotten that Ottawa story of the bleeding lodgepoles, Papa!" Robert called after Joseph, as persistently as ever.

"See here!" said Joseph, swinging around impatiently.

It was all right for the child to be odd and sensitive, but Joseph simply mustn't let the sensitiveness grow until Robert became a "girly" man. If there was anything Joseph couldn't stand, it was a delicate-minded man. You could have a delicate streak in you, all right, that loved sunsets and flowers and all beautiful things. Joseph had seen plenty of that, even in the gruffest, burliest Nor'-westers, and he knew that he had a big wide streak himself. But you'd got to cover it over with a lot of sand and strength in this coarse-textured world.

"Come here, Robert!" he commanded, and there was a harsh edge in his tone that Robert didn't often hear.

"Come, take this ax. I know it's heavy. Take it. *Take it,* I say!"

"What are you going to make me do, Papa?"

"Now. Chop!"

"I can't! I can't!"

"A Bailly never says 'can't.' Chop! Chop, I say!"

Robert shut his eyes tight, swung the huge ax feebly, and hit the bark of the tree ten inches from the groove that Joseph had already made.

"Very bad. Do it again!"

From the other side of the tree, Jean Baptiste pointed to his own eyes with both forefingers and then pointed at the child. Joseph leaned down and looked. Robert's eyes were closed again.

"Open your eyes, Robert!"

"Oh, Daddy, I don't want to see it *bleed!*"

"It doesn't bleed! For St. Christopher's sake, don't be foolish. Stand up, there! Open your eyes, and chop like a man!"

Robert opened his eyes, took aim, and turned his head away. Jean Baptiste, on the other side of the tree, was muffling his mouth with brown hands. "Bailly against Bailly!" he was chuckling, "Ze boy got a will of hees own." This time the awkward ax struck the groove and knocked out a chip not much bigger than a flake of sawdust.

"More!" urged Joseph. "More! At this rate, it would take a hundred years to chop that tree down! Go at it like a big woodsman, Robert! Down with the tree! Go on! Go on!"

This time, Robert kept his eyes open and his gaze on the tree; but his face was tense, and a tear slipped down his cheek. He lifted the big ax, swung a small arc, chopped, lifted the ax, swung, chopped, until the effort grew pitiful to see, and his father relented.

"All right, Robert. Very good! You see the tree doesn't bleed. Aren't you glad you helped a little to build our house?"

"Do I have to answer that question, Daddy? Ask it some other time!"

And Robert ran off, trying to hold back the unmanly tears that *would* come. As he ran off down the slope towards the river, where Marie and the three girls had gone to hunt for spicewood, yarrow, and calamus root, Joseph could hear Lucille's taunting voice in the distance:

"He's crying! He's crying! He's crying! Little Baby Robert, baby, baby. . . ."

With a troubled heart, Joseph resumed his work.

"All right, Jean Baptiste!"

The two men worked rhythmically, with alternate strokes, on the thick oak tree. Joseph's strokes cut deeper. As the wedges of split wood approached, Joseph gave the order:

"We'll alternate now on this side, Jean Baptiste. The tree must fall to the east in order to destroy as few of the young maples at the edge of the bank as possible."

The music of the axes continued. Never before, in all the thousands of years of the existence of Calumet marsh and dune, had this strange song of the settler's ax been heard. The quick splintering of tomahawk against saplings, to fashion the lodgepoles—this staccato sound had been heard, and the guttural music of Indian voices under the trees, as the Ottawa or the Potawatomi camped in the sugar grove at the north end of the wooded plateau, or as the Sauk and the Fox, the Winnebago, the Menominee, and the Sioux, passed gorgeously in single file along the old Sauk Trail. Even the voices of white men had been heard here, for the great La Salle and Father Marquette and Father Hennepin and many lesser explorers and priests had passed along the ancient trail. The trumpeting of the elk, the scream of the panther, the howl of the timber wolf, the barking of the fox, the screech of the Carolina parrakeet, the echoing blast of the trumpeter swan, the storm of the passenger pigeons settling in the beech trees, the gobbling of wild turkeys, the drumming of partridges, the splashing of muskrats in the water, the wild cries of wild death and wild life—these had been heard in the heart of the Calumet.

Now the wilderness echoed to a new vibration, the thud of man-swung weapons, the multiple crash of trees. Everything else was still. The birds had retreated, in consternation, to the shrubbery along the Calumet or the tangle of smartweed, celery, Spanish needles, arrow head, rose mallows and pond lilies in the swamp below.

Joseph and Jean Baptiste continued to make their rhythmed music, pausing only once in a while to wipe their foreheads or to exchange a merry comment. Suddenly, very quietly, a shadow, shorter than the shadow of a tree, stood across the open space that they had already cleared. Joseph looked up. Still as a tree, his arms (wrapped in a scarlet blanket) folded across his breast, his bronze head held high, his eyes steadily regarding Joseph, stood the Potawatomi chief, Leopold Pokagon. Joseph dropped his ax, strode over to the Sauk Trail where Pokagon stood, and extended his hand. Pokagon waited for a full half-minute before taking the proffered hand. As he did so, he spoke solemnly in Algonquin.

"In friendship I take your hand. I take fast hold of it. God sees us take hold of each other's hands and will be witness against him that shall deceive."

"In friendship I take your hand," replied Joseph. "Come and sit down in my humble house."

He led the way to a spacious tent set up in the open center of the maple grove at the east end of the wooded knoll. From a pouch hanging from one of the lodgepoles, Joseph immediately took a quantity of tobacco, which he presented to Pokagon who received it with an almost inaudible:

"Me-gwuck, me-gwuck, Monami Bailly."

Pokagon slowly filled the calumet that had rested in his belt along with tomahawk and hunting knife, and Joseph filled his own Indian pipe. The two smoked in silence for a long time. Joseph wondered why Pokagon's face was so stern and unsmiling today. Some hidden trouble, doubtless, that would come out in the course of a long, cryptic conversation, like a harmless fox pelt drawn from the concealment of a blanket, or like any Indian emerging from ambush at the end of a day's crouching.

At last Pokagon said: "I see you are cutting down trees—trees too large for lodgepoles."

"Yes, my friend Pokagon, trees too large for lodgepoles but not too large for a white man's roof and cabin walls."

"Ugm-m-m-m," Pokagon grunted, and smoked on. Joseph began to sense the drift of Pokagon's meaning.

"Perhaps I should have consulted you first, my friend Pokagon. Am I setting my house down in the midst of your hunting grounds or your trapping preserves? If so, I am sorry. But I have here a paper signed by the Big Chief of Michigan Territory, Governor Cass, who is a subchief of the Great Father at Washington, and he gives me leave to trade with your people, the Potawatomi, and to build my cabin here."

Joseph got up and took from a deerskin bag lying on the ground at the back of the tent a document with a large red seal attached to it, and opened it up for Pokagon to see.

"Yes, I see," said Pokagon. "It is like the paper of the Treaty of Greenville that I saw when I went with my father. It is like the Treaty of Saginaw. I know those papers. Yes—the papers are signed, and the white waves of the sea move on, taking here a little piece of beach, there another . . . We have not yet given *all* of this land away by treaty, but it will soon be gone from us. If there *must* be a first white settler, here, I am glad it is you, Monami Bailly. We all like you, and the Wing Woman. The Great Spirit has touched you, and you are our friend."

"Thank you, my father."

"But did you know that you have chosen a sacred spot, Monami Bailly? a place loved by us for hundreds of years? We have camped near here in the spring for the blueberry picking and the sugaring and the Sweetwater Dance. Many of our dead are buried on that oak ridge across the marsh half a mile to the northeast."

"I am sorry, Pokagon, if I have chosen the wrong place for my home. But I imagine that any place from the Little Vermilion River to the Grand River is sacred to the Potawatomi."

"They are all sacred. But this place especially so. Why did you leave Parc aux Vaches?"

"For many reasons, my father. This is a new and untried place where I may help my brothers the Indians. It is near the crossing of two great trails rather than the one Sauk Trail. It is nearer Lake Mitchigami. It is nearer the life at Fort Dearborn for my boy and my girls. It is more beautiful. I do not intend to stay here forever. But for a while, it is the best place."

"Good reasons. Monami Bailly is still as cunning as the black-snake, as shrewd as the wolverene."

"You will allow your people to trade with me as before?"

"Yes. Why not?"

"What would you and your people like, my father, in payment for my use of this site for my cabin and storehouses and my use of the beach for my boats and boathouses?"

"I will talk to Chief Topenebee and Black Partridge and Raccoon and Shavehead and a few of the others, Monami Bailly. You are willing to pay, then, for these rights, for as many years as you stay, a fair price in merchandise or money?"

"Certainly, my father."

"I have heard of white men along the frontier who were not willing to pay money or merchandise or even courtesy to the red men. Their hearts have made good targets for arrows."

"You know me better than that, Chief Pokagon. You will protect me and my family. And I will give you and your people a fair price, as I did at Parc aux Vaches, and many good things in trade."

"If all white men were like you, Monami Bailly, there would never be any trouble, but the white race and the red race would hunt together and play bagataway together, and sit around the campfire and smoke the pipe of peace forever."

"Some day that will happen, my father."

"Perhaps. It happened in the happy days when the French were here and built Little Fort over there on the dunes. My father has told me that the Frenchmen were like brothers to the Indians, that the Great Spirit had touched them all. It is so always with the Frenchmen. It is not so with the Americans."

"No? They are rough and in a little of a hurry. But they are a brave people and a wise people. I am an American now myself, Pokagon."

"No," said Pokagon, placing his hand on Joseph's stomach and then drawing his hand down the length of Joseph's body to the toes of his boots. "No, Monami Bailly, you can never be an American. The blood and the flesh of you are French. A little piece of paper like this"—he scrunched Joseph's government permit contemptuously in his hand—"cannot make you an American. I hate those pieces of paper. I shall have one in my hands in a little while. You know of the great treaty gathering to be held at Checagou in the Moon of Whortleberries?"

"Yes. The council that General Cass has called for August."

"You are going?"

"Yes, I am going."

"In that council they will give me a little piece of paper like that to sign, and they will promise my people money, and they will take away miles and miles of our hunting grounds and our trapping grounds, our wild-rice fields and our blueberry marshes, our council grounds and our burial grounds, as they have done before. And what can we do? Nothing. We shall put the dead goose feather to the paper. And we shall be dead geese ourselves . . ."

Joseph was silent, for he too felt like an intruder.

"They will squeeze us in at last between a single marsh and a single dune. Perhaps they will drown us in the lake—"

"Oh, no, Pokagon, they will give you much money. They are very rich."

"Yes—they are very rich and very cunning—like crows, and numberless as the leaves on the trees."

Pokagon waited a moment, his eyes narrowing over a tense thought. Then he said:

"But these white waves of people cannot go on forever, moving towards the west. There are sands that will drink up the water . . ."

Joseph waited for an explanation but acknowledged after a long silence:

"I do not understand you, my father."

"There are sandy plains far to the west, as you know, Monami Bailly."

"Yes, I have never been there, but I know."

"And living there is a mighty nation of Indians, wiser than the bear, craftier than the beaver, stronger than the elk, swifter than the storm winds of Lake Mitchigami. They are descended from a mighty nation that ruled from many-terraced tepees of stone far to the south, thousands upon thousands of years ago, whom men call the Aztecs. They know strange music, more powerful than the magic of De la Vigne, strange herbs, strange things. They have power to stop the white tides—"

"There is no danger, father, that the tides will move farther west—"

"There *are* white men who have dared to go far beyond the great Father of Rivers to the Ocean of the Sunset."

"Yes, I know," said Joseph, remembering the long journeys of Lewis and Clark, of Stuart and Crooks and M'Dougal, and his own desires towards the west.

Pokagon stared through hawk-eyes into the eyes of Bailly, down to the last fluttering finch of a dream.

"You have almost dared it yourself, Monami Bailly. The desire is not dead."

Joseph involuntarily lowered his eyes.

"Do not dare it, Bailly. You must not find the trails across the plains. Those are buffalo trails and Indian trails. They must never, never be white trails. Even you, whom the Indians love, will be killed, if you dare it."

"I no longer wish to dare it, my father. My trails are to the south, to the bayous, and creeks and swamps at the end of the Great River. . . . Now, I remember, I have seen strange Indians in the market place at New Orleans with sealskins from the Great Western Ocean—"

"You do not have to go so far to find the Indians from the West, Monami Bailly. Now and again an Indian from the west rides, more swiftly than the wings of the Thunder Bird, into our encampments, delivers his messages or his tokens, and is gone again. Many a stranger in camp, whom you take to be a Winnebago or a Fox or a Shawnee, is really a messenger from the sandy plains. Their message is often death—death to the white man."

"Why do you tell me these things?"

"Because you are gradually pushing out your trapping grounds,

Monami Bailly, farther and farther all the time, deeper and deeper into the woods and wider and wider along the prairies. Even you must stop, Monami Bailly. Even you must be careful."

"Thank you, Pokagon. I shall be very careful."

"De la Vigne is a friend of the Indians of the plains. He has been to the plains. He has studied their magic. He comes down now almost every spring with the Ottawa of Arbre Croche, to this very sugar bush here, this grove, this swamp, where he gathers his strong medicines and his poisons."

Joseph was stunned. He thought that he had chosen a place utterly remote from enterprises of De la Vigne and Rastel. He understood now the import of the two messages that Pokagon had come to deliver to him—the necessity of his making devoted friends of all the neighboring Potawatomi, by payment of a generous annuity, and a warning that this was territory frequented by De la Vigne.

"I thought that the Ottawa of Arbre Croche went always to the sugar bush at Rivière des Raisins."

"They used to go there. But the settlers are coming in there as thick as ants. Since that last war of the British and the Americans, many of the soldiers who fought there have brought their families from Kentucky and Ohio to live there, as you very well know, Monami Bailly. The maple trees are being cut down to make log cabins. There is no more sugar bush. It is very different from the little village that the Wing Woman knew. For the last three years, the Ottawa and De la Vigne have been coming *here*."

"Thank you for telling me, Pokagon. But it doesn't change my plans." Joseph put out his hand, and thanked Pokagon again with the strength of his grip. The two men rose.

"Let's go find the Wing Woman. It's time she set Magama to preparing a fine supper for you."

The gold of afternoon had deepened against the tree trunks, the living trees and the fallen giants. A rich tapestry of light and shade lay over bark and grass, the trillium leaves, the Solomon's seal, and the torches of the Indian paintbrush at the knoll's edge. A parrakeet flashed its lightning of green and yellow wings across the newly made opening.

"Beautiful here," said Joseph, "but—you can't escape the wolves . . ."

Pokagon turned and regarded him intently.

"No," he said, "you can't escape the wolves."

"But you can be ready for them, mort de diable! I think I hear voices. You haven't ever seen my little son, have you, Pokagon?"

Chapter XXIX

INDIAN BORGIA

IT WAS a midsummer day of 1823. The cicadas were shrilling in the oak trees on the summit of Bailly's ridge. Everything else was tense as a mirror about to break. Earth was waiting for the storm to muster the electricity lurking over the molten lake, the shimmering marshes, the hot crystals of the dunes, and crash it down in spearing flame.

There was only one figure stirring on the ridge. The fifty Ottawa Indians who had remained at the Calumet for the herb gathering, after the rest of the Arbre Croche band had departed north for their spring planting and crop tending, had dispersed in the cool of the dawn to their various tasks, the squaws and the medicine men to gather herbs, the braves to fish at the lake. One medicine man remained behind, standing over an iron kettle suspended from a rustic tripod, in which some decoction smoked to an already simmering sky.

The Bailly cabin, thirty rods away, the servants' cabins, fur sheds and work shed, six log structures in all, showed no signs of life; but from the main house, the voices of two children lifted now and then in play or protest. They sounded petulant, dulled by the heat.

The medicine man stirred his brew with a long hickory stick. He was naked except for a loincloth and a deerskin belt, with a wolf tail suspended from the back and a silver-handled hunting knife, a tomahawk and a medicine-pouch fitted into the front of it. Two turkey feathers and a small green parrakeet's feather were twisted jauntily into the curling clusters of dark hair at the top of his head. De la Vigne's eyes seemed to reflect the sinister sparkle of his decoction, as he stirred. Perspiration oozed from every pore of his yellowish brown skin, but satisfaction, above bodily ordeal, showed in every line of his face, from thin, upswerving lips to thin, upswerving eyebrows. The mixture was deadly, and De la Vigne delighted in its lethal beauty. So Circe must have watched her caldron with narrow eyes, or Caesar Borgia his. All the varieties of noxious plants of the Calumet marshes (any one plant sufficiently potent to cause the death of an enemy), and various snakes' heads, which the Indians wrongly believed to be potent also, were here being boiled together: mandrake root, poison sumac, deadly nightshade, monk's hood, poison ivy, and the pounded heads of rattlesnake and copperhead. A beautiful brew! More destroying than a cluster of lightning bolts in the hand of Motchi Manitou, the Demon of the Sky.

Although for many years no invading Sauk bands had rushed in with a hail of arrows from the west, and for many a long moon no Iroquois had slipped in on stealthy snowshoes from the east, every Ottawa encampment had its poisons ready. The juices had been used on arrow tips in the British and American feud ten years before, and many a drop of poison had found its winged way to a paleface settler's heart in the same way before and even *since* then. Some of the evil medicine was used against demons in combating disease, and when mortal patients or mortal enemies were lacking it was delicious now and then to watch an animal die by drugged degrees.

De la Vigne had been thinking of the multiple possibilities of his pot. But here, in this environment, so close to the hated Baillys, the abstractions were narrowing, narrowing at last into one definite, personalized vision. Wonderful, delightful, if he could convey this poison to the mouth or the heart of just one of the Baillys. Triumph supreme. The woman who had scorned him, the man who was his employer's rival. But the Baillys were on their guard, Chief Blackbird was watching, and even his own disciple, Neengay Lefèvre, seemed to be queer, disaffected, suspicious, since she had come down here to the Bailly region. Impossible plot! Yet how Rastel would applaud and reward him with a shower of gold! Rastel was gone for longer and longer intervals now, spending most of his time at the gay post of New Orleans, letting his agents collect as they could in the North, and returning only once every two years or so for a reconnoitering, a gathering of furs, and a pay-off. He was a rich lord now, with affairs of the cities on his hands, but De la Vigne doubted if Rastel would ever be so pre-occupied as to forget his hatred of Bailly.

De la Vigne stopped stirring for a moment, and let his concen-trated picture of Joseph Bailly float on the surface of his bubbling pot. Bailly had gone off with the fishermen; but his face was here, distorted with heat and agony, his mouth twisted with pain, his blue eyes bulging, his red hair swirling like autumn leaves . . .

A child's voice interrupted, in Algonquin:

"What are you doing?"

De la Vigne turned and looked down, startled. He knew that the Bailly children had been forbidden to come anywhere near the encampment, and whenever he had sauntered down the Sauk Trail they had fled, like startled quail, into the thickets or the log cabins. Beside him was a vivacious little girl about eight years old, with yellowish skin, large black eyes, and masses of black, curling hair. She was holding fiercely to the hand of a boy slightly younger than herself, who was struggling to get away. The little boy looked as if he were of a different breed entirely, with a pale, olive skin like the Wing Woman's, delicate features in the upper part of his face and the determined chin and startlingly blue eyes of his father. De la Vigne conceived an instant loathing for him and a momentary feeling of kinship for the girl who was taking such delight in dragging her brother to the forbidden encampment.

The obvious reply had sprung to De la Vigne's lips: "Mixing poison", but he checked it, made a mumble out of it and remade the answer: "What am I doing? Making a drink. Yes, making a drink." All the lines of his face tensed in the concentration of creative thinking. "Making a *magical* drink that will make all the spirits, the *good* spirits come and talk with you. The 'little men,' the Puckwees, will come and play with you! If you wish, you will be able to see Pau-puk-keewis dancing on the white shore of Lake Mitchigami, as he sings his songs among the sand grains. The spirits of departed braves will march down from the Great White Path in the Sky and make a brave warrior out of the little boy there."

"I don't *want* to be a great warrior! Let go! Let go of my hand, Lucille! Maman told you not to come here! And Papa told you not to come here!"

"Well, well, well! Why should they have told you not to come here?"

"Never mind! They said it was dangerous here!"

"Dangerous?" De la Vigne laughed contemptuously. "Dangerous among your Ottawa friends? Doesn't your grandmother live here in the encampment? and Chief Blackbird, who's related to you, too? You can see it's not dangerous here. Can't you?"

"Yes!" declared Lucille. "Pouf! You're just a little coward, Robert. You'll never be a brave! Give us some of that magic medicine, will you?"

"Yes. I'll dip some maple sugar in it and see how you like the taste of it. Wait here a minute."

De la Vigne stopped his stirring and hurried to his tepee to get some cakes of maple sugar that the tribe had made in the spring at the Bailly grove. He was grinning from ear to ear. Wonderful! He couldn't have planned it better himself. All he had to do was to dip two small cakes of maple sugar in the mixture, give them to the children, to do their lethal work, then hurry away on a belated herb-hunting trip and not return until the next day. Meanwhile, it would seem obvious to everyone that the children had helped themselves to the juice that had been left cooling in the pot. Motchi Manitou, the Evil Spirit himself, couldn't have devised a better plan! Bailly's only son, of whom he was so ridiculously proud that even the Indians jested a little over it; and the girl too. Two birds with one arrow! Revenge was sweeter than the sugar of the maple, sweeter than roast raccoon, sweeter than the rum of the English . . .

De la Vigne sliced off two slabs of maple sugar from a full mocock that hung in his tepee, the silver-handled hunting knife quivering in his excited hands as he worked. Not even taking time to replace the knife in his belt, but carrying it in his right hand, the sugar slabs in his left, he glided out of the tepee, trying to compose the evil rapture on his face.

Returning to the pot, he leaned down, pulled out two unconsumed twigs from the fire to make a platform for the sugar, placed the maple slabs on these twigs, then lifted the hickory stick out of the simmering mixture and dripped the juice over the predestined funeral cakes. The entire process took several absorbed

minutes, during which Neengay Lefèvre happened to be passing first through the clearing and then through the oak and
maple grove which lay between her daughter's house and the
Ottawa encampment. As she came to the edge of the grove and
the second clearing where the Ottawa tepees stood, she stopped
suddenly. Lucille and Robert were standing in rapt attention beside the medicine pot of De la Vigne, who was dripping dark
streams of a liquid very carefully from a stick on to some invisible
object on the ground. He was very much preoccupied, for he,
who was usually as wary as ten foxes, allowed Madame Lefèvre to
stand there entirely unobserved. The gnat of suspicion buzzed in
her ear. Something was wrong. Something more than medicine
was brewing. After a short interval to allow cooling, De la Vigne
stooped, picked up with a skewering twig one of the objects on
which he had poured the black liquid and handed it to Robert.
The boy's grandmother could plainly see the smile of triumph
pressing up De la Vigne's lips, the gleam in his eyes.

On soft, moccasined feet, Neengay Lefèvre crossed the thirty-
yard space that separated her from the children. De la Vigne had
just skewered the other object, which Neengay guessed from its
shape must be a maple cake, and had passed it to Lucille. Both
Robert and Lucille had already taken small nibbles of the cakes
when Neengay loomed over them and knocked both confections
out of their hands, shrieking: "No, no, no! Run! It's—"

Before she could utter the word "poison," De la Vigne seized
her by the back of the neck with one hand and clamped her mouth
shut with the other. Neengay struck out wildly, her hands clutching at De la Vigne's hair. The parrakeet feather and a bunch of
black hair came out in her left hand. The children were running
as fast as their feet could carry them towards the cabins. Robert
kept running, but Lucille looked back over her shoulder. She saw
her grandmother lying on the ground, with De la Vigne stooping
over her.

"Take it! Take it, I say!" De la Vigne whispered in a hoarse
voice that carried all the way to Lucille through the stillness.

Lucille realized that some violent, dark drama was impending.
She hid behind an oak trunk, her black hair mingling with the color
of the bark, her eyes peering out like an excited squirrel's eyes.

De la Vigne's first impulse had been to use the hunting knife that gleamed on the ground where he had laid it when he started preparing the cakes. But that was the unthinking impulse of the typical Indian. De la Vigne was craftier, more farsighted, quicker than the adder's tongue. No, this witness should die of poison, also as if by her own mistake!

Neengay Lefèvre was trying to get up. De la Vigne squatted down over her stomach and, pinioning her arms with his knees, now tried with both hands to force open the jaws that he had, a moment before, clamped shut. Opening them at last, he inserted, before a cry could issue, one of the poisonous cakes dropped by the children, pushing it far into his victim's mouth. In her struggle, Neengay took several unintentional gulps, the mandrake and the ivy and the sumac-juice pouring death into her body.

As the sugar melted and diminished in her mouth and her struggles increased, it became obvious that she was attempting to say something final, something important to De la Vigne. He put his hand into her mouth and pulled out the small cube of sugar that remained unconsumed. Her poison-burned throat was now free for speech:

"You've tried—to murder—to murder—your own—daughter— De la Vigne . . ."

De la Vigne thought that the poison had already gone to the old lady's head. "You my daughter? You old witch!" He let out a cackle.

"No—you fool—no! The child, the little girl with the—black hair that curls like a nest of snakes—like your own . . .

Lucille was straining to hear, but Neengay was speaking in a hoarse whisper too feeble to carry. What was this secret? What *was* it?

"At the Crooked Tree, Marie's baby died. . . . Lucille is the child of—Enewah—"

"Who knows this? Who knows? Do the Baillys know?"

De la Vigne literally squeezed the answer out of Madame Lefèvre with his cruel hands.

"Nobody knows—but Chief Blackbird—and Running Cloud— and Shingebiss—and I. The other squaw—at the birth—and old Nee-saw-kee—are—dead."

With the last word, Neengay's breath began to come thickly, her brown eyes to bulge out of their sockets, her face to turn splotchy and purple like the berries of the Solomon's-seal, the foam to come to her lips, the terrible convulsions of the poison pain to twist and torture her body.

"O Gitchi Manitou—I have worshiped the wrong God!" cried Madame Lefèvre, in the Indian tongue. Then, in the French which she had not used for almost thirty years: "O God—of the Christians—O God—of the good Father Marquette—O God of my daughter—the Wing Woman—O Christ—have mercy on my soul . . ."

There was thick foam at Neengay's lips now. De la Vigne rose and watched the last contortions of her body.

When at last his victim lay still, De la Vigne picked up the second poisoned cake and placed it in her partially open right hand, closing the fingers over it. The left hand was clenched tight, from pain, as if already in rigor mortis. Then De la Vigne snatched his silver-handled knife off the ground, slipped it automatically into his deerhide belt, looked for any other traces he might have left, beat out the embers of the fire, and glided away on the Sauk Trail northeastward, in the direction opposite to that taken in the morning by the hunting parties and the herb gatherers.

De la Vigne's only thought was of self-rescue. That thunderbolt of intelligence that the crafty-faced child was his own daughter, he would consider at his leisure. If she were not killed by the poison—he thought it likely that she would be, before she could speak a word to anyone—he could use her to advantage in new schemes against the Baillys. Both children were probably dying at the threshold of their home. Nobody, he thought, had been left at home to look after them except their grandmother, Neengay Lefèvre. Neither child would reveal the forbidden trip to the encampment, and death would seal their lips too soon for any explanation. He was perfectly safe.

He padded up the Sauk Trail, the still leaves of the groves along the Calumet ridge throwing mottled lynx-shadows on his yellow skin. He was deep in the dark whirlpool of his own thoughts. His eyes looked down, not taking those quick glances of cognizance around him that Indians turn on the landscape without moving their heads or seeming to look. Suddenly, another Indian figure loomed out of the shadows and stood before him. It was Chief Pokagon. For several seconds Pokagon had been watching him approach. He had noted that De la Vigne was hurrying, head down, like a hunted animal. De la Vigne looked up sharply.

"Forest on fire, De la Vigne? I smell no smoke."

"No! Oh, no! I left a bundle of herbs in the marsh a few miles from here, forgot all about them. Must go back and get them and take them to camp before sundown."

"You're losing your turkey feathers."

De la Vigne put up his hands to his head and found both feathers hanging down almost over his ears. He fumbled around for the parrakeet feather, but it was gone. He tried to compose his twitching fingers, his twitching voice.

"I'd got back to within a mile of camp when I remembered the herbs. I've been out all day gathering 'good medicine.' No place better than these Calumet marshes, is there, Pokagon? Good place."

"A good place for *good* medicine. Well, goodbye."

Pokagon swung off down the trail. De la Vigne stood still a minute, quivering with unaccustomed fear over that last phrase: "A good place for *good* medicine"! Why had Pokagon had to come along just then? Why had he, De la Vigne, let himself in for Pokagon's hawk scrutiny? Why hadn't he cut down along the marsh at the foot of the ridge, out of sight? He left the trail immediately and plunged into the underbrush.

At the Bailly cabin, events had been occurring contrary to De la Vigne's expectations. The steady purr of her spinning wheel had kept Marie from hearing anything until Robert entered the open door, and she looked up to notice instantly his deathly pallor. She rushed to him.

"Robert! Robert! What's the matter?"

"I don't know. I feel sick."

"What have you been doing. Tell me! Tell me!"

"I—I— Oh, Maman, Lucille dragged me to the encampment. She held me by the wrists, like this—"

"Never mind! Never mind! What *happened?*"

"That man—that medicine man—"

"Oh, Robert, what did he do? Tell me quickly!"

"He gave us a little, little piece of maple sugar dipped in a juice that he said would make us see wonderful things. Oh, Maman, he said it would make us see Pau-puk-keewis dancing on the shore—"

But Marie had dashed to a shelf beside the fireplace. Dipping out water with shaking hands from a birch-bark bucket into a cup, she added to the cup almost a handful of salt. "Drink this, Robert! Drink it—quickly!"

She forced the nauseous liquid into the child's mouth, then hurried him outside the cabin. In ten seconds he had vomited. She then carried him to his bed, laid him down, made a fire in the fireplace and swung a kettle of water over it. There was no one to help her. Joseph and Jean Baptiste and the Indian menservants had gone fishing with the Indians. Rose and Esther and Magawa had gone off on the herb-gathering expedition. Her mother had just left for the encampment. Lucille was nowhere to be seen. Marie rushed to the door again and began to call loudly:

"Maman! Maman! Maman!"

No answer. In reply, Lucille came stumbling across the clearing, dragging her feet and very nearly falling. Many a time she had pretended to be sick or to faint, just to tease, but this was more than dramatized. This was real.

"Lucille! Did the medicine man give you a poisoned maple cake, too? Did he?"

"Yes. And he gave one to Grandma, too. She's dead!" said Lucille, studying her mother's face for every quiver of agony, even through her own blur of weakness.

For a snake-in-the-grass second, Marie was agonizingly reminded of De la Vigne's face. Then, as in moments of intense human emotion, Marie's mind became crystal-clear above her tortured heart. It was as if the soul or whatever we choose to call that essence which seems to endure through all identities, took charge above the stricken individual that was Marie Bailly. First, she must save this child who was yet living, then rush to her mother. Perhaps Lucille was dramatizing again, or "lying," as Joseph ruggedly insisted upon calling it. Marie hurriedly administered the same vigorous salt-water remedy to Lucille, laid her in her bed, and took a look at Robert, whose cheeks seemed pinker, and who was able to smile back at her faintly. Then she ran, like a deer, across the opening to her mother.

Marie listened for the beating of her mother's heart, but there was no sound. There was no lift of breath. There was only the look of a stagnant pool in the pain-bulged brown eyes. Foam was on the lips. The legs and arms were twisted in the grotesque curves of the body's protest against pain. Marie wept and called out the one word "Mother," over and over. Then, chokingly, she repeated the only passage that she could remember from the masses for the dead. It did not matter to her that she was no consecrated priest. Her desire was to save the soul of her mother who had sinned against God.

" 'Be favorable, O Lord, to our humble prayers on behalf of the souls of thy servants and handmaids, for whom we offer to thee the sacrifice of praise; that thou mayest vouchsafe to grant them fellowship with thy saints. Through our Lord . . .' "

Marie attempted to fold her mother's stiffening hands across her breast. She noted, as she did so, a small maple-sugar cake in her mother's right hand, a small green feather clenched tightly in the other. She shrank from drawing the eyelids over her mother's staring eyes. Someone else would perform that office for her. With one agonized last look, she turned and ran back towards the cabins. There was one more thing she must do, one more antidote she must try for the children. On the lower west ridge, just above the edge of the marsh, grew masses of goldenrod and purple blazing star which were just coming into bloom. Marie knew, from past experiences of accompanying her mother on many an herb-gathering expedition, that blazing-star was used as an emetic, and an antidote against poison. Rushing down the slope, she gathered an armful of the lavender spikes, plucking up as many of the flowers as she could by the roots. Returning to the house, she quickly cleaned the bouquet, then dropped the whole mass, roots, stems, flowers, into the kettle of boiling water. At intervals during the afternoon, she gave the concoction to her two children.

When Joseph and the Indians returned at sunset Lucille and Robert, though still very weak, seemed to be out of danger. All night, the great medicine drum of the thunder crashed over the encampment.

It was late afternoon of the next day, just before sunset.

If De la Vigne had thought to cover his wolf tracks, he had never done a more bungling job in his life. The children had not taken enough drops of the poison into their systems to affect either their minds or their bodies. They had reported everything.

In spite of a lurking fear of medicine man's magic, the Indians had rallied fiercely to the cause of the Baillys. They had sent out searchers, as soon as the storm had cleared at dawn, along all the ridges and marshes, to find the criminal and bring him back to camp. Pokagon had arrived at the Bailly encampment a half-hour after Marie's discovery of the tragedy and had reported the general direction of the fugitive.

But De la Vigne was not found until the next morning, far off along the banks of Trail Creek, where he was padding along like a lynx in the footsteps of golden-haired Ginsey McCoy, who was utterly unaware of his presence behind her and who was frightened into hysterics by the discovery of him, his capture, his squirming efforts to free himself, and his threats of evil to all concerned. He was brought back over the Sauk Trail, bound with deerskin thongs that cut deep into his flesh.

The Ottawa demanded an instant trial. Although it was the custom of the Indians to allow a murderer a few months in which to collect a sufficient number of furs or ponies "to cover the blood" of the slain and to redeem his own life from the incensed relatives of the victim, the culprit, in a case of especial atrocity, was tried immediately, while anger and resentment ran at sizzling pitch. Such was De la Vigne's situation. He had argued and wrangled and threatened for a postponed trial. He had promised a thousand pelts of the finest beaver and a hundred pelts of rare Pacific seal to Bailly, the son-in-law, and to Chief Blackbird, the remote cousin of the dead woman. Bailly had refused the ransom and had also refused to press the immediate trial, at Marie's request, although he would have welcomed the chance of throttling De la Vigne.

Marie had tossed in a sea of emotions all that sleepless night, struggling between the black, eye-for-an-eye Indian sense of justice that surged deep within her, and the surf of her spiritual nature, flowing over and above the dark undersurge. The unforgiving Ottawa stood back and allowed Indian justice to take its course, under the supervision of Chief Blackbird. No great council wigwam was built for this occasion. No feasts were held. No medicine man was appointed as mediator, for the medicine man was himself the criminal.

In the Indian encampment, the fifty Ottawa, Joseph, Marie, and Jean Baptiste seated themselves under the maple trees at the edge of the clearing. It was like a gathering of tropical birds, for the Indians were dressed for a ceremonial occasion, the many-colored feathers in their hair, red calico shirts, red and blue and white blankets, the dark blue skirts of the squaws, the luster of silver earbobs and necklaces and bracelets making a seething mass of color under the green maples and the white oaks. The tepees and the bark shelters formed a semicircle across the way. De la Vigne's tepee was in the center of the semicircle. The black pot and its black contents still swung on the tripod, as mute evidence at the trial. Five or six feet to the left of the pot, on a low platform of logs, rested the body of Neengay Lefèvre in a crude, open rustic coffin.

Chief Blackbird gave a sign for the culprit to be brought. Asa Bun and another young brave entered De la Vigne's tepee and led him out. He was no longer wrist-bound, but his ankles were loosely hobbled. He tried to stand straight, like the typical courageous Indian, but there was a curve of fear over his lean shoulders and fear in the hypocritical sneer on his face. He had blackened his entire body with charcoal, except for three zigzags of yellow across his chest, probably to strike the terror of lightning and of a wizard's power into the spectators. There were three blackbird wings in his hair. His medicine pouch, his gourd rattle and six scalps were at his waist thong. He had, of course, been deprived of his tomahawk and his knife.

He was led to the middle of the small open space between the big medicine caldron and the coffin of Neengay Lefèvre. Asa Bun and his companion stepped back. Chief Blackbird came forward and stood beside De la Vigne, facing the tense company. In a loud, monotonous, nasal voice, Blackbird stated the accusation, much as accusations are proclaimed in paleface trials:

"Neoma de la Vigne, you have been accused of murdering Neengay Lefèvre, my kinswoman, mother of the Wing Woman and mother-in-law of Monami Bailly. You have also been accused of trying to murder the only son and the youngest daughter of the Wing Woman and of Monami Bailly. Is there any reason why you should not suffer death? You, as the medicine man, are your own mediator. Speak!"

De la Vigne took the gourd rattle from his belt and shook it dramatically. In spite of themselves, in spite of their hatred and contempt, the group quivered as always, in response, like the dried corn kernels in the gourd. De la Vigne knew his power. Twice he shook the gourd. Then all was doubly still. Fixing the audience with his hypnotic gaze, he spoke:

"My brothers, you have dragged an innocent man to the border of death. You are deceived. Listen, my brothers, and I will tell you the strange story of what happened to Neengay Lefèvre. Early in the morning, after you had gone to the hunt, I set my pot to boil over a low fire. Then I remembered that I must have an antidote for the poison that I was making, lest someone in camp should accidentally taste the brew. I remembered the great patch of blazing star that grows on the dry hill of sand near the mouth of Trail Creek—"

Marie impulsively cried out:

"Why did you not gather the blazing star that grows at the foot of this ridge? I used it yesterday as a cure for my children!"

The Algonquin exclamations of surprise ran around the group like a sudden wind in the trees, the men ejaculating, "Ataw-a! Ataw-a!" and the squaws, their own feminine syllables of "Nia! Nia!"

De la Vigne thought quickly and answered:

"The blazing star that grows at Trail Creek is of a darker purple, a richer power, as the Wing Woman well knows. As I was saying, I left my pot simmering and hurried to Trail Creek."

"How was it," asked Pokagon in a deep, steady voice, as he rose from his place, "that I met you hurrying down the trail, your face to the east, when the western sun was beginning to paint the trees red, hurrying like a hunted deer?"

For the moment, De la Vigne had forgotten the explanation that he had given Pokagon at that time. Here was an unexpected hitch. He tried to remember:

"I had come almost back to the camp, as I told you, Chief Pokagon, when I remembered the silver-handled hunting knife given me by Monsieur le Marquis Maurice Rastel, that I had left five miles back on the trail. . . . Shall I not go on and finish my story, Chief Blackbird?"

"Had you something to say first, Chief Pokagon?"

"Only that the silver hunting knife was in De la Vigne's belt when I met him on the trail."

More exclamations of surprise from many throats.

"Continue, De la Vigne."

"I think that Father Pokagon was blinded with the sunset light. I will say no more of that. So I hurried on. Night came on, and the storm. I decided to camp near the Potawatomi of Trail Creek. You found me and dragged me back this morning, like a murderer. It is plain to be seen that Neengay Lafèvre thought I was making good medicine. She felt ill. She came to my pot while I was gone. She got a piece of maple sugar from her tepee to make the medicine taste better. Her grandchildren came along. She gave them a taste of sugar and juice—"

"Oh, no, she didn't! Oh, no, she didn't! *You* did! *You* did! *You* did! You know you did, too!"

It was Lucille, run away from Rose and Esther, whom Marie had put in charge of the children to prevent their coming to this gruesome trial. Lucille jumped up and down with excitement, pointing her finger at the man who was her natural father. The hearts of Running Cloud and Blackbird, who alone in the group except for De la Vigne held the secret of Lucille's birth, beat loudly under their brown skins as they watched this strange, accusing drama.

De la Vigne's eyes opened so wide that the whites showed all around them. Then he narrowed his eyes and tightened his lips and rasped out:

"You're not going to believe a child, are you—a little lying girl? That's no proof! That's false, false, false! Br-r-r-r-r!" He took the strip of scalps from his belt and flipped them in Lucille's face. "Br-r-r-r-r!"

Marie went to the child and took her by the hand. Lucille jerked away. She wanted to see the whole of this spectacle. Marie picked her up. She became a kicking, screaming mass of protest; but Marie held her firmly, carried her back to the cabins, delivered her again to Rose and Esther and returned to the trial.

When Marie returned, De la Vigne was trying to obliterate the effect of his tactical slips by threatening and frightening the group. Curses are the white man's prerogative. But De la Vigne was approaching malediction pretty closely:

"May Ah-nim-o-kee, the Thunderer, send down his lightnings upon you and destroy you all, you and your people and your dogs and your ponies and all your possessions, if you dare even to think of destroying me. May the Thunder Birds and the Water Panthers make war where you walk! If you destroy me, I will destroy you!"

Again De la Vigne flourished his gourd rattle. No one would have dared to speak except Blackbird, Pokagon, or Bailly. Chief Blackbird spoke:

"It is not a question of what will happen afterwards, my brothers. It is a question of what must be done now. He says he did not commit the crime. Did he commit the crime, or did he not?"

"Kaw! Kaw! Kaw!" came the Algonquin *No's*, like the voices of many crows over the encampment. De la Vigne had used his mesmerism well. The *Kaw's* became stronger and stronger as each barbaric advocate gave supplementing courage to the next.

But Blackbird, the kinsman, was not satisfied.

"You believe then, my brothers, the story of De la Vigne, the magician? It is true that no one except the children saw him commit the crime. But it is true also that his story has spots in it. Is there no other testimony? Monami Bailly, speak to us and help us make clear this case."

Joseph Bailly rose from his place.

"If my father wishes me to speak, I will speak. First I will ask a question. Does anyone remember what feathers the magician, De la Vigne, was wearing in his hair yesterday morning?"

The Indians looked surprised. A few of them nodded their heads negatively. Then a young girl, Three Stars, who was half in love with De la Vigne and did not realize that what she said would be used as incriminating evidence, cried out:

"Yes, a parrakeet's feather, green, and two turkey feathers."

"Hoh! Hoh!" (Yes! Yes!) came many murmurs now. "A parrakeet's feather and two turkey feathers!"

"He had only two turkey feathers hanging down crookedly when I met him," said Pokagon.

"Open the hand of Neengay Lefèvre," suggested Joseph, in a ringing voice. "Perhaps you will find something in it."

More exclamations of surprise.

De la Vigne let out a somewhat hysterical laugh and cried: "It means nothing, nothing, *nothing*, my brothers! Perhaps Monami Bailly put something into the squaw's hand himself!"

There were protests at this, for Joseph's honesty was well known. Remembering the technique of the marshaling of evidence at his own trial in Detroit, Joseph spoke more vigorously, warming to the subject:

"If the parrakeet feather means nothing, what would you say if you should find clutched in the dead hand of my poor mother a few strands of dark hair, dark hair that *curled*? There is no one here who has dark curling hair except the magician, De la Vigne."

"And your child! Your child has dark, curling hair!" cried De la Vigne. "The girl, Lucille! Perhaps it was she! Yes, it must have been *she* who gave the poisoned cake to her grandmother!"

The resemblance of the hair and even of the faces of these two suddenly struck Joseph like a blow! He must think of this later, not now. He heard the Indians angrily protesting the accusation of the child and then crying out:

"Hoh! Hoh! Yes! Yes! That would be proof, if the curling hair were found, proof that De la Vigne is the murderer! Let Monami Bailly open the hand!"

"Joseph, you are condemning this man to death!" protested Marie, in a low voice. "Should we who try to teach the Indians about Christ condemn him?"

"Would you have De la Vigne go free to murder our children, Marie?"

"I wish with all my strength that he were dead, but not through us, Joseph, not through us! That dark blood upon us!"

Joseph turned to the company and declared: "This is a trial, a just trial. We have set out to find the murderer. I do not necessarily demand his death, but his banishment from the tribe forever, my brothers. I ask, for the sake of justice, that the hand of Neengay Lefèvre be opened. But I would rather not open the hand of my mother myself."

"I'll do it!" cried the ruthless Asa Bun, coming forward.

"Very well, Asa Bun," agreed Blackbird.

Asa Bun leaned over the coffin and applied his strength to Neengay's hand, clenched like a hand of stone. In a moment, he held up triumphantly a parrakeet's green feather and a small handful of black hair.

"Bring the hair here," directed Blackbird. While Asa Bun looked on, the Chief studied the strands of hair in the palm of his hand. Instantly, he announced: "It curls!"

The Indians stood up and shrieked. They brandished their tomahawks at De la Vigne and made rushes in his direction. The sneer on his face faded, and he stepped back, almost into the arms of Asa Bun, who had resumed his place behind him. Marie covered her face with her hands.

Blackbird raised both his arms for silence. The Indians fell back. Some of them sat down again.

"It is murder then? You agree it is murder?"

"Hoh! Hoh! Hoh!" (Yes! Yes! Yes!)

"Very well then, Joseph Bailly, you are the nearest male relative of the slain woman. Plunge your knife into the murderer's heart! Or tomahawk him!"

Joseph stood up, but did not, for a second, step forward. He was deliberating what to do. Every nerve in his body stretched towards the avenger's knife. Here was the murderer of his wife's mother, the would-be murderer of his children, the would-be murderer, in times past, of his wife and of himself, the greatest menace to the Baillys existing in the world, with the exception of Maurice Rastel. Joseph could have plunged the knife into De la Vigne's breast as easily as he could have knifed a wolverene caught in one of his traps. He would be considered a coward if he did not do so. Yet something held him back, that element which differentiated the white man, with his restrained morality and controlled wrist, from the Indian, with his wolflike lust for killing and his immediacy of trust. Before Joseph could move, Marie, who had become more and more revolted by the demonstrations of vindictive savagery all around her, and had been swept by a counter-wave of high emotion, had risen and had slipped quickly to a place beside Blackbird.

"Chief Blackbird," she said, "as the nearest blood relative of the slain woman, I ask the right to speak."

Chief Blackbird paused. Women were never admitted into the councils of men. They were weak in mind, and stained in body, with the pollution of many moons. He did not speak. Marie, without waiting for permission, turned towards the spectators and raised her hands for silence. There were many guttural protests, many murmurs of dissent. Marie held her hands in the half-lifted position and looked steadily at the Indian audience, with the strange pour of beneficent power that she knew so well how to use in quieting the suspicions of animals. In her beaded deerskin dress—for she had wisely chosen the Indian costume for this occasion—her beaded moccasins, her hair drawn in two braids over her shoulders, her cheeks deathly pale, her face bright with a strange zealotry, she looked like some French-Indian Jeanne d'Arc. She waited until the last murmur had subsided, and not a whisper disturbed the quiet July air. Not a leaf stirred. Not a squirrel frisked the stillness.

"My brothers," Marie began, in a clear musical voice, "a life has been taken. Let no more lives be taken. The Great Spirit looks down on this peaceful grove and says: 'Let there be no more death in this quiet place. Let no more murder be done. Let no more blood stain the earth.'

"Remember the twenty-one commandments, my brothers. Does not our fourteenth commandment say: 'Thou shalt not commit murder, unless it be while on the warpath'?

"We are not on the warpath, my brothers, and killing the medicine man would be but a second murder.

"Do not our second and third commandments say: 'Thou shalt not commit any crime, either by night or by day, or in a covered place: for the Great Spirit is looking upon thee always, and thy crime shall be manifested in time, thou knowest not when, which shall be to thy disgrace and shame. Look up to the skies often, by day and by night, and see the sun, moon and stars which shine in the firmament, and think that the Great Spirit is looking upon thee continually.

"It is hard for me to say these words, my brothers, here in the grove where my mother lies dead and my children also might have died. It is harder than pulling the teeth from the jaws of a living wildcat. I have struggled all night with the wildcat, here, inside of my heart. The Great Spirit and the God of the Christians have conquered it at last. It lies dead.

"Surely you know, my brothers, that the good Father Marquette, whose memory is so close to us all at the Crooked Tree and here at Marquette Springs, would have counseled mercy, like Christ whom he served and who is the underchief of the Lord of us all. And you know, too, that our beloved Father Richard would also counsel mercy.

"Let your hearts be turned to kindness. Use your knives on the black bear and the deer, if you must, but do not stain your hands with the blood of a man!

"Send the magician De la Vigne far, far away. Let him be a wanderer among other tribes. He has done much harm along the shores of Lake Mitchigami. Send him to the Sauk and the Fox, never to return, on pain of death. But do not kill him. Your son, Chief Blackbird, who is studying to spread good words and good deeds, would say the same thing. Do not kill him! *Do not kill!*"

Marie dared not turn her head to look at the dead face of her mother, for fear she herself might weaken or arouse pity and vengeance again in the crowd. She walked back to her place. Joseph took her hand and clenched it tightly.

There was silence, then a rising murmur of protest from the death-hungry Indians.

Joseph rose and said: "The Wing Woman has well spoken. Let there be no more death. Let the magician be banished forever."

Then a middle-aged Indian with a scarred, deep-lined bronze face rose. It was Black Turkey, the father of Enewah. He had always suspected, though he had never for a certainty known, that De la Vigne had been the seducer of his daughter. As a result, he had for years hated De la Vigne with a corrosive hatred.

"Let there be death!" cried Black Turkey, in a raucous voice. "Your hearts are pale. Let the Wing Woman have the heart of a bird. Not you: You are petticoat-men! You are cowards! Kill him!"

This appeal struck a roaring, responsive chord in the Indians.

"Kill him! Kill him!" cried Asa Bun, who had supposedly

always been a friend, a partisan, and a partner in crime of De la Vigne.

"Kill him!" came from more and more areas of the camping ground, until at last the communal demand for death was one united, barbaric roar.

"Death is demanded. Death it shall be!" shouted Blackbird, finally. "We-ho! We-ho! We-ho!" (So be it! So be it!) shouted all the Indians.

De la Vigne saw that it was too late for the council pipe of peace, smoked at so many Indian trials. All were against him except Pokagon and Joseph and Marie Bailly, and he was as good as dead.

"Let me sing my death song!" he cried. "My drum! My drum!" For it was the Indian's privilege to sing his own funeral song, giving himself courage for the journey to the land of departed spirits.

Asa Bun brought the drum from the tent. De la Vigne placed it in front of him, paused, then began to roll out the deep, dismal sounds. In a high voice, at first quavering with fear, then growing stronger, he sang:

> "I go to the land of departed spirits,
> Where I shall be a great Magician,
> Where I shall be the medicine man of Motchi Manitou!
> I will strike the lightning down on my destroyers!
> They will burn like little beetles in a forest fire!
> I will send the tempests
> And blow their cornstalks down,
> And blow their tepees down,
> And blow their birch-bark lodges down!
> I will blow the Ottawa from the earth!
> They will be as gray and forgotten as dust.
> I go to the land of departed spirits.
> I am brave. I am brave. I am brave!"

The last echo of the voice, the last vibration of the drum died away. Only a vesper sparrow swinging on a red osier-bush in the marsh below broke the dreadful stillness with its pure, thin song.

De la Vigne laid the drumsticks down, and stood erect for death. The song had strengthened him. The defiance had returned.

The idea of punishment by poison had occurred both to Marie and to Joseph, but not to the Indians. They preferred violence.

Chief Blackbird took the hunting knife from his belt and, turning from the spectators, faced De la Vigne, whose eyes burned fiercely into and beyond Blackbird, whose jaw was tense, whose head was high. Blackbird put his left hand firmly on De la Vigne's right shoulder, made a short, quick, preparatory gesture with the knife, a second stab which did not yet cut the flesh, and then, while every breath was held, plunged the knife, with an echoing thrust, deep into the heart of De la Vigne. Pulling the knife out, Blackbird steppped quickly to one side. For a few terrible seconds, De la Vigne stood, while the blood spurted from the wound, in separate jets, with each gasping breath that he took. Then his knees began to give way. The defiance slipped from his mouth. The threat vanished from his eyes. The face was empty. De la Vigne fell to the ground.

Chapter XXX

THE BALL FOR LAFAYETTE

They were all waiting for General Lafayette to come downstairs. He was undoubtedly weary from the prolonged ceremonies of the day.

He had stepped from the New Orleans boat at exactly noon. Twenty-four guns had been fired from old Fort St. Charles, as his foot touched the soil of Baton Rouge. Léon Bonnecaze, consular agent of France, splendid in a red velvet cloak heavy with gold embroidery, his white-silk-shirted chest sparkling with starry decorations, his diamond shoe buckles frosting the air, had stepped forward, had removed his three-cornered white hat, bowed so low that the powder from his hair fell like snow on the ground, and had delivered the formal welcome. The General had responded with that force and charm and bonhomie which, together with his courage and passionate love of liberty, had brought America to his feet three times before this final triumphal tour of 1824. Silk handkerchiefs had waved in the air. "Vive Lafayette! Vive Lafayette!" had echoed and echoed and added surges of sound to the ripples of the Mississippi below. The musicians had struck up the "Marseillaise." Powdered heads had bowed low again on both sides of the wharf road, as Bonnecaze had escorted the distinguished guest to the gilded coach, with its four white horses, waiting proudly to make the brief journey to the town hall.

Baton Rouge had changed greatly from the unprepossessing village of sixty log cabins that Joseph Bailly had visited ten years before. The new town hall was of brick. There were half a dozen fine French manors now lifting their gables over the magnolia trees. There were two churches. There were dozens of new cabins. There were two new taverns, but none equaled Madame Le Gendre's in permanent popularity.

At the town hall, Lafayette had made a more elaborate speech. Then the white horses had taken him to the barracks, and from there to the sumptuous home of his host, Monsieur Bonnecaze. He might well be questioning the truth of that admirable adage, "Rien de plus estimable que la cérémonie."

Now the ball guests were waiting for Monsieur Bonnecaze to bring his famous guest down to the lower floor; Madame Bonnecaze, in a full dress of sea-blue gauze trimmed with puffings of blue satin and small roses of pink satin, was, in the meantime, doing the honors downstairs most graciously. She was being especially courteous to Joseph Bailly, for Joseph had not visited his post for two years, and there were newcomers to the rapidly growing town to whom he must be introduced, as well as a number of gay French people from New Orleans who had followed up the river to enjoy the festivities at Baton Rouge, after the whirl of festivities in the metropolis. Joseph had already greeted all his old friends: Duplantier, who was acting as aide to Lafayette in Louisiana, Monsieur de Boré, whose snow-white hair at eighty needed no powder, Dr. Cousso, and the Lanzins. Joseph had just remarked to Dr. Cousso:

"Now that Napoleon is dead, it seems as if all the homage we ever had for the Emperor, in his best days were now being added to our old love for General Lafayette, to make a new affection for him. I declare my blood raced like a boy's when I first saw General Lafayette this morning. Hero worship, if you will! I'm not ashamed!"

"Neither am I, Bailly! I'm older than you, but I feel just the same. The man's got magic!"

"He's a symbol, too," said Joseph. "A symbol of all that's brave and fine in France, and friendly towards America. A splendid link between the two greatest countries in the world! Mon Dieu! What I'd give to be such a link!"

"In your way you are, Bailly. You're a good Frenchman and a good American!"

"I hope so, but—"

The graciously importunate voice of Madame Bonnecaze broke in:

"And here, Monsieur Bailly, are some delightful people from

New Orleans who've just driven up for the festivities—Monsieur and Madame Maurice Rastel!"

Joseph turned from Dr. Cousso and looked into the faces of the two people whom he had first met at another ball many years before.

Corinne was still beautiful, amazingly so. She was slim as a girl and carried herself with a conscious patrician erectness. Her complexion was still lovely, in spite of the use of the rouge of "Spanish paper" through the years. There were lines only about her eyes—very small ones, almost imperceptible. Her eyes were still brilliant, with an almost artificial brilliance. Her eyelids were gilded. Her lips bore the suspicion of tinting. Her lustrous, black hair was unpowdered, piled high on top of her head in numberless rolls and curls, and set off with a single, large crimson rose. Her dress was of crimson velvet, with the neck cut very low, and the slim waist held with a golden girdle, the buckles being in the shape of golden hands possessively clasped. The dress was richly embroidered down a front panel and around a wide hem with golden fleur-de-lis. On her hands and arms were long white gloves. Joseph noted that on the backs of the hands of both gloves the name "Lafayette" was embroidered in gold thread and pearls. In spite of the fact that her costume and hair arrangement were at once youthful and audacious, Corinne carried it all off with a dashing charm which was entirely successful. Certainly every masculine pair of eyes turned towards her with the concentration of eyes focused behind opera-glasses at the theatre. Certainly every woman looked double daggers in the direction of Corinne and in the direction of the involved husband.

Corinne smiled devastatingly at Joseph.

"Ah, Madame Bonnecaze, you don't need to introduce us! I met Monsieur Bailly in Quebec when he was just a charming, callow boy—and I was a little girl!"

Joseph flushed, in spite of himself ("little girl," indeed!) and, to cover his confusion, bent low over Corinne's hand and gave it a prolonged kiss. When he rose, he discovered on Rastel's face the very expression that he had caught on that envious night at Quebec thirty years before. He made a stiff, short bow, without extending his hand, and Rastel responded with a bow so curt that it was scarcely more than an inclination of the head. Madame Bonnecaze noted the scant courtesy and remembered that Léon had told her that Monsieur Bailly had known Madame Rastel in Canada years before. Monsieur Bailly must know by this time how lucky he is! she thought with that jealousy-cloaked-in-piety which is sometimes called self-righteousness.

At this moment, the fiddles and the drums and the harp in an embowered corner of the room broke out wildly into the "Marseillaise." Every French heart beat like the drums of the army of Ardennes. The crowd in the Bonnecaze ballroom gave way, the men at attention, and made a path for General Lafayette to the side of his hostess as he came slowly down the stairs with his host. The colorful Monsieur Bonnecaze was resplendent, as usual, this time in a gold-embroidered green velvet surcoat, white brocaded waistcoat, green velvet knee breeches, white silk stockings and the same shoes with diamond buckles and the same glittering decorations that he had worn in the morning. Monsieur de Lafayette was a blackbird walking beside a parrakeet, for he was dressed in quiet black broadcloth, edged with white satin, with white silk ruffled shirt, white, ruffled sleeve ends, white silk cravat, black knee breeches, white, silk stockings, silver-buckled shoes, his only decoration being a medal presented to him by the grateful American people on his visit in 1784. His long, gray unpowdered hair was clubbed back and tied with a small, black velvet ribbon. In spite of his homeliness—and Joseph had to admit that the odious man-in-green at his father's masque-ball had been right about Lafayette's forehead, froggy eyes, and a froggy chin, the guest of honor looked distinguished from the top strand of his gray hair to the toes of his silver-buckled shoes. He was erect as a soldier, all the five feet nine of him. The deep lines of his face were characterful, from the two trenches that ran down the center of either cheek to the seams of his thoughtful forehead. His protruding eyes were luminous. His large mouth drawn together with difficulty over jutting teeth was yet upcurved at the ends with humor and affability. Love of humanity shone about him like a visible aura. Every Frenchman in the room felt an almost irresistible impulse to bend on one knee and kiss the hem of Lafayette's broadcloth coat.

For once, Joseph did not defer gallantly to others by yielding his place near the hostess, but stood exactly where he was, in order that he might be among the first to meet the man whom his imagination had adored from earliest childhood.

But Rastel thrust himself forward and Madame Bonnecaze was forced to present him first. He bowed low, with a Louis XVI swirl of body and arms that took his thickly powdered topknot almost to the ground, and Lafayette responded with an affable half-bow. The medal that Napoleon had presented to Rastel blazed on his lavender silk coat and in the mirror of his self-conscious eyes.

"We have had the honor, General Lafayette," he said, "of meeting you more than once in New Orleans, and now, unwilling to let you go, we follow you in your triumphal course up the river."

"Thank you, monsieur," answered Lafayette unencouragingly, for long since, in New Orleans, he had caught the specious nature of the man.

"And now may I present, general," interrupted Madame Bonnecaze, "the charming Madame Rastel."

"Enchanted to see you again, Madame Rastel. The roses of New Orleans are as beautiful as ever, I see, madame!"

"I picked the choicest I could find in your honor, monsieur!" answered Corinne, with mock ingenuousness, touching the rose in her hair.

"I had not noticed it. That is an invisible rose, madame, surmounting the visible."

Lafayette bent low to kiss Corinne's hand, suddenly caught sight of his name embroidered in pearls and gold, drew back and relinquished the hand with a smile.

"I am sorry you have deprived me of the pleasure of kissing your hand, madame, but grateful—for the golden recognition."

"I am sorry, too, mon général—but think how many fine gentlemen will be kissing your name tonight."

"Sans doute, madame—no doubt." As Lafayette straightened up again, Corinne was aware that she had overstepped the line of delicacy.

Rastel moved close to Corinne, squeezing her elbow, and making a barricade between Lafayette and Joseph Bailly.

"I should like the privilege of showing you the country hereabouts, general," said Rastel. "Could you not ride with me to-morrow? I know every creek and bayou and wooded ridge. My fur-trading operations come up almost to Baton Rouge—and I'm extending them all the time." He raised his voice on the last sentence, crescendo to the final phrase, so that Joseph might absorb every syllable. Joseph understood, in a flash, what he had long suspected, that Rastel was at the bottom of the diminution of his Louisiana fur intake in the last two years. But, through the thoughts that rioted in his mind, he was able to hear the firm, polite voice of the Marquis de Lafayette replying:

"Thank you, monsieur, but I believe that Monsieur Bonnecaze has already planned for every hour of the morrow. Has he not, Madame Bonnecaze? I deeply regret—"

"Yes, General Lafayette, you are right. The day is filled from dawn till midnight," agreed the courteously collusive hostess. "And now, where is Monsieur Bailly? I saw him here only a moment ago. Ah, Monsieur Bailly!"—beckoning to him over Rastel's shoulder. "General Lafayette, let me present one of our most famous fur traders, known from New Orleans to Quebec—the very flower of France in America—the Seigneur Joseph Bailly de Messein."

Rastel's eyes narrowed, and he bit his lips. Corinne after a momentary embarrassment let her eyes rest on Joseph with a look of pride that changed to artificial contempt, as Rastel darted his glance towards her.

Joseph, his heart thumping, bowed very low and said:

"General Lafayette, I consider this the most historic moment of my life, for I am meeting the man who has done more for the related causes of France and of America than any other living man. I love both countries with all my heart, and I honor what you have done."

"Thank you, Monsieur Bailly!" answered Lafayette, looking, with genuine admiration, into Joseph's honest face and grasping his hand with enthusiasm. "I gather that you yourself have done much for the two loved countries. I shall want to hear more of your work and your adventures. Can you not drop in tomorrow for a quiet chat perhaps? Eh, Bonnecaze?"

"Why not for dinner, Bailly?" urged Bonnecaze.

"I shall be honored and delighted to come for dinner tomorrow!" answered Joseph, lifting his resonant voice sufficiently for Rastel, three couples away by now, to hear.

After a half-hour of presentations, the music for the dance began. The large living room and entrance hall had been turned into a sizable ballroom. Tall vases of roses and althaea and festoons of lustrous magnolia leaves decorated the mantelpieces and the walls. A polished floor, gold-framed pictures, and French tapestries here and there suggested Versailles rather than a small trading-post town on the lower Mississippi. Whenever a courtly Frenchman created his quarters he created a miniature court. Whenever a coureur de bois set up his lodge of branches in the forest he lived, suitably, like an Indian. Both types displayed Gallic flexibility.

As the dances began, the sparkle of gold and silver and jewels flashed in the taper-light from a hundred gracefully moving figures. After the minuets and the reels and the "French fours," the music of the comparatively new "waltz" struck up. Joseph had learned the steps at officers' dances at the new Fort Dearborn during the last year, and had enjoyed the spirit and the rhythm of the dance and the opportunity it gave to converse with a partner held steadily at close range. In spite of his height and strength, he was a graceful dancer. He was eager to try the waltz with Corinne, who had always been airy as a ballet dancer and was, of course, the most arresting performer on the Bonnecaze floor. He was not unwilling to converse with the lady, either—in memory of that other night of thirty years before. The bitterness of his feeling at the court-martial in Detroit had strangely worn away. Only the earlier emotion seemed to return this evening. He danced the first waltz with Madame Bonnecaze, in order not to excite too early the jealous notice of Rastel. Madame was as light as a mud-sunk Mississippi alligator. When he had escorted his hostess to her gold chair by the wall, and had murmured a desolated farewell, he crossed the floor quickly to Corinne, who was surrounded by half a dozen buzzing gentlemen.

"Pardon, Madame Rastel, but may I have the honor of the next waltz?"

"Half a dozen have asked me for it—but I've promised nothing. Promises are dangerous, are they not, Monsieur Bailly? Yes, I am inclined for very old friendship's sake, to give it to you, the last comer. I see that tramping the woods has not impaired your dancing step, monsieur!"

"I understand you knew Monsieur Bailly in Quebec years— No, not years ago, madame, for you are very young," remarked Dr. Cousso, with stumbling gallantry, "but before this time—"

"I knew Monsieur Joseph Bailly when—"

"If you say 'when he was just a callow boy' again, I'll—" Joseph substituted a hearty laugh for the threat.

"You'll what, monsieur?"

"I'll tell what you were like when you were, as you said, 'a little girl'!" There was more than a faint reproof of Corinne's age-concealing dissimulation in the phrase.

"Why, what was I like, monsieur?"—the eternal feminine forever in pursuit of her own portrait. Corinne evidently trusted her ex-lover's gallantry.

"You were devastating! You were— Wait a minute. Let me remember my schoolbooks. You were, what Aeschylus said of women:

"more dangerous than all dangers
Of skies above and seas below—"

"And now I suppose I'm harmless and safe as one of Monsieur Lafitte's old boats sunk in the mud of Barataria! Is that what you imply, monsieur?"

"My dear Madame! You did not allow me to complete my tribute. If you were devastating then, you are the destroyer of all fleets, the Circe of all mariners, the end—or the beginning—of all hearts now!"

"Good, Bailly! Well done! Well done!" exclaimed Cousso, patting him on the back.

Old De Boré merely smiled a faintly quizzical smile. The pattern was becoming clear to his astute, ancient eyes. These two had once been in love with each other. Each had found marriage elsewhere. But there still lingered, under all the light and spurious bantering, an ember of that first romance. The man was scarcely aware of it. The woman was.

The lovely melody of the waltz undulated from the violins.

Joseph placed his right arm around Corinne's waist, his left hand over her hand and carried her out into the room. Thirty years slipped away like sun-thawed snow. He was young again. Corinne was young. He drew her close. She curved into his arms unresistingly. A strange, oriental perfume came up from her dusky hair. There was no word to be said, only the beautiful, impassioned, rhythmic moment to be enjoyed. Old De Boré, on the side lines, smiled again.

"Bon Dieu! They dance like two beings merged into one. As if they had done nothing but dance together for thirty years! Rastel is watching them out of the corners of his eyes, enchanted though he is with the charms of Madame Duplantier. Look out, Joseph Bailly! Peril is made of such reckless rapture as yours!"

When the waltz was over, Corinne said to Joseph: "We have not talked at all. I have so much to say to you. Do let us step out into the garden."

"And Rastel?"

"He's simply captivated with Madame Duplantier. But perhaps it might be better for us to wait until the music begins again."

Accordingly, they talked with a group of ladies and gentlemen gathered at the end of the room, then, the instant the music began, while Rastel's back was turned and he was ready to begin the next waltz with Madame Duplantier, they slipped quietly to the glass door leading to the rear garden. The front of the house had a large whale-oil lantern hung over the portico, but the rear was unlighted. There was only the pale glow that came from a quarter-moon and the southern stars. Corinne found her way adeptly to an ideally romantic wooden bench under a magnolia tree. The trickle of water from an only half-successful fountain in the near distance added the final touch to the histrionic setting. Joseph smiled over Corinne's characteristically artful preparations. But he assured himself: "You're too old to get caught again now, my boy! And so is she too old! Circe, at fifty, though she may look thirty, by means of her magic, is still—past youth!"

But as soon as Corinne's rich, emotional voice began to stir the shadows, the old, irresistible spell began to work. Joseph realized that, even in utter darkness, that blood-warm voice would set his heart pounding.

"Joseph, how good it is to see you again, how good, how very good—"

"How can you say that, Corinne, when you have wished me ill for so many years?"

"Wished you ill? Why, Joseph!"

"Certainly. Contrived with your husband how you could defeat me on all the frontiers of the Northwest—"

"You don't know the whole story, Joseph. I have had to stand by my husband, of course, but I have worked for you quietly, too, as I have told you before, deviated the course of Maurice's projects many and many a time so that they would not cross your projects. *I have helped you as much as I have helped him.*"

Joseph debated whether this statement, so throbbingly spoken, so plausibly stated, was just another of Corinne's enchanting fables.

"For anything you may have done for me, I thank you. . . . I remember now. I do thank you for restoring my trading license at the trial at Detroit. That was very good of you, madame."

In the form of address, Corinne quickly recognized man's injured pride.

"Oh, but I do not mean, mon cher Joseph, that your magnificent, independent business is in any way indebted to anyone but yourself. I was merely trying to tell you that a little injury might have been done to it—had I not been watchful of your welfare. For instance, your trade at Arbre Croche was never injured, was it?"

"There was good reason for that. I won't remind you of the physical encounter at Mackinac Island. By the way, your friend —and agent—De la Vigne, is dead."

"Dead? That—that remarkable man?"

"Yes. That remarkable man is dead."

Joseph related the story briefly but dramatically.

"Maurice will be much perturbed," commented Corinne.

"Doubtless," rejoined Joseph.

"And, Joseph, do you realize how untouched your work at the Rapids of Grand River has been? I am responsible for that. I diverted Maurice to the Maumee instead—"

"*You* did? You never heard the story of the near-debacle at the Rapids?"

"Not your version, Joseph."

Again Joseph told a swift, dramatic tale.

Corinne saw that her arguments were drifting against her.

"But, come, Joseph, let us not talk of the fur trade any more or of Maurice. Maurice is a brilliant man, and he is my husband. He has given me wealth and power. Whether he loves me or I love him is quite another question."

Joseph did not interrupt the significant silence that followed. Corinne resumed, richening her voice even more:

"There is only one man I have ever loved. Only one *good* man who has ever loved me."

In the darkness Corinne slipped her hand which she had ungloved, into Joseph's. His large palm closed over it slowly.

"I'm sorry if the wealth and the power haven't brought you happiness," sympathized Joseph. Commiseration was beginning to do its deadly work, as Corinne had hoped. "You deserve happiness."

"Thank you, Joseph."

Corinne was too shrewd to allude to Joseph's own happiness or unhappiness. That other world of his, that domestic sphere, must be entirely shut out from his remembrance on this enchanted night in Louisiana. For tonight, all his memories, all his thoughts, all his world, must be hers.

"Thank you, Joseph. You've always been so gallant, so kind. You don't know what cruelty and ruthlessness are, how they can use friends as pawns, kinsmen as pawns, even a wife on the chessboard of business or political intrigue. You can't guess the things I've been forced to do. If I hadn't, Maurice would have tortured me in one way or another. Oh, Joseph, how many times I've longed for your kindness, for your understanding, for your chivalry! How many times!"

Joseph began to wonder whether perhaps he had not always misjudged Corinne, whether his hurt pride over her marrying Rastel had not bitten into his interpretation of her, whether he had not foisted Rastel's ruthlessness upon her charming, ingenuous shoulders. Even her adverse machinations preceding the trial at Detroit slipped out of his memory under the beguilement of magnolias, the moon, and Corinne's strange, imperishable magic. There was no one to bind him to the mast lest he should succumb to the voice of the siren. Even the chuckle of Jean Baptiste might have saved him. But Joseph listened and was lost.

"Parbleu, but I'm sorry, Corinne! If only I might have known—" Joseph's voice went several notes deeper with feeling. Corinne knew the exquisite, exclusive triumph of women, the subjugation of the giants.

"Have you thought of me at all, Joseph, during all these years?" she asked, in order to bring that feeling to the exposure of expression.

"Yes, I have, Corinne—"

"Often?"

"Yes. . . . Often."

Joseph did not intend to say any more. But Corinne waited. And the silence, as she intended, was like a taut drumhead waiting for the burst of revelation.

"Yes, often," Joseph rushed on. "You have been carried in my memory from Quebec to the Pays d'en Haut, from Montreal to Mackinac, across the shining lakes and down the rivers to New Orleans! You have gone on many splendid journeys with me, Corinne!"

"Joseph, my Joseph!"

In the starlit darkness, Corinne lifted her face at the most perilous of all angles—and Joseph leaned down, put his strong arm around her, and kissed her. How long that kiss or that series of kisses lasted, they never knew. Directly over them, a rapier-sharp voice asked:

"*Who's poaching now,* Joseph Bailly?"

Joseph jumped up to face a familiar silhouette in the semi-darkness.

"This calls for a duel, Monsieur Bailly. Not a guttersnipes' fist fight, but a gentlemen's duel! Now! As challenger, mine are the terms as to weapons and place. Follow me!"

Joseph felt automatically at his belt, but all his weapons, of course, except a small knife in a brocaded sheath, he had left at Madame Legendre's, when he dressed for the ball.

"You are mistaken. As the challenged, I could dictate the choice of arms, as you well know. But I surrender the privilege."

"My dear Bailly, how noble of you—as usual!"

"But surely not into Monsieur Bonnecaze's house? To disrupt the ball on private matters?" asked Joseph, as Rastel opened the door through which Joseph and Corinne had entered the garden.

"Why not?" Rastel was more than eager to make himself the center of a dramatic spectacle in which he should triumph in the presence of Monsieur de Lafayette. No need to go through the rigmarole of the exchange of notes, long-previous appointment of seconds, selection of place and all that! Here was the place! And the foil which he had left at Grandpré's Tavern was already tipped with a poison so obscure and slow-working that no suspicion could possibly arise this time.

Rastel dramatically sought out Bonnecaze and told him of his injured honor and of the duel that must be fought immediately.

"But *not in my house*, Monsieur Rastel!"

"So I told him, monsieur," corroborated Joseph.

"Then just outside the house, in the light of the door lamp at the front. Surely you have no objection to that, Bonnecaze? It will not disturb your dancers. It should be as easy to settle a question of honor there as under the great lantern of the Orleans Theater in the city! Do you forget the two duels that were fought there last week after the ball for General Lafayette?"

"Very well, Monsieur Rastel. Make your preparations. My foils are in my office at the back of the house."

"Thank you. I prefer my own foils. I shall ride to the inn to get one."

"Very well," assented Bonnecaze, amused at this obstinate alteration of dueling custom.

General Lafayette had joined the group by this time, and Rastel had the effrontery to turn to him, bow low, and ask:

"General Lafayette, will you do me the honor of acting as my second in this affair?"

Without the slightest hesitation, Lafayette replied:

"Thank you for the honor, my dear Monsieur Rastel, but I feel it is not for me to involve myself, as a foreigner, in American private affairs."

"Then you, Monsieur Bonnecaze, will do me the honor?"

Bonnecaze hemmed and hawed before he replied:

"No offense, Monsieur Rastel—but—but—as host—of this evening—you understand—I cannot—"

"I see. Very well."

Rastel turned on his heel to seek for a second.

Lafayette immediately spoke to Joseph.

"I would gladly have acted as *your* second, Monsieur Bailly, but now, you see, I'm committed to noninterference! Good luck to you!"

"Thank you, general. I would not have dared to dream of such support, much less ask for it. Your words will carry me to victory!"

"No doubt of that!" put in Bonnecaze.

"I'm terribly embarrassed," apologized Joseph, "to have caused you all this trouble, Bonnecaze."

"No trouble at all, my dear Joseph." Giving Joseph a resounding slap on the back, Bonnecaze laughed and concluded: "I'm not surprised at the dénouement, Joseph! Picked up the old romance, did you, in my garden? Gad, but she's pretty! I don't blame you!"

"I did nothing but kiss her—because she wanted to be kissed!"

This seemed to strike Bonnecaze as even more amusing, and he called out to Cousso, who was talking to Madame Lanzin near by:

"Come here, Cousso! Come here! Do you know what's up? Rastel's going to fight a duel with Joseph here because he kissed Madame Rastel in the garden! And what do you think Bailly says, by way of excuse? He says: 'I did nothing but kiss her—because she wanted to be kissed!' "

Cousso joined in Bonnecaze's laughter. Then, suddenly, Cousso became quiet:

"See here, Joseph. Is it a duel with guns, broadswords, rapiers or foils?"

"Foils."

"Gad! Do you remember that hushed-up scandal of years ago about Rastel and the poisoned foil?"

"Why, yes, I do. You were telling the story the night I first met you all at Madame Legendre's tavern ten years ago."

"The two seconds could rearrange a duel with guns."

"No. Let it stand. Rastel insists on foils—and on his *own* foil for his *own* use! Queer dueling—but I'm not afraid."

"I'm the only doctor here. I'll doubtless officiate as physician to both parties. Meanwhile, I'll ride home as fast as I can and prepare a few antidotes, though Heaven knows what Rastel's latest venom is. He's gotten hold of a lot of Indian secrets. Hold him off as long as you can." And Dr. Cousso slipped away as inconspicuously as possible.

"You have a foil, doubtless, that I can use, Bonnecaze?" asked Joseph.

"Oh, surely, surely! Come back to my office."

"And, for my second, do you think Duplantier would serve?"

"Second? Second? Oh, Monsieur Bailly, do you need a second? Take me! Or am I not old enough?"

A young, slim, aristocratic-looking fellow of about nineteen had caught the last words of the conversation between Joseph and Bonnecaze. It was Charles Gayarré, the grandson of old Étienne De Boré. Joseph looked at young Gayarré with a sudden jump of the heart, for it was as if he were confronting his own image of thirty years before—a flaming-eyed youth eager for every kind of glorious adventure! This was the kind of young man that Robert, his own son, would be in a dozen years!

"Why, of *course* you're not too young!" answered Joseph, putting his arm around the boy's shoulder. "I'd be *delighted*, Charles! Perhaps you'd better go ask your grandfather's permission. If he says 'Yes,' it's arranged!"

Joseph smiled indulgently as young Charles walked away, two inches more vertical with pride than he had been before he blurted out the question.

Half an hour later, the musicians were playing to an empty floor. Every guest, man or woman, was standing outside in the shadows, just beyond the fifteen-foot circle of light cast by the whale-oil lantern on the gravel roadway leading up to the Bonnecaze door. Joseph had already taken off his blue broadcloth coat and his flowered waistcoat, and young Gayarré was holding them proudly over his arm. Joseph was flexing the foil in the gravel, testing its resiliency. Rastel made more of a slow, spectacular scene of removing his handsome canary yellow, gold-threaded coat and vest, which were bowingly received by his second, a local Spaniard of doubtful reputation, Don Antonio Silva. In receiving the clothing, Don Antonio held Rastel's foil loosely under his right arm. In that watched-for instant, Corinne, who had been standing behind Don Antonio, reached forward and deftly rubbed the end of the foil for a distance of eight or ten inches with her handkerchief, which she had just drenched with a quarter of a glassful of wine from the Bonnecaze sideboard. Keen old De Boré was the only person who saw and, seeing, understood.

The two men took their places, the white ruffled shirts blue-shadowed in the lamplight, the foils gleaming intermittently as the rays slashed along the edges.

Rastel's postures were, at first, theatrically elegant, as if he were playing to his audience; Joseph's were unconsciously graceful. Rastel was as sure that his astuteness would render him a quick victor as Joseph had been sure of the triumph of his bodily strength in the fist fight on Mackinac Island. For some minutes the thrusting and parrying led nowhere, Rastel's quick shifts of direction towards various parts of Joseph's body being met with equal astuteness by Joseph. Then Joseph took the offensive, as vigorously as if he were again using fists, thrusting and thrusting towards Rastel's heart and driving him back at last into the circle of shadow, as women screamed slightly and gave way in a billowing mass. Rastel, losing his theatricality and, with it, much of his elegance, began to fight tensely for his existence. At last he gave a thrust that tore Joseph's shirt and grazed his skin six inches under the right arm-pit. There was a single feminine shriek. Joseph recognized in its tone, deeper than the most feminine outcries, the voice of Corinne. The sound gave him a strange courage. He drove Rastel to the opposite rim of the circle of shadow, clashing his foil so quickly and so often on the other foil that the incessant sound was like that of rain and wind on palmetto leaves in a southern hurricane. At last, Joseph gave a quick, side-swiping stroke as Rastel came close to his heart, and the foil flew from Rastel's hand. Rastel waited, arms half raised, his face as white as his ruffles, for Joseph's final gesture. But Joseph surprised Rastel and everyone else by stooping, picking up Rastel's foil, keeping it in his own hand, and handing his own foil to Rastel.

"Change foils—and continue! Permitted?" asked Joseph of the two seconds, who had stepped forward into the circle of light as soon as Rastel had been disarmed.

"Bueno!" approved Silva, never dreaming of poison on his protagonist's foil.

"Bien!" echoed young Gayarré, eagerly.

The sighs of relief uttered by Joseph's five old friends were distinctly audible. Corinne and these five all noticed that green shadows of fear had come out under Rastel's eyes and down the mid-channel of his cheeks and at the edges of his tight lips. Nevertheless, he straightened his shoulders and prepared to sharpen his motions against death.

As they stood there, before Silva gave the sign to begin again, Joseph shouted out, " 'Avec les loups il faut hurler!' " *

Rastel shuddered, wondering whether, by this, Bailly meant to convey that he knew of the poisoned foil tip. " 'Pro pelle cutem!' " he cried, using the Hudson's Bay Company motto.

The signal was given. Again there was fruitless parrying for several minutes, each man wary as a wolf. The two foils, clinched up to the hilt, stopped each other a dozen times, and were disentangled only to become involved in new entanglements. The loud breathings of each contestant could be distinctly heard in the brief intervals of clinching. Then Joseph drew back and thrust straight towards Rastel's heart. As the foil was about to hit, Rastel swerved his body, cried "Touché!" jumped aside, and struck his own foil into the gravel. Life had suddenly become dearer even than honor-in-the-presence-of-Lafayette. For Rastel had remembered, with sudden nausea, the death he had watched a Choctaw Indian die in Lafitte's camp down at Bayou Barataria ten years before. The Indian had betrayed the location of one of Lafitte's hide-outs, and Lafitte had cunningly administered to him one of the poisons made by the Choctaw themselves. Rastel remembered the green, foaming lips, the tortured eyes, the squashed-worm writhing of that Indian traitor. This was the poison, always carried in his portmanteau, that Rastel had chosen for Joseph. This was the poison that he, the plotter, had just escaped.

Rastel put out his clammy hand to Joseph. In a loud yet quivering voice, he announced:

"My honor is avenged, sir. You may go—unscathed."

* "When one is with the wolves one must howl"—the battle-cry and maxim of the Nor'westers.

"By Gad, I'm ready to fight to the death!" cried Joseph, angered by the superciliousness of that release.

"Come, come, gentlemen." Bonnecaze came into the circle of light. "The duel has reached its natural conclusion. You're both avenged, I'm sure. What do you say, Monsieur Silva, Monsieur Gayarré?"

"Acabado."

"Fini!"

"Good! Then—on with the dance, ladies and gentlemen!"

"We're always so damned inconclusive, aren't we, Rastel?" remarked Joseph to Rastel, as the others moved away. "Can't kill each other off—*to save our lives!*" And his laugh rang out.

Two hours later, the guests stood singing "Le Drapeau de Carillon," which served as the stirring finale to almost all French festivities:

> "Mes compagnons, d'une vaine espérance,
> Berçant encor leurs cœurs toujours français
> Les yeux tournés du côté de la France,
> Diront souvent: reviendront-ils jamais? . . .
> Réveillez-vous! Apportant ma bannière
> Sur vos tombeaux, je viens ici mourir!"

As Joseph stood singing at the top of his voice, one hand behind his back, there was slipped into that hand a crumpled piece of paper. Over his shoulder Joseph saw Corinne following Rastel in the direction of General Lafayette and Monsieur and Madame Bonnecaze, to make her adieux. Joseph put the paper somewhat guiltily into one of his trouser pockets.

Half an hour later, he read it by candlelight at Madame Legendre's tavern. Corinne, not finding any paper, had ruthlessly torn a page from *L'Esprit des Lois* of Montesquieu, one of Monsieur Bonnecaze's prized volumes, and had written in the margin:

Bravo, my duelist! M. goes to the Bayous on Friday for a week. Meet me at the Absinthe House on Bourbon Street on Saturday at four. Six happy days together! Love ever!

C.

Joseph turned the page over. There was no writing on the other side, but the printed page was the beginning of Chapter I of Book XXIII: "Of men and of animals," followed by the beautiful poem of Lucretius, "O Venus! O Mother of Love!"

Joseph could not help wondering whether Corinne had torn off that particular page by accident or by design. He returned to the more important note. One more reading was enough to memorize it forever. His head swam with the prospect. He was too weary, too excited to think. It was all a dream, a delightful dream of youth returned. He fell asleep in semi-enchantment, as he had so often done in those far-off days at Ste. Anne de Beaupré.

Five days later, on the appointed Saturday afternoon, Joseph was walking southwest down the Rue Royale towards Bienville Street. He was walking slowly, for he was debating with Joseph Bailly. He had had several days in which to cool off, several days in which to listen to the bantering laughter of his friends in Baton Rouge, several days in which to remember his family on the Calumet. What if this were an ambuscade, with Rastel waiting? He wasn't afraid. Corinne drew him, as she had always drawn him. The sirens' music was in his ears. The Absinthe House was only four "islands" away. Life was so short. This was doubtless his last adventure. Why not?

He stopped suddenly before the windows of Amédée Fortier's Boutique des Armes. The same kinds of foils, swords, battle axes, pistols, and muskets were there that had bristled with threat for as long as he could remember. He recollected suddenly how he had stood there ten years before and had coveted the small silver sword with the figure of a naked boy leaning back along the handle, coveted it to take back to an unborn son! He searched the window for it, but it was gone, of course, sold long since. But the unborn son was flesh and blood now. Robert! His affection went northward in a great tide sweeping away the unnatural love of Corinne. He went into the shop.

"Good afternoon. Have you, by any chance, a sword for a small boy? I remember seeing one in your window years ago—of silver —with the figure of a boy along the handle—"

"That was a beauty, wasn't it, monsieur?"

"You remember it?"

"Yes, out of all the hundreds of swords I've sold, I do happen to remember it, for its beginning, monsieur, and for its end."

"I almost bought it myself, although I didn't have any little boy then. Tell me about it."

"That sword, monsieur, was made for Napoleon's son, the King of Rome, by Bonfils, the great silversmith of Paris. But Napoleon said that the figure on the handle was too weak, too delicate-looking. The silver boy must be a strong boy such as the King of Rome must be. So Bonfils made a new sword for Napoleon, and I bought the discarded one."

"And what was the end of it? Who bought it of you?"

"Monsieur de Boré bought it about eight years ago for his grandson, Charles Gayarré. Monsieur de Boré is not superstitious."

"He's a wonderful old gentleman. I saw him at the ball for General Lafayette at Baton Rouge five nights ago, and he danced three cotillions and three waltzes!"

"Nom de Dieu! He's eighty years old, but nothing ever tires him—and nothing ever escapes him."

"Je suppose. Now, about swords—"

"Yes, monsieur. Now, you'll scarcely believe me, but I have another sword here that belonged to the King of Rome. It's not quite so beautiful as the first, to be honest with you, but it's very charming."

"And how do you happen to have so many of the Emperor's belongings?"

"Fortunes of war—and death, monsieur. Everything was dispersed three years ago, you know. They say the young prince is locked up in the Castle of Schönbrunn at Vienna, almost a prisoner. Some of his belongings were sold and scattered with those of his father. Here is the sword, monsieur, if you wish to see it."

Fortier took down from a shelf a morocco leather case, with a huge N in gold painted on the cover, and opened it on the counter in front of Joseph. The sword handle was of gold. A golden eagle, wings half spread, gripped it with its claws. The design had strength, beauty, vivacity. Joseph took in his breath sharply. For the son of the Wing Woman! For Penaci, the Bird Boy! For Joseph's Aiglon!

"You don't like, monsieur?"

"It is interesting," said Joseph, his trader's instinct dulling the near enthusiasm in his voice.

He had gasped instinctively, because it was the perfect, made-to-order gift for Robert, for the child who loved animals and trees as passionately as he loved people, for the child whom the deer often followed on woodland trails, as they followed Marie, for the child upon whose shoulders the birds sometimes paused in their flight. Joseph dickered for the sword, paid half the price he would have been willing to pay, and walked out, the leather case under his arm, his heart singing. He could hardly wait to give that sword to Robert! Five days ago, he had talked with Lafayette. Today, he owned the sword of Napoleon's son! And now he had a son of his own! Life was very rich.

If he took one of the new steamboats up the river he could be home in less than a month. No slow schooner or barge this time! He must find out when the next steamboat was due to leave.

He turned southeast towards Front Street and the Mississippi River.

Chapter XXXI

A PAGE FROM MONTESQUIEU

JOSEPH disembarked at Evansville, after the swiftest, noisiest, dirtiest river journey he had ever made, rode up to his trading post at Vincennes, gave careful directions to his agent, Gilbert Dubois, and posted up the old Wabash Trail to Lake Michigan as fast as Veillantif, the chestnut Arab that he had left at Vincennes, could carry him.

When Joseph was a quarter of a mile from home, Robert, sailing leaf boats on the Little Calumet River, heard his father's lusty voice singing in the distance the old canoe song of the voyageurs:

> "Le fils du roi s' en va chassant,
> En roulant ma boule,
> Avec son grand fusil d'argent,
> Rouli, roulant, ma boule roulant,
> En roulant ma boule!
> En roulant ma boule!"

Letting his leaf boats loose, in the hurricane of his excitement, Robert flew up the bank and past the house and along the Sauk Trail, until Veillantif and his rider bulked brown and gold and red among the leaf shadows. Joseph was wearing boots, buckskin leggings, a brown broadcloth riding coat, red sash, and brown beaver cap. He leaned down and swept his son up joyously to his customary place in front of him on the saddle. They rode into the yard, singing together at the tops of their voices:

> "Three beautiful ducks a-swimming go,
> The prince he would a-hunting go!
> Rolling my ball! Rolling my ball!
> The son of the king, the king his son,
> He comes to hunt with a silver gun.

With his gun of silver, silver-bright,
Aims at the ducks and they all take flight,
Aims at the ducks and they all take flight!
Rolling my ball! Rolling my ball!"

By this time, Marie was out of the house, and Esther and Rose came flying, with Lucille at the end of the excited family group, and Jean Baptiste twisting his cap with nervous joy.

Joseph had forgotten how beautiful Marie was. The flush of happiness on her cheeks and the luminousness of her eyes gave an added beauty to the pattern of her face. There was no duplicity on this face. A pang went through Joseph, as from a poisoned foil thrust, at the recollection of his encounters with the Circe of the Mississippi.

"But what's this? What's this?" asked Joseph, after all the embraces were over. "What's happening here?"

Half a dozen men were scattered over the grounds, and two surveying instruments had been set up on the trail south of the house.

"Government men, Joseph, surveying for a road from Checagou to Detroit to be built over the old Sauk Trail. They've found our 'solitary place' too soon, haven't they, Joseph?"

"Yes, they have! We'll have to see about this! The road runs too close to the house. All right to have our friends the Indians, filing quietly down the Trail, and a very few palefaces, but millions of Yanks—that's different, isn't it? You should see them down at Vincennes! The covered wagons going through to the west! You should hear the hubbub, the swearing, and the shouting, the cracking of the whips, the screaming of the children, the yelping of the dogs. It's pandemonium. That mustn't happen here! I'll go to Washington, if necessary."

" 'The wilderness and the solitary place' ! Oh, Joseph! By the way, they tell me we're in *Indiana* State, not Michigan Territory."

"Mon Dieu! How can that be? Not *Michigan* Territory, our dear, old, lucky Michigan Territory? Well, let's forget about it now. I'm so happy to be home! Nothing else matters! Come, and I'll show you the presents I brought you all from New Orleans! Couldn't carry much on a saddle horse, but I hope you'll be satisfied! And you, Jean Baptiste, how are you, mon cousin?"

"Glad, mon frère—ver' glad to see you back!"

Joseph and Jean Baptiste unstrapped the saddlebags. Before Joseph went into the house, he strolled over to the surveyors with an attempt at Yankee familiarity.

"Hel-lo there! Building President Monroe's highway, eh? Well, I'll come out and talk to you fel-lows later."

Then he went in, impeded by the affectionate gestures of his family. It struck him that the log cabin was getting too small for such a lively family. He must build a beautiful homestead like that of Monsieur Bonnecaze at Baton Rouge. Perhaps, even, they might move to Baton Rouge or New Orleans or some such place where life for him and his family might be more festive, among French people.

In a few minutes, Joseph was spreading out the packs on the cabin floor, the carpetbags containing his clothes, the mysterious packages containing the presents.

"Oh, Joseph, there's a wine stain on your flowered vest, and the sleeve of this ruffled shirt is all torn to pieces! What kind of a party was it? You need your wife, I think."

"I wore those clothes—at the ball for General Lafayette!"

"The ball for General Lafayette? Really? Oh, oh! Tell us all about it! How wonderful!" came the cries from all directions.

"Yes. I went to the ball. And I do need my wife!" Joseph put his arms around Marie and hugged her.

"Tell us! Tell us!"

"Presents first—and then I'll tell you all about it."

Somehow, at this distance, Corinne looked like a very small siren sitting on a very small rock. Only Lafayette retained his gigantic stature.

"For you, Marie, this ruby and silver necklace to be worn at the next ball at Checagou or Detroit or Fort Wayne—and at the next ball at New Orleans, for surely the children will be old enough next year for you to leave and go with me!"

Joseph thrust into a side crevice of his mind, and jammed it down with incorporeal fists, the annoying thought of a possible encounter between Marie and that new Corinne, more deadly flirtatious than ever with the desperation of middle age.

"Oh, Joseph, how gorgeous! From Paris, of course? The necklace of an Empress, who knows?"

"Of course it's the necklace of an Empress—now!" Joseph laughed gayly as he clasped his gift around Marie's neck, above the awkward line of her linsey-woolsey dress.

"And now for the girls! Let's see! *Little* packages. They had to be. Couldn't carry doll houses or toy spinets on horseback! You should see those shops in New Orleans! Fairyland! I'll take you all some time! And from New Orleans we'll sail to Paris! And then—"

"The presents! Why don't you show us the presents?" interrupted Lucille.

"Be more polite to your father, Lucille," admonished Marie.

"Well, here's some more jewelry for the older girls. How do you like this, Rose?" And Joseph held out to Rose her first string of pearls.

"Oh, lovely, Papa, *lovely!* A *million* thanks!" Rose flung her arms rapturously around her father's neck.

"And Esther—a string of coral for you. You shall have pearls when you're fifteen, like Rose, my dear."

"Thank you, Papa! Thank you!"

"Oh, Esther!" lamented Rose. "What a shame that Fort Dearborn is closed again, just as we're growing up and might be going to military dances! Mamma says there used to be such wonderful dances there!"

"Nobody there, in Checagou now, but the Kinzies and the Beaubiens and Dr. Alexander Woolcott of the Indian Agency."

"Oh, but Robert Kinzie and Médor Beaubien would be grand on a ballroom floor, I think!"

"You little minxes! Don't you think of anything but beaux and dances? You certainly are growing up faster than I realized. Time to send you off to school with Thérèse, or somewhere else."

"Pokagon came through the other day, Joseph, with a message from the Reverend Isaac McCoy. Mr. McCoy has moved his mission and school over to the St. Joseph River, near Parc aux Vaches. It's to be called Carey Mission. There's quite a flourishing school and he wants us to send the girls there."

"Not a bad idea! Not a bad idea for a beginning. We'll see."

"The McCoys have just lost their sixth child."

"Sixth child? My God! And I suppose McCoy just bows his head and accepts it! 'The Lord giveth and the—'"

"Joseph!"

"Forgive me, Marie. Now let me see. My little Robert, your present."

"You forgot me! You forgot me!" shrieked Lucille.

"Oh, no, I didn't. You want your present next? All right."

And Joseph drew from a carpetbag a package about eight inches high. It was a little French doll, a court lady of the eighteenth century, perfect in every detail.

"Oh, how adorable! How darling!" cried Esther and Rose.

"Don't you like it, Lucille?" asked Joseph.

"Yes, but I wanted some jewelry."

"I'm very sorry," said Joseph, taken aback. "I did bring a ring for Agatha's little girl. I don't know just where I put it. Perhaps I can give the doll to Sally and the ring to you, when I find it. Would you like that?"

"Yes."

"Yes, *thank you*, Papa," admonished Marie gently.

"And now, *Robert!*"

"Yes, Papa!" Robert's eyes were shining.

Joseph drew from the carpetbag the largest package of all and laid it in Robert's lap.

"This," said Joseph, "is for my little son, who is as supple as steel, as strong as a young eagle, as precious as gold!"

Robert breathlessly unfastened the clasp of the leather holder and brought to light the eaglet-handled sword.

"Oh, Papa! It's the most beautiful thing in the world! The *most beautiful thing!* I don't dare touch it, it's so wonderful!"

"Touch it! Handle it! Use it! That's right! Flourish it, like a man!"

"It's not dangerous, Joseph?" asked Marie.

"Oh, no!" laughed Joseph. "Anyway, men must learn early to handle dangerous things, without fear! Swords and women and such!"

"It's fit for a prince, Papa!"

"It belonged to a prince. It's from the collection of Napoleon's little son—the Eaglet. We shall call the sword L'Aiglon, n'est-ce pas—for my Little Eagle of the Calumet!"

"Oh, yes, L'Aiglon! L'Aiglon!"

" 'Le fils du roi s' en va chassant!' " sang Joseph, his voice ringing with joy.

> "Three beautiful ducks a-swimming go.
> The prince he would a-hunting go!
> Rolling my ball! Rolling my ball!
>
> . . . .
>
> "He comes to hunt with a golden sword
> With his sword of gold, his golden sword.
> Aims at the ducks and they all take flight!
> Aims at the ducks and they all take flight!
> Rolling my ball! Rolling my ball!"

Robert marched around the room, flourishing his sword in rhythm with his father's song, his shoulders set back proudly, and looking quite martial, much to Joseph's satisfaction. The dreamer-aspect of Robert had always worried his father. The sword was just the thing to harden and strengthen the child's spirit.

"And now, Jean Baptiste, did you think I'd forgotten you?" cried Joseph.

"No, mon cousin! I t'ink you remember always Jean Baptiste."

"Here, Jean Baptiste—a little gift to help you slice your way in the world!"

From a small leather sheaf, Jean Baptiste pulled out a hunting knife, with a handle worked in bronze and silver.

"But, mon cousin, how could I use a t'ing so beautiful? Too good for Jean Baptiste. Too good! Jean Baptiste, he ees made of wood and steel, not all zese shiny t'ings."

"Jean Baptiste is made of gold!" cried Robert.

"That's right!" echoed Joseph. "It's not good enough for you, Jean Baptiste. Keep it and use it—and good appetite to you!"

"Now, tell us all about your journey, Joseph, everything!" urged Marie, settling back on her heels like an Indian.

"Not just now, Marie. It will take days to tell the whole story. I'll just say it was a pretty successful journey. I'll tell you everything later. I must go out now and talk to those surveyors. I've a dozen questions to ask them. What are we having for supper?"

"Ah, my hearty Joseph, I thought you'd ask that! We *were*

having lake perch and water cress and wild plums. But I see we'll have to do better than that, with you home again! Jean Baptiste, do you think you could go out and shoot a young turkey for us? You remember that huge flock that went chattering down the banks of the river an hour ago? They can't have gone far."

A half-hour later, everyone was out of the cabin except Lucille. Joseph had gone to talk to the surveyors. Marie had gone to the bakehouse, at the rear of the main cabin, to give instructions to Magama. The other children were staying as close to their father as they could.

Lucille was rummaging around the carpetbags and clothes and wrappings that still lay on the floor, in search of the coveted ring that she had so skilfully wheedled out of her father. Where could it be? If it were anywhere to be found, she would find it. She spread out all the papers that had come around the gift packages, chiefly old sheets of the *Moniteur de la Louisiane*. She searched every corner of the carpetbags. Then she began on her father's clothes. Pockets of trousers. Pockets of vests. Finally, in the pocket of Joseph's flowered vest, she found a paper, a page from a book, with some flourishing handwriting on it. The phrase "Meet me" caught her eye. She read, slowly but surely.

Bravo, my duelist! M. goes to the Bayous on Friday for a week. Meet me at the Absinthe House on Bourbon Street Saturday at four. Six happy days together! Love ever!   C.

The import of the note did not at first take possession of the ten-year-old girl. But, as she held the paper in her hand the meaning seeped gradually into her precocious mind. She rejoiced in the discovery almost as much as her own father, De la Vigne, would have rejoiced. Here was a weapon to make her mother unhappy, to bring trouble tumbling around her father—and to usher drama into the too quiet household! Nothing really exciting had happened since De la Vigne had been put to death for murdering her grandmother the year before.

Marie was the first member of the family to return to the cabin. She was eager to straighten things out, to put Joseph's clothes away, to make the living-and-dining room tidy for the evening meal.

"I guess Papa had a good time in New Orleans," commented Lucille as Marie began to pick things up from the floor.

"Yes. I guess he did. He looks fine, doesn't he? He'll tell us all about everything as soon as he can."

"I wonder if he'll tell us *all* about it," remarked Lucille cryptically.

Marie gave the child a quick look, and went on with her work.

"I wonder if he'll tell us about the duel."

"Duel?"

"The duel and the lady whose name begins with C, and whose husband's name begins with M."

"Why, what *are*—" Marie, of course, was about to ask, "What *are* you talking about?" when the two initials suddenly filled out into names in her astonished mind. Lucille watched the changes and then the sudden control on Marie's face. Instinct told her that her mother would not pursue the subject. So she thrust the paper into Marie's hand.

"Look at this! I found it in the pocket of Papa's flowered waistcoat."

"I don't want to look at it. Put it back exactly where you found it! You have no right to look at your father's private papers—and neither have I."

"All right. But I know it by heart. It says:

"Bravo, my duelist! M. goes to the Bayous on Friday for a week. Meet me at the Old Absinthe House on—"

"Stop! Stop, Lucille! Stop!"

But before Lucille ran out of the house to the refuge of the woods, she screamed at Marie the rest of the message:

"Meet me at the Absinthe House on Bourbon Street on Saturday at four. Six happy days together, Love ever!   "C."

Marie had taken Lucille aside before dinner, and had warned her that if she betrayed to her father or to any member of the family so much as a single hint of the note that she had found in her father's vest pocket, Marie would keep her in bed for a week, fasting on bread and water—a punishment to which she never resorted before. Only once during Joseph's recital of his adventures, at the wild-turkey dinner that night, did Lucille touch danger. He was pausing for a breath and a morsel after his description of the Lafayette ball when she suddenly asked:

"And how about duels, Papa? Didn't you see any duels in New Orleans?"

Marie cast a look almost as furious as one of Neengay Lefèvre's in the direction of Lucille. Joseph paused, for one perturbed instant, his fork in the air.

"No, I saw no duels—in New Orleans," he answered firmly, But, with a pang, Marie noticed a slight quiver of the muscles at the corners of his lips.

"By the way," put in Marie, talking very fast, "do tell us more about the steamboat that brought you up the Mississippi. Does it look like the *Walk-in-the-Water?* Who remembers the time the *Walk-in-the-Water* first came to Mackinac Island, and how frightened and excited the Indians were? How they shook their tomahawks at the boat and shouted out: 'Skiuta Neu Bequin! Skiuta Neu Bequin! Fire boat! Fire boat!' Who remembers . . ."

A few weeks later, Joseph was returning up the ridge trail across the marsh from the shore, where he had gone to see whether the waves driven by the first autumn storms had reached as far as his boathouse. The grounds of his establishment were deserted, except for Lucille, who had pilfered a long black silk skirt and a plumed riding hat of her mother's and was standing in front of one of the fur sheds like an elegant lady à la mode, the finger with the ring which her father had given her extended ceremoniously, as if to an imaginary beau. Her back was turned to Joseph and she was talking in mellifluous tones to the invisible hero. Joseph walked towards her and became gradually aware of the words she was repeating over and over again:

"Bravo, bravo, my duelist! M. goes to the Bayous on Friday for a week. Meet me at the Absinthe House—you know, the Absinthe House on Bourbon Street, on Saturday at four. Yes, on Saturday, at four! Six happy days together, my love! Kiss my hand, my love. Six happy days!"

Joseph drew a breath of staggered astonishment. Lucille turned around. His voice was harsh and grating:

"What are you talking about, Lucille?"

"Oh, oh, I'm just pretending. Just pretending I'm a lady in New Orleans!"

Joseph seized one of the child's wrists firmly.

"*How do you know* what a lady in New Orleans thinks?"

Lucille became panicky.

"I read it in a note."

Joseph let go of the wrist. He remembered the page from Montesquieu left intact in a flowered vest pocket.

"Have you told your mother?"

"Yes. Yes. I have!" Lucille gloated in the sudden, sword-cut lines of pain on Joseph's face, the tragic depth in his eyes.

It was not until they were in bed, that night, that Joseph opened the perilous subject with Marie.

"I want you to go with me, Marie, the next time I visit the post at Baton Rouge."

Marie choked inwardly and was silent.

"In fact, I had thought we might care to settle some time in Louisiana. We might fulfill our mission to the Indians as well in the remote post of Baton Rouge as here."

"Oh, no, oh, no, Joseph!" cried Marie, like a frightened child, and flung her arms around his neck. He drew her close.

"There's no danger in Louisiana, Marie, I assure you. No danger of any kind."

In the deep silence, two wolves could be heard far out on the dunes baying to the hunter's moon. Marie quivered in Joseph's arms. He knew just how deeply she was suffering, and wished that she would ease herself, like most women, and speak. He admired more than ever her restraint, her self-sacrificing loyalty. The garrulous protestations of Corinne came back to him in windy echoes. There was no help for him. He must himself explain.

"There's no danger, Corinne, from swamps, poisons, alligators, hostile Indians, false traders—or false women," he said, and did not know that, in his prepossession with the temptress' name, he had used it.

Still, Marie was silent. Joseph would rather have fought Rastel with bare fists from Mackinac all the way down to New Orleans than proceed on this tragic emotional journey. He fortified his soul again, and went on:

"I saw Rastel . . ."

Silence. He stumbled on:

"I also saw Corinne . . ."

There was the slightest intake of breath from Marie. No other sound. Joseph rushed headlong, leaping the intervening barricades:

"I fought the duel, Marie. I fought it and won it! But I want you to know that I *did not go to the Absinthe House!* And I want you to know that I love you with *all* my heart . . ."

Chapter XXXII

LITTLE EAGLE OF THE CALUMET

IT WAS late in the summer of 1826. All of the Bailly children had returned from school. Thérèse had made the long journey from Quebec, a charming and "finished" young woman of twenty-one, eager to remain with her family until her long-planned marriage to William Blackbird, who was returning in the autumn, after six years of schooling in the East. Rose and Esther, now seventeen and fifteen years old, were back from Mr. and Mrs. Bazeley's Boarding School, in Philadelphia—Rose bubbling over with joy and with red-headed enthusiasm at being home again, Esther strangely aloof. For Esther had picked up from the Philadelphia Biddles (who had been reluctantly polite to Edward's sisters-in-law and had invited them to tea and dinner the precisely necessary number of times, no more) a feeling of shame for her Indian blood. This shame came to the surface in the form of a wounding contempt for everything that her mother said and did. Marie understood perfectly and, adding this new grief to the grief over the never receding image of Corinne, went on her way, with the same serene smile, suffering deeply, but still in absolute silence.

Lucille and Robert had been attending McCoy's Mission School in its newer location, where Marie had visited them as often as wintry trails allowed. Joseph had journeyed as far south as Vincennes, leaving the Baton Rouge post unvisited except by his skillful southern agent, in spite of the possible machinations of his old rival. He felt vaguely uncomfortable about Baton Rouge—not afraid, for fear had no place in his rugged nature, but uneasy, burned-by-the-fire.

The summer had, nevertheless, been one of the happiest that Joseph had ever known. The children were all developing delightfully and were as healthy and happy as any parents could desire. Even Lucille was becoming more amiable and attractive.

Robert had grown into a fine sturdy boy of nine years. To make things perfect, Agatha and Edward and six-year-old Sally had come down from Mackinac Island in a fur barge on a July day and had spent three weeks with the family.

The mission work with the Indians was progressing well. Several Indians were ready for baptism whenever Father Richard should come along the Sauk Trail. Joseph had made a complete translation of the New Testament into Algonquin. He was also giving lessons in history, science, and mathematics to the braves, and Marie was teaching the squaws reading, writing, and needlework. The Indians were slow but agreeable pupils. Other things were going well enough, too. Business, though good, was not so flourishing as in the opulent days at Parc aux Vaches, and Joseph, foreseeing the dwindling of the fur business as the streams came gradually under the settlement and dominion of the Yankees, was already turning to other projects. He saw, in his sturdy imagination, villages springing up all along the Detroit-Checagou Road. He had successfully turned the course of that road, so that it made a wide, escaping curve three-quarters of a mile north of the house, although it followed the Sauk Trail in the main; but he saw benefits from the neighboring road, even while he preserved his privacy. He also saw possibilities in that shore whose every indentation he knew so well from Checagou to Mackinac. He had, long before, secured a mile strip of shore land on either side of the mouth of Trail Creek and half a mile of land along the banks of the river, as well as tracts near the present Tremont, Gary and Miller, Indiana. He began to write letters to the old French friends in Detroit and Quebec, urging them to come and settle, to buy land where great harbors and cities would develop shortly along the prairies and the dunes. He entered partnership with Oliver Newberry, the "Commodore of the Lakes," that new, bustling Yankee citizen of Detroit, and became part owner of three vessels, named for a hero who was as dear to Newberry's American heart as to Joseph's French enthusiasms (and for various occasions in the life of that hero): "the *Corsican*, the *Austerlitz*, and the *Marengo*."

During this summer, too, Joseph began building the fine French homestead which was to take the place of the old log cabins. Ever since the discovery of the "page from Montesquieu," Marie had passionately urged the building of the homestead here, in Indiana:

"When the children are older and you've made all the money you will ever want to make, and our work among the Indians is done—then it's time enough to go back to the cities. Don't you think so, Joseph?"

Joseph, remembering that his trading journeys yielded him many a festive hour in the ballrooms or the fiddle-resounding log cabins of New Orleans, Baton Rouge, Vincennes, Checagou, Fort Wayne, Detroit, Mackinac, Montreal, and Quebec, that his children were at the best schools in America, that Marie's rustic phase was coming to predominate as she grew older, had promptly answered by beginning the homestead. The house was only half finished, a handsome, gabled, balconied, three-story house of Quebec stone foundations, the frame of cedar and white-oak timber from Bailly's own woods. Joseph was still using one of the smaller log cabins as his office.

Late on a drowsy Sunday afternoon in August, Joseph sat at a crude table in this office trying to compose two letters, one to Monsieur de Boré, one to Corinne, to whom he felt it necessary to write because of some information recently received from Monsieur de Boré. For, at the conclusion of many charmingly loitering pages, which discussed the condition of the sugar plantations, the fur trade, the appalling growth of New Orleans, the river "crowded with boats as thick as needles on a pine tree," the situation in France, the development of his grandson Charles Gayarré (who was growing to be "quite a wit and an inveterate reader of all the newest books from Paris, the charming loafer!"), some philosophical paragraphs on old age, life in general, death, the old gentleman had written these words:

I'm growing old, Bailly, but I've decided that death is only life—with a difference. I'm not afraid. . . . As a plagiarist of King Francis I, I'd carve on the windows of life: "Toujours *la vie* varie, et fou est qui s'y fie.". . . Everybody fails you in the end, through perfidy or death. But just the same, Joseph, life is interesting and splendid. There are surprising bits of heroism all along the way, dramatic displays of human nature that make the whole sorry spectacle worth while.

Perhaps I shouldn't mention it at all, but I saw one minor bit of heroism and devotion, the night of your duel with Monsieur Rastel, that I think I ought to tell you about before I slip out of this world.

That dashing wife of Rastel has her good points, Joseph, or perhaps it's simply that she loves you still. Just before the duel, I saw her in Bonnecaze's dining room drenching her handkerchief with wine, and a moment later she was out under the trees frantically wiping off the end of the foil her husband was going to use on you. You get the idea? Rastel has poisoned the foil. Madame suspects it and wipes it off, running a great risk to save the life of her lover. A rather nice picture, n'est-ce pas? Just to prove there's a shining streak somewhere, even in the heart of every flirt! Don't take it too seriously, but I thought you'd be flattered to hear of this little attention.

Do come down our way again soon. Did you know you made quite the "coup" of the Bonnecaze ball? General Lafayette said that you were one of the finest men he'd met in America, with all the gracious qualities of old France added to the brisk and enterprising qualities which have come to seem so characteristic of the Americans! Bravo for you, Joseph Bailly!

Joseph read the last paragraphs again and tried to recommence his letter to Corinne. Jean Baptiste, whom he was sending down to New Orleans on business, would deliver it personally in a few weeks. It was a difficult letter to write, first, because he was not sure that it was necessary to write the letter at all, in spite of the irresistible urge of what he thought was gratitude, and secondly, because Robert, who was playing outside on the grass with Lucille, had been bothering him for a full half-hour to take him over to the lake shore.

"Come on, Papa! Come on! It's so warm today, and the lake will be beautiful! Maybe I could get Maman to fix up a supper for us to eat on the beach, so that we might see the sunset together. The sunset and the herons flying home! Oh, Papa, do come!"

"If you'll be a good boy and leave me alone for one half-hour then I'll take you over to the lake!"

"The sun's halfway down. I love you, Papa! Hurry!"

"Robert, be quiet! You mustn't interrupt me. I've a very important letter to write." And Joseph rose and closed, with something of a bang, the door of the tiny log cabin. The brief glimpse of Robert had shown the boy with his treasured sword, "L'Aiglon," strapped to his belt.

"Dear Corinne," wrote Joseph. He stopped to address the envelope, then resumed:

I did not intend to write to you again, ever, but I have just learned something which gallantry urges me to acknowledge and appreciate. We are both growing old—even you, ever youthful and beautiful Corinne—

There was a sound of quarreling outside, half heard through the partially open window. Lucille was vociferating:

"No, give me the sword! You use a sharp stick! Then you can have the sword, and I'll use a sharp stick!"

"I can't let anybody use my sword, my precious sword! No!" said Robert.

The sword had certainly strengthened Robert in every possible way. The youngster had rarely dared before to defy his taller, stronger, wilder sister. Joseph went back to his letter with a smile:

and so I feel that I want to tell you, before it is too late,

The sounds of stick on steel outside. Then a final smack and a pause in the battle.

"Ah, bravo, my duelist!" cried Lucille, and Joseph felt vaguely uncomfortable. "But I've won! I've won! I've knocked the sword from your hand!" Then Lucille's voice changed. She was evidently impersonating a grande dame. "Ah, my duelist! Won't you meet me at the Absinthe House tomorrow at four? You will, my love? Ah, how happy I am! Kiss my hand!"

Joseph suddenly tore into shreds the envelope he had just addressed to Corinne, and was about to tear the letter itself when the voices of the children became more imperative:

"It's my turn now with the sword!"

"I said you couldn't have the sword!"

"I will! I will! It isn't fair! Give it to me! Give it!"

Joseph sat still, between the two excitements, the remembered duel at New Orleans and the minor duel outside. He mustn't let himself get so excited. The past duel must be forgotten. The present little conflict must be overlooked. The children were certainly old enough to take care of themselves. He turned back to the letter:

that I thank you with all my heart

There were only the small sounds of struggle outside now, grunts and exclamations as the two children apparently struggled for the possession of "L'Aiglon." Joseph hoped that Robert would win and keep possession of the inanimate object that he seemed to love best in all the world. Suddenly there was absolute silence, that alarming silence of children which, in the midst of clamor, usually means trouble. Joseph took one stride to the door and opened it.

Robert was lying almost straight forward on the ground, the little sword under him, thrust at an angle through his chest. Lucille, her eyes wide with terror and excitement, was standing over him, her legs spread apart, her hands stretched open, statue-still.

Joseph rushed to his son, turned him face up, tore open the little homespun yellowish shirt, pulled out the sword point, clutched with his great right hand the edges of the wound, so dangerously close to the heart, and, with the other arm, lifted the child up and carried him into the house.

"It's nothing, nothing, Marie," protested Joseph, his stricken face denying the words.

When they laid the child down on the sofa in the main room of the cabin, he had already lost consciousness. It was forty miles to Checagou and to the nearest physician, Dr. Alexander Woolcott, but Jean Baptiste, wringing his hands in the doorway, offered to go.

"Wait, Jean Baptiste," said Joseph. "Wait just a minute."

Marie brought towels and stanched the outer bleeding. But the inner bleeding could not be stopped. The auricle of the heart had apparently been pierced by the tip of the little sword. Robert had never looked more beautiful than now as he lay with his fine young head thrown back against the folded buffalo rug. L'Aiglon himself, Napoleon's son, was never handsomer. Joseph watched his son closely as Marie worked over him. Slowly, the flame that had always belonged on that eager face turned to ashes.

With a great choking cry, Joseph sank on his knees, beside the couch.

Two days later, the Bailly family and a few friends stood on the oak ridge a half-mile to the northeast of the homestead. They were consecrating the first pioneer cemetery in northern Indiana, on the ridge where the Indians, for untold years, had buried their dead.

Since it was a twelve-day ride to Detroit and Father Richard could not therefore be summoned, Jean Baptiste had dashed off to Niles and brought the Reverend Isaac McCoy, to perform the ceremony, and Mrs. McCoy. Another voyageur had ridden to Checagou to bring the Kinzies; but Dr. Woolcott alone, Kinzie's son-in-law, came to represent the family, for John Kinzie himself had died only the day before Robert's accident. With the doctor came Alexander Robinson and Billy Caldwell, the Sauganash. Except for these and Ginsey McCoy from Trail Creek and Joseph's half-dozen voyageurs, all the group assembled on the ridge top were Indians: Chief Pokagon and some thirty Indians from Pokagon's village, who had been devoted to Joseph from the old days at Parc aux Vaches and had learned of Joseph's trouble from Jean Baptiste on his way to McCoy's Mission; thirty more Indians from Trail Creek, and Chief William Blackbird, who had ridden in unexpectedly from Arbre Croche, unaware of Joseph's and Marie's tragedy. Among the Parc aux Vaches Indians were Topenebee and Shavehead and Weesaw. But today Weesaw was not wearing his scarlet turban and scarlet sash, his silver nose ring and his silver amulet as big as a dinner plate, nor was Topenebee magnificent with imperial blanket and eagle-feathers, nor Pokagon in his chief's dress. Today all were as naked as Shavehead, except for the breech-clout. Today all the Indian faces and bodies were blackened with charcoal, the heads were gray with dust, and the chieftains were stripped of bangles and the distinguishing eagle feathers, for all were united in the identity of death, the democracy of mourning.

Jean Baptiste and three of the voyageurs had borne up the hill the small coffin that carried Robert, wearing the little sword he had so fatally loved. Joseph and Marie and the four daughters, all in black, had followed with slow steps.

Joseph and Marie had never known or dreamed of such torment as they had endured during the last two days. Joseph was sure that no victim tortured on the rack could ever have suffered more. How *could* Isaac McCoy accept such torture as this with a prayer and a smile and a "God's will be done"? All the long years of waiting for his son and the nine beautiful years of the little boy's life had become so passionate a part of Joseph's strong nature that the sudden destruction of the dream, the reality, and the hope were, in spite of his vitality, as the death-in-life of himself. Added to the intensity of his love and grief was a lesser anguish that screwed and twisted itself into the torn nerves of the larger torture. This was the realization that, if he had not been busy with a letter to Corinne de Courcelles Rastel, which he probably never would have sent, but which betrayed to himself a weak and miserable disloyal area still existing in his heart, the son whom he loved might not have met with his fatal accident. Moreover, if he had not been on his way to a rendezvous with Corinne at the Absinthe House, he would not have passed the armorer's shop and had been moved to buy the sword, in the first place.

Joseph was not sufficiently detached at the moment, and aware of humanity in general, or of that law of averages which we call fate, or of that law of capricious exceptions which we also call fate, to realize how unextraordinary was the malicious circumstance that seemed to trail a sequence of enduring tragedy out of momentary misdoing. He was convinced, beyond even the reason which, like the rocky substratum of Quebec, had always underlain his faith, that he and his transient deviation were chiefly responsible for his son's death. Lucille, to be sure, moved in and out of his agony, a black little figure, twisting the fatal sword towards her brother's body. Joseph wanted to believe that the desperate struggle and the lurching bodies and Robert's fall had caused the peculiar accident; but he wished that he might have pushed away the letter and opened the door in time to see, to know—to prevent. He had found the letter this very morning on his table in the office cabin exactly where he had left it, and had burned it immediately. But how could he be sure that Lucille had not seen this letter also, adding another anguish to the stricken heart of his wife? He strengthened his grip on Marie's arm as they reached the summit of the ridge.

The wooded plateau was a beautiful place, with oaks and maples and sassafras and a thick matting of wild ivy and trillium, hepatica and violet leaves; Indian paintbrush, goldenrod and blazing star gave the first autumnal brilliance to the universal green. Below, to the northwest and the southeast were the colorful, rank marshes (marbled now with the rose mallow), with hard-packed trails running across, connecting the ridges of the ancient Valparaiso moraine. To the southeast lay the ridge of the homestead. A mile to the northwest, just above the domes of a few Indian mounds, lifted the dunes, some of them tree-topped, others as white as the shoulders of women. "Trois monts," the three mountains, stood up white and green and glistening against the intense, collar-of-a-peacock sky. On one of those dunes had stood, not so long before, the palisaded Petit Fort of the French that had echoed to so much adventure before it had weathered down into gray oblivion.

Here again today was France on a hilltop, but France spreading into the land through peaceful settlement, not fortified invasion. All this domain was Joseph Bailly's, as far as the eye could see, marsh and river, ridges, dunes, and shore beyond. But he knew, in his empty heart, that fearful cry of humanity in the midst of its most earnest endeavors: "A quoi bon? A quoi bon? What for? What for?" In the midst of success, he confronted the old skeletal fact that every man suffers defeat, for even success suffers the certainty of the defeat of death.

As soon as the listeners were all assembled, Isaac McCoy began an interminable prayer. Then, seeing an opportunity for further missionary work with the Indians, he began to preach an equally interminable sermon on the subject of resignation, and humility before the Lord, ineptly taking as his text the passage from Obadiah: "Though thou exalt thyself as the eagle, and though thou set thy nest among the stars, thence will I bring thee down, saith the Lord."

Since the service was Protestant, allowing more latitude than the Catholic, Joseph wished that McCoy had chosen instead to speak of the child, Robert. He found himself rebelling against the remoteness of the Bible and of its brave, impossible adjurations. In the midst of the tides of grief, he could cling only to the shining pebble of Robert's identity clutched in the desperate hands of memory; the rock of God was too gigantic, too slippery for his hold.

But McCoy was long accustomed to grief and death, and the

loss of children, and with each loss, as Joseph well knew, he had merely bowed his head in submission. This Thy-will-be-done attitude governed the whole tone of his prayer and his endlessly long funeral sermon. In his tremendous vitality, Joseph rebelled. There was a surge within him which almost bore him to his feet to say:

"This is the funeral of my son, my son Robert. Let us speak of him! I cannot lose him in such abstractions. Bring him to life again, in words! He was a fine, strong, beautiful boy. He was . . ." That shining pebble of Robert's identity—so soon to be lost in the sand.

In his monotonous voice the minister prepared to utter the words of commitment. He had just cleared his throat to begin, when a figure stepped forward from the group of blackened Indians. It was Pokagon.

The chief raised his hand and, speaking at first in English, then, in Algonquin, said:

"Man of Prayer, I beg you to let me speak for myself and for my Indian brothers, of the little boy, the little Bird Boy whom we all loved, before you put the sand over him. He was the finest little boy we have ever seen among the red or the pale people. He was quick as a deer, strong as a young panther, graceful as a sea gull shining on the waters that break on the shores of Lake Mitchigami. The birds and the animals loved him. The Indians loved him. For the Great Spirit, whom the palefaces call God, had touched him, as the Great Spirit has touched his father, Monami Bailly, and his mother, the Wing Woman. He was never known to do a treacherous thing or a thing that the palefaces call unkind, yet he was strong, as a man should be. He would have been a great man in the land of the living. He will be a great man in the land of the dead. He has run ahead of us, along the White Roadway of the Many Stars to the happy hunting grounds that lie beyond the western sky. The spirits that are there will say, 'Bon jour, bon jour!' and they will love him, as we have always loved him. O Great Spirit, O God of the palefaces, be kind to the little Bird Boy . . ."

No biblical words, no remote comfort had been able to touch Joseph and Marie as these simple, heartfelt words touched them. They wept.

The minister committed the child to the earth. A great wooden cross, which had been made by Jean Baptiste and Toussaint Pothier, almost as tall as the cross of Marquette at Cross Village, almost as tall as Father Allouez's cross near Parc aux Vaches, was lifted up by the two voyageurs, and embedded over the first white child to be buried in northern Indiana. On the cross, a few words selected by Marie had been carved with hunting knives:

ROBERT BAILLY

1817–1826

Bienheureux les cœurs purs, car ils verront Dieu.*

But the course of tragedy was not yet finished. Joseph was to learn of the clustering quality of human sorrows.

The next morning, Joseph had gone to his small log-cabin office where he sat blindly at the table, trying to map out a plan for the fall journeys to the fur posts which must soon be undertaken. "A quoi bon? A quoi bon?" He leaned his elbows on the table, cupped his chin on his hands, and pressed his fingers hard against his temples, as if they could, with physical violence, push out of his brain the long procession of pictures of Robert that kept marching through it. There was a shadow in the doorway, felt rather than seen. Joseph looked up. Chief Blackbird stood there, framed against the sunlight. His body and his face were still covered with the charcoal of mourning, and his face was as stricken as if he had lost his own son. Joseph placed a rustic chair on the other side of the table, for there was scarcely room in the small cabin for them both to sit cross-legged on the floor. Then he drew tobacco and a calumet from the table drawer and offered them to Blackbird; but the Ottawa chief shook his head. For a long time, neither man spoke. Joseph noticed how old and lined and down-dragged the face of Blackbird had become, and how the fierce light in his eyes had smoldered to a spark. An old chief now. Many birds had flown through the trees since the upstanding days of long ago at Arbre Croche!

At last Blackbird spoke, in Algonquin:

"It is a hard thing for any man to lose a son."

* Blessed are the pure in heart, for they shall see God.

Joseph nodded his head slightly and tensed the betraying muscles of his eyes and mouth.

"I know how hard it is, Monami," continued Blackbird.

"Thank you, my father."

"I know, Monami Bailly—for I have lost my son."

Joseph looked up quickly into Blackbird's face. The chief had only the one son, betrothed to Thérèse. Was he affectionately referring to Robert, or was . . .? The question in Joseph's eyes was answered.

"Yes. William, my son."

"My father. Oh, my father!"

Joseph stretched out his large white hand and closed it over the wiry bronze hand of the Indian, as it lay on the table. The two bereaved fathers did not move for some time, compassion flowing from hand to hand and carrying every message that needed to be carried.

Joseph knew that, after a time, Blackbird would tell him all the things that Thérèse would long to know. At last, the Indian father spoke in Algonquin:

"I had a message from New York. Mr. Ferry, the minister on Mackinac Island, brought it to me. In June, William was to finish his studies. He was the highest in his class, the best of all the young men who had come to study from all over the world. My son! The morning of the day he was to graduate, he was found lying in his bed in a pool of blood. He had been stabbed to death."

Joseph groaned.

"Your son, too? But, how, my father? Why? Oh, God, why?"

"I do not know, my brother. Only this I know. William was the only Indian in his class. Four years ago, when the great treaty council with the Potawatomi was held in Checagou, William sent me the message that he was having many quarrels over Indian rights with the American students. He was writing many letters to Washington, many letters to Detroit to protest against the long injustices to the Indians. He said he was afraid the Americans hated him. 'But we, my father, we were the *first* Americans. I am not afraid of these last Americans,' he said. Then, early last spring, when he learned of the treaty council that Governor Cass is calling at McCoy's Mission in the month-of-gathering-wild-rice this year, he wrote to Mr. Ferry to tell me that, on his way home in July, he was going to stop at Washington and talk to the Great Father there about this new council that would take more land, almost all the remaining land from the Indians. I learned this in June when I was last at Mackinac Island. I think, Monami Bailly, that the Americans murdered him so that he would *not* get to Washington!"

"How terrible! How terrible! Yet it looks as if that might be true, my father. We must find out."

"Thank you, Monami Bailly. But it is too late when a man has lost his son."

"Everything," said Joseph, "is too late when a man has lost his son."

"Tell me, Monami Bailly, if it is not too hard to tell, how the Bird Boy lost his life. They say, a sharp thing. I do not understand."

"From New Orleans I brought my son a sword. He loved that little sword more than anything in the world—except birds and animals and trees. He was playing with it—out there on the grass. Lucille wanted to play with it. The two children struggled. The point somehow got turned towards Robert. I think he fell against it. Lucille is not able to tell me just what happened."

"It was Lucille, then?" Blackbird spoke the child's name so strangely that Joseph looked up. The chief's eyes were dilated, and his parted lips revealed his teeth.

"The magician's daughter!" said Blackbird, looking through and beyond Joseph, still with that look of frozen violence on his face.

Joseph wondered if the old chief had suddenly lost his mind from excess of grief.

"She is not your child, Monami Bailly!"

"Come, let us not talk any more, my father," said Joseph. "Let us go in and see what Magama and the Wing Woman have prepared for us to eat."

"Sit where you are, Monami Bailly. I have a long story to tell you. You do not believe me. But you will believe me when I have finished. Three who knew the secret are dead: Neengay Lefèvre and old Nee-saw-kee and one of the squaws who took care of Enewah. Of the other three, Running Cloud and the squaw Shingegiss and I are growing old, and the truth must not die with us, lest more disaster descend upon you through the child that is neither yours nor the Wing Woman's."

Joseph held his breath and seemed to listen not only with his ears but with every pore of his body. Blackbird began with Marie's arrival at Arbre Croche from the Menominee village eleven years before. He told of Enewah and of her dying confession of her seduction by De la Vigne. He told of the girl born alive and of the infant son of Marie and Joseph that lived for only a few minutes. He told of the daughter of De la Vigne substituted for the son of Joseph, as a temporary exchange, to draw Marie back into life from her own abyss of death. He told of Marie's adoration of the child and of how the two midwives and Madame Lefèvre and Running Cloud and old Nee-saw-kee had decided to keep the secret and allow Marie to have the child forever. He added that Madame Lefèvre had not realized, until some time after the substitution, that the infant's father was De la Vigne, but that it was too late then to destroy Marie's illusions.

"That is all, Monami Bailly. It is time, as I have said, that you should know the truth, if the child of De la Vigne is bringing disaster upon you."

Joseph closed his eyes and dug his hands into the auburn hair above his temples.

"If this is so, I have lost not one son," said Joseph, "but two. No! Not two, but three—for William Blackbird also was to have been my son!"

Then suddenly he got up, tipping over the chair.

"Let's go on a wolf hunt, Blackbird! If I think any longer, or feel any longer, my head and my heart will burst! Let's take our swiftest horses! Wolves against the moon! We'll kill every wolf in Michigan Territory and Indiana!"

Chapter XXXIII

THE STORM AND THE SKELETON

JOSEPH was astonished at Marie's reactions to Blackbird's story of the substituted child, which he told her on his return from the futile wolf hunt.

"You *can't* believe that for a *moment*, Joseph? I don't believe it, and I *will not* believe it! It is, of course, a legend spun by the story-tellers of Arbre Croche around the evening campfires. There is no word of truth in it. Do I not remember the birth? Do I not remember Running Cloud and my mother and the laying of the child in my arms? Do I not remember the long journey? It was Lucille who was my companion of the long journey!"

"But, Marie, don't you see how different she is from our other children? As different as the blackbird is from the sea gull. Can't you see it?"

"If she is different, she is different because she suffered with me the hunger and the backbreaking miles and the frozen body and the frozen soul—and the torture I endured over your being taken prisoner, Joseph. All the other children were conceived and born in luxury and happiness. Lucille is the child of my sorrow. Lucille is my child!"

"But she looks like—"

"No, no, no, no! Don't say that! What a dreadful story for Chief Blackbird to tell! He is crazed with his own grief! He does not know what he is saying!"

"Marie, it is well to consider it a little."

"No, no! I don't want to hear such a wild story mentioned again! As if our sorrow were not already as great as the sea! As if a new storm needed to come up over that sea!" She bowed her head and wept uncontrollable tears.

He went away, pondering that strange thing which is a mother's love, arching forever over the disinherited and the deficient, the abnormal, the pitiful or the contemptible.

The equally difficult task confronted Joseph of telling Thérèse about William Blackbird. He found her sitting under a maple tree by the river bank, making lace by a pattern which the nuns in Quebec had taught her. She was wearing the same black dress, with white lace at the neck and cuffs, that she had worn at her brother's funeral. The sunlight poured through a rift in the leaves directly on her golden hair.

Joseph stopped for a moment, his heart giving way at the thought of destroying Thérèse's happiness, then advanced, feeling like a murderer. He was able to come quite close before she stirred slightly and looked up.

"May I sit here beside you for a moment, Thérèse?"

"Yes, indeed, father. Do come!"

Seeing the lines of suffering in her father's face, the strong yet sensitive mouth dragged down with sorrow, the eyes from which the light had vanished, Thérèse laid her hand in his. He tried to prepare the way for her, and, holding her hand very tight, said:

"You are a brave girl, Thérèse."

"I think you are very brave, father."

"We must all be that. It takes the courage of lions sometimes."

"Yes, I know."

"I wish I could take all the sorrow *you* will ever have, and bear it for you, Thérèse."

Not quite understanding, she looked up into his eyes and read, in their compassionate gaze, a message beyond the inadequate pattern of words. She turned as white as the lace in her lap.

"Father! Has anything happened to—to—"

Joseph nodded.

Thérèse sat very still, while her father told the story, her face white, her eyes like blue marble, seeing through and beyond anguish. Such, thought Joseph, must have been the eyes of Mary, before the crucifixion.

Now and then, she closed her eyes or put her hand to her throat, but not a tear came.

"My life is over," she said simply, when Joseph had told every detail.

"Oh, no, Thérèse—not over! Just begun. We all reach stopping points in our lives, places where the path is suddenly blocked by a skeleton. But the path goes on! Even now, for us both, it must go on."

Joseph remembered, all at once, his walk in the pear orchard with his mother, thirty long years before. He remembered how her recital of her own disappointment in love had helped to assuage the disappointment which, at the time, had filled his being. He paused a moment; then, thinking that he might help his daughter, said:

"There was a time, Thérèse, long before I met your mother, when I loved a very beautiful woman in Quebec. I thought, of course, that she was made for me and I for her, inevitably. We planned to be married as soon as I returned from a journey into the Pays d'en Haut. For three years I dreamed of nobody else. Her voice was in the streams. She walked beside me in the snow. She waited for me in the pine forests. Then at last I returned to Quebec —and found that she had married someone else. My life, too, seemed to have come to an end."

"But she was a remorseless woman, anyway, father, and my William is—was—a saint."

Joseph looked intently at Thérèse. Could she possibly know the identity of the woman of whom he spoke? Or was this a shrewd feminine surmise? She went on:

"Madame Rastel, father dear, begging your pardon, can hardly be spoken of in the same breath with William Blackbird. Why, father dear, you're not offended, are you? Or did you think I didn't know who it was!"

"I didn't dream you knew! Who told you? Lucille? Surely, your mother hasn't spoken of her?"

"Why, no, darling, of course not! Mother never mentions her. But I first began to think about her in connection with you when you came back from the court-martial in Detroit, and talked and talked about her, bitterly, but *far too much.* I was only nine at the time, but I remember noticing the color that crept over mother's cheeks so often, and the very sad look that darkened and deepened her eyes whenever you spoke of Madame Rastel. It was clear, even to me, that a little corner of your heart, and mother's, was still troubled by her. Then I knew that you must have run into her again in New Orleans last year. There were all sorts of little signs, long before Lucille went around shouting about the duel and the fair lady! But I think I'm the only one, father dear, except mother, who's pieced together the whole story. And we both know that it is really mother you love."

"Thank you for saying that, Thérèse." Then, after a pause: "You're a fine girl, Thérèse. You've never given your mother or me one moment of unhappiness. And my heart breaks that such suffering should have come to you. But, by and by, the deep, terrible wound will heal, and some new happiness will come to you."

"Not to me, father. William was my one, my only love. I think I shall devote my life, in memory of him, to some form of benevolent teaching."

"Here with us, then, among the Indians."

"Perhaps. . . . But I'm really thinking, father, of the Ursuline Convent in Quebec."

"Oh, no, oh, no, Thérèse! Not that! A living death!"

"What can life be, after this, except—a living death?"

Joseph sought desperately to swerve Thérèse from the thought. It seemed best to divert her attention, for the moment, by presenting the problem of Lucille. Possibly she would understand this situation as adroitly as she had understood the Corinne situation and would confirm his own belief in Blackbird's story. He needed something besides the prejudiced maternal reaction to that strange story. Best to tell it now, before Thérèse's grief had overwhelmed her and she could no longer see or hear any other tragedy. He told her the long tale in detail.

When the story was all told, Thérèse waited a moment, in silence, as if to reconsider every detail of it. Then she said:

"I believe it is true."

"Your mother does not believe it."

"No. She would not. She has never seen the things that the rest of us have seen Lucille do. She has been divinely kind—too kind. I have never understood how mother could have stood up and defended De la Vigne, the murderer of her own mother! Do you think I could defend William's murderers? Not now. But perhaps, after I had been in the convent a long time, I *might* be able to do it. I believe mother is a kind of saint—"

"I know she is—or how could she have stood *me* for so long?"

"Father? You may be no saint, but you *are* a colossal dear!"

After a pause, Joseph said: "I wonder, Thérèse, if it has crossed your mind—the thought—oh God, I hate to say it . . . but the thought that Lucille was—was—intentionally responsible for Robert's death."

Thérèse took her father's hand between hers.

"It is too late to wonder about that, father. Yet I don't think so. But I do think this story of Blackbird's should be thoroughly investigated. You will never rest until you find out the whole truth about it. I know you well enough to be sure of that. And, when you go to Arbre Croche, I want to go with you, and from there, father, to Quebec—to the Convent of the Ursuline nuns."

During that autumn of 1826, Joseph had delayed the journey to his trading posts. He was usually well started long before the equinoctial storms. But he had stayed on at the Calumet for almost a month, supposedly to attend the treaty council called for early September by Governor Cass at McCoy's Mission, but mainly in the hope of dissuading Thérèse from her quiet, determined purpose of entering the convent of the Ursuline Nuns of Quebec. From the day that he had told her of William Blackbird's death, the "idée fixe" had taken hold of her, and no argument could influence her. Marie was somewhat more sympathetic towards the idea, her religious spirit surmounting the maternal. If her child wished to devote herself to God, she, the mother, would acquiesce, would lay what she loved upon the altar. But Joseph, always more active, always more worldly, the religious occupying only a portion of his spirit, rebelled against immuring his daughter forever even in a prison of saints. The picture of the altar flame guarded for a hundred years by the white nuns of Quebec seemed no longer beautiful. Thérèse was too young, too attractive, too likely to love and to be loved again. During that month, Joseph had paced endlessly back and forth across the puncheon floor of the cabin home—for the homestead was not yet ready for occupancy—shaking the little structure with his booted feet and his loud protests, his copper hair flashing rebelliously in the sunlight each time that he passed the open door. But Thérèse had stood like a church statue, quiet as a nun already, in her white-collared black gown, her hands folded, her steady blue eyes as far away as Quebec. There was no moving her. On the final day of argument, Joseph had said:

"But at least I want you to promise—to promise—that you will wait a year—promise . . ."

His voice had suddenly faltered, for with those words there had flashed blindingly back on him the memory of the deathbed of his father, and deafeningly the echo of his father's words, almost the very words that he himself had just used.

With Joseph's own firmness in refusing Michel's wishes, Thérèse had answered, in a quiet voice, which, nevertheless, thundered in Joseph's ears:

"I am sorry, father, but I can promise nothing, absolutely nothing—"

"Merciful heaven! Ciel!" exclaimed Joseph, one hand in his flaming hair. "I'm not—I'm not commanding you to do it! I guess this is *your* Pays d'en Haut!"

"Pays d'en Haut? What do you mean, father?"

"I'm telling you—I'm telling you my protests are at an end. You may enter the convent—if that's what you want most in all the world!"

And before Thérèse could fling her arms around Joseph's neck, he had rushed out of the house and off towards the lake to let the west winds blow in his hair!

So it happened that on this twenty-fifth day of September, the Bailly family and all the voyageurs were down on the beach to launch the boats for the trading journey to Mackinac Island, which was to end in the longer voyage to Quebec. Joseph did not tell Marie that he planned to stop on the way at Arbre Croche, to investigate Chief Blackbird's story.

Now that she was leaving, Thérèse's eyes were suddenly blurred with tears, and she clung to her mother desperately, and Marie clung to her with all the passionate love of the long years of happiness and the intensity of the loneliness to come. As Joseph looked at them, he wondered why the Great Spirit, or God or whatever the Great Something might be called, allowed so much sorrow to come down on the shoulders of so good a woman as Marie—the death of Robert, the departure of Thérèse, the scorn of Esther, the tragedy of Lucille, the shadow of Corinne. Something blinded him, and he turned to the boats and shouted the old cry of the "bourgeois" of the voyageurs:

"To boats all! To boats all!"

There was a scurrying, a pulling off of red toques by the voyageurs, handshakes, cheers, the last desperate embracing of Thérèse by her mother, her sisters, the sliding of the two long birch-bark canoes into the pale blue water, the dip and slap of the red paddles— and the boat song led by Toussaint Pothier. With an added displeasure, Joseph heard the insouciant Pothier slide into the refrain of the "Prisoner of Nantes," for Joseph could not keep back the thought that he was delivering his daughter into a kind of sanctified prison. The prisoner of God! He could not, for the life of him, this time, join his voice to the voices of the voyageurs:

> "Dans les prisons de Nantes,
> Dans les prisons de Nantes,
> Lui-ya-t-un prisonnier, gai, faluron, falurette,
> Lui-ya-t-un prisonnier, gai, faluron, dondé!"

The progress over the lapis water was swift and sure for several days. The air was warm. September rehearsed the dreams of summer. The trees on the dune tops were magnificent bouquets of color, swirls of gold, plumes of crimson, arrested flames. The creeks ran like gold beneath them. The gulls, in great ermine flocks, rested on the water or rose ahead of the canoes, tracing curves of continuous beauty in the wing-cleft air. All was serene, poised, beautiful. Even Thérèse, with her eyes already penetrating beyond the boundaries of beauty, turned back to the earth and found it good. More than once, a pang shot through Joseph, as Thérèse pointed out some fiery tree, some lion-shouldered dune, some incredibly shining stream or the dark blue shadows of the gulls moving like ghosts of birds across the sand.

Each day, the little company of canoeists moved farther into the lake, beyond the second sand bar, beyond the third, finally a half-mile out, to cut the shore curves, avoid the promontories and make better time.

The three canoes were pausing, on the first gray day of the journey, far out, opposite the point where the Grand River debouches into the lake. The voyageurs were enjoying the respite of their pipes, and Joseph and Jean Baptiste were laughing over the remembrance of their encounter with the Indians at the post up the Grand, eleven years before, just before Rastel had retaliated with Joseph's arrest.

"Have I ever told you that story in detail, Thérèse? You were only a little girl and couldn't appreciate it at the time. It was really quite exciting—eh, Jean Baptiste?"

"Sacré tonnerre, yes! Ze two wolves had been at eet togezer wiz ze Indians!"

"I would have gif my fiddle and my red sash to have been with mon bourgeois that day!" declared Toussaint.

"Tell me what happened, father."

"Well, once upon a time there were two gray wolves who were always suddenly appearing on the trail. One day at the Forks of the Grand—"

Joseph was looking down at the water. There was a ripple, as if a shark had just passed under the boat, and at the same time a breath of cool air from the west. Joseph instantly broke off and turned to look at the horizon. A low cloud bank, blackish green, had formed.

"Arrachez, mes gens! To shore! To shore!" shouted Joseph, at the top of his lungs.

The voyageurs snuffed out their pipes, jammed them into their pockets, picked up the paddles, turned the canoes at right angles to the shore and dipped with all their might. The sky darkened suddenly. The lake became pale green, with long, light rustling waves slipping to shore. Then, as the black clouds on the horizon mounted, the colors on the lake glided into a translucent emerald-green, shot through with yellow streaks like an enormous cat's eye. Gigantic rumblings began to come from the edge of the world, then staccato flashes of lightning from half a dozen different areas of the west, followed instantaneously by another sweep of wind across the water, that bent the blades of the sword grass and the leaves of the bittersweet and the sumac and the willows on the dunes. A low shiver of trees and land things went out to meet the sound of the freshening waves.

The voyageurs paddled frantically. Their faces grew gray. At first they uttered the usual exclamations of surprise, the "Sacré tonnerre!" and the "Enfant de l'enfer!" But now they began to call on St. Anthony, on Ste. Anne, on Father Marquette. The names of the saints mingled with the swish of the waves.

The boats had not yet reached the third sand bar, where the water was over a man's head, when the Great Wind, to which all the lesser impulses of wind had been but feeble preludes, struck. The Thunder Birds and the Water Panthers fought. The trees on the tops of the dunes roared. The waves mounted into milk-white crests. The rain came, horizontal, sharp as arrows. The gulls, glinting gray-white against the black clouds, screamed madly, striving to breast the wind, veering, turning, retreating, plunging now into the lake, now into the sky, in wheeling, desperate spirals. The sea roared, and the fixed land answered back.

"St. Antoine! St. Antoine! Have mercy on our souls!"

"Ste. Anne! Ste. Anne! Have pity!"

"Père Marquette! Help us!"

For some moments, the voyageurs, who could steer their boats through the most desperate rapids in Canada, took the slopes of the mounting waves with skill. The first boat, containing four of Joseph's voyageurs, had almost reached the shore, and the second, with Joseph, Thérèse, Jean Baptiste, and Toussaint Pothier, was between the third and the second bars, when a huge diagonal wave washed completely over the canoe and overturned it. Joseph reached out towards Thérèse and caught her by the skirt. He could see Jean Baptiste struggling in the waves, trying to turn the canoe over. He caught a glimpse of Toussaint's white face and saw rather than heard his scream: "Sauve moi!" Toussaint could not swim.

Joseph found he could not touch lake bottom. He took Thérèse under one arm, and tried to swim back towards Toussaint, but the great, pounding waves were too strong. He was borne towards shore, until, as he reached the second sand bar, the dangerous undertow began to drag him back. It took all his tremendous physical power to battle against this reverse current. At last, he reached the second sand bar, found he could stand, and made his difficult, buffeted way, walking, dragging Thérèse, who was barely conscious. He pulled her to shore and was met by the four voyageurs who had reached the beach in safety.

"Take care of her. Carry her up under the trees. I'm going back for Jean Baptiste and Toussaint," said Joseph.

"No, no, no, Monsieur Joseph. No! You will drown!"

But Joseph was off through the water. He could see a dark object still clinging to the overturned shell of the canoe, as it rose and fell on the great crests and in the troughs of the waves. The wind had become such a hurricane that Joseph could scarcely move against it. The waves broke with gigantic force as he inched his way through them. The canoe, borne towards the shore with each successive surge, was moving diagonally southeastward, and Joseph had to double his energies to catch up with it. He had almost caught up with it in shoulder-high water, when he saw, through the gray rain, that the dark body of Jean Baptiste was no longer there. Toussaint, of course, had disappeared long since. A great misery went over him. He searched the near-by water with his eyes, and through a white crest caught a glimpse of vanishing dark clothing. He plunged towards it, reached out, clutched something, was borne down by a gigantic wave. The pageant of his past began to slide before him, precisely as it had done on a moonlight night long before at Great Slave Lake, when he had begun to freeze slowly to death. He knew that he was drowning, but this time he did not fight to live, for something kept repeating in the dark abysses of his soul: "A quoi bon? A quoi bon? . . . My son is dead. . . . My son is dead. . . ." He let the pageant slide: his first pony ride at Ste. Anne de Beaupré . . . his first dance at Quebec. . . . Corinne de Courcelles in a mask . . . his mother saying, "I hope you'll find the Great Adventure." . . . Jean Baptiste saying, "I join your bateau, mon cousin, because you're as soft as a baby-otter and you need leetle-fox Jean Baptiste to look after you—*Jean Baptiste had saved him so often!* He *must* save Jean Baptiste. . . . He tightened his grip on the cloth that was in his fingers. He struggled with his body and with his soul. He lifted his head above the water. He choked. He breathed. He stood up. He pulled Jean Baptiste's head and shoulders out of the water. He took a step towards shore. Another. A wave went over him. But by using every ounce of energy he remained erect. Step by pounded, battered step, he moved towards shore on a journey that seemed a dying mile in length, but was, as a matter of fact, a distance of only three hundred feet. As he reached the sodden-gold shore with his burden, he thought he was going to lose consciousness; but he knew he must not, for his strength and intelligence would be needed to restore Jean Baptiste to life. What if Jean Baptiste were already dead? What if he had dragged a dead body to shore? He pulled Jean Baptiste out of the reach of the dragon-green waves, kneeled down, turned him over, face forwards, took off his drenched buckskin jacket, rolled it, shoved it under Jean Baptiste's stomach and began to move him back and forth over it, as over a barrel. He had seen such methods used twice on half-drowned fishermen on the beach at Mackinac Island.

The four voyageurs offered to help, but Joseph nodded his head negatively, although he felt more dead than alive. The rain lashed over him. But he kept moving Jean Baptiste back and forth, back and forth, unflinchingly. After some ten minutes, Jean Baptiste coughed and moved one hand. Joseph worked on. Jean Baptiste muttered—"Mon cousin—"

Joseph turned him over on his back and motioned the voyageurs to carry him up under the trees, where Thérèse lay.

Two hours later, in the woods back of the dunes, where Joseph had ordered a brush shelter and two linen tents, saved from the first boat, to be put up, Jean Baptiste said shyly to Joseph:

"Why you bother bring in leetle good-for-not'ing Jean Baptiste, mon cousin? Too much bother for not'ing."

"Because you're the damned best man in the whole Northwest, Jean Baptiste!" answered Joseph, unreservedly.

Poor Toussaint Pothier had been found, two miles down the beach, the day after the storm. Joseph and Jean Baptiste and the four voyageurs had dug a grave in the sand on a high dune, where the winds could play in the pines over him as beautifully as Toussaint had fingered the strings of his fiddle. They had made a cedar cross for him, not so high and not so broad as Father Marquette's cross at Arbre Croche, but plainly visible so that, hereafter, all the voyageur-friends could doff their red toques as they passed and offer a prayer for the singing soul of Toussaint.

In three days, the lake had calmed again, the swamped canoe had been repaired and the little company had again embarked, minus one man and half the baggage.

The newest encounter with disaster and death had set Joseph wondering, in spite of himself, whether Thérèse had not chosen wisely a career which placed her beyond all predicaments. He was able to look at her with less anguish and a little more understanding. She would be tending the altar flame, beyond the reach of all storms on the Great Lakes and all tempests of the human heart and mind and soul.

In seven days, they reached the shore of Arbre Croche. Chief Blackbird had already gone off, with the braves, for the fall hunting and trapping, but Joseph had all the information that Chief Blackbird could give. It was Running Cloud whom he wished to see, and Shingebiss, the second surviving midwife.

When camp had been made at the edge of the village, Joseph took Thérèse with him, but sent Jean Baptiste and the voyageurs off into the back country to get a supply of deer meat for the rest of the journey. He did not want even Jean Baptiste to know what was in the wind. He and Thérèse went at once to Running Cloud's lodge, with a supply of beads and silver ornaments, without which Joseph would no more have thought of traveling than a man travels today without a pocketbook. They seated themselves on the log floor and accepted Running Cloud's refreshments of venison broth and corncakes. She herself was fasting on water and boiled corn, and would continue to fast for many a month to come, in her mourning for her dead son.

Joseph spoke of the hunting and the fishing at Arbre Croche, of Chief Blackbird's visit to the Calumet, and, at last, of young William Blackbird. The tears ran unashamedly down the black charcoal that smudged Running Cloud's face, and fell on the rags of her mourning. Thérèse put her arms around the old squaw who was to have been her mother-in-law and wept with her. When Running Cloud's Indian reticence was thoroughly dissolved, Joseph opened the subject which he had journeyed so far to investigate.

"You have lost your son whom you loved, Running Cloud. And I—I have lost *two* sons."

The idea was a little slow in penetrating Running Cloud's grief-blurred mind. Joseph said nothing further. Running Cloud at last looked up.

"*Two* sons, Monami Bailly? *Two* sons? I knew of the going away of the little Robert, but I did not know that Monami Bailly had another son to lose—"

Joseph looked deeply into Running Cloud's eyes as he repeated slowly, in Algonquin:

"You did not know that Monami Bailly *had ever had another little son to lose?*"

Running Cloud tried to keep her eyes steady before Joseph's gaze, but could not. Joseph repeated the question, with increased emphasis:

"*You did not know that Monami Bailly had ever had another little son to lose?*"

"What has some little linden bird whispered in Monami Bailly's ear?"

"A strange story, Running Cloud. The linden birds have not forked tongues. They tell the truth. Running Cloud will also tell me the truth. Have I been the father of two sons?"

"Yes, Monami Bailly. You have been the father of two sons."

"I want the whole story, Running Cloud, from beginning to end. I *must* have it. Do you understand?"

"Yes, Monami Bailly."

And Running Cloud told of Marie's suffering, of her near-loss of life and the absolute necessity that had arisen of keeping her alive by placing some substitute-child in her arms—essentially the same story that Blackbird had told. She added the story of old Nee-saw-kee's baptism of the dying child, and of his bestowal of the name "Little White Fawn" upon it.

"I am glad that my son was baptized by Nee-saw-kee. Do you know where the Little White Fawn was buried?"

"Yes."

"Could you show me the place?"

"Yes. The child was buried at night, far outside the village. For it was supposed to have been Enewah's illegitimate child."

"Buried with no ceremony?"

"Again old Nee-saw-kee said over the little grave what he could remember of a paleface prayer, the one that goes: 'Our Papa who lives in the Happy Hunting Grounds—' "

"Thank you, Running Cloud. Keep these silver earbobs in remembrance of the Little White Fawn. Now I want to see Shingebiss, the squaw who was the midwife of Enewah. Then I will come back and get you, and you will take me to the place where my son was buried. If there is a shovel anywhere in the village I want it—also an extra tomahawk, very sharp. Have them ready for me."

"Yes, Monami Bailly."

"Where is the lodge of Shingebiss?"

"Over there, Monami Bailly. She is very old."

Fortunately, Shingebiss had a large admixture of cupidity, for she was prepared to hang on to the secret like grim death until she saw Joseph's assortment of silver bangles. It took four of the most expensive ornaments from Campeau's shop to extract the story, bit by bit; but it matched the stories of Blackbird and Running Cloud in every detail.

Joseph strode back to Running Cloud's lodge. It was near sunset, but he was determined to finish his task on that very day. Running Cloud had collected the implements that Joseph had requested. It became the duty of Thérèse to provide entertainment by distributing a few more beads and bangles to the group of curious squaws who had gathered around Running Cloud's lodge, certain that some mysterious event was brewing. When the squaws were all squatting around a small heap of vermilion beads, Joseph and Running Cloud slipped out of the lodge, the shovel concealed under the squaw's blanket, the tomahawk under Joseph's jacket.

Running Cloud led Joseph almost half a mile along the bluff to a large cottonwood tree that had stood contrastingly among the pines, as a vivid landmark, for many years. Joseph thought back on the endless times that he had passed that tree in his voyages to and fro on the lake, without realizing its significance to him, without knowing that it marked the grave of his son. At this hour, the trunk of the tree was not white, but Indian-bodied, and all the trunks of the trees in the woods below were smitten with undevouring flame. Even the gulls, as they floated past on a level with the high dune, took the color of the sunset and once more became flamingoes.

Joseph knelt down with the sharp tomahawk, and began to shear off the goldenrod and the asters and the bittersweet vines that had grown over the sandy sod at the base of the tree. Then he stood up and began to shovel away the gold-brown earth. About a foot and a half down, the shovel struck something more substantial than sand. Joseph knelt again and, loosening the flower-root-tangled sand, brought out the earth with his hands. In a short while, the outlines of a partially decayed birch-bark box began to show. By digging all around it and putting his hands deep in below it, Joseph was able at last to bring up the tiny coffin. Fragments of birch bark fell away as he lifted it. He laid it on the ground and removed the rest of the cover of bark. A mildewed cotton wrapping surrounded the tiny body. But the skull was uncovered and tiny tufts of reddish hair still clung to the bones on either side.

"Little White Fawn! Nin-gwis! My son!"

"That is just what the Wing Woman kept saying over and over and over!" said Running Cloud. "Nin-gwis! Nin-gwis!"

How long Joseph looked down on the tiny skeleton, he never knew. It seemed to clothe itself with sturdy flesh, as he looked, the sockets to become living eyes and the auburn hair to cover the tiny head.

It was only when Thérèse, who had escaped at last from the squaws, stood beside him, that Joseph laid the tattered box back in the grave, replacing carefully every piece of protecting birch bark. As Joseph smoothed over the last handful of sand, Thérèse, kneeling beside him, began to repeat the Lord's Prayer: "Notre Père, qui es aux cieux, ton nom soit sanctifié . . ." Joseph's voice joined hers, while Running Cloud stood silently.

As they went towards the village, through the twilight, Joseph asked Thérèse:

"Do you think I should tell your mother, Thérèse? Or should it all remain a secret between you and me?"

"I think you should tell mother everything, father. There is no possible doubt any more. Even the red hair, father, like yours. But if she does not wish to believe—well, she will not believe."

"You are a wise daughter." Then, after a moment: "All my sons and all my daughters seem to be leaving me. I shall miss you, Thérèse."

Chapter XXXIV

GREEN GROW THE RUSHES

It was a late April afternoon of 1830. There was a kind of happiness in Joseph's heart, though he did not think that he could ever sing "Malbrouck s'en va-t-en guerre" at the top of his voice again. Robert's death seemed to have killed his exuberance at its source. Yet Joseph gave the outward impression of vigor, health, enthusiasm. For a man of fifty-six, he was singularly youthful in appearance. There was very little gray in the copper of his hair, his cheeks were ruddy, his eyes sapphire, his back straight as a cavalryman's.

Joseph had determined to make as joyous a thing as possible of this expedition. He and Marie, Rose, Esther, Lucille, and Jean Baptiste were riding to Detroit for purposes both of business and enjoyment. A letter from James and Sarah Abbott, received three weeks before, had brought an invitation to attend a housewarming reception and dance, to celebrate their occupation of the new home on the corner of Griswold and Fort Street. It had needed no clamorous pleadings of the three daughters to persuade Joseph to take them. For he was intending anyway to make a business trip, to conclude arrangements with Oliver Newberry, the Yankee shipbuilder of Detroit, for partnership in the construction of two new lake vessels.

Joseph was energetically keeping pace with the times. If the beaver and the mink and the otter were dwindling away, other enterprises were developing as fast. Since the opening of the Erie Canal, settlers were beginning to pour over the Detroit Road, in a steady cavalcade. Checagou, now platted as a pioneer village, its harsh, pungent old Indian name subdued into the more civilized syllables of "Chicago," was growing into a sturdy settlement and the rebuilt fort was again occupied. There were almost enough settlers to justify the Trail Creek harbor, and Joseph was writing steadily to his Canadian friends to urge the establishment of a French-American settlement near the proposed site of this future harbor. But his present interests centered in Detroit. Oliver Newberry's business was booming; he could hardly construct enough vessels to keep up with the demand. He welcomed Joseph's offer of capital, and the addition of his business acumen to the enterprises. The *Napoleon* and the *Lafayette*, to which Joseph was contributing, were about to be laid down on the stocks.

As Joseph turned his thoughts vigorously towards the future, he felt almost like singing out again. Instead, he shouted out to Rose, who was the best rider, except himself, in the family:

"I'll beat you to the first cabin, Rose!"

They were within sight of the first little settlement they had seen since leaving White Pigeon three days before. It was the new cluster of log cabins marking the site of the future Ypsilanti.

They pounded off down the trail-road. Veillantif brought Joseph in only a horse's length before Rose! Rose swept up, her plumed hat gone, her auburn hair flying in the wind! They slowed down, and the dozen settlers came to their doors and waved and called out to them to stop and "have a bite" and "stay the night." Joseph and Rose and, a little later, the rest of the family dismounted in the cause of friendliness, for no invitation on the frontier could be refused, without offending.

The old town of Detroit was a day's journey farther on. After a meal of "hominy and hog," and a night spent on puncheon floors, the Bailly family rode out of "Ypsilanti" next morning, on the road to Detroit.

The settlers had drained a considerable acreage of the marshes around the village, and the purple loam looked rich. The makers of the Detroit-Chicago Road had also drained the marshes in channels, along the gouged borders of the first crude highway, and the going was much easier now than it had been in the old days. But the soggy ground still stretched in at least a Twenty Mile Swamp, if not the old Thirty Mile Swamp, from "Ypsilanti" to Detroit. A thousand birds flicked to and fro, bluebirds, meadow larks, red-winged blackbirds, orioles, finches, resting now and then on the dried sedges of last year or coming down to drag the first worms of spring out of the lush ground. The world was alive with wings and the ever deluding hope of spring.

"I'll wager you a penny, Jean Baptiste, that Campeau's ponies are browsing on that ridge, as usual!" Joseph cried out, as they drew towards the junction of the Upper and Lower Rouge.

"I no bet, Monsieur Joseph! Of course ze ponies are zere! Zey or ze fathers or ze grandfathers been zere for ze last forty years!"

Sure enough, the ponies dashed in all directions as the Bailly cavalcade galloped up, then returned and eyed the group curiously. Joseph drew up on the ridge where he had always paused for the view. The prospect had changed more than a little since that day before the fire in 1804, when he had looked down on the sixty whitewashed log cabins. Detroit was now a city and the capital of Michigan Territory. It had almost two thousand inhabitants, and there were five times as many houses—some square New England houses, many still in the old French style, with steep, slanting roofs and dormers. But now there were also a few buildings of stone or brick, most conspicuous of all, the tin-roofed cupola of the Capitol, the Mansion House Hotel, and Father Richard's almost-finished stone church of St. Anne, with its two steeples tipped with the iron crosses lifting joyously into the blue sky. But the white picket fence that once surrounded the town was in ruin, only a few weather-beaten patches showing where it had once been a shining, continuous line of defense. Old Fort Shelby was gone. The tall sycamores still thrust above Savoyard Creek, below the site of the fort, but Joseph knew that the creek had disappeared and that the fleur-de-lis growing in the mud indicated the blue trace of its ancient course. The great pear trees marking the ribbon farms still towered along the river, and here and there the arm of a windmill stretched out from the foliage. But down among the wharves smoking chimneys indicated Newberry's shipbuilding yards and the ironworks and the places where many another distiller and builder and manufacturer, besides Abbott and Campeau, had set up their busy enterprises. There was smoke on the river too, for the steamboats were pushing in among the sails, dragons devouring the Andromedas of beauty.

Joseph's eyes shone as he looked. He had always loved Detroit, and he loved it more than ever as it exhibited the doughty signs of progress. "Grand little town!" he said. "Give her a hundred years, and she'll be as big as New Orleans!"

"It grows too big!" commented Marie, wistfully.

"Oh, my little Marie! My old-fashioned little Marie! It must grow like your children—big!"

"I don't like to see my children grow too big either. Soon my Rose and my Esther will be finding their husbands, and away they will go!"

"But Médor Beaubien lives in Chicago and that's not far away!" remarked Lucille, giving Esther a teasing look.

"I'm not going to marry Médor Beaubien. I wouldn't for the world! He's half Indian!" declared Esther emphatically.

"Why, Esther! He's the nicest and handsomest man in the Northwest, except Papa!" championed Rose.

"Why don't you marry him yourself then!"

Joseph moved his horse closer to Marie's, for he knew how much Esther's remark about Indians must have hurt her.

"But soon there will be more grandchildren, Marie, as our children go away. Think how wonderful that will be! More Sallys! And we *must* have a grandson, Marie. We *must* have a grandson!"

"Yes, Joseph." Husband and wife looked into each other's eyes and read the same thought. The old sorrow rose up in Joseph's heart like an unbearable tide.

"Come, Rose!" he cried. "I'll race you to the gate. Mon Dieu, I forgot! There isn't a gate any more. And there isn't any fort. I'll race you to that first white house!"

"All right, Father! Here we go!"

This time, Joseph purposely reined Veillantif back a little, in order that Rose might have the joy of arriving first. Her horse almost climbed the whitewashed walls of the first house before she could stop him!

"Ah-h-h-h! Joost like your Papa! Joost exactement!" exclaimed a white-haired old gentleman, in a black, swallowtail coat, black suit, white cravat, and plug hat, who was strolling towards the open country, and whom Rose had very nearly knocked over.

"Oh, Monsieur Campeau, how do you do? Look! look here, Papa! It's Monsieur Campeau!"

Joseph dismounted, and the two old friends embraced heartily.

"You're going to stay at my house, Joseph, as usual?"

"Not this time, Campeau, thanks. I've brought the whole family along. We'll be staying at the Mansion House; but I want a good, old-fashioned talk with you as soon as possible. Suppose you come down to the Mansion House in an hour, and we'll have a little 'quelque chose,' eh?"

"Ah, bien, my good friend! Not'ing would pleese me more! I was going out to see my ponies, but I will see them later."

After Campeau had greeted the rest of the family, the little group on horseback turned down the road to the river. They had gone only a short distance when Joseph saw another familiar figure driving a wagon down St. Antoine Street and dashed ahead.

"Ah, Beaubien, Beaubien!" he shouted.

Antoine Beaubien reined in his horse and gave back the greeting: "Ah! Bon jour, Joseph! Bon jour! Bienvenu! Comment ça va?"

"It goes well—and with you, Antoine?"

Antoine spread his hands with that expressive gesture of accepting amiably a malign fate; and answered in French:

"Oh, fair, fairly well, Joseph. But think what a magnificent farm I might have if the town hadn't crossed it with their new-fangled streets and cut it up into their newfangled lots!"

"Well, it seems to me the farm's producing pretty well still, from what you told me last year about the crops!"

"Oh, yes, but think what I'd have if I still had the *whole* of my dear old farm!"

"See here, Antoine! Didn't I hear you'd sold those lots for ten thousand dollars?"

"Yes. Yes, I did, Joseph. But it's not the same dear old farm!"

"Dear old farm be hanged! You did the right thing! Times change, and you're getting rich with the change. Praise God from whom all changes flow!"

"You're still the same old Joseph, aren't you? You old Yankee!"

"I'll bet you wouldn't sell your house if they offered you seven thousand dollars, you old snail!"

"You're right, dead right, Joseph! They've offered me nine thousand—and I *won't sell!*"

"Ventre bleu! You won't sell? Snail, I say, snail—carrying your house on your back!"

"Mon Dieu, where would I live—without a house?"

"Impossible Antoine!"

"Impossible Joseph! No, sometimes I think you're not a Frenchman, but a Yankee pig. But a very *nice* pig, mind you! Ah, here come Madame Marie and the pretty, pretty daughters!"

Antoine was really referring to Rose, for Rose was a beauty. Esther was rather plain, with her straight brown hair, brown eyes, and over-large French nose. Lucille, except for her masses of curling, dark hair which she had learned to draw concealingly over the left side of her face, her snapping black eyes, her sinuous grace, and the expert manner in which she utilized her charms, could not be called a "raving beauty." But she had undeniable fascination, that strange lure, that animal pull, that aroma of sex that had also belonged to her father. Ever since the death of Robert, and Joseph's return from the exploring expedition to Arbre Croche, Marie had refused to admit, by any spoken word, that it had been definitely proved that Lucille was not her child. Yet Joseph felt sure, by many a hidden sign and many a searching look that Marie laid upon Lucille, that her heart knew what her mind refused to admit.

"Come and see me, Joseph, and bring Madame and the daughters," suggested Antoine, as he started to drive away.

"I will, Antoine, tomorrow. Suppose you come and have a 'bonne bouche' with me at the Mansion House, as soon as you finish your errand. In an hour or two? Bien?"

"All right, Joseph. All right."

"By the way, is Peter Navarre in town?"

"No, he's scouting off in the direction of your Door Prairie for a place to settle down. You'll probably see him over there."

"Peter settle down? Sacré tonnerre! What's the world coming to!"

"Why, Peter's getting old, Joseph, and so are you and I. He's forty-five!"

"Pouf! Forty-five's still young!"

"Impossible Joseph!"

"Well, see if you can get hold of Pierre Desnoyers and bring him along—impossible Antoine!"

"Eh bien, I will. Au revoir!"

The Mansion House or Grand Hotel was a magnificent new

building on Jefferson Avenue, constructed in large part from the stones of the demolished Fort Shelby. It was three stories high, a giant in one-story Detroit. A low veranda, supported by immense pillars reaching to the roof and approached by a flight of stone steps, extended along the entire front. Directly below, were Oliver Newberry's shipyards, then the sweep of the boat-rippled river, and, across the way, the houses and gardens of Windsor.

Joseph made his arrangements with the proprietors, Mr. and Mrs. Boyer (recently come from Pennsylvania) as jolly and round-natured as they were round-shaped. When the family were well established in two large rooms on the second floor, overlooking the river (Jean Baptiste had gone to bunk with some old voyageur-cronies at Campeau's), Joseph went down to wait for his friends in the bar: a low-beamed room to the left of the hotel entrance and opposite the huge dining room, with windows that looked out on the porch and, between the pillars, to the river. Boyer was officiating. The only patron, a stooped figure in wrinkled brown broadcloth, turned, and Joseph recognized Abijah Hull. Abijah gulped his last mouthful of whisky so fast that he coughed, spluttered, and lost his breath completely as he set down the glass. Joseph laughed aloud.

"Well, how do you do, Abijah?" he said, putting out his hand. "Won any more cases recently? or fought any more duels? How *are* you?"

"Fine, fine—ungk—fine!" answered Hull nervously. "No, Boyer, no—ungk—I won't take that second order—ungk. I've got business, business right away!"

"Oh, is the Sieur de Rocheblave in town again?" asked Joseph, still baiting him.

"Oh, no, no, no, no, no, no!" sputtered Hull. "Good day! Good day! Good day!"

He trotted out of the room. Joseph's laugh echoed through the open window and hurtled against the fifty pillars of the veranda. When Hull was well out of hearing, Boyer joined in heartily with the laugh.

"Sort of made him nervous to see you, Mr. Bailly, eh?"

"You weren't in Detroit in '15, Boyer. But I guess you've heard the story of my court-martial?"

"Oh, yes, Mr. Bailly! I guess everyone in the Northwest knows that story and how you came out clear, on every point, and made your enemies 'lick the dust' as the Good Book says. Mr. Rastel's never set foot in Detroit since, so I hear, and Abijah Hull's never been able to make any money to speak of, since that day—just scrapes up enough to keep his gizzards together. Comes in here to drown his disappointments in drink twice a week regular. Yes, you've made and unmade a lot o' men, Mr. Bailly!"

"Oh, no, Boyer, it's just circumstances."

"Well, what's circumstances but the doin's of men?"

"They're also the 'doin's' of God or Fate or the Great Spirit or whatever you want to call it, Boyer."

"The Great Spirit, eh? You think those Injuns know what they're talkin' about?"

"I *know* they know what they're talking about, Boyer."

"Well, maybe. Maybe not!" Boyer suddenly remembered that Mrs. Bailly was said to be part Indian. There was only one outlet for his embarrassment.

"Have a drink, Bailly! Have a snort of brandy on the house! Consignment from Quebec that came in on the last boat! Great stuff!"

"Thanks, Boyer. I think I'll wait. Ah, here comes my good old friend Campeau."

"Nice fellow, Campeau." Then, as if to himself, as he turned toward the bottle-shelf: "Wee bit old-fashioned, but a nice fellow, just the same."

Joseph began to feel as if the sun were going down on all the French Canadians in America. He himself was still out in the strong daylight, but he had to make an effort to stay there. Twilight would be so much more restful. But twilight was—the enshadowed beginning of the end.

Campeau came up the veranda steps, all smiles.

"We'll sit at this little table by the window, Boyer. More comfortable. And Campeau and I have many things to talk over together. Antoine Beaubien and Pierre Desnoyers may be joining us in a little while, so we'll be draining many a glass of your good beverages this afternoon, Boyer."

"Good! I always like to see a few Frenchmen sit down at my

tables for a long afternoon chat. They sip this wine and that, and a bit of brandy and a liqueur or two; and before you know it, they've run up a nice enough little bill. Not extravagant, you know, but—enough. The Americans come in and gulp down a strong whisky and wabble out again and that's all there is to it! Too much in a hurry. But you Frenchmen know how to enjoy life."

"Well, I'm an American now myself, Boyer, but I still cling to the old French ways of enjoying life, pardieu! Now, for instance, we won't start with an absinthe this time. Can you, by any chance, serve us that nice old Canadian dish of drink—l'eustrope? I haven't had it for a devil of a long time! You know? Distilled peaches in rum?"

"Do I know it, my dear fellow? How long do you think I could have stayed in business in Detroit without knowing how to make l'eustrope?"

"Ah, Bailly! There isn't anything Boyer doesn't know about drinks!" said Campeau, seating himself at Joseph's small round table by the window. "And there isn't anything Mrs. Boyer doesn't know about cooking! That's one of many reasons why the place is so popular!"

They had scarcely finished their first eustrope when Antoine and Desnoyers came up the steps. Desnoyers was as straight, handsome, and well groomed as ever, but when he removed his hat his curling hair showed gray, without benefit of powder. Joseph remarked something else too about the dressing of that head:

"See here, Pierre, mon ami. What's this you're wearing?"

"What's what? Oh, my silk hat? Why, silk hats are all the rage in Paris and London. Didn't you know?"

"Oh!" said Joseph, and sat back speculatively in his chair.

Pierre was puzzled. "Why, don't you think they're just as fine-looking as the old-fashioned beaver hats?"

"No, my dear Pierre, I don't!" said Joseph, with unexpected emphasis. "Don't you see that you're ruining my business?"

"What? Ruining your business?"

"Why, surely, Pierre! If silk hats become the rage throughout all the fashionable world—London, Paris, St. Petersburg, New York—why, then, the beaver hats go into the rubbish heap, and with them all the beaver trappers in North America and all the magnificent business that has maintained the great fur companies and the independent traders for a hundred years! Your silly little fashion, Pierre, ruins me and a thousand other traders!"

"Why, my dear Joseph! I'll throw this cylinder to the dogs and promise never to wear another silk hat as long as I live!"

"Never mind, Pierre. Calm yourself. I've seen the handwriting on the wall for a dozen years. That's why I'm here in Detroit today—to try to build up my declining income in another business. Four more eustropes, please, Boyer—and make them strong!"

"Yes, sir!"

"Yes. I saw the streams being trapped out a dozen years ago, and the settlers coming in after the late war and draining the marshes and planting the crops over the beaver huts—the white tide of pioneers that the Indians have tried to push back with their poor, feeble brown hands. The white tide! If we're not going to be swamped, if we're going to ride on the crest of that tide, we've got to be prepared for it with boats, with good strong arms and with our wits!"

"Oh, Joseph," said Campeau, in French, "you're still so young, my friend! So full of energy! I've always suspected you of having a little American blood in your veins! Are you sure you're all from Canada?"

"All from Canada! All from Artois! But, surely, you understand, Campeau, you with your enterprise, your shrewdness?"

"I understand, my boy. But eventually one gets tired, you know. I'm sixty-two, Joseph. And at sixty-two one is willing to drift, to let the tides carry one along a bit."

"I'm sorry to hear it, Campeau! Sorry to hear it!"

"Wait till you're sixty-two!"

"Oh, Joseph is hopelessly hopeful!" remarked Beaubien. "He's never going to grow old. He's going to be maddeningly young at eighty. Here's to the hopeless hopefulness, the perennial youth of Joseph Bailly!"

They lifted the glasses and sipped the brandy.

"I'd hate to die. Wouldn't you, Joseph?" asked Pierre, suddenly.

"Well, it's my favorite world," answered Joseph. He wanted to add, "It's easier to die, when you've lost your sons," but thought better of throwing this shadow on the party.

"Well, I haven't dreaded old age quite so much," commented Pierre, "since I read somewhere that Richelieu was irresistible at eighty. Here's another toast! To Richelieu!"

"Our glasses are getting disgracefully empty, Boyer," cried Joseph. "How about some champagne?"

"Very good, sir!"

"Well, you'll still be a beau at eighty, Pierre! No question of that!" said Joseph. "Shall I ever forget how you and Campeau trailed Madame Rastel to my cell the day before my court-martial! She certainly had you bewitched!"

"How about yourself, Joseph? Eh?"

"Not I!"

" 'Qui s'excuse s'accuse! Oh, Joseph! By the way, how is the lady?"

"I haven't seen her since the ball for Lafayette in Baton Rouge six years ago. She was quite beautiful even then. Amazingly so!"

"Another candidate for eternal youth, n'est-ce pas?"

"Well," said Joseph. "I've heard that Ninon de Lenclos still had admirers when she was eighty."

"Ah, 'eighty' again! Here's to 'eighty'!" cried Pierre.

"Wait for the champagne, that sparkles like youth! Ah, here it comes! Here's to 'eighty'!"

"Here's to 'eighty'!"

"Well, as for me," cried Pierre, "when the time comes for me to die, my wish is to die somewhere around a woman!"

"Sh! Pierre! Suppose some one should repeat that to your wife."

"Well, all I'd have to say would be that I *meant* my wife! My wife's 'a woman,' n'est-ce pas? Ah, how good this champagne is!"

"Did you read that little item in the *Detroit Gazette* a few days ago," put in Campeau, "about the Parisian who'd always been a good drinker—like us? At last he lay on his deathbed, with his friends all around him. Suddenly, what should he ask for but a glass of water? 'Water? Water!' echoed his friends in amazement. 'Yes, *water*,' repeated the dying man. 'That surprises you, mes amis—but didn't you know that, in order to be saved, one must, at the last, become reconciled with one's enemies?' "

"Bien! Bien!"

"Another bottle of champagne, Boyer!"

"Yes, sir."

"See here, Joseph! You'll ruin yourself," protested Campeau. "Think of the beverage tax! Let me treat!"

"No, no! Taxes to the devil!"

"That's what I say," echoed Campeau. "Taxes to the devil! The government at Washington and the Michigan legislature put on so many taxes, we die of them! From the swaddling clothes to the shroud, everything is taxed. What do the lawmakers live for except to tax, tax, tax! In England, they tax only seventeen luxury articles, like the wines, tobacco, silks, jewelry, carriages. Here in Michigan Territory, we pay the tax on the bread we eat, the water we drink, the clothes we wear, the house we live in, the grave we're buried in! It is ter-rible! Ter-rible! And the public officers—they steal at least a third."

"Why should *you* worry, Campeau?" asked Joseph. "You're rich. Besides, all you have to do is to sell a little more land to the greedy Americans, and you're richer still."

"That's what he tells *me!*" protested Antoine. "Sell! Sell! Sell! What is the *money*, Joseph, when you lose the land, the good, good land?"

"Why, buy *more* land outside the city, Antoine! Cash in on your city land and move your farm to the outskirts!"

"He is hopeless!" declared Antoine, raising his hands in the Gallic gesture of despair.

"Yes. He does not understand," agreed Campeau. "The land it is the heart. You would not tear out the heart of a man, eh? The Americans, they come to us. They say: 'Ten thousand dollars for the strip of the land next to your house!' It is aw-ful! Aw-ful!"

"And what do you say, Campeau?" asked Joseph.

"I say, I say: 'Well, if it is worth ten thousand dollars to you, it is worth ten thousand dollars to *me*. I keep it!'"

Joseph shook his head.

"Here's to keeping it! Here's to the old ways!" cried Antoine.

"Ah, bien, bien—here's to the old ways!" echoed Campeau.

Joseph was the only Frenchman who did not lift his glass.

"And here," cried Joseph, "here's to the *new* ways!"

From behind the counter, Boyer winked at Joseph, and lifted a sympathetic, progressive glass.

At that moment, there was a terrific clatter on the veranda outside, and two dashing young men rode their Canadian ponies up the flight of stone steps, straight through the door and up to the bar.

Joseph was dumbfounded, but Boyer and the others seemed not in the least astonished. The same thing had evidently happened before.

"We've come to sample your mint juleps again, Boyer. Want to see if they're better than those at Woodworth's Hotel today," announced the older of the boys. He was a dark-haired fellow, with very blue eyes, ruddy cheeks and a deep dimple in the chin, a dashing youngster if ever there was one. The other was blond, equally ruddy, equally handsome, a little inclined towards stoutness.

"Can those be the Abbott boys!" exclaimed Joseph.

"Yes, the Abbott boys, Madison and Bob. The most rollicking boys in town! Smart as whips, both of 'em!" replied Campeau. "When they settle down to business, they'll be as important as their papa. But, just now, they're busy having a grand time and cutting all sorts of capers. They ride up Boyer's steps once or twice a week, to sample a second julep, à cheval. And he has to stand for it, and passes out the stirrup cup as merry as you please, good-natured cuss that he is!"

Joseph rose from the table and introduced himself.

"By Jove, I didn't recognize you boys—you've grown up so fast! Join us over here at the table, won't you? I'm not inviting the horses, but I *am* inviting you! Have the juleps on me!"

"Thank you, Uncle Joseph. I wonder if you like the julep as we always order it—Monongahela whisky, fresh mint, and, on the brim, peach brandy and honey! All right?" asked Madison.

"More than all right!"

"Fine! Thanks, Uncle Joseph!" said Bob. "Sorry you're not inviting the horses, though. Well, we'll hitch them to one of the veranda pillars, and join you."

"I know what your *horses* eat!" Joseph shouted after them, as they rode towards the door.

"What?" asked the boys, grinning back over their shoulders.

"Wild oats!"

True to his pledge to progress, Joseph went down the next day to Oliver Newberry's shipyards. It was like a meeting of the giants. Newberry was a Goliath of a fellow, and almost as Titanic a legend on the inland seas as Paul Bunyan was in the bordering timberlands. "Admiral of the Lakes," they called him. Ugly as Polyphemus, with a gnarled forehead that jutted in front and a brain bag that jutted behind, grooved cheeks, deep-set, almost hidden black eyes, eyebrows that were black forests in themselves, straggling black hair that fell untidily over forehead, neck, and ears, an immense, loose-hung figure. Newberry's manager of the shipyards was Captain Chesley Blake, another giant, tawny of hair, with crimson-splotched cheeks, sea-blue eyes, a magnificent frame, and such a voice that it was said that when he issued his orders and shouted his magnificent oaths on board his vessels, during the storms on the lakes, the very masts trembled, the sea shuddered, and the competitive thunder ceased.

Blake roared a welcome to Joseph, and even Joseph's voice sounded small in comparison. Then Blake bellowed:

"Oliver! Oliver! Here's the Fur King, Joseph Bailly! Come out and see him!"

Above the din of the hammers of the shipwrights, Newberry heard the call in his office and ambled out to see Joseph, putting on his soiled beaver hat as he came. Half a dozen papers fell from it, as he lifted it to his head.

"Well, Bailly, just in time! How do you like our ship? There she is. Isn't she a beauty?"

"I'll take your word for it, Newberry. Doesn't look as if she could weather a storm yet."

"She'll weather every storm from here to Fort William!"

"Fort William! Ha!" roared Captain Blake, and the exclamation was a hurricane in itself. "You numbskull of a Newberry! You chowder-headed donkey! She'll weather every storm from here to Siberia!"

"All right, you blithering, blustering, blankety-blank Blake!

All right. From here to Siberia!" echoed Newberry, with a laugh that revoked the invectives.

"I'm wondering about the name," put in Joseph, to deflect the quarreling that might become serious (and never did). "Napoleon foundered on an island. Perhaps it's a bad name for a vessel, after all. Why not *The America*, or *The Yankee Gull*, or something like that?"

"You? You, a Frenchman, say that?" protested Newberry, who cherished a fanatical worship of Napoleon. "Dang my hide! I'm amazed at you!"

"Well, I used to idolize Napoleon; but, after all, Napoleon failed, and this ship has got to succeed! No Waterloos for her!"

"No. No water-loose, but water-tight, my boy, water-tight!" And Captain Blake released another hurricane.

"Oh, go blast yourself, Blake!" But Newberry laughed again, and it was easy to see that the two men idolized each other through all the fulminations. "Come into my office, Bailly, and look over the papers, will you? I've several things to talk over with you."

"I've several ideas myself," declared Joseph.

"That's what I like about you, Bailly." Newberry clapped Joseph on the back resoundingly enough to knock an ordinary man over. "You're full of ideas, full o' ginger! Kind that makes the world go round. Now, most o' these Frenchmen in Detroit— nice fellows, all of 'em, mind you—don't want no more than a canoe, some fishin' hooks, a rifle and a couple o' dogs. You're different. Dang it, you're different as hell!"

The fiddles were already singing their high songs in the hand-some new brick mansion of the Abbotts, when Joseph banged the door knocker. He had only time to look proudly down at his wife and remark, "You've got three pretty fine daughters, Marie, but you'll be the belle of the ball just the same!" before Pompey, in the usual green uniform, swung wide the door. The tufts on Pompey's head were white now, but he was the same old darky, deferential to all his master's friends and to the master himself.

"Massa Bailly! Massa Bailly! Wel*come!* And the Madame

Bailly! And the young prin-cess-es! Lawdy! Lawdy! How many hearts will be a-broken tonight! Um! Um!"

Indeed, the girls did look pretty, Rose in yellow silk and white lace, Esther in blue with pink satin rosebuds, Lucille in a deep lavender, the most favoring color for her complexion. Her black eyes sparkling with excitement, her black hair billowing closely over her cheeks, an artificial iris tucked into her curls, Lucille to-night looked the part of a real "charmer." But Joseph had not been far wrong in giving the palm to his wife. Marie wore a red velvet rose in her coiled braids, a ruffled black silk dress, and new red slippers, upon which her husband had sentimentally insisted. Her skin was still smooth and beautiful, her expression serene, her eyes deeper than depthless. Joseph was well pleased. He had no reminiscent envy of Joseph-at-the-ball-for-Lafayette.

A few moments later, the family entered the drawing room. There were at least a dozen officers in the room, with their bright blue uniforms, white crossbands, gold epaulets, bullet buttons, and black polished boots. There were lawyers and doctors and busi-ness men, representing the newer enterprises that had turned De-troit from a frontier village into a city. Joseph heard, even before he saw, Oliver Newberry and Captain Blake. In their evening clothes, they looked stiff as giants in armor. Father Richard was moving about, an amiable spectator, and Governor Cass was min-gling genially with the thickest crowds. Most of Joseph's French friends were present, with a few of the younger generation, Cam-peau's son Timothy, Pierre Desnoyers's boys René and Armand, young Antoine Beaubien and his cousin Médor, visiting from Chicago, and Sarah Abbott's nephew John Whistler, whose father, Captain William (son of the builder of Fort Dearborn), was now stationed at Fort Howard on Green Bay. Bob and Madison Abbott were already making love to all the girls in the room, but straight-way dashed to the middle of the room and took on the Bailly girls without a qualm. Joseph smiled, as he saw his girls swept into the center of a group of young beaux. But the thought that had entered his mind before, pierced it again with one swift stab:

"That's the beginning of the end: marriage—my girls—empty house . . . No, no! Perhaps the beginning of the beginning: grandsons!"

He turned back towards Sarah Abbott, whose hand he had just shaken:

"Those are fine boys of yours, Sarah! Fine boys!"

There was such a wistful tone in his voice, that Sarah, understanding his sudden memory of the loss of his own son, said:

"Those are beautiful daughters of yours, Joseph. My Sarah would be twenty-four years old, if she had lived. This is her birthday."

Joseph took Sarah's hand again for a moment.

"We've had a strangely similar fate, haven't we, Sarah? Worldly goods, love, joy, sorrow—the human portion. But, on the whole, luckier than most—perhaps."

Joseph noticed Abbott looking at him as he held Sarah's hand, the same proprietary look that Abbott had worn on his wedding trip, a quarter of a century before. Joseph released his old friend's hand.

"God bless you, Sarah. 'En avant!' Forward!" he said.

The company having nearly all arrived, the fiddles struck up the famous old promenading song. Joseph rushed over to Marie, who was talking to Madame Campeau, bowed, took her by the arm. Madison Abbott seized Rose by the elbow with hardly a by-your-leave, and Timothy Campeau took Lucille. Médor Beaubien was politely asking Esther for permission to promenade with her, when Joseph, to his dismay, saw her straighten up and turn her back. She stood haughty and unescorted for several minutes until John Whistler marched across the room, made a military bow copied from his father and his grandfather, and received permission to take her proud young arm. Joseph decided to make it a point to be especially pleasant to young Médor during the evening. His thoughts went back over the long and genial associations with the Beaubiens, in Detroit, at Grand River, at Chicago. Things were coming to a pretty pass, in American society, when his own daughter, with her good eighth of Indian blood, could turn up her nose at a handsome and charming half-Indian like Médor Beaubien! Joseph felt like turning Esther over on her blue-silk-covered bottom and banging the bumptiousness out of her. No more Philadelphia schools for her, if that was the result!

"We're all a-marching to Quebec!"

The whole company began to march and sing, James and Sarah Abbott leading the way:

> "We're all a-marching to Quebec;
>   The drums are loudly beating.
> The Americans have gained the day,
>   And the British are retreating;
> The wars are o'er and we'll turn back
>   To the place from whence we started;
> So open the ring and choose a couple in,
>   To relieve the broken-hearted."

The company widened out into a large circle. Only Father Richard and a few of the older officers of the fort remained on the outside. Every single French person, man or woman, was in the circle, for age could never keep a Frenchman from the dance. Campeau marched as spryly as his young son, Timothy.

Madison Abbott was the first fellow thrust into the center of the circle.

> "Green grow the rushes, O!
> Kiss her quick and let her go!
> But don't you muss her ruffle, O!"

Lucille Bailly was directly opposite Madison, her black eyes shining. Madison took Lucille's arm, drew her from the moving circle, crushed her to him, kissed her hard upon the lips, and released her. In that wild second, Lucille knew what all her pent-up energies had desired all her restless life long—the drama that she eternally craved. This was it at last! The lips of men! The arms of men! The "scalps" of men to fasten to her sash!

Madison retired from the circle. The group sang:

> "There's a rose in the garden
>   For you, young man,
> There's a rose in the garden
>   For you, young man!
> Now pluck up courage and
>   Pick it if you can!"

Lucille circled the group with her bright, dark eyes. Médor Beaubien was, by all odds, the handsomest young man there. Although she felt a trifle of the same hauteur that Esther so conspicuously displayed, there was something indescribably potent about Médor that drew her. She summoned him into the circle. He pressed her close to him and kissed her, hard and lingeringly, while the group sang:

"Green grow the rushes, O,
    Kiss her quick and let her go!"

Joseph and Marie had a sudden, severe realization of their newest problem. None of the other daughters had ever shown such signs of unrestrained passion. The situation was in Joseph's mind all evening, as he watched his three girls dancing. When the fiddles swung into the waltz (Abbott had given orders that this comparatively new, too-close-embracing dance should not be allowed more than once during the evening), Joseph noted how Rose and Esther managed to be held at a distance of at least twelve inches from their partners, while Lucille allowed herself to be embraced so tightly that not a page of the Bible could have been slipped in between. He was somewhat relieved when refreshments were served and the dancing temporarily stopped.

In the center of the dining table, on an immense silver platter, was displayed a masterwork of the chef's art, a cooked, spiced, stuffed deer standing on its own legs and looking at once lifelike and appetizing. On other platters lay hams, turkeys, chickens, pheasants, passenger pigeon squab, buffalo tongues, beaver tails, elk steaks, lobsters, oysters, pickles, hickory nuts, black walnuts, French pastries, doughnuts, and pies and cakes of all kinds and stripes. On the buffets were bottles and jugs and bowls without number, of French brandy, Jamaica rum, Monongahela whisky, claret, sherry, Madeira, Canadian shrub, apple toddy, eggnogs, and hot Scotch punch.

The general conviviality became louder. Joseph's laugh resounded. Captain Blake's and Oliver Newberry's shook the house. Joseph was in a corner of the dining room, telling a story to his French cronies, when Marie came across the room. She waited until the end of the story.

"Joseph, come here a moment, please. I can't find Lucille. She's disappeared. I'm worried."

Joseph would have dismissed the situation in a matter-of-fact way; but his eyes had been opened that evening, and he left his cronies and went hunting. The search took him upstairs and downstairs. No Lucille. He even went to the kitchen, where Pompey had gone to get another tray of refreshments and old Tetro and a few new negroes were at work. He pretended to want a glass of water, which seemed to amuse Pompey greatly and set him cackling and protesting: "Water, water? Yes, sah! Yes, sah! Old Pompey knows what kind of flu-id Massa Bailly wants!" Then Joseph escaped, unobserved, out of the back door, and walked as quietly as an Indian down a brick walk into the rear garden. As his eyes gradually became accustomed to the starlight of this first mild evening of early May, he heard voices and walked even more cautiously until he came behind two figures half reclining under a tree.

"Hug me, hug me tight, tighter," he heard Lucille saying.

"You bet I will, you little charmer!"

"Kiss me! Kiss me!"

Joseph remembered a garden in Baton Rouge. As much in anger at himself as at Lucille, he shouted:

"Get up, Lucille! Get up, I say! Oh, it's you, Médor, is it? You ought to know better, you young idiot!"

"Sorry, sir, but nothing serious—"

"Next minute, it *might* have been serious. You both ought to be taken to the old whipping post out in the Square! I'd gladly administer the cat myself!"

"But I love him," cried Lucille, "just as you love Cor—"

Joseph gave Lucille such a swift box on the ear that the syllable was broken off.

"Of course I love *cordial*. But what has that got to do with you, you little witch? March into the house, and we'll be going home!"

"Sorry, sir, dreadfully sorry!" protested Médor again.

"I've no doubt it was Lucille's fault. No doubt whatsoever!"

When they got back to the house, the fiddles were playing "Dan Tucker."

"Oh, don't take me home! Let me dance! Let me dance!" begged Lucille, clutching Joseph's arm.

"Dance! Dance?" Joseph found himself answering. "Dance to perdition!"

Chapter XXXV

THE BLACK HAWK

THE Indians still padded along the moccasin groove of the old Sauk Trail, in front of the new, large, many-gabled, Colonial-yellow Bailly house. Although Joseph had been successful in deflecting the course of the Detroit-Chicago road of the whites a mile to the east, two soldiers, with knapsacks on their backs, rode up to the Bailly house once a week, with mail from Fort Dearborn or Detroit, and now and then, in spite of the fact that Joseph was building an inn on the road to take care of the increasing number of hospitality-seeking travelers, a white wayfarer sauntered up to the door. But, on the whole, visitors were few at the homestead.

Then, in 1831, a tremor of excitement swept, like a premonitory wind, over the quiet old Indian trail. Little bands of Potawatomi or Ottawa filed up to the house, sat on the floor or under the trees with Joseph, smoked his tobacco, and murmured of Black Hawk, of proud, dark hearts, rebellion, turbulence along the Rock River, danger along the Mississippi. Joseph could see that old wounds had not healed, that old sores were festering. There was little laughter around the circle, little telling of Indian tales. The talk was of the white man's ruthlessness, seizing, seizing, pushing, pushing, crowding, crowding; and of Black Hawk, the newest incarnation of Indian freedom, Indian protest, Indian rebellion, the new Pontiac, the new Tecumseh.

"As soon as the leaves of the coming spring are as large as a squirrel's ear," said the Indians, "the Sauk are going to sweep eastward over the land, even as far as the Great Lakes. They are going to push every white man and every white woman into the Lakes!"

Joseph said little, satisfied that he was considered a brother, not an enemy, and trusting to the sweep of inevitable circumstances and the white man's power to clear away these final dangers.

Then, on an early autumn day of 1831, a splendid Indian figure, accompanied by thirty braves, rode up to the Bailly homestead. More than once this Sauk warrior had passed along the trail, at the times when the great processions of Menominee, Winnebago, Fox, Sauk and Sioux from the west stalked gorgeously towards Canada to receive the British annuities. Joseph instantly recognized Chief Black Hawk. Not tall, but very straight, with exceedingly dark skin, a Roman nose, high, intelligent forehead, and magnetic black eyes, he was a man to demand and command instant attention. He rode a white pony, was dressed in the uniform of a colonel of British cavalry; his silver sword dangled at his side, and he carried a blood-red banner.

A handsome young Indian rode beside Black Hawk, his scalplock twined with splendid feathers of many colors, his face and chest painted with the dangerous war colors of red and black, a red blanket calculated to fly gorgeously in the wind behind him, and countless ornaments, including many glass bugles and silver bells jingling about his ankles, wrists, neck, and ears. This was Black Hawk's son. The other warriors were only a little less imposing—red aristocrats, all of them.

Any ordinary white man might have been alarmed by such a company at such a time. But not Joseph. His daughters fled into the house, but Joseph extended his hand and offered an unflinching welcome.

"We camp here!" announced Black Hawk, not deigning to ask permission but regally declaring the fact.

"Good!" answered Joseph, in a loud voice. "Welcome, my father! Welcome! My house is yours. My grove is yours. Spread yourselves out. Make yourselves at home. My women will prepare a feast for you."

Even Marie, who was accustomed to Indians, was alarmed. To be sure, it was autumn, the time of dying leaves, and it would be long before the new leaves were as large as a squirrel's ear; but possibly Black Hawk had decided that the season of death for the leaves should be the season of death for all those who were related to the persecuting palefaces.

Marie hurried her daughters upstairs to put on the deerskin leggings and the blue cloth skirts of the Ottawa, and the beaded

jackets and many bead necklaces—anything to bring them closer
to the guise of Indians. She herself drew from a chest the beautiful
white deerskin suit that she had worn at her wedding. It was a
little tight now, but Rose pulled and tied her into it. Doubtless
Black Hawk would consider the ceremonial costume a worthy
honoring of his chiefly visit.

Then Marie and the daughters, and the squaw servants, whose
teeth were chattering with fright—for the Sauk were famous as
the fiercest tribe between the lakes and the Mississippi, fiercer even
than the Winnebago—set to work on a feast such as they had not
laid out for many a day; great keetles of min-dah-min-ah-boo (corn
soup), Ottawa tamales by the dozens, roast corn, roast deer,
batches of corn bread, hickory nuts, and bowls of the comparatively innocuous pioneer drink, metheglin, made from honey.

In the midst of the proceedings, Lucille disappeared. Marie interrupted her work long enough to call through the house, then
to go out on the lawn and look in every direction. The sound of
high laughter directed her towards the Indian encampment. In
the grassy space where De la Vigne had met his death, Lucille was
playing ball with Black Hawk's son. Marie's first impulse was to
call Lucille home; but, on second thought, she decided that
Lucille's boldness might this time be turned to advantage. Let her
be as affable as she cared to be towards any or all of the Sauk!

Joseph invited Black Hawk and his son and ten braves selected
by Black Hawk himself to dine in the house, while the other
braves were served in the encampment by the Bailly servants.
Everything went off well. The Sauk never knew that Jean Baptiste Clutier stood guard on the narrow staircase (purposely designed only eighteen inches wide for resistance in case of frontier
attack), gun in hand, with an arsenal beside him and two of the
voyageurs watching on the landing above. The servants shuddered as they passed the staircase on their way from the bakehouse
and the kitchen into the dining room and out to the lawn. Joseph,
at the head of the table, kept up a series of stories of adventure and
jokes in Indian style, and Black Hawk responded with more stories,
and the other Indians ate and spilled their food and grunted. Marie
came in now and then, or sent one of the daughters with an extra
dish. Only Lucille lingered fearlessly, and it did not escape Joseph

that Black Hawk's son pierced her with his eyes, and at several such times, said things to his father in a low voice.

After the dinner Joseph and the men adjourned to the encampment for a smoke, more stories, and Black Hawk's discussion of his troubles on the Mississippi. Joseph, suspecting that Black Hawk had come into the Calumet region chiefly to secure Indian allies, spoke long and tactfully of the peaceful intentions of the Ottawa and Potawatomi and their friendly agreement with the whites, and used every argument he could summon against active hostility and bloodshed and in favor of coming to terms with the palefaces. He was glad when, close to midnight, Black Hawk seemed to wish to terminate the discussion.

"Well, we can never agree on this, Monami Bailly. The Great Spirit has looked on you; but you are forever white and I am forever dark, and a river of blood runs between us. Let us not talk of this any more! Let us talk of your daughter!"

"My daughter?" gasped Joseph.

"Yes. The daughter with the Indian skin. I wish to buy her for my son. He wants her for his squaw."

Joseph thought fast. He must in no way offend, but the thing must not be allowed to happen.

"I am honored. My family is honored by the request, Chief Black Hawk. But the child is young, too young, for a paleface, to marry."

"She is a woman."

"Yes. But she is too young."

"I give thirty ponies."

"I am honored. Come back next year, and we will talk about it."

"Forty ponies then." The old look of hardness was coming into Black Hawk's face. "You do not like Chief Black Hawk's son?"

"Chief Black Hawk's son is one of the finest young men I have ever seen—a strong man, a handsome man, a great warrior!"

"But you refuse to take my son as your son?"

There was stone in every line of the chief's face. His hand was at his tomahawk. If he killed Joseph, it would rouse the ready blood lust of his braves. It would be the beginning of a massacre. There was only one way out. Reluctantly, Joseph took it.

"De la Vigne, the sorcerer, long ago cast his spell upon my daughter-who-looks-like-an-Indian. She is bewitched. She is bad medicine."

Black Hawk's hand ungripped the tomahawk.

During the night, Joseph sent Jean Baptiste galloping across the marsh road and along the Chicago-Detroit Road to apprise Pokagon of Black Hawk's coming. He remembered well Pokagon's attitude when Tecumseh had ridden into the Potawatomi village near Parc aux Vaches almost thirty years before, and he knew that Pokagon would be a strong influence for peace.

The next day, Joseph said a ceremonious goodbye to Black Hawk and his braves on the lawn in front of his home. Then he hurried into the house, where Marie had waiting for him a complete Indian costume, brown walnut juice for darkening his face, and vermilion paint. The transformation into a Potawatomi was made as quickly as possible, and Joseph mounted Veillantif and galloped away, at full speed, across the marsh, to the beach, along the hard wet sand at the waves' edge, to Trail Creek, between the tall dunes that guarded the entrance, and up the river to the Council Grounds near the ancient springs of Father Marquette. Pokagon and Topenebee, Shavehead, Weesaw, and a hundred Potawatomi from Parc aux Vaches were already there, and Trail Creek scouts were just riding in with the message that Black Hawk and his braves had already been sighted coming along the Sauk Trail and would be in the village in a moment. Joseph had just time to make himself known to Pokagon and Topenebee when Black Hawk rode in magnificently with his braves.

During the confusion, Joseph had time to perform one small service. A glimpse of Ginsey McCoy crossing the campground decided him to go instantly to Ginsey's Indian husband and advise him to keep the girl closely concealed until the departure of the Sauks. The roving eye of young Black Hawk might easily come to rest on the startling, golden-haired girl, and, although the Indian codes were usually strong against buying or abducting squaws already married, there was no telling what Black Hawk might do, if the Potawatomi should refuse to join his conspiracy. The husband of Ginsey grunted his approval of Joseph's suggestion, the girl was shoved into the wigwam, and the tent flaps were dropped.

The remainder of the day was consumed in the enjoyment of feasts, smoking, Indian lacrosse, shooting, and arrow play. It was not until night came down, and the supper fires were gleaming in the darkness, that Black Hawk finally planted a vermilion-painted post in the center of the encampment.

Then, one after another, the young Sauk braves began to dance around the post, shouting their war cries and hurling their tomahawks into it until it bristled with blades and handles, like a gigantic porcupine. Then, in unison, they began to repeat their war song, their strength-of-eagles, fierce-as-panthers, death-to-the-paleface song, rising in a crescendo of yells at the end of every stanza.

Black Hawk watched the circle of Potawatomi intently—there were two hundred all together—in the hope that the younger and wilder braves would become heated with the martial excitement, join the dance, and hurl their blades.

There was fire in the eyes of Shavehead. He was jumping up and down in the front row of the circle of Potawatomi, nearest the firelight. Joseph saw the danger of his incendiary influence and moved forward from the shadows in the rear, to seize his arms, if necessary, to prevent him from joining the battle group of the Sauk. Joseph did not trust Shavehead nor relish the idea of his penetrating his own disguise; but he was determined, at all costs, to keep him from starting a general defection of the younger Potawatomi. Shavehead started forward. Joseph reached out his arms to stop him. But, at the very instant, Pokagon, seeing Joseph's danger, leaped out of the ranks, seized Shavehead's arm, twisted him around, and brought him back to the circle of the Potawatomi. At the same moment, Pokagon signaled to Joseph, with his head and eyes, to return to the shadows in the rear.

Black Hawk saw that the time had come for some of his eloquent personal persuasion. He signaled to the war dancers to stop, and every sound in the camp ceased. There was breathlessly respectful silence. The dancers formed a circle in front of the Potawatomi. Black Hawk moved close to the war post. He raised his right hand towards it and towards the dark sky beyond the post:

"O Great Spirit, we give thanks that Thou hast given us strength to fight for the earth that belongs to us. Give us more strength, the strength of a thousand prairie wolves and ten thousand buffalo! Give us strength, O Great Spirit! Let our brothers, the Potawatomi, join with us to drive the palefaces across the prairies into the Great Lake, where they shall be drowned, and disappear forever!"

Black Hawk lowered his arm, paused, then addressed the Potawatomi, his voice at first low and slow, then rising higher and becoming more and more heated with savage fire:

"The white men are taking your lands from you, inch by inch," he said at last. "They are taking the food from your mouths, the water of the streams from your lips, the campgrounds from under your feet. The graves of your ancestors are being plowed up to make crops for the white man and for the white man's horses. The earth is beautiful. It is our earth. The Great Spirit gave it to us. Shall we not fight for it? Or shall we lie down and let the white man walk over us and cut up our lands and our bodies into little pieces for his pleasure? Shall we not fight for the earth that is ours? If you will join with us, I will have an army like the trees in the forest, and I will drive the palefaces like autumn leaves before an angry wind!"

"Hoh! Hoh! Yes! Yes!" came the cries from Shavehead and his neighbors. Now Pokagon stepped forward and, standing beside Black Hawk, began to speak:

"My brothers, Chief Black Hawk has spoken strong words and brave words, but they are not wise words. The black hawk from whom he takes his name does not pounce on a pack of prairie wolves that would tear him in pieces. The hawk is wise and pounces on a field mouse or a gopher or a prairie chicken!

"The Great Spirit has willed that the white men shall be given a portion of the land we love so well. We do not understand, but the Great Spirit is wise. The Great Spirit declares that the white men and the red men must live together side by side. It is possible to do this. There is nothing so good as a good white man—men like Joseph Bailly and John Kinzie (whom the sands have covered), and Alexander Robinson and Billy the Sauganash and the good Father Richard. Let us have peace. Let us not have war, for war will destroy us. Black Hawk says he will have an army like the trees in the forest. Yes! But the palefaces will soon bring an army whose numbers are like the *leaves on the trees*, and will sweep you and your army into the great ocean beneath the setting sun. It will be the end of the red man. Take heed, my brothers. Make peace, and live. Or make war, and die—you and your old men, *your squaws and your papooses*."

The last sentence was a stroke of genius, bringing a sudden vision to Topenebee and Shavehead and the aggressive party they led of their own squaws and papooses lying in lakes of blood similar to those that they themselves had poured around the whites at Fort Dearborn and the Raisin.

Black Hawk rose and cried: "Throw your tomahawks at the war post, my brothers! Let the war post be filled from the top to the ground! Let the tomahawks sing!"

But not a Potawatomi stirred, not even Shavehead. Black Hawk's strong face darkened. There was an ominous pause, and the Sauk braves watched their leader. If there had not been a proportion of two hundred Potawatomi to only fifty Sauk, the sullen lightnings that flashed from Sauk scalp to scalp might have fired destruction into the camp.

"You are not worthy to be our friends! We will go!" cried Black Hawk, and he drew his own tomahawk from the post. The other Sauk moved forward and pulled out their weapons also. Then Black Hawk swung at the post, near the ground, with his tomahawk, and in a few furious strokes, brought it down. He then marched away towards the tethering place of the horses.

Pokagon and the Trail Creek chief followed him, spoke to him, and urged him to stay and spend the night in the encampment; but Black Hawk refused:

"No, we will ride back in the darkness, southwest towards the Illinois country, towards Shabanee's village, where there are other Potawatomi, braver Potawatomi, who will join us!"

Joseph Bailly spoke out from the darkness. "Do not ride along the Sauk Trail in the darkness! It is a path hard to find. It is easier to ride to Chicago along the beach, in the starlight." He wanted no sulking Sauk Indians riding past the homestead or camping in the grove. But he had failed to disguise his voice.

"Who are you? *Bailly, the white man?*" cried Black Hawk, fiercely.

"White man?" retorted Pokagon scornfully. "Did you think we would allow a white man at our council, Chief Black Hawk? But Red Fox is right. The trail on the beach is good. It is hard-packed

after high waves. I will lead you along the river trail to the beach."
Joseph raced home along the Sauk Trail.

If Black Hawk was unable to win over the Trail Creek and Parc
aux Vaches Potawatomi and Shabanee's braves at Paw Paw Grove,
he left a swirl of influences behind him, that became more and more
tumultuous as the year 1831 passed into the epic year of 1832. As
rumors came back from the Mississippi that Black Hawk's warriors
were massing in great numbers for final revenge on the whites, who
had driven them from their fields and their homes, the Potawatomi
seethed again. There was a surge of sympathy towards Black
Hawk's brave, insulted people. At Parc aux Vaches, Pokagon
again addressed his warriors and held them from battle. At Chicago, Alexander Robinson, now chief of the Chicago Potawatomi,
called a council, and it required the eloquence of five white men
to hold the headlong braves in leash: Joseph Bailly, Alexander
Robinson, Billy Caldwell, Noël le Vasseur, Gurdon Hubbard.
Bailly told them of the council at Trail Creek the year before and
of Pokagon's eloquence and of Pokagon's arguments. Then he
distributed a hundred silver bangles from Campeau's, and considered the money well spent as a bribe for peace on the frontier.
Sullenly, the Chicago Potawatomi disbanded, promising not to
fight.

On April 6, Black Hawk crossed back east over the Mississippi
with five hundred warriors, and on May 14 he startled and overwhelmed Major Stillman on Sycamore Creek. The rumors spread
like runners of prairie fire: "The Indians are massing by the tens
of thousands." "They are sending their squaws and papooses into
Canada." "The British are sending them aid again. The redcoats
are marching down from Canada to join with Black Hawk." "The
Indians are sweeping like a great red tide east, east towards the
lakes. They will wipe out every white settlement."

Panic swept over the Middle West, a genuine hysteria. It was
at the same time tragic and comic. The tiny settlements were far
spread out—a few clusters at Dixon's Ferry, Plainfield, Peoria, in
Illinois, whose terrified inhabitants galloped towards Chicago
breathless, with white faces, leaving their possessions behind, even
their clothes, some appearing without shoes, others without hats;

a few clusters to the northwest of the Bailly homestead, at Gull Prairie, Gull Corners, Niles, Parc aux Vaches, two families at Marshall, five families in Kent County, two in Allegan County. Those to the east fled towards Detroit. Many of those in the southwest of Michigan and northwest of Indiana fled towards Door Village, five miles from La Porte, thirteen miles from Baillytown. Two hundred men organized a tiny army, and began frantically to build fortifications at Door Village, a stockade 125 feet square, two blockhouses, ditches, embankments. The rumor that Shavehead was organizing the fiercer Potawatomi into a massacre band added terror to the motion of the spades! Other forts were flung up at South Bend and on Terre Coupée prairie. The guns of all the Indians on Prairie Ronde were taken away from them. Near Danville, some friendly Indians tried to signal a band of whites on the road, but the hysterical settlers raced on, almost killing themselves and their horses, in their effort to escape.

Joseph Bailly sent his family to the fort at Door Village, and he and Jean Baptiste and his voyageurs and Indians moved back and forth between the village and the homestead, in an effort to protect both places. Joseph dug and hacked and helped with the building of the fort, like a good soldier, giving the energy of ten men, though he doubted that Black Hawk would ever be seen along the lakes again.

On June 10th, a regiment of United States infantry marched down the Sauk Trail from Detroit to Chicago. Among them was young John Whistler, who sent his best wishes, through Joseph, to Esther. At the same time Lieutenant William Whistler, his father, was moving towards Chicago under the command of General Winfield Scott, on the steamer *Henry Clay*, unaware of the spectral guest on board which was to spread even greater terror over the lakes and the prairies than the Sauk and the Fox Indians.

Chapter XXXVI

DEATH IN DETROIT

As JOSEPH rode into Detroit on that July day of 1832, his thoughts were all of business and of the future. His head was full of a thousand plans. At fifty-eight, he still had the energy and the enthusiasm of youth. He still rode his horse like a straight-backed soldier. He was still a magnificent specimen of a man (with weather-beaten cheeks, keen, sea-blue eyes, ruddy hair into which only the touch of iron-gray was beginning to creep, and the strong chin and forehead formations and fine middle-face lines that suggested the contrasts in his personality). He was dressed well, as always, in the compromise costume of a gentleman-trader, well tailored suit, ruffled shirt, high boots, bright sash and today a voyageur's cap, for comfortable summer riding.

He was planning partnership with Oliver Newberry in a new vessel. The *Napoleon* was a great success, carrying more trade up and down the lakes than the partners had dared to hope. The project for a Trail Creek harbor was developing, and must necessarily ride through to eventual success. Joseph had already planned a litttle town on the brink of the harbor, had platted the streets and given them family names and historic French names: Robert Bailly Street, Marie Lefèvre, Geneviève de Gaspé, Sister Thérèse, Napoleon and Lafayette Streets. He had registered the plat at the new La Porte County office in the recently incorporated village of La Porte.

More and more settlers were coming down the Erie Canal, riding down the road from Detroit to Chicago. One of Joseph's plans on this particular visit to Detroit was to talk to some of the old French friends even more persuasively than before and try to get a group from Detroit and Frenchtown-on-the-River-Raisin to come and settle on the Trail Creek harbor site and form a French-American colony. The Baillys would still have a wilderness home, but would have, sufficiently near, a congenial French group to be very happy and gay. And there would be justly earned money for the shrewd founder of the community!

No, Joseph wasn't an old man yet. He had recovered much of the old buoyancy and hope. His son was dead—but there would be grandsons soon! And there would still be a great Bailly estate and many enterprises for the grandsons. There was gold in other things besides furs. There was gold in the land—in the tawny sand and in the black earth of the marshes. There was gold in ships. There was gold in harbors . . .

The town of Detroit was nearer now by several fractions of a mile to Ypsilanti. More houses pushing out the frontier of Cadillac's ancient stockade settlement! No more need now for the palisade and the blockhouse towers and the sentries listening for Indians. It was a safe American town now.

Joseph rode into Detroit, eyes alert to greet the friends whom he was sure to see walking or riding or driving the old French carts through the widened streets. But there was absolutely no one to be seen today. Outer Detroit was like a deserted village. However, when Joseph rode into the market square, where the old whipping post had stood until very recently, there was sudden commotion! A stage coach was drawn up at the curb. People with bags, cloth bundles, parrot cages, family portraits, Bibles, leather chests, jewel caskets, fiddles, flutes, silver teapots (as if they were running away again from the fire of 1805), were climbing aboard, pushing past the driver who stood guarding the coach door, climbing up to the top of the vehicle, and almost pushing one another off the roof and the wheels in their eagerness to find a place. In fact, one fellow actually did fall off as Joseph reined in his horse and watched: a plump, stuffed-goose-looking chap, who finally picked himself up and vented imprecations at all the passengers and the driver together! The stage driver climbed aboard, clucked to his horses, and the overloaded vehicle crawled off, while the fallen passenger waved futile arms and shouted threats and a woman ran wildly out of a side street, dragging two children and two portmanteaus with her, and added her useless shrieks to the vanishing coach. Joseph wondered why Detroiters should be so desperately eager to get to Pontiac or Mount Clemens, or whatever the destination of the coach might be. Certainly, there were no smoke and no scarlet flames in the air, as there had been on that June morning so long ago. A land sale, perhaps. But why take your parrots along to add to the confusion?

As Joseph reached the stranded man and woman, the woman cried out:

"You can't loan me a horse, sir, can you, me and my poor children? We've missed the coach!"

"But there'll be another coach tomorrow, madam. And I don't live here. I've just arrived. I'm sorry I can't help you. What are the people hurrying for, if you don't mind telling me?"

"My God, man, don't you know what's happened?"

"Why, no, what *has* happened?"

"The cholera, sir—the cholera's broken out! Came on the *Henry Clay* with General Winfield Scott. Boat's gone on to Chicago, but it's left death behind it. Fifty cases already! It'll be getting worse! Go back where you came from, sir! Go, before they close the town and forbid folks to leave!"

"Thank you for telling me. Good luck! Good day."

Joseph rode slowly on. He was not afraid. He doubted whether the disease would pounce upon a man who was as strong as an ox, although, to be sure, diseases sometimes had a whimsical way of taking the strong and leaving the weak. However, it might be wise not to take too many chances. He would transact his business quickly and get back home as soon as possible. Just as well that Marie and the girls were not with him this time, or even Jean Baptiste.

As he rode past Ste. Anne Street, he looked down the widened vista of the street to Father Richard's beautiful stone church. It was even yet not quite completed, for there was still scaffolding at the rear. For twenty-seven years Father Richard had been raising the money and building that splendid successor to the little old wooden church, the little "lodge with bells."

Joseph rode on to the Mansion House. There was no stableboy to take the horse, and so, for the moment, he fastened the lines to a hitching post and went up the veranda steps. The entrance hall was deserted. Mr. Boyer was not at the desk or the bar. Joseph stepped across the hall and looked into the dining room. He was just about to step into the kitchen, when the door opened and Mr. Boyer came out, his face the color of paper, beads of sweat standing out on his forehead, his eyes bulging.

"Oh, Mr. Bailly, Mr. Bailly!" he gasped. "It's Mrs. Boyer! She's fallen on the kitchen floor. Can't move. All the servants dropped everything and ran the minute she fell. I can't get her up! I can't get her to her bed! Can't get anyone to help me! Oh, God, what shall I do?"

"I'll help you," said Joseph quietly.

"But it may be the cholera, Mr. Bailly. It may be the cholera! I'm not afraid. If my good wife dies, no use *my* living any longer. But you, Mr. Bailly, you—"

"I'll help you."

Joseph pushed into the kitchen. Mrs. Boyer was lying on her back, her head propped on Mr. Boyer's coat, which he had folded under her for a pillow. Her face was plum-colored, her glassy eyes were so withdrawn into the sockets that they semed to focus backwards; her mouth was open, her lips and nose were pinched, her breathing was alarmingly rapid and loud. But she was still able to speak, in a harsh whisper:

"Never mind—John. Never mind. Never mind, Mr. Bailly. . . . Don't—bother—about me. . . . Leave me be. . . . You mustn't catch it—"

"Of course we'll mind!" declared Joseph reverberantly. "We'll get you to bed, and you'll be well, in no time! Boyer, get a chair. It will be easier to lift her into a chair and carry her that way up the stairs."

Mr. Boyer was forced to place a cholera placard on the Mansion House, and Joseph took rooms at Woodworth's Steamboat Hotel. As soon as he was settled, he went down to the wharves to talk to Oliver Newberry and Chesley Blake.

For the first time, the shipyards were empty. Where before there had always been the jabbering of hammers, there was now complete silence. Nor were the thundering voices of the giants echoing today against the warehouse walls and the half-finished hulks of Napoleonic vessels. Joseph wandered aimlessly over the stocks, noting the kegs of nails open to the rusting air and the hammers and saws and work-aprons dropped on the ground where terror had swooped down and put the workers to flight. Joseph walked to Newberry's office. The door was open. Newberry, with his paper-stuffed stovepipe hat on his head, sat staring at his desk, his motionless quill pen in his right hand, his left elbow on the desk, his left hand supporting his head. He started violently, as Joseph blurted out:

"Hello there, Newberry! Hello!"

In a subdued voice, which was no more like Newberry's than the hum of a gnat is like the bellowing of a bull, came the answer:

"Oh, you, Bailly? Sit down. How do you happen to be here in this City of the Dead?"

"City of the Dead! Come now! You and the other Detroiters are taking this thing too damned seriously! Pluck up! Disease can't get you down, Newberry! You're as strong as one of your own storm-bucking ships!"

"This is too big a storm, Bailly! Look out for yourself!"

"Oh, come now! Let's forget about it and talk business! I came to see how the new ship's getting along. Where's Blake? I'd like to see him, too."

Newberry gave a ghost of a laugh far back in his throat.

"Blake? He cut and run at the first case of cholera two weeks ago. Took the first vessel headed for Lake Superior. Wouldn't believe it, would you? Thundering giant! Scared out of his boots! Look at this letter, will you? Came in this morning on a vessel from Sault Ste. Marie, with twenty-five cents postage due! See if I don't dock that off his salary when he comes back!"

Newberry took his hat off, fumbled among the papers and handed Joseph the letter:

Sault Ste. Marie, July 8, 1832.

Dear Oliver,

I rejoice to tell you that I am well. As the old bore of a preacher used to say from the prattling box back in Maine, when I was a boy: "I am snatched as a brand from the burning." Oh, Oliver, how I wish you might see the folly of staying where you are and would follow me up the Lake!

By the by, you have not paid me my salary for four months. You asked leave to borrow the money for that new boat you and Bailly are building. But now that the pestilence is among you and you know not how soon you may go, please make a note of my overdue salary and leave the I.O.U. in a noticeable place on your desk. You ought to prepare for death, and you certainly ought to prepare that statement at once. I hope that all is well with you and the other friends at Detroit. Remember me to Bailly when he comes, and tell him I have gone on a little trip up the lakes and will be back when business is better in Detroit. By the way, don't forget to make out that note about the salary, at once.

Business seems to be good up here at the Soo! Saw Henry Schoolcraft this morning. Says more vessels have touched at the Soo in the three months since the ice has been out of the channel than in the whole of last year. Better come up and look things over up here.

But before you leave, don't forget to write out that I-Owe-You, will you, Oliver?

Your devoted friend,

Chesley Blake.

P.S. Don't put the I.O.U. in your hat, but on your desk, please, Oliver. I'm sorry to suggest it, old fellow, but they might bury the hat with you.

"Can you beat that, Bailly? The blithering, bellowing bottle-head! The—the—"

"Come, come, Newberry! He's just suffering from panic."

"I'll pour his wine for him, when he comes back! I'll make his blood run!"

"I've heard you threaten each other before. It's like two giant oaks shrieking at each other in a storm, but never crossing branches with each other. Come on, Newberry, let's forget the cholera and talk business."

"Talk business? Who's going to be left to do business in this plague-stricken town?"

"You and I, Newberry. *You and I!* Now, about this new ship. How about naming it *L'Aiglon*—for—for the little son of Napoleon, you know, the king of Rome."

"The kid's just died, hasn't he?"

"Yes. But what difference does that make? People can remain almost as alive—in memory—"

"No! Too much death around here. No, by Gawd, no! Let's name it—for a change let's name it the *American!*"

"Good! That suits me! The *American!* Splendid! But I *would* like to name the next one L'Aiglon. . . . Now, let's see those quotations on lumber. . . ."

The cholera, after all, was like that other fire of 1805. Its purple flames leaped from house to house, devouring the structures of human lives indiscriminately.

Joseph was caught in the conflagration. The authorities closed the city. No one was allowed to leave. It seemed, therefore, just as necessary to Joseph to help, as it had seemed in the actual fire of twenty-seven years before. He was again absolutely fearless. He had a towering faith in his own strength and his own immunity.

Father Richard and Father Kundig were working night and day with a little band of nurses, the Sisters of Mercy, organized under their leadership, who were making every sacrifice of time and labor for Catholics and Protestants alike. Among them were two daughters of Joseph Campeau, a daughter of Antoine Beaubien, a daughter of Pierre Desnoyers. Under the same leadership, it became the task of Joseph Bailly and of Jacques Beaugrand, who was at last pathetically redeeming his reputation with this humane work, to visit as many houses every day as possible, to report the needs of each family back to the priests and the nurses, to see that the houses were placarded where necessary and to notify the old sexton, Israel Noble, who, followed by the death carts, rode through the streets at all hours, ringing his bell and calling out his terrible cry of "Bring out the dead! Bring out the dead!"

Joseph had thought that the plague would last only a few days, but it ebbed and raged and ebbed and raged. At first it failed to touch the company of his acquaintances.

One afternoon, he went hurriedly to Ste. Anne's Church to summon Father Richard to Campeau's slave headquarters for the purpose of administering extreme unction to old Crow, whom Catherine Campeau, one of the Sisters of Mercy, had been vainly nursing. When Father Richard arrived, Joseph and Campeau followed him out to the "quarters." Crow was lying on a bed of straw in the corner of a little cabin which he shared with three other unmarried slaves. He was dressed in a dirty blue calico shirt and blue cotton trousers. The red silk houseman's uniform, of the kind which Crow had proudly and vividly worn for thirty years, hung on a peg above the bed. Crow smiled faintly as Father Richard entered the room, and murmuring the "Pax huic domui," knelt beside the bed.

"I've come to pray with you, Crow," he said, as he placed on the floor a cruse of oil and a small vessel of holy water.

"Dat's mighty good ob you, Father. Habn't been inside yo' church for nigh thirty years, ebber since Ann died—"

"I know. I know, Crow. But you've been all over the outside of it, eh, my boy? The new steeples were harder to climb, though, weren't they?"

"Yes, Father. Did you build 'em dataway on purpose—to keep old Crow off'n 'em?"

"No, Crow. Oh, no! Just to get them up a wee bit nearer heaven—"

"Dat's where I's goin'—"

"Yes, Crow."

"I's not sorry. Ann's been waitin' for me a long, long time."

"Yes, Crow."

The old darky's breath began to come fitfully, his eyes to darken.

Father Richard hastened with his work of absolution. Very quickly he sprinkled the cabin room with holy water, and, in the old Latin words, bade the "evil spirits and all malignant discord" be gone and the "angels of peace" enter the room of the dying.

The remembrance of the scene in the prison cell at Fort Shelby came back over Joseph, and the words of the psalm that Father Richard had used to give him comfort, words even more suited to this ordeal than to that ordeal of long ago: "I will say of the Lord, He is my refuge and my fortress . . . Surely He shall deliver thee from the snare of the fowler, and from the noisome pestilence. . . ."

Father Richard returned to Crow's bedside and knelt down. Joseph and Catherine Campeau slipped to their knees, and, at last, even the unorthodox Campeau knelt down also beside his old slave's bed. Father Richard dipped his thumb in the sacred oil and made the sign of the cross over Crow's faintly stirring eyelids:

"Per istam sanctam unctionem indulgeat tibi Domino quidquid per visum deliquisti."

On all the gateways of the five senses, Father Richard laid the final seal of the cross, closing them to mortal use, sanctifying them to eternity, eyes, ears, nostrils, lips and hands. Then came the last beautiful Latin prayer:

"Respice, quaesumus Domine, famulum tuum, in infirmitate sui corporis fatiscentem, et animam refove quam creasti!" ("Look down, O Lord, we beseech Thee, upon Thy servant, failing from bodily weakness, and refresh the soul which Thou hast created.") "Per Christum Dominum nostrum. Amen."

Crow's lips seemed to murmur, "Amen," or, perhaps the word was "Ann."

All was still in the room. Joseph and Campeau and Catherine Campeau rose to their feet. Father Richard tried to get up also. But a cramping pain had suddenly seized him, and he fell, cholera-stricken, beside the bed of his last communicant.

There was no human being in Detroit or in all the territory between Saginaw Bay and the River Raisin who failed to come into the city and into Father Richard's beautiful, almost completed Church of Ste. Anne to kneel before the bier of the beloved priest. Cholera or no cholera, all plague restrictions, all health rules, all panic, all terror were overridden, as the worshiping crowds passed before the high altar and looked into the kind and smiling face of Father Richard, as he lay on his slanted coffin. Not all the laughter wrinkles around the corners of his eyes had been smoothed out even by the tranquilizing hand of death. He looked as if he might be smiling at one of St. Peter's jokes.

Sixty-seven tall tapers, representing Father Richard's age, burned around three sides of the bier. The words "The Father of the Fatherless" were written in roses on a blanket of white field daisies that had been gathered by all the girls in town.

The funeral, conducted by Father Kundig, lasted for hours, and the procession that accompanied the body to the cemetery was endless. There were no sincerer mourners than Joseph Bailly and James and Sarah Abbott who walked together in the procession.

Following the funeral, there was, of course, a new outbreak of the disease. An eighth of the population of Detroit was swept away. Justice, human and divine, did not seem to function. The lawyer, Abijah Hull, was kept as busy as a cormorant plucking the bones of the estates and residues of the dead.

At night, it seemed as if the city were on fire. Bonfires of tar and rosin burned at the street crossings and, in the middle of the square bounded by Jefferson and Woodward avenues, a huge iron potash kettle was kept filled, night and day, with the same supposedly beneficial ingredients. The actual and the invisible flames raged.

At the Mansion House, Mrs. Boyer had succumbed to the plague. After a lapse of days Mr. Boyer reopened the house, and after a lapse of still more days his patrons began to drift back to him, to sample the mint juleps. But the customers drank less abundantly than before, for it had been observed that the bibulous were the first to drown in the tides of the plague, and that the abstainers were apt to be survivors.

Nevertheless, a gay group gathered there in the afternoons as before: Timothy Campeau, youngest son of Joseph Campeau; René and Armand Desnoyers, Pierre's dashing heirs; young Antoine Beaubien; and Bob and Madison Abbott, who invariably rode up the stone steps and laughingly demanded their stirrup cups at the bar.

Then one day, when the pestilence had struck against the group and carried away Armand Desnoyers, young Antoine Beaubien suggested that the rest of the comrades band together in a so-called "Mutual Insurance Society," to serve one another until death. Boyer turned over to them the third-floor ballroom of the Mansion House. Cots were put up, and there the ten young men remained, away from the world, living out their till-death-do-us-part pledge.

Just before leaving for home (during an apparent cessation of the cholera, when the authorities had temporarily let down the city bars), Joseph Bailly went to say goodbye to Boyer and to the boys in the ballroom whom he knew so well.

He knocked on the always shut door of the ballroom, and, as he entered, paused for a minute to watch from a distance the characteristic activities of the various members of the little group. Timothy Campeau was sitting on the floor, against the wall, playing a fiddle, René Desnoyers and three other French boys were playing

euchre, Jean Marsac and Tom Smith were wrestling in the middle
of the floor. On a bed in the corner, one of the boys was lying,
while Bob Abbott and young Antoine Beaubien were standing
chatting rather earnestly beside him. Joseph went over immediately to the bed, where he found Madison Abbott propped up, with
his clothes on.

"What's the matter, Madison?"

"Nothing, I think, Uncle Joe. I was just fool enough to eat
cucumbers yesterday with three mint juleps, and I've got a bit of
indigestion."

Joseph looked at him carefully in the shadowy light, and recognized the same purple look that he had seen on the faces of Mrs.
Boyer, old Crow, and Father Richard. Evidently Bob and Antoine had recognized it, too, for they looked at Joseph with contracted brows and questioning eyes.

"Have you had a doctor yet, Madison?"

"Oh, no, I'll be all right! The doctors are so overwhelmed, you
couldn't get one if you tried."

"Well, just to make you feel more comfortable, we'll get one
for you a little later, I think."

Joseph tried to make his voice seem casual and unanxious, but the
white rabbit of fear suddenly looked out of Madison's face.

"Almighty God! You don't think I have—"

"I think as sturdy a boy as you is going to throw off indigestion
or whatever-it-is, in no time at all!" answered Joseph vigorously.

"For God's sake, don't tell my mother!"

Joseph patted Madison's shoulder and strolled away as unhur-
riedly as he could, pausing to chat and joke with all the other boys
before he finally left the room. Then·he raced down the stairs.
In the entrance hall, he ran full tilt into Sarah Abbott, who was
coming in with a napkin-covered basket over each arm.

"Sarah!"

"Why, Joseph, why are you hurrying so? What's the matter?"

"Nothing! Nothing! I just have some business to attend to,
Sarah. I'll see you later. By the way, where are *you* going?"

"Upstairs, with some fresh-baked cherry pies and French doughnuts for the boys."

"Let me take them up for you, Sarah."

"You can carry one basket, Joseph."

"Let me take both!" He spoke very fast. "And I wonder if I can ask an immediate favor of you in return—to take a little note to Oliver Newberry right away for me! I'll write it out at the desk!"

"Joseph!"

Joseph had been avoiding Sarah's eyes. Now Sarah compelled him with her voice, and held his gaze with a look from her great brown eyes that searched the very depths of his soul.

"Joseph, *what has happened?*"

"One of the boys is ill, Sarah. And I don't want you to go near that ballroom. There may be no danger—and again there may be danger."

"Which boy is it, Joseph?"

Joseph hesitated a fraction of a second overlong.

"Oh, Joseph, we've always understood each other, deep below the words. Oh, Joseph, tell me the truth!"

"The boy begged me not to tell his mother—"

"Joseph! *Which one is it*—Madison or Bob?"

The name stuck in Joseph's throat. He could not speak. Sarah thrust the baskets into his hand, to check his pursuit, and fled up the stairs.

Joseph stayed in Detroit long enough to give every possible assistance to the Abbotts. Somehow, losing Madison would be like losing his own son over again. He spent much time in the ballroom, helped the doctor with the bloodletting, gave calomel at regular intervals, kept hot-water jugs packed around the patient at night, after he had forcibly sent James and Sarah home, and did everything that a father might have done. Madison's strong young constitution and Sarah's and Joseph's unremitting care pulled him through. By a miracle or possibly by Joseph's rigorous banishment of them to the other end of the great room, none of the other boys caught the disease. Nor did Sarah. Nor did James. Nor did Joseph.

It was definitely time now for Joseph to go home. After the final goodbye to the Abbotts, Joseph went down once more to Newberry's warehouse. A few men were hammering away at the growing skeleton of a boat. Newberry was standing beside it, giving orders with peremptory gestures, but in so low-pitched a voice that Joseph could not hear him until he was almost at his side. Where were the thunders of yesteryear?

"The *American*'s getting along, Newberry. Grand work!" said Joseph.

"Walk along towards the office with me, will you Bailly?"

Newberry was silent so long that Joseph looked sidewise at him, scrutinizingly. Newberry was getting old. Yes, decidedly, he was getting old.

"Mind if we change the name of the boat, Bailly?"

"Why, I think *American*'s a splendid name! Couldn't be better!"

"Yes. It *could!* Could be more definite. Sort of commemorate a special American. Got a message from a lake captain this morning who's just come down from Superior. I'd like to call the boat the *Chesley Blake*, if you don't mind."

"Blake's dead?"

Newberry nodded his head.

"Cholera?"

Newberry nodded again.

Chapter XXXVII

POWWOW AT CHICAGO

JOSEPH rode towards Chicago, heavy with many thoughts, on a September day of 1833. He knew very well that his friends the palefaces were going to take the last acres from his friends the Potawatomi, for a mess of pewter money. There was nothing he could do about it. The forces were too great for one man to stand against. It would be like a sandpiper strutting against the waves of Lake Michigan in a September storm. All he could do was to watch every phase of the treaty council and to stay as close as he could to his friend Pokagon.

As he rounded the southernmost curve of the lake he loved so well, he thought of Pokagon and his braves in the days of Pokagon's youth (which were the days of his own youth, for the two men were, in age, only a year apart) galloping over the prairies in pursuit of the thundering herds of buffalo. These vast prairie acres now belonged to the white man. Only the deer and the foxes, the prairie wolves, the grouse, and the snipe hunted through the tall grasses now. The Indians rode quietly now, on their way to Chicago, to traffic with the white men.

To the west Joseph could see the dark oasis of Blue Island jutting up out of the light-colored prairie, and, far to the north and west the line of trees that marked the running of the Des Plaines and Chicago rivers.

From a point seven miles south of the Chicago River, where the shore makes one white horn of a long sweeping crescent, that ends at the river mouth, Joseph sighted the whitewashed walls of the rebuilt Fort Dearborn. From that distance, and even from a little closer, when the bark-colored roofs of the log cabins began to show, the place looked peaceful enough. But as Joseph approached still nearer he observed a variety of structures, a vast multitude and a seething commotion such as he had never seen before in the

517

vicinity of Chicago. Stretched out a mile to the south of the town, on the beach, and a mile to the north and all along the river and on the surrounding prairie, were the bark lodges and the painted wigwams and the helter-skelter shelters of five thousand Indians. The recently incorporated town itself had acquired half a hundred new cabins since the year before. The little streets were seething with all kinds of people, commissioners and real estate men and little-big businessmen in silk hats, trappers and fishermen, voyageurs, peddlers and merchants, tavern keepers, interpreters, and the human sharks that follow the crowds as surely as the big fish follow the lesser fish; and thousands of Indians, with all their gaudy paraphernalia of paint, feathers, glass baubles, beads, silver medals, and jingling bells. In the open prairie spaces beyond the settlement, the Indians were racing their horses or tilting at one another with long spears, wild knights of America, or practicing their exciting game of lacrosse or merely riding up and down and yelling at the tops of their lungs, as a result of good spirits and good old Chicago whisky.

A hundred different scenes of drunkenness were being enacted, a hundred different episodes of gaming and sharking.

As Joseph rode up the river trail, he felt sick at heart. Always the contact with the palefaces degraded the Indians, reduced them to the brute beasts they were *before* they were Indians. These were not the proud, shrewd, splendid, free Indians of Trail Creek and Parc aux Vaches, the Rapids of the Grand and the Crooked Tree. These were brown beasts already trapped and twisted, hobbled and neck-wrung by the whites.

Joseph rode up to the fort to pay his respects to Major William Whistler.

Two days after Joseph's arrival, on the 15th of September, the guns of the fort boomed out to summon the chiefs to a preliminary council. The council lodge, a large open shelter, had been constructed on the north side of the river at the corner of Rush and Kinzie streets, not far from the old Kinzie house. It required hours to prod the reluctant old chiefs into the council chamber. They knew the deed that was about to be perpetrated by the palefaces, and they walked unwillingly to their doom. One by one they came, wrapped in their blankets, red sphinxes: old Topenebee, young Topenebee, Pokagon, Black Bird, Black Partridge, Weesaw, Shavehead, Shabanee, and twenty or thirty others, who held the fate of their people in their hands. The half-breed chiefs, Alexander Robinson and Billy Caldwell the Sauganash, were there, in positions of importance, as mediators between the two races.

Dozens of interested whites who expected to make claims in the apportionment of the lands were also there: Jean Baptiste Beaubien and Mark Beaubien, John and Robert Kinzie, sons of Joseph's old friend John Kinzie, Antoine Ouilmette, Jean Baptiste Chandonnais, Joseph Bertrand of Parc aux Vaches, William Burnett, Joseph's old rival, and Robert Stuart of Mackinac Island, present on behalf of the American Fur Company; two interested travelers who were later to write picturesque accounts of the proceedings: Patrick Shirreff and Charles Joseph Latrobe; and other interested spectators, Major William Whistler, young John H. Whistler, Gurdon Hubbard, John Wentworth and officers and soldiers from the fort. The Commissioners were Governor George B. Porter of Michigan, William Weatherford, and Thomas J. V. Owen, the Indian agent at Chicago, successor to Dr. Alexander Woolcott.

Joseph smiled sardonically as he stood, with arms folded, against a post at the back of the council lodge. Watching the sphinx-faces of the Indians and the apparently casual but too eager faces of the whites, he knew that it would be many a tedious day before any conclusion was reached or any one of those calm Indians placed his brown hand and symbol-signature on the parchment documents that were waiting in Governor Porter's breast pockets.

The great council fire in the middle of the lodge had been lighted and kept burning since noon. It was now almost sunset.

When the thirty Indian braves had seated themselves on one side of the council fire and the commissioners, secretaries, and interpreters had seated themselves on the other, and the council pipes had been smoked in silence for a long time, Governor Porter cleared his throat, with ostentatious resonance, and rose, assisted by a secretary, from his place on a mat on the ground. Extending his pudgy hand in an amicable, semicircular gesture to include the group of Indians seated at his feet, Governor Porter began:

"My red brothers! The Great Father at Washington, whose

ears are always open to every thought and desire of his red children, heard from his far-off lodge in the great White City, that his Indian children on the shores of Lake Michigan wished to sell their remaining land, from the lake to the Rock River, and receive in return many bushel baskets of silver dollars, many clay pipes, many kegs of tobacco, many warm blankets, and many, many acres of land (far better than these poor prairie acres), on the green shores of the Great Father of Waters. The Great White Chief at Washington has therefore sent his subchiefs to treat with the chiefs of the Potawatomi. This is good. Very good. Let the Commissioners hear what the Indian chiefs have to say on this happy subject."

His face beaming with benevolence and facile hope, Governor Porter eased himself down on the mat again, with the help of his secretary.

There was utter silence in the lodge. Not a soul stirred. After a number of tense moments, Mr. Weatherford coughed uneasily. In a moment, Mr. Owen echoed the cough. It seemed as if a trial of speechlessness had begun. Then, when the dome of silence began to bear down and crush, Pokagon rose, in one graceful, elongating motion, from his place on the ground. He stood with dignity for a moment, then said:

"We thank you, Governor Porter, for any kindness that may be hidden in your strange words. But we wish to say that the Great Father at Washington must have seen a bad bird which has told him a lie. For, far from wishing to sell the *last* of the good land that the Great Spirit, who is far greater than the Great White Father at Washington, gave us so long ago—we wish to keep it."

With these simple words, Pokagon sat down again, to an accompaniment of many Indian grunts of approval. Then the two other white Commissioners, in turn, rose and spoke, with vigorous but unpersuasive eloquence. Governor Porter called upon Topenebee, upon Blackbird, upon Shabanee of the Illinois Potawatomi. Quietly these others repeated Pokagon's words. Then Governor Porter tried to appoint another council for the next day. No, said the Indians, clouds were gathering in the sky. The weather would not be propitious. Joseph, still standing with folded arms at the back of the council house, smiled again.

As twilight was coming down over the prairie, Governor Porter adjourned the council, but suggested that the Indians wait for a distribution of gifts. Then, dozens of boxes of clay pipes and barrels of plug tobacco were brought into the council house and distributed to the chiefs and to hundreds of Indians gathered outside.

Along the river and the beach and the prairie, the campfires were soon lighted. Chicago was a place of fallen stars.

After the preliminary council, day after futile day passed. The signal guns of the fort were fired without result. The chiefs stayed away from the council lodge. Excuse after excuse was given by the wary Indians. The weather was not favorable. The moon was not favorable. Two of the important chiefs had not yet arrived. There was nothing to be discussed.

The Commissioners, the agents, the interpreters, a few of the halfbreeds, and the sharks, worked unceasingly with the Indians, persuading them of the fabulous riches that would be theirs, and the fabulous acres that would belong to them on the Father of Waters. More clay pipes, more plugs of tobacco were distributed. Whisky was poured out in streams rivaling the flow of the Chicago River.

At last, the pressure of the white tides became so great that the beaver dams of Indian resistance broke. On the 21st of September, the council fire was lighted once more in the lodge; the Indian chiefs filed in, and the hundreds of braves, squaws, and all the town hangers-on gathered in a dark mass outside.

Joseph knew that the ultimate moment had come. The impassive faces of the Indians betrayed to his keen eyes the intensity of their emotions. A tightening around the firm jaws and in the forehead muscles, a lessening of the angle at which the heads were carried, a fire gone from the eyes—these were the signs by which Joseph knew the measure of their ordeal. A few had lost all dignity and were befuddled with drink.

Again, Governor Porter spoke first. But this time, he adopted the evasive and indirect methods of the Indians:

"The Commissioners wish to know why the Indian chiefs have summoned them to this council?"

But if he expected a direct answer to this indirect question he was mistaken. The red man answered question with question. Pokagon replied:

"The assembled chiefs wish to know why the Great Father at Washington is calling his red children together at Checagou?"

Governor Porter then took the buffalo by the horns, and spoke vehemently, threateningly, declaring that the Great Father at Washington had come to the end of his patience, that he had been endlessly kind to his red children and would continue to be just and kind, but that he would not be trifled with any longer! There must be no more beating about the bush. Would the Potawatomi exchange their strip of grass and sand for the magnificent gifts and the magnificent territory that the Great Father was so generous as to bestow upon them, or would they not? Would they be great, rich chiefs, or wandering beggars? Come, what was their decision?

Billy the Sauganash and Alexander Robinson, who had long since realized that there was no opposing the westward march of the white man, rose and spoke to their Indian brothers and gave the final touch to their persuasion. The papers were made ready. Pokagon was asked to sign first. He rose from his place at the east end of the lodge and asked permission to say a few last words. The red light of the sun, setting over the Potawatomi prairies, colored his hair, kindled his splendid face, and gave an epic significance to his figure.

"It is of no use protesting any more," said Pokagon. "The white tides sweep on, bearing all before them. The palefaces come, and the red man is driven towards the setting sun and the evening star of death, west to the shores of the Great Lakes, west to the shore of the Great River, west to the shore of the Great Ocean, in whose waters he will sleep forgetfully at last. The land that was ours is slipping from us, the last strip of land that we loved. Soon the St. Joseph River and the Checagou River and the Calumet and the Grand will no longer know the dip of the red man's paddle. Where once I moored my canoe to the shores of Lake Mitchigami, now the great steamers are already at anchor. Where the war dance made the air ring, is now heard the piping fiddle of the paleface playing 'Yankee Doodle.' The brick walls lift on the spot where once the deerskins were spread, and the great oak trees are cut down. No more will the flint-tipped arrow fell the deer, and the woodlands will soon resound no more with his bounding step upon the brink of the river. The bones of our dead are given to the wolves. Where the great chiefs held their councils and where the pipe of peace was smoked by the great warriors, the towers of the towns are rising up against the sky. All has changed except the sun, moon, and stars; and they have not, because the paleface God and our God hung them beyond the white men's reach! I seek for the wigwam of my people! O Great Spirit, forgive the paleface for what he does to my people . . ."

Then the onlookers saw a strange thing. They saw tears flowing down the cheeks of Pokagon, as he bent his head, and took the quill pen from the hand of Governor Porter.

The final negotiations required several more days. There were many complicated arrangements to be made, many claims to be settled against the transferred estates of the Indians.

Then, just before the Indians broke camp and scattered to their various homes where they were to be allowed to live for two or three years longer, before the actual resettlement was made, the vanquished Indians broke forth in one last desperate, magnificent celebration.

On the morning of the 25th of September, eight hundred warriors gathered at the council house and formed themselves into a spectacular procession. They wore only their loincloths and, in their hair, hawks' and eagles' feathers; but their faces and bodies were brilliantly streaked and circled and zigzagged with all possible patterns and all colors, chiefly the warlike vermilion and black. The hideous designs on their faces, of enlarged mouths and extended and multiplied teeth and encircled eyes, gave the participants the aspects of monsters. Most of them carried tomahawks and war clubs. A large band of wild-looking musicians started the forward movement of the procession. These were equipped with Indian drums, Indian pipes, and sticks and clubs to clash resoundingly together to make more din than music. As this savage band struck up and incoherent yells rose from all parts of the multitude, the snaky procession began to wind west, up the north bank of the river Chicago.

Joseph, standing beside Elinor Kinzie on the balcony of Mark

Beaubien's Sauganash Hotel, watched, with fascinated eyes. This, he knew, was the last Indian procession, the last Indian dance, in the village at the old Chicago Portage, the village that had belonged to the red men long before the days of Father Marquette and the Sieur de La Salle and the unnamed voyageurs of long ago. It was a splendid, defiant pageant!

As the Indians progressed, their motions became faster and more furious, their drums more thunderous, their yells more terrible, their gestures more menacing. At the bridge that had recently been thrown across the north branch of the river, the long procession crossed, turned south to the log raft bridge across the south branch, turned east and approached the Sauganash Hotel. As the Indians came nearer to the group of palefaces gathered in front of the hotel and on the balcony, they played up theatrically to their audience! The wild leaps into the air became higher, the stoopings to the brown earth lower, the yells more deafening, the brandishings of clubs and tomahawks more terrible, the twistings and shakings and leanings forward and backward, the writhings and snakings more amazing.

Several women on the balcony screamed. One plume-bonneted woman, standing on the other side of Elinor Kinzie, cried out:

"They're going to murder us! It's another massacre! Oh! Oh-h-h-h!"

Elinor quietly took the woman by the arm and said:

"Don't be afraid! It won't be another massacre. I know these Indians well. I was in the Fort Dearborn massacre myself."

"You were in the Fort Dearborn massacre!"

"Yes. This is just the last celebration of the Potawatomi. It may seem a fearful sight to you. To me it's just very pitiful."

"Pitiful? Well, I declare! Pitiful! It's the most horrible sight I ever saw in my life. I'm glad those terrible creatures are going away, never to return. Thank goodness, our Government knows what it's doing!"

Elinor raised her eyebrows, in the same hopeless curve with which one shrugs one's shoulders, and looked up at Joseph, who returned her glance with comprehension.

The long procession, at this moment, extended back from the hotel all the way to the bridge over the north branch of the river.

Joseph concentrated for a time on the individual figures in the seething mass, to see whether he could recognize any one. Through the dust that had been raised and through the perpetual motions of the yelling, perspiring, corybantic throng, it was difficult to pick out persons. But Joseph was able to single out Shavehead, with his single scalplock, long hawk's feather, unearthly yells, and foaming lips. It seemed as if all of Shavehead's long accumulated hatred of the whites were being exposed in the wild contortions of his body and in the shrill scream of his throat. His tomahawk flashed in silver arcs of death, as if he were cutting off the scalps of a thousand new enemies. Elinor Kinzie clutched Joseph's arm and held it tight, as Shavehead went by!

Joseph recognized no one else until the very end of the long procession. There, not running or leaping or dancing or brandishing, walked Shabanee and Pokagon, in strange, contrasting dignity, wrapped in their scarlet blankets.

As the terrible noise receded towards the fort, Joseph turned to Elinor and remarked:

"*We* know that they're not all heroic, and that they're not all savage, don't we, Elinor? We know that there are just as many differences among them as there are among us. We have our scum-of-the-earth and our John Kinzies! They have their Shaveheads and their Pokagons!"

"You're right, Joseph. They're just people—and I can't help wondering whether we, who are driving them from their ancient camping grounds at Checagou, are really a better people than they are. Are we going to make a better, happier village on the river than they did—I wonder."

"Well," said Joseph with a quizzical smile, looking down on the river from the fifteen-foot-high balcony, "our wigwams are a bit higher!"

Chapter XXXVIII

DE LA VIGNE'S DAUGHTER

It was April of 1834. The Ottawa were encamped again on Bailly's oak knoll. The last flocks of geese were swinging northward. The hylas were shaking their castanets in the marshes. The tight green umbrellas of the mandrake were unsheathing in the woods. The arbutus was in bloom. Last year's nests swayed in the trees. But all the nestmakers were in the woods again, orioles and yellowbirds, bluebirds and cardinals, parrakeets, and all the rainbowed throng. The red-black earth was rich and expectant.

For the first time since the coming of Joseph Bailly, that earth had felt the gash of the plow, and the passing of men in long, horizontal patterns over it. The prairie that bounded the marsh on the north, the prairie that had once been marsh itself, had been plaited into dark, velvety ripples. There were cabins all around it; the cabins of Jesse Morgan from Virginia, of Reason Bell from Ohio, of Adam Campbell from Indiana, of Thomas Gossett and Theophilus Crumpacker and Jerry Todhunter and John Spurlock and Hosea Gosling and a dozen others with names as gnarled as their frontier-battling bodies. The soldiers returning from the Black Hawk War had reported the rich undeveloped prairie and marsh and timber lands; and the Fort Wayne Road and the Detroit-Chicago Road had felt the trampling of hoofs and heels and covered-wagon wheels; and the Erie Canal had known the stirring of many boats prow-pointed towards the west.

The first house to go up near the Baillys had been that of Jesse Morgan, three miles to the northeast. Joseph and Jean Baptiste and the Bailly Indians had helped with the cabin raising. It had constituted the most exciting event for years. Neighbors! Something besides wolves and Indians! Now there were dozens of neighbors, and the stagecoach ran through once a week from Detroit to Chicago. Michigan City, at the mouth of Trail Creek and at the terminus of the old Indian Trail from the Wabash, had been platted and settled two years before. There were a few prospective purchasers of lots for Joseph's Baillytown at the mouth of Trail Creek. The world was growing.

Now that there were neighbors, it was possible to borrow and make exchanges. One morning, Running Cloud, wishing some potatoes to throw into the soup pot, sent the young girl Three Stars to the Bailly homestead for the desired article. But Marie's answer was that the Baillys too were out of potatoes, and that she understood that Hosea Gosling had some for sale at his house.

"Run along to the Goslings' with Three Stars and buy potatoes for me, too, will you, please, Lucille?" called out Marie to the youngest daughter, who was out at the fur sheds talking to the voyageurs who had just returned from the winter's trapping. Lucille answered with an instant affirmative, for young Raoul Gosling was as handsome a six-footer as had come into the country for a long time, and Lucille was glad of every chance to tantalize him with her charms. There were, of course, Jerry and John Morgan, living a mile north of the Goslings, and Thad Todhunter, but Ruel was, by far, the handsomest of the near-by settlers' sons. Lucille took, with alacrity, the silver coin that her mother slipped into her hands and started off with Three Stars.

"I'd like to go back to the encampment to ask Oshogay to come with us," suggested Three Stars. Oshogay was a grandniece of Chief Blackbird and Three Stars' best friend among the young squaws.

In a few minutes, the three girls were on their way across the fields, two in Indian dress, one, who yet looked quite as Indian as the others, in linsey-woolsey. They talked in Algonquin as they went, laughing and telling stories and making gay, inconsequential remarks about the spring and about the young paleface men and the young braves. As they came onto the plowed tract of the Gosling domain, they saw, at the far edge of the field, Ruel Gosling and Jerry Morgan and Thad Todhunter walking up and down and, with splendid, immemorial gestures, sowing the Gosling acres.

"We'll go over and talk to them when we come back," said Lucille, and she waved her hands to them.

All three young men responded, and Ruel dropped his work and ran towards them.

"What can I do fer you, girls?"

"Nothing, Ruel. Isn't your mother at home? We want to buy some potatoes."

"I'll attend to it fer ye. Mom and Pop have gone over to La Porte to tend to some business. I'll fix ye up."

"All right."

Ruel looked with pleased eyes at the two Indian girls. Lucille noted the look that swerved away from her, and the smile that went away with it, and decided that she wasn't going to have any competition. She was going to have Ruel's undivided attention.

"I'll go in with you, while you get the potatoes."

"Oh, I've got some sacks right out here beside the house waitin' fer sech as you."

"Oh, all right. Thanks, Ruel. How about your carrying them for us a little way? They're plenty heavy, you know!"

"Heavy fer *you?* Yer as tough as a plow handle, girl! But I'll carry 'em fer ye a mite of a ways."

Lucille looked up sideways at Ruel with a warm and drawing glance. "My Gawd!" thought Ruel. "She'd do to flirt with! Mighty purty, and hot as a tomato in the sun!" He let Lucille brush up against him as they walked. The Indian girls chattered on ahead of them across the fields.

Jerry Morgan and Thad Todhunter had reached the end of a furrow at the south end of the field, close to the footpath that edged a small creek and a strip of wood. The Indian girls hurried a little to get past, but the boys set down their seed sacks and came up and said: "Hello!"

"Boo-joo!" said the Indian girls.

" 'Boo-joo'! What does *that* mean? Trying to scare us?"

Three Stars and Oshogay shook their heads. They understood only a few words of English.

"Oh, that just means 'Hello'!" explained Lucille, coming up. "Hello, boys. How are *you* getting along?"

"Oh, we're not getting along. We're *staying!*" said Thad, winking at Ruel.

"Fine, Miss Bailly!" supplemented Jerry genially. "How's things at your place?"

"All right! The voyageurs have just come back. Pretty lively over at our place! Come over and dance some night! We've got plenty of good fiddlers now, besides Dad."

"Dang my buttons if I don't!" said Thad. "Do them squaws dance too?"

"Mercy, no!" answered Lucille, emphatically. "Just Indian dances, you know! Not French and American dances, like you and me!"

Again Lucille rolled her eyes. Ruel winked now at the other two boys.

"Walk along with us a way, why don't you?" urged Lucille.

"All right. To the end o' the field."

The two boys took their places beside Three Stars and Oshogay. They tried to loop their arms through the girls' arms, but the squaws pulled away in alarm. The boys thought that was good fun. They put their arms around the squaws' waists. Then the Indian girls began to run. They ran very fast towards the encampment. Jerry and Thad laughed and pursued. This was more fun than hunting deer!

Lucille hurled herself against Ruel and laughed too. Ruel set down the sacks of potatoes, and put his big arms around Lucille, drawing her vigorously close. Then Lucille put up her lips and gave kiss for wild, young kiss. A meadow lark sang as it lifted from a near-by furrow. The world throbbed with irresponsible spring. Lucille was as the young, brown earth, rich, expectant. She leaned back. Ruel laid her on the ground, under a red maple tree. She did not resist as he sowed his seed in his neighbor's field. . . .

Three Stars was a faster runner than Oshogay, faster even than Jerry Morgan. She ran all the way to the encampment, while Jerry was turning back and Thad Todhunter was struggling with Oshogay. The first person whom Three Stars encountered was Joseph Bailly, who had just arrived with Jean Baptiste to cut firewood at his sassafras grove on the edge of Morgan Prairie.

"Oh, Monami Bailly! Monami Bailly!"

"Three Stars! What *is* the matter?"

"The palefaces! The palefaces! The bad young men! They caught Lucille and they caught Oshogay, but they didn't catch me! They— Oh, it's awful, Monami Bailly! They—"

But Joseph had already started off, on a run, with Jean Baptiste following after. It was not long before they could hear sounds like the thrashing of a wounded deer, with human exclamations mingled in the scuffle, at the edge of the woods ahead of them. Joseph ran panther-swift. He came upon Thad Todhunter and Oshogay rolling over and over on the ground, Oshogay fighting like a demon, Thad trying to get her fastened down.

"Get up, Thad Todhunter!" shouted Joseph. "Get up, you almighty fool!"

The two stopped rolling. Thad got up, by inches.

"You ought to be horsewhipped! I'll take this up with Mr. Todhunter—and so will the Indians. You can be sure of that! I hope they scalp you! Jean Baptiste, take Oshogay home and report that no harm's been done her. I'll be along soon. Get along!" he said to Thad.

As the boy started to go ahead of him, Joseph gave him a kick that sent him sprawling on the ground and not desiring to get up again for some time. Joseph hurried on more cautiously. There were no more sounds of scuffling, no screams. But, in another moment, Joseph could make out the sound of a girl's shrill laughter at the edge of the thicket. Joseph moved slowly now. In a few moments, he came upon Lucille entangled with Ruel on the ground.

Joseph pounced on Ruel and dragged him off De la Vigne's daughter, pulled him to his feet, and then knocked him down with a blow on the chin.

"Now"—when Ruel came to himself again—"you shall marry this girl!" (Joseph could not manage to say: "My daughter".)

"I don't want to marry him! I won't marry him!" screamed Lucille. "I want to marry a rich man and live in the big cities! I won't marry this country fool! I've had what I want of him!"

"You'll marry him, all right," said Joseph.

"B-b-but Mr. Bailly, I'm—I'm g-g-going to marry Celia Bell. This ain't my doin's, Mr. Bailly. Your girl wanted this. She *wanted* it, Mr. Bailly! She—"

"You're going to marry Lucille, if I have to horsewhip you all the way to the justice of the peace at La Porte! Get up! We'll go and talk to your father. Get up, you cussed young fool!"

Hosea Gosling was disgusted with his son, but he was equally disgusted with the idea of that son's being forced to marry the daughter of a squaw and a French Catholic. For the first time, Joseph ran up against the hostile Protestant Yankee, as neighbor. Words ran hot and high. Joseph heard the epithets, "God-damned Catholics!" "Tarnal Frenchmen!" and "Stinking squaws!" and let fly with his fists. When the six-foot Gosling picked himself up from the floor, he was a trifle more wary of his phrases.

"Can't ye give a fellow time to think it over, you Jo Bailly, you?"

"No! This affair is to be settled right here and now! Your son marries my daughter or, by Heaven, I *will* horsewhip him all the way from here to La Porte! Wait and see if I don't!" Then Joseph had a sudden inspiration as to how to handle this American neighbor. "It's not such a bad match either, my good fellow, from your American point of view! I'll settle twenty thousand dollars on the young people, as soon as they're married!"

"Tw-tw-*twenty thousand dollars!*"

"Yes. You didn't know I had that much money, did you? Money talks to you Yankees, doesn't it?"

"Talks, man? It *shouts!* Would ye mind puttin' that down in writin'?"

Several things happened, to delay this horsewhip-wedding for a few days. In the first place, as soon as Joseph returned across the fields from his interview with Hosea Gosling, he was met by Rose, who came running to tell him that some old friends had arrived in a covered wagon. And, secondly, the Indians had begun to seethe over the affront to their young squaws, and all of Joseph's and Marie's efforts were required on the knoll to avert massacre.

The old friends, to Joseph's great joy and astonishment, proved to be Rebecca and Nathan Heald (now honorably discharged from the army) and their seventeen-year-old son Darius, who were moving their household goods to some of the rich territory west of St. Louis recently explored and glowingly described by the soldiers returned from the Black Hawk War. The Healds consented to stop with the Baillys for a few days. But there was little time at first for amenities, because of the seething in the grove.

As soon as Three Stars had brought in her news the hundred Ottawa had set up the war post in the center of the camping ground and had started to dance around it. The girl had gone directly to the encampment, so that Marie had been unable to talk to her and calm her down; but Jean Baptiste had shrewdly taken Oshogay first to Marie, still in the cloth skirt and beaded waist that had become shredded and mud-covered in her struggle. Marie had washed her, clothed her in new Indian garments, and talked to her long and persuasively before permitting her to go back to the Indians; but Three Stars, in her panic, had already stirred up the hornets' nest. It did not matter that neither girl had been successfully attacked. That they had been touched at all by the hated whites was sufficient. The Indians began to dance. The war drums began to roll. And, to make matters worse, half a dozen of the Ottawa went down to Peter Pravonzey's newly built tavern, half a mile east of Bailly's small inn, on the Detroit-Chicago Road, and achieved complete drunkenness on the horrible brew that Pravonzey served out to them.

Joseph and Marie went out to the grove immediately to see what they could do. Unfortunately, Pokagon, with his moderating influence, was not there. Asa Bun and Shavehead, along with the relatives of the affronted girls, were acting as the chief stirrers up, and were reveling in the imminent glory of blood. Blackbird did nothing to restrain them, for Oshogay was his relative and he felt personally outraged as well as vengeful for the tribe's sake. Joseph tried to speak to the assembled group, but they would not even stop to listen to him. The drums rolled. The gourds rattled. The knoll shook with pounding feet. The war songs resounded:

> "The palefaces have attacked us,
> They have attacked what is dearest to us!
> They have attacked our young girls!
> We will go to their lodges.
> We will burn their lodges to the ground!
> We will scalp every paleface
> For miles around!
> We will tear off their flesh!
> We will drink their blood!
> The palefaces have attacked us.
> They have attacked our young girls!
> We will make black ashes and blood,
> Red blood and black ashes!
> Hoh! Hoh! Hoh! Hoh!"

Joseph and Marie returned to the house to wait until the energies of the Indians should die down. Toward evening, the war dancers would be wearier. Later, when the supper fires were lighted, they might try again.

Accordingly, at dusk, when the drums had stopped for a few moments, Marie went alone to the encampment. She took her place near the war post and begged for silence. Shavehead and Asa Bun and some of the younger braves shouted angry interruptions at her, until Blackbird stood up and told the Indians that it would do no harm to listen to the Wing Woman. Marie spoke of the pioneer boys as being young and mischievous, as not having known what they were doing. No real harm had been done. So why all this excitement? Hereafter, the Indian girls must not wander away from the encampment; then all would be well. There was a ring of paleface cabins all around, and every cabin had guns and fighters in it. And the Indians must not forget that Fort Dearborn was occupied again, and that Major William Whistler, the brave son of the brave builder of the first Fort Dearborn, whom many of them remembered, was there with all his soldiers, ready to come galloping down the Checagou Road with death-spouting guns at the first sign of Indian trouble. "Peace, my brothers, peace! Again, remember Father Marquette! Was he not a good man? Was he not also a white man? Father Richard—was he not also a good man, and a white man? Joseph Bailly is a brother to the Indians. All know that the Great Spirit has looked down upon him. Peace, my brothers, peace!"

At this moment, Shavehead lifted his hand and something struck Marie in the face. It was a scalp from Shavehead's belt.

"She has a forked tongue!" cried Shavehead. "She is protecting the palefaces. She is also protecting Captain Heald, who is at her house, the man who destroyed the guns and the whisky at old Fort Dearborn, in order that we should not enjoy them! We failed to kill him at the massacre. Let us kill him now—and all the palefaces!"

Shavehead threw another scalp and another. Marie turned and fled towards the house.

Thus the gruesome scalp dance began. The Ottawa went through the motions of ripping off one another's scalps, drinking one another's blood. Shavehead's scalps were thrown, like rags, from hand to hand. The braves shrieked. The squaws screamed. The drums boomed. By midnight, there was such a deafening uproar that Joseph feared that, at any moment, the Indians might rush off to massacre all the whites. He was not at all sure that his own family would be exempted from the slaughter. He begged the Healds to take the road for Chicago, but all three of them refused to desert, in this crisis. There came upon Rebecca's face something of the grim, brave look that she had worn at the Fort Dearborn massacre. She asked Joseph for a gun, and clenched it as tightly as she had clenched her riding whip on that terrible day in 1812. Major Heald was all for galloping off to summon the soldiers from Fort Dearborn. But Joseph knew that, if that happened, the soldiers would simply shoot down the Ottawa and create an even more desperate situation. Joseph had to hold Heald by the lapels of his coat to keep him from going. Heald then began to apply his military tactics to the barricading of doors, windows, and staircases, and the preparing of the guns and ammunition to be used in the last desperate resort. After some persuasion, Joseph did at last consent to send word to Billy Caldwell and Alexander Robinson at Chicago and to Pokagon at Parc aux Vaches. He was not sure that he could trust any of his own Indian servants in this emergency, for the old savage hatred of the whites might be stirring in them too, in response to the excitement in the grove. Jean Baptiste was the logical messenger to ride through the night to Pokagon, but who could be spared to go to Chicago? Marie offered, Rebecca offered. Then Rose spoke up and declared emphatically that she was the one to go, that her little Arab was as swift as the lake winds and knew every inch of the trail.

Joseph agreed. He saddled Rose's horse for her and led her part way across the marsh road. It was two o'clock by now, and a three-quarters moon was just rising, so that the going would be easier a little later. When they were a mile from the encampment, and the drums were no louder than the hylas singing in the marshes all around them, Joseph kissed his daughter goodbye.

"Remember, Rose, don't act as if you were bringing any alarming message into Chicago! Find Alexander and the Sauganash as soon as you can, and give the message to them—and to them alone. Ride back with them as fast as you can. I trust you! Good luck! Goodbye!"

Rose kissed her father, mounted her little Arab, and was off towards the pine woods, the dunes, and the shore. She knew that she would not be able to make any time until she reached the beach, and not even then, unless the sand were hard-packed from recent, long-running waves. Her heart beat fast, for she had never ridden unaccompanied at night before, and she was leaving her family in terrible danger. Fears for her own safety were groundless, she knew, for a few words in Algonquin and the name of Bailly would quiet any wandering Indian, and there would probably be no palefaces until she reached the cabin at the mouth of the Grand Calumet ten miles from Chicago (unless some covered-wagon caravan should be camping on the beach), and the scant danger from wolves and wildcats would be over as soon as she reached the open shore.

Yet the rising moon made the pine woods ahead look deep with unrevealed perils. Rose remembered with a slight shudder the Indian belief that the moon was made to give light to the dead. An owl screeched as she entered the woods. Was it an owl, or an Indian? She dug her riding boots into her Arab's flank; but the snow had only recently melted, and the trail of wet leaves and mud was impossible for galloping. In the woods, the light of the moon was deep blue, almost sapphire, and the April stars were like snowflakes in the bare trees. But Rose was scarcely aware of the night loveliness, for she was still tense and kept turning her eyes in all directions, without turning her whole head—like an Indian hunting for danger. At last she reached the inner slope of the dunes. It was still slower going now, through the sand mixed with leaf mold. Then, she was at the summit of the dunes, where the crown of trees came to an end, and the white west slope swept down in terraces to the beach.

Rose did not dare to sacrifice an instant to pleasure, but, as her horse went through the fetlock-deep sand to the beach, she tossed her fears to the cool wind and gave herself completely to the joy of the scene before her. The shadows of the pines were long black figures, prone Manitous, on the beach. The small waves had already caught the glint of silver. The sand was gray-blue in the moonlight, the lake black-blue. Over the water, to the south, Orion, the last of the winter constellations, was setting in pale splendor. As Rose reached the last terrace of sand, she noticed how incredibly sharp and black were the shadows that the moon had thrust under the dry sword grasses.

In a moment, she was down on the beach. The singing waves had been just long enough in their reach to make a yard-wide strip of hard, ridable sand. Again, the girl dug her boots into her horse, and now the little Arab responded and raced full speed down the beach. Rose's plumed riding hat came loose, and her auburn hair fell down and blew behind her in the April wind. But she threw her head back, and rejoiced. The lake sang in her ears.

In the momentary pools at the waves' edge, the moon and the stars were reflected; and every creek that poured into the lake was bright with silver. The pebbles were fallen moons. Even the sand facets gave back the light. Thousands of small toads jumped away from the horse's hoofs. There was a smell of earth and a faintly discernible fragrance in the cool air. Petals and wings were not far off! It was a beautiful world—edged with danger, like a sword shining and sharp, like the fine blade of "L'Aiglon" that had carried death to her brother. Never the perfect thing for long. Never the full-orbed joy. Always, as her parents said so often, there seemed to be wolves against the moon!

She could almost hear, from this distance, the drums of the Indians beating their songs of death. She rushed on. But the little Arab could not gallop forever. Now and then she let him walk, or pause to drink from some star-drenched pool held between furrows of sand. Orion went down, and the Swan, the constellation of summer, flew up over the pale dunes.

It was still dark when she reached the cabin of Andreas Zirngibl, at the mouth of the Grand Calumet. Andreas was a Bavarian, a one-armed veteran of the Battle of Waterloo, who had once claimed the fishing rights over two miles of the River Danube, but whose fishing preserve now was the whole of southern Lake Michigan. Rose pounded on the door and routed Andreas out, for he was ferryman as well as fisherman. Three silver dollars slipped into his hand helped to silence his deluge of questions.

"Ever'thing all right, Miss Rose, at your place? Sure ever'thing all right?"

"Oh, yes, Andreas! It's just business. I'm going to Chicago on *business*. But you will hurry, won't you?"

Andreas, however, never seemed more deliberate, nor more awkward at poling the barge over the swollen river with his one arm.

The morning sun was just rising as Rose finally rode into view of the little settlement that had just been incorporated as a town. How it had changed in the last year! Rose was astonished. The place seemed to grow overnight. Ever since the Indian treaty of the year before and the opening up of new tracts to the palefaces, the pushing of the Illinois and Michigan Canal, and the harbor improvements, as her father had explained to her, people were pressing in from all sides. Coming up the beach towards the town, she had to thread her way through several covered-wagon encampments. The pine-tree knoll where the Fort Dearborn massacre had taken place was completely covered with wagons, Hoosier travelers, screaming children, and puppies. The river no longer wound in a long loop almost to the knoll. A spring freshet of the year before had caused it to burst across the sand bar that separated it from the lake and leap past the fort and the Kinzie house straight into the waters of Lake Michigan. Government engineers had already constructed a lighthouse and part of a pier east of the fort. Gone were the days of the four simple structures, the fort, Dr. Alexander Woolcott's agency house, the Kinzie house, and Ouilmette's cabin. Now there were five hundred houses, over two thousand people, and lots were selling for the unbelievable sums of a hundred, two hundred, even three hundred dollars apiece!

Rose rode up the south bank of the river, past John Croft's warehouse, Gurdon Hubbard's meat-packing house, the store of Jean Baptiste Beaubien, past the fort, and over the marshy trail, straight on to Wolf Point, at the forks of the river, and Mark Beaubien's hotel, The Sauganash (which he had named in honor of his admired friend, Billy Caldwell). Robinson's trading post and Billy's cabin were across the south branch of the river. Rose thought it prudent to stop at Beaubien's hotel first, for Billy and Alexander might very well be there having breakfast or hobnobbing with the guests. As she rode, Rose let the reins slacken for a moment while she adjusted her hair and put on her plumed hat again. She looked very handsome, with her bright red hair and red cheeks flaming against the background of her stylish dark green hat and riding habit. But she cared very little about her own appearance that morning. She was desperately eager to seem casual, while getting hold of Billy and Alexander at the earliest possible moment.

The large two-story, brick-chimneyed wooden hotel looked gay in a fresh coat of white paint and sea-blue trimmings and window shutters. Outside the door hung a wooden sign, over which Rose did not pause, for she already knew its information by heart:

Lodging for one person over night...... $.12½
Horse feed .... $.25
Supper and breakfast .... $.25
Dinner .... $.37½

Rose gave "Bon jour" to two blanketed Indians who were sitting in the dirt outside, and knocked on the door. It was immediately opened by jolly Mark himself, the younger brother of Joseph's old friend, Antoine Beaubien of Detroit and of Jean Baptiste Beaubien, his former agent on the Grand River. Mark was a tall, paunchy fellow, stuffed with the good comestibles of his own hotel. He had a high forehead, bushy eyebrows set low over the eyes as in so many French faces, a large nose, a small chin, the usual wide flexible French mouth and mobile cheek muscles. His eyes were large and brown. He was dressed in a brilliant blue uniform to match the hotel shutters. Brass buttons gave the final touch of splendor.

"Nom de Dieu! Mademoiselle Rose! What you doing here so early in ze morning? No trouble at ze Papa's place?"

"I have a message, Mark, a most important message for Alexander Robinson and Billy Caldwell. Where are they?"

"Ah, too bad, too bad! Zey off on ze wolf-hunt as soon as ze light she break zis morning!"

"Oh, dear! When will they be back?"

"Zey be back by noon for Mark's apple pies! A man, he brought a wagonload of apples from Detroit yesterday and Mark he make ze best apple pies in ze whole Nor'west! You, too, will have?"

"Oh, no, Mark! I must be getting back; but I *must* get hold of Billy and Alexander first."

"Come een! Come een, Mademoiselle Rose! You not ride all ze way from Bailly Place zis night?"

"I'll come in, Mark," answered Rose evasively.

"You have ze coffee, n'est-ce pas? and ze ham—Gurdon Hubbard ham, ver' good—and ze eggs?"

"Just a cup of coffee, Mark, please."

"Here, you, Pierre, take Mademoiselle Rose's horse. Come een. Come een, Mademoiselle Rose."

Mark led Rose into the large living room, with its fireplace at the right, its hotel counter and bar at the left. All the furniture was made of rough logs. There were no rugs on the floor. Four men, who were standing at the bar, immediately turned around as Rose entered. One of them took off his silk hat, with instant politeness; one removed his raccoon cap, the others remained covered. A man near the fireplace, who was reading a copy of the town's first newspaper, the *Chicago Democrat*, rose from his chair and made an almost imperceptible bow. Rose responded with a smile which was more than perfunctory, for the man was young, handsome, well dressed. He had the bluest eyes, except those of her father, that she had ever seen.

"Come out to ze kitchen, Mademoiselle, and warm up. Zen we will have ze breakfast."

"Only coffee, *please*, Mark, for I *must* find Alexander and Billy right away."

Mark shrugged his shoulders.

"They probably all ze way to Joliet by now! No use!"

"Pardon me, will you present me to the young lady, Monsieur Beaubien? I have something to say!" requested the young man of the sea-blue eyes.

"Mademoiselle Bailly, zees is Mr. Francis Howe of New Haven, Connecticut, clerk of Mr. William Ogden. Mr. Howe, Mademoiselle Rose Bailly of ze Bailly Seignory, forty miles up lake."

"Charmed, mademoiselle! May I say that nothing would delight me more than to gallop off and try to find Mr. Robinson and Mr. Caldwell for you—if you will permit!"

"Indeed, I *will* permit, monsieur! This is most kind of you. It is really *most* important—I mean, a small personal matter, but most important to me!"

"Then—I hope you will not consider me one of those forward Yankees, mademoiselle—it is also of the utmost importance—to your newest acquaintance!"

In an hour and a half, Francis Howe was back with Billy and Alexander, and in half an hour more Rose and the two half-breeds, who possessed so much influence with the Indians, were galloping south along the shore. Francis Howe had implored Rose to be allowed to go with her, but she had refused, with what small amount of flirtatious laughter she could summon in those anxious moments, and had suggested that he ride out to the Calumet on some later day.

As the three riders turned across the marsh road towards the Bailly place at sunset, Rose listened for the distant sound of the Indian war drums. There was no sound. Did it mean that massacre had begun?

"Hurry, oh, hurry!"

They raced across the marsh road, and turned up the Sauk Trail towards the encampment. The sound of an enormous voice came to them, echoing over the Bailly ridge. It was Joseph, using his tones of thunder to the Indians. The three travelers dismounted, fastened the reins to the hitching posts in front of the homestead, and crept to the camping place. The Indians were standing, in sullen circles, around the war post, their tomahawks still clutched in their hands, resentment on their vermilion-streaked faces. Joseph, dressed in his fur trader's outfit of buckskin leggings and jacket, red sash, red shirt, was standing in the very center, beside the war post. His shoulders were set back, and he was gesticulating violently. His face was flaming and perspiring, from the vociferous effort he was making; he was obviously using all his resources of physical and mental power. It was apparent that he had been speaking for some time, and was now coming down from general persuasions to some sort of personal appeal:

"I know how you feel, my brothers, for was not the child who was raised in my house among those who were followed across the fields? I am tearing my heart out to tell you the truth. You are eating my heart. You are having your vengeance—on me! For I am telling you that it was she, and not the young man, it was she alone who was responsible for the pursuit. It was she who drew the young men across the fields, who excited their passions, who called to them to come. It was she, the child whom I have raised in my house."

There was a murmur of renewed vehemence around the circle, a lifting of tomahawks a notch or two higher in the air. Joseph was playing with fire, but it was the only recourse left. All his other arguments had failed, and he had been speaking for an hour and a half, at this time (and twice before, since the departure of Rose). He did not intend to sacrifice Lucille to the general anger, but to shift responsibilities to her from the pioneer boys and thus to avert the general massacre. Then, in order to save her, it would be necessary to transform her into one of the Ottawa and to confess her Indian origin. But he knew that he must not mention De la Vigne, for that also might be disastrous to her. He must save all the white settlers for miles around, through Lucille, but he must also save Lucille, the child whom he and Marie had forever protected, but who had marked a trail of disaster—a wolf-trail—across their lives from the beginning.

"But I will not have you blame the child, for she was born out of great sorrow and sin."

There was a murmur of surprise, for how could the Wing Woman have been guilty of sin?

"Again I tear my heart out and give it to you to eat. The child is my child. The child is not the Wing Woman's child!"

The swish of surprise was like the night wind stirring in the upper branch tops. Then there was absolute silence.

"Nineteen years ago, my brothers, the Wing Woman lay at Arbre Croche. Running Cloud and Neengay Lefèvre attended her. A son was born to the Wing Woman, my brothers—a son! At the same time, in the next birth hut, Enewah—Enewah, the daughter of Black Turkey—gave birth to a daughter!"

There was not a sound anywhere on the bluff. Black Turkey's eyes protruded like the beady eyes of his animal namesake.

"Enewah and the son of the Wing Woman went away beyond the evening star together. The Wing Woman lay at the gates of evening. The living child was laid in her arms, with the counsel and sanction of old Nee-saw-kee. The child Lucille is not a paleface. The child Lucille is an Indian. She is Black Turkey's granddaughter!"

There was a great murmur and a great talking now. The tomahawk hands went down. The blades of death were forgotten. Joseph saw that his difficult battle was won. He let the Indian gossiping, which so much resembles the white man's gossiping, lick, like tongues of flame, over the encampment. Then he spoke, loudly again, his last words:

"Go, my brothers! There has been much sorrow here, in this camping place along with the many joys, sorrow for you, sorrow for Monami Bailly and the Wing Woman: the murder of Neengay Lefèvre, the attempted murder of the children, Robert and Lucille, the punishment of the sorcerer, De la Vigne, the death of Monami Bailly's *second* son, the folly of Lucille and the paleface boys, the fright of Oshogay and Three Stars. Motchi Manitou has cast a spell on this encampment. Gitchi Manitou tells you to pack your tepees and your camp pots and kettles and go back to Arbre Croche, where the air is sweet, and where there are no evil spirits and no palefaces. Pack your things, my brothers!" shouted Joseph. "And be gone, before more disaster happens! Quickly, lest Motchi Manitou strike like the Water Panthers!"

Chief Blackbird stepped forward:

"You have heard what Monami Bailly says. Every word he has spoken is true! Pack your things. At dawn, the canoes must be launched on Lake Mitchigami!"

Chapter XXXIX

SHAVEHEAD

WHILE the Indians began to break camp, Alexander Robinson and Billy Caldwell remaining on the grounds to see that nothing went wrong with the departure plans, Joseph returned to the house with Rose. It was now necessary to tell Lucille what all the Indian world knew, no matter how much the revelation might hurt or disturb Marie: the true story of her birth. The greater evil, massacre, had been averted. The crimes of De la Vigne had, by the strange justice of destiny, been expiated through his daughter.

As Joseph told his story to the family, Marie sat like marble. De la Vigne's daughter crumpled under the blow. For, although she had never known what real affection was, in any relationship, and had therefore never really loved any of the Baillys, she had apparently enjoyed a certain unconscious pride in belonging to them. Suddenly to realize that she belonged only to Black Turkey and the Indians, was abysmally humiliating.

"If this is true," she said, "—and I don't know whether it's true or whether it's been made up to punish me—I'll go! I'll not go to the Indians. But I'll go to Ruel Gosling. I'll marry him right away, Papa, I mean—I mean—Mr. Bailly—and we'll leave for some other place—for the west, where the Healds are going, perhaps—unless"—she cast a sly look at Darius Heald, who sat, looking rather embarrassed, in a corner of the room—"unless Darius wants to marry me!"

"Lucille!" exclaimed Joseph. "This is no time for such impudences! You're marrying Ruel Gosling, and you're settling down and turning into a good wife! And don't call me Mr. Bailly, for God's sake! We've been your parents for nineteen years . . ."

Early the next afternoon, the Baillys and the Healds and Ruel Gosling and his father rode the twenty miles on horseback to the little log-cabin courthouse at La Porte, for the marriage ceremony of Lucille. Ruel Gosling was as sullen as if he had been going to the county jail. Father Gosling was not so sullen. He had thought of a kind of blackmail, a way of getting money for himself out of Bailly: on the condition of his (Gosling's) keeping the secret of the real reason for the forced marriage. He sidled his horse up to Bailly's and was as unctuously agreeable as possible all the way to La Porte. If Bailly could give such a dowry. . . .

The tiny little log-cabin settlement of La Porte had suddenly grown into a certain local importance. It had recently been made the seat of the new county named for the famous Commodore David Porter. Towards noon, as the Baillys and the Healds and the Goslings rode along the prairie trail towards the village, they noticed signs of considerable activity in the settlement, covered wagons drawn up on the outskirts, many horses tethered under the oak trees, many people swarming in front of the courthouse. The first person Joseph encountered solved the mystery of the crowd:

"Land sales, sir. Big land sales going on. The deals are over for today, but there'll be more tomorrow. Better buy some property. Good land! Good buy!"

Joseph shook his head. He had enough land. So the property bought by the Government from the Potawatomi at the Councils of 1828 and 1833 was being sold and parceled now, in small bits, to the oncoming whites. Gone were the wide prairies of the Indians, where they could roam free as the golden winds!

Joseph tethered his horse to a tree near the courthouse and looked about him. The place was swarming with pioneers, in homespun pantaloons, red, blue, or butternut-dyed shirts, Wellington boots and homemade straw hats, traders in their deerskin outfits, and real estate agents and business men from the East in black frock coats, cambric shirts, and cravats. Most of the women were in calicoes, dark-colored shawls and straw bonnets. A few Indians in their scarlet blankets and bright feathers contrasted colorfully with the more somber pioneers. Several of the Indians had imbibed too freely of the peppered whisky of the whites and were reeling up and down the grassy road or sitting helplessly against the log walls of the courthouse.

One of these Indians lurched rudely against Rebecca Heald, as she was hitching her horse to a tree near Joseph's. Rebecca looked into the Indian's face and screamed. It was unmistakably Shavehead—the lean, cruel-faced Shavehead, with the single scalplock dangling from the crown of his bald head. Rebecca's last glimpse of him had been at the Fort Dearborn massacre, as Shavehead had held aloft the severed head of her uncle, Captain Wells. Although Shavehead's mind was misty with drink, the scream sharpened his senses and his recognition for a moment. He let out a wild, reminiscent yell, using Wells' Indian name:

"Hi yi! Apekonit! Apekonit!"

Joseph and the Major were immediately at Rebecca's side.

"Go away, Shavehead, go away!" insisted Joseph fiercely, in Algonquin, and put his hand threateningly on his hunting knife. "Why did you come here to La Porte? Why didn't you go back to Parc aux Vaches?"

The Indian slunk away, but not without one more yell of "Apekonit!" which made Rebecca shudder with the hideous memory.

As Shavehead retreated, Joseph turned towards a disheveled, bearded pioneer, in torn clothes and a torn hat, hand-woven of reeds:

"Do you happen to know, sir, where Judge Samuel C. Sample may be found this afternoon? Is he at the courthouse or at his home?"

The pioneer's eyes were following Shavehead, with a strangely concentrated look, and he did not seem to hear a single word.

Joseph repeated his question.

The bearded man turned his flashing gaze on Joseph. "Judge Sample is in the courthouse," he said. Then he suddenly pulled the reed hat down over his face and walked hurriedly away.

Joseph stood bewildered. He could not identify the man's face; but the voice he had certainly heard before, under some dramatic circumstance.

"Rebecca, will you do me a favor?" asked Joseph. "Follow that man, please, without letting him know he is being followed. Find out who he is. I must know. Then join us at the courthouse."

At the courthouse, Judge Sample performed the prosaic civil

ceremony for Lucille and Ruel, with dispatch. The fond father of Ruel had to punch his son in the ribs once or twice to get the responses out; otherwise everything went off in dull, though apple-pie order.

When the ceremony was over, Rebecca, who had returned in time to witness the procedure, said to Joseph:

"I think the man I followed prefers to remain unknown, Joseph."

"Then you didn't find out?"

"I *recognized* him, Joseph."

"You recognized him? Do I know him?"

"Indeed you do. But he's changed, so changed, Joseph, in twenty-two years. He's nothing but the rag a soldier's uniform becomes in the end, when—"

"Soldier's uniform? I simply can't recollect—"

"Why, Joseph, it's Louis Pettle!"

"Good God! I must go speak to him."

"I wouldn't, Joseph. If he wants to recognize you, that's time enough. But I've a strong feeling that long ago he set out to forget everything associated with the old Fort Dearborn days. No wonder! I must tell Nathan not to seem to know him, unless Louis gives a sign. He's already recognized us, I'm quite sure."

"I'll tell Marie," said Joseph.

A crowd was gathered in the roadway before the courthouse, and in the center of it was Shavehead, shouting drunkenly in English at the top of his voice. The crowd was laughing and jeering; but, as the Bailly group approached, the titters were slipping off into silence. The recent sight of Rebecca Wells Heald had set something stirring in Shavehead's tipsy brain. He was beginning to boast about his part in the Fort Dearborn massacre. The name "Apekonit" arrested the attention of the Healds and the Baillys, and they came to a halt at the edge of the circle. Across the way, Louis Pettle was also standing, his arms folded somberly across his chest, the same gleam in his eyes that had burningly followed Shavehead down the road a half hour before.

"Apekonit! Apekonit!" Shavehead was shrieking, as he reeled. "Captain—Wells! I take the ax. Me, me, Shavehead! I chop the head off—zlick! I eat the heart. It make me brave! Red is my tomahawk! My scalping knife is red! I climb up the white-covered wagon! I climb in! I scalp one little boy! I scalp two little boys! Paleface babies! I scalp them all! Two mothers fight like cougars! One brown-hair. One black-hair. Ten fresh scalps at Shavehead's belt! Me, me, Shavehead! Great Potawatomi brave! Shavehead!"

The listeners had become frozen into silence. Only Joseph moved. By dint of vigorous shoving, he made his way from the back of the circle of listeners to the front, pushed into the center of the circle, and took Shavehead fiercely by the arm.

"You're drunk, Shavehead! Go home—back to Parc aux Vaches! No room for you here!"

The crowd gave way. Joseph pulled and dragged Shavehead all the way to the crossroads, where the trail to Michigan City and the trail to Niles joined, shook him vigorously to bring him to his senses, and set him facing northeast, on the trail to Niles. As Joseph returned to town, he met Louis Pettle, who did not even see him through the fumes of his own thoughts. Joseph stopped, as if to speak, but Louis walked on.

Half an hour later, the Baillys and the Healds and the Goslings rode out of La Porte. They had just reached the crossroads when Joseph drew rein and said:

"I'll join you all later. There's something I want to find out. I'll follow the road to Parc aux Vaches for a short distance. Then I'll gallop back and be with you—in less than an hour! Au revoir!"

He was gone before any one could follow. The others rode slowly on towards Trail Creek. Joseph dashed, faster than tumbleweed in a prairie gale, over the trail to Niles, his keen eyes searching everywhere for signs. There was no man on the road, going or coming, as he had expected there would be.

But a mile from town, he found what he had half feared, half hoped, with some retributive instinct, to find. A swath freshly made through the roadside leaves and grasses by a dragged object led to the warm corpse of Shavehead. The brown back was riddled with bullets. The single lock of hair was missing from the scalped head.

Instead of scouring the prairie for the murderer, who could not possibly have gone far, Joseph turned and rode back to the Trail Creek road.

Twenty-two years after the massacre, Fort Dearborn had been avenged. So be it.

Chapter XL

THE BROKEN WINEGLASS

In the fall, Joseph made his last journey to Baton Rouge. Only once since the night of his confession-of-the-duel had he cared to broach to Marie the subject of building another house, in the South. With the first mention of the name of Louisiana, Marie had again turned to marble. For this emotional reason, with all its ancient implications, and because his business was centering more and more in Detroit, Chicago, and the Calumet region, and distance made it impossible to defend his interests at Baton Rouge with success from the gradual encroachments of Maurice Rastel, Joseph decided at last, with more than a little reluctance, to pull up stakes entirely at his southernmost trading post.

There was a world of meaning in Marie's eyes as she said good-bye to Joseph on the lawn in front of the homestead and watched him ride away, northeast along the Sauk Trail towards Trail Creek and the Wabash Trace. Joseph, for once, did not go away singing gayly:

"Malbrouck s'en va t'en guerre!"

He went away silently. He could feel Marie's eyes piercing his shoulder blades, through, to the heart.

The little settlement of Baton Rouge was more crowded than ever, full of refugees from the plague. For over a year, the Asiatic cholera had lapped at New Orleans in successive waves. By the time Joseph arrived, the last livid wave had almost subsided, but the refugees were hesitating to return to the city.

Madame Le Gendre's Auberge was so crowded that the weekly meetings of Joseph's old cronies no longer took place there. They met, of an evening, around the dining table and the well stocked buffet of Léon Bonnecaze.

548

Joseph stayed at Baton Rouge for two weeks. He had come to close his trading post on the Mississippi forever, and he had not yet closed it. The old fighting spirit had risen up in him. The things that his agent, Antoine Larocque, had told him about the machinations of Rastel in all the territory around the post and about the subtle bribes that Rastel had held out to Larocque, and certain apparent attempts to do away with him, had made Joseph's blood boil. "Mort de tous les diables!" Was he to give up and slink out of the country like a whipped dog or a wounded fox? No! A thousand times no! He would hold on to the end! Nothing could make him give up this symbolic post! He tried to push from his mind the remembrance of Marie's look on that last day when he rode out of the yard. What would she think? Never mind—a man's business was a man's business! All his life he had fought for his independent trading rights. For many years of his life, he had fought against Rastel's encroachments. Was he to give up now—like an old, defeated man? The thought of Marie beat against his brain. One evening, he walked very fast to the home of Léon Bonnecaze, in an effort to outstrip that pursuing thought. But it was ever nicking at the heels of his brain.

The old cronies, all except Monsieur de Boré, who was too tottering to get about now, sat around the table of Léon Bonnecaze. Joseph took more drinks than usual, and talked a little louder than usual. But nothing seemed to ease or blur the trouble that whirled in his troubled mind.

A great many stories were told, many witty Gallic remarks danced like shuttlecocks over the table. At last there was a little pause, and Dr. Lanzin said:

"Dr. Antommarchi is in town, worn out with attending the cholera patients in New Orleans. The plague's over, and he's come up to rest."

"Plague's really over?"

"Yes. At last!"

"Dieu soit bénit!" The exclamation was repeated sibilantly around the table. Then Cousso remarked:

"The Doctor must have seen a sight of human nature!"

"Yes. Plenty of queer stories. Antommarchi told me one today.

He didn't use any names, but I think I can guess the characters. Pretty gruesome. Want to hear it?"

"Oui, certainement."

"Oui."

"Oui."

Joseph tipped back his wineglass, drained it, and settled back for the story. Dr. Lanzin began:

"Well, about two weeks ago he was called to one of the handsomest houses in town, rich husband, beautiful wife, all that sort of thing. Husband lay ill of the cholera. Antommarchi had so many cases he didn't stay long—let the man's blood and gave the wife instructions as to what to do or have done. He said the husband never let his wife leave the room for an instant. Antommarchi got the impression that there was no love lost between the two, and that the wife was imprisoned there against her will. The man seemed to have some strange, hypnotic power over her."

Joseph began to twirl the stem of his empty wineglass nervously between his thumb and forefinger, as his hand rested on the table.

"Antommarchi was not called to the house again, and more or less forgot about the case. Then, one day last week, the wife, in deep mourning, came to the Doctor's house. When they were alone in his office, she cried out:

" 'Doctor, you said my husband was *dying*, didn't you? *Didn't* you, Doctor?'

"She sounded a little hysterical. Antommarchi cautiously answered:

" 'I didn't commit myself, madame. I said the case looked pretty serious. Why do you ask? You never called me again.'

" 'Oh, Doctor, Doctor, he *would* have died, wouldn't he?'

" 'One can never tell, madame. More than a third of my patients have recovered.'

" 'Merciful God!'

"The Doctor waited. There was utter silence for a moment, then the woman said:

" 'Oh, it's horrible, horrible! I knew I was not a good woman, but I didn't know how utterly bad I was until now! The man I loved was *fortunate* not to marry me when he came back from the Pays d'en Haut! He was fortunate! Fortunate!' "

Dr. Lanzin permitted himself one quick look at Joseph, who had stopped twirling the glass but was clenching the stem so tightly that his knuckles showed white.

"Antommarchi let her ramble on. He thought it would be a cure for the sickness of her mind.

" 'Oh, Doctor, let me tell you what happened! If I don't tell some one, I shall go mad—absolutely mad!

" 'The morning after you left, my husband stopped breathing, turned purple. I swear to you he stopped breathing! I swear it! I swear it!

" 'I heard the bell of the death cart out in the street. I escaped from the room where I had been kept for a week. I ran down the stairs. I called to the driver of the death cart and told him to call for a dead person next day, that my husband had just died.

" ' "I'll come right in and get 'im!" he said.

" ' "Not now! Not now! He's only just died!"

" ' "I'll get 'im! City health law says 'e must be carried right out!"

" ' "I must prepare him!" ˙

" ' "Prepare nothin'. Stay where yuh are, lady!"

" 'The man and his assistant pushed past me, with a stretcher, and went up the stairs. I leaned, half fainting, against the doorpost. I saw the cart only fifty feet away, in the street, with the bodies of eight or ten people thrown every which way into it. As I looked I thought I saw an arm move.

" 'When the man came down the stairs, with the body of my husband, I said:

" ' "You have a living person in that cart! I saw an arm move!"

" 'The man laughed and said:

" ' "Don't worry, lady! If he ain't dead now, he'll be dead afore I throw 'im into the cholera pit!"

" 'My husband was taken out just as he was, in his nightclothes, without even a sheet thrown over him, and was thrown into the cart. All I could see of him was one of his arms hanging over the side. The two men got up onto the driver's seat. Just before they started off, I saw my husband's arm move, then I saw his head lift for an instant above the sideboard of the cart! During one awful instant I stood there! My conscience told me to shriek to the driver to stop—that my husband, too, was still alive, that he might still be saved! But, in that very same second, all the long years of my unhappiness, all my hatred of the man, all my horror at the thought of returning to the old life surged over me in a black whirlpool and drowned my voice. I *could not speak.* As the cart rattled off, the devil repeated in my ears the words: "If he ain't dead now, he'll be dead afore I throw 'im into the cholera pit!"

" 'I think I fainted. I hope I did. Or perhaps it was just my conscience that fainted—or my soul—if I have a soul!

" 'Oh, Doctor, Doctor, do you think he would have died anyway before he reached the cemetery? Or—oh, God—do you think—he was *buried alive?*'

" 'I think,' Dr. Antommarchi answered, 'that you were so tired that you imagined everything! I'd forget about it and go home and have a good rest. It's all over now anyway.'

"But Dr. Antommarchi told me that, knowing what he did about those two, he wouldn't be a bit surprised if the lady *had* let her husband be buried alive! She's a very strange woman, Antommarchi said. He never could make her out, never could tell whether she was good or bad or a little of both. A beautiful, strange woman! Kind of seemed, said Antommarchi, '*to wear a mask.*' "

In the silence after the story, there was a sharp crackle. Joseph's clenched hand had suddenly broken the stem of his wineglass.

Chapter XLI

WOLVES ALONG THE OLD SAUK TRAIL

JOSEPH closed his trading post at Baton Rouge. Rastel was dead. The long fight was over. The zest was gone. Joseph emphatically missed the smoke of conflict in his nostrils, the howling of the hostile wolves on his horizon.

He wondered about Corinne, wondered how much of a conscience she had, how long she would be troubled over the grim finis that had been written (or that she perhaps had written) to the life of the man who had loved and tormented her for thirty years, wondered what the proportions of good and evil really were in her strange nature, wondered if she would give *him* a thought. But he turned his back on New Orleans and took a boat straight from Baton Rouge to Evansville.

Before he left, he took some live-oak acorns and some locust seeds from the ground near his trading post. Bonnecaze offered him a small magnolia tree from his garden. Joseph flushed, said something about snows of the north and "snows of yesteryear" that Bonnecaze failed to catch, and courteously refused the gift.

When Joseph reached the Calumet in October, he found that events had been occurring rapidly in the lives of his three youngest daughters. Lucille had dealt the family its final blow. On a day only two weeks before Joseph's return and only five months after her marriage, when she had gone to shop at La Porte, she had encountered a dashing character from New York who had come to look over Indiana real estate, and, after spending the day with him in town, had disappeared completely. The Goslings had stormed the homestead, not for grief over the loss of Lucille, but in the hope of collecting some sort of consolation money. Marie had, of course, deftly postponed the matter until Joseph's return.

"Well, that's the end," commented Joseph. "I'm not going to try to find her! I'm sorry to hurt you, Marie, but Lucille would only bring back a new trail of disaster across our lives. As far as I am concerned—c'est fini!"

To Joseph's amazement, Marie looked at him with entirely unperturbed eyes and repeated:

"As far as I am concerned, that is the end, too."

"Why, Marie, I thought—"

"I've known for a long time, Joseph—that Lucille did not belong to us. She has shown herself a true daughter of De la Vigne. I even suspect— No, no! I *must* not say that! . . . I am ready now to have the little White Fawn brought down from Arbre Croche and placed in the cemetery beside *our other son.*"

News of the other daughters was happier. Rose and Esther were bubbling over with excitement, like the Little Calumet in a spring freshet. Two young men had been riding over to the Calumet every other Saturday from Chicago, Francis Howe and John Whistler. Both young men had received their promises for life. The girls wanted to be married at the homestead, on the same day in the spring.

"Well, well, Marie, our last cubs! And what do you say to OUR going to Paris in the spring?"

"Later, Joseph, later it would be marvelous! But Agatha is having another baby in the early summer, and I must be with her on the Island."

"Wonderful! Our *grandson!* How proud we shall be!"

"Yes, Joseph."

The surge of memories. He broke in on his own thoughts abruptly:

"I have news for you too, Marie. The old wolf is dead."

"What do you mean, Joseph?"

"Maurice Rastel is dead! But you know, Marie, I'm just a little —disappointed."

"Disappointed?"

"Yes. There's so little left to *fight* against!"

In November, Joseph went to Indianapolis to bring his harbor project before the state legislature. He came home, his pockets filled with insubstantial promises.

During the winter, he reached the conclusion that, just as surely as the Anglo-Saxon palefaces were driving the Indians out of the country, just so surely they were crowding out all of the French traditions, if not the French people. Not only were his French friends of the old régime in Detroit feeling the pressure, but he and his family were beginning to be subjected to it. The only one of his neighbors who was altogether friendly and sympathetic was Jesse Morgan. Many of the others were crude, inhospitable, and openly impudent. They did not hesitate to make remarks to his face about the "fiddlin' French," the "heathen Catholics," "squaw men," and "half-breeds." Joseph's flaming temper and forthright fist did not help matters. As for Marie, she found the settlers' cruelty to animals unendurable. The manner in which they slaughtered the wild deer by the hundreds and the passenger pigeons by the needless thousands (resorting to perpetual gunfire, poles and lanterns, shrub fires, clap-nets and blind decoys, collecting the beautiful birds by the cartloads and selling them for twenty-five cents a bushel) was beyond her sympathetic comprehension. She had even found Thad Todhunter and Ruel Gosling and some of the other settlers' sons skinning a live wolf on Morgan Prairie one day (while Lucille had stood by encouragingly), then releasing it and yelling with savage delight, as it staggered to its death.

Joseph wrote back to his friends in Quebec and Detroit and Frenchtown-on-the-Raisin:

Stay where you are! This is no place for the French. Until these rough pioneers raise up a better, politer breed of men, there will be no real understanding between the French and the Americans. The day will come, as it has come in Canada and in the larger American cities. But not here, on this frontier,, where the plowing of the bare earth gives no space for the flowers of gracious living to grow. The fleur-de-lis never ceases to grow in French hearts. But out of *these* American hearts—only the corn grows!

Stay where you are. The harbor project is at a standstill anyway. I am opening my tract to the Americans.

It had been a bitterly cold winter and a bitterly cold spring, with hoar frost every morning and frequent snows. Rose and Esther had planned a double wedding out-of-doors on the old camping ground of the Ottawa Indians, but the weather was so sharp that, on the afternoon of the 20th of May, the ceremony was performed indoors with Father Badin, of the Diocese of Vincennes, the first priest ever ordained in the United States, officiating. A few of the old friends from Chicago rode over for the ceremony, Major Whistler and Elinor Kinzie and the young Kinzies and Gurdon Hubbard and the Beaubiens, even the handsome, repudiated Médor Beaubien.

Just before the departure of the newly-weds on horseback for Chicago, the two young couples went down to the bank of the Little Calumet and, under Joseph's supervision, planted an oak and an elm sapling, with twigs intertwined, as symbols of the happy occasion.*

As the young people rode southwest, an hour afterwards, with all the Chicago friends, down the Sauk Trail towards the marsh road and the lake, Joseph and Marie stood side by side, watching until the leaf shadows took them entirely.

"The happiest procession the old Sauk Trail has ever seen!" said Marie. "But, oh, Joseph—the last of our little ones!"

"Yes. But we must think of the grandchildren now, Marie! Agatha's son! How soon can you get ready to leave? Five days? Six days? Close up the house and everything?"

"Close up the house? Why, Joseph? I'll be back in a few weeks!"

"Oh, no, you won't, my Marie!"

Joseph fumbled in his pocket and pulled out a letter.

"We're sailing from Quebec on the first of August for Paris!"

"Paris? Oh, Joseph, I can't *believe* it! How *wonderful!*"

"Here's a letter from the City of Dublin Steam Packet Company of Great Britain!"

"Steamship? Oh, Joseph! Not those terrible new contraptions —on the *ocean!*"

"Certainly, my Marie! The *Royal William*, the very second steamship to cross the Atlantic!"

The next day was even colder than the double-wedding day. The young May buds clung closed and blighted to the trees. There was not a wild plum or cherry or crab-apple blossom anywhere. The trillium flowers were frozen marble on the knoll.

Marie was in the house with Magama, covering the furniture

* The two trees are mirrored in the river to this day.

and taking down the curtains. Joseph was supervising the voyageurs in their airing and beating of the last of the fur packs, before the journey to Mackinac Island. He was closing his entire fur business forever. The gold of the rivers and the marshes of the old Northwest was almost gone. The pioneer's ditches were turning the marshes into meadows. The pioneer's plow had taken the place of the traps.

Suddenly there was the sound of many hoof beats coming from the northeast on the old Sauk Trail, a shouted command or two, the cracking of whips.

Joseph and Jean Baptiste and the voyageurs straightened up from their work and waited, wondering. Then, through the aisle of trees to the east of the camping ground and across the open area, and past the fur sheds, rode two United States cavalrymen, sitting stiffly in their dark blue coats, their brass buttons shining in the sunlight. Touching his cap, but without any further salutation, one of the soldiers called out:

"Where the hell's the Detroit-Chicago Road? What kind of a road is this anyway?"

"This," answered Joseph, "is the old Sauk Trail, the road of the Indians from the Mississippi to Canada, for hundreds of years."

"Road! Huh!"

"Cut across the marsh at the first turn to the right, for the Detroit Chicago Road."

"Humph! Thanks."

In a moment, there followed the outriders a long line of horse-drawn carts, not unlike the death carts used during the cholera plagues in Detroit and in New Orleans. In these carts Joseph saw, to his horror, hundreds of Indians, with their wrists and ankles bound. In some cases, batches of eight or ten were bound together, like cattle headed for the butcher. Soldiers rode in long lines on both sides. After these, came straggling Indians on foot, not only the young braves, but old men, old squaws, young squaws with papooses strapped to their backs. To make matters worse, a cavalryman now and then rode back and lashed the laggards with a whip, some of the flanking infantrymen prodded them with bayonets. This, obviously, was the disinheriting, and the drive of the Indians towards the west, according to the terms of the Chicago treaty of 1833. Joseph recognized the Indians as belonging to the Ottawa and Potawatomi tribes. His blood boiled, as he was forced to watch helplessly. Here were his friends, not only being dispossessed of all they owned and loved but being treated like wild beasts as well. He began to single out individuals whom he had known for years. There walked Weesaw, the once-proud peacock, of the red sashes and turbans and the silver bangles, stripped now to a loincloth and shivering on this cold May day. With his bangles had gone his vanity, his pride, his dignity. An Indian cannot long survive humiliation or loss of freedom. Weesaw's head was down, his back sagged. He was a dying peacock indeed. He did not even look up as he passed Joseph's well known house.

"Courage, Weesaw! Courage!" Joseph called out in Algonquin. "You'll be a great chief in the new land! Courage!"

Weesaw passed stolidly on, without looking up, as if his sense of hearing and of seeing were gone along with his sense of pride.

There were not many of the Parc aux Vaches Indians, whom Joseph strained his eyes to find. But the Trail Creek Indians were there, in full force. Joseph was able to find Ginsey McCoy very easily, because of her golden hair and white skin. She was walking slowly and painfully, carrying a baby not in the Indian manner, strapped to her back, but in her arms. Her Indian husband, his hands tied behind his back, was walking beside her, grim as death. Ginsey looked around her desperately as she passed, and, catching sight of Marie in the doorway of the house, held out her baby towards her and called out. Marie came closer.

"Take my baby, Wing Woman! He is dying! Take him and care for him! Please, oh, please! He is only three days old, and he will die on the journey!"

Marie tried to reach towards Ginsey and take the baby, but a cavalryman rode up, lifted his bayonet over Ginsey, and said:

"Hey, you! What you tryin' to do?"

"She wants me to take her baby and care for it!" said Marie, pleadingly. "Can't you see she's a white woman? Let me have the baby!"

"No! Get out o' here! She married an Injun, and an Injun she is! Every man jack of 'em's got to go—braves, squaws, and brats! Them's orders!"

Ginsey cast a despairing glance at Marie over the head of the tiny infant, and walked on, weeping. Marie hurried into the house, returned with blankets and bread in a hastily tied bundle, ran down to the marsh road which Ginsey had just reached, and tied the bundle around Ginsey's neck. From that moment, Marie busied herself with bringing from the house blankets, clothes, and food and throwing them into the carts, as they passed. Joseph, on the other side of the moving line, tossed in dozens of fur pelts, wondering how much use of them the well clothed soldiers would permit to their shivering victims.

After the Trail Creek Indians, came a group from the Kalamazoo region with whom the Baillys were not quite so well acquainted. But at the end of the long procession, which kept passing the homestead for over an hour, came Noonday and the Ottawa of Grand River and, at last, the Ottawa of Arbre Croche. To Joseph and Marie, but especially to Marie, who had grown up at Arbre Croche, this final spectacle was almost beyond endurance. Old friends of her mother, old friends of hers without number, walked past, with grim, downcast faces, except when some old warrior, like Yellow Thunder or Black Turkey, lifted his head and spread out his arms and seemed to entreat the Great Spirit for mercy upon him and his people. Asa Bun, the cruel, vindictive Asa Bun, walked like a wounded wolf, head down, tail dragging in the dust. No one would have laughed now at Sassaba, who had wanted, so long ago, to be baptized "Cursed Toad," or at Wab-she-gun, who had wanted to be baptized "Blockhead," or at Petosega, the "Child of Hell," indeed!

Only a few of the young people looked about them with something of their natural buoyancy. Among these were Oshogay and Three Stars, who were walking arm in arm, heads up, smiling furtively and talking. But a sudden stop was put to their subdued chatter when one of the cavalrymen, who had long been observing Oshogay's charms, came alongside, swooped down and lifted her to his saddle, with the cry, "Come here, my pretty squaw!" The capture and the hug that accompanied it must have reminded Oshogay of her experience with Thad Todhunter, for she screamed like a trapped panther and struggled with such terrible desperation that she slipped from the cavalryman's grasp and fell from the horse, one of whose hind hoofs came crushing down upon her face. The cavalryman rode on, as if he had merely lost a button from his coat.

"My God!" shouted Joseph Bailly, rushing forward. "Aren't you fellows going to do anything for this poor girl?"

The Indians were crowding forward towards Oshogay, and the soldiers were beating them back with whips and bayonets, and trying to move forward over the wounded body of Oshogay, as if nothing at all had happened.

"Give this girl to me to take care of! I demand it! She's hurt—terribly hurt!"

"Oh, you demand it, do you? Who are you anyway?" A cavalryman gave Joseph a cut over the shoulder with the butt of his whip.

Joseph looked up—into the face of Lieutenant Higgins, who had arrested him at Cœur de Cerf and opposed him at the court-martial at Detroit.

"Oh, Bailly, the jailbird, wants it! Lecherous, too, eh?" said Higgins. "Pick up the girl, Private Billups and Private Stacy, and throw her into the nearest cart! *He can't have her!*"

"Yes, Major!" The soldiers lifted Oshogay, whose face was an unrecognizable bleeding mass, and threw her with a resounding whack into the nearest cart.

"Go get me my shotgun," said Joseph in a low voice to Jean Baptiste, who had come up and was standing beside him. "This passes all human endurance."

"No, mon cousin. I disobey for once. You be shot down by soldiers. No use! No use!"

"Yes, of course, of course! No use! No use! I know just how these Indians feel, how darkly their blood boils. I feel like killing all these beastly soldiers, all of them! Mort de tous les diables!"

"Get along! Get along!" commanded Major Higgins.

There was disorder in the line, both forward and back, due to the interruption, and Major Higgins rode forward to straighten out the line. Joseph turned towards the rear. At the very end, which was guarded by four infantrymen, Joseph saw Chief Black-bird and Running Cloud holding on to each other, as if each could hardly stand. Taking advantage of the momentary halt, Joseph hurried up to them. Marie also had seen them, and was approaching on the other side of the line.

"My friends! My friends! I would do anything in the world—" said Joseph.

"I know, I know! It's of no use, Monami Bailly. The end has come," answered Chief Blackbird.

"No! Not the end! You will have a new life on the Mississippi, Chief Blackbird!"

"Running Cloud and I will not live to see the Mississippi. We will soon lie down beside the road and sleep, and even the bayonets of the soldiers cannot waken us, then!"

"No, no, Chief Blackbird! You are a brave! Fight to the end!"

"The long fight is over, Monami Bailly. They burned our village at Arbre Croche. They trampled our graves. They leave our dying and our dead by the roadside, without even giving them burial. Shingebiss, old Shingebiss, who saw the Wing Woman's first son born, was left dying on the banks of the Grand. And Loonfoot died on the St. Joseph. And Oshogay will be thrown from the cart on the banks of the Little Calumet, and Running Cloud and I will not live to see the green waters of the Illinois—"

"Get along now! Line's movin'," cried one of the guards.

"Get along! Get along!" echoed the three other guards.

"Here! Take these!" said Joseph, thrusting some silver coins into Blackbird's hand.

"No, Monami Bailly! What should I want with the white man's silver?" Blackbird spread his brown palm and dropped the silver on the ground. Two of the guards swooped down, like turkey buzzards, picked up the coins, and stuffed them into their own pockets.

Joseph and Marie walked alongside for a minute.

"Where," asked Joseph, "where are Pokagon and Topenebee? I haven't seen them."

"They tell me," answered Blackbird, "that Topenebee drank too much of the white man's firewater at La Porte a few days ago and fell from his horse and was killed. Pokagon, whom the white men love, is being moved to Rush Lake, on the Paw Paw River, with a few of his braves. He does not have to go to the Mississippi."

"Get along! Get along!"

"Goodbye, Chief Blackbird! Goodbye, Running Cloud! God bless you! The Great Spirit protect you!" cried Joseph and Marie.

Blackbird bowed his head and walked on, and Running Cloud, the tears streaming down her face, limped away beside him. The last that Joseph and Marie saw, as the procession passed out of sight, was one of the guards prodding Blackbird in the back—not with the flat but with the point of his bayonet.

"That," said Joseph, "is the end of our Indians of the old Northwest. That is the end of the old Sauk Trail."

Chapter XLII

FULL MOON

WHILE Joseph and Marie were closing the homestead and the fur sheds, there came two more groups of travelers along the Sauk Trail, before the grass and the ferns, the mullein and the thistles and the heal-all should grow over the ancient moccasin-grooves.

First, Pokagon and his little five-year-old son, Simon Pokagon,* came to say goodbye. Pokagon looked like the child's grandfather rather than his father. Although the "Great Father at Washington," recognizing his active friendship for the whites, had granted him the special dispensation of remaining in Michigan Territory with a few of his braves, he was a grieved and broken old man. The Indian villages all around him had been burned, the graves of his ancestors desecrated, and his people bound and tied and driven west. The horrors that he had witnessed lay in the black pools of his eyes. Nothing that Joseph could say could restore the old light. The only meager satisfaction that Pokagon had, lay in the news that an escaped Potawatomi had brought him from Chicago, that three good half-breed friends of the Indians had met them at Chicago and had determined to share their fate in the west: Alexander Robinson, Billy the Sauganash, and Médor Beaubien. Otherwise, Pokagon's words were all of defeat and death.

"No, Monami Bailly," he kept saying, "I am ready, very ready to see the Great Spirit . . ."

Four days after the Indian trek, Isaac McCoy and his wife, and the two children remaining now out of his twelve, and a few of his teachers and servants drew up in covered wagons in front of the Bailly Homestead. They were following the Indians to the west, to establish the McCoy Baptist Mission near Independence, Missouri, a mission which was to become a famous landmark to the

* Who, after studying at Notre Dame and Oberlin, was to become the author of many books.

563

covered-wagon trains pushing ever farther and farther towards the sunset. McCoy did not linger long at the homestead. The stories that Joseph and Marie told him of the atrocities that they themselves had witnessed in the short span of a quarter of a mile of the Indian procession's progress set spurs to McCoy's horse and motion to the wheels of his wagons.

"Goodbye! Good luck!"

"Goodbye! God bless you!"

As Joseph and Marie turned once again towards the house, Marie asked:

"Does the McCoys' journey towards the west stir your blood, Joseph, as the journey of Wilson Hunt and Ramsey Crooks from Mackinac Island to Astoria did so long ago? How you *did* want to go with them!"

"Why, Marie, how did you guess? How did you know?"

"Oh, my dear boy! You're as easy to see through, sometimes, as the shore waters of Lake Michigan on a smooth day or a calm moonlight night!"

"Am I so simple as all that?"

"No, not simple: strong and splendid as the whole lake; but sometimes the shells and the pebbles and the river grass and the frantic fish do show through—to your wife!"

"I guess you've understood many things, Marie, ma chère."

"Yes, Joseph. I've understood many things. And I've *always* loved you."

The barges reached Mackinac Island on the 10th of June. On the 1st of July, a son was born to Agatha and Edward Biddle, to whom they immediately gave the name of Joseph Bailly Biddle. Joseph recaptured a little of the old joy that he had known at the time of Robert's birth. Here was a new cycle beginning: flame and shadow, shadow and flame. New moon, waxing moon, full moon—wolves against the golden disc—waning moon, darkness, new moon, full moon, wolves . . . So it had always gone. So it would always go. Grandchildren. A new moon. A new cycle. Joseph's heart was full of all the joys and all the sorrows of a life three-fifths of a century long.

At the island, Joseph closed his Mackinac fur accounts forever.

John Jacob Astor was also giving up his fur interests there. Ramsey Crooks, now a full-faced, paunchy, hearty, middle-aged gentleman, had still enough "go" left in him to buy out Astor's interests and stick it out for a few years longer. But Robert Stuart was retiring and moving to Detroit. Uncle David Stuart had died long since. As for the voyageurs, there lingered around the old Astor Trading Post only a third of the number that had sworn and tussled and sung and lounged and fiddled and beaten the furs there in the old days. And the Indians were almost gone. A few relics of the island Indians, a few from Point Ignace, instead of the hordes that, for a hundred years, had crowded in by the thousands, in all their gaudy finery, during the roistering summer months!

When Joseph and Marie boarded the sailing vessel for Quebec, it was a comparatively small group that came down to the wharf to wave them off—Edward Biddle, Ramsey Crooks, Madame La Framboise, Samuel Abbott, Henry Schoolcraft, Dr. William Beaumont and his patient, Alexis St. Martin. Joseph's own dozen voyageurs, six Indians, and, last and dearest of all his comrades, Jean Baptiste. There were undisguised tears in the eyes of Jean Baptiste:

"Goodbye, mon cousin! Bon voyage! And come back to ze woods sometime. Jean Baptiste will be waiting!"

"I'm coming back, Jean Baptiste! And we'll conquer new woods and new worlds together, n'est-ce pas? Good old Jean Baptiste!"

The two held hands firmly, then kissed each other on both cheeks. Joseph turned to Edward.

"Goodbye, son! Take care of Agatha—and my grandson!"

"Yes, mon père. It's hard to lose you—but good to see you going off for a lark at last, instead of working and planning!"

"To tell you the truth, I feel like a lazy fool. I'm beginning to miss the work already! I'll have to set some traps in the ocean!" Joseph shook the masts above him with his sentiment-disguising laughter.

He and Marie gave their son-in-law a final embrace, waved to all the company, and stepped up the gangway to the deck of the *Chesley Blake*.

At Quebec, there were four days to spend before the departure of the steamship. Before taking the stagecoach for Ste. Anne de

Beaupré, Joseph and Marie left their baggage at the stage office, and walked up the hill to the Convent of the Ursuline Nuns for a word with Thérèse behind her sacred grille.

As Joseph walked up Mountain Street, all the memories came trooping back: the night of the Mask Ball (a fascinating girl, that Corinne de Courcelles—but what a faint and far-away figure she had become in his life, like a figure seen through the small end of a pair of spy glasses!); the night that he and Raoul went galloping out of town to their father's death; the day he left for the Pays d'en Haut; the day he came back; the day he and Marie spent in Quebec, on their wedding trip, buying the yellow silk and the green-plumed riding hat and the red slippers! That was the happiest day of all!

Joseph gripped Marie's arm.

"Do you remember, Marie, that happy day we spent here, after we were married, shopping for riding clothes and red slippers?"

"Do I remember? Oh, Joseph! Let's stop here a minute, and just remember! I'm out of breath! Aren't you?"

"No!"

"Sturdy Joseph! That was a happy day indeed—except for the little lady in green silk, who met us at the wharf and tried to spoil it!"

"Lady in green silk?"

"You don't remember?"

"Oh, yes—yes, I do."

"She's tried to spoil it for us a great many times. But she's never quite succeeded—has she, Joseph?"

"No, ma chère."

"Do you realize, Joseph, that she's the last wolf?"

"Why, what do you mean, Marie?"

"Well, we've outlived all our enemies, all the wolves along our trail: my aunt and uncle Lefèvre, De la Vigne, Shavehead, and Monsieur Rastel—all except one, Joseph."

"How about Abijah Hull and Major Higgins and Pélégor and William Burnett, and Lucille?"

"The important ones, I mean. We'd have to be Mr. and Mrs. Methuselah to outlive them all! After all, there's only one sleek and beautiful and important one left."

"That one is as good as dead, I think. She's probably not beautiful any more. And when a woman like that has no beauty left, she has nothing at all."

Marie looked up with a quick sidewise glance at Joseph, and felt fairly well satisfied that he meant what he said. They continued mounting the hill, talking all the rest of the way of Thérèse.

They pulled the bell at the convent door, and, after a long pause, a white sister noiselessly opened it. They asked for Thérèse, who, since her name was already that of a Catholic saint, had simply chosen to become Sister Thérèse.

"If you will wait on that bench near the grille, please, I will go and find Sister Thérèse immediately."

Joseph and Marie passed from the sunny street into the cool stone hall of the convent. The only light came from two leaded windows at the end of the forty-foot hall directly above the open chamber marked off by the iron grille. They moved towards the bench.

A novice, in a black gown and a white guimpe and veil, was just coming out of a small side door, near the grille, with a wooden bucket in her right hand and a scrubbing brush in her left hand. Joseph and Marie had come within twenty feet of her when suddenly she did a strange thing. She stopped, looked at them steadily, then set down the bucket with a great splash, and turned to retreat, in unconventional haste, through the door from which she had just come. But before she had made the complete turn, the light from the leaded windows had fallen full on her strangely familiar face, her incongruously pale cheeks, her long, sinuous red lips, the duplicating line of her long, sinuous black eyebrows, her interminable lashes, her peculiarly beautiful blue eyes with yellow circles around the centers. It was a face across which the world had written many experiences, and which displayed a greater variety of vivid emotions in that single instant than the faces of most nuns are supposed to betray in an immured lifetime.

Joseph gripped Marie's arm with a violence which revealed his sudden inner turmoil. Marie laid her other hand quietingly on his arm. There was not time to speak of this other sister yet, for Thérèse was suddenly there behind the grille, beautiful in her black gown and black veil, and in the serenity of her face. Joseph and

Marie forgot all disturbances in their joy of seeing her. They talked with her for a long time about her work, about the marriages of her sisters, the birth of her first nephew, the deportation of Blackbird and the rest of their Indian friends to the Mississippi, and about their own imminent journey to the Continent.

Before they finally turned away from the grille, Marie asked:

"What is the name of the novice who came out to scrub the floor, Thérèse, and then went away and never came back?"

Thérèse gave her mother a deep look and answered:

"Sister Marie."

"Sister *Marie!*"

"I see," said Marie quietly. "For Mother Marie of the Ursulines, or Mary, who was so fortunate as to be *the wife of Joseph.*"

"Or Mary Magdalene," said Joseph as he drew his wife to him and kissed her fervently.

As the Baillys descended at twilight from the coach at the gate of the old home at Ste. Anne de Beaupré, they saw Antoinette's two grandchildren, the children of her daughter Anne, playing tag among the pear trees at the east side of the house. From an upper window, Antoinette caught sight of her brother, who had been expected for several days, and exclaimed to Madame Geneviève, who was lying in the same old four-poster bed in which Michel Bailly had closed his eyes to the world:

"Oh, Maman, it's Joseph!"

"Quick, quick, Antoinette! Help me out of bed! Put me in the chair. Fix my cap! Put on my slippers. Joseph must not know I'm dying."

"You mustn't say that, Maman."

"Of course I'm dying! You know it. I know it. That young whippersnapper of a Dr. Campion knows it. But he won't say it— thinks he can fool me. His father, old Dr. Campion, wouldn't have been afraid to tell me the truth. Come, Antoinette, hurry, hurry! And you must tell Charlotte to put supper back on the table again."

"They've stopped to talk to little Michel and 'Toinette. Don't hurry too much, Maman. It isn't good for you. You shouldn't be doing this, you know."

"I'm not going to spoil Joseph's journey to France. He's worked hard all his life. He's going to have a good time! And he's not going to worry about *me*. I'm going to sit up as long as he's here, if it kills me! There, how do I look? Oh, I know what I need to make me look ten years younger! Bring me some of Anne's Spanish paper. There, on the mantel. Dab a lot of it on my cheeks. Now rub it off a little. Do I look rosy and well?"

"You look very pretty—and young, Maman."

"Well, eighty-one isn't very old. After all, Uncle Baptiste lived to be ninety. I'd like to live to be a hundred. It's a good world—I love it! Every person and bird and flower of it, and every stone of it. A good world!"

"Where do you want to sit, Maman—by the south window or the east?"

"The east window, looking into the pear orchard. There! That chair feels good! Mon Dieu, but those rose beds down there need weeding! And the grass is too long in the pear orchard, and some of those heavy pear branches need propping. Good gracious, Antoinette! Why don't you keep your eye on things? What will happen to this place when I'm gone!"

"There they are! I hear their voices at the door!"

"Come, hand me your knitting, Antoinette! I want to seem busy! I haven't knitted for so long I've almost forgotten how!"

"Yes, Maman, you've been too sick to knit for six months. Here you are. Here's the knitting."

In a minute, Joseph and Marie were in the room.

"Maman, Maman! How well you look! Not over thirty! A little thin. But such good color—such bright eyes! Ma mère! Ma mère! And Antoinette! You've gained the flesh that Maman's lost. A good, substantial sister! Good old 'Toinette! Who else is here?"

"Anne and her children and Raoul and his wife. But all except the children have driven over to Point Lévis today to see the soldiers drill. Raoul's son's regiment is stationed there for a month."

"Your grandchildren are adorable, Antoinette!" exclaimed Marie. "Sweet enough to hug forever! Especially the little boy."

"Run down now, Antoinette," urged Madame Geneviève, "and see that Charlotte puts supper on the table again for these poor, starving children."

"Thank you, Maman. We're as hungry as bears!" declared Joseph heartily. "Well, Maman, you should see *our* newest grand-child—a grandson, mind you, Maman, named Joseph Bailly Biddle!"

"How nice of Agatha and Edward to name him after you!"

"Yes, isn't it wonderful?" Then: "I'm glad Raoul's son will carry on the Bailly name."

Madame Geneviève slipped her hand over Joseph's.

"I know. I know how much you and Marie have suffered. But now will come more grandsons. And then you'll never know *real* pride until you produce *great*-grandchildren, as I have!"

"It's good to see you surrounded like this, Maman. You must be very happy."

"Yes, I *am* happy, Joseph. I still miss your father, as I've missed him since the day he died. But my life is very full."

"You'd make any kind of life worth while, Maman, even if your home were a bear cave on Great Slave Lake!"

"Why not, mon fils? The adventure is in us, not in the distance we cover or the places we see. Your life has led you northwest to the Pays d'en Haut, south to New Orleans, now east to the old world. I've lived it all with you—and I'll wager my adventures have been just as thrilling as yours!"

"Then we've *all* had quite an exciting life on the Northwest frontiers, haven't we?"

"Certainement! And what a *good wife* you've had to share them with you!"

"Thank you, ma mère," said Marie. "But you mustn't forget that it's very easy to be a good wife to a good husband."

"Ah, *has* he been a good husband?" asked Antoinette laughingly, as she came back into the room. "A long while ago, there was a greenish-eyed French girl on his trail, who worried us a little. What became of her, Joseph? She married the man Papa wanted me to marry, didn't she? Then what?"

"A very exciting life on the frontier and a very lavish one in New Orleans. Your would-be husband died a ghastly death of the plague in New Orleans last year. I'll tell you a story about it some time."

"And she?"

"Sh! Antoinette, you have the unrestrained curiosity of a schoolgirl. Be quiet!" remonstrated Madame Geneviève.

"Madame Rastel is a middle-aged woman now," answered Marie. "She's just entered the Ursuline Convent in Quebec."

"Oh, so you know all about her, daughter?" asked Madame Bailly, who had been watching Marie closely with her steel-blue eyes.

"Oh, yes! These men—you know, these men are so transparent."

The three women laughed knowingly together.

"You looked so much like your father when you laughed then, Marie—so very much like him! He was a dear man."

Madame Geneviève lingered a little over the recollection, and then added, with a kind of feminine transparency: "And so was Michel!"

"You still think Papa would have forgiven me for going into the Pays d'en Haut, Maman, and trading on the frontiers all my life instead of staying here?"

"Of course he would, Joseph! Who could possibly imagine your staying here and pruning pear trees all your life! Your father admired men of action. He would have admired you tremendously, everything you've done—developing one of the largest private fur businesses on the continent, fighting the battle of independence for yourself and others on all the frontiers, becoming a power for good among the Indians, among the French, among the Americans, wherever you've settled, helping in the good growth of a good, growing country."

"Maman, you take rather a large view of my activities, I'm afraid! Where did you get such notions? I've merely done my foolish best each day, as you taught me to do so long ago!" And Joseph laughed with the pride his Mother's words had given him.

"My dear boy! What *is* success, but doing one's foolish best each day? I'm very proud of you! What are you going to do next? For I'm sure you haven't finished yet."

"No, I'm not through yet, Maman! The fur trade is dead. But there's plenty to do in those booming little towns of Chicago and Detroit."

"I'm sure of it! En avant, Joseph! Now what *is* that lazy Charlotte doing? If only Nicolette hadn't become so rheumatic that she had to be put out to pasture with her relatives! Old Nicolette's costing us a pretty pension, Joseph, but she was worth it! Tell Charlotte to open a bottle of Burgundy and anything else you want, Joseph."

"Aren't you coming down to sit with us at supper, Maman?"

"Not tonight, Joseph. I've had my supper. I think I'll just stay here and watch the moon come up over the orchard. It's a full moon tonight."

"So it is," said Joseph, rising.

In the east, from which the pale bands of the twilight had not yet entirely faded, the great gold disc was coming up over the sweep of the St. Lawrence River and over the shrines and the gabled houses and the fruitful orchards of Ste. Anne de Beaupré— the beautiful but too tranquil scene that Joseph had so long ago forsworn. Here he was, at the full moon of his own life, in the place from which he had started out, forty years before, to the Pays d'en Haut on the way to all his adventures.

Marie joined her husband at the window. Joseph put his arm around her.

"Full moon!" said Joseph.

"And no wolves!" They uttered the words at the very same instant, and Joseph's laughter rang out over Marie's, as they turned from the window and followed Antoinette down the stairs to supper.

THE END